Open and Shut

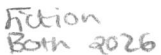

Mark Hamilton

About the author:

Mark Hamilton works as a freelance copywriter and lives in Bristol with his wife and family. *Open and Shut* is his third novel, following on from *Heaven Scent* (2019) and *Crackle & Pop* (2022). He has published several collections of poetry, including *In Badock's Wood and Other Poems* and *Wengerball at The Arsenal*. You can find him on X (Twitter): @mhamilton1509

All characters in this publication are fictitious and any resemblance to real persons, either living or dead, is purely coincidental.

The right of Mark Hamilton to be identified as the author of this work has been asserted in accordance with the Copyright Designs and Patents Act 1988.

All rights reserved. No part of this publication can be reproduced, stored, or transmitted in any form without the permission of the author.

Copyright © Mark Hamilton 2024

1.

No, wait, what...?!

Alice scrabbled increasingly desperately in the bathroom cabinet. Where were they??

They were here.

They *had* been here.

They weren't here anymore.

Shit!

She slammed the mirror door shut and double-checked around the rest of the bathroom. Had she moved them somewhere else? No. She saw herself clearly (through her early morning haze) taking one yesterday. Right here, in front of the mirror, by the basin. Then putting the packet back where she always put it. Nestling on the left-hand side, with the paracetamol and aspirin and small bottle of mouthwash next to it.

And now – it wasn't there. And already she was feeling the need. Her mouth was sticky. Her skin was dry. There was a shakiness and an irritability rising. She needed a tablet!

She was pointlessly hunting around in the kitchen when her phone beeped from the bedroom. A message from Tony. Who, not twenty minutes ago, she had kicked out of the flat.

"Just to say, so long and thanks for the Mng! ☐"

The bastard! Should she phone him and demand he bring them back? He wouldn't come, would he. And even though she'd probably never see him again, she didn't want to seem too desperate for them. So instead she typed:

"Hope you don't choke on them. Tosser."

Then she blocked him from her contacts. What a low scumbag. But it was just the sort of thing he'd do. Based on her limited experience of him (three evenings, two nights). Conceited, self-satisfied kind of a guy. With a nasty twist to him – like a bad cocktail. Well, pour him away...

But, more importantly, where was she gonna get some more bloody Mng?

Alice sat down on the end of the bed, considering this problem. Then she sprang up to make herself a strong coffee. That would help a bit. Plus her vape, too.

She would be all right for a while anyway. The physical symptoms would only gradually increase. While the mental symptoms might not emerge for a day or more. So if she could get hold of some tablets that evening...

That shouldn't be difficult. She knew of a pub near the river in the centre of town where dealers were rumoured to hang out. Mng (pronounced by the letters, m-n-g) was everywhere these days, even though in theory it was only available on prescription. It was an epidemic. She hadn't procured any from a dealer before because her GP was willing to prescribe them for her – there being extenuating circumstances in her case.

She was a special case… Alice screwed her face up into an ironic scowl as she reflected on this.

Still, for now, she was OK. The coffee was good, the vape too. Of the days, it was Saturday. The sun was shining. She was going into work for a couple of hours in the morning – having notes to write up and admin to catch up on – and then she was seeing her friend Mel in the afternoon for some retail therapy. And perhaps she'd phone Lewis later on too.

Yes, she'd phone Lewis later on too. She'd already decided that she'd do that a couple of days ago, while she was technically kind of seeing Tony.

What an idiot she'd been to start technically kind of seeing Tony. She had called it off with Lewis a month ago – he was a sweet guy and pretty fanciable, but she'd decided they needed some time apart to take stock and reflect. He'd agreed, albeit unwillingly. Then she'd gone out for a few drinks with a couple of friends, got pissed, and had started being chatted up by a tall, dark guy at the bar. One thing had led to another… Not that night, but when they had met up again a few nights later.

End result: he'd stayed the night twice. They had never gelled though. She'd never even particularly liked him. He was decent-looking, but had that strain of arrogance and complacency that should have been a red light flashing. He worked in sales after all – what more did she need to know?? It was why she'd got drunk each time, to make her eyesight blurry and pretend that red was green.

But colours were clear in the morning. And that morning, they'd got into a petty squabble when she told him she needed to go into work. He'd been expecting a lie-in, a lazy breakfast, some more lordly attention (no doubt). His face dropped, he made a disparaging remark about this not being the service he'd paid for (?) – and that was when, finally, she *did* see red. And took the opportunity to fan the flame into a nicely blazing argument and get rid of him.

However, he had had the last laugh, as she now saw. Taking nearly a whole packet of Mng with him – two months' supply. She remembered telling him that she had some, although she'd played it down as an occasional thing.

An occasional thing! There was no such thing as occasional once you were hooked on Mng. You had to take a tablet every day, or every other day minimum. The only saving grace – for some – was that it took a little while to get hooked, as it wasn't especially strong from a pharmacological point of view. It built up over time. There again, given what most takers of Mng were escaping, they were virtually certain to need to keep taking it – and so were almost certain to get hooked. Nice one, Alice! She scowled at herself again.

The thing about Mng – a composite of magnesium, zinc and codeine – was that it was designed to help people addicted to other things to overcome their addiction. So it was kind of ironic that it turned out to be addictive in itself...

At least Alice wasn't in any kind of emergency state. For the moment, her symptoms were only mild. But it would be good to keep busy and active – so she got ready to go into work and set out on the short drive not long after 9am. She decided, as usual, to drive herself. Like most people, she didn't trust the self-drive function. She liked to do things for herself in any case.

She headed in towards the centre of Knott – the small, mid-Somerset city where she had lived for nearly five years now – and then turned off towards the clinic. As she went, she passed almost in view of the Mng factory on Mill Lane. Ironic in a way that she lived so close to the Mng epicentre… The factory, owned by SmartLab Pharmaceuticals, had been operational for several years now. It had started off producing generic drugs, then switched entirely to Mng when it had received approvals two years ago. The site itself was something of an iconic place in the Knott landscape – having formerly been the home of Crackle Confectionery Ltd and its famous Crackle Bar. But when that family firm had been sold to Shark Snacks plc, it had promptly been closed down in the early 2020s and production of the Crackle Bar had been switched to one of Shark's bigger sites in the north. It had been a local trauma to see the factory close and 100 jobs go. The site had lain empty through most of the 2020s, rusting away amidst tall mourning weeds, before SmartLab had ridden to the rescue – investing heavy sums in turning the old factory into a state of the art pharmaceutical production facility.

Alice drew in to her place of work – Clear Minds Clinic. It was a smart, modern place, two floors, all clean angles of precise metal and glass. It was appropriately green and peaceful in its surrounds, with blossoming cherry trees and limes breathing quietly in the strong early May sun. It was already in the mid-20s, forecast to reach 30° by mid-afternoon. God only knew what full summer held, each year getting hotter than the last... Meanwhile, winters were mild and stormy with frequent flooding across the country; interspersed with sudden deep freezes and blasts of snow. Even in 'temperate' Britain, the climate twisted and flailed like a cat chasing its tail.

It was pleasant to step with a whoosh through the automatic sliding doors into the cool air-conditioned reception area. Alice greeted Sam the receptionist with a cheery 'Morning!' and proceeded to her consulting room. It was quiet around the place – there were never many consultations on a Saturday and most staff only formally worked one in every three. Alice herself was 'off' that day. But she liked to keep on top of her workload and didn't mind coming in just for a couple of hours.

She had some case notes to write up. She could have done it from home, but she liked to be in the work environment. Being in her consulting room put her 'in the zone'. She liked to be in the zone, because she liked her work. God knows she was no case study herself (!), but that didn't mean she couldn't be a good therapist. It was all about listening anyway – gently encouraging, prompting and coaxing the patient to talk. That was what most of them, ultimately, wanted – to be heard. *Validation is what we're looking for...*

Clinically speaking, most of her patients had relatively mild conditions. Clear Minds Clinic was not a centre for the acutely mentally ill. It was one of those private treatment facilities that had proliferated across the country in recent years as greater awareness of mental health and wellbeing led to multiplying levels of self-diagnosis and a desire to be treated. Every second person, it seemed, was having therapy of some sort. Any kind of mental health professional had a guaranteed lifetime of work ahead. This was one of the reasons Alice had chosen a psychology degree some fifteen years ago. The breaking tide of mental affliction had already been apparent back then.

Alice's patients had the usual run of issues – depression, anxiety, phobia, bereavement, relationship breakdown, addiction, dependency (including some to Mng...). They were real issues. Some of them were deep-running, with their roots in trauma. They were few and far between who came for some 'designer' therapy to idly pass the time.

No, the mental health pandemic was genuine. Alice had formed the view that, underneath, we are all ailing. Stick out your tongue and the spots of mental imbalance are there. It's just a question of degree and how many protective layers the sickness is hidden under. Indeed, that was true of her as much as anyone. She was addicted to Mng, she drank too much, she had a problem with commitment... Maybe she needed counselling herself. In fact, she felt that her role as counsellor was what kept her within stable bounds. Listening to and helping others was a form of therapy for herself as well. If she wasn't a therapist, she'd probably be sitting on the other side of the desk...

She set to work writing up her case notes. Although, in fact, what this actually amounted to was feeding the recordings of her consultations through her AI app, which then wrote them up for her in a matter of seconds. All she had to do was read the texts through and make a few small edits to finish them off.

The notes were spookily good. It was as though the artificial intelligence really understood her patients; as though it had lived through a range of penetrating mental problems of its own and could empathise from the depths of its machine-coded heart. The write-ups were concise but complete; objective but individualised. They were also scattered with useful references, such as: "The patient exhibits a tendency to construct false behaviour trails as a distraction and to protect his true self – see Winnicott's theory of the True & False Self for more context." Or: "The patient appears to have accepted her inability to overcome her fears and anxieties, and is therefore trapped in a repeating cycle. Seligman's notion of 'learned helplessness' may be relevant to this case."

With AI so good, it was no wonder that increasing numbers of people didn't even come to see a human therapist anymore. There were a multitude of AI apps available that you could 'chat' with either textually or verbally and receive analysis, advice and support. Some patients grew weirdly attached to their AI consultant – there had even been cases of people seeking help (from either a human or a different AI) to overcome what had turned into an insidious emotional dependence! Recognising the direction the trend was heading in, some clinics – including Clear Minds – were developing their own apps for patients to access on a cheap subscription basis. The future of human psychologists wasn't so assured after all…

Still, Alice welcomed it because it took away so many tedious tasks. She was confident that there would always be *something* for qualified human therapists to do.

Notes completed, she attended to a few other bits of admin. It was pleasant to do so on a quiet Saturday morning in the peace of her consulting room. It was a generous office, with a large desk, lots of space for bookshelves and cabinets, and a number of comfortable chairs for patients to choose from. It gave onto the rear side of the clinic's grounds with plenty of waving green in view and the twittering of birds drifting in through the open window. She couldn't complain about her set-up here. She enjoyed her work. It was just a shame that were other factors that unsettled her…

Her work done, she moved quickly on. She needed to keep busy to hold those withdrawal symptoms at bay. She could feel the ticklish irritability rising as the headspace she was housed in thinned; like a pilot in an ascending plane.

Before leaving, she decided to go upstairs on the off-chance that someone from Finance was in. She needed to check whether one of her patients had settled their overdue bill. It was unlikely that anyone would be there, but you never knew…

There was no one in. The whole of the second floor was empty in fact. However, walking back towards the stairs she noticed that there were two people in the meeting room – one of whom, she saw through the glass wall, was her boss, Clear Minds owner Eric Smythe. As she passed, he lifted his head and saw her. An enthusiastic, dapper, energetic man, he gestured to her and she went to the door.

"Hi Alice, how are you?" Dr Smythe asked. "Didn't think you'd be here today."

The other person turned round towards her in their chair – and she saw that it was none other than Kevan Monk, CEO of SmartLab. "Hello Kevan," she said as he nodded at her. "What's with the Saturday meeting!" she added, half-jokingly.

"Oh well, you know, we workaholics never stop!" Eric replied.

"In fact, we're just catching up on a semi-significant development," Kevan Monk injected in his low tones. "The regulator has informed me that it plans to carry out a review of Mng. They're concerned about levels of addiction, they say. They're going to announce it next week."

"Really? Oh my!" Alice exclaimed. "Well yes, that *does* sound significant."

"We don't think it's anything to worry about. It's a formality really," Eric said with what felt like a forced brightness. That was his way – positive, sanguine, glass half-full.

"Hmmm. If that's the case, why would they publicly announce it?" Alice asked.

Kevan Monk tipped his head to one side and shrugged. "Well, they want to be *seen* to be acting. There is a minor dependency issue, for a very small number of patients. It's nothing serious. They're taking the opportunity to assert their image as a tough, proactive regulator. But it won't lead to anything. I'm very confident about that."

"You think so? Good. I suppose…"

"You suppose? What, you think they *should* be reviewing?" Monk raised an eyebrow and held his gaze on her, as though daring a response.

"To be honest, it could be more than a 'minor issue', Kevan. You know I think that. I've got a number of patients right now who have become addicted. It's not as serious as their original addiction, granted, but it *is* an addiction… with some acute withdrawal trauma attached. I suggested at the time of the trial that longer-term study and analysis was needed."

On that at least, Alice's conscience could be clear. Three years ago, Clear Minds had been one of the centres running final stage clinical trials for Mng on behalf of SmartLab. Alice had led the work. She felt certain that further study on dependency issues was needed. She had said so in her report. That was good. But pressured by Monk, she had eventually toned her wording right down. That was not good. She hadn't been proud of herself for that…

"All opioids are addictive!" Eric cut in, keen it seemed to prevent any kind of a disagreement developing. "Mng is mild compared to other products. And ongoing monitoring and analysis *is* happening. As the regulator knows. Like Kevan says, it's a PR exercise."

"Well, you're obviously much closer to it than me. So – fair enough!" Alice replied. Then she couldn't help adding: "Sales seem to be going great guns for sure, and not just through GPs… Mng is everywhere!"

Monk fixed her with his dark-eyed, steady gaze. That was how he was – there was something still and watchful about him. When he looked at you, his eyes seemed to rest on you for an extra second or two compared to the norm. His manner and movements were deliberate and had a strange stillness, too, as if gravity exerted an additional force on him. Everything he did seemed pre-considered, pre-planned.

"Hmm. Yes, sales are very positive. Demand is high," he said, drily.

"Clearly! I just don't know how so much of it is getting onto the streets given that it's prescription-only…?" Alice mused. Getting no response, she continued, "So anyway, what's the plan then? That's what you're discussing now obviously."

"Indeed. What plan can there be, Alice?" Eric said, spreading his hands. "We'll provide them with anything they ask for, give them full access to historical and current records. There's nothing to hide, after all."

"It's more a case of managing the public and media reaction. That's what we're discussing in point of fact," Kevan Monk added, stroking his black, close-cropped beard. Alice had never liked that beard. It was like a mask painted across his face.

"Sure, I see. Well then – I'll let you get on as I guess you have plenty to discuss!" Alice threw out. "I'm sure you can devise a strategy to manage it all…"

"Needless to say, please keep this to yourself for the time being, Alice. We're telling you in strictest confidence," Kevan added.

"Of course. Understood. All right then, I'll get going. Nice to see you again, Kevan. See you on Monday, Eric."

She made a quick getaway towards the stairs. As she descended, she realised her legs were weak, her body trembling. All of this was bringing back bad memories. Her capitulation, her sense of guilt. She had allowed Monk (and Eric) to steamroller her. Monk was desperate for a speedy license, having taken on considerable debt to fund the development of Mng and all the clinical trials. Eric, she was sure, also had skin in the game. And hadn't a brand new Mercedes coupe suddenly started occupying Eric's space in the Clear Minds car park only a few weeks after Mng's approval had been obtained?

In fairness, it was also true that she had been paid a significant bonus herself at the end of that financial year…

Yuck. Quite frankly. She despised herself, when she thought about it. And it was why she was now so keen to move on from Clear Minds, to find a new role somewhere else, far away from Knott. She had decided at the time to stay for at least another three years, for the sake of her CV. Those three years were now up. That said, it was complicated by other factors, such as her love life – Lewis – who, in one of those little twists of circumstance, worked here in Knott for none other than... SmartLab Pharmaceuticals!

Half-smiling, half-grimacing to herself, Alice emerged into the strong sunlight that was simmering in the carpark. As she got into her car, her phone pinged.

"Looking well. We should meet again."

Bloody hell! Gross. It was from Monk. That was the first time she had seen him in person for over a year. During the clinical trial period, they had been lovers for a while...

She wasn't alone in that. As it were. Monk had a reputation – a deserved one – as a philanderer. He was good-looking in his way, and loaded, and didn't lack confidence to put himself forward. But he was creepy with it. Women didn't stay with him long. She remembered the night when a group of them had gone out to a bar. She had been sitting next to him. As he spoke to someone else, she had felt him calmly put his hand on her thigh under the table. Without breaking his speech. Without even looking at her. She had been so shocked that she hadn't reacted. He had taken it from there. For some reason, she had let him...

She shook her head as she drove, trying to scatter the memories. She certainly wasn't going to go *there* again. She wouldn't even reply to his message. Which he must have sent even as he was discussing the Mng situation with Eric. Yes, *creepy*... He had funny habits too. He was dominating in the bedroom. The memories weren't good. In fact, when she thought about it all from this distance, it almost seemed like an abusive relationship... She hadn't consciously seen or thought that at the time. There had been fun moments too, and the glamour of a semi-secret relationship with a wealthy CEO, and she had just let it all carry her along. Which was probably what he had been counting on as he pursued his own selfish ends and desires. Underneath she had known, even if she hadn't articulated it to herself. And the poison of it had kind of seeped upwards until she couldn't ignore it any longer. So then she had broken it off, after it had been going on for a couple of months. Actually, it hadn't been hard to shake him off because by then he'd started looking around again. That was how he rolled.

How he rolled... In his huge house – almost a complex – on the edge of Knott. In his huge bed, super kingsize. All those cold sparse rooms with white walls and minimalist furnishings.

But there she was, remembering it all again. Put it away, pour it away. Like Tony this morning. How much men tended to lead only to disappointment... After Kevan, she'd stayed single for a year. And had enjoyed it. Then she'd met Lewis through a friend... And it turned out he worked at bloody SmartLab! But she forgave him for that and their relationship had been so much better. Not perfect, but worth something. She'd phone him later. They'd been going out for nearly two years, until their present hiatus.

It was nearly midday when she got home. Two hours until she was meeting Mel. So she threw herself into cleaning her flat – wiping away all traces of Tony. She needed to keep it clean because her landlord was so damn fussy. He invited himself round every couple of months on various pretexts but she knew he was checking. If only she could buy her own place. But that was just a dream, as it was for nearly everyone of her generation and younger. You'd need a lottery win just for the bloody deposit. There she was, nearly thirty-five, a solid earner, and her festival-going tent was probably the extent of the 'property' she'd ever own! Well, until her mother passed on perhaps. Her mother was a mess all right – but she *did* have the distinction of being a mess in her own faded surroundings. She'd got lucky when a spinster aunt had died and left her her flat. Although that had meant moving to Weymouth. But there she'd gone and decided to stay rather than sell it. It gave her new fields of men to comb through after all, new bars and pubs to sit in... Good old mum. She must phone her too, later on. It had been a while since they'd spoken. Easter, was it?

The brisk cleaning and vacuuming was good for her, pushing away some of the dry tingling that was gathering. Then a quick sandwich, another strong coffee, some hungry sucks on the vape. She'd be fine! Who needed Mng? Not this cognitive therapist, oh no no no! Not until she could get down to that pub in any case.

Alice took the short bus ride into town for her rendezvous with Mel at 2 o'clock. She'd met Mel at a gym class a few years ago: they had instantly hit it off and become friends. Mel was an administrator in the NHS, a similar age to Alice – but was married with a two year old daughter. Today was a 'release day' with her husband looking after the little girl. So Mel was in party mood and keen to enjoy her free time. The first thing they did was to go and buy frappes and cake and have a good catch-up.

Alice was struck by how tired Mel looked. The rigours of having a baby... Would she ever have one? Only time would tell. But suffice to say that she didn't feel too much of a maternal clock ticking.

Mel pumped her about Lewis. "Are you still apart? Do you still chat? You know what I think, Al! He's a great guy. You make a really good couple..."

"Yeah, I know, so people say... We do, I guess. I'm not sure Mel... I don't know quite where we are to be honest."

"But you hooked up with this other guy then? What did you say... Tony?"

"Ha! He's history already darling. In fact, I got fed up with him this morning and threw him out!"

"Like a piece of trash! You go, girl. Oh to be free again and do things like that!"

"Well, but *you* get... a husband you can order around... stability... a beautiful little girl beaming up at you..."

"Before she's sick all down my front, yeah!"

They headed off round the shops with no particular intentions. Just to browse and see what they came across.

In one store, Alice saw a summer dress that caught her eye and went to try it on. The dark blue cotton set off nicely against her dark hair and blue-green eyes. As she looked at herself in the changing-room mirror, she felt that it gave her a fresh and sexy look, fitting snugly around her trim figure.

Without thinking about it, she found herself suddenly video calling Lewis...

"Hello Alice?"

"Hey sweetie, how are you doing?"

"Yeah, I'm good thanks. Just in the park actually, having a kickabout."

"Oh yeah?"

"Yeah. You just caught us on a break. We're all knackered!"

"Oh cool, well I won't keep you. I was just trying on this dress – what do you think of it?"

Alice moved the phone around her, up and down, giving him all the angles...

"It's err... It's really nice, Alice. It suits you."

"Suits me?"

"You look great, Al. You look...hot!"

"*That's* what I wanted to hear! Thank you, Lou. I guess I'll buy it then."

"Glad to be of service."

"What are you doing later? Tonight."

"Tonight? Oh, a few of us are going to the Freemantle. There's a band playing, etcetera..."

"Oh right, enjoy. I was just going to say, I'm at home tonight. Come round if you want? *Later* I mean. Any time really. If you want..."

"Ah! Really? Well... that may be possible to arrange..."

"Up to you of course, Lou. No pressure. I mean, if you score elsewhere or whatever..."

Lewis laughed. "What kind of a guy do you take me for, Alice! I mean... yeah, I'm sure I'll probably... you know..."

"Brill. Well, *probably* see you later then. Better run. Enjoy the game sweetie."

She blew him a kiss and cut the call. She'd gone and surprised herself there. Really hadn't envisaged that. But it was done now!

She bought the dress and hooked up with Mel again. After a couple more hours, they had an early supper as Mel wanted to get back to help her husband put their daughter down. "A mother's work is never done!" she joked, downing her second glass of Chardonnay.

Alice matched Mel with the wine, because her Mng symptoms were really beginning to gather now. It was hard to concentrate and she had to fight to conceal her distraction...

Bloody Mng! It was a simple concept: when someone becomes addicted to their poison of choice — hard drugs, alcohol, gambling, pornography, sex — a contributing factor is often an underlying emptiness they are trying to escape. The theory was that, if you could fill up that sense of emptiness through a powerful sense of meaningfulness, you could reduce the patient's addictive need too. This is what Mng did. Its ingredients induced a powerful sense of presence in the taker. The extracts of magnesium and zinc, combining, increased the mental alertness of the patient, flicking a switch that seemed to put everything into a special and as it were highly charged focus. It wasn't a high as such — rather, an exhilarating on-the-level where the patient was completely keyed into everything around them.

"And so I said to Peter, how on earth do you think I'm going to be able to do that if I'm also trying to double-check all these spreadsheets?"

Underneath or around the edges of that was the action of the opioid, codeine, which induced an analgesic warmth and a gentle glow. The combination of that with the sharp focus of the magnesium and zinc was a deliciously seductive sensation. Like floating through clouds on a bed of steel...

"But I just couldn't get through to him, Alice. You know what I mean? When something's just not going in? Anyway, that was last week's boring work drama... Who knows what next week's will be!"

The result was — quelle surprise, actually — that takers became addicted to Mng itself. It wasn't physically kicking it that was hard – compared to cold turkey or alcohol withdrawal it was nothing much – but mentally. That rich infusion of meaningfulness inverted itself into an awful vacuum of meaninglessness when Mng was withdrawn. The meaninglessness was hugely amplified compared to pre-Mng levels – a deepening, intensifying black hole that prostrated the sufferer, even made some suicidal. Luckily, the deepest depths of this only lasted for a few hours before it began to wane. But a handful of people, reportedly, had not pulled through…

"The thing is to just not let work get to you. It's life outside work that really matters. Don't you think?"

Despite all this, Alice wished more than anything that she had some Mng in her bloodstream right now… She was smiling and nodding at Mel, but had no idea what she was actually saying. She gulped at her wine, like liquid oxygen that might save her.

"Don't you think, Alice?"

"Sorry, what?"

"I thought so! You've been miles away, darling. Sorry – I know I've been rabbiting on. Don't get the chance very often! Anyway, tbh I'd probably better be going. It's been lovely catching up!" Mel said.

"Oh, I'm so sorry, hun! I lost the thread for a second. Think the wine's hit me. I need to get home myself – flop out on the sofa!"

Smiling, apologising, reconnecting as they prepared to disconnect, they gathered up their things, paid the bill –

and parted with a volley of good wishes in the warm and honeyed evening air.

Spinning away towards the bus stop, Alice suddenly realised that she was not in fact far from the Mng-proffering pub. Mentally, she had been envisaging going there under cover of darkness – but, in fact, why not go there now and just get it done?

Ten minutes later, having diverted herself via an ATM (she could hardly remember the last time she had used one), Alice was approaching The Dog and Duchess, which was situated in a kind of hinterland between the centre of the city and a run-down suburb of ageing apartment blocks and council flats. The atmosphere changed intangibly as she walked, becoming laced with a harder and rougher edge. Litter flittered. People hung around. The river to her right seemed to slow and thicken, swollen with unease. It bounced the sun back off its surface in harsh, dazzling waves.

She felt nervous as she pushed through the pub's doors. She didn't know what to expect – never having been there before – and of course didn't know what the protocol was for what she was about to do (for what she was about to receive). She was met by the view of a faded interior, worn carpets, tatty walls. A long black counter served as the bar. Groups sat around, a mix of ages, but the place was only medium busy at that hour. An old rock song was playing.

What should she do?? She went to the bar and decided to order a vodka. The walk had cleared her head and she felt fine to take another drink on board. It was moral support, of sorts, and she wanted something that she could down quickly and get away... Mobility seemed important in a situation like this.

Having received her drink, she moved off to find a table. Deliberately, she looked around her as she went – making a show of looking like she was looking. So that, if anyone was looking, they would see...

Sure enough, in a corner by an antiquated fruit machine of some sort, sat a couple who seemed alert to comings and goings. Alice's eyes flicked across theirs, held the woman's gaze for a significant second... She sat down and took a glug of her vodka and tonic. She play-acted looking in her handbag for this and that, scrolled through her phone, ate up a couple of authenticity-lending minutes. Then, led by a kind of instinct, she got up and headed for the ladies. A flicker of concern crossed her mind about her bags of shopping, but she'd just have to chance it. The woman seemed to acknowledge her with a faint movement of the head as she passed. She seemed to be on the right track!

She went into a cubicle and sat on the seat, her heart pounding. This was weirdly scary, weirdly exciting. She heard the door to the ladies open, close. A soft cough. A running tap...

Alice quickly flushed the toilet and came out of the cubicle. Yes, it was the woman. Girl, really. Early twenties probably. Tough looking, thin, pale. She was puckering her narrow lips in the mirror and dabbing at her cheeks with a puff. A cheap make-up case lay unzipped.

As Alice moved to a basin to wash her hands, the girl turned to her and said quickly: "Are you looking for something? If you get my *meaning*."

Alice nodded. The girl stepped away and into a cubicle, produced a packet of what Alice could immediately see was Mng from the thin jacket she was wearing. Alice moved forwards, readying her cash inside her pocket. The girl held her phone up, right into Alice's face – she had opened the calculator and entered 100 in big figures.

In a couple of seconds, the exchange was done and Alice found herself stumbling out of the loos. The girl's partner was standing outside the door – presumably prepared to block or hold up anyone going in there while the deal took place.

She sat down at her table and realised she was shaking. She downed the rest of her vodka, wishing that she'd asked for a double. Her bags, she was glad to see, were still there. Well, there was no point in hanging around. She got up and went to the bar; ordered another vodka (neat); downed it in one draught; and exited swiftly without looking back.

Then she ordered a taxi through her phone; only two minutes to wait. Carefully, she eyed the packet that was nestled inside her handbag. Yes, it was genuine, sealed. 64 of the sweet little things would be packed tightly inside. She'd been having one as soon as she got in…

Alice found herself garrulous in the taxi, buoyed by adrenaline and anticipation. She was talking a load of nothing, about the weather, about congestion in Knott, whatever passed through her head. The driver didn't say much back – he was one of those quiet ones – but that didn't matter. The point was simply to get back; talking seemed to speed the turning of the wheels.

Once inside her flat, she wasted no time. Straight into the bathroom, where with hands atremble she tore open the packet and popped out a shiny yellow pill. It looked like a little sweet... In it went, slurped down with water, some of which in her haste dribbled down her chin. Oh, she was an embarrassment, was she not?! She signalled her disapproval by avoiding her eyes in the mirror.

It would take about an hour before the magic started to happen. She pulled down the blinds in the living room and fell onto the sofa, tired from the shopping and sleepy from alcohol. You weren't supposed to mix Mng and alcohol, but she had never found it to be a problem. In fact, a couple of drinks added to the pleasurable vibes. She stretched herself out and it wasn't long before she fell into a doze, warm and close and fuzzy. She wished she'd opened the window. She should get up to open the window. But she was pincered and held there on the sofa, in this sticky well of sleep... Kevan Monk was there, somewhere in the shadows, like a toad, beady-eyed, watching – but so too was Lewis. So that was better. She shifted in the well, looking for the best position. Then, water was running. Sweat into her eyes. At last, she managed to wrench herself up into a sitting position. She raised the blind and opened the window, letting in warm curls of air. Then she went to the bathroom and stripped down and freshened up, splashing water on her body.

Cooler again, she thought she could feel the warmth beginning. Yes, here it was. It was the codeine beginning to act, spreading a warmth along her limbs, smoothing away the edges of things. It was so lovely, so relaxing, this soft internal infusion…

She sat down, now in her silky pyjama shorts and top, and waited. A smile opened on her face as she expected the moment when the metals of the earth, magnesium and zinc, would kick in…

And here it was! Yes, here it was – this popping of the mind, like the pushing of a reset button, causing a wonderful, clear-edged refresh; this opening up and stepping through, this passing across an unseen boundary, into a new and rare and precious zone.

She looked around the zone – a place where suddenly everything was so focused, so full, so real. Her living room, now, was a place where she really was *living*. She was alive, organic, pulsing… Her thoughts were incredibly clear, translucent. It was like the warm, crystal waters of the Caribbean or the Aegean, compared to the cold and turgid North Sea…

Nothing had changed, but everything had changed. It was an almost mystical transformation. Now, just sitting on the sofa in her living room was a significant act imbued with meaning. *Everything* had meaning! This was why they called it Mng of course – a half-play on magnesium backed up by the product strapline of *"A supplement for enhanced meaning"*. Still, she was surprised the regulator had allowed it. It surely set a bad precedent, opening the door for prescription drugs to become hijacked by marketing and spin and branding. But there it was – done now.

Oh, this was *gooood*! Now, there was no need for anything to be justified by a point or a purpose – just being was purpose enough. Consciousness was a cup filled to the brim...

She could sit here – for hours! – and thrill to this sense of wholeness, completeness, *density*. Things had weight and substance; her mind, her perceptions, were hard and solid and sharp. It would rise to a peak over the next hour and then, although gently subsiding, would stay with her in the background for hours to come...

So Alice sat, thrilling to her state, doing nothing. Eventually she did get up, and moved out onto the small balcony she was lucky to have as the sun went down. She felt as though, just by sitting there, she was participating in the sunset herself. She was involved in the deepening of the light, the lengthening of the shadows, the echoing trills of the birds that hymned it... Almost, she could cry. Almost, she could let a tear slide down her cheek at the beauty of the evening and her mind's involvement *within* it, stitched into the fabric of its airy insides.

But she didn't *need* the sunset. There was the same meaningfulness everywhere. So, in fact, she went back in before the show was done and got a snack and a cold drink and turned on the TV. She flicked across the channels as darkness deepened outside and night took over.

It didn't matter what she watched – it was the consciousness sharp and alive inside her that was important. It didn't have words but, if it did, she felt that what it would say would quite simply be: "I *am*!" Perhaps, she thought, those were all the words that, translated, we ever speak…

Time passed without her even realising it. All of a sudden, it was nearly midnight. She wondered whether Lewis would come…

As she watched an old music programme – bands from the eighties; so long ago but, there in front of her eyes, still so present – she began to fall into a pleasant drowsiness. The peak had passed. She just felt a satiated repleteness and relaxation. Her eyes began to close…

Then the intercom sounded. She jumped up, instantly recalled to the moment. It was almost 1am. Lewis had come, and she was ready for him.

2.

When Lewis woke up, for a second he wasn't sure where he was. Then it all came back to him, with a sweet rush of recollection...

He glanced over at Alice who was still fast asleep. She looked as lovely and desirable as ever, her long limbs splayed over the thin sheets, her hair an artistic fan on the pillow. She breathed slowly, deeply, as though carefully constructing the answer to a question. He smiled down at her, a little gift she'd never know she'd received.

It had been a good night. She had certainly been *on* it! Lewis had happily gone with the flow, counting his extraordinary blessings. The month they had spent apart hadn't been fun. He had missed her so much and now, all of sudden, they were back together again. It seemed. You could never quite be sure, with Alice. She was unpredictable, strong willed. She'd do what she wanted. Had she seen anyone else during their separation? He couldn't rule it out...

He wouldn't get upset about that, and he wouldn't probe. He didn't want to look jealous. That would make her feel restricted. He knew that she liked him. Clearly, she had some feelings. Just go with it then, and let it move in its own direction.

It was after eight o'clock. Lewis got up, went to the toilet and then into the kitchen. It didn't take long to go anywhere in Alice's flat. He closed the kitchen door so that the kettle boiling wouldn't wake her in the bedroom.

He made himself a cup of tea and then went through to the living room and out onto the tiny balcony, where there was just enough room for two chairs. It was in the shade at that hour. He sat and surveyed the peaceful Sunday morning. It was going to be another hot and sunny day by the look of it. He wondered whether Alice had any plans... He had no real plans of his own.

A shadow caressed his head. He turned and there was Alice in the doorway. "Morning, early riser!" she said. She took his hand and gently pulled him in...

Later on, they made breakfast together, albeit only cereal and toast because Alice didn't have much in. (She never seemed to have much in; she had no interest in cooking.)

"So, how have you been?" she asked him. "We've hardly even chatted!"

"Yeah, I mean, OK... It was a nice surprise to hear from you yesterday."

"It was probably the shock of running into your glorious leader."

"Kevan Monk? Really? Where'd you see him?"

"At the clinic. I went in to do some admin. Him and Eric were having a little one-to-one meeting."

"On a Saturday?"

"Yeah. Have you heard anything, at work?"

"What do you mean?"

"Kevan said the regulator has told him they're launching a review of Mng. Due to its addictive qualities."

"No, really!" Lewis lowered his loaded spoon from his mouth. "Not heard anything about that."

"I think Kevan had only just been told himself, on the Friday probably. So it was a kind of emergency meeting with Eric. I guess he'll tell you internally at SmartLab this week. Please keep absolutely shtum about it until he says something."

"Of course. But, jeez... So, what did he say?"

"He played it down. You know – just a PR exercise by the regulator, nothing to worry about. The addiction problem only affects a minority, benefits hugely outweigh the drawbacks. That sort of thing. His main concern seemed to be managing the media when the news breaks."

"Yeah, well that will be crucial of course. Looks like I'll have a busy week then!" Lewis worked in the marketing team – and there were only four of them. Then he seemed to rally. "But there's nothing to be worried about, is there? Overall, Mng is a brilliant product. So, it's all good." Lewis believed in SmartLab, Kevan Monk, Mng.

"Well, you know what I think, Lewis. The regulator *should* be reviewing. There's so much Mng dependence around. It's an epidemic."

"Yeah but, Mng and all the others, Alice! They're *all* addictive – from bloody OxyContin down! Lots of other drug classes are too – anti-depressants, other types of painkiller. I mean, where do you start – and why Mng??"

"There's a window for them to do something about Mng because it's so new. More thoroughly weigh the benefits against the downsides. Make the guidance around it more restrictive. There's definitely a need, Lewis. It's spreading so fast."

"No, I'm with Kevan on this," Lewis said, pointing his spoon into the air, seemingly at evidence. "It's the regulator wanting to look tough, score some PR points. Nothing will come of it. There's a lot of backing for Mng. At the highest levels, I mean. I know that for a certainty."

"Because Kevan's told you?"

"Because *he's* been told. In senior level meetings. Whitehall, and so on."

"Oh, the corridors of power, hey?"

"Yes, the corridors of power! They do actually exist, Al."

"Well, I still have my doubts. They didn't need to announce anything… And there's so much of it around, Lewis! It's supposed to be prescription-only. So where's it all coming from?"

"That's a different issue. Distribution, logistics…"

"I have patients who've got hold of it. They say you can just find it on the streets. How is that happening? Something's not right…"

"Yeah, I admit, that *is* a puzzle."

Alice sat forward and looked directly into Lewis' eyes. "Can you look into it, Lou? There must be something you can find out at work? Distribution records or, I don't know, commercial agreements, supply chain information? There's a *hole* somewhere, and Mng is pouring out of it!"

Lewis looked non-plussed. "Ummm… I don't know Alice! What could *I* find out? I'll have a think."

"Please do, Lewis. Please do. Like I say, something isn't right. Something doesn't add up. And people are getting addicted as a result. While – sorry to say it – SmartLab is getting richer."

"Richer?!" Lewis snorted. "That's all relative, Alice. You know how much goes to the private equity investors?"

"All the more reason to pump out as many pills as possible then."

"Ha ha! I'll tell Kevan about your concerns."

"In your next one-to-one catch up, you mean?"

"Miaow," Lewis said with a grin. "I know I'm junior. But I'll make my way up the greasy pole in good time."

"Yes, but at SmartLab?"

The question hung in the air between them. Lewis got up from the table to make the toast…

It was an old bone of contention. Alice wanted to leave Clear Minds and make a new start somewhere else, probably London. But Lewis didn't want to give up his job at SmartLab. Where did that leave them? It had been a major factor in Alice's cooling off period.

"For now, yes," he mumbled. What could he say? He owed so much to SmartLab. To Kevan. They had given him a chance when he had still been at a low ebb. He wanted to repay that. And he was learning and developing all the time. It was too soon to think about leaving.

They had taken him on at the end of the wilderness years of his twenties. That had followed the trauma of his late teens – when his best friend had died from a bad tab he had taken at a party. That tab should have been taken by *him*. But Dan had begged him, offered to pay him over the odds, and had swallowed it himself... So it should have been Lewis that went, but Dan had taken his place. Poor innocent Dan. His cheeky, fun-loving, madcap best mate. It should have been him! Not *him*. It was a sacrifice Lewis didn't deserve. From which, even, he had made a profit. How disgusting was that?

The investigation, by the police and by his parents, and Dan's parents, and his school – all of that lay across him like a deep scar. He wasn't sure he'd ever get over it. He had retreated into his shell. He hadn't applied to university. He'd just stayed at home, under the shield of his confused, disturbed, loving parents, and done nothing. He went to the weekly counselling sessions that his parents had arranged for him. He didn't go out. He didn't drink or take drugs. He lived a life of lonely, sober self-loathing. Eventually, he'd got himself a job. Just stacking shelves and loafing around in a supermarket. A suitably nothing occupation. But he'd been able over time to save enough money to eventually move out. He'd rented a room in a shared house. Left the supermarket eventually and drifted into another crap job. Six months later, another.

But time does, slowly, heal. His counselling sessions stopped after a few years, his therapist judging him to have made good progress. Lewis himself was pleased to let them go. He'd found that, in fact, counselling almost held him back rather than helping him. Because somehow he had less incentive to get over things and push himself back into the world when he knew that he could hide in his shell and then spill it all out again to his therapist. The sessions were like a buffer that protected him. Stripping them away had actually been part of his recovery. Maybe that was the psychologist's cunning plan all along…?

By his late twenties, he hadn't exactly come to terms with the tragedy, but he saw that he shouldn't let it curse his whole life. In his sessions at Dan's grave (he had never been able to give those up – they were like therapy embedded into actual real life), he talked it through obsessively with him under his breath. And eventually one day decided that the signs Dan was sending – the rising spiral of those dead leaves blowing along the path, the hopping of that crow, this shaft of weak sun on Dan's headstone – were telling him to at least try to move on.

He began to look around him more. He began to mix more with the people in the house he shared. And he looked at more substantial jobs – one of which was for a marketing assistant at SmartLab. Kevan Monk himself had interviewed him. He interviewed for most non-operational roles in fact, the company consisting of less than two hundred people. Lewis liked that about him. There was lots, in fact, he liked about Kevan. Starting with the fact that he had given Lewis a chance.

"It's a junior role, Lewis. A starter role. But I think it will be good for you. I think it's what you need," Kevan had said, with those strangely piercing eyes of his. It was as though he could see right inside Lewis, right in to his real self – and was taking him on nonetheless.

Over the last two years, Lewis had got into the role and indeed had been promoted. Now he was number three of four instead of four of four. Progress!

It wasn't long after starting there that he'd met Alice. Needless to say, his twenties had been a romantic desert. After the various wild seeds he'd sown during his chaotic teens. So he was badly out of touch, out of time. But somehow, she seemed to be attracted to him. Maybe it was pity or a mothering instinct or something? She certainly liked to be in charge. And she was. She was also a couple of years older than him, which seemed to reinforce it. Somehow, age always seemed significant. At least until you turned forty or something. Whatever, he was happy with it that way. He was besotted with her. He was in love with her, he guessed he'd say…

So, his life had actually begun to properly turn itself around. He enjoyed his job and he had a beautiful, clever, fascinating girlfriend. He didn't deserve it, but it was where he was. He still visited Dan regularly and explained and wrestled and listened. He felt that he had Dan's blessing. Incredible, supernatural Dan. He liked to think that under the ground lay the huge, wordless wisdom of the dead, which Dan had become a part of. A consolation, of sorts...

But, now, just when he felt he was turning a corner, Alice kept talking about moving away, finding other jobs. Lewis couldn't leave Knott, not yet, maybe not ever. He'd have to keep visiting Dan. He didn't *want* to leave, anyway. He may have been submissive, but he could also be stubborn!

"Well, I'm planning on starting a proper job search," Alice threw out. "I've already seen one in London I'm gonna go for. There are a couple of recruitment consultants I'm going to register with too."

Lewis shrugged as he waited for the toast to pop. What could he do? "OK, if that's what you've decided..." he said.

"But while you *are* at SmartLab, Lewis, please can look into all this? There must be something you can turn up."

"I don't know what you're expecting to find. But yeah, I'll talk to someone in Distribution as a starter. There are monthly sales sheets I think I can access too."

"Brilliant! Thank you Lewis. You never know, there might be *something*. I can't just stand around while people up and down the country are getting addicted."

"No worries. I agree it's a concern. Of course I do. But it's just one more addiction amongst a whole sea of them at the end of the day. That's my point really."

"Doesn't mean we shouldn't try to do something about it."

"What about you? Are you still, you know, taking it regularly?"

"Oh, on and off," Alice lied. "Yeah, I take it now and again. Not that I really *need* it. Just because it gives you a good feeling."

"That's what every addict says!" Lewis blurted. Then he quickly added, "Sorry! I didn't mean that *you* are an addict, Al. You know…!"

Alice leaned back and exhaled exaggeratedly. "Watch your step boy!"

She said it jokily and didn't seem fazed – but nevertheless, the atmosphere between them had fallen. They spread jam on their toast and munched in silence.

"Anyway, what plans for today?" Alice asked. "I need to do some food shopping this morning. I could drop you home on the way if you'd like?"

"Oh… sure, thanks." He masked his disappointment. Something that had been discussed but then dropped provided him with a quick answer. "Yeah, I promised I'd help Gav this afternoon tidying up the garden, cutting the grass and that. Not much else."

"Cool. Well, you can catch some sun while you do it, have a beer or two…"

"Exactly. And probably a barbie this evening. You?"

"I'm going to Glastonbury this afternoon. With Chloe. Bit more work to do this evening though."

"Poor you. Still, if you *will* be a high-powered professional and all that..."

They carried on with a general pleasantness, but were both aware that they were holding each other at a distance. Getting back together seemed to be a little like skimming stones across water – it took a few bounces before things came to rest.

Alice drove Lewis home mid-morning. It wasn't far – only ten minutes – but they lived in very different surroundings. Alice's flat was in a block in its own grounds, mainly inhabited by young professionals and families. Lewis lived in a terraced house amongst narrow streets that were home to students, low-paid workers and assorted drifters.

They pulled up a little in advance of Lewis' place, taking advantage of a parking space.

Alice turned a smile onto her boyfriend. "Good to see you again, sweetie! See you again soon, yeah?"

"Of course. One evening this week?"

"Sure. We can decide your place or mine etcetera..."

She leaned forward and gave him a warm and tender kiss.

"You can come in now if you want!" Lewis croaked.

"I'm afraid we've both got jobs to do my dear! Why don't we say… Tuesday? Not sure I'll be able to wait any longer."

"Ha, me too! OK then gorgeous." They kissed again – then Lewis levered himself out into the rising heat of the cramped city street.

He whistled on the short walk to his door, gave a warm wave to Alice as she moved off past him. It had been a confusing morning. He didn't understand Alice, women, relationships. It was a constant swinging to and fro, an oscillation on a weird frequency. Maybe what he'd do today was pay a visit to Dan, try to tune into all that wisdom stored on the other side of the grave.

3.

The murder that shook Knott was discovered early on the following Sunday morning.

It was shortly before 6am when Martha Gonzalez pulled into the Dark Lane car park. This was a very small facility – with room for only 30 cars – that was somehow little known about and usually had spaces. It seemed to have escaped notice and avoided change over the years, tucked away as it was off a minor side street in between other bigger roads. A small enclosure behind crumbling stone walls, with faded markings and outbreaks of weeds, it seemed to be a place the council itself had forgotten. There had been no modernisation, no electric charge points installed – but it was only a five minute walk to the hospital where Martha worked in the kitchens, and it was free parking on a Sunday.

Sure enough, there was plenty of room. Martha parked up and stepped out into the damp morning air. It was dull and overcast – would it rain later, or would it clear away to become yet another hot sunny day? No matter, she'd be shut up in the kitchen until mid-afternoon anyway.

Walking briskly towards the exit, she suddenly noticed a pair of feet sticking out from under a car near the payment machine. Was someone fixing their vehicle? A mobile mechanic perhaps? But the feet and legs looked anything but mobile… Oh! She smiled to herself. Probably someone who'd had too much to drink last night and was sleeping it off. Dead drunk! She tutted indulgently. Then, stopping by the car – old, rusted, scarred – something really didn't feel right. She noticed dark staining on the tarmac, glistening angry clouds... She got down on her knees, as though to pray, and peered, trembling, under the vehicle... A second later, her cries bounced against the closed sky and she stumbled up and away, feverishly crossing herself.

It wasn't long before the car park was a crime scene, taped off and tented. The whole of Dark Lane was sealed off. Multiple police cars sat with their lights silently flashing. Two ambulances. Officers and forensics teams. Her statement taken, a weeping Martha was given a lift home from the shift she'd never make.

Murder was a rarity in Knott. Not much of any note happened there, in truth. Technically a city due to its small cathedral (and, more lately, its agricultural college which had expanded to become a university-level Centre for the Study of Sustainability and Climate Change), it nevertheless had a population of only 30,000. So it was Britain's second smallest city after its nearby neighbour of Wells (population just 10,000). Knott lay ten miles east of its more famous cousin, and about the same from Glastonbury. The three places formed a triangle that some deemed of mystical significance, although it wasn't clear exactly how. But the majority of any mysticism that floated in the mid-Somerset air remained centred on Glastonbury with its Holy Grail, its Holy Thorn, its famous Tor. Knott had nothing to rival those. In fact, its main fame was as a spillover for accommodation during the mayhem of the Glastonbury festival.

But back to murder. Those that did take place in and around the city of Knott were usually by crazed, sadistic men in domestic disputes. This one was clearly different. The victim was a man in his forties. Stabbed multiple times in the back and side, deep slashes through his thin shirt. Then, it seemed, pushed under the car while the blood poured out of him like oil. No ID, no wallet, no phone.

Was this his car that he had been stowed under? A search of DVLA records showed the owner was a Martin Silverwood with a registered address, sure enough, in Knott. His photo on the Passport Office system showed a near-certain match…

By mid-morning, Detective Inspector Jim Sharp and Police Constable Ayesha Kaur were on their way to the address. Sharp chewed his gum irritably. He had been just about to set off to watch Somerset play a one-dayer in Taunton when he'd had the call. He'd been looking forward to that game. He'd put in a full claim for overtime and expenses all right.

Mind you, he liked to spend a bit of time with young PC Kaur. Pretty girl. Young. Malleable. Learning. As old and cynical as he was, he liked to try to teach the new generation coming into the force. Pass on the knowledge and all that. He glanced down – she had good legs in those trousers, too.

"So, what are you thinking, PC Kaur?"

"Sir?"

"About what we know so far. What we've got to go on."

"Well, sir – we shouldn't even try to draw any conclusions yet. Too early. Not enough evidence."

"No. But still – no wallet? No phone?"

"No, sir."

"So… points towards robbery, wouldn't you say?"

"It's amongst the range of possibilities, sir?"

Christ, she was young and textbook! He nodded, chewed harder. "So we think there's a wife?"

"Yes sir, from the electoral records."

"Assuming it wasn't her wot done it – although of course, we have to keep that within your 'range of possibilities' – this will be one hell of a shock."

"Yes, sir. If that is the case. Poor lady… I shudder to think of it…"

Her nickname at the station was 'Hard Kaur' but DI Sharp knew that she had plenty of softness and compassion to her. She had been a good choice for the assignment.

They pulled up at the house – a faded looking semi. In need of some TLC. Aka, money. This wasn't a wealthy area. The car had been, what? fifteen years old. No. The dimes they had not been a-flowing for Martin Silverwood esquire…

"OK then. Let's do this, constable," he said, spitting his gum out as they got out of the car. "Nice and easy does it…"

There was a short, cracked path through a ragged front garden. Mournful, grimy-looking front door. DI Sharp rang on the bell. But it didn't seem to work. He rapped on the door, a little harder than intended. They stood and waited... It took a good minute before there was a rattling of the lock and the door opened.

A small, slight woman in her early forties stood in front of them. Her eyes were drawn by PC Kaur's police uniform.

"Mrs Silverwood?" DI Sharp asked politely. She nodded. "I'm Detective Inspector Sharp and this is Police Constable Kaur, from Knott Police. I wonder whether we could come in to talk to you about an important matter?" Almost apologetically, they showed their badges.

"Is it Martin? It's Martin..." she said. "What's happened?"

"Why don't we go inside and sit down, Mrs Silverwood? We can talk about it better inside," Sharp said gently.

"Right. OK." The woman backed inwards, letting them step across the threshold. She led them down a musty hallway with peeling wallpaper, before turning right into the living room.

Or at least, they *assumed* it was the living room. There was almost no furniture in it – just two old wooden chairs, a small TV on a rickety display unit, and books in piles around the floor.

"Let me get another chair. I do apologise. Not really set up for..." Mrs Silverwood mumbled, then disappeared out of the room. Sharp and Kaur exchanged glances. They stood, for the moment, at the side of the chairs, like awkward sentries.

Mrs Silverwood came in with another old wooden chair. They sat in a little triangle.

"Mrs Silverwood," DI Sharp began, clearing his throat. "I'm afraid we may have some bad news. When was the last time you saw your husband?"

"Yesterday. He was in the house. Then he went out in the evening. What's happened?"

"Do you know where he went? Did you speak to him?"

"No. But it was probably to the casino. That's where he spends a lot of his night times, I think."

"But you don't know for sure?"

"I'm afraid not. We... don't talk much, officer. We are estranged really."

She spoke with effort, as though she were infinitely tired and this was the limit of what she could manage. "Why? What have you... What's happened?"

"Mrs Silverwood, I'm afraid that a man has been found this morning. In a car park in the centre of Knott. He was lying next to the car that is registered to your husband. The man was deceased. I'm so sorry to say..."

PC Kaur lifted her chair and moved it next to Mrs Silverwood. She squeezed the woman's hand. They sat for a minute as Mrs Silverwood fumbled for a tissue from her sleeve.

"We need you to come with us, Mrs Silverwood," PC Kaur said gently. "For a formal identification. Do you think you'd be able to do that?"

Jane Silverwood nodded her head. A tear began to run down her cheek. She looked like someone who was already used to living with grief. "How did he...?" she whispered.

"I'm afraid it was a stabbing. I'm so sorry. We strongly believe it is Martin. We wouldn't have come if not. But we need a formal identification," PC Kaur said.

Jane leaned back, letting out a long breath, and held her hands against her eyes, shutting out the light. "Oh, Lord. Oh, Martin!" she cried. "We lived like strangers but still... but still... I loved him... I used to love him. I loved him..."

The tears began to come. PC Kaur put an arm around her. DI Sharp sat stoically, looking around the room. He wondered whose the books were. Then he got up and went to find the kitchen. It was a kitchen-cum-dining room – similarly bereft of furniture in the dining area: one very small round table and one chair, sitting in empty space. How did they live like this?

He brought a glass of water back in and handed it with a supportive grunt to Jane. "When you're ready, Mrs Silverwood," he said. "When you're ready. There's no hurry."

She sipped at the water. "A stabbing, you say? A stabbing! Oh, poor Martin. It's unbelievable. Who would… Why would…?"

"He had no wallet on him. No phone either. Would he usually have those on him?" DI Sharp asked. She nodded. "There's a possibility that was the motive, Mrs Silverwood. We shouldn't speculate… But maybe he had won some money at the casino?"

"That would make a change!" Jane said with a snort.

"Maybe you could try calling him? Just in case…" DI Sharp suggested.

Jane got her feet and went to get her phone. Then she took a deep breath and dialled. A second later: "Straight to voicemail," she said.

"Could we take down the number actually?"

Jane held up her phone and PC Kaur wrote the number in her notebook. "Did you try phoning him at all last night?" she asked.

Jane shook her head. "I spoke to him briefly… yesterday in the afternoon, I think it was. In the kitchen. We spend most of the time in different rooms. Mostly upstairs."

"Did he seem OK yesterday? And recently in general? Anything wrong, worried about anything?" PC Kaur questioned softly.

"It's difficult to say, officer. We spoke so little. I would say he has been pretty much as usual recently. Drunk most evenings, passive-aggressive, you know..." She gave a wan smile.

"Oh really? Did he – does he – work?"

"Yes. Health & safety officer at the council."

"Knott Council? OK..." PC Kaur wrote that down. "So, was he usually out at work in the week, in the daytimes? He was. I see..."

"Well then," DI Sharp cut in, "perhaps we'd better get going? If you feel ready, of course, Mrs Silverwood?"

They got up and Jane Silverwood gathered a couple of things. Then they led her out and into the police car outside, while neighbours twitched at the net curtains...

*****

A couple of hours later, a car dropped Jane back. She walked slowly into the house, then drifted like a ghost into the kitchen where she sat down on the chair. The other one was still in the living room, but she wouldn't be needing that. It was just her now...

Oh, Martin! What an end, so horrible...! No one deserved that. What a hideous, vile, unspeakable thing. The poor man. She had loved him once, he had loved her.... And now, all of a sudden, from nowhere, he'd been brutally torn out of his life. Left to die, in a car park, gurgling out his blood. Who could imagine what that was like? Her hope was that the shock was so great, and the bleeding so rapid, that he had quickly passed out of consciousness. Maybe, in fact, he had barely felt a thing after the first stabbings. Had lain there in a weird kind of sleep until his soul had slipped away.

He looked like he was asleep anyway, when she had seen him on the slab. They had done a good job of composing his features. There was a kind of serenity. Did that come to all of us when we finally move beyond the physical life dumb show?

Stephen.

She was drained from the tears she had shed over the last few hours, cleaned out, empty. She wiped at her face and got up to turn the kettle on for a cup of tea. She needed something. She hadn't eaten anything all day. As usual, she was hungry, but not hungry. Why, how, should she care about feeding herself? Tea would do, a biscuit. If biscuits there were. Were there? There were.

Tea then. Biscuit.

She turned on her trusty portable radio. An antique from about 2000. She always had her radio on. Noise in the background. She'd carry it around with her in the house. She didn't mind what it was – music modern or classical, news, talk show, radio play, adverts. She'd randomly twiddle with the frequency and find something that appealed in the moment. Today it was – a commemoration service for something from somewhere. That seemed to fit. *The day thou gavest, Lord, is ended*... She began to cry again, sobbing into her clump of wet tissues.

She would have to pull herself together, though, that she knew. There would be so much to do, now. A funeral to arrange. People to tell. She'd have to phone Martin's parents. Or his sister. One of them would do. Work as well, she supposed. Neighbours. Other things – bills, finances. The thought of it all made her faint.

Not because she didn't *want* to do it. They may have argued, and fought, and hated each other but of course he deserved a proper funeral. Of course she'd get it done. And honour his memory. But where the energy would come from – that she didn't know.

What did energy feel like? It had become something she only briefly knew when passion flared up against Martin. Otherwise, she couldn't remember. Otherwise, she just felt so tired in body and soul. Energy belonged to that time before. That different life, that was gone.

Stephen.

She made her tea and sipped at it, chewed dutifully through her biscuit. She would have to steel herself to phone either his parents or his sister soon…

Poor Martin! Poor, bad-tempered, alcohol-soaked, gambling-addled Martin. It had been his way of dealing. Needless to say. So in a way it wasn't his fault. He hadn't been like that before.

What do you do when the meaning drops out? When the bottom suddenly has no bottom? When suddenly there is all-consuming pain and nothing to live for?

That had been Martin's way of dealing. Her way of dealing had been to become a shadow of herself. To withdraw, turn away, to lay herself down inside herself and let the mourning flow. Grief is a river that never runs dry.

That's how she had been for five years now. While Martin had blustered and floundered and raged. He'd barely held down his job with all his hangovers and bad tempers. But he'd managed to keep it, at least. So he could piss and spin all the money away in the night times. And then slowly sell off all their furniture and possessions for additional stake money and to pay back loans.

She hadn't put up a fight about it. What did she care about furniture, now? In a sense, she wasn't in a position to resist anyway, seeing as she'd never returned to her teaching job and brought in little more than pocket money from her cleaning work.

Initially, there had been mutually shared grief, tears, agony. For a few months, they were closer than ever. But slowly, as the dead sickness set in, a widening channel grew between them, until they didn't know each other anymore. Until they deeply annoyed each other, to the point of screaming hatred and shouting on the landing and sleeping in separate rooms.

For the last three years, they'd lived like strangers. Tenants in a house neither wanted to live in (but couldn't leave). Ghosts in the same cage.

Stephenn.

4.

Alice and Lewis were lying at opposite ends of the sofa, twiddling their feet in each other's faces as they spooned ice cream from their bowls. They had half-watched the news, as almost everyone did in those days. The procession of political dogfights, international flashpoints, climate change emergencies and disasters, extremist crimes, hate movements, domestic murders, rapes, child stabbings, abuse, neglect, racism, mental breakdown, mass suicides, rocketing costs, unemployment and unaffordable homes – became rather too much for anyone.

When the local news came on after the national bulletin, Alice was about to turn it off. "Wait a minute, let's watch it," Lewis said. "There'll probably be something about that murder."

"What murder?" Alice asked. She didn't have to wait long – it was top item. It was quite a short report, however, given that there wasn't much to go on. Martin Silverwood, aged 46, council worker, had been found brutally stabbed to death in Knott early on Sunday morning. Police were working to establish his movements that night. A grim-faced, old-school looking officer called Detective Inspector Jim Sharp appeared on screen appealing for anyone with information to come forward. He said that Mr Silverwood was believed to have spent some time at the Regency Casino on Market Parade that night. They were working to establish how long he had been there, and where else he had been. Martin had been found in Dark Lane car park. DI Sharp was particularly interested in anyone who had seen Mr Silverwood between midnight and 2am on Sunday morning. Enquiries were ongoing.

"That's the one!" said Lewis. "People were talking about it at work today. That guy was an inspector at the council. Apparently he inspected both SmartLab sites a few weeks ago. He was a real arse, they said."

Meanwhile, Alice was lost in a little cloud of her own. She closed her eyes, thinking. "You know what? I think he was a patient of mine. Maybe two years ago? Perhaps three? Martin Silverwood... I'll have to look up my records tomorrow. I'm pretty certain. Oh my God, the poor guy. He only came for a few sessions I think. His baby son had died. Grief, depression etcetera..."

"The usual tricks of your trade."

"Err, I try to *cure* them. Instead of manufacturing chemicals that make them worse."

Alice went on her phone to see what more she could find. There was a slightly fuller story on *Knott News*. When she saw his photo – fleshy-faced, hang-jowled, a lick of dark hair across his forehead – she knew it was him.

Married but with no children, the story informed readers, Martin had spent most of the night in the Regency Casino where he was believed to be a regular customer. The health & safety inspector, who had been employed at Knott Council for over a decade, had left at circa 1am. It was not known whether he went directly from there to his car. Regrettably, there was no CCTV along Dark Lane or in the car park itself – something the council had been promising to rectify for several years. Death was thought to have occurred in the 1-2am timeframe. Searches around the area were continuing. The car park was expected to be closed for another couple of days. There were several alternative car parks nearby, including Green Street and Wincanton Square. It was thought that a particular focus of police searches was Martin's phone which had not been on his person but which he was believed to have had with him that night. Anyone with any information or who had seen Martin on Saturday night/Sunday morning should contact Knott Police on [XXX].

"So how was he an arse at SmartLab?" she asked Lewis.

"Well, apparently he was half-pissed for one thing. They could smell it on his breath. And I think he was just, you know, throwing his weight around. Demanding to see this document and that certification. And also stuff that didn't have anything to do with health and safety. Rubbed everyone up the wrong way, basically."

"And now he's dead."

"Yeah, I think people were feeling kind of guilty for bad-mouthing him!"

The next day in between patients Alice looked up her records. Here it was – she had seen Martin Silverwood around three years ago. He'd only come for six sessions. His son, Stephen, had died two years prior, just five months old. It was a case of 'cot death'. Completely out of the blue, they had put Stephen down one evening, checked on him at bed-time – and found him lifeless in the morning. It was a devastating tragedy, Martin said, that he and his wife Jane simply hadn't been able to come to terms with. Everything was ripped apart. They had had NHS counselling, but had recently been discharged. He was on anti-depressants. He had started drinking heavily. He had begun to smoke weed. He wouldn't lie, occasionally he did coke too. His wife Jane was also distraught, but at least she stayed off any substances. She was strong in that way. Although she wasn't outwardly strong because, formerly an English teacher in a secondary school, she had still not gone back to work. She couldn't face it, she said, she couldn't face the world when there was no meaning left. She had withdrawn completely. They had begun, increasingly, to argue. They had begun, indeed, to despise each other – stuck together in a curse and hating it.

Martin, Alice remembered, had been a proud man. Not one naturally given to talking. Of a large build, he would sit with slumped shoulders in his chair and mumble his feelings out almost unwillingly. But he knew he still needed help, so forced himself through the sessions. However, he really couldn't afford private counselling which was why, after six meetings, he had stopped coming. He wasn't a big earner at the council and Jane was earning nothing. He also mentioned gambling and online gaming – a habit, she surmised, that was just starting up and quite probably had got worse.

She wondered how else things had gone. Had Jane recovered, gone back to work? Had their marriage healed? It said in *Knott News* that there were no children.

Jane had been relatively old when she had Stephen, Martin had told her – nearly forty. After the first months of shock and despair, they had begun to try for another baby. But this raised all sorts of conflicts and traumatic emotions. Physical relations had broken down altogether. To both of them, the thought of another baby seemed part-blessing and part-betrayal. It seemed very unlikely there would ever be another, Martin said. So it seemed to have turned out...

Alice also saw in her notes that Martin said he'd recently opened a social media account, under the pseudonym SilverWolf, on the popular platform KittyWake. He thought this might help him, giving him a channel, as he said, that he could 'vent' in. She had observed at the time how his avatar name showed that he felt like a lone operator, an anti-hero protagonist in a hostile world.

She didn't have time in the office – but when she got home that evening, she looked up Martin's profile on KittyWake. This was one of the second generation social media platforms that had replaced the initial wave of the likes of Facebook, Twitter, Instagram and TikTok. Unlike most others, it was mainly text-based rather than multi-media and immersive. As such, it felt quite suited to Martin, who didn't strike her as an alternative reality or metaverse type person. KittyWake was popular with older users, even if, like every other platform, it was flooded with bots and AI and fake profiles. It really had become impossible to know who you were interacting with. AI could hold real time conversations full of quirks and tics and 'real person' oddities. Some iterations had been trained to lie with 100% conviction. If you asked them 'Are you a bot?', they would deny it without compunction.

This was why no one paid any attention to social media anymore. It was an entertainment, a pastime, a diversion. Which, of course, was how it had started out in the first place. Now, you could play some cool 3D games and pretend you were in a parallel universe; you could have fun meetings and interactions with people you actually knew; and meet others if you were careful and made sure they weren't a bot or a honey trap. But after social media's brief flirtation in the late 2010s and early 2020s as a serious messaging and influencing medium, that mirage had all but evaporated. Politicians, commentators, activists and pundits concentrated more on their own channels now and on the hyper-corridors between linked websites that was possible under the latest iteration of the internet.

Anyone with a serious point to make on social media found themselves shouting into the wind. It was indeed a wind tunnel, an echo chamber, a Pandora's box bringing the lid down on itself and its bloated blaring contents. As a result, anyone trying to peddle a message was forced to express it in ever more extreme terms in order to get noticed – which meant that most users ignored it even more. It was hopeless. Or rather, the clue really *was* in the name: it was media simply designed to be social...

True to his comment about venting, Martin didn't seem to have used it for the purposes of socialisation. He didn't have a photo in his profile, or post any photos; he didn't give any precise details about his personal life; and he only had a handful of connections. Most of his posts generated no interaction, had seemingly no traction. They were just shots into the void.

Alice scrolled back to his earliest posts (this didn't take long, because there weren't many of them) and it was clear from the outset that he had used KittyWake as a place for digital shouting. How depressed he was, how pissed he was, how much he hated everything. A couple of early entries were interesting:

"Not telling my wife or anyone else about my profile on here. SilverWolf is *top secret*. It's a secret between you and me, babe! Let the good times rolllll…"

"How I wish I hadn't started this online f***g gambling. What a prick. Pissing money away. Hope they choke on it. Maybe it tastes nice. What am I fucking talkkking about? What's wrong with me? Well – have another spin, hey? Maybe I'll win big and all will be forgiven. Forgiven… that's what we're all bloody seeking for, ness pa? #GambleResponsibly"

And one that had made Alice smile:

"Have given up my private therapy sessions, dahhling. Too f***g expensive. Can't afford it, mate. I mean, if I had enough money to afford private bloody counselling, I don't think I'd need counselling!!! #IronyAlert"

Martin had generally only posted a couple of times a month, with occasional more concentrated flurries, so it didn't take long to get towards the present. In truth, the entries were getting quite repetitive. Alice was beginning to lose interest – when a post from eight months ago caught her eye:

"Anyone else into Mng? I'm a fool, I know, but have started popping a few. Got offered, thought why not? I liiike it. Not a druggy high. But gives you a lovely, clear, concentrated feeling. Supposed to help wean people off their addictions apparently... Will it help me stop drinking or gambling? Doubt it. But hey, I'll go along for the ride ☐ #Mng"

This was followed about two months later by:

"Why, how, is there sooo much Mng on the streets? It's everywhere. Can't get away from the stuff! #Mng"

About another two months after that, Martin made another Mng-related post:

"Been trying to come off the Mng... The thing that's supposed to cure addictions is itself addictive! Brilliant, huh?! And f***g hell, it's hard. The low you get coming off it... Slammed between the eyes by a horrible, grim, monster emptiness. Couldn't handle it. Too depressing. So, took another tablet. Shelving the clean-up for now. #Mng"

Other assorted posts followed until around six weeks ago Martin had written this:

"Heyyyy, @SmartLab. How's it going! Pretty well, I expect. Sooo... why IS there so much #Mng everywhere? The explanation must surely lie with you? Let me know xxx"

That one really made Alice sit up... Even if, on checking, she found that SmartLab had no KittyWake account. Martin's @ went nowhere. There were a couple of likes but no follow-up posts or interactions that she could see.

When was it that Lewis said he had inspected SmartLab? A few weeks ago? Not long at all after this post...

Ah! Here was another one – from only two weeks ago:

"Fun Question: Why are there so many cans of coke in the world?

Answer: Because Coca Cola make a shedload and then distribute them!

Second Fun Question: Why is there so much #Mng in the world?

Answer: Use your f***g imagination, @SmartLab

Isn't it curious how a prescription drug that's only meant to be sold to GPs and hospitals is somehow ending up in the hands of dealers on the streets?? #JustSaying"

That one must have been posted after his SmartLab inspections. It had been Martin's penultimate post. Scrolling quickly upwards, his last one was in front of her now, dated ten days ago – less than a week before he died:

"Hi there, @SmartLab! How ya doing! What can you tell us about Primegate Pharmacy Supplies then? They your new best friends? Big kisses xxx #Mng"

The rest, as they say, was silence... A few days later, Martin lay stabbed to death on a car park's faded tarmac. Poor sod. Alice lingered on the text, re-reading it like a poignant epitaph. Martin would have had no idea as he typed it that it would be his last ever KittyWake entry...

Her heart beating hard, Alice looked up Primegate Pharmacy Supplies. But the drum beat began to settle: there was an unremarkable website – shots of an office building – some blurb about proudly supplying to independent pharmacies around the UK – a premium on value for money and quality of service – product pages – an interactive ordering facility – contact details, an address in Swindon. Dull as.

She sat back, her head spinning. What did this all mean? Was it just a coincidence that soon after Martin had started writing about SmartLab on social media (and physically inspecting their sites), he was dead?

Surely, the implication of what he had written was clear: he suspected SmartLab of distributing Mng themselves directly to a network of dealers and sellers. Which she had had some suspicions of herself. And which would have been completely illegal...

So what if, what if... Martin's posts had in fact come to SmartLab's attention? Or what if he'd even contacted them himself and confronted them with his suspicions?

And when she said 'them', she meant, of course, Kevan Monk... Martin would doubtless have gone straight to the top of the business. He'd want to confront the boss with it, not the workers.

From there, it was easy to imagine that he'd wielded whatever he knew – or thought he knew – as a threat. As blackmail. Clearly, he had financial difficulties, debts, a gambling habit to service…

Oh God, was this what the murder of Martin Silverwood was all about?! Or was she just losing the plot?

Come off it, Alice! What was she thinking? Kevan may have been objectionable but surely he wasn't a knife-slashing killer!

Was he?

And what was this about Primegate? There seemed to be nothing at all remarkable about the company. What had Martin been driving at?

No, she had to keep things in perspective here. Martin was a mess – an Mng addict, a gambling addict, a semi-alcoholic. A destroyed, bereaved father with a broken-down marriage. Full of grief, bitterness and anger. No one listened to him anyway. He had hardly any followers. No one was picking up on his messages or re-kittying them. He was shouting into the wind, a deranged drunken prophet. So why would Kevan Monk take any notice?

Well, he might do if it was all true… Imagine what he had to lose. If he was indeed illegally distributing Mng to generate more revenue so he could keep the show on the road (and also get a whole new raft of people hooked), he'd be ruined if it came out. SmartLab was the culmination of his life's work, he'd put everything into it. She knew he'd run various businesses through his twenties – mobile phones, gaming consoles – and then had switched to pharma when he'd amassed a pile. "The barriers are high – but the rewards can be off the scale," she remembered him saying to her once. Everything would come crashing down if he was unmasked. SmartLab would collapse, he'd go bankrupt, he'd probably go to prison. Personally, he had so much that he'd lose: his multi-million pound house in Knott, a swanky flat in Chelsea, a villa in Spain with a big shiny boat in the marina. He travelled around the world going to conferences and seminars, he holidayed in the Caribbean, Florida, Monaco. He hobnobbed with executives and influencers, he was featured in lists of the UK's top entrepreneurs. No, exposure was something he simply could not allow.

And of course he wouldn't have had to do the deed himself. Alice remembered various shady men who hung around Monk's place – associates of an unspecified nature, halfway between bodyguards and fixers for whatever he needed doing. Slip one of them a few grand in a brown envelope and she was sure that he could get almost any 'problem' removed…

But Christ, come on Alice! Would you listen to yourself, she asked? Surely it was far, far more likely that it was just a coincidence Martin had died after these posts. It was almost certainly just a robbery or some kind of psychopath attack. Martin had been horribly unlucky, the victim of a random crime. And why was she even thinking about it? It was for the police to work out, not her.

But – should she tell the police about these posts? No one knew of his Kittywake account as far as she knew. His posts would probably never come to light if she didn't come forward…

She needed to sleep on it all. Calmly reflect in the morning. Ah, it was almost certainly nothing…

Before she went to bed, however, she phoned Lewis.

"Hey babe… Look, I wanted to ask you another favour… There's a company called Primegate Pharmacy Supplies. I think they must buy Mng from SmartLab. Could you look into them? Anything you can find out. Are they a big customer, do they buy big volumes – that sort of thing?"

"Errm, sure. Why do you ask though?"

"Just a name I've come across. I've become kind of curious. Would that be OK?

"All right then. Name doesn't ring any bells, I have to say. Primegate Pharmacy Supplies? Leave it with me."

"Thanks, Lewis. Speak tomorrow evening? And you were going to find out about SmartLab's distribution more generally? Any joy with that?"

"Nah, it's been so hectic with this regulatory review being announced and all that! But I will, I promise."

"Cool. Thanks babe. Sweet dreams…"

Alice took herself off to bed, the darkness around her reverberating with all sorts of confused images of blister packs and car parks and frenzied blood-lust killings.

5.

There was no CCTV. They had no murder weapon. There were no fingerprints or DNA. They hadn't found Silverwood's mobile phone. They really had nothing to go on.

DI Sharp was not happy. He'd been planning on taking early retirement next year after thirty-five years in the force, fifteen in Knott. He didn't want to go out with a failure against his name in one of the highest profile murders seen in Knott for decades.

He'd already experienced the bitterness of a failure that was unfairly held against him earlier in his career, which had held him back ever since. He should have made Superintendent at least, Chief Superintendent, maybe even higher…

However, when he was an inspector in Leeds, attached to the narcotics unit, he'd led a case involving a drugs cartel. Everyone knew that Jimmy Bender was its leader, its mastermind. Everyone knew that he was running a cannabis ring and laundering the proceeds through various betting shops and car washes. There had been high confidence that he'd finally be brought to book after a carefully planned sting operation and coordinated dawn raid. But the case had never even come to court after Jimmy's lawyers found a technical breach of procedure with an informant that, they alleged, broke human rights and privacy law. It wasn't DI Sharp's fault – it wasn't even his part of the operation – but he'd been tarred with the failure simply because it was his case. There was an instant change in the weather around him; he could feel it and smell it. His career in Yorkshire fatally stalled.

That was when he'd moved down to Knott. His wife Mary hailed from the south west and her health had never been good. They decided a move to cleaner air and quieter surroundings would make sense. But while he'd become DI, that had proven to be his ceiling. The past was held against you, never fully forgotten. Once you took the rap for something, it was permanent. Those were the bloody breaks. So he'd ploughed on, minding his own business, getting the job done, towing the line. He tried not to think about the pay rises he hadn't had, the bigger bonuses he hadn't been given. Instead, he helped himself to the little side benefits of the job where he could, carefully inserted his fingers in various local pies…

He was determined that there wouldn't be another miss against his name, not now, not when he was so close to the finishing line, the saloon bar, the golf course. This case was looking tricky – he'd just have to make damn sure he turned something up.

The Superintendent was already pressing him. She had called him in for an update and grilled him. To be honest, he wouldn't mind her big hands on his balls – but not when they squeezed cold and hard like this.

"We need to provide a public update soonest," Superintendent Odutola said, sitting massy and grave behind her desk, silhouetted against the window. "I've had the Avon & Somerset Commissioner asking. What have you got, Jim?"

"Well ma'am, we're going flat out, looking at every angle."

"Such as?"

"There's no CCTV in the car park or along Dark Lane as you know, so that's obviously a hampering factor…"

"Yes, I've already discussed that with the Leader of the Council… But, spilt milk, Jim. What *update* do you have?"

"I've had divers in the river. Teams searching along the banks and surrounding area. Looking for the knife or other evidence such as the victim's phone. Nothing yet. We've been reviewing extensive amounts of CCTV footage around the city centre. And in the casino of course."

The Superintendent raised an eyebrow, waiting.

"We've established that Silverwood was there from 10pm until 1am. He ate. Played some slots, then roulette, then blackjack. Came out £200 up. He cashed that in and left shortly after 1. We've identified a couple of people who left shortly after him – although not *immediately* after – and are following up on that."

"And anyone who left shortly before, Inspector?"

"Yes, that too," he added quickly. (Note to self…). "I've personally interviewed the casino manager too, as well as staff who were working there on the night. Silverwood was a regular. But a small fish, small stakes. No one noticed anything untoward that night. He was there on his own. Just quietly gambling. Drank quite a lot too.

Would have been considerably over the limit if he *had* made it to his car, ma'am."

"Hmm! Well, let's not release *that* information. Disrespect to the victim and all that. But £200 you say… Not, I think, enough for a murder?"

DI Sharp shrugged. "Who knows. It might be enough for someone who was desperate. Who needed a fix. Or the killer may have thought it was a bigger amount than that."

"Yes…" The Superintendent leaned forward and moved a paperweight on her desk, thinking. DI Sharp found his eyes on the flexing of the juggernauts that lived beneath her blouse…

"The Council Leader told me that Mr Silverwood was a fractious man," the Superintendent said. "Not universally liked by his colleagues. Or some of the businesses he inspected. That needs looking into."

"Of course, ma'am. We're on that already. We're poking around good and hard, you can be assured of that. There's a lot to go at ma'am. Frankly, Martin Silverwood was a mess. He wasn't popular. He was also quite heavily overloaded, financially – there were a number of loans, credit cards. We're looking to see who he'd fallen behind with… He had drink issues, drug issues too. The usual type of stuff – cannabis, cocaine. Some of that Mng stuff too, sources say… Quite a cocktail of ingredients, ma'am!" He didn't get much back. He added: "I've also sent PC Kaur out to speak to the wife again this afternoon. Now that the initial shock has subsided a little. I'm hopeful she can use her impressive soft skills to loosen something out of her…"

"OK. Good. But I need more than this, Jim. I need something concrete, something hard by the end of the week." (DI Sharp smiled inwardly to himself.) "A specific line of enquiry, a specific area of interest. Something solid we can release or appeal to the public over."

"Yes, ma'am. And you'll have it. Don't worry."

"I don't worry, Inspector. *You're* the responsible leading the case."

A sudden broad smile. A blade catching the sunlight.

"Yes, ma'am…"

When PC Kaur came back to the station towards the end of the afternoon, they had a debrief at DI Sharp's desk.

"A couple of useful things, sir," PC Kaur reassured him. "It was hard work though. Mrs Silverwood is so withdrawn. Really in a world of her own. I'm sure the murder has made it worse, but she's probably been in a heavy depression ever since their son died. She's never got over it, sir."

"Terrible thing Constable, of course…"

"It's heartbreaking sir. She showed me the baby's bedroom upstairs. It's completely untouched, everything just as it was. The cot, the musical mobile thing, teddy bears, the wallpaper… So sad," PC Kaur seemed quite emotional at the memory of it.

"Absolutely… But what did you get then?"

"Well, on the subject of furnishings. The reason the house is so empty is because Martin started selling all their furniture off. About a year ago it started, sir. To generate money for gambling and also for loan repayments. Poor Mrs Silverwood just didn't have the spirit to stop him. Just let him carry on. She showed me their two bedrooms upstairs – both almost completely empty as well. Just a bed each, sir, clothes basically in piles on the floor."

"I see. Loans, you say?"

"Yep. She wasn't very clear about who the loans are with. They've been struggling to make the mortgage payments as well. That said, I think that Martin's passing will mean the mortgage is cleared off. That will be a relief for Jane, I am sure."

"Is that right? And is there any other life insurance?" DI Sharp asked quickly.

"I asked of course," PC Kaur said. "She wasn't very clear. But thinks that if there was any, Martin cancelled it when they started to get into financial difficulties."

"We must check that out. I'm sure she had nothing to do with Martin's death. But we should tick that one off."

"Of course, sir. On it." She made a note on her pad. "The other thing I learned sir – Martin had been getting around. Other women, sir."

DI Sharp perked up at this. "Oh really? Get any names, details?"

PC Kaur shook her head. "Jane tried to ignore it, block it out. He would only occasionally bring a lady friend back to the house. Usually he'd come home himself afterwards, in the early morning, or just stay out and not come home for a maybe a day or two. She thinks he had at least two 'girlfriends' during the last couple of years but says she had no idea how serious they were or whether the women were married or had partners and so on. It was pretty tough getting anything from her at all really, sir."

"Well, good work Constable… We really *have* to find that man's damn phone! It will be a treasure trove of messages, of that I'm sure… Suppose he was knocking off someone's wife. Kids maybe in the mix, too. A jealous husband, build up of rage, red mist descending… Bob's your bloody uncle."

"I asked her, sir, whether there had been any odd or unexpected visitors to the house asking for Martin – husbands, debt collectors etc. No joy, unfortunately."

Still, perhaps they were starting to make progress. "OK, let's reconvene and review first thing in the morning," DI Sharp said. "I've had the Super on my back today. We need rabbits, Constable. Out of hats. Sharpish."

"OK sir, understood. Keeping very close to the incident room too, sir."

"Good job, Constable. We'll get the bastard who did this before long," DI Sharp said, giving himself a generous look at PC Kaur's behind as she walked away.

He finished off some paperwork and then headed out into the city centre. He was going to conduct some private investigations of his own that evening. There were various Knott lowlifes he wanted to press on a one-to-one basis.

He had a bit of time before he was meeting Anton the Bulgarian at the Regency casino... So he took himself off to a grungy pub, The Sunken Armada, where Dave the Flick was often to be found. Unfortunately, though, there was no sign of said mean bastard. It had been thirsty work making the fifteen minute walk in the still-hot early evening sun so he got himself a long cold pint and stepped outside for a fag.

DI Sharp was one of the few smokers left in the United Kingdom. He wasn't going to give in to those fuckers in Government who kept on and on relentlessly piling more tax on a packet of smokes. Twenty quid a throw now. Well, he'd show them. He'd keep on grimly at it. Even if he only allowed himself a couple a day and had to make do with sweet-smelling poisonous vapes the rest of the time, like all of the kids and the benefits scroungers. He'd be a smoker until the day he died.

He lit up and took a heavy pull. Ah, that was better. Sandpaper my throat, baby, coat my fucking lungs with your love... Sod you, Mr Chancellor!

He was nearing the end of his cigarette – and was halfway down his pint – when he noticed a pock-marked teenager at his elbow.

"Mng, mate?" the lad said in a hoarse whisper.

"Excuse me?"

"Mng..." The kid flashed a packet at him inside his sleeve. "A hundred mate..."

DI Sharp reached into his pocket and flashed his police badge in return. "You're asking the wrong man, pal." The kid froze. DI Sharp whipped the packet from him. "But yes, I'll have them. Thank you very much. Now fuck off!"

"Whaaat?" the boy exclaimed. "Give me my... That's a hund..." Then he turned on his heels and shot away around the corner.

So these were Mng... DI Sharp smiled to himself and stowed them in his pocket. Who knows, maybe he'd try one at some point, see what all the fuss was about...

He made the short walk across the centre to the Regency. Nothing was very far from anything else in Knott. As he turned into the casino entrance, he knew it was four and a half minutes at an average walking pace to the Dark Lane car park where Martin Silverwood had met his end. That had still been too long for him to make it alive...

It was cool inside the casino, and pleasingly quiet at that early hour. It wasn't a place that DI Sharp normally frequented. He wasn't one to throw his hard-earned money away chasing a house-loaded dream. But it seemed that there was no shortage of dewy-eyed punters left in the world. It was an irony that the nickel-hard thugs he had to spend much of his time watching seemed to be the most susceptible of romantics. Or maybe they just had cash to recycle...

He walked past the hyperactive flashing slot machines towards the restaurant area at the back. Yes, there was Anton, seated and ready. He was conscientiously studying the menu he'd probably looked at a thousand times before. Even in the loamy air-conned air, DI Sharp could see that a thin bead of sweat was coursing down the side of Anton's fat head. He couldn't have been more than five foot five but he probably weighed nearly twenty stone…

"Good evening, Mr Rostanov," DI Sharp said, pulling back a chair.

"Detective Inspector! How nice to see you again," Anton said, smiling widely. He held out a fleshy hand. DI Sharp shook it, then wiped his palm off on the edge of his chair under the table.

Anton instantly sprung into host mode (this was understood between them, even though it had been DI Sharp who'd called the meeting), clicking his fingers for waiter attention, pouring some water into DI Sharp's glass, and asking him what else he'd like to drink.

Sharp took a beer while Anton carried on sipping at his mineral water.

"A terrible business of course, Detective Inspector. Very terrible. I understand he leaves a widow…" Anton said gravely. He dabbed at his mouth in sympathy. "I do not believe there has been a murder like this in Knott for many years. We have been blessed to be free of violent crime. This must be a credit to yourself and your colleagues."

"Thank you Anton – but you can spare the flattery, you know."

"Oh, I am not flattering, Detective Inspector. You know that I have the highest opinion of you. The very highest."

"That's kind of you, Anton," said DI Sharp, draining his beer. That one had gone down fast – he'd need to pace himself a little... Anton, however, was on it already, waving at the waiter for another.

"So, what do you know?" Sharp asked, leaning forward. "Was Martin Silverwood a... client?"

Anton sat back and dabbed again at his mouth. This time it seemed to indicate that there was such a thing as client confidentiality. Then he gave a small, mournful smile and said: "He was, Detective Inspector. Although of course I can't..."

"And was he up to date?"

"Ummm, well Inspector, you know it would be..."

"The man is dead, Anton! Sliced through his lungs and kidneys. You don't need to worry about confidentiality now. Please just tell me..."

"He was... not. No. He had fallen behind. He owed nearly three thousand pounds including charges if I am not mistaken," Anton said quietly. Then he added: "Which is all the more reason, Detective Inspector, why I would want him to stay *alive*, is it not!"

"Of course. Needless to say. I wouldn't be speaking to you like this, Anton, if I regarded you as a suspect."

"I am pleased to hear you say that, Detective Inspector. Very pleased," Anton said, raising his glass of water. "He was not a model customer. Not like *you* were. But believe me that I was sad when I heard the news. Martin was not a friend, but he was… OK, you know? I was very sad."

"Three thousand pounds sad, perhaps?"

There was a little silence, then Anton broke into laughter, his small dark eyes twinkling. "You have a wicked, English sense of humour, Inspector!"

Anton always found a way to work that reminder in, whenever they had a conversation. Three years ago, Sharp had had to take a loan himself. When Mary had been diagnosed in the early stages of an aggressive cancer. He hadn't been able to leave it to chance and NHS waiting lists. Too many people died nowadays holding on in the queue. Anton had given him a special 'police discount' with an interest rate of 'only' 25%… It had been painful, but Sharp had managed to meet every repayment and clear it off in the agreed 48 months.

He firmed his tone. "Help me out here, Anton. I need leads, information. You must have heard something? On the grapevine. There must be some speculation doing the rounds?"

"What do you think I will have heard, Detective Inspector? I am a quiet man. I mind my own business…"

"You know, Anton, next month I'm attending a digital crime and money laundering course. There will be several delegates there from HMRC. Plenty of time to exchange tips and information during the coffee breaks…"

Anton carefully removed a strip of fat from the edge of his steak, a precise surgical operation. A bead of sweat hung at the end of one thick, black eyebrow. He wiped his face.

"I don't say that Martin Silverwood had enemies exactly, Detective Inspector Sharp. But I wouldn't say that he was popular either," Anton offered. "His work, of course, meant that he offended some people. When he didn't give them a good inspection report."

"Such as?"

"Well, last year – when was it? – in the spring perhaps, he gave a very negative report about a restaurant on Denmark Street. The Cod Café. Do you remember it?"

"Hmm. Yes, I do."

"It had to close down. Health and safety violations, poor food hygiene too. The owner, Peter Franks, was very unhappy. As you can imagine. He protested that the report was unfair. He appealed but was unsuccessful. He blamed Martin Silverwood for this, even though Mr Silverwood's report was only one part of the process. It was food standards that really got him closed down."

"Right…"

"Peter Franks opened a new place. The Fish Fryer. But it's further out in a quieter area. He couldn't afford anywhere in a good location because he had lost a lot of money when the Cod Café had to close. Now, I believe the Fish Fryer is losing money. It is a tough business in your chippie trade."

"And you're telling me this because…?"

Anton looked around him, lowered his voice. "Peter Franks was here on that Saturday night. I saw him. I also saw him, at one point, speaking to Martin Silverwood. Not in a friendly way, you understand. Neither was it a fight or an argument. But it looked like – what would you say? – a prickly exchange, Inspector…"

"But surely you're not saying that he would stab Silverwood to death because of his fish and chip business?" DI Sharp asked, lowering his voice too.

Anton levered the last of his steak and chips into his mouth and chewed with slow deliberation. Then he leaned in close to DI Sharp.

"No, Detective Inspector. Not only for that. I do not think so. But you see, in fact there is more. The rumour has it that Mr Silverwood has also been involved with Peter Franks' wife… It is a – how shall we say – a *live* engagement…"

Bingo! DI Sharp put his knife and fork down, sat back and bestowed an unofficial smile on Anton Rostanov.

"I see…! Now, that is interesting, Anton. That's very interesting. Peter Franks you say…"

"Of course, I know nothing about it directly, Inspector. I throw no stones. I am simply passing on to you things that I have heard spoken of," Anton said, dabbing daintily at his mouth. "Coffee, Detective Inspector?"

DI Sharp celebrated his possible catch with a double brandy alongside his coffee. Now he really had something to go at! Anton excused himself to speak to someone on a 'business matter' at another table. Sharp sat there contentedly imbibing his twin drinks, taking his time. He had been going to visit another bar to see if he could run down another lowlife contact who had a line in ketamine and weed. But he didn't need that now…

A pleasant fuzziness began to spread through DI Sharp as cognac met lager. He looked at his watch – coming up to nine o'clock. He had told Mary he'd be home late ('surveillance operation'). She was always in bed by around half nine anyway and her medication would send her straight to sleep.

It looked like he'd be able to squeeze a visit in to Mrs Bright. Yes, he had to say, he fancied that all right. He'd better call her though. He'd been in trouble with her before, banging on the window unannounced. She'd given him a right old bollocking. And then come down on him real hard the next time he'd been. God, that had been good…

He hailed the waiter, ordered one last brandy ('Thanks, Anton…').

He smiled. He dialled. He crossed his twitching legs.

6.

"Mum, look at you!" said Alice, tutting, as her mother sat slumped woozy in a chair. The side of her head was bandaged and she had a livid black eye. "You look like you've been in a fight!"

They were in Weymouth hospital, where her mother had been waiting for her in a discharge room. Alice had been at work when she picked up a voicemail from the hospital in between patients. Valerie had fallen over and cracked her head on the pavement. They'd held her overnight and now she could go home. But they wanted someone to be with her for the next 24 hours at least to monitor her recovery. Alice had managed to cancel her last appointment and get down to Weymouth by late afternoon.

"I didn't want you to come," her mother snapped. "No need. But they said otherwise they wouldn't let me go."

"Yeah well, here I am, mother dear. You'll just owe me one, that's all."

"I gave them Bill's number first," Valerie sniffed defensively. "But I think he was down the pub. Useless old soak…"

"I wouldn't go too far down that line, Mum. Sounds like you were pretty soaked yourself."

"Pavement was uneven. The council will be hearing from me, I can tell you."

"Hmm. But I'm sure they'll check with the hospital. The nurse told me you were singing like a good 'un when they brought you in."

"I was fine, Alice, really. I'd only had a couple. Was just trying to keep my spirits up. That was all."

"Right... Anyway, let's get you up and out of here. You're coming with me."

"You're going to drop me home?"

"No, Mum. We'll pick up some things but then I'm taking you back to Knott. You can stay with me for a few days."

"What? Why? I don't want to do that!"

"Well, I can't stay down here, Mum. I've got appointments that I can't cancel. You can rest and recuperate with me. I'll bring you back at the end of the week. It will be nice..."

"Oh really Alice, I'm not a child! That's really not necessary."

"Don't worry, Mum! I'll get some wine in. Which you can drink *in moderation*. I'll cook for you, look after you, make a fuss, you know..."

Her mother harrumphed but seemed in fact, on reflection, not to dislike the idea too much.

"Well, I suppose it's a long time since I've seen your place. Maybe a change will do me good..."

Alice helped her up and they moved slowly off along the corridor. Valerie's mobility was good but she was evidently still somewhat weakened and shaken by her fall. Holding Alice's arm, she was thin and bony as a bird.

"Does it still hurt? Looks like you really whacked yourself, Mum."

"Throbs a bit. I'll be OK. My mouth's hellish dry though. Could do with a little something to take my thirst off..." She looked up at Alice and gave a cheeky smile.

"Ha! A small night cap will be all!"

It had been a horrible worry when she picked up the message. Relief now made her indulgent. This was the first time her mum had hurt herself, although it was by no means the first time she'd drunk herself into a stupor. Her mum was a semi-alcoholic, she had to face that fact. Now, into her late sixties it was set to become increasingly problematic. Her system was packing up, her body had no strength left. All the years of intake, and smoking, and under-eating were having an effect. Mentally and emotionally, her mother had been shot for years already of course...

That was no surprise when you considered that her father had walked out when Alice was aged just three and Valerie was already struggling to cope. He took himself off for an easier ride elsewhere. Mum was left in that small dingy flat in Bristol trying to bring Alice up alone on benefits. Eventually, some maintenance began to come through once her dad had moved to Gloucester, settled himself with another woman and found a new job. But still, it was hard. She wasn't a natural mother, as she'd always readily admitted. From her teenaged years, she'd liked a drink. Money had always been scarce. Keeping body and soul together was a kind of daily conjuring act.

One way of trying to pull off that trick was to find healing in the comfort of strangers. There had always been plenty of strangers. From about the age of six, Alice had vague memories of them. Most of them were very transitory – a few weeks or even just a night – but a few had developed into longer relationships. There was one man – Ken – that her mother had come close to actually settling down with properly. He hung around in their flat a lot. He had a droopy moustache and smelled of tobacco smoke. But it had never actually reached the point of proper cohabitation.

That was the closest Alice had come to having a father figure. Her own father had kept very fitfully in touch for about ten years. She'd seen him a few times – park, ice cream, fizzy drink. That then petered out to a birthday or Christmas letter or email. Which then petered out to nothing at all. In his last email, she remembered, he had told her that things were "complicated". He had a new life, a (new) new partner (but no children), they were planning to move north, it was difficult to fit his old life in. Maybe when she was an adult they could meet and become friends. He would like that. He hoped she understood. She hadn't replied. As far as she was concerned, she had no father. He was dead to her, and that was all.

They made their way out of the hospital and Alice helped her mother into the car. Then they drove to her flat to pack a bag. It was an airy, high-ceilinged flat with views towards the sea front. But it was messy and unkempt, in bad need of a deep clean. Empty wine and spirit bottles lay around. At least there weren't any ashtrays – Valerie had finally managed to give up smoking a few years prior, which had been a relief.

"Mum!" Alice scolded. "Look at the state of this place. I'll give it a good clean when we come back..."

"Oh stop fussing, Alice! Now, can you find my nice little red party dress? It's a silky number with little tassels at the neckline," Valerie said, sitting on her bed and gesturing weakly towards a wardrobe.

Soon they were done and on the road heading towards Knott. It was a beautiful sun-shot evening. Warm air raced at the windows. Summer greenery wrapped around them in a thick effusive roll. Here and there, banks of wind turbines added their mechanistic poetry. Her mother seemed to enjoy looking at it all – but it wasn't long before her head had sunk forward and she was held in a rasping, dribbling doze.

Alice glanced at Valerie's aging features, feeling a twinge of love. Her own face was in her mother's – they shared something around the eyes, the set of the nose. Both were tallish and thin, dark-haired. People could always tell they were mother and daughter. Is this how Alice would look in thirty years? Probably, although Alice hoped she wouldn't have that tracery of red veins on her cheeks, the cracked rosacea of the long-term drinker.

Their relationship had never run smoothly – they had always bickered and disagreed – but in fact, as Alice saw at that moment, that was a form of closeness in its way. The fact of being an only child and single parent created an involuntary bond in itself, a cord that might stretch but could never actually be broken. Because no matter how much they argued and fought, they were in a sense each other's only option. Alice had become a rebellious and difficult teenager – Valerie's response had been to apparently care less than Alice did. She didn't check where Alice was or track what she was doing. Then intermittently she'd let fly at her, as though she suddenly cared, as though Alice's wellbeing suddenly mattered. Which incensed Alice even more and made their fighting worse…

But although she was unruly, Alice was bright and did well at school. She did A levels and got accepted for university. She couldn't wait to get away. She grabbed the opportunity with both hands, never moving back.

However, one way or another, they always stayed in touch. They met up, kept up with each other's news, loved each other in their own flawed and unsatisfactory way. Alice mellowed through her twenties: her mother had done the best she could. There was a bond there underneath everything that simply was. She was grateful for it.

She had also picked up quite a lot from her mother's template. Especially in her relationships with men. Like Valerie, Alice found it hard to settle with another person. She could be peremptory, demanding, inconsistent. It was her way of keeping distance. She needed to break that cycle. She wanted to get into a relationship that lasted and bore fruit. She had hopes that Lewis might be the one...

They drew up outside Alice's apartment block and she gently woke Valerie up. "Where are we?" she said thickly. Then she grimaced, reaching at the side of her head. "Ow!"

Inside, she settled her mother on the sofa and turned the TV on. Then she prepared a light meal. Her mother picked at it, eating only little wisps. "I'm very tired, Alice," she said. "I think I'll go to bed. I can probably even leave that night cap after all. I'll just take one of my painkillers instead."

Once Valerie was 'down' (it was weirdly like having a baby...), Alice poured herself a big glass of wine and phoned Lewis. She filled him in on her maternal drama – but the real reason for calling was because she was couldn't stop thinking about Martin Silverwood and the SmartLab business.

"What have you got for me, Lewis? Turned anything up?"

"Well, it's hard to say. I can't ask people things too directly. Might look odd, you know... But I did establish that when he went to inspect the distribution warehouse, he kept asking about a big consignment he saw, for that company you asked about. You know – what was it – Primegate Pharmacy Supplies?"

"Oh really?"

"Yeah. Kept coming back to it apparently. Wanting to know about how frequently we dispatch there, what quantities. Even though there was nothing to do with health and safety. That's what pissed the shift manager off."

"OK. That's interesting."

"Is that why you asked me about Primegate? But then – how did you know?"

"Oh, just came across them. When I was googling. Coincidence really," Alice said vaguely. "Anyhoo… when shall we see each other again? I'm tied up with my mum until the weekend obviously. How about Saturday evening?"

They talked on for a bit and said their good nights. Wine downed, Alice felt sleepy too and made up the sofa. She could hear her mother snoring from her bed, sending up little reedy whistles. It made a rhythmic background accompaniment and it wasn't long before she was asleep herself.

Alice had managed to cancel her appointments for the next two days, so was able to devote herself to her mother. On the first day, they got up late and had a slow breakfast. Valerie seemed a bit better – clearer in the head – and was quite happy just sitting on the sofa idly flicking through TV. But by the afternoon she was starting to ask more insistently about a 'little snifter'.

"Not in the middle of the afternoon, Mum! 6pm embargo earliest," Alice said.

"Little bloody Hitler!" her mum shot back.

They went out for a short walk to a nearby park, mainly to kill some time. Her mother was getting much better. Her balance was fine and, she said, her head wasn't hurting anymore. When they got back, Alice replaced the bandage. The cuts underneath were healing well already. Her black eye still looked bad but would clear itself up with time. There was nothing really wrong with the old bird now.

It wasn't possible to hold back the tide any longer. By five o'clock, her mother had the wine flowing. She could certainly knock it back. Soon, she was halfway down the bottle without any discernible difference…

By eight o'clock, she was sozzled and slurry. She insisted on starting a second bottle. Alice refused. She turned her campaign efforts to vodka instead. "Just a couple of small ones," she snapped. "Plenty of orange. Hardly make any bloody differensh."

They argued back and forth. Alice felt trapped and claustrophobic. So did her mother. Eventually Alice lost patience, lost the will. "Fine! Have a bloody vodka! But go and sit outside on the balcony, will you? Then I can pretend you're not here."

"That's a nice way to speak to your bloody mother," said Valerie, going to the kitchen where she slopped plenty of vodka into a glass and added a small amount of orange juice. She sniffed meaningfully on her way back through the living room. But Alice kept her eyes steadfastly on her laptop. "Sometimes I really wisssh I'd had the other one."

"What do you mean?" Alice asked.

"I wish I'd had the other one. That's what I mean…" Valerie continued on her way and went out onto the balcony, keeping the door open.

"What other one? What are you talking about, mother?" Alice said angrily.

Her mother's voice came floating in, as though a ghost off-stage. "I wish I'd had the other baby. The one I didn't have. *That's* what I mean, if you mussht know!" Then she began to sob.

"What!? What baby? What do you mean, Mum?" Alice jumped up and stood in the doorway, her eyes fixed urgently on her progenitor in the chair. "You were going to have a baby? When?"

"I never told you, did I?" Valerie said wistfully, blearily, looking away towards the trees. "You were about… seven? I was expecting. But I didn't have it. In the end."

"You…" Alice felt suddenly weak and faint. "You had a… *termination*? Is that what you're saying?"

Valerie turned and looked up at her daughter, tilted her chin in defiance. "Yes. That's right. A little secret all these yearssh…" Then her chin collapsed and she wiped feebly at her tears.

"So I could have had a… But you didn't… And you never even…" Alice felt like she had lost the power of speech.

She couldn't process this news, slapped at her like a fish on the table. She had always wished she'd had a brother or sister. She had always so regretted being an only child.

"You could have fucking *told* me, Mum! Properly, I mean. Rather than like this!!"

Alice slammed the balcony door closed and hurried through to her bedroom where she threw herself down on the bed. She stared up at a watery ceiling. So she could have had a brother, or a sister, after all! How many weeks had it been alive? She *had* had a sibling, a living sibling – even if only a half one – for a couple of months at least! She wasn't against abortion – it wasn't something she'd ever even really thought about closely – but now the sadness of it felt overwhelming. She *had* a phantom half brother or sister, who had briefly existed, in her mother's womb. There was a genetic companion piece to her somewhere in the invisible, impossible spirit world...

She lay there, reflecting. How things might have been. What it could have been like, growing up with a young sibling, another half, someone to share all the difficulty and frustration with of having Valerie as a mother... It was like pulling apart her own ribcage and peering in... The loss of it was horrific. Tears bathed her face as she moaned and sniffed. Then she turned over and buried her face in her pillow, breathing out hot frustration and misery.

After maybe half an hour, Alice began to feel a little calmer. It could have been, but then wasn't... It hadn't happened. A million things didn't happen, every single day. Close up that hole, move on...

In a way, she realised, she couldn't blame her mother too heavily. It must have been completely unwanted, unplanned. Maybe she hadn't even been sure who the father was... The point really was that she should have *told* her, at some point, in an appropriate way and at an appropriate time! It had come as such a random shock, almost by accident, out of the evening bloody blue...

Eventually, Alice sat up. She blew her nose, did some deep controlled breathing, and went to make herself a cup of tea. There was a knocking on glass. Then her mother, opening the balcony door, asking in a child-like voice: "Can I come in again now? I need to have a wee."

"Go on then!" Alice cried. Valerie shuffled in. "I don't suppose you know whether it was a brother or a sister?" Alice asked.

Her mother shook her head. "They couldn't tell back then. I was ten weeks." Then she said: "I'm sorry, Alice."

She went into the bathroom. Alice hovered outside, listening to the toilet and faucet sounds that were like a strange submerged music. When her mother came out, they looked each other in the eyes. Then they shared a long, silent hug. "Let's get you ready for bed," Alice said.

Alice tossed and turned on the narrow sofa for a long time, confused thoughts and feelings and images whirling around in her head. One moment she felt traumatised and hurting, the next moment she felt normal again... This would take some time to process, for sure. She had suffered a loss, genuinely an awful loss, but at the same time it was now entirely historical, in the past, a smudge really of something that hadn't happened, back in time. What to make of that? It just made her sad. It conjured a sadness, that rose up like a mist out of things, that seemed to undermine everything, shaking at the foundations as with a pair of tiny, clenched little fists… Oh! She heaved suddenly and gave out a yelp of pain. She went to the kitchen and swayed at the sink, gulping down some milk for comfort…

Eventually in the small hours, she fell asleep. She woke up early the next morning and immediately took some Mng. It wasn't long before a calm, focused concentration spread like warm syrup through her. The sense of self-sufficiency it induced was a help.

Before last night's news, she had already decided on a course of action for that day and she wasn't going to change it. So after breakfast and a period of quiet sitting and internet-browsing, Alice told Valerie that she was going out for an hour or two. "Just stay here quietly and for god's sake don't get pissed," she said.

It wasn't far to the SmartLab distribution warehouse – it was only a few miles outside Knott on the Glastonbury road. Alice wasn't sure what she was looking for or what she would actually do when she got there, but she felt it was something that she had to pursue. Now it also had the bonus of getting her out of the flat and away from her mother for a while.

Once out of Knott, the Somerset countryside quickly surrounded her: green fields, thick hedges, little burry side lanes. It soothed her spirits a little. She focused on the road ahead, trying to push thoughts away. This gave her a kind of tunnel vision, which was exacerbated when she entered an avenue of overhanging trees. Light and then shade came at her like a rapid flickering film, seemed to transpose her somewhere else. Suddenly, everything felt strange, as though she had entered another world... She shook her head, trying to clear the oddness away. But she still felt herself to be shuttered somewhere else, held somehow on the underside of things...

Here was the distribution centre. Obviously, she couldn't go in. Her vague idea was to park somewhere nearby, see how close she could get from the outside, and try to get a decent look in through the binoculars she had brought.

She came to a lay-by about half a mile later. So she parked up and began the walk back. She realised how hot it was. The sun beat down. It was a ferocious, breathless morning – it was surely set to be the hottest day of the year so far. Sweat began to run down her temples, she felt her T-shirt sticking to her back. She wished she'd brought a hat.

Cars raced past her intermittently, shuddering her with gusts of hot wind. She lifted her hand to shield her eyes from the glare of the sun. The depot was still several hundred yards away. This was no fun.

But eventually she reached it. She walked on past it a little way, then ran across the road so that she was on the correct side. From the narrow strip of pavement at the road's edge, there was a path that cut through some fields towards a copse of trees that stretched down one side of the warehouse site. She reckoned she could get a good view in from there...

She walked a way along the path, then cut across an area of field until she was in amongst the trees. It was dry and hot and parched. Cracked grey leaves lay about on the floor, even though there was a green waving canopy above. She wasn't sure what kind of tree they were – birches, maybe?

Tramping her way in between the tree trunks, Alice saw that she could get quite close to the depot. A high wire-mesh fence surrounded it, but she had a good line of sight in. As luck would have it, she was looking directly at what appeared to be the main dispatch bay. There were a few lorries parked up, a few men milling around. Inside a hangar-like opening, she could see conveyor belts and racks of shelving.

She crouched down next to a bush. Alice through the binoculars zoomed in to focus and everything became very big, like in a story. It felt very odd. What was she doing here? What if someone saw her? She was perhaps 100 metres from the depot. How visible would she be to the naked eye? Her heart was thumping. She manoeuvred herself further into the bush, right in, so that the greenery enveloped her. But the branches were stiff and sharp, they scratched her arms and legs. She was, again, sweating heavily. There were rustlings in the leaves on the ground, like lizards. She felt as though bugs were crawling down her neck and along the backs of her legs. She flapped at them with her free hand, almost losing her balance. She felt she might faint. She was so thirsty! She had also failed to bring any water...

She managed, though, to refocus. Yes, here was the dispatch bay. She could see men's faces up close, ugly and large. They were like magnified play-figures or animations, imaginary creatures. Was any of this real? Where, again, was she?

There were a few comings and goings as vans from a national courier firm were loaded and headed off. It all felt quite humdrum. After about twenty minutes, she was considering giving up. But then an unmarked white van drew up. A man got out. She fumbled around, trying to find him, getting at first only a hit between the eyes of grey industrial unit. Then she got him. It was another hit between the eyes. This man was one of Kevan Monk's 'associates' who lingered around his place in Knott! She couldn't remember his name, but she definitely recognised him. He was immediately recognisable after all – a huge man, maybe six foot four, almost as wide, with a bald head, a neck thick as a tree trunk festooned with dark tattoos. As mean-looking as he was ugly... There had been another smaller man, wiry and weaselly, who was almost always with him. Like a non-twin version of Tweedledum and Tweedledee. But this time, Dum was on his own.

Before long, a pallet of boxes was brought out by a forklift and placed near the van. Was that... did that say... yes, it did! A big printed label said Primegate Pharmacy Supplies! In a matter of minutes, the consignment was loaded into the van. The man jumped in and was off.

Alice, like a bird in the bush, let out a whistle. This was a turn up for the books! Primegate again... the connection with Kevan Monk... However unreal all of this was, it was nevertheless beginning to make a weird kind of sense...

She stayed there with her binoculars for a while longer, until she was satisfied there was nothing more worth seeing. Then she crawled stiffly out of her bush and made her way back through the crackling copse, out into the burning sunlight. Slowly, unsteadily, pantingly, she retraced her steps to the heat-box of her car. She had overlooked, of course, to park it in the shade.

She fired up the air-con and moved off. Her mind was a blur. Monk, Mng, SmartLab, Primegate... Also, her lost brother, her lost sister, her sibling that wasn't to be... Alone in the car, she pressed her way on, back down the country road, back through the tunnels of the wavering trees, as though she was racing towards an urgent destination. What was her destination? But perhaps that was something no one knew until after they had reached it or even until they had accidentally arrived somewhere else.

What was all this nonsense? She needed to pull herself together. She hoped she wouldn't find her mother sprawled and singing on the floor...

But no. On the contrary, coming into the flat she found Valerie quite calm and composed. Indeed, she was sitting neatly on the edge of the sofa with her bag packed and by her feet.

"I want you to take me home," she said, with a tight little sniff, like a queen. "I'm fine now. My head doesn't hurt. My eye is healing. Bill phoned and said he's been missing me."

"But are you sure, Mum? Is that sensible yet?"

"Absolutely. It's too hot in your flat. My place is much cooler. Bill will come over and stay the night. I'll have company. Don't worry."

Alice considered. Her mother was right. She had to go into work the next day anyway. It made good sense.

"Fine," she said. "Give me ten minutes and we can be on our way."

Alice slugged down plenty of water and then had a piece of bread and cheese to keep her going, spooned some salad that was in the fridge. Then she was on the road again, this time heading southwards to Dorset. It was only an hour to Weymouth – they would be there soon after one. It would be a bit of a round-trip, but she should be able to get to Swindon by about three…

They didn't talk a lot on the way. Both sensed that it was best to leave things fallow, let the news, the revelation, brew. But they discussed her mother's friend Bill a little ("a lovely man who lost his wife, still full of love and fun") and then Valerie asked about Alice's situation.

"Oh well, I'm kind of on again with Lewis. Remember, you've met him a couple of times?"

"Yes. Seemed like a nice boy. Well, that's good. And what about work? You've been saying for ages that you want to leave the clinic?"

"I know, I do... But, I don't know, that would mean leaving Knott, moving somewhere else. Lewis is very attached to Knott. Where he grew up and everything."

"All the more reason for him to get away! A nice boy but... a bit docile, dear? Lacking, what shall we say, *oomph*?"

Alice smiled. "Hmmm..."

"Don't let him hold you back, Alice. Never let one person do that. Especially not a man. What they've got downstairs, you can find anywhere you know."

Alice shot a glance across at her mother at this somewhat bizarre statement. Was she OK? She was sitting there calmly, gazing ahead, the rushing road reflecting in the small pools of her eyes.

"Okayyy, thanks Mum!"

They got back to the flat in the heat of early afternoon. Alice immediately opened some windows for her mother and the sea-scented air began to move through.

"I would have cleaned the place up if we'd come on Saturday, Mum, but I don't have time now I'm afraid," Alice said.

Valerie tutted. "What are you trying to say, Alice? It's really not that bad. Bill's coming later. I'll set him to work. Earn his corn..."

"OK then."

"Thank you, Alice. You've put yourself out for me. Rearranged your work. I appreciate it."

"No problem. It's been good to see you. We ought to spend more time together anyway."

"Yes." Valerie paused. Then she said: "You know, the names I had in my head were James if it was a boy and Catherine if was a girl. What do you think?"

"So, you *did* consider having it, for a time?"

"Briefly... I know it's been a shock to you. I hope you understand."

"Of course. Your decision, Mum. Water under the bridge a long time now."

They embraced, more tenderly than they had done for years. Once again, Alice realised how thin her mother was, what a fragile old organism she had become. However tough she also was.

Then Alice left, thoughts and feelings moving around inside her like drifts of ragged cloud. But soon, she put them away as she concentrated on the journey ahead. She plugged the Primegate postcode into her satnav and submitted to the hard, clean instructions of the bot. There was a restfulness in being so held.

The journey passed without pain or incident and by mid-afternoon Alice was on the outskirts of the Wiltshire town. It seemed that Primegate was situated on a trading estate on the edge of Swindon, within easy reach of the motorway.

"In one hundred yards, turn left. Turn left. Turn left. Now, TURN LEFT! You have reached your destination," the robot woman informed her.

It was a small estate that essentially consisted of one winding road with offices and units on either side. Alice nosed along, looking for Unit 27. It would be on the left. On the left. Here was 17. Here was 19. On the left. You have reached your... On the left. Number 27.

Here was 27. It clearly said so on a little plaque at the front of the forecourt. Was there some mistake? This was not the office in the website photos! Instead, it appeared to have shrunk right down to become a small, low unit – more of a garage than anything else. The first units on the estate had been offices and bigger buildings, but from about 20 onwards they seemed to reduce in size, shrivelling to lock-ups. The neighbouring one, for example, said A1 Plumbing; the one opposite was Wiltshire Ballet Wear. They were for micro businesses. Room for one little office area on the side, the rest just storage space. She hadn't seen the name of the business written anywhere at all on Unit 27.

Feeling a sense of déjà vu, Alice continued on past. She followed the road round a bend and saw that the trading estate finished not far ahead. She parked outside a unit that was clearly unoccupied and walked back towards 27, on the opposite side of the road.

She was pleased that she'd thought to bring a hat this time. Both to shield her from this burning sun and also because it made her feel a little more concealed. She began furtively looking across as unit 27 came into view. There had been nothing going on when she drove past but now a scruffy van was outside.

She carried on walking, peering to left and right as though looking for a specific place. She kept this up for a while further, until she was nearly at the entrance to the estate. She saw a board that listed all the businesses — sure enough, against Unit 27 it said Primegate Pharmacy Supplies.

Alice turned around and walked back, keeping to the other side from Primegate. When she got there, she saw that the unit doors had been opened and two men were carrying boxes out. She didn't recognise either of them. But it was no surprise to see the SmartLab logo on the side of the boxes in their hands...

Woah, OK! she thought. So that's what it is. Open and shut, surely? Primegate is a front, a fake, and what Monk is doing is simply distributing Mng directly from here to a network of dealers around the country. That's why there's so much of it on the streets. Because SmartLab is supplying it, dumb ass! Like Martin Silverwood had implied in his point about Coke. All so simple. Hiding in plain sight. No one asks any questions because no one's bothered. Mng is not that serious, it's not like heroin or crack or coke. And in fact it's doing good — bringing the UK's addiction problem down overall. SmartLab makes millions extra — which Monk needs to keep his private equity investors happy – and it goes through the books as sales to Primegate. Which no one's ever heard of, but as no one cares anyway, no one asks. She'd bet a million dollars that it was the same accountants doing the books for the two companies. All nicely audited and signed off, thank you very much and, oh yes!, that extra payment on the side...

So, surely this proved that she was right, about Martin and his Kittywake posts, about blackmailing Kevan Monk... He'd demanded hush money. Monk had only given him the first part...

As she turned this over, a sickness rose inside her. She stumbled back to the car, fumbled at the door and fell inside. Hellish hot again. She slurped at the lukewarm water she had with her. She brought the air-con roaring on. At first it was just more hot air though. She threw one car door open, like a bird with an injured wing. Tears came to her eyes. What was happening, what had she stumbled across? This was insane. She must have fallen down a rabbit hole...

The first thing was to get out of there. She had a sudden fear that those men would have noticed her walking past twice and looking across, and that they'd come down the road to find her. She took some deep breaths, tidied her hair in the mirror and started up the car. Then she turned around and drove out of the trading estate, forcing herself to keep her eyes fixed ahead as she passed unit 27.

She began to feel a bit better when she was out of the immediate vicinity and on the way back towards Knott.

But it wasn't long before the questions began to surface again. Should she contact the police? Would they listen to her? She didn't have any firm evidence... Although perhaps those KittyWake posts were evidence of sorts. What did one do in a situation like this?

She phoned Lewis. He couldn't talk long – he was at work at SmartLab of course – but she arranged for him to come over that evening. She'd lay everything out in front of him and see what he made of it...

When she got home, she was tired from what had been a long day. It was still very hot. When would this heat break? It felt like something had to break.

Lewis arrived at around seven o'clock. Coming in, he was very amorous, not having seen Alice for several days, but she held him off. "I need to talk to you about something really serious," she said.

"Don't tell me you want to break up already!" he cried, his expression a mixture of fear and disgust.

"No, no, no! It's not that, Lewis. Not at all! Now, just hear me out..."

She told him everything, calmly and in order from the beginning. Having initially kept interjecting and asking questions, Lewis fell increasingly silent. Alice got to the end, then stopped. Lewis said nothing. "Well?" she asked. "What do you make of all that?"

He was silent for a few more seconds. Then he let out a long breath. "Alice, are you feeling all right?" he exclaimed. "I mean, you can't be serious!"

"But why not? Doesn't it all add up?"

"Silverwood might have had an issue with SmartLab, I get that. And this Primegate thing *is* odd. But – murder? No way, Alice, no way!"

Of course, Alice had been expecting some resistance. Lewis admired Monk and felt very much in his debt, she knew that. He also enjoyed his job at SmartLab and believed in the company. It would be hard for him to take on board.

"You know, Primegate is 100% a fake," she said. "I submitted a random order for some goods through their website when I got back today. Surprise surprise, got an automated reply saying the system is temporarily down, please try later. And I noticed, there isn't even a phone number on the website. Just a generic email address."

"Yeah… that's all pretty strange. I'll look into it some more at work. There must be some kind of an explanation. But anyway, that's separate. The main point is – Kevan is not a murderer! I'm sure of that."

"I had a relationship with him, Lewis, as you know. And he's a strange guy. I saw that up close. I wouldn't rule *anything* out…"

"But *if* everything you're saying is right, there are other things he could have done, surely? He wouldn't have to bloody stab him to death!"

"Such as?"

Lewis considered… "Such as, such as, I don't know, pay him some money and make him sign a non-disclosure agreement? Hmm. Maybe not. Such as, stop the operation for a while, cover his tracks, and start it up again later? I don't know! But there would have been other possibilities. You can't make me believe that Kevan is a killer."

"I hope he isn't. Really. But *someone* killed Martin. And Kevan Monk certainly had a motive."

"Spoken like a true detective, Inspector Carlisle! I mean… I think we both need to sleep on this, reflect on it, don't you? It's too early – too fresh – to act on anything yet."

"But… I called Knott police station just before you came, Lewis…"

"You WHAT??"

"The officer on the phone took down all the details and seemed very convinced. Asked loads of follow-up questions."

"Alice, what the fuck have you done? You're joking, right??"

Alice's shoulders gave her away first, as she subsided into giggles. Lewis thwacked her with a cushion and they began to roll around on the floor in a play-fight, burning off all the nervous energy they had built up.

Sleep on it they would. After they had more fully relieved their tension and their need, brought themselves to a sweet, lingering precipice in one another.

Later, lying in the sticky darkness trying to find sleep, Alice reflected that she hadn't even told Lewis about her lost half-sibling. *That* was a measure of just how upside-down things had been that day.

7.

Jane propped her bicycle in the driveway and let herself into the house. It was such a nice house – her favourite of the three she cleaned. Light and airy, a period property that also felt contemporary and up to date. The owners were a lovely couple, young professionals who were going places but had no airs or graces. They always spoke to her nicely, treated her with respect. One of them a solicitor and the other an accountant. Early thirties, she would guess. Earning enough between them to buy this four bedroom Edwardian semi. No children yet to fill it with but, she suspected, they would be on the way in the coming years. Then this really would be a delightful family home...

Stephen.

She took the radio out of her bag and set it down on the mantelpiece in the living room. She turned it on and there was some kind of discussion programme going. Fine. She began to dust.

It was nice work, cleaning. You could just switch your mind off and do it. It was rhythmic in its way. Therapeutic. You could see the results, which was satisfying. It was nice to imagine that she was providing a service that her customers appreciated, coming home to a clean and tidy house. "Oh good, Jane's been in. What a good job she's done." That sort of thing.

So what was she saying? That she liked to be appreciated? Perhaps she did. Even if, at the same time, she liked to be ignored and left alone.

Cleaning ticked all the boxes therefore, because her work was valued (she hoped) while she hardly ever actually saw her customers. It was a solitary occupation, performed when no one was around. The only way of knowing that she had been there was through a kind of negative deduction: the removal of dirt, the smoothing away of disorder. Yes, the cleaning sprite must have visited…

Jane preferred her new career to her old one. Although, as she recalled, she had loved her old one when she was back there, in those days. The thought of it made her shudder now. To stand in front of a classroom of children, teenagers, young adults, and talk and direct and control, and seek to inspire and motivate and illuminate, at the same time as imposing discipline and order and respect – she couldn't believe that was something she had done! If she had to go back there now, she felt that the waves of youthful energy would sweep her away, blow her clean out through the windows! She would *want* it to. It would be intolerable to stand there. To set herself up as 'teacher' running the show. To pretend that everything was important, that the words coming out of her mouth like spaghetti hoops mattered.

She would also have to pretend that the books she was reading with them had significance. This was something she had once passionately believed! In the old days, she was always reading a book, whether it was a text she was teaching or something she was reading for herself. Literature meant everything to her. Books classic and modern added something to life itself, supplemented, amplified her. A good book added meaning and resonance, brought a sense of depth, reassured her somehow that there was a significance to things. Whereas in the rare periods when she didn't have a book on the go – or was not engaged by the one she was reading – she felt a depletion, a flatness, a sinking of the spirits.

It was strange to think of that now. Now, if she attempted to read a book, the words wouldn't register, she couldn't take anything in. She veered off to one side, like a vehicle leaving the road, bumping through the bushes. Besides, what did any book matter when there were so many of them? They kept coming, on and on and on. Why, right now, she realised, this radio programme was in fact an author discussing her latest book. Next week it would be someone else. Then add all the films and dramas, music, art, animations, AI creations – whatever else! The world was a mad, incessant factory of creation, brilliant but insane. It was too much, it hurt her head, her eyes, her insides. It was something she didn't believe in anymore.

Her inability to get back to her old life was something Martin had never forgiven her for, she knew that. He despised what he saw as her weakness and self-indulgence, which also made a big difference to them financially. So he saw it as a huge act of selfishness too, and a kind of vandalism towards their marriage. Why couldn't she just get back in the f***g classroom and earn some bloody money?? *He* had gone back to work, he kept ploughing on and pulling himself through. Why couldn't she?

It was a fair question. But she'd forgotten the answer long ago. She just knew she couldn't. It was an impossibility. Part of another life, another path, that had just disappeared.

She could have tried harder to rediscover it, through therapy for example. But when the will is gone, how do you get it back again? Once they had been discharged from their NHS counselling, she had been happy to let it go. Martin had persisted, booking himself in for some (extortionately expensive) private counselling. That hadn't lasted long. The mathematics of the numbers had simply been too steep; he had slipped down to the bottom and roiled around there on his own. But he could at least say he'd tried. Whereas she had retreated into herself at the first opportunity, wandering around silently inside her own walled garden. Martin called to her over the wall. She didn't reply. He began shouting, louder. But she wanted more than anything simply to be left alone, to drift among the dead stalks and withered blooms, anticipating some kind of final release. Not that she would ever… No. Her mind, her soul, didn't move her in that direction. She would do no violence to herself. In that sense, she was strong and stable. She wouldn't force her end. But, beneath her daily consciousness, she was aware that she was athirst for that final letting go that would one day, eventually, come…

At least she had made herself go out and find some cleaning jobs. For a couple of years now she'd been doing this. Usually three customers a week. It brought in around £900 a month. Better than nothing, no?

But it wasn't anything like enough of course. Their previous life had been built around reasonable dual incomes. The mortgage, the bank loans, the credit card balances. When she had stopped work, it put them in a difficult position. She wasn't proud of that. But it was just numbers. Like everything else, it didn't really *mean* anything. Luckily, Martin had somehow managed to get a promotion at work, a pay rise. There had been a small legacy left to Jane by a distant relative. Martin had even won £5,000 on a scratch card once – she could still remember him whooping with delight in the kitchen. They'd cut back. He'd cancelled policies, such as their life insurance. He'd sold her car. (She didn't mind this; she preferred the clean self-sufficiency of cycling and didn't want to go far anyway). Then he'd started on the furniture.

She was pleased that the wake following Martin's funeral was due to be in a community centre rather than their house – there would have been nothing for anyone to sit on. Martin's parents and sister had taken over the arrangements and that was what they preferred. It was out of her hands. As soon as his body was released, a date could be set. She was dreading it. Seeing everyone on his side and hers. She hadn't seen her own parents for at least a year, her brothers for longer. At least she didn't have any friends left to worry about! That almost made her smile.

Her parents lived in Cheltenham (where she herself had grown up), as did one of her brothers while the other lived in London. She didn't know – she would have to broach the subject soon – whether they were expecting to stay with her for the funeral. How to explain that there were no beds, no sofas, nothing to sit on! She hoped that they would all want to stay in a hotel anyway. After all, they had become like strangers to each other. Gradually, they had stopped excusing her distance and remoteness. They had become exasperated, taken it personally. That was a sadness to her. But there was nothing to be done. Maybe the funeral would help build bridges. Her parents had liked Martin. They had been shocked and deeply upset at the news. They had kept in touch with him intermittently after she had stopped responding, although that too had petered out as Martin descended ever further into his self-destructive hole. But they would certainly come to the funeral. It would be painful to see them. Her brothers too, if they came. She had never been so very close to them due to a few years' difference in their age – their bond had always been to each other as they grew up, playing football, riding bikes, being boys. Would they come? They had got on OK with Martin. Half of her hoped they would and half of her hoped they wouldn't. Whatever happened, the whole thing was going to be a trauma that she'd have to shut out even as it was taking place around her.

She finished the dusting and started on the kitchen – wiping down the surfaces, cleaning the oven and the hob. Bringing out a shine. She could see her reflection in the brushed steel, a dark suggestion of herself.

Dark suggestions… There had been a few of those from that police constable. Nice woman though she was. She had gently but insistently pressed. Asking about finances and insurance. Wanting to know all the details of Martin's life. How much did he drink, how often did he gamble, did he take drugs? She didn't even know the answers with any accuracy! Nor did she know the details about Martin and his lady friends. Just that there had been a number. Occasional traumatic noises through the bedroom wall. Comings and goings, bumps in the night. But not often. He had at least had the decency to generally play away from home. They had never talked about it. He knew that she had moved beyond any question of physical relations; she knew that he hadn't; the rest followed. She didn't blame him and she didn't feel any anger. He could screw whoever he wanted, the dirty old sod. No, she didn't mean that! He was free to fulfil his needs and look for love and affection where he could find it. The rutting old goat. The pathetic riddled old addict. The – but no, she didn't mean it. Maybe she did. Oh, whatever. Just leave it. Poor Martin. And what a horrible, horrible, awful end he had come to. RIP.

Stephenn.

She moved upstairs, blitzed the bathroom with bleach and brilliancy, then cleaned the master bedroom. The other three were empty, so they didn't take long. Three empty spaces – it was almost like home… She ironed the clothes that Mr and Mrs Purcell had left out for her (this earned her an extra £25), then brought the vacuum up and created a dust-sucking whirl of noise.

Then, a retreating force, she backed downstairs to vacuum there, starting at the rear and working forwards. She would finish in the hallway, stow the vacuum under the stairs, and step lightly out of the house to leave it pristine and unbroken, like freshly fallen snow. Her job was humble, it was fatuous like everything else, but she liked to think that she did it well.

Now it was time to go and visit her son. The Purcells lived nearest to the cemetery of her three customers so she usually visited him each week when she was done there. She pedalled away from the house, humming lightly to herself. It was only a fifteen minute ride and there was a florist along the way. She stopped there to buy some new flowers – tulips on this occasion.

It was a big cemetery with extensive grounds. She had been there so many times she could find her way around it blindfolded by now. She left her bike near the entrance and proceeded on foot – past the old Victorian era monuments ranged at the front, towards her son who was located in a middle plot. As always she marvelled, half in horror, at some of the gaudy outsized Victorian erections, many of which were in a complete state of disrepair. Some of the graves' stone casings had cracked and collapsed inwards – you could see earth and dusty cobwebs inside although she never looked too closely. She imagined rats and other creatures must have made them their home. The once-proud monuments looked sad and misguided now, but who was there left to do anything about it? Eventually one day, she imagined, the council would have to respectfully dismantle them and come up with an alternative, low cost solution, whatever that would be.

Some of the modern graves were also badly neglected. It amazed her how much it varied. Some plots were just bare piles of earth, overgrown with weeds around the edges, and faded or barely legible lettering on the stained and/or leaning headstones (some of which were actually just wooden crosses) – while others were immaculately kept and tended, like cemetery show homes, festooned with fresh flowers, balloons, candles, photo frames. Who got what? The more loved, the less loved? Or did it just depend on a random interplay of factors? It made no difference anyway, she realised that. It only appeared to, on this side. But still, she was glad that her son, for however long she was here, would have a fitting, immaculate grave.

Here he was. Near the intersection of two paths, in a corner of the left middle plot. There was a lovely chestnut tree nearby that provided shade at certain times of the day, two yews a little further off. He was here, he would always be here, quietly reposing.

Stephen.

The sun lit up the black marble and glinted off the silver lettering on his headstone, little shooting jewels. Stephen Paul Silverwood. Born 03/02/30. Died 28/07/30. "May flights of angels sing thee to thy rest."

That was all it said. They had opted for simplicity. Her sweet prince...

She took the old roses out of the holder and arranged the new tulips, orange and yellow and pink. Then she took her cloths out of her bag and wiped down the headstone and then the casing of the grave itself. She rubbed and rubbed until everything shone – a black mirror.

She began to talk, as she always did – anything that came into her head. She had given up trying to say profound things quite early on. Now, she just told Stephen about what she had been doing, what she had cleaned, what she might have for tea, what she had heard on the radio. She had briefly told him about Martin after it had happened. But she had excused herself from saying much, because he would already know everything if it was possible to know. *Did* he know? Did he exist anywhere still, in another form? She thought perhaps his spirit had joined the great mass of the life spirit, that resided somewhere, invisibly, in another plain or dimension… Sometimes she thought of it in terms of a raindrop falling into the sea. But she didn't know. How could anyone know? She wasn't a believer in 'God' and heaven and hell, she knew that. As to anything else – it was guessing and groping and hoping, was it not?

So where was her son? He was with her, inside her thoughts as she spoke to him now, listening and smiling and reaching out a perfect curled little finger to touch at her hair. That's where he was. O her chevalier!

Stephenn.

Well, he was in splendid shape, shining in the sun, graced by abundant flowers. He'd be a fine catch for a lucky girl.

She said her goodbyes and assured him she would be back soon. The moment of turning away was always the hardest. It never got any easier.

But there, it was done, and he was still in her thoughts so in fact it didn't make any difference. He knew that. Stephen…

Soon, she'd have two graves to visit. She *would* visit Martin, although not as often. It hadn't been decided where he would go. The other of Knott's two cemeteries was easier for his family and she had already told them that that was fine by her. Putting him 'in' with Stephen was out of the question of course.

She made her way back towards the exit. It was relatively quiet in the cemetery as usual, although she could see in the distance a small huddle of people outside the crematorium and a hearse parked up: another service about to begin.

Then she spotted a young man standing at a headstone who she had seen before. She had seen him several times, in fact. There was something about him that caught her attention and especially today, although she didn't know why. She took little notice of anyone these days, hardly saw the people she moved past. But she felt something when she looked at this man, a kind of sympathy, a stirring. He had a gentle face, hair the colour of corn, hipster sideburns that seemed, somehow, whimsical relics of another time. He was tallish and of a trim build, quite smartly dressed – had he come from work? – although she had seen him before in jeans and T-shirt, shades.

His shoulders were hunched forwards as he stood in front of the grave, and she could tell that he was talking.

But then he sensed her along the path and stopped, flicked a brief glance in her direction.

Amazed inwardly at herself, Jane found she was coming to a halt and taking a step towards him. It was as though something was gently pushing her from behind. The man looked at her again and their eyes met. She saw that his were a beautiful sky blue.

"I've seen you here before," she found that she was saying. "I'm sorry for your loss."

"Thank you," Lewis said, concealing his surprise. "It's fine though – it was a long time ago."

"Is he your brother?" Jane asked, looking at the inscription: Daniel Richard Flynn.

"My friend. He was my best friend, when we were growing up... Taken too young, you know!"

"Yes, I know about that..."

Jane was standing quite close to Lewis now, facing towards the headstone, as though she too were honouring Dan's memory.

"It's a comfort to come and visit them, isn't it?" Jane said. "So you're still coming after all the years that have passed."

Lewis shrugged, smiled. "I find it helps, you know? Helps me. And I want Dan to know that I still remember."

"Absolutely."

"Not that I really know whether he's watching or is aware or not. But, at least when I'm here, I think so…"

They stood silently for a few seconds and looked at the headstone. It was a grey granite one with black lettering. Several bunches of artificial flowers were in place, bright and convincing.

"And you?" Lewis asked eventually. "Who are you here for?"

"My son. He died five years ago. He was very young. He's back over there," Jane said, briefly pointing in Stephen's direction.

"I'm very sorry," Lewis said.

"Thank you. But it's fine. It's the only thing that matters. So it doesn't give me any pain."

"Not while you're here, you mean?"

"It's like an invisible thread, isn't it. That's with you all the time. That's what we need to remember."

Lewis wasn't sure he followed this but just as he was trying to process it, the woman had stepped slightly back. "Well, it's been lovely to say hello. But I mustn't hold you up," she said. "I am sure that we'll see each other again?"

She smiled at him, and nodded, and moved away. Lewis nodded back, raised his hand. "Thank you. Yes, I guess we probably will."

Then she turned and was walking swiftly along the path, illuminated in the sun. It seemed almost as though, wisp of a woman as she was, she was being carried. Lewis raised his eyebrows to himself, and turned back to finish off his conversation with his best friend Dan.

8.

PC Kaur pulled up outside The Fish Fryer. More accurately, she pulled up about 100 metres after The Fish Fryer because immediately outside was a no parking zone. She walked back past various other places – a launderette, a betting shop, a kebab house – and peered in through the window. It was 4pm and it was shut. A sign in the window told her that opening hours were 12-2pm and 5-10pm every day (closed on Mondays).

However, she thought she could detect movement towards the back of the interior, so she banged on the glass and waited. There was no response. She banged again, a little harder.

She was just about to give up when a shadow appeared and gradually formed itself into a person as it approached the door. A short man with a big belly. His shirt was unbuttoned, revealing a dirty looking white vest and a hairy chest sprouting out over the top of it.

The man unlocked the door and looked at her. "Closed until 5pm, officer."

"I'm not here for chips, sir. Is it Peter Franks? Could I come in for a minute?"

"Oh. OK..."

He stepped back and let her in, then relocked the door. PC Kaur looked around – it wasn't big. Just a few feet to the counter, with a couple of chairs that customers could sit on as they waited.

"Come through if you want officer? I'm in the back doing prep."

He lifted the flap in the counter and she followed him through to a small area at the back where there were a couple of fridges, a freezer, a sink. There were big buckets of water filled with bobbing potatoes.

"Just a few more to peel," Peter Franks explained, picking up his peeler. "Not that I probably need to do them," he added.

Then, as if an afterthought, he said: "So how can I help you officer? Nothing serious I hope?"

"Well Mr Franks, it's about a murder that took place ten days ago. You may have seen about it in the news? The victim's name was Martin Silverwood?"

"Oh yes, I've seen about that."

"Mr Silverwood spent most of the night before his death in the Regency casino. We're speaking to people who were there. We know from the casino's lists that that included you, Mr Franks?"

"Right... Yes, I think I was there. Because it was a Saturday night, wasn't it?"

"That's right. Saturday night before last."

"Yeah, I closed up here a bit early as a I recall – it was dead, surprise surprise – and went down there, I think."

"And you knew Mr Silverwood, I believe sir? We have some CCTV footage. A conversation."

"Oh." Franks started peeling harder. "Yes, I knew him."

"I don't want to take up your time now, sir, as you're busy. And we're doing interviews properly, in the station. Can we arrange a time for you to come in?"

"Umm…"

PC Kaur flipped out her phone. "I'm looking at my calendar, Mr Franks. How about tomorrow morning, 10am? You don't open up here until 12?"

"There's prep to do though, officer. And I don't have anything to tell you. Don't know anything about it."

"It shouldn't take long, sir. And like you said, you may have some unused spuds from tonight if you're lucky. Or unlucky. Whichever way you look at it."

"Yes I expect I will. Don't know why I bloody bother!" he said, raising half a tired smile. "10am? I suppose I can manage that, yes."

"Thank you sir. You *do* need to come though please. Although it will just be an informal conversation, not a formal interview. I can send you an email reminder now if you give me an address?"

Soon she was gone. Peter blew out his cheeks as he dried his hands on his shirt. What the fuck. He had to go in and talk about Silverwood. He'd hated the man. But he hadn't done anything. He'd been as surprised as the next man when he saw the news. He had nothing to hide. But it didn't look good. On the face of it. On the bloody face of it. The man who had got his business closed down, the man who had been shagging his wife – now dead.

Well, he'd go in. He'd answer whatever they wanted to know. He hadn't done anything. It would just be a pain in arse, taking up his time. But then it would be done.

He had to start getting the batter ready, cook up some fish. In this bloody business he'd tied himself to. What a prick he was.

He had thought – he'd really thought – there would be money in it. Wished he'd never listened to that twat of a cousin of his, who'd told him one time how much money chippies make. Rolling in it, he'd said, fish like bloody gold bars, he'd said, printing bloody money.

Should have stayed in normal, clean retail. With no stink of bloody fish or oil. Or he should have stuck at the couriering he'd got into after that. Although that was bloody hard work, one damn drop after another, endless bloody targets.

But he'd seen gold, he'd been blinded. He'd promised Mandy it would only be for a few years. He'd make a mint and then get out. But it had been shit right from the start. Because he'd had that damn loan in the first place, eating up his profits. Along with the rent and the rates and the price of bloody electric. Nothing left after that. Just the smell and the heat and the hassle.

But Cod Café – it could have worked. If he'd just been able to get through the first few years. Then bloody Silverwood had come. Said that the place was unsafe from a fire regulation point of view. Big and expensive changes needed, new venting, everything moved, clearer exit routes. Then the food standards people had come, two months early. He knew – he just knew, even though Silverwood denied it – that Silverwood had got them on the case. Why? What did Silverwood have against his business? It was vindictive, that was all. Then the food people found faults too, mice droppings, poor hygiene conditions. He'd tried to keep the vermin out! God knows he'd tried. But pest control was expensive. And it put the customers off. They'd notice. He'd blocked holes up, put things down, but whatever he did, they still got in. He wasn't good at that side of it. Safety and hygiene and food standards and all that. He'd done his best. He'd always done his best. What the fuck could he do about it if his best was no bloody good?

Peter wiped at his face with his battery hand, smearing his cheek. God, he wished he could just go home. He'd probably take barely a hundred quid tonight. And he had to pay 20% of that to the owner, who he was renting off. And cover all the expenses himself of course. It sucked. It sucked so much. Like the whole of his bloody sinking life.

He knew all too well that if he couldn't turn it around soon, Mandy would be off. The writing was on the wall. She'd been playing around for the last two years or more, while he'd been frying fish and chips until ten every bloody night. Including with that arsehole Silverwood. Although he wasn't the only one. A laughing stock, he was. The sad battered fishcake of fucking Knott.

Talking of which... He put some fishcakes in to fry and some sausages. Opening time in twenty minutes. He wondered when he'd get his first customer. Some nights, it wasn't until after six. The kebab place nearby was popular, and it did chips as well. There was a popular chippie about five minutes away. And there was the parking problem of course. He'd known all this, and it was why Stav the owner had set the rent so cheap (although the 20% was steep) – but it was all he could afford as he tried to get back on his feet after the closure of Cod Café.

But, Silverwood... He hadn't liked the guy from the first. Arrogant, he was. Looking for an argument. Poking and prying and trying to find things wrong. Throwing his weight around. As if he amounted to anything, working for the council! And then one day, when their dispute was midway through, he'd come in and Mandy had been there. Began flirting with her, right under his bloody eyes. And acting softer towards him, as if he was actually a decent guy. And Mandy had responded. He could see that straightaway. Something you knew, when an attraction was there. It was in the body language. And there wasn't anything you could do about it. To stop it.

He knew what the police would say. He knew what they'd be thinking. And it didn't look good, did it? They'd exchanged a few words in the casino when they'd run into each other. What had he said? He couldn't even really remember, having been pissed at the time. Just another warning to keep his dirty hands off his wife. Nothing big and it was over in a minute. Then of course he'd walked home that way... Well, that was the bloody way home, wasn't it! But it felt like everything was somehow falling into place to point at him. It was as if God or someone *wanted* him to look guilty. Maybe he even *was* guilty then, in a way. If God wanted it. Maybe he was! If wanting someone dead made you guilty. Although he would never... No, he wouldn't, he couldn't, he'd never go *that* far.

Silverwood may have been a wanker, but he didn't deserve to be cut open and gutted, like a fucking fish.

9.

"OK, I'm gonna do it!" Alice said.

"Really? Are you sure?!" cried Lewis excitedly.

"It's the only way," she said. "Gotta be done…"

She picked up her phone and found the message from Kevan Monk.

"Right, what shall I say?" She bit her lip, considering. "OK… *Hi Kevan… Sorry I didn't get back to you. It came as a bit of a surprise seeing you again… But I've been thinking… it would be lovely to catch up… Fancy a drink or something one night soon?*" She looked at across at Lewis. "How does that sound?"

He nodded. "Yeah, fine I guess…"

"Cool. I'll add an A and one kiss." She re-read it carefully. Yep, that would do. She pressed send. "Done!"

"Oh my God!" Lewis said. "You've sent it? OK. It's all good… But like we said, you'll have to go at it gently, indirectly, yeah? Just subtly probe around a bit."

"Of course."

"And an absolute bottom line is that you won't go back to his place, or invite him back to yours. And I'll be waiting somewhere nearby. On hand."

"Yes, Lewis, understood!" It was ironic that, even though Lewis still refused to believe that Kevan Monk could have had anything to do with Martin Silverwood's murder, he was so jumpy and excitable about the prospect of this rendezvous.

"Oh! He's read it!" Alice said. "And he's writing a reply..."

In it came. *"Nice to hear from you. Sounds good. Wednesday evening? Kx"*

A few minutes later, it was all agreed. Kevan said he would book a table at Don Carlo's, an upmarket Italian in the centre of Knott, for 7.30pm.

"So he's going full monty straightaway," Lewis observed. "Swanky meal not just a drink..."

It was Sunday evening so there wasn't long to wait. They watched a film together and had an early night. Before they went to sleep though, lying close together in the dark, Alice told Lewis about the news she'd had from her mother... She began to cry, she couldn't help it, it all came pushing through, and Lewis responded with a wonderful and immediate tenderness. He asked her gentle questions, sensitively helping her probe her feelings. He talked a little, again, about his friend Dan. They found deep comfort in each other, physically, emotionally, and what seemed like an oddly mutual pain... They fell asleep with their fingers touching, almost intertwined.

Monday and Tuesday were busy days with back-to-back appointments, so before she knew it Wednesday had come round and Alice was contemplating seeing Monk again. One on one, tete a tete. It sounded almost sweet. If you didn't know who Kevan Monk was.

She made sure to time her Mng taking so that it would peak in the evening. As she left work, she felt the effects beginning to come through – her mind was a warm animal living in the moment; she was sharp, focused, alert. She got home and got ready with brisk efficiency. She'd already planned her outfit – an expensive, tight-fitting black dress, black shoes, matching clutch. Looking in the mirror, she thought she approved.

Her cab arrived. She had decided against driving herself as then she could have wine if she felt she needed it and Lewis would bring her home in any case. As they travelled in, she messaged him. He was already in situ, in a pub across the road from Don Carlo's.

"Agent Inman is ready and in place! Can be with you in less than two minutes if needed!"

So that was all good, then. She had to confess, she had no idea at all how this would pan out. Whenever she'd tried to think out what she'd say, her mind had clouded over and she had formed no kind of plan. She was trusting to her instincts. She'd be bold or cautious depending on what signals she picked up from him. He wasn't the type to flare up though – he'd be cool and composed whatever she said and however he felt inside. That was a comfort. It wasn't as though everything would explode into a violent scene, remonstrations, angry shouting. And they would be in a public place, after all. As the most expensive restaurant in Knott, he would probably know some of the other diners there which could inhibit him from getting openly worked up.

The cab pulled up outside at just a couple of minutes after half-past – perfect timing. All was good, she told herself, although she could feel her heart skittering inside her chest as she walked into the cool, air-conditioned restaurant. It had been a venue in Knott for years. An American diner for a long time which eventually folded, then briefly a restaurant/night club which collapsed within less than six months when its opening unfortunately coincided with Covid. The site had lain dormant for a couple of years and then Don Carlo's had opened. It had been a fixture in the city for over a decade now, renowned for its suave atmosphere, impeccable service and excellent food.

Announcing herself at the reception desk, Alice was shown upstairs to the second floor, and then on up to the roof terrace. She had eaten at Don Carlo's a few times, but never up here as it was usually booked solid. It was a lovely spot, with views out over the city towards a green haze of hills beyond. The sun was getting lower in the sky, diffusing an early evening orange. Awnings and trellises with vines and greenery provided shade. Alice took all this in as she simultaneously scanned for Kevan Monk. Then she spotted him sitting at a table in a quiet corner as the waiter led her towards him. He looked up and saw her, rose politely to his feet. He looked very smart in dark trousers and a tailored open-necked shirt. What passed for a smile passed across his features. "Alice, lovely to see you," he said, and they air-kissed on each cheek. "You look stunning," he added as they took their seats.

"Well, I didn't expect this!" Alice said. "How did you get a table up here at such short notice?"

"I know the owner and he owed me a favour. It seemed like a good time to call it in," Kevan said drily. "Now then, shall we get a little aperitif?"

They ordered martinis and sipped on iced water as they waited. "Nice up here," Alice said approvingly, looking around. There were perhaps fifteen other tables of varying sizes, most of which were already occupied by other diners. Theirs was set back a little in a nook, affording plenty of privacy.

"We'll get a good sunset in a bit too," Kevan said. "On some evenings it's really spectacular."

"I didn't have you down for a nature man."

"Oh, I appreciate all beauty, Alice. As you know…"

It was the usual Kevan Monk. Everything delivered deadpan, with the minimum of variation, eyes closely watching. He was handsome, though. She had forgotten how much so. The sun was bathing his face in an apricot light, bringing out the smooth healthiness of his complexion. There was a strength to his face, a well-moulded symmetry and balance. The dark furze of his beard underlined a kind of potency. And of course she knew that under that expensive clothing was a hard and muscled body. Monk kept fit, watched what he ate, worked out every day. He had his own gym at home.

"So, it was good bumping into you the other week at the clinic," she said. "It had been a while, hadn't it?"

"It had indeed."

"And apologies once again that it took me so long to reply to your message. But yeah, I thought it would be good to reconnect, as they say. Catch up again, as friends."

She didn't expect him to react to her closing addendum, and he didn't. Instead, he raised a martini which had now arrived and smiled. "Absolutely," he said, as they clinked glasses. "A toast also to Mng, that you played such an important part in bringing to market," he added.

Alice smiled. "Of course! And how's it going? No end of demand, it seems!"

"It's going very well. We're close to obtaining licenses in several countries overseas now. Going international."

"But what about the regulatory review? Anything more on that?"

Kevan sat back. "Oh, it's in hand. They've made their announcement. But I think we've contained it pretty well."

"Oh right, good. Hope it stays that way."

"That depends on the outcome of course. But I'm confident we'll be OK. After all, if the regulator came to a bad conclusion, it would reflect almost as much on them as on us…. Now, what do you fancy having?"

They inspected the menus, placed their orders.

"So, how long will it take do you think – the review?" Alice asked.

"Oh... Six months at least. They'll do it thoroughly, go through everything again. Including your report, of course."

"Yes."

"But don't worry, Alice. There's nothing in there that we can't defend."

"No..."

"You don't sound sure. But don't forget, we now have two years' user data and results. Yes, there is a small addiction problem. But it's nothing in the scheme of things."

"Yes... I have to say though, Kevan, that seeing at first hand some of the addiction issues amongst my patients, I'd describe it as more than a 'small problem'."

"Even compared to addictions to other opioids? And other drugs? And alcohol, and all the rest of it? Keep your perspective, Dr Carlisle!"

"Well, there have been cases – although admittedly not among any patients of mine – of really severe withdrawal problems..."

"Let them stay on it, then! It doesn't do any harm." Then he added: "I have a mild addiction myself. But it doesn't make any difference. It is entirely manageable."

Alice laughed, despite herself. "I do too, to be honest!"

"Admirable loyalty to the brand. I thank you."

"But also, I mean, it's becoming another recreational drug, Kevan. You must be aware of that? Mng is being bought and sold on the streets. It's a real concern – although no one seems to be paying much attention."

Kevan raised an eyebrow. "But why should anyone be worried, when Mng is so mild? It's not worth the time and effort compared to heroin and crack and everything else. It's as nearly harmless as weed."

"Except it's not! The withdrawal symptoms, Kevan… And where's it *coming* from, that's what I can't work out…?"

"Well, we know there have been illegal operations to manufacture counterfeit product," Kevan said, shrugging. "Both in the UK and overseas. The general composition of Mng is open source."

"But that's even worse! If they're fakes, they could be dangerous. People could *die*."

"The samples we've obtained have in fact been remarkably good. No dangerous impurities. So that's not an issue, Alice. You can rest assured on that."

Their starters arrived – and Kevan seemed pleased at the interruption. Although he had remained calm and unruffled, Alice sensed that he wasn't relishing the conversation so far. She had an urge to drop Primegate into it and see how he reacted. But how? She couldn't think of a way that wouldn't be cack-handed and forced. So she changed tack instead.

"Wasn't that terrible, the murder here in Knott?" She tossed it out casually, in the way of making topical conversation.

"Oh yes, awful. Horrible to think about," Kevan said. "Wine?"

He filled her glass and they drank. It was an immaculate Italian chardonnay, reassuringly expensive...

The sun, with a blush of red, was sinking below the horizon now, while the orange light around them had darkened to a steel blue. Kevan was a figure in shadow, lit in flickers by the candle that sat between them on the table. But then so, presumably, was she.

"Have you heard anything about how the investigation's going?" Alice asked, quickly adding: "I mean, you're very well connected here aren't you, you probably know people in the police?"

"I do," he said. "But no, I haven't heard anything. If anything, I think they're struggling for leads. But I'm sure they'll turn something up before too long. A murder like that leaves a trail."

"Yes... It was very violent, wasn't it? The poor man..." Alice shuddered. "He worked for the council, didn't he?"

"I believe so."

"I read that he's left a widow, and that five years ago their baby son also died. I mean, can you imagine what that poor woman is going through? Just appalling..."

"Indeed. It is difficult to think about."

"But this man, Martin Silverwood, I think he came in and did an inspection at SmartLab not long ago? Lewis told me. We're friends, as I expect you know?" Kevan inclined his head in acknowledgement. "And Lewis said that he kind of fell out with people – seemed to be asking lots of persistent questions about something or other? It just sounded quite... strange?"

She didn't get any reaction. "Is that the case?" Kevan said. "I really don't know about that, Alice. You know, I don't get involved with things at that level. I expect it was nothing." Then he said, finishing his plateful: "I can't believe it would have been enough for one of my employees to murder him, if that's what you're suggesting!"

"No, no!" she cried. "I was just mentioning it, as a kind of curiosity really. That's all. I get the impression that Martin Silverwood was that kind of man – a bit difficult, easy to fall out with, you know?"

"That may well be. Obviously, someone had a grudge against him. Either that or he was just unlucky. Jumped on and knifed and robbed. It could have been as simple as that?"

"It could have been, of course... I just hope the police bring the killer to justice. Whoever did it deserves a long, long sentence."

As Alice said this, the lighting around the terrace came on, supplementing the candles. Suddenly, they were more present to each other. They eyed each other silently for a second, then looked away as the waiter came in to clear their starters. They looked back at each other, smiled.

"It is indeed nice to see you again, Alice," Kevan said, raising his glass. "It's funny how you forget the details of how someone is. But as soon as you see them again, you remember it all straightaway."

What exactly did he mean by that?! She simply smiled and nodded in response. He knocked his wine back. That was his second glass already.

"No," he continued, wiping his mouth, "I don't get involved at that level, Alice. I can't. There is too much to do. Keeping our investors on side. Reports, forecasts, roadshows. Preparing for another funding round. I am in London a lot. It's demanding – but exciting. Working towards the vision."

"And what's that, then?"

"The Mng we have now – that's just the start, Alice. It's only the beginning, the first iteration." Kevan Monk leaned forward, his eyes gleaming. "I have scientists and chemists working right now on the next phase. Mng2 will take it to new realms. We're strengthening the metals, the magnesium and zinc, and working the codeine down to trace levels. That way, the mental hit will be huge while the addictiveness will disappear. New Mng will give a sense of absolute meaning. It will be exhilarating, intense. It will make the taker feel absolutely complete and whole. No need for anything else. It will become as simple and natural as drinking water – everyone, everywhere, will take Mng. It will just be something we do every day –

taking the medicine, like brushing our teeth. And after the first couple of years, it will be so cheap that everyone can afford it. Like paracetamol. It will only be in the early years that I, that SmartLab, will make serious money. But that's fine. I want to change the world, Alice. That's what I'm doing this for. It's not about my personal gain."

"OK… sounds exciting," Alice offered, somewhat weakly.

Their food arrived. But Kevan Monk rolled on, ignoring the waiter. "I know I used that word myself – but it's more than exciting, Alice! It's my mission in life. It's everything to me. Think about it: a non-addictive supplement that takes mental alertness and wellbeing into the stratosphere. That virtually guarantees… happiness! Makes us feel whole and part of a meaningful framework of things. It will decimate drug use. Alcoholism too. People will only drink because they like the taste and as a pleasant social activity. Depression will become a thing of the past. It may even contribute to combating mental illness – there are signs that the stimulation to the brain will improve cognitive health. And religion too. It will loosen the hold of dogmatic creeds and institutions. Because we won't *need* religion. We will realise that God is inside us, Alice. Mng will make the connection. It will reveal to us the God inside our own minds, like a sun coming up. Everything will be changed."

"You're serious, Kevan? You really believe all this?" In fact, Alice felt a flash of excitement herself. "It's a hell of a vision!"

"It is. It's got to happen. Another great thing? Those who are struggling with any addiction to Mng1 right now will be able to transition to Mng2. In a short period, their addiction should therefore be broken. Not that they'll want to stop taking it of course. But it will deal with that issue too. I'm putting everything into this, Alice. But it requires money. For the R&D, the development, the trials. And it means I've got to keep the profitability of SmartLab up, to keep investor confidence and give them some early returns. Realistically, Mng2 is several years away. So I have to keep the sales and the funding coming in. Nothing, no one, can be allowed to get in the way of that. I won't let that happen."

He paused, beginning to eat his food. Alice's mind was racing. It was both thrilling and faintly scary. This prophet-like zeal.

"And the profits are holding up? Enough to keep funding it all?"

"Sales are good and increasing. And whisper it quietly, but I've got a major pharma, and I mean a *global* one, interested in coming in and taking a stake. Discussions ongoing, watch this space, etcetera. And like I said, we're getting close to obtaining some licenses overseas, in Europe and Australia. The US is looking harder. But we're off to a great start. It's about keeping up momentum and not letting anything slow that down."

"I can imagine. Too much at stake."

"The future of humanity, Alice. I mean, look where we are. Look at the chaos of the world – the violence, the unhappiness, the misery. Mng2 will be immense. It will be a cure. It will transform. It will be like turning the brightness up, on a screen. At the moment, we're set too low. It's as simple as that, Alice – we are dimmed. But Mng will turn us up, it will restore us to how we're meant to be. We will become like new beings, like angels! I mean it when I say the world will be a different place. It's bigger than... the invention of the internet, than AI, than anything! It can't be over-stated. That's why I'm so passionate, Alice."

Kevan sat back, seemingly replete of both food and words. He rested his hands on the table. Glancing at them, Alice had a sudden flash of what they may once have done... 'No one can be allowed to get in the way'... A chill went through her, despite the clammy warmth of the night air.

"Do excuse me for a moment, Kevan," she said, getting to her feet. "Popping to the ladies."

Her head was spinning from Kevan's intense monologue. What was one to make of all that?! From a humble tablet to the solution to life itself... She grabbed the space she had given herself, breathing in and out deliberately as she went. As soon as she was in the toilets on the second floor, she got her phone out and dialled Lewis. He answered straightaway: "What's happening? Everything OK?" he asked breathlessly. "It's fine, Lou. All good. Just wanted you to know. We should be finished soon. I'll call you as soon as I've left," she told him.

She took her time on the loo, came out, washed her hands and freshened up. She looked at herself in the mirror. "Not long to go now, girl. See it through!" she said to herself.

Back up on the terrace, she saw that Kevan was nearly at the end of another glass of wine. The bottle was finished – and she'd only had one glassful and a top-up…

"All good? Would you like a dessert?" Kevan asked, a faint slur to his words. Alice shook her head as she sat down. "I'm stuffed! It was delicious."

"I'm pleased. It's always good here." Then he sat forward, as though decisively: "You know, Alice, I'm really trying to be good too. I've changed. I'm becoming a different man. My vision for Mng has given me a new purpose. I want to help the world, to change the world! I know I have issues that I need to deal with. Behavioural, I mean. Anger and… forcefulness and so on. But through Mng and through the purpose it's given me, I'm changing. I wanted you to know that…"

"I see… That's cool…" Alice floundered. "I'm pleased, Kevan! Just don't let your vision for Mng lead you to extremes, that's all I'd say."

"Extremes?"

"Extreme acts… I don't know. Nothing is worth getting completely obsessive over, no matter how well motivated the vision."

"Perhaps not…"

The conversation tailed off, their empty plates and glasses reinforcing the sense of an ending. "Well, I'll get the bill then," Kevan said, gesturing at the waiter.

Before long, they were making their way across the terrace towards the stairs. Alice felt Kevan's hand on the small of her back as they went, but she gently moved herself out of his reach, hoping this would be a sufficiently clear signal...

When they got outside, they turned to each other with an air of mutual hesitation. "Well, would you like...?" Kevan began, but Alice quickly shook her head. "Sorry, but I need to be getting home, Kevan. I've got a full day of appointments tomorrow." Then she looked at her phone. "I've just requested a cab – it's one minute away. Thank you for a fabulous meal. A lovely evening!"

"You're welcome. Your company is always special. I hope we'll see each other again soon."

He kissed her on the cheek, a real kiss this time not the airborne sort. She didn't mind.

As her cab pulled away, she could see him in the mirror for a bit, watching her recede, then she lost sight of him. She sank back, letting out a big sigh – of relief? confusion? anxiety? She wasn't sure...

Then she phoned Lewis. "Sorry babes, you'll need to make your own way to my place! Well, I couldn't let him know you were waiting nearby, could I? Yes, yes, don't worry – I'll fill you in on everything as soon as you come!"

10.

DI Sharp waved goodbye to Mary in the living room window and got into the car. He felt zippy and raring to go. Those Mng tablets were amazing! He wished he'd discovered them sooner. They were so good, he'd been taking several each day even though it said to only take one. The effects were brilliant. They made him feel so present in the moment. He was able to bring the full weight of his intelligence and experience to anything he was doing. They enhanced his sense of wellness too. He had to confess, he'd been feeling his age a little in recent times – a bit of aching here, a tiredness there – but these babies seemed to dispel that as well. They gave his whole system a lift. Which seemed to last almost the whole day, ready for him to take some more in the morning!

He'd have to congratulate that CEO of SmartLab if he saw him again. What his name? Kevin Monk. He'd met him at a drinks do a while back for the great and the good. The guy was friendly with Superintendent Odutola and she'd extended an invitation. Of course, Monk was something of a local VIP being the leader of Knott's jewel-in-the-crown business that put the city on the map. Mind you, how would he explain away taking Mng himself? OK, on second thoughts maybe not...

His Mng boost would help him today as he prepared to grill his number one suspect Peter Franks. They'd called him back in for a formal interview. His answers to PC Kaur in the informal questioning had been far from satisfactory. This was his man, he could feel it in his bones! Boy, would he nail him that very morning. And when the case was swiftly and satisfactorily closed, all would be set for his early retirement. Maybe, after all, life wasn't so bad.

DI Sharp whistled as he went, navigating the Knott traffic on his way to the station where he'd been based this last fifteen years. He suffered no fools in the car. He hooted and gestured at a couple of dithering drivers. They, like Peter Franks, were obstacles to be batted away. The intelligent man will always cut through to reach his goal.

When he got to the station, he had a debrief straightaway with PC Kaur. Her legs looked particularly fine that warm and bright morning – it was skirt and tights today – catching rays of sunlight under the desk. But he kept his mind on the job.

"So, Franks will be here at ten? I want you to lead the questioning, Constable, but I'll probably jump in quite frequently too. You can be mainly neutral, even sympathetic. I'll weigh in harder. We'll see if a few sudden knocks throw him off balance. Make him open up."

"OK sir," PC Kaur nodded. "So, you think he's the prime suspect?"

"He has all the motives, does he not?"

"Yes sir," she nodded again. But then she added: "There *are* a few loose ends though, that don't seem to quite fit."

"Well, it's our job to connect those loose ends and tie them up. Is it not, Constable?"

"Yes sir."

"Good. I'll see you in Room 3 at 10 then. That's all for now."

Peter Franks arrived on time and, at ten o'clock sharp, the DI of that name accompanied by PC Kaur strode into the interview room to get started.

Franks was huddled nervously in his chair, blinking in the bright light of the small, windowless room and repeatedly sipping at the water he'd been given. He gave off an odour of fish, chip fat and anxiety.

"Thank you for coming in again, Mr Franks," PC Kaur said. "You know me of course. This is Detective Inspector Sharp, who is leading the investigation. We'll be recording this conversation as it's a formal interview." She clicked the recorder on. "The time is 10.04 on Thursday 24 May, 2035. In the room are Peter Franks, DI Sharp and myself, PC Kaur. Now then, Peter, can you tell us your movements on the evening of Saturday 12 May, from 6pm onwards?"

Peter Franks cleared his throat noisily. "Yes OK. It's the same as everything I've already told you though."

"Could you tell us again please, Peter?"

"All right then... I was at work in the Fish Fryer that day. We open at 5, so I got there at around 4. I worked there all evening. I was on my own because I don't employ anyone else. Don't need another person, unfortunately, not at the Fish Fryer. It was quiet, so I actually closed up early, at about half-past nine. I cleaned up and went down to the Regency casino. Usually go there once or twice a week. I think I got there at about half-past ten. I had a few drinks, played some slots. Then some roulette. I left at about 1am. I walked home. Got in at something like 1.20am. That's it, officer. I didn't see anything unusual. I know nothing at all about Martin Silverwood's murder."

"Right," PC Kaur said calmly. "Did you talk to anyone you know at the casino?"

"Well, yeah… I know quite a few people there, regulars like me, you know. Chatted to a few people at the bar. There was, let me see, Dave Sawyer, an old friend. Malcolm Hunt. A guy called Anton. Anton Rostanov who has a finance business. Just casual chat, you know…"

"And, correct me if I'm wrong, but I think you said you also saw Martin Silverwood? You spoke to him?"

Peter shifted on his seat. "Well, yeah, I did, yeah. Like I told you before. We exchanged a few brief words."

DI Sharp cut in. "The CCTV, Mr Franks, suggests that your words were not friendly. You didn't like or get on with Martin Silverwood, did you?"

"I mean, officer, I *didn't* like him, no. I admit that. But there's no way I'd ever kill a man. It's just not something I could do. I'll tell you that for nothing."

"Why didn't you like him, Mr Franks? Can you explain your relationship please?"

"I've told all this to PC Kaur already… But, OK. He inspected my old business, the Cod Café, and gave it a bad report. He got food standards involved too. We argued about it. In the end, I had to give the business up. That was a while ago, mind, a year ago..."

"And is that all?"

"Excuse me?"

"Is that the only reason you didn't like Martin, Mr Franks?" DI Sharp persisted.

"I mean... there were other things. Like I've already told the constable."

"And they were?"

"He was... my wife and him were... seeing each other, you know. On and off, like. I knew about it. I found messages on Mandy's phone. I had it out with him a while back."

"Had it out?"

"I saw him in the pub a couple of months ago. I told him to leave my wife alone."

"Did it become physical?"

"No – just words. He didn't say much. Didn't deny it. Mumbled a few things about there was nothing in it. But I know they saw each other again."

PC Kaur broke in more gently. "And so, Peter, is that what you spoke to Martin about on that night in the casino?"

"I told him to stay away from Mandy, and keep away from her this time," Franks said. "That was all. It was very brief. But I wouldn't... I would never..." He trailed off, dropping his head, eyes fixed to the floor.

"The CCTV shows that you put your hand up to his chest and pushed him back. It was quite an aggressive confrontation, was it not?"

Peter bridled at this, raising his head. "Hardly aggressive in the scheme of things, officer! I barely touched him! What would you do if another man was sleeping with your wife!"

"*We* ask the questions here, Mr Franks," Sharp said with a cold, affronted dignity.

PC Kaur took over again. "So you had what we may describe as a brief altercation? The CCTV shows that was at about 11.30pm, around an hour after you arrived. Did you run into or speak to Martin again that night? You didn't? And then you left at 1am."

"How many beers did you have that night, Mr Franks?" asked DI Sharp. "How many had you had when you spoke to Martin Silverwood, and how many more did you have before you left?"

"I don't know officer! I wasn't very drunk. I think I had five. I can take eight or nine on a good night."

"So you'd had... a couple maybe when you argued with Martin. And then three more?"

"Something like that."

"And you left at 1am, only a few minutes before Martin. Did you sense that he was getting ready to leave? Thought you'd get in position maybe, wait for him outside?"

"No, officer! How could I know when he was going to leave?"

"CCTV also shows us that you collected a jacket from the cloakroom on your way out. It was a very warm evening – why did you have a jacket with you, Mr Franks? Was there anything *in* the jacket?"

Again, Peter bridled at the questioning. "Nothing in it, no officer! If you must know, I wore a jacket because it helps mask the smell. From the chip shop. But I got hot walking to the casino, so I gave it in when I arrived. That's all."

"So you walked straight home?" PC Kaur asked. "And your route was to go down Dark Lane?"

"That's right. It's the quickest way home, to go down there. Left out of the casino, left again, and then down Dark Lane. That's the way I *always* go."

"And did you see anything, notice anything unusual, along Dark Lane? In Dark Lane car park specifically?" she asked.

"I didn't. It was quiet. I don't think I passed anyone. Of course, I wasn't looking for anything anyway. It was just a normal night, a normal walk home, officer."

"And when you got home, was your wife there? Was she up?"

"You know that already officer. You spoke to Mandy, didn't you? She was in bed, fast asleep. She'd had a few I think. I got into bed quietly and went to sleep myself."

DI Sharp cut in. "So she can't vouch for the state of your clothes? She can't give an eye-witness statement that they were clear of any blood, for example?"

"I hung them up in the wardrobe, officer! You can come and look at them if you want. You can take them away and examine them! They're as clean as a whistle. Relatively speaking."

"We may do just that, Mr Franks... So, let me put an alternative scenario to you and see what you think. You had five beers – you were drunk. You sensed that Martin was going to leave shortly. Perhaps you also knew that he had parked in Dark Lane. You left and waited in a concealed spot outside. You followed him when he came out, down Dark Lane. You had a knife in your jacket. When he turned into the car park, you pounced. You killed Martin, then took his wallet and phone to make it look like a robbery. You have either hidden them somewhere or thrown them away. Likewise your clothes and the murder weapon. Why should we not believe that *that* is what actually happened, Mr Franks?"

"Because it's not true, officer! None of that is true! I am not a bloody murderer!"

"But you have a history of violence, Mr Franks. A suspended sentence three years ago for grievous bodily harm?"

Franks sat back and let out a whistle. "That was just a fight that I got into in a club, officer. A random incident. You know that, if you've read the notes."

"Yes I have. And they tell me that the fight was about your wife. The man you attacked was making advances to her on the dance floor."

"It was completely different officer. He was pissed, obnoxious, he started coming at me when Mandy pushed him away. It was a one-off."

"But it shows that you're capable of violence. You hated Martin Silverwood. He had ruined your business. He was sleeping with your wife. You couldn't deal with it any longer. Your rage reached a point where you decided to act…"

"No, Inspector Sharp! No, that's not right!"

DI Sharp changed tack. "How *is* your relationship with your wife, Mr Franks? Was she, I don't know, planning to leave you, for Martin Silverwood? Had she started talking about splitting up?"

"No, officer. She has been unfaithful, but that's the way our relationship goes. She wasn't in *love* with Silverwood or anything. It was on and off, a casual thing. To be honest… to be honest, there have been other men too. It's her way."

"Her way?" DI Sharp raised an eyebrow.

"When she's had a few especially. It comes out in her. She looks for, I don't know, comfort. She gives comfort. She's a loving woman."

"Does she give *you* love, too?"

"Look, I don't need to… what business is that of yours! We have our own private relationship, officer. I'm not going to talk about that. We're man and wife. We're married. We're staying married. That's it."

"Yes, understood. I don't want to unnecessarily pry, Mr Franks. But it helps to establish the context of things," DI Sharp said, softening a little. "Can I also ask, Mr Franks, about your financial position? You must have taken a hit when the Cod Café closed. Are you solvent, would you say?"

"I have some financial pressures. But I'm managing."

"The Fish Fryer doesn't do very good business though, as you yourself have said?"

"Not really. But it might pick up. I'm planning some changes."

"Does Mandy work?"

"She does some part-time shifts in a hairdresser. As an assistant, like. Doing the hair washes and that."

"So she doesn't bring in much. It must be hard then."

"But what are you getting at Inspector? What does my financial situation have to do with anything?"

"Just that it would fuel your anger against Martin Silverwood, no?"

Peter snorted. "Yes but his death isn't gonna change anything money-wise, is it? Come on, officer. Give me a break…"

"I will give you a break, Peter, I will give you a break," DI Sharp said, nodding. "We're nearly done. For now, I think. Tell me – if we were to ask for your phone would you give it to us? And a search of your property?"

"Of course, I have nothing to hide," Peter said defiantly. "Go ahead. You can look at anything you want."

"OK, good. We'll get back to you on that, Mr Franks. Rest assured."

They brought the interview to a close and PC Kaur led Peter Franks out. DI Sharp sat in the interview room ruminating with satisfaction on what had taken place. When PC Kaur returned, he looked up at her and said: "OK constable, let's get the wheels in motion. We arrest him by the beginning of next week. Get to work on a warrant to search his property and seize his phone."

"Yes sir. So… you think we've got enough?"

"I do. My instincts are telling me, constable. Thirty years in the service teach you things, you know."

"OK sir…" PC Kaur said, unable to keep the doubt out of her voice.

"What, you don't agree?"

"Well, sir... I agree he had the motive. And he was in the right place. But if we don't find any physical evidence – the knife, blood, DNA on his clothes...?"

"The only way we'll find them is if we do a search, is it not? Surely you can see that, PC Kaur?"

"Yes sir. I believed his wife when she told me that his clothes were all normal and in place. Nothing missing from his wardrobe. That could be a problem, sir?"

"She was asleep when he got home. He could have hidden them in a bag, destroyed them the next day, replaced them with others? Who knows how closely she monitors his wardrobe? She doesn't sound like the most up-together of women!"

"Yes sir. The CCTV evidence is not very well-focused and it's in black and white. But of course, we'll have our experts compare the contents of his wardrobe to the CCTV, see if they believe they are the same. We'll also scan the CCTV footage along the main road after Dark Lane again. He would have had to walk along there for a short distance before crossing over to get to his house. We might pick him up there, and there might be a good enough view of his clothes to detect for signs of blood."

"OK, good. Whatever the *details* are, PC Kaur, I can feel Peter Franks' guilt. I feel it in my gut. He's our man."

"Right then, sir. I'm on it..."

DI Sharp was annoyed at her uncertainty but there again she was callow, inexperienced. She had so much to learn. In this job, you just had to go by instinct most of the time. If you waited for all the little pieces of evidence to fall into place, you'd never solve anything. You'd be waiting until bloody Christmas to solve a crime at Eastertime. Get your stockings all mixed up with your bleeding eggs...

A bit later, he went to give an update to Superintendent Odutola.

"He's our man, ma'am. I can feel it."

"I will trust your experience, Detective Inspector. But we still haven't found the murder weapon, or the victim's phone, or his wallet, I believe? Do you have any physical evidence that links Mr Franks to the crime?"

"Not yet ma'am. But we will. His motive is so clear, it's screaming out. He was in the casino that night and confronted Mr Silverwood. Barring evidence, it's an open and shut case."

Superintendent Odutola arched her back and sat up to her full height in her chair, eyeing DI Sharp intently. "Is that so? Just don't make fools of us all, Detective Inspector. This case is too high profile for that."

DI Sharp, who had been enjoying his view of the hills, gave a confident smile. "I know that, ma'am. I wouldn't risk anything here if I wasn't sure. We'll arrest him as soon as we're ready and bring him in. I guarantee you the whole thing will be done by the middle of next week."

"I will hold you to that."

"You can hold me any way you'd like, ma'am."

"DI Sharp! Do *not* get over-familiar!" the superintendent cried sternly, although with just enough of a hint of irony to keep DI Sharp at ease.

"With your permission ma'am, I'd better get back to my desk? I have a lot to get done."

"I want *very* regular updates. Thank you, Detective Inspector…"

DI Sharp stayed working until after seven o'clock. He'd been in before nine. That was the police officer's life – long hours and devotion to duty. And he still had one more thing he wanted to do on the way home…

He knew he shouldn't. It was a risk. It was craven and indefensible. But he just had that itch. *She was a loving woman.* When he got that itch, there was nothing he could do about it – except scratch.

He got in the car and drove off. He took a little detour so that he passed the Fish Fryer. Yes, lights were on. Franks was there. He had a couple of customers too. That was good then. He wouldn't be home for about three hours.

It was certainly useful to have an unmarked car and not to wear a uniform – he could operate incognito. He parked quite near to Franks' address and walked back under the sycamore trees that lined the road. The area was a bit scruffy but OK. Houses dating probably from the 1950s. Now, where was number 37?

Here it was. A little sign by the bleary front door directed him round the corner to flat 2. He walked along the cracked path and came to another, equally faded door. He took a breath and rang the bell. It was another hot evening and he felt himself sweating as he waited. But was that the warmth or nerves? Nerves? He must be getting old...

A light came on and he heard steps down the stairs. The door opened and there she was in front of him. Yep, what he'd picked up on the grapevine was true. Mrs Franks was a proper woman all right. She wore a loose-fitting cotton shift, one piece. He could sense the ample contours beneath. She was bare footed with bright red toenails.

"Can I help you, love?" she said. She had a thick, handsome face, if a little worn by the years. Dyed blonde hair piled up in a coif. She had the air, somehow, of a husky backing singer, a seasoned performer in the late-night clubs and the bars.

"Good evening madam. It's DI Sharp from Knott Police." He held up his badge. "I wondered whether I could have a word?"

"Oh God, is it about Peter *again*? What's happened now?"

"It's nothing to worry about, Mrs Franks. No new developments. But could I come in perhaps, for a short chat?"

She paused, then nodded. "Come in." She held the door wider and he squeezed past her into the small vestibule. He got a whiff of alcohol on her breath. She closed the door and preceded him up the stairs, giving him a decent view of her plump, stretching calves as she went.

She led him into the kitchen where on the table were some glossy magazines and an open puzzle book. A bottle of vodka sat next to a glass. It looked like she was drinking vodka and coke.

"I spend most of my time in here in the evening," she explained, gesturing towards the contents of the table. "It's cooler because the sun's on the other side. So hot recently, hey? Anyway officer, how can I help?"

"The first thing I have to stress is that I'm here in a personal capacity, Mrs Franks. Or, may I call you Mandy? Thank you. I'm here in a personal capacity, Mandy. This is not an official visit. It won't be recorded anywhere. My phone is turned off. This is between us."

"I see. But why...."

"You know your husband has been questioned regarding the murder of Martin Silverwood. Who you also... knew. I believe? I always feel great sympathy, Mandy, for the spouses and families in serious cases like this. It must be very hard."

"It is, officer. It certainly is."

"Please, call me Jim."

"Jim."

"The whole thing must be very hard to process."

"It is. But I know Peter's innocent. He didn't do it, officer. Jim."

"Losing Martin must also be a big shock."

"Oh absolutely. It's just awful. So awful…"

"You were close, I think?"

"Well… as I'm sure you know, we had a…what can I say? We kept each other company sometimes. A hot and cold kind of thing."

"Was it… I don't know, serious?"

She took a gulp of her vodka. "It was just a… what can I say, just a thing. I liked Martin but it wasn't 'love' or anything, officer. It was what it was…" She tailed off, dabbing with her finger at some crumbs on the table. There was a pleasing opening through the loose buttons in her shift as she leaned forward, a hint of dark crevice.

"And your husband? Peter?"

"You're a nosey one, aren't you Jim! Why are you asking me all this?"

"Because like I said Mandy," DI Sharp said, upping the earnestness, "I feel great sympathy for people in your position. Great sympathy. You're usually overlooked. The stress, the toll it takes. So I wanted to tell you that if you can think of *anything* that would help Peter, anything at all, you must let us know. At the same time, if you know anything else, you must let us know that too. You've got to do whatever is best, for you, as well as him."

"Like I said, I know he's innocent, Jim. I've already been through everything with another officer. Told her everything I know. Which is not a lot, I'm afraid." She drained her glass. "Drink?"

DI Sharp shook his head as Mandy poured herself some more vodka, then went to the fridge to retrieve the coke.

"I know I drink too much, Jim. But sometimes it feels like all I've got. I mean, I love my husband but... Well, I don't need to go into it. I'm on my own a lot. He doesn't get home until late. Tired, smelling of fish. Straight to sleep."

DI Sharp smiled sympathetically. "Yes, that must be hard. You've got it hard, Mandy..."

"But I don't know what I'll do. I mean, if he's arrested, if he's put away! What will happen if he goes to prison? How will I get by, the rent. It's bad enough already."

"That's why I'm saying Mandy that you need to tell me anything that might help. If there's a way to help, Mandy..."

"I don't know anything, Jim! I was fast asleep that night. Woke up in the morning, everything was normal. Peter got up and was completely normal. All of a sudden, the police keep wanting to question him!"

"There are reasons..."

"As if he'd actually kill Martin! Stab him, with a knife? Never. And poor Martin. Poor, poor Martin. Someone, some beast, did it. But it wasn't Peter, I know *that*."

"So, can you think of anyone else with a reason to do it? Did Martin say anything, tell you anything about any enemies he had, arguments he'd got into – anything like that?"

Mandy sat back in thought. "Well... not really that I can think of. Although, I mean, he had a bit of a temper on him. He wasn't a *happy* man. Could be quite argumentative. So, I wouldn't rule out that there were people out there, that didn't like him."

"OK. But we need leads Mandy, something concrete, you know? Otherwise, I'm sorry to say it, but your husband is suspect number one..."

They went round the houses for a while as Mandy tried to recollect anything that would help. Martin had told her once about a disagreement with someone who ran a fitness centre. He'd been verbally abused on a building site near the centre of town. He'd given what-for to a traffic warden who'd given him a ticket...

Eventually, DI Sharp leaned forward, peering into her eyes. "Look, Mandy, these are all potentially of some use. But I really need *more*. Is there anything *else* you can think of, Mandy, to help me? So that, maybe, afterwards, I can help *you*?"

He brought his hand forward and rested it lightly on her thigh. There was a pause...

A tired smile passed briefly across her face. Then Mandy brought her own hand down and laid it gently on DI Sharp's. This man wasn't attractive. He had small, hard eyes and a hard face and thin grey hair. But it didn't make much difference. Lock yourself away. Then see if it will help.

She squeezed his hand and smiled, then got to her feet and led him out. He bumped against her as they went, pawing at her hips, slobbering at the back of her neck. They went into the bedroom, where she pulled the curtains to. Then she turned and slowly pulled her shift up and over her head, as DI Sharp frantically fumbled to get his trousers down.

Not long later, he was tipping almost drunkenly down the stairs. What a feast! She had got quite into it too, he thought. And was pretty relaxed afterwards. Seemed most interested in another drink. That was all good then. And, who knows, maybe something to come back to again...

It wasn't yet nine. He'd go and have a drink somewhere because he didn't want to get in before Mary was asleep. That cheap perfume Mrs Franks wore – it would be reeking off him, he knew. So Mary had to be asleep. That was something he so admired about Mrs Bright. She never wore perfume, because she understood. That attention to detail, that awareness of the small but important things. Such professionalism. Yes, Mrs Bright was the best. But as he pulled heavily on his cigarette next to the car, he would give a pretty high rating to the wife of Peter Franks, too.

11.

"Hi babes, how's it going?" Lewis asked.

"Yeah, not so bad," Alice said, getting up to make her way outside so she could hear him. "We've had some food and now we're just having a couple of cocktails. I'm pretty tired so I don't think it will be a late one though. How are you getting on?"

"Yeah we're going fine. We're in between Swindon and Reading. Traffic's not too bad really."

Lewis was going to London with some friends for the long bank holiday weekend. A group of four of them were driving up – she could hear the music and lively chatter in the background. They were going to a gig on the Saturday night and planning to spend most of the rest of the time slobbing in parks and pubs, coming back on the Monday evening.

That was fine by Alice. He'd arranged it during their time apart and it was fair enough to carry on with it. She didn't fancy squeezing herself along with them. Instead, she was quite content to have a quiet weekend. In fact, it would be a good opportunity to get down to some proper job searching. She was keener than ever now to leave Clear Minds and move away from Knott. Whatever Lewis had to say about it. She thought she might also nip down to Weymouth on either the Sunday or the Monday to see how her mother was getting on.

"Oh cool. Well, I hope the rest of the journey's OK."

"Yeah. Fingers crossed. You still haven't heard anything from Kevan then, I take it?"

Her meal with Monk had been three nights ago now. Alice had downloaded everything to Lewis afterwards – although she really hadn't known what to make of it.

"So, is Kevan the slasher killer of Knott then??" had been Lewis' question as soon as he had got in through the door of her flat.

"I don't know, Lewis. I just don't know!" she had replied.

"Well go on – tell me everything then!"

"Really, Lewis, I've come away with nothing really! I couldn't ask him anything directly of course. We kind of fenced around it a bit, about the murder, about Martin's inspection of SmartLab, you know. Also about all the Mng on the streets. But he didn't offer anything up. Obviously enough, I suppose."

"Did he seem uncomfortable at all?"

"Not really. But you wouldn't expect him to, would you? Being such a confident and self-contained kind of guy. BUT, he did get weirdly passionate about Mng. How it's going to change the world when he brings out the next version. He said something about not letting anyone or anything get in the way."

"Oh yeah? Hmm… What next version? There hasn't been any communication about that at work."

"A new compound with less codeine in it to reduce the addictiveness, and more magnesium and zinc. He seems to think it will fix all the problems of the human race. Make us all completely happy and fulfilled, that kind of thing...!"

"Okayy. Fair enough. He's keeping that a closely guarded secret then."

They had talked on, kicking it around for a while. But where could they get to? All they could conclude was that they didn't have anything to take it further with at that point. They would just have to keep their eyes open and see if anything more emerged.

"Have a great time then sweetie," Alice said. "Maybe speak at some point over the weekend but don't feel obliged. Just don't get to stomach-pumping stage!"

"All right then, you too babes! Love ya, have a good one."

"Byeee."

Alice went back inside. She felt a little guilty, but what could she do? The truth was that she *had* heard from Kevan again. He had messaged the very next day, telling her that he was throwing "a little party" on the Saturday night at his place. It was something of an annual event apparently, every late May bank holiday weekend. From a follow-up conversation they'd had, it appeared that it would be quite a do. The great and the good of Knott would be there – business people, bankers, private equity investors, lawyers, council leaders, police chiefs. Kevan was smart all right, she knew that, and he appreciated the importance of making connections with the people that mattered. She'd know a few people there, he assured her – Eric Smythe for one, another consultant from Clear Minds. "I'll make sure you have people to talk to. And of course, I'll talk to you myself!" he said, before adding: "Oh, you can stay the night too if you want. There's plenty of spare room around the place."

She had decided not to tell Lewis because he couldn't back out of going to London so what was the point in letting him know? He'd be deeply uneasy about it. He'd want to come too. Or he'd insist that she didn't go. He'd be jealous and difficult. Better all round just to wave him off and then let things unfold.

She went home quite early that night, tired from the week's exertions. After a good night's sleep, she was up early on the Saturday morning and got straight into looking for other jobs. There were various things around – no shortage of demand for counsellors to fix the creaking human mind – and she made a list of possibles. She started a couple of applications and saved them as work in progress. One was in London, the other in Bristol. There was indeed life beyond Knott!

It was fiercely hot again. Her phone showed 32° at lunchtime. The heat was just piling up, layer upon layer, like a tower of hot bricks that, it felt, would eventually have to come tumbling down. Weather forecasters had started to talk about a break in the weather coming. It couldn't arrive soon enough...

She had a doze on the sofa in the early afternoon, grasping at the healing of a little cross-breeze that flowed between living room and bedroom. But still she boiled in the warmth, and was soon feeling sticky and oppressed. After a while, she jumped up and got in the shower. Flowing cold water was the only real relief.

From around four o'clock, she began to get ready for the evening – the party started from six. She chose a light, strappy summer dress. She picked some comfortable pumps to wear. She put a few things into an overnight bag. Then she had a sandwich and some fruit, unsure of how much food there would be.

Just as she was leaving, she realised that she'd forgotten to take any Mng in the morning. So keen had she been to start her job search! She hesitated in the stairwell – should she go back and take one or bring the packet with her? But she really wanted to cut her dependence down. She'd be back tomorrow lunchtime latest and could have one then. No. She left it. Power woman that she was, she thought, smiling to herself.

It was only twenty minutes' drive to Reacher's Point which was situated just outside the southern edge of Knott. It had been built, Alice believed, in the early 2000s, designed by an architect who then made it his own home. It was quite a structure. Low-slung and full of angled glass, it seemed to crouch on a hillside like a spaceship that had landed. At night, lit up, it glowed. Downstairs, an enormous living area gave onto huge french doors that could be thrown back to let in all the air and the light, leading to large gardens that sloped gently this way and that and gave great views of the city of Knott. On the other side of the ground floor were further rooms – a study, a library, a second living room, toilet, kitchens. All was minimalist and sleek, white walls and ceilings, uncluttered, with just a modicum of expensive furnishings, paintings and accessories to make the place feel like a home rather than an office or an institution. Upstairs, as Alice knew, were five bedrooms, two bathrooms, and access to a small roof terrace. Only Kevan's bedroom was occupied. The rest sat immaculate and empty most of the time.

Outside, on the other side from the gardens, were a number of outbuildings and annexes – guest rooms, a lab, workshops, storerooms, garages. These Alice had never properly seen or explored. Her visits to Reacher's Point in the past had been largely confined to the main living room and Kevan's bedroom, with a couple of steamy clinches and 'workouts' on the roof terrace for good measure. This time around, she was hoping to see more…

It was true to say that she was going to this party on a mission. She was determined to hunt around for evidence when the opportunity presented itself. Whatever that might be. Anything linked to Martin Silverwood. Anything linked to Primegate. Anything she could find. She didn't have any clear notions of what those things may be. But here was an opportunity that she was not going to pass up.

She pulled into the big, gravelled parking area of the house shortly before six thirty. It was getting pretty full already. Prestige cars stood recharging themselves on the many charge points Monk had had installed. Kevan's sporty black BMW was there, complete with its number plate of KM1 MNG. Alice squeezed her modest two-door ride in between a long Mercedes and a sleek Alfa Romeo. Insecurity purchase, anyone?

Music was drifting back through the hot static of the evening air as Alice walked up the steps towards the house: a smooth, funky kind of jazz. At the front door, a smooth funky kind of event worker stood in smart dark shorts and light linen shirt, greeting her to the evening. She politely indicated the way inside. Alice thanked her and moved into the house, remembering it more and more clearly as she went. It had been two years, but stepping back in made it feel like only two weeks somehow. How the past lives within the present, ready to resurface at any time...

That said, it was very different on this occasion with so many people there. Approaching the living area which was down a staggered series of steps from the marble-floored vestibule, she could see quite a crowd below. Waiters and waitresses, all in the same shorts and linen shirts, were hurrying around with trays of drinks and canapes. Tables down one side of the room also held lots of hot dishes, salads, breads, sweetmeats, desserts. Big buckets full of bobbing beers. Massed ranks of wine bottles uncorked and ready. Spirits and chasers hovering in the wings.

As she moved down the steps, Alice scanned closely for Kevan. She needed to work out whether he was with anyone that evening – or whether his plans centred on her. She hoped the latter – it would make it easier if they slept together and she knew where he was. If she stayed in a guest room – maybe off in one of the annexes – it would obviously be much harder, and maybe even impossible, to rootle around during the night.

First signs were promising. She could see him outside in the garden, speaking to a small circle of men. They looked like professional types in leisure mode, smartly casual, intelligently mingling – bankers or investors or lawyers perhaps.

Then she saw Eric Smythe standing with his partner Tom inside the doors, chatting to another couple. She made a beeline over and they all greeted each other and made introductions, carried on talking about the weather and the party and the food. No sooner had Alice joined them than a waiter was at her elbow, offering her a tray of drinks to choose from. She mustn't get pissed, she'd have to be careful – but a cold white wine was irresistible. She'd drink it slowly. She set a limit to herself of three.

Another tactic, of course, was to eat plenty of food. It wasn't long before Alice was at the tables, helping herself to a generous variety of edibles. She realised that Eric and Tom were at her elbow.

"So, how's your mother?" Eric asked. "Is she making a full recovery?"

"Oh yes, I think she's OK thanks. Must give her a ring. I may pop down and see her on Monday in fact. Check that she hasn't been overdoing the sauce!"

"Good. Yes, well we're fine ones to talk aren't we?" he said, raising his glass. "Tom drew the short straw and is driving us home, aren't you Tom? So a few large ones incoming for yours truly, I think!"

"Bear in mind that I don't accept rowdy or disorderly passengers in my cab, dahhling!" Tom joked.

Suddenly Kevan materialised through a crowd of people. "Should have known the Clear Minds crew would be freeloading at the food table!" he said. "How are you all?"

Alice turned and made sure to rest a hand on Kevan's hip as they air-kissed. She let it linger there for a few seconds. He seemed content for her to keep it that way, briefly putting his own hand on the small of her back where her dress opened, his fingers little probes against her skin.

"Good turnout Kevan," she said approvingly.

"Well, this is the third year running now. It's become an item, it's in people's diaries. As you know, I just *love* to give back."

"Oh of course. Big-hearted philanthropist that you are."

"Seriously, though, I like to bring people together like this. It's a nice thing to be able to do."

"And it buys you and SmartLab so much currency with all the people that matter in the community…"

"That too, of course. That too…"

They talked on for a while, her and Kevan and Eric and Tom. The body language was good, even if, as host,

Kevan's eyes were continually roaming around the room, making sure that everything was going smoothly. He looked very dapper in smart trousers and shirt. The first buttons of his shirt were undone, revealing the top fuzz of the chest that she had already known and, she hoped, would know once again later on that night.

"I must circulate," he said to her after a while. Then he turned and semi-whispered: "You've brought an overnight bag?" She nodded. He smiled and quickly squeezed her hand as he moved away. Bullseye, she thought.

The evening rolled on like the sky across the Somerset hills. As sunset approached, more people moved into the garden where their voices and laughter rose like the midges that danced in the warm strawberry-tinted air. Eventually, a blush of fire graced the view over Knott, lighting the world in an ethereal parting glow. Then night began to thicken around the garden, reaching its fingers into the trees and the flower beds, slowly deepening itself, a mysterious well.

In contrast, as nature slowed the music quickened, becoming livelier and more contemporary. The dance area in the living room began to fill. People lost their inhibitions as their alcohol levels rose.

For Alice, this was an opportunity to reconnoitre downstairs. She remembered it from before, but it would be good to refresh her memory so she could be really focused later on. Yes, there was Kevan's study opposite the second living room. Next to it was what she supposed you would call the library, full of books and various pieces of art. Further down the hallway was the huge kitchen with its dining area attached. Here was the downstairs bathroom which was her pretext for nosing around.

Emerging from the toilet, there was a man waiting to use it – it was Dum from the distribution centre! It was curious that, now she was back in situ where she had seen him before, his name instantly came to her: Janko. She thought he hailed from the Balkans or somewhere like that. She had a feeling that in fact he might even live here, somewhere on the complex. Along with the smaller second man, whose name she recalled now was Piotr. Doubtless he was somewhere around tonight too. She glanced up at Janko as she passed him and gave a brief smile. The man mountain returned the faintest flicker as he stepped back to let her pass. She wondered whether he had seen her putting her head around all the various doors down here? But that surely didn't matter, as lots of other guests would be doing the same. Normal, nosey human behaviour...

Her phone buzzed and she saw it was a message from Lewis. He had sent her a blurry, bouncing video clip from the gig he was at, with the message *"Wish you were here!!"*. She replied, with a twinge of guilt: *"Enjoy, babes! I'm all good, just having a quiet one."*

Coming back to the party, she saw that Kevan was on the dancefloor with what looked like his group of banker mates. She stood and watched his somewhat stiff and awkward grooving, then became conscious of a large black woman in a bright floral dress next to her with a much smaller man in suit and tie. They were watching and chuckling at the japes going on. Alice turned and nodded and introduced herself. The lady replied: "It's very nice to meet you, Alice. My name is Patience and this is my husband Henry."

"And what do you do? How do you know Kevan?"

"Oh well, I am superintendent at Knott Police. I have met Kevan at various functions, you know how it is? We are good acquaintances."

"The police? Fascinating! You must have a lot to deal with. So many problems these days."

"You're telling me!" she laughed.

"So of course, I must ask you about the matter of the moment… That murder in Knott. How's the investigation going?"

"Oh well, it's going…"

"Any breakthroughs yet? Any prospect of an arrest? There's so much public interest in it."

"Of course, I can't divulge any details to you, Alice. But let me just say that we are making progress. You should watch this space as they say."

"Oh really?"

"Definitely watch this space. Over the coming days. That is all I can say!"

"Well, that sounds encouraging. Such a shocking murder. I knew him, in fact, Martin Silverwood. He was a patient of mine briefly. A couple of years ago."

"Is that right? It's a shame then that Detective Inspector Sharp is not here this evening. You could have given him some insights. He's leading the investigation. Of course, that is why he's not here. Too much to do to be here drinking beer and dancing!"

She smiled down at Alice, a broad and friendly smile. Alice liked this woman. She had a warm and positive vibe. "And what would you have told DI Sharp, if he were here?" the superintendent asked.

"I mean… he had problems obviously. He lost his child aged only a few months. Cot death. He was hugely torn up. But other issues too. A lot of anger and frustration as I recall."

"Yes, I imagine. You must see a lot of that. We do too."

"Well, we're both investigators of the human mind, are we not! Anyway, I'll certainly stay tuned to the investigation. I'll watch for announcements with interest."

They talked on for a while, then Alice excused herself to get another drink (three of three, doing OK…). It sounded like they were on the verge of making an arrest, then. She really did need to act fast and see if she could unearth anything. Superintendent Odutola had given nothing away but one thing seemed certain – the suspect in their sights was not Kevan Monk!

Alice went outside to get some air. There were a number of people strung around, laughing, a few smoking vapes or cigarettes. Alice pulled her own vape out and took some puffs. It was coming up to midnight already.

Some guests had already left. She wondered how long the party would go on...

She found that she was standing near a middle-aged man in cords and a jacket who was one of the few hard core cigarette smokers. He looked pretty old school all round. Their eyes briefly connected, so Alice introduced herself.

"Nice to meet you. Yes, I've known Kevan for some years. Alan Harbridge. Accountant. We do the SmartLab accounts."

"Oh right. What's your firm?"

"Harbridge and Little. We're just a small outfit in Knott. Very pleased and proud of course that Kevan has entrusted his business to us as a local firm, rather than one of the big national practices."

"Of course. Are there many of you?"

"Just myself and my partner, Stephen Little. A few support staff. We only have a handful of key accounts."

"So, how's it doing? SmartLab I mean?"

"Well... The accounts show, what can I say, a true and fair position. Put it like that!" He tittered at what must have been some kind of accounting joke.

"Is it, you know, profitable? Doing OK?"

Alan drew himself up, in the shadows. "Profitable... That depends on the basis of measurement, I hardly need say. The revenue recognition model employed. Certainly, turnover is *very* healthy. Going great guns."

Alice thought she may as well give it a shot, there in the dark. "Good to hear. Tell me, do you also do the accounts for another company called, what was it again, Primegate?"

There seemed to be a slight stiffening in his stance, although it was hard to tell. "Primegate? Why do you ask?"

"Oh, just a business that I came across recently, at work. We're thinking of placing an order. They do pharmacy supplies, medicines, equipment. It just randomly popped into my head to ask you, that's all."

"Primegate... I can't place it... Possibly my partner... It's rather late in the evening – and long in the glass if you know what I mean – to be juggling company names!"

With that attempt at humour, he stubbed his cigarette out and mumbled an apology about needing to find his wife. Then he was off. Alice raised her eyebrows to herself, and went inside herself to see what was what.

Gradually, the party began to thin out. The waiting staff had packed up and left at midnight. The food had all been cleared away. Increasing numbers of people, including Eric and Tom, thanked their host and made an exit. Approaching 1am, Kevan's extensive play lists had exhausted themselves and looped round to start again. He turned the music off and there were a few minutes of restful silence in which people just sat quietly and chatted and chilled. Then Kevan announced: "Three slow songs to end the night folks!"

The romantic numbers came on. Kevan approached Alice and took her by the hand. He began to talk but she wanted to avoid dialogue as far as possible and so rested her head against his shoulder and they swayed gently in a peaceful silence.

At the end of the trio of tunes, a few sidelights came on. Blinking and tired, the people who remained made their moves. Alice went out to collect her bag – most of the cars had gone, although a handful remained belonging to guests who were staying the night. Kevan had told her that all of them were staying in annexe rooms – they would be alone upstairs in the main house.

She came back in and saw that Kevan (assisted by Janko and Piotr) was politely ushering guests out and showing them the way to their rooms. She caught Kevan's eye and gestured that she was going upstairs. She made her way to his bedroom that she knew from previous visits two years ago. She found it unchanged: big, bare, hard-floored. There was a super-sized bed, built-in cupboards with mirrors, very little other furniture. Big windows, and skylights in the ceiling, were designed to let in lots of light – sunlight, moonlight, starlight, whatever was on offer.

Alice went into the ensuite bathroom and cleaned off her make-up, brushed her teeth, got ready for bed. She changed into her pyjama shorts and top. Then she got into bed, turned off the main lights and switched on the bedside lamp. She waited...

Kevan came in about twenty minutes later. "Sorry!" he said. "It was like herding bloody cats. Everyone's safely in their places now…"

He skipped forward and sat on the bed. "I've missed you," he said. "Me too…" she answered, breathlessly. She sat up and began giving him a long, penetrating kiss. She had two objectives: 1) get it over with as quickly as possible, and 2) avoid any talking that would lead to avowals of affection.

Her approach seemed to work. Kevan responded immediately – as she could feel when she directed her hand downwards. She gripped, stroked, teased. Soon, he was tearing at his clothes as she pulled off her top and bottom and switched the sidelight off. They got to energetic, wordless work, rolling around on the playing-field of a bed under the faint glimmer of the hazy stars.

As she had hoped, with so many guests nearby even if not inside the house, Kevan kept it straightforward and functional, so that it was quite soon over. Alice acted her part appropriately – although it wasn't all fake. "Thank you," she breathed. "Thank *you*," he replied. "Just the 'climax' to the night I was hoping for!"

She went to the bathroom and, when she came back in, saw a spot of light in the darkness and noticed a pungent smell: Kevan was smoking a joint. This was great news – hopefully it would knock him out into a deep sleep.

"Wanna drag?" he asked. She shook her head. "I'm done. Think I'll fall straight asleep!"

With that, she got into bed under the thin sheet, rolled onto her side and waited. She had to make sure she didn't in fact fall asleep because she hadn't been lying, she was completely bushed. The aromatic weed instilled a sleepy aura too. She began to pinch herself in order to stay awake.

After a few minutes, she heard Kevan stubbing out the joint. Then he went to the bathroom. That oddly child-like, tinkling waterfall of wee that all men seem to make reached her. Then a toilet flush. Noisy clearing of throat into the basin. Buzz of electric toothbrush. Spit-spat-spot. Ah, here he came… She closed her eyes and feigned rhythmic breathing. Kevan made sure the windows were open for airflow, fiddled with the curtains and pulled down the blinds on the skylights with the cords. Eventually, he was in bed next to her and settling down to sleep.

She waited… He seemed to be asleep within about ten minutes, but she wanted to be sure. Better to be safe than sorry…

After what she judged was around twenty minutes more, she felt she was in the clear. Kevan's breathing was deep and steady; he hadn't moved a limb. She made a couple of test twitches with her legs, turned over onto her back, coughed, scratched… Nothing. This man was off with the fairies all right.

Slowly, carefully, she levered herself out of bed. Picking up her phone, she saw that it was 3.30am. A suitably dead time of night. She got to her feet and tip-toed silently out of the bedroom.

It was lucky she knew the house, because there was thick darkness everywhere. But she would be sparing with the use of the light on her phone. She was getting low on charge in any case. The stairs were easy because they were solid stone with a strip of carpet down the middle. Down she went, holding her breath, step by slow step.

She really didn't know exactly what she was going to do or what she was looking for. But Kevan's study was the obvious destination. She crossed the hallway and came to the door which luckily was ajar. It was a heavy wooden door and made no noise on its hinges as she eased it a fraction wider and slipped inside. She turned on her light and looked around her, feeling like a burglar, a thief, an assassin… She had only been in here briefly once or twice but she remembered the general layout. There was a desk where Kevan worked, a low coffee table and a couple of easy chairs, some cabinets ranged around the wall. Advancing to the desk, she sat in the chair and turned on the table lamp. She was sweating in the sudden blaring light, heart thumping. She kept stopping to check for noise. But all was silence…

She tried the drawers. The top ones were locked but the lower ones on each side were not. Looking inside, she saw various sheafs of paper, folders. She wouldn't have time to look through properly. Instead, she did some quick random sampling – and found nothing very revealing. Minutes and board papers and reports… Feeling the need to keep moving, she got up and tried the cabinets: all locked.

She turned the light off and left the study. The second living room was next. She wandered around inside like a sprite with a lantern, casting pools of light over the furniture and artefacts. She half-expected things to spring shockingly to life once illuminated, rising up in recrimination and protest. But everything remained inanimate and dead. Then she caught a big flatscreen TV on the wall, which glared her light back at her, capturing her in her pyjamas like a phosphorescent ghost inside the screen. Her heart jumped. She expected something awful to happen, a crash, a smash, the outbreaking of a terrible creature or a spirit hell-bent on vengeance or retribution or death… But nothing happened. And there was nothing to see here.

Next, she'd take a look in the library. That old game Cluedo suddenly came into her head. Could she roll a six and get herself across the hallway and into the room? Perhaps she was, who was it?, Miss Scarlet? *"I would like to see… Colonel Mustard… in the library, with… the candlestick!"*

Her rolling was successful – here she was. Shit! The library door had sent up a definite creaking. She crouched inside, heart racing in her ears… Then she carried on, performing a quick tour. Just bookcases, display cases, a snooker table strewn with balls, a few chairs. She briefly inspected the books – some old hardback 'display' volumes which she bet he'd never looked at (encyclopaedias, reference works, Shakespeare, Dickens); a couple of cases of paperbacks, which were a mixture of scientific/biochemical works, business, philosophy and a little fiction (mainly, she noted, thrillers and crime). There were heavy curtains drawn to, here as in every room: Mr Monk certainly liked his privacy.

That was it... What should she do? She hadn't properly looked through those drawers in Kevan's desk. The thing to do was to roll herself back to the study, she decided.

Creeping slowly down the hallway, she stopped a couple of times to listen... Then she skipped quickly back into the study and hurried over to the desk. She turned the table light on again and opened the left hand drawer. There had been a large bundle of loose papers that she'd hardly looked at... Leaning down, sweating, she pulled it out and flicked quickly through it. Wait, what was that?! Was that the Primegate logo? She'd gone past it, where was it? She reverse-flicked, trying to locate it, fumbling at the pages.

"What are you doing, Alice?"

Her blood froze. She bolted upright, dropping the papers back into the drawer.

"Kevan! I... I was just..."

"Are you looking through my things?" he asked angrily, advancing towards her, hair tousled, in his boxer shorts and a T-shirt.

"I couldn't sleep! Well, I woke up. Then I couldn't sleep. I was just..."

"You were just going through my private papers! Is that right?!"

"Jesus, Kevan, it's not what it looks like… I promise you, I…."

"Yes??" He glared at her, visibly furious, fists clenched, trembling.

It was hopeless. She had to just let it out.

"You did it, didn't you Kevan? You did it!"

"Did what?"

"The murder. Of Martin Silverwood. You murdered him, or had him murdered, I don't know which."

"What the FUCK are you talking about, Alice? You think I… you're saying that I…" He spluttered out, seemingly too shocked to finish his sentence.

She pressed on. "Look, I know Kevan, all right? I know. About Mng and how it's being distributed, about Primegate. I think Martin Silverwood tumbled to it too. He was trying to blackmail you, is my guess. So you had to shut him up. You went ahead and murdered him! Am I right?"

"Alice, Alice, Alice…" Kevan said, shaking his head and smiling. "WHAT are you saying? I mean, listen to yourself. Are you feeling all right?"

He was slowly getting nearer to the desk. Alice, by instinct, had risen to her feet and was slowly moving back in tandem.

"You've obviously had one apple juice too many," Kevan continued. "Or maybe you're ill. That's it, in fact, that's what it is. It happens a lot, Alice. To counsellors and shrinks. They see so much madness they go mad themselves. The sickness spreads, Alice."

He was at the desk now, but Alice had moved round, behind the back of an easy chair, and now in fact had her back to the door, less than ten feet behind her. Kevan didn't seem bothered. Maybe she could make a run for it. Was the front door locked? What did she need? She had her phone. But the car keys... Damn it! The car keys were upstairs...

"Look, don't worry Alice – I'll arrange some help for you, OK? Things have obviously been getting too much. You're sick, Alice. You don't know what you're thinking... It's sad, but I'm sure there's a path through this. I'll help you, I'll be here to give you all the support you need..."

As he said all of this, gazing towards her, Alice suddenly realised that in fact he was looking *past* her, beyond her, at something behind...

With a sudden lurch of the heart, she turned her head – too late! A dark figure was looming at her shoulder, wrapping a powerful arm across her chest like a vice. A big hand came up and pressed something against her face. An awful chemical reek enveloped her as Janko smothered her with some kind of cold, damp cloth. He pressed it tighter and tighter, relentless, without pity. Alice was suffocating, drowning, she was disappearing down a hole that was closing over her head... A massive inaudible scream was trapped inside her, but she couldn't get it out! She felt sick and dizzy, she was slipping away... She gave a desperate kick of resistance and almost managed to break herself free. But she was too groggy, she couldn't loosen herself. Janko reasserted his grip. She was going now, going, the tide of a nauseous unconsciousness was rolling in…

Eventually, Alice's body went limp and Janko eased his hold. She slumped to the floor like a lifeless ragdoll.

12.

Alice realised that she had opened her eyes. A white blur swam in front of her. Her head was heavy. She turned it from side to side on the pillow and it seemed to follow a second afterwards. She felt sick. Where was she? What was going on?

She tried to remember... As if she was thinking back to things that had happened long ago, she began to recall the party at Kevan Monk's house. The people she had talked to. The garden, the sunset, the dancing. Oh yes, upstairs with KM... Oh yes! Downstairs looking around... It all came back, including the horrible details at the end...

She sat up, her head trailing her body. Ouch. Yuck. Headache and nausea. She looked around her as her vision gradually came together. A very bare and plain room. White walls and ceiling. Greyish laminate flooring. Perhaps 12 x 12 feet. She was on a single bed, in the pyjamas she had been wearing. The only other furniture was a wooden chair by the bed and another one in the corner of the room.

There was a piece of paper on the chair next to her. She had to focus hard to make out the words: *"I will come when I can and we will talk. K."*

Slowly, she got up. She felt a little unsteady at first but soon was moving OK. She went to the door but was unsurprised to find it locked. She shook at the handle but the door hardly moved or rattled: it was incredibly solid. She banged on it, but only succeeded in hurting her fist. What was it made of – steel?

Then she shouted: "Hello? Hello?" Then: "Help me! Somebody help!"

She felt like she was in a sound-proof vacuum. No one would hear. She pressed her ear to the door – couldn't detect a thing. There was also a buzzing in the room which made it hard to hear. She looked up – it was from an air-conditioning unit that was running with an uneven purr. At least it was keeping the room cool. Then, near the unit up in the corner, she saw what was surely a camera. Fucking hell. Was she being watched?? And why did Kevan have a room like this at all? It felt like a cross between a prison cell and a hospital room…

There was a small sealed window near the bed. But the glass was frosted and it had a grill secured in front of it. She couldn't get her hand through. She could tell it was daytime outside; it was probably bright and hot again although it was difficult to tell. She looked around – no, none of her things were here. No phone, no watch. No way of telling the time.

There was another door opposite the bed that was open and she could tell it was a bathroom. She looked inside: a toilet, a basin, a shower cubicle. She realised she was incredibly thirsty so she turned the tap on and had a long drink. Then she sat on the toilet and had a wee. There was a full roll of toilet paper in the holder – it looked like it had never been used. She wondered – had anyone else stayed in here? When was the last time? It could have been a guest room, she supposed, however bare and austere. She looked down between her legs – her urine had come out cloudy and dark. But her drink and her wee had made her feel a little better. She blew her nose too, always a comforting ministration.

However, then she realised that the after-effects of whatever they had knocked her out with were not her only problem. She was also feeling prickly and dry… Assuming it was Sunday morning(ish), she hadn't had an Mng tablet for 48 hours now. She had to have one soon. She had to get out of here!

She couldn't believe that Kevan had locked her in here. Well, there again, given that she'd come straight out with her accusation, maybe she could. And it proved beyond doubt that she was right. The man was a murderer, the man had blood on his hands! Bloody hell…

A cold sweat crossed her, she twitched and shuddered. What might he do to *her* then? Was she safe? Would he murder her too? Kill her here, then load her into the back of his car and dump her somewhere far away? Janko and Piotr came into her mind. Two grim stooges capable of almost any act. Oh fuck, what had she got herself into…??

Maybe she was in one of the annexes. Maybe there were still guests around from last night… She went to the door again and banged and banged and shouted and cried. But it was useless. It was like banging on a cliff-face. She felt tears beginning to come. She went back to the bed and lay down. She needed to rest and regather her strength and think. She needed to stay calm. Kevan would surely come before too long.

She closed her eyes and soon began to doze. She was very tired. She lay in a kind of half-conscious stupor for a while. Her need for Mng became steadily clearer, piercing its absence through the fog. Her thoughts felt thin, her system was weak, her mouth was dry, there was a tremble inside her limbs. Since she'd started taking Mng, she'd never gone more than 48 hours without one. This, as much as the circumstances she found herself in, raised a pitching kind of fear within...

She must have dropped into actual sleep without realising it because all of a sudden she found herself starting awake as a key turned in the lock of the door. She eagerly levered herself up – and saw Piotr coming in with a tray.

"Food," he said, putting the tray down on the second chair in the corner.

"When's Kevan coming? How long are you going to keep me here?" Alice demanded shrilly, jumping up off the bed. "You can't keep me here! This is illegal, this is disgusting, this is wrong!"

Piotr looked at her blankly. He had a straggly horseshoe moustache which came right down to his jawbones, giving him a mean kind of look.

"He will come. Later."

"When later? When? I must know!"

He shrugged. "Later. When he is able. You eat now."

Then he turned and slipped back out of the door. She heard the key turning again in the lock. She banged and kicked at the door and shouted after him – but he was gone and didn't come back.

"Fuuuck!!" Alice shrieked in frustration. This was just crazy, unbelievable. This couldn't actually be happening, could it?

She looked at the tray which sat on the chair, a real thing. Yes, this was happening…

What had room service brought then, she asked herself with almost the trace of a smile. Actually, she could really do with some food…

There was a boiled egg, some toast, a few slivers of cheese, a miniature pot of jam. A small pot of tea, some milk. She would have preferred coffee, but beggars couldn't be choosers.

She sat on the bed and ate. It was a strange experience in fact, because she had no phone, there was no TV, there was no music. How often do we just eat without distracting ourselves with other things? It made her feel stripped back, disassembled, denuded… She was very conscious of her jaw, chewing, her throat, swallowing. Munching and drinking in silence (except for that bloody aircon). Alone on this creaky bed in a weird, empty room. Was anyone watching her, she suddenly wondered. She flashed a glance up to the camera in the corner. Then she raised her middle finger and swore. "Fuck you Kevan," she mouthed with deliberately rounded enunciation.

Maybe that would bring him skittering to her door…

Her meal done, she belched in the camera's direction and put the tray on the second chair. Now what to do?

She wished she'd asked Piotr the time. She would really have liked to know. Not knowing left her feeling adrift, anchorless. Her guess was around lunchtime. 1pm, maybe 2? But she had no real way of knowing. Maybe Kevan would come when all the overnight guests had gone – which might be early afternoon?

She went back to the bed, plumped the two pillows up against the headboard and lay back against them. She would wait then...

Then she picked up the piece of paper and re-read Kevan's note. Looking up at the camera, she screwed the paper into a ball and tossed it to the floor.

All these petty, defiant gestures... But what else could she do?

There was nothing else she could do.

Before long, she was very bored so she got up off the bed and began pacing up and down the room. She could at least keep her step count up... Up and down she went, ten steps up and ten steps back. If she did it a hundred times, that would be 2,000 steps.

But she got fed up with it after thirty laps and sat back down on the bed. Then she slumped down to a lying position, closed her eyes and began to drift off.

At last, there was a jangling at the door. She sprang up – and Kevan came in, holding a small tray on which two mugs steamed. He nodded at her cheerily, threw out a hello and locked the door from the inside. Then, carefully balancing the tray, he picked up the second chair and brought it over to within a few feet of the bed.

"Alice, how are you?" he said with a friendly tone. "I've brought you a coffee – milk no sugar, I think that's right? Some biscuits too…"

She was in no mood for banter. "When are you going to let me go? You can't hold me like this! It's *illegal* Kevan. You're breaking the bloody law. And you drugged me last night. You could get years in prison, just for this."

"I don't want to do this to you Alice – but you left me with no choice. Snooping around last night – illegally, I may say – and then coming out with those outrageous accusations. What did you expect me to do?"

"Not this! And so – you deny it, do you?"

"I do."

"But you've locked me away in here and are holding me against my will. Hardly the actions of an innocent man."

"Alice, think about. I'm the CEO of a significant business. I'm a prominent member of the business community. I can't have you wandering around throwing out wild accusations about me. These things can gain traction, however ridiculous and outlandish they are. So, I decided to bring you here. So that we can have a sensible chat and reach an agreement."

"An agreement?"

"Yes. Exactly that."

As angry as she was, Alice was also desperate for caffeine. Reluctantly, she picked up her mug and drank some coffee. It tasted good. She took a biscuit to accompany it.

Kevan took a couple of sips of his coffee. Then he said: "Until we've reached a satisfactory understanding, you're going to stay here. I need to be clear about that."

"What?" Alice snorted. "This is outrageous. I *will* tell people about this, Kevan. The police, the media. You see if I don't!"

"Well now, let's think about this," Kevan said calmly, with the hint of a smile. "If you persist in accusing me of these things, the first thing that will happen is that you'll lose your job. Eric is very much on side. He believes in the Mng vision, like I do. And he won't want to keep you in his employ. The reference you get won't be worth having."

Alice stared at him, disbelieving. Was Eric in on this too?

"Secondly, there's the regulatory review. Remember that I have all the documents from the clinical trial, including a complete trail of the versions of your report and the changes you agreed to make. If I go down, you come down with me, Alice. I'll make sure they're fully aware of the role you played. And there's the bonus you received after the trial – that wouldn't look good, would it? I expect you'd be struck off the psychologist's register. You'd become unemployable."

"And you think these threats will shut me up about the murder in cold blood of an innocent human being?" Alice shook her head vigorously. "You've got me wrong there, Kevan. Not everyone is like you, you know."

"Maybe, maybe not, Alice. I'm just telling you how it would be, that's all." Kevan eyed her with his flat, unreadable eyes. Then he added: "Oh, and how's your mother keeping these days?"

"What do you mean?" she said sharply.

"It's just that I heard she had a fall recently. One glass too many, I think? It would be awful – wouldn't it – if she was to have another fall. People can really hurt themselves, Alice, if they lose their balance when drunk."

Alice jumped up from the bed at this and stood glaring down at Kevan who remained calmly seated, draining his coffee.

"If you so much as touch a hair on her head, Kevan! If you dare... If you go anywhere near her – you or your bloody cronies – you'll regret it, I swear!"

He looked up at her and laughed. "Oh Alice, help me, I'm frightened! Look, I'm just talking, what shall we say, worst case scenarios. There's really no need for any of this to happen. You just need to come to your senses, drop these absurd allegations, and be reasonable. Capish?"

Alice, shaking, raised her hand as if to strike Kevan... But then she relented, stepping back and slumping down onto the bed. "You bastard," she said.

"I'm sorry. I didn't want it to be this way," Kevan replied, inspecting his fingernails. "But like I said to you before, I will do anything – whatever it takes – to protect the future of Mng. It's going to change the world, Alice, it's going to bring so much good! So much improvement to everyone's lives. It's worth everything. And you can choose to play a part in it all. It's an opportunity for you to do some real good, Alice."

She laughed, discordant and semi-hysterical. "Some real good! Bloody hell, your logic is so twisted, so sick! You're one sick fuck all right."

"There's no need for rudeness," Kevan sniffed. "Well, I've said all I needed to say. So I'll get on and leave you to have a think…"

"Wait, Kevan, can I ask you one thing? I really need some Mng… I haven't had one for two days. Could you bring me some tablets? Please?"

"Haha! I'm afraid not, Alice. That's not part of the service here. Maybe it will help you see more clearly what you need to do."

"Kevan, please! I'm begging you!"

"No, Alice. No Mng."

He picked up the tray and got up from the chair.

"At least can you or someone bring me my vape then? It's with my things. Can I have my things?"

"Your vape, yes. You'll get some supper in a couple of hours. We'll bring it then. Obviously though, you can't have anything else like your phone."

"Jesus, I really am a prisoner here. And I notice there's a fucking camera up there too. Are you waiting for me to do a striptease of something?"

Kevan smiled, shrugged. "It's just for security, Alice. No one's watching you all the time. Occasional checks that's all."

"Brilliant, thanks so much Kevan. Lovely to know... Anyway, yes please, my vape would be a start. It would help. The Mng withdrawal is starting to kick in. You know, the withdrawal I warned about in my report all that time ago?"

"The withdrawal that in the vast majority of cases is completely manageable, you mean? You'll get your vape. See you later."

"So what time is it by the way? Mid-afternoon?"

"It's coming up to four. We'll bring supper around six."

"And it's Sunday? Just to make absolutely sure."

"Yes, it's Sunday."

"OK. I know you won't give me my watch because it's smart. Could you maybe bring a clock or something? I can't bear not knowing the time."

"Vape and clock. Done, Alice. Until later!"

Then he was gone. The key rattled in the lock from the other side – the side she was not allowed to be on. She fell back on the bed with a groan. She couldn't believe she was negotiating for supplies and equipment. She couldn't believe any of this whole damn situation!

What to do, what to say, how to behave? Was Kevan bullshitting with her in any case? What if she said she agreed to forget her accusations – how would he know she'd stay true to her word? Was he actually planning to let her go at all, or did he have another fate for her in mind?

She couldn't think straight. Not in these bizarre circumstances, and not with her Mng withdrawal rising. She could feel it getting worse. A sickness was growing. Her head felt like it was going to fall off.

Maybe it would fall off! That would solve a lot of problems actually.

Then she realised the aircon had been turned off. Monk economising on the electricity... Quite quickly, it began to get very warm. She fanned herself, splashed water on her face. This was the last thing she needed. Of course, control of the aircon was another weapon at Monk's disposal...

She paced up and down, creating her own draught, refusing to think about all the things Kevan had put to her. She wouldn't get drawn into it, she just wouldn't go there. Let him do what he would. There would be no surrender, no capitulation. She would just hang in there, whatever it took. He was a murderer and she wouldn't allow herself to deny that fact.

Soon, the heat in room became oppressive. It was so airless! She knelt down by the door and put her head on the floor: there was a tiny current of air coming in. She stayed there for a couple of minutes, feeling a little relief. Then it began to feel too absurd; she got up and drifted back to the bed.

She realised that sleep was in fact her best potential defence against all this nonsense. So she curled up in the foetal position, making sure her bum was sticking defiantly in the direction of the camera, and tried to drop off. She tried to soothe her mind, clear everything away, focusing only on the here and now of her breathing. It was something she often advised her patients to do when they experienced moments of high stress or panic.

She was almost surprised to find how well it worked. Within a few minutes, she could feel herself easing into a half-unconscious doze. It was like moving along a slide, down through some velvety rushes that brushed against her face. And then she was below the warm surface and breathing deeply and at ease...

When she suddenly snapped to, out of what was now a steamy uncomfortable swamp, she felt that around an hour must have passed. She doused herself with water in the bathroom. She came back in and angrily mouthed 'Aircon' at the camera. Then she sat and waited - it would surely be supper time via room service – in this weird alternative hotel – soon. Her stomach told her this too, not just her mental clock. She had the strangely disorientating sensation of feeling simultaneously hungry from a lack of food, and nauseous from a lack of Mng.

Time dragged on. This whole situation was mad, intolerable. She had to get out of here. The thought crossed her mind that she could perhaps try to escape when supper came. If it was Piotr that brought it, he was quite a small man... She could charge at him or smash him over the head with the chair? But she wouldn't know where she was, where to go. He'd probably catch up with her in no time. And if it was Janko, she'd have no chance at all. She hoped it wasn't Janko. She didn't want to see him ever again. Not after what he'd done. The memory of him squeezing her remorselessly until she'd nearly burst, suffocating her with that foul cloth soaked in chloroform or whatever it was... She wanted to erase that whole episode for evermore.

Eventually, finally, a key turned in the lock. Janko hulked into the room bearing a tray. Alice looked down straightaway, determined to act like Dum wasn't even there.

"Your food. And in the bag, your vape. Also a clock," he said. Then he paused with the tray and added: "I am sorry. About last night. It was boss' orders, you know? I hope you OK now?"

She nodded briefly, keeping her head down.

"OK... Enjoy your meal." He put the tray and a small plastic bag down on the chair next to her. She glanced at it, noticed a cup of tea.

"Can I have coffee in the morning, please? Instead of tea. You keep bringing me tea. I prefer coffee," she said, feeling like she really was in a hotel.

She got the impression Janko smiled, although still she didn't look directly at him.

"Coffee? Of course. I will tell the kitchen. Good evening."

And then he was gone. She inspected the contents of the tray: the mug of tea, a plate of what looked like spaghetti Bolognese, some crackers and cheese, an apple. Also a plastic bottle of water. Not so bad…

In the bag was her vape and a mechanical clock. She also saw with a small internal celebration that her toothbrush and toothpaste were there. Yes! She would at least be able to brush her teeth. This was huge. As for the time, it was apparently half past six. She put the clock on the chair next to her bed. It felt so much better when you could tell the time. When time became invisible, it was an awful miasmic foe.

She began to eat. But her hunger and her nausea continued to battle with each other and she only ate about half of the spaghetti, one cracker, the apple. Then she drank the tea and took big intakes from her vape.

All of this made Alice feel better – but only a little. She still felt like shit. She had a horrible fear that the night was going to be an ordeal as her Mng withdrawal intensified.

Neither did she have anything to do... She sat on the bed and stewed. It was getting very warm again. She could tell from the glazed blaze at the window that it was another hot evening. The sun wouldn't go down for a couple of hours yet.

Once her food had gone down a little, she decided to cool down with a shower. There was only a hand towel in the bathroom and a small bar of soap at the basin – but they would have to do. So she got into the shower and ran cool water over her limbs, working up a thin lather with the soap. Then she patted herself dry with the towel as best she could. It wouldn't take long to dry out in any case. Next she gave her teeth a vigorous, sweet-relief brushing.

Coming back into the room, she saw that her tray had been removed. She hadn't even heard anyone coming in. But that was good news because in the fetid air of her cell the Bolognese would have made an unpleasant smell. The service around this place was perhaps picking up, she observed wryly to herself.

Refreshed and fresh-teethed, she sat back on the bed. Would Kevan come that evening, she wondered? Or would he leave her hanging? She had a feeling it would be the latter...

It was coming up to eight o'clock. The blaze in the window was fading and it had become murky in the room. Getting up to turn on the light was an event.

An event that was instantly over. Christ this was hard! With no phone, nothing to read, nothing to watch, nothing to listen to... There was no sound from anywhere that she could hear. Was the room sound-proofed perhaps? In the oppressive stillness, she was vaguely aware of her own heart, beating a drum under her ribcage. She could watch the clock, she supposed. So she regarded the second hand as it moved inexorably round the clock face. Round and round it went, silent and relentless. The unstoppable passing of time... She ate up a couple of minutes in this way. Then she averted her gaze and left the clock to it.

She got up and began walking. It seemed like the only activity open to her. It would also help hold off her awareness of her nausea, her headachey-ness, her trembling. It wasn't long before she felt weak and tired, but she pushed herself on: twenty laps, fifty, seventy-five, a hundred! She looked up at the camera, as though asking for her prize.

Then she fell back on the bed, quivering and faint. She felt, in fact, that she may be able to get to sleep. It was only nine o'clock – it would be the earliest she had gone to bed for years – but it was the best way of all of passing the time.

She had a wee, washed her face, pulled the thin curtains to across the window, turned off the light and got into bed. It was very dark. She held her breath for a few seconds – absolute silence apart from the wobbly thrumming of her heart in her ears.

She lay in the warm, close air, staring up at a ceiling she couldn't see, waiting, hoping, for sleep to come. All of a sudden, there was a clicking and a whirring that made her jump in shock. Then she realised – it was the aircon! This was a blessing. Gentle rivulets of cool air began to reach her, dimpling over her limbs. It had a great, relaxing effect. Alice turned over so she was facing the dark blank of the wall, and soon drifted off to sleep.

It turned, however, into a horrible night. She soon entered a phase of vivid, fractured dreams that she would wake from and then dip down into again. The aircon turned off after a few hours and the room became increasingly hot. Alice was roiling on a wet and sweaty bed, she was a ship labouring in hostile tropical seas. She began to shake and quiver, turning over from one side to the other, again and again.

In one dream, she was a teacher walking along a corridor conscious that she was late for her lesson. She needed urgently to get to the classroom where, she knew, the kids were rioting ever more wildly. But as she tried to speed her way to the class, it was as though she were walking through heavy drifts of sand. She couldn't get any traction, she was slipping and stumbling, she was going nowhere fast. A desperation rose inside her. She was going to get punished by the head teacher – probably caned, then sacked. She began pulling at her clothes as though that would help her break out of this terrible quagmire of sand that she was trapped in. But it was hopeless. Tears began to rise, she cried out in the corridor as the noise from the young voices in the classroom grew unbearable to her ears.

That dream suddenly ended as she briefly flicked awake. Her relief was tempered by how lousy and weak she felt. She stumbled up out of bed and went to the bathroom where she splashed water on her face and had a wee.

She came back to bed and saw from the clock that it was half past two. Then she slipped back under the surface into sleep. The next dream she had any memory of later was of her mother. Valerie had put on weight – she stood, in fact, bloated and flabby in an absurdly ill-fitting bikini. Water seemed to be running down her. She held a wine bottle in her hand, and was randomly spilling red wine onto the floor. Alice realised she was doing it deliberately – because she had lost a baby and had then lost her wits. She was dousing wine everywhere so that she could set the room, and herself, on fire. She tried to call out – "Mum, don't do it!" – but nothing came out of her mouth. She was forced to watch her mother carry on, turning and turning, white flesh rippling, casually sloshing wine in a circle of blood around her, a crazed smile fixed on her face like a mask...

Panting and tearful, Alice jack-knifed awake. She peered through the darkness at the clock: 4am. She couldn't bear to go back to sleep, although she felt crushingly, miserably tired. Instead, she turned on the light and drank some water from her bottle and took a series of deep puffs on her vape.

Then she got up and began walking. She walked and walked, up and down, back and forth, hoping she could somehow stride all the shittiness out of herself. Leave it behind, discard it in her wake, like afterbirth. But still, the trauma of her dreams, especially the second one about her mother, her lost sibling – her lost sibling! – thrummed sickly through her.

Nevertheless, after a while she thought – although she couldn't really tell – that she felt a little better, physically. A little less sick, less faint, and with only a mild headache now. But there was a horrible dullness crouching inside her, like a toad. This must be the onset of the mental withdrawal from Mng. It didn't feel good. It didn't feel good at all...

What time would it get light? Around 5am was her guess. Not too long now. Maybe daylight would help.

After half an hour of walking, she felt tired. So she turned the light off and got back into bed. The darkness was indeed just beginning to thin. A new day was coming. But the hint of daylight somehow made her feel more tired than ever. She turned over, facing the wall again, and fell into a light doze.

When she awoke, the room was in a watery nascent light. It was six o'clock. Alice went to the window and lifted the curtain – there was a kind of grey effulgence against the thick frosted glass of the window.

She let the curtain drop and stood there. Let the sun rise, let the day begin – what was it to her? She felt disembodied, disconnected, unconcerned by anything that happened to be. She turned and moved stiffly back to the bed. She lay down, pulling her knees up to her chest, and stayed there, eyes open, seeing nothing and almost empty of any thought at all.

For a long time, she remained in that position. She vaguely noticed the aircon coming on, and was almost something like grateful. She lay.

Finally, there was a jangling at the door. She flicked her eyes to the clock: 9am. It felt like about 25 o'clock. Piotr came in with the tray. "Good morning," he said. "Your breakfast." She made no reply, just watched him as he put the tray down on the chair in the corner. He turned and looked at her. "Are you OK?" She made the faintest of motions with her head. "OK then... Enjoy your breakfast." Then he was gone.

She lay there, unable or unwilling to get up. She had no appetite. But after a while, the aroma of coffee reached her so she lifted herself off the bed and took the mug. She also broke off a small corner of toast. Then she sat back on the bed and drank the coffee. She munched slowly on the toast. It took a long time to eat, as though it was a sheet of thin cardboard she was trying to ingest.

Breakfast done, she lay back down again in the same position. It seemed the best option, amongst all the options she didn't have and wasn't interested in.

After a while, the door opened again. Kevan Monk came in. He brought the chair from the corner of the room and set it down next to the bed.

"So, how are you today?" he asked. "Not looking so great to be honest..."

"No."

"What's wrong?"

"What do you think."

"You're fed up. That's understandable. Have you thought about our conversation yesterday?"

"No."

"Not at all?"

"No." She looked at him, for the first time. "I don't care about any of it. What you did, what you didn't do. It doesn't mean anything."

"So what does that mean?"

"It means I don't care. It means I just want to be left alone."

"I guess you're suffering from a bit of Mng depression?"

"Your Mng is killing me. Making me feel like shit, yes."

"It will pass, Alice. It doesn't last long. Hang in for a bit."

"Great, thanks. Will do…"

"So, what am I going to do with you? I need to know what you're thinking, Alice."

"I'm thinking – whatever you want me to be thinking. I'm thinking everything, I'm thinking nothing. It's all the same."

"Very cryptic…"

"Well, shall I be direct instead?" Alice suddenly pulled herself up. "Do you want to fuck me? Is that why you're here?" She pulled her pyjama shorts off, then her pants, dropped them to the floor. "Come on then! Let's do it."

She pulled her knees up and opened her legs, closed them, opened them again. Kevan's eyes involuntarily watched.

"Alice! Put your things back on. That's not what I'm here for." He got up and turned away.

"Really? You're sure? Because I don't mind. Frankly, I don't give a fuck…"

"No, Alice!" Kevan said firmly. "Put your bloody pants back on, will you?"

Alice let out a long sigh. "You're no fun," she said, picking her pants and shorts up from the floor. When she'd put them back on, she lay down and turned towards the wall. She started to sob.

"Like I said, you'll come through this soon enough. It won't take so very long," Kevan said gently.

She didn't answer. She just lay there, looking at the wall from the distance of a few millimetres, taking its uniformity in. She was pointless like this wall – her body, her mind, her feelings. Her only-childness. She felt insubstantial, unreal, an imaginary ghost. Everything, inside her, outside her, was empty, a thin illusion; everything could be blown away, like paper screens on a stage, and it would make no difference at all.

She expected Kevan to go, but he stayed seated beside her. She could feel him, watching over her. After a while, she closed her eyes. She fell asleep.

She woke up – he was still there. It was midday. The room was bright. The aircon was on.

He smiled at her. "You had a good snooze. I have to go in a minute. But later I'll come back."

"Do what you want."

She still felt awful. If there had been a gun, a knife, she would have loved to use it on herself. She sat up and dropped her head and let out a long hopeless stream of breath.

"That good, huh? Remember Alice, new Mng will cure all of this. You could switch to new Mng and feel no withdrawal at all. Take it for as long as you want, give it up whenever you want – no problems, no downsides." She glared at him. "Only upsides, honest Alice. I swear. I promise. It will usher in a whole new world. It's coming, Alice."

Then he got up, put the chair back, picked up the breakfast tray, and left the room with a little wave. She sank back onto the pillows.

A bit later, someone new came with a lunch tray but she turned them away. The afternoon slowly passed, the seconds ticking on. Intermittently, she got up to walk a few laps or to go to the toilet. She had a wash. The aircon came on and off – someone playing mind games, weaponising cool air.

It was nearly seven, Alice slumped on the bed in a hopeless pile, when Kevan came in with a supper tray. "You need to eat something," he said.

There was some soup. He picked up the spoon and held it out for her. She shook her head, refusing to have him feed her. She took the spoon herself and had a few mouthfuls along with a piece of bread. Then she had a banana and drank a cup of tea. That was all she wanted. It didn't matter that her body felt hollowed out and pathetically weak.

Kevan left her. She sat. The light in the room began to mellow, taking on a darker gold. It would be night-time soon.

Just after nine, Kevan came back. She raised her eyebrows at him, then closed her eyes. He sat down.

"Obviously, you won't be at work tomorrow. But don't worry, Eric has it all in hand. Your patients will all be contacted to let them know you're unwell," he said.

Her patients... They felt like something from a different life, a thousand miles or years away.

"OK," she said.

Her eyelids began to droop. Had there been something in the soup? Or was it just tiredness and ennui? She let herself drift...

Soon she was lying down in a half-sleep. She could feel that Kevan was there. He remained sitting by her side. She felt him to be a watching spirit, some kind of dark angel emanating a mysterious presence, with a suggestion of dark, untrustworthy wings. She didn't know whether she welcomed him or not. She felt that it probably made no difference. Eventually, without knowing it, she was properly asleep. This time, her sleep was deep and dreamless. She remembered waking and seeing that Kevan was no longer there – the clock showed midnight. She turned over and went back to sleep again.

13.

"No! That's not right. I didn't!"

Peter Franks sat slumped over the table, head down, looking at the scratched surface. He sat inert and hopeless, big and brawny like a boar or a bear, exuding misery. He was sweating. He gave off a pungent stench. It was only 8.30am.

He'd been woken at 6am with a thin breakfast. Hauled back into the interview room at 8am. Why had they woken him at six if they weren't going to start the interview until eight? It was all part of the warfare, that's what it felt like. He was under attack, under siege, accused of something he hadn't done. Why wouldn't they bloody believe him??

They'd come to his house the day before, on bank holiday Monday morning, banging on the door shortly after eight. Another early morning thing. He and Mandy were still in bed, turning in their separate sleeps. The noise pushed its way into his uneasy morning dreams, the banging on the front door below, the persistent ringing of the bell. What the f- ? Going to the intercom – the sodding police. Down he'd gone – a little crowd of them, two cars, lights going.

"Peter Franks, I am arresting you on suspicion of the murder of Martin Silverwood."

Then that stuff you hear on crime dramas on TV. "You do not have to say anything... but anything... court of law." Whatever it was. He'd had that once before, of course, after that night club fight. But this was different, another bloody level. Murder! At his house, crack of dawn, neighbours watching through their curtains. The gossip starting up, the murmurs. Mandy coming out, wrapping her dressing gown around her, asking what was going on. The humiliation, the powerlessness. The, what was the word? The impotence.

So they'd taken him away, clapped him in a cell. Then started the questioning. It had gone on and on, all of Monday, through the afternoon, into the evening. The same questions over and over. He wanted to stand up and scream at them, sweep them all away, just fucking blast away the lot of them!

But he couldn't do that. He had to try to keep his calm. They wanted to rile him. They wanted him to lose his cool and say something stupid.

The lawyer they'd given him had told him to just 'no comment'. But wouldn't that make him look guilty? He'd done nothing wrong, he had nothing to hide. There was no question he couldn't answer. So he was answering, mostly, and no commenting some of the time.

That arsehole DI Sharp was eyeing him coldly again, fixing him with his unpleasant stare. The inspector didn't look so great himself. He was sweating too. There was a kind of monotonous dullness to his tone as well.

"So, where is the knife, Peter? What did you do with it?"

"I don't know anything about no knife. I didn't have one. I didn't do it."

"Did you throw it in the river? Take it home and clean it? Put it back in your little kitchen knife set? Dump it somewhere?"

"I didn't have a knife."

"What did you do with the clothes you were wearing? Did you try to wash the blood out or did you throw them away somewhere?"

"There wasn't any blood. I didn't do it."

"What about Martin's phone? What did you do with that, Peter? Where is it?"

"I didn't take his phone. Because I didn't do it."

"You didn't do it? But you did send Martin a message six weeks ago that read, and I quote, 'Stay away from Mandy or I'll fucking kill you'. Isn't that right?"

"No comment."

"Look, Peter, the game's up. Game set and match. You may as well confess. You'll get a more lenient sentence if you own up to what you did."

"I didn't do it! I didn't do it, officer."

"You beat a man into unconsciousness three years ago over your wife. You have it in you, Peter. That's obvious."

"I am an innocent man, officer. I didn't do it."

"Your business, Peter – it's not doing very well, is it? We can see from your bank records that you've piled up big debts. You don't have enough coming in. You blame

Martin Silverwood for that, don't you? You blame him for the Cod Café being closed down. He started all your financial problems, didn't he?"

"No comment."

"It's a creaking old ship all right, isn't it Peter? How long before you go bankrupt do you think? One month? Two?"

"I will go bankrupt if you keep bloody holding me here!"

"Oh, I think you can forget about getting back to the Fish Fryer, Peter. That's over. And so yes, it's looking pretty grim I'm afraid."

"You can't do this to me! I am innocent. I didn't kill him! I didn't touch him! I need to get back to work. This is... this is a bloody crime against *me*, that's what it is!"

"You should have thought about the consequences when you knifed Martin to death, Peter. Did you really think you'd get away with it?"

"I didn't do it."

"It's as clear as day, Peter. You hated Martin because of your financial problems. And because he was dipping his wick in your wife. Which one made you more angry, Peter?"

He didn't bless that question with an answer. He kept his head down, shaking, trembling, on the verge of hyperventilation.

"I bet it was Mandy that upset you more," DI Sharp continued. "I mean, who could bear the thought of another man shagging an attractive woman like your wife? I don't say I don't understand what you did, Peter. I understand the rage that built up. The hurt. The humiliation. Eventually, it all just exploded, didn't it? You couldn't help yourself. That's understandable. There'll be a bit of sympathy for you in some quarters, I expect."

"I... didn't... do it!!"

"Fine. Keep denying it, Peter. We'll see what our search of your property turns up, shall we? Right now, as we speak, officers are going through everything, your clothes, possessions, tools. Your laptop, the internet searches you've made. Examining everything, every inch. Your car too, of course. The Fish Fryer. We're enjoying your phone as well. All the messages you sent Martin. The exchanges with Mandy. It's all very revealing, Peter. You haven't got anywhere left to hide, son."

Perhaps it was the slightly softer tone of DI Sharp's last sentence that finally got Peter to look up. He slowly lifted his head, his eyes bleary and full of tears, sweat glistening on his stubble, his skin a fiery mottled red. He glanced at his solicitor who, as ever, was eyes down scribbling notes. He looked beseechingly at DI Sharp, and at PC Kaur sitting po-faced beside him.

"But officers, I swear to you, on my life, on Mandy's life, on anyone's life you want, that I didn't do it. I just didn't do it. Why won't you believe me?"

"Everything's pointing your way I'm afraid, son. You're really in a fix. If you didn't do it, you'll need something pretty special to convince us," DI Sharp said. "Do you have anything?"

"Like what?!" Peter exclaimed. "How can I prove I *didn't* do something! It's supposed to be the other way around."

"You mean, for us to prove? Oh, have no doubt that we're on the case there, Peter. Like I said. Officers and forensic specialists crawling all over. It's amazing what they can find, Peter. You wouldn't believe."

"Jesus!" Peter cried, his head slumping down again. His big shoulders heaved.

"We're speaking to Mandy again too, of course. And other people you know. Who knew Martin too. The casino crowd. The net is closing in, Peter. Think about it, Peter..."

DI Sharp sat back, crossing his arms. A silence filled the room. Peter felt it growing, like gas expanding, pushing against the walls. It was like a pressure cooker. Getting ready to blow.

"I need the toilet," he blurted.

"Oh come on, Peter, we've only been going an hour!"

"I need the toilet, I said! It comes on quick. Do you want me to piss myself?"

"You can wait a bit longer, I'm sure."

"Officer, I have a bloody prostate condition if you must know. Please can I go to the loo?"

DI Sharp sighed. "Interview suspended at... 9.27am."

A male officer came in and escorted him to the toilet. He locked himself in the cubicle and hung his head. He was in hell. This was the worst thing he'd ever known. He was an innocent man but he was trapped. What could he do? If they would just bloody believe him...!

How he hated Martin Silverwood. He had hated him in life, but he hated him even more now! Silverwood was like a curse on him. A curse that was getting *worse*, not better. He hadn't deserved to die in the way he did, but even so Peter cursed him back. Fuck off and leave me alone, Silverwood... It was a poison running through his veins.

The lawyer had told him the police had gained an extension from 24 to 36 hours before they either had to charge him or let him go. That was still about... 10 hours away. 10 fucking hours! What would he do, how would he survive it, if they just kept on and on questioning him through all of that time?

But, as a faint dribble of piss came, what he had to remember was – that he hadn't done it! He was INNOCENT. So there was nothing they could find. No knife, no phone, no bloody clothes. If they had no physical evidence, they couldn't charge him. That's what the lawyer had said. And there was no evidence. They wouldn't find anything. They'd have to let him go... wouldn't they?

And then he'd have to go home. He'd have to face Mandy, her questions... The neighbours, everyone else around and about the place... Oh God. What was happening. There was work too. Some big payments imminent. Nothing to pay them with.

Christ, this was hard. This was so fucking hard! He sniffed and sniffled on the toilet seat, gulping for air, trying to keep the panic and hysteria down. He never imagined that life could get like this. His head was fizzing, he felt dizzy, he felt sick, he felt disgusting. This was all disgusting. Where was the way out of this??

He pressed the flush and the toilet gurgled into ugly life. Then he pulled his trousers up and took a deep breath. He had to man up. He just had to brace himself to deal with what lay ahead, to face down all the waves and waves of whirling, swirling questions.

14.

Jane leaned forward on her bike as she pedalled up the hill that led to Reacher's Point. It was always quite hard getting up the incline at the end of the ride but there was a satisfaction in making it and she liked the warmth it spread in her calves.

It was hot work too. Even at nine o'clock it was warm and sultry again. However, the weather was forecast to finally break that day. She could see the clouds beginning to gather in the west, grey silhouettes banking on the horizon. She had heard something on the radio about thunder and torrential rain. That would make a welcome change after all these days of endless sun and heat.

Here, she'd made it. She stopped at the big metal gates and put her thumb on the key pad. The gates swung open and she wheeled her bike in. There were a few cars in the parking area as usual. Most of them she recognised, although there was one small red vehicle she hadn't seen before. Mr Monk's car wasn't there. He was not usually home when she cleaned, given that she always came during the week. He was a high-powered business executive, they told her, who ran that company SmartLab with their big factory in Knott. Medicines and pills.

He would certainly have to be successful to own this place! Reacher's Point was so big. Endless rooms and outbuildings. The main house so smart and minimalist and modern, so much glass and airy space. She didn't like it much. She'd much rather be in her own house which was empty in a different way but at least it felt like a *home*.

Stephen.

Jane went up the stone steps to the front door where again she placed her thumb on the pad and let herself in. She went to her pigeon hole as usual to see whether there were any instructions. All the staff – the housekeeper/cook, the other cleaner, herself, the handyman, the gardener – had a pigeon hole. Oh yes, there was a note for her.

"Jane - Please clean the main house today. There is no need to clean Room 1 in the near annexe. Please do NOT go in there. Kevan."

She knew that there had been a big party at the weekend and so was expecting a lot of work to do, even though she'd been assured that the catering company would clean up inside themselves. She wasn't expecting their standard to be very high, however. But she was pleased that she didn't have to worry about the outbuildings and annexes – the other cleaner Pat must be doing those.

But why was she not supposed to clean Room 1? That was down at the end of the main house, in a kind of annexe after the kitchen. She believed in fact that that 'annexe' had already been there, part of an original building with thick walls and floors. There were a couple of storerooms down there along with Room 1, which was occasionally used as an overflow for guests or by a member of staff when they needed to stay over.

It was odd – Mr Monk didn't usually leave her notes or give her direct instructions. Notes were normally from the housekeeper Mrs Davenport who came in three times a week, meaning sometimes they coincided and sometimes they didn't. Mrs Davenport's role was to oversee and coordinate the domestic staff and their shifts, and also cook meals for Mr Monk which she would prepare and then leave for him in the fridge or freezer along with notes and cooking instructions. It was Mrs Davenport who had advertised the position and hired Jane. She'd only met Mr Monk a few times. She didn't believe he even knew her surname. She had never warmed to him very much – he seemed like a cold and distant man. Rather like his house. In fact, she had never really liked the whole Reacher's Point job. She had considered giving it up once or twice. She could surely find something else without much difficulty – there were plenty of cleaning jobs around.

She began to assemble her cleaning materials so she could get started on the hall and some of the smaller rooms first. She'd leave the main living room and the upstairs until later. She stuck her head into the kitchen to see if Mrs Davenport was there. But the only person in there was that strange man Janko. Another thing she didn't like about Reacher's Point – there were odd characters like him and Piotr who hung around the place. She didn't know what they actually did. There were a few others that milled around now and again – all men – but Janko and Piotr actually *lived* at Reacher's Point. They had a room each in one of the annexes. They had to clean their living quarters themselves, so she'd never actually been inside. That would be the last thing she'd want to do anyway – she wouldn't want to get any closer than she had to. There was something unpleasant about them, a faint air of menace.

Janko looked up from the breakfast bar where he was spooning a bowl of cereal into his mouth and grunted a rough kind of greeting. Jane raised a hand and backed out.

Stephenn.

Then she began dusting the hallway before giving it a vacuum. The positive aspect about Reacher's Point was that, in fact, it was very light work. The house always seemed barely lived in. Everything was kept pretty much spotless. As for Mr Monk, he seemed only ever to use the kitchen (where he ate his meals), his study (where he'd work on his computer), and his bedroom. The living room was generally only used when there were guests – which didn't seem to be particularly often. What *did* happen more frequently, it seemed, was that Mr Monk would have a lady friend to stay. Jane would sometimes find lipsticks in his ensuite or discarded make-up items in the waste bin; now and again, a hair band or forgotten piece of clothing in the bedroom.

She turned on her portable radio (Mahler symphony) and worked her way down the hallway, doing the study, the library, the downstairs toilet, the kitchen. She had to turn the lights on in each room as she went, because it was starting to get quite dark: those clouds were steadily rolling in, filling up the sky and shutting out the sun that everyone had become so used to over the last month or more of unbroken heat. It was going to break now, all right. It looked like it would crack imminently. In fact, there were one or two very low rumblings that also made themselves felt, as though someone was adjusting a piece of furniture upstairs.

She pressed on with her work, moving along the corridor into the near annexe as it was known with its storerooms and, of course, Room 1.

So, what was it about Room 1? For some reason, she felt very curious. Whereas usually she was no longer curious about anything at all; nothing concerned her anymore, everything was merely space she moved through. This shouldn't be any different. She should leave Room 1 alone and just carry on with what she needed to get done. But there was something about the way Mr Monk had written NOT in capitals that, perversely, made her really want to look.

She almost tittered to herself at this perversity. This was unlike her! To have her interest in something aroused. Well, maybe she would just have a quick peek…

She approached Room 1. Was she actually going to go in? She hesitated, and instead stood outside and listened… But the walls were very thick, the door too. There was no sound that she could make out at all. It was either go in – or leave it.

All of a sudden, she found herself knocking on the door. But the door was so solid it made almost no sound at all – it just hurt her knuckles.

She'd have a look then. The door was locked. She took out her keys and found the right one. Here we go…

Softly, slowly, Jane pushed the door open and looked inside. To her surprise, there was a woman sitting on the bed!

"I beg your pardon. I didn't mean to disturb you," Jane said.

The woman, who was wearing pyjama shorts and a top, jumped up and came towards her, reaching out a hand. "No, no, it's OK!" she said.

"But I can't…. I don't think I was supposed…" Jane stammered, backing out. "I do apologise."

"Please, wait! Don't go!" the woman cried.

Jane stopped her backtracking. So this woman had been locked in here? What was going on? The woman looked like she had been through duress. Her hair was dishevelled, she was pale and drawn, she looked very tired. The air in the room was fetid and stale. It was a sad sight, especially as Jane could see that, in normal circumstances, the woman would cut an attractive, intelligent, confident kind of figure.

The two women looked intently into each other's eyes, examining, exploring, probing what they found. In the background, from the corridor, came the faint sound of the Mahler symphony peaking. A kind of understanding passed between them.

Without speaking, Jane nodded and held up the key. Then she moved out of the room and shut the door. She put the key in her pocket and moved briskly away, back along the corridor towards the main house.

Stephennn.

15.

Alice stood staring at the door. Had that just happened? She wasn't sure what was real and what was imaginary anymore.

She moved to the door, holding her breath, and put her ear against it. It was too thick to make anything out. Slowly, cautiously, she put her hand on the door handle and tried it... Yes! As she had thought and hoped, the woman hadn't locked it! Freedom beckoned! Bless you, cleaning lady, whoever you were...

But she had to be quick. Who knew when Kevan or Janko or Piotr might come. Was Kevan around today? It was Tuesday, a working day, of course. Hopefully he was elsewhere. But his two sidekicks were likely to be on the scene.

She began to rapidly gather up her things. Someone had brought them last night. Who knew when – she had been asleep from early evening, in and out of wakefulness, with Kevan at her bedside much of the time. She had woken early – about 6am – and had noticed her things on the second chair in the corner. There was a plastic bag with the dress she had worn, a thin blouse she had brought, her wash stuff and make up, her clutch containing her purse. On the floor, her pumps. Everything except for her phone, her watch and her car keys.

The crucial thing was her shoes. She put them on. Yes! She was out of here...

She went to the door and opened it as noiselessly as she could. The cleaning lady had gone. In front of her, a corridor, a few closed doors off it. It was quite dark down here, no lights on. Accentuated by the cloud that had rolled in over the last couple of hours.

Alice sensed that the main house was to her left. So she turned to the right and moved with quick light steps along the corridor. Her heart was in her mouth in case anyone appeared... But it seemed empty and silent down here. The signs were good – as long as she could actually get out.

Soon, she rounded a bend in the corridor and saw that it came to an end. There was a fire door with a bar across it that you needed to depress to open. Would it open? Would it set off some kind of alarm?

Wishing herself luck, Alice took a breath and pressed down on the bar. The door made more noise than she would have liked – but it opened. No alarm sounded. She was suddenly in the open air! But where was she, and which way was out?

She was standing on a stony path that wound its way around the house. She knew that up to her left was the main garden in front of the living room. To her right was the way to the parking area and gate. So, if she went straight on, across this stretch of grass and down through those bushes and trees that stood on a slow gradual slope, she should hopefully come to some kind of perimeter wall or fence that she could climb over and away...

Crouching low, feeling like some bizarre kind of commando, Alice scooted forward under the bruised, lowering light of a cloud-filled sky towards the greenery. It was only about thirty yards and soon she was there. She wrapped herself into a leafy bush and caught her breath, her heart thumping.

She felt very tired. Even though she had slept from early evening through to morning, she felt drawn and wan and her limbs lacked any kind of strength. She hadn't eaten much over the last couple of days. Breakfast had come at nine, delivered by Janko, but it had only been a small helping of cereal and one piece of toast.

But the main thing was that she felt more herself today. That awful, sluggish Mng withdrawal depression had receded. Yesterday had been terrible. The memory of it was itself depressing. Her spirits had been so low, it had been like a kind of mental and emotional death, leaving her an inert lump inside her own shell. But it had passed. On waking in the morning, she had known straightaway that she'd turned the corner. It was Alice waking up again, not some blasted vestige of her spirit. Maybe, she hoped, she could actually give up Mng now.

She remembered too that Kevan had sat with her. As though silently willing her recovery? There had been no need for him to stay there. She had felt him to be there for several hours. Could that be right? Why would he? She could almost say it had been a factor in her improvement. She had felt him there, a hovering presence, brooding over her, helping her through.

But what was she saying, she had asked herself as she sat up in bed on waking up that morning. That man was not her friend! Look what he had done to her! Knocking her out, holding her captive, making dark threats even including the implied harming of her mother! It was monstrous, deeply wrong. It showed who he really was. The lengths he would go to as he pursued his Mng mania.

And that had included the very worst crime of all... The taking of another life. Whether it had been at his hands directly, or those of Janko, Piotr or some other low-life associate, Monk simply had to be brought to book. Justice had to be done, for Martin Silverwood's sorry sake.

Tired as she was, she had to drive herself on. She turned and moved into the outlying reaches of the garden, through a row of willow trees that draped their long dry rustling fingers, in between thick rambling bushes and banks of rhododendron, until at last she could see a wall.

It was about six feet high but there were ridges and grooves in the stonework that meant she was able to clamber up. She looked out – there was a field of what looked like barley or wheat, a group of trees beyond. It wouldn't be far after that until she'd come to the outskirts of Knott.

She slung her bag over and down onto the ground, then launched herself off after it. She landed with a jarring jolt to her ankles, but rolled over and seemed OK. She listened – she was half-expecting to hear a hue and cry from the house, the mobilisation of a mob, the yelping of hounds. Like a fox in a chase. But there was only silence...

Quickly, she got to her feet and started walking along the edge of the field. She would obviously have to stay away from the roads in case they realised she'd escaped and came in pursuit. That was OK. She reckoned she should be at Knott police station within an hour.

Suddenly, there was a flash followed by a tremendous crack. She thought that a tree had fallen, or even – in the altered reality she was now caught up in – that a meteor had hit the house. Then she realised it was a storm. Thunder rang out in deep rumbles, reverberating around the field. A wind started up, blustery and fresh. A few seconds later, more lightning sheeted across the sky. The barley or wheat was illuminated like a ghostly image of itself, waving. Then a torrential rain began to fall. It came down in a drenching mass, huge fat drops whipped by the wind. The breath was almost knocked out of her; in seconds, she was soaked. She took her blouse out of her bag and put it on over her pyjamas – better than nothing, but not much. It wasn't long before the blouse was drenched too, hanging heavy and distended. She preferred that though to looking like she was entering a wet T-shirt competition.

Runnels and funnels of water were soon sloshing around her feet as the rain came down and the thunder rolled. More lightning cracked across the sky. She began, suddenly, to laugh. This was actually good fun! She was pretty sure that she was OK now, she'd slipped Monk's clutches. She looked around behind her – nobody there.

In a few minutes, she reached the bottom edge of the field and slipped into the safety of the trees. It was only a small grouping and led, she could see, into an area of scrubland skirted by a path. Beyond that, a housing estate that marked an outlier of Knott.

Alice caught her breath in the din of the rain that was battering the leaves, like a percussion orchestra let loose, raising hell. She leaned against a dripping tree. After the heat of all these past weeks, the coolness of the air that blew around her was a blessing. *Anything* was a blessing, after what she'd come through.

She squelched forward, her eyes fixed on the city ahead, determined to make it to the station as quickly as possible. There, she would set out everything that had happened and lay down her claims against Kevan Monk of Reacher's Point, murderer, fraud, and creator of the curse that was Mng.

16.

"Hello, Clear Minds, Sam speaking. How can I help?"

"Oh yes, hello. My name's Lewis. I'm a friend of Alice. Alice Carlisle. I wondered, is she there? Can I speak to her if she's free?"

"I'm afraid Alice is unwell. We've cancelled all her appointments for the next couple of days. Could anyone else help?"

"Oh. No, it's a personal call really. It's just that I can't get her on her mobile. I haven't been able to raise her for the last couple of days. Maybe that explains it…"

"Yes, I suppose it does."

"It seems odd though. Do you know what's wrong with her?"

"I'm afraid not. It must have come on quite quickly though. She was at a party on Saturday night that a few other colleagues here went to. Kevan Monk's party – you know, from SmartLab?"

"Oh, is that right! Well… Yes, came on quickly then."

"Can I take a message for her, for when she's back?"

"No, it's all right thanks. I'll keep trying her mobile. Maybe she'll turn it on again soon. Thanks very much."

"OK great, thanks. Goodbye."

Lewis put his phone down on his desk, his mind whirring. Kevan Monk's house? Party? But he'd messaged her on Saturday and she said she was having a quiet night in. That was the last time he'd heard from her...

He'd messaged her a couple more times over the weekend but had got no reply. He hadn't thought too much of it and had decided not to message her again himself – he didn't want to look needy and over-bearing. But then he'd phoned her when they were on the road back from London on Monday afternoon and it had gone straight to voicemail. He'd begun to think there was something odd. When they'd got back to Knott, he'd tried again. Then he'd driven round to her flat: her car wasn't there and nobody home. He'd begun to really get worried...

And now this. What should he do? He had to do something! But damn it, he had a meeting in twenty minutes, at half past nine, that he couldn't get out of.

Lewis decided that straight after the meeting he'd claim to be feeling really sick and say he was going home. Then he'd drive out to Kevan Monk's place and check it out... He knew that Monk was (apparently) in London in meetings that day. But could Alice possibly be at his house – voluntarily or otherwise...?!

The meeting dragged on for the full appointed hour. Lewis began to try to show signs of being unwell – wiping his forehead, coughing, cricking his neck. As soon as it was finished, he told his boss that he had a bad headache and felt aches and pains coming on...

Then he was off. He knew where Kevan Monk's house – the famous Reacher's Point – was. It should only take about twenty minutes to get there.

Tension and nerves grew as he drove. What was he going to do? He was convinced that Alice must be there. And he just had that gut certainty that she was there against her will. Why would she turn her phone off? Why would she not contact him at all to let him know where she was? Especially after they'd been so close recently. She'd told him, so movingly, about the revelation of her lost half-sibling a few nights ago. She had wept and cried, she'd let it all out, and he had found whole waves of love welling up inside him in response. They had been more tender and open with each other than ever before. He'd revisited with her the whole subject of Dan… They had wrapped themselves tightly in each other, healing and hurting at the same time, cleaving one to another, passionate, overcome. It had been the most beautiful thing he'd ever known. And now, silence? No way. Something bad, something deeply *wrong*, was afoot…

Without any doubt, this was a time for decisive action. This was a test of his manhood. Of the strength of his love, his passion for Alice. He would just force his way in there if he had to!

Soon he was getting close to Reacher's Point. But as he began to climb the hill that led to the house, the skies suddenly opened and a massive downpour of rain began. Thunder rang out, lightning sizzled. Even with the windscreen wipers on at top speed, he couldn't see a thing. These were hardly ideal conditions.

Nosing slowly up the road, he could eventually see the house about fifty yards ahead. He pulled over and parked where there was a small space next to the gate to a field. Then he took some deep breaths and prepared himself...

The rain certainly didn't help. He was wearing some smartish trousers and a shirt – and was soaked within seconds as he strode up to the house. Wiping his eyes, he peered through the wall of water at the gate. There was no way through, only an intercom to ring. He didn't want to do that. So he moved a little further up the road and then levered himself up over the stone wall and into the hedge that ran along inside it. He closed his eyes and mouth against the sticks and leaves that jagged themselves against him as he pushed himself through. He landed in an uncomfortable heap, in the earth that was already waterlogged mud, then crawled his way out.

He stood up, wet, muddy and scratched, and looked across at a parking area in front of him. There stood Alice's car! That confirmed it. That was it. He stared up at the house like an enemy he had to take down. There was no time to stand and think. Let's bring this on!

Lewis ran towards the house, bounding up the stone steps two at a time, as the rain pelted down. His clothes by now were wet cloths plastered against his body, his hair was matted to his head, water running into his eyes as the world around him roared. Adrenaline coursed like madness through his veins.

He reached the front door. He couldn't, he mustn't, stop now, not even for a second! He held his finger on the doorbell, he hammered with his other hand on the door. He began to yell, "Hello! Hello! Let me in!"

After perhaps thirty seconds, the door swung open. There in front of him was someone he recognised, a woman, who was it – the woman from the cemetery!

"Hello!" Lewis stammered in his surprise.

"Hello?" the woman said. "We met before...?"

"I'm looking for my friend, Alice. I have reason to believe she's here. You must let me in!"

"The young lady perhaps..." The woman nodded. But Lewis, discarding manners, was already moving past her into the house.

"Where is she?" he cried. "Please, tell me where she is!"

Then he turned as he sensed someone approaching. A huge man, almost as wide as he was tall, stood in the hallway in front of him.

"What you want?" the man barked.

"There's a woman here. Alice. She's being held against her will. I know it!"

"Leave. You cannot come in," the mountain intoned.

This was the moment. Lewis steadied himself, raising his fists like a boxer. "Let me through!"

The man gave a sneer in response and came forward, swinging a massive fist at Lewis' head. Lewis, remembering his childhood boxing lessons, ducked with a flowing, silky movement and piled all his strength, all his passion, all his will, into a full-throttle punch of his own.

Crack! He landed flush against Janko's jaw. The problem was that the crack seemed to come from Lewis' fist rather than Janko's face…

Lewis gave a yelp and shrank back as a screaming pain shot through his hand and up his arm. Janko meanwhile stepped fractionally back – then quickly recovered. He sneered again and advanced, ready to teach this young idiot a lesson he wouldn't forget.

Suddenly, however, there was something tangling Janko's feet. He tripped on the cord to the vacuum cleaner which Jane had yanked tight, bringing it a few inches off the floor like a tripwire. Janko's foot clipped his heel, he tottered, staggered – then fell like a mighty tree. As he came down, he banged his head with a dull thud against a side unit by the wall.

Lewis and Jane looked at each other as Janko sprawled inert on the floor. "Where is she?" he cried.

"This way!" Jane said, running down the hall.

Lewis followed her, panting, his hand throbbing, his vision blurred. But when they got to the room and Jane opened the door – no one was there.

"Look, she was here but I left the door unlocked for her. About half an hour ago. She's got away."

"Where to? Her car's still here?"

"On foot of course. The only option. She would have gone out of the back door down there. Then I guess she went through the garden and out over the wall."

"OK..."

"I imagine she's walking back to Knott right now."

"Right! I'll see if I can find her then," Lewis said, turning straightaway. Then he stopped: "Thanks so much! You obviously helped Alice out. And you were right, when you said we'd see each other again!"

"No problem. I'm glad to help. But you go – quick! Before he gets back on his feet..."

Lewis nodded and sprinted back along the corridor, past Janko in the hallway, and out of the house towards his car.

When Jane followed him, Janko was recovering, sitting against the wall, rubbing his head.

"Are you all right?" Jane asked.

He nodded. "I will be OK. But she is gone?" He grimaced. Then he said, "You, Jane. You better leave. I know what you did. There is no place for you now."

Jane shrugged, mimicking surprise. "What do you...?"

"I mean it. Go now. Before I get angry. Why you trip me like that? How did the woman get out?"

"I really don't... OK, you're right. I'll pack up and go."

A short while later, Jane was on her way. She had no regrets. She had never liked working there in any case. And clearly, something deeply unpleasant had been going on.

Meanwhile, she had helped not one but two people that day! It had felt *good*. It made her feel restored in some way, reconnected. And she'd see Lewis again, without any doubt at all. He may even become a friend, the girl perhaps too.

It was still sheeting down with rain when Jane pushed her bike out through the gate. Good job she'd brought her waterproofs. As she free-wheeled down the hill, the water coursing along the road shot up from her tyres in a great whooshing arc. Water, water everywhere! Water and wind and thunder and fire! Jane threw her head back and let out a loud laugh as she gathered speed, faster and faster, shooting down the hill.

Stephennnnnnnnn!

17.

"Was your wife shagging lots of men then, Peter, or just Martin Silverwood?" DI Sharp asked.

"Sod off."

"Language please. But was she?"

"No comment."

"I guess Martin was her favourite then, eh? Is that why he riled you so much? Is that why you killed him?"

"Didn't kill him."

"Are there other men you'd like to kill too, Peter?"

Peter looked up pointedly and stared at DI Sharp.

"For the record, Peter is now eyeballing DI Sharp," said DI Sharp.

This was murder. Peter couldn't take much more of this. They'd actually called a halt to the grilling at around half ten and given the impression they'd be stopping for a while. But only ten minutes later, he'd been hauled out of his cell and brought in again. It was a deliberate tactic, he knew that. Premeditated. Warfare, is what it was. Mental and psychological warfare.

Now it was PC Kaur's turn to chip in.

"Peter, look, I know you're tired and fed up with this. Just tell us what you did and it will all be over."

"I didn't do anything!"

"Where's the knife, Peter?" she asked.

"Don't know."

"Where's the mobile phone, Peter?" asked DI Sharp.

"Don't know."

"Where's Martin's wallet, Peter?" – PC Kaur.

"Where are your bloodied clothes, Peter?" – DI Sharp.

"How long did you spend planning the murder, Peter?" – PC Kaur.

"Did it feel good, when you stuck the knife in, Peter?" – DI Sharp.

Peter kept himself hunched forward, eyes down. He put his hands over his ears and began rocking back and forth.

"Look, son, there's no need for the baby routine, OK?" DI Sharp said brusquely. "It's not gonna get you out of this. We're here for the long haul, Peter. We'll keep asking these questions all bloody day if we have to. Understand?"

Peter shrugged.

"Do you understand?"

"I'm not stupid, Inspector! Yes, I understand! But why can't you? Heh? Why can't any of you? I'm not fucking guilty! I didn't kill Martin Silverwood!"

"Oh... Oh, I see. Well, forgive me then Peter. I didn't realise it was as simple as you denying it and us packing up and going home! What do you make of that then, Police Constable Kaur? Shall we call it a day then?"

There was a brief silence, and then DI Sharp started again. "Right then, Peter. Can you please run us through your movements again on that Saturday? Starting from around lunchtime."

"Inspector, how many times do I have to tell you all this?"

"As many times as it takes, son."

Peter closed his eyes and shook his head. Maybe if he kept shaking, everything would vanish. Maybe if he kept his eyes closed long enough, when he opened them again he'd be somewhere else. He couldn't bear this. There was about another seven hours left until they had to charge or release him... It might as well have been seven centuries. He'd never felt more hopeless, more alone...

Just then, a low rumbling reached them. It grew in volume, making the table shake, until it cracked like a branch snapping. Then there was the sound of rippling gunfire, bullets against the walls in a crazy battering of noise – torrential rain. There were no windows in the interview room but the light seemed to change its texture for a couple of seconds as lightning flashed outside. The striplight on the ceiling went out, then came crackling back on. The storm was in full cry.

"Come on then!" DI Sharp said. His voice was thin in the din around them.

Suddenly, Peter felt a breaking inside him. Like the storm, it welled up and quickly took on an irresistible force. It came pouring out of his mouth.

"I did it! I did it, officer..."

They all sat up. "You did what, Peter?"

He could feel his solicitor staring at him in shock, but he ignored him and carried on. "I killed Martin Silverwood. I murdered him. I did it."

Peter hung his head again, but inside he could already feel the difference. Even if it wasn't true, it was such a release, like opening a sluice gate and letting the waters flow.

"Now – this is very serious. Highly serious, Peter – do you understand me? You're saying that you committed the murder?"

Peter nodded, looked up. "Yes, officer. I did it. I'm sorry I didn't confess to it straightaway."

"That's OK, son. As long as we get to the truth in the end. So – in your own time, nice and calmly, step by step, can you tell us what happened that night?"

"Yes. I'd been thinking about doing it for several weeks. Knowing that he was sleeping with Mandy. Knowing that my business was going down the drain – all his fault. I knew he almost always went to the casino on Saturdays. So, I went there too. I had a knife in my jacket, taped into the inside pocket – you were right about that, Inspector."

Peter felt himself warming to his theme. The words began to come faster. He kept on pushing the words out against the hammering of the rain and the clattering of the thunder, this end of the world. "I went inside, I saw him. We spoke. I told him to stay away from Mandy, said I'd break his fucking bones if not. He just smirked at me – arsehole. I hung around, keeping an eye on him. I drank quite a few pints, began to feel quite pissed. Then I could see that he was getting ready to leave. So I got out first. Took my jacket and got outside, waited in a doorway. I thought he'd probably parked in Dark Lane because I'd passed him there before. I had checked and knew there was no CCTV either."

He took a breath, gulping for air. It was surprisingly easy, making all this up, telling them what they wanted to hear.

His lawyer seemed to have stopped trying to get everything down, was just sitting with his arms folded, grimacing in the din of the storm. Well, who cared? He pushed on, into the maelstrom. "I followed him down Dark Lane, making sure he didn't notice me. Stayed back about 20 yards. I put some gloves on. When he turned into the car park – I pounced. Sprinted up, grabbed him round the neck and with my other hand, plunged the knife in. I stabbed him four or five times. I could hear from his gurgling that he didn't have long. I took his phone and his wallet so it looked like a mugging. I turned the phone off straightaway so it couldn't be tracked. I pushed him under his car so he wouldn't stand out. Then I got out of there as quickly as I could. Didn't see anyone as luck would have it."

"OK very good Peter. What then?" DI Sharp asked, roaring into the wind.

"Well, I got home," Peter shouted back, trying to make himself heard. "Mandy was asleep. I washed – there was a bit of blood. I hid my clothes and the knife and the phone and the wallet. There was a bit of money. I took that. Then I waited. A couple of days later I drove somewhere. Can't remember where exactly. Just went around and around and eventually stopped. Some scrubland. I burned my clothes there to a cinder. His wallet too. I'd already smashed his phone up with a hammer and thrown the bits away. Threw the knife somewhere. That was all. Then I went and bought some new clothes and put them in the wardrobe. I knew Mandy wouldn't notice anything. She never pays me much attention…"

Soon, Peter was back in his cell. If he didn't feel so horrible, he'd actually say he felt good! He had cleared it all out, got it all out of himself, all the shit, all the crap, all the tangled rotting debris of everything. It had come flooding out, a river that had burst its banks, carrying all the random rubbish with it. Watch it go! Left behind was a kind of cleanness. Or blankness. Or emptiness. He had confessed, he had agreed with them that he had done it – what more was there to say? Now it was just about taking his punishment. Living a life inside. Mandy would be OK – she was a survivor, she would always find someone to help her on her way. Now, he could just give up on all of that, all the stuff he'd been failing at over all these years, his cod and chips life, his unfaithful wife, his sorry sinking struggles. Goodbye to all that. Yes, this was better, this was peacefulness, this was sanctuary. He so much preferred this.

The storm had waned a little. It was just hard rain now rather than a mad torrent from hell. It was quieter in the cell.

Peter dropped his head onto his chest and suddenly began to snort great tears, as though he had violent hiccups. Gouts of snot and saliva slopped down his face, clinging to his skin. Sad, mottled creature, he trembled, he shook, he was overwhelmed by misery, by confusion, by relief.

18.

Alice began to relax as she reached the outskirts of Knott and was surrounded by housing and built-up life. She was surely safe now. She strode quickly on, through the driving rain, wrapping her blouse around her for what protection it gave. That wasn't much: she was soaked through and dripping wet. Cars sent up great plumes of water, the few pedestrians that were around scurried along under umbrellas, bending into the wind. At least no one really took much notice of her, in her strange state of dress, given this cataclysmic meteorological burst.

It didn't take long to reach the police station, which was near the centre of town. Alice marched in and went to the reception desk, where she stood creating a puddle of water on the floor. The officer behind the desk looked at her and raised his eyebrows.

"Caught in a shower of rain, hey? How can I help you madam?"

"I need to see Detective Inspector Sharp," she said. "It's urgent."

"Right. And what is it concerning?"

"It's about the murder of Martin Silverwood. I have important information that I need to give."

"Is that so, madam? And your name is?"

Alice gave her details. The man didn't ask any further questions, but said he'd see if DI Sharp was available.

Kindly, he procured a towel from somewhere. She went to the toilets and dried herself off as best she could.

She had to wait about twenty minutes, steaming softly in the warm air of the station, watching the comings and goings as people milled in and out. These were a welcome distraction – if she closed her eyes, she realised that her heart was racing and there was a kind of fizzing in her brain. It had been a weird and draining couple of days...

Eventually, an officer came and led her into an interview room. She sat and waited, nervously chewing her lips. Five minutes passed, ten... Then finally a small, wiry, unsmiling man came in.

"Miss... Carlisle, I believe?" he asked. "I'm Detective Inspector Sharp. You wanted to see me?"

He sat down and looked across the table at her. He had a thin, tough-looking face. Something dead about the eyes in their ungiving gaze.

"Yes, officer, that's right. It's about Martin Silverwood. The murder that I think you're leading the investigation on?"

"That is correct."

He waited. So she went on: "I know who did it, officer! I've come here as soon as I could."

"All these days later?"

"It's complicated. And I had to be sure... It's a man called Kevan Monk, officer. He murdered Martin Silverwood."

DI Sharp lifted an eyebrow. "Kevan Monk? As in, the CEO of SmartLab here in Knott?"

"That's right, that's it. It was him officer. Him or someone working for him."

"Oh, you don't know which? That suggests you may not have any actual evidence or proof then, as to who did the deed?"

"Not as such officer, no. But I know for sure that Kevan Monk was involved. That he made it happen."

"And why would Mr Monk want to do such a thing? What was his motive, Miss Carlisle?"

She sensed a fair amount of scepticism coming off DI Sharp. But that was no surprise.

"It's all to do with Mng. You know, the drug that SmartLab produces? They've been flooding the market deliberately, illegally. Martin Silverwood realised what was going on. He started to blackmail Kevan Monk. Monk had to shut him up. So he – "

DI Sharp cut in. "Okayyy. You have proof of this? As in, evidence, documentation, anything of that kind?"

"I mean, no, not as such. Nothing I can show you. Although there are some posts Martin Silverwood made on social media."

"Right... And what about you, Miss Carlisle – do you know Kevan Monk? Are you... personally acquainted or anything?"

"Well… yes, we're friends. Of sorts."

"Of sorts?"

"I mean, we were kind of… lovers, a couple of years ago. It rekindled a bit recently. But that was only because –"

"It *rekindled*. What do you mean exactly?"

"I mean, we've had something of a relationship. I went to a big party he held at the weekend, for example. But then, I mean, get this, he actually held me hostage. At his house. I managed to escape today. That's why I'm soaked. I came straight here."

"Hang on, hang on. He held you hostage? You mean, forcibly?"

"Yes! You see, I stayed the night after the party. Then he caught me looking around his house. I was trying to find evidence about Mng and everything."

"You were looking round his house? At his personal things? Had you… slept together, that night, if you don't mind me asking?"

"Well, yes, we did sleep together as a matter of fact. But that was only because I planned it. Because I wanted to get access to his house. I got up later in the middle of the night and – "

DI Sharp held up a hand. "OK, look, Miss Carlisle, this is all getting rather… tangled up, if you know what I mean. You are or were in a relationship with Mr Monk. You began snooping round his house in the middle of the night. He found you, was obviously upset at this, and some kind of argument followed."

"No, what followed was that he – or one of his sidekicks – knocked me out, with some chemical like chloroform or something, and he locked me in a room…"

"Whatever the case, we're getting quite a long way from the murder of Martin Silverwood here."

"It's all connected, Inspector! Believe me. I can take you through all of it, step by step."

"Look, Miss Carlisle. There's something I should tell you at this point. We are holding a man, right now as we speak, in a cell in this police station. He admitted to the murder this morning."

"What, Martin Silverwood's murder? Who?"

"We haven't released his name yet. But will do shortly. He has nothing to do with Kevan Monk. He had clear and compelling motives for killing Martin, and we have CCTV of him in the same venue as Martin on the night of the murder."

"Really?"

"Really. He has confessed to the crime. We already have our killer, Miss Carlisle."

"Well… I don't know what to say. Could there be some kind of mistake? Is this man mentally together? Clear about what he's saying?"

"He is. And he has a motive that's as clear as day. So when it comes to Kevan Monk, Miss Carlisle…" DI Sharp raised his palms into air, as though he was letting a bird fly away.

"There's a mistake here!" Alice cried. "There must be! I know, I *know*, inspector, that Kevan Monk did it. Or caused it to be done."

"Miss Carlisle, we deal in facts here. Proof. Your very uncertainty there shows us that you don't have much of either. We receive allegations and tip-offs all the time. It's hard facts that we need."

"What are you saying? You don't believe me?"

"I believe that you believe it, Miss Carlisle…" DI Sharp glanced at his watch. "Look, I'm very busy, I have a lot to do. A man has just confessed. However, here at Knott police we are of course relentless in our pursuit of the truth. So, I will ask a colleague to come in and they'll take a statement from you. OK? We will follow up on it as appropriate."

"What does that mean? You must… interview Kevan Monk, grill him, bring him in!"

"We will take your statement, Miss Carlisle, and then we will proceed as appropriate. That may well include speaking to Mr Monk. But you will have to leave decisions over our investigation to us. Do you see?"

Alice nodded. She saw. This was going to go precisely nowhere…

But what could she do? Someone else had gone and confessed! Could it be... could it be that Kevan was NOT, in fact, guilty? Could she somehow have been horribly mistaken about the whole thing? She sat back and rubbed her face. She didn't know what was going on anymore, what was true, what was false, what was somewhere in between.

"Well then, thank you for coming in, Miss Carlisle," DI Sharp said, getting to his feet. "I'll send an officer in. If you don't mind me saying, you look tired. Wrung out. I'd recommend you go home straight after this and get some rest."

"Thank you, officer. Maybe I will." She gave him a mournful smile.

A little while later, a female officer came in to take her statement. Her manner was hurried and less than enthusiastic. Alice found that her own belief and conviction had been punctured too. Her own words sounded stretched and incredible to her ears. She left out the hostage element entirely, stuck to her suspicions about Mng and Martin Silverwood's KittyWake postings, his inspection at SmartLab. She mentioned Primegate too.

"That's all?" the policewoman said. It was unclear whether she meant that factually or as a matter of judgement.

"Yes, that's all," Alice said.

The policewoman told Alice that they would follow up fully and appropriately and would keep her informed if anything significant transpired. Moderately reassured,

Alice gathered up her things and tramped out. Well, it was essentially all in the hands of the authorities now...

There was one more thing to do before she could go home and sleep. She flagged down a taxi in the rain. "Clear Minds clinic, please."

When they reached the clinic, Alice jumped out and marched straight in. Sam the receptionist looked at up her in surprise. "Alice! I thought you were unwell."

"I probably am," she said. "Don't worry Sam, it's nothing catching. Look, is Eric in?"

"Yes, he's upstairs. In a meeting I think, but – "

Alice didn't wait. She squelched off and began racing up the stairs. She knew she looked wild and extraordinary, but there was nothing she could do about that.

Yes, there he was, in the meeting room with two colleagues. An internal meeting. That was OK then.

She went to the glass door and loomed. Eric saw her and his face instantly changed. She could see him wrapping the meeting up; the two consultants in there came straight out, giving her surprised looks as they went. She didn't have time for explanations though – she just smiled at them and headed straight in.

"Alice! You're ill, I thought. What are you doing here? And why are you... dressed, like that?" Eric asked, getting up from his chair.

"You know where I've been, Eric. Don't play innocent with me."

"What do you mean? I thought you were at home in bed."

"Yeah, right! You know that Kevan's been holding me at his place. You know everything. You're in with him, aren't you?"

"In with him? In what way? Alice, you're not making sense," Eric said, shaking his head.

"Oh come on, Eric! Mng, illegal distribution, Martin Silverwood..."

"Martin Silverwood? Isn't that the man who was murdered recently?"

"The very same. The man that *Kevan* murdered. Or had murdered. Whichever is the case."

"Now you really are worrying me, Alice! What on earth are you *talking* about?"

"It's OK, Eric. Don't worry. I've just been to the police. Told them all about it."

"The police? What?? Jeee-sus!".

"Well, it's true isn't it? And you're in with him, Eric, I know you are. From things Kevan's said. Plain as day."

"Alice, honestly, I don't know what you're talking about... Truly!" He came closer to her as she twitched and fidgeted, a concerned look on his face. "Are you OK? You look... if you don't mind my saying, dishevelled, *bedraggled*, agitated. What on earth's been going on?"

"You *know* what's been going on, Eric. I know that. OK?"

"Look, Alice, sit down, take a breath. Maybe you need to go home, get some rest. Mind you, that's where I thought you were anyway..."

"Bullshit," Alice fired back, glaring at him. "You know that Kevan's been holding me in his house. *That's* where I've been. But I managed to get away this morning. I went straight to the police station, I laid it all out to them. Be assured of *that*."

"But this is extraordinary, Alice! Honestly. I don't know what to say! But, so,... what did the police say?"

"They said another man has just confessed! But they're gonna look into it, into Kevan, SmartLab. They've assured me."

Eric smiled, opening out his arms. "But there you are then! Someone else has confessed? So Kevan *can't* have done it, surely... Alice?"

"I don't know... But I *do* know that Kevan's been holding me these last three days. In a room, in his house, behind a locked door. Illegally. I *do* know that, Eric!"

"Can that really be true, Alice?"

"What, you think I'm making it up? For fuck's sake, Eric. I'm telling you – HE'S BEEN HOLDING ME CAPTIVE!"

"But Alice, I... What can I say to that?" Eric stammered, an imploring look on his face. "I just don't know what to *say* to an allegation like that. It's too extraordinary. I mean, *why* would Kevan do that? You'll need to explain it fully to me, properly, from the beginning…" Then he quickly added: "But unfortunately, I'm really sorry, I just don't have time right now." He glanced at his watch. "Honestly. I have a call starting in a few minutes, that I *have* to join. I'm sorry. Maybe we can speak later…?" He turned to face her and shrugged his shoulders, as though in sympathy, giving her a despairing, quizzical look. She half-expected him to pull out his empty trouser pockets next.

Alice gave out a sharp sigh. "I mean, OK Eric, fit me in when it's convenient, as your diary permits, whatever…! It's Kevan I really want to talk to anyway. Where is he today?"

"He's in London. An investor meeting."

"Will you tell him please that I *demand* my phone back, and my watch, and my car. Straightaway, as soon as possible. I would phone him myself but, well, he's got my phone, hasn't he!"

"Umm… Of course, I'll tell him, Alice. I'll tell him that."

"And in the meantime, Eric… I can't work here anymore. Everything has changed for me. I resign. With immediate effect."

"No! Really, Alice?" Eric stepped forward and put his hand to Alice's arm, peering into her eyes. "Are you sure that's what you want to do?"

"I don't want to desert my patients. I feel bad about that. But I have no choice. We can work out a handover schedule of course," Alice said determinedly, returning Eric's gaze.

Eric paused. Then he smiled. "Well, if you're sure that's what you want, Alice. If that's how you feel. It's unfortunate, but I can see that, given what you've been *saying*, you might feel that that would be for the best... Nevertheless, sleep on it at least will you... Yes?"

She knew that he wanted her gone and was only keeping up appearances. As soon as she'd said about someone else admitting to the murder, he had visibly relaxed. She could see straight through him.

"Well, I might as well go now then," she said. "I'll get out of your hair, Eric. But one last thing – tell me, do you believe in what you're doing too? Like Kevan does?"

"What, you mean in Mng? Absolutely! I know all about the development of Mng2 if that's what you mean. It's massively exciting, Alice. It's going to be transformative, revolutionary."

"And as a shareholder in SmartLab, I guess that's great news..."

"Oh, this goes far beyond money, Alice. Far beyond. It's not really about that at all. It's about the happiness and contentment of the human race!"

"No matter who gets hurt or murdered or traumatised in the process?"

There was a stiffening in his smile, before he said: "Do give some further thought to your resignation, Alice. I'll be prepared to keep you if you decide you want to stay. You're a highly talented psychologist. A valued member of the team."

"You know I won't stay, Eric. You know I can't. And I really don't know how *you* manage to live with it all either."

It was as though she hadn't just spoken. "Well, why don't you go and get cleaned up, have a shower, get some rest," he said brightly. "I'm sure you'll feel much better." He was beginning to lead her out, his hand pushing firmly at her elbow. "I'll speak to Kevan for you. And we must speak soon, for a proper chat. Why don't you speak to Sam on the way out, get a slot in my diary? I should have some time available soon… Take care of yourself, Alice. Goodbye…"

And so she went. She didn't bother about a meeting with Eric, but instead simply asked Sam to call her a cab. Then she went outside to wait, trembling, looking at the thick curtain of incessant rain…

A car approached. But didn't she recognise this vehicle? Her heart gave a massive leap. It was Lewis!

She ran out into the rain towards him. Lewis saw her and screeched to a halt, leaving the car skewed across two parking spaces. He threw the door open, clambering out.

"Alice! Here you are! Where have you been?"

"Lewis! Oh, I'm so glad to see you! Lewis – my love!"

They hugged and rocked each other to and fro as the rain came down, pelting them with a sweeping wet confetti. They kissed and cried as the relief and the joy surfaced, they held each other tight, palpitating heart to heart through their drenched, second-skin clothes. *This* is where human happiness lies, Alice thought, in this unstoppable charging of sweetness and love, right here...

They got in the car to drive to Alice's place. They had so much to talk about, so much to catch up on, to share.

19.

Normally, he'd have been swaggering around the station, chest puffed out, lapping up all the praise and applause. Then he'd have been down the pub, getting a skinful, going large. And of course, he'd have been booking himself in, rat-up-a-drainpipe style, for a visit later on to the bountiful boudoir of the goodly Mrs Bright.

But not this time. DI Sharp just didn't feel right. In fact, he felt deeply *wrong*. He wasn't himself. He didn't know who he was. And it was that bloody Mng that was to blame.

He'd run out of tablets three days ago. That little shit that he'd bought – OK, taken – the Mng from outside the pub had sold him a pup. The second blister pack in the packet had nothing inside! He'd opened each and every one of the 32 blisters and they'd all been empty. Love and air, nothing more.

He knew he'd been taking too many of them. He'd been popping them like caffeine pills. Because he loved the burst of clarity they gave him, the focus, the lift. They gave him a sharpness like his own name, helped him cut through everything, like a knife. So he'd been chucking them down, thinking he had another 32 up his sleeve, enough to last him over a week, ten days. Maybe because he'd been taking so many, the withdrawal was that much worse. He'd been caught with his pants down all right.

He went out for more, like a fucking shot. But he went round all the pubs, rattled the cages of all the little wasters and pimps and snivelshucks – and there was no

Mng to be had. It had just dried up, they said. The supply had suddenly stopped. Maybe it would come back, maybe it wouldn't. Who knew, they said. Would he like some speed instead?

It had been the same each day since. He'd been out night-times, lunchtimes, early mornings, like a desperate punter prowling the kerbs. Not a fanny on offer, old or young.

He'd kept going, like a proper professional. Despite feeling faint and shivery and sick. Weak and sweaty and shit. He'd pushed that aside, battened down to the job. He had to – the investigation was coming to a head. He had to nail Franks, get himself a mug he could say was shot.

Today the difficulty level had really stepped up. As soon as he'd opened his eyes that morning, he'd known he was in trouble. Because he just felt so dull, so grey, like he was lost on an endless flat sea... There was no substance to anything, no meaning at all. He could barely get himself out of bed. He was a two-dimensional cutout going through the motions. He was something, he was nothing – what difference did it make?

At least he'd managed to force himself on, punching out the questions, until Franks finally cracked. That had been a relief. He didn't think anyone had even noticed that he wasn't really DI Sharp anymore. Then he'd dealt with that strange woman who had come in, throwing around accusations about Kevan Monk. That had been an irony, seeing as how it was Monk's product pushing him now towards all this...

In usual circumstances, he might have taken an interest in what the woman had to say. There could have been something in it. And there was nothing he liked more than to sniff around the great and the good, see if there was a way to bring them down. If it was a question of cutting someone successful down to size, he'd be right there, at the front of the queue, brandishing his hammer and his chisel.

But today – what did he care? He couldn't bring himself to take an interest. They already had someone after all. Did it matter if it was this person or that person? As long as there *was* a person, that was enough. Justice was served, even if the plates had got mixed up...

So there we were. DI Sharp had his man, he'd bullied a confession. But it felt like it was *him* that had been sentenced.

The superintendent had called him in to give her congratulations. "Well done, Detective Inspector, well done!" she boomed, smiling broadly. "I always had faith that my star man would come through. Congratulations, sir. Now let's just make sure we get an appropriate conviction."

She shook his hand and then pulled him to her in a quick, back-patting hug. But instead of ensuring he leaned forward and got maximum contact with her woman-mountains – a good sensation to store up for later – he found himself standing limp and listless inside her arms, then falling back, mumbling his pathetic thanks.

What was wrong with him? This wasn't him... It was the Mng of course. If he could get another fix, he'd be fine. But he couldn't get one. He could try his GP of course, come up with some story about why he needed a prescription – but it took weeks these days to get an appointment. It would be so far off as to be pointless. And so, he was caught in this whirl of blank, hopeless misery and didn't have the strength to get himself out.

It was as though something had taken control of him, moving him along, steering him relentlessly in one direction. He could see the end it was taking him towards. He had no will to do anything about it.

He hung around in the station, staring at his screen as if he was doing something productive. Then Mandy Franks called him. He'd ignored a couple of her calls already but felt he had to answer this one. She wailed and whined down the phone – he'd used her, he'd abused her, she'd make damn sure it all came out. She'd go to the press, she'd go on social media, she'd let the whole world know what a corrupt and dirty old man he was. He told her that, genuinely, he was sorry – he'd done what he could, he'd tried his best for her. But her husband had confessed, of his own free will. What could he have done? There was nothing he could do. He'd see to it that she got all the support, all the assistance, the force could muster. He gave her his word on that. He almost blubbed, himself, down the phone (having taken himself swiftly to a quiet spot at the end of an empty corridor when her call came in). And he almost in fact *believed* his own tears. She seemed pacified, began to snivel more tenderly, a breathy huskiness entering her tones. He said he'd be in touch soonest, he really wished her all the best at this most difficult and traumatic of times…

It was a good job he had such a good team around him. PC Kaur had everything in hand. That woman would go far. She deserved to. And he wasn't only thinking about her legs.

He did indeed go to the pub after work, at the insistence of PC Kaur and some of the rest of the team. He sipped at a beer and tried to force a smile. PC Kaur asked him if he was OK. "You don't seem quite yourself, sir. I expected you to be full of celebration. Are you tired, maybe?"

He agreed that he was, and then tried to move the conversation away from the personal as quickly as he could.

"Now then, Ayesha, about the lady who came in this morning. Those allegations about Kevan Monk… I want you to get in touch with Monk tomorrow. Arrange a time to talk. There's nothing in it, I'm sure of that. Just run through a few questions, get some answers and then that's box ticked, matter closed. OK?"

He didn't stay very long: he had to get home before Mary went to bed. He settled the tab for everyone at the bar, asking them to add another £50 for further drinks – and then even paid with his own personal bank card! Something was clearly very wrong. Everyone was shocked when he left so early. But he turned away from them all, eyes down, making his excuses, and drifted out into the rain.

This rain... There would be flooding, around and about, in Somerset and beyond. All day it had come down. It seemed appropriate. He'd driven home, staring dully through the windscreen as the wipers wiped, through these streets where he'd lived and worked for so long. So long, everything seemed to say...

He'd got back just in time. Mary was on her way up. He kissed her, gave her hand a squeeze. "Goodnight, sleep well love. Goodbye..." His voice had almost caught in his throat.

And so now, here he was. Sitting in the kitchen, having a last couple of drams. He swilled the whisky in his glass, watching it pointlessly go round.

He got up and went out into the back garden. A last cigarette. He lit his fag and pulled the smoke in, deep into his lungs. And then out. And then in. And then out. How many times had he done this in his life? Eventually, it was over. He stubbed the butt out, looked at the last of the smoke as it diffused itself into the wet night air. Somewhere in the darkness, a bird was singing. Why, sometimes, do birds sing at night? Are they lost? Disorientated? Confused? It was a small question...

Then in, to the kitchen again. One more thing to do. He went to the living room and found a pen and piece of paper in the bureau there. Then he went back to the kitchen and sat himself stiffly down. He wrote:

"My dearest Mary,

I'm so sorry. I hope you can forgive me. I have suddenly found that I can't go on. I don't know why – it just seems that there is no meaning left. It has taken me by surprise, but I don't feel there is anything I can do. It's too strong for me, Mary. That is all.

All the insurance and pension information is in the top drawer of the desk in the living room. I know you'll be OK. You have lots of friends and people who care for you, after all.

You have been the best thing in my life, Mary. The only thing that really matters. But now it's time to say goodbye.

If there is such a place, I will certainly see you on the other side.

Your loving husband,

Jim."

He hesitated as he re-read the note, was on the verge of scrunching it up and throwing it away. What a load of snivelling bullshit. But as a matter of fact, it was true. She had been the best thing. She was too good for him, he knew it. Faithful and kind. She had tolerated all his excesses, forgiven him his sins, turned a blind eye. Even though, if he was honest, she had stopped loving him years ago. He couldn't blame her for that. What was there to love? It had become a matter of companionship, an arrangement they shared, in separate rooms. Since her illness, she'd moved beyond physical relations in any case. She became free of all that. Whereas he… he'd well and truly fallen into that pit. No, he had never really deserved her. He was pleased that she'd be well provided for by his pension and the life insurance (he'd double-checked the terms). She had a good support network in Knott. She really hardly needed him, if truth be told.

His hand was shaking as he poured himself one final shot. He gulped it down, feeling its parting smack. He became aware of tears on his face. That was a turn-up for the books. When was the last time he'd cried? It must have been nearly forty-five years ago, when his mother had passed. He'd been thirteen. Left with just his father, his angry moods, the bruising edge of his hand. His mean-spirited older brother, too.

Well, he thought, forget what did. Where had that phrase come from? He didn't know.

Shakily, DI Sharp turned his phone off. Then he pulled himself up from the table and turned off the light. He stepped through the side door at the end of the kitchen into the garage. He never had fixed that hinge, he thought. Never mind.

He pulled the light cord and then found the hose that he'd bought years ago and carefully stored. Oh yes, he'd had something like this in the back of his mind, as a contingency, for a long time. With the kind of life he led, you needed an emergency exit in case it all came crashing down – a sudden exposure, a scandal, a disgrace. Well, he'd managed to avoid that all these years. But now, things had got him in a different way, a way that he'd never foreseen. Events had caught him out eventually, outmanoeuvred him, ambushed him from behind. Things were just carrying him along, towards that fall, and there was nothing he could do about it. Never mind.

He attached the hose to the trusty old Ford Mondeo that he'd been the owner of for twenty-five years. He'd never liked those damned electric vehicles, had held on proudly to his traditional petrol car. It was still in good condition, even if it had developed quite a smoky exhaust in recent times. Well, that was no bad thing right now. He almost smiled as he wiped at his eyes and fed the hose through the window. He dropped himself like a stone into the driver's seat and turned the engine on.

It wouldn't be long before he was out of it, at peace, miles and miles away, or just nowhere at all.

20.

"I've got it, I've got it! How about we take out a loan and buy an ice cream van!" said Lewis, eyeing the rackety tootling old van a hundred yards further down the seafront. "They're a bit of a relic but we'd make a fortune, I betcha!"

"Hmmm, yeah, that's quite a cute idea Lou," replied Alice with a smile.

They were sitting on a bench in Weymouth overlooking the beach. Ten days had passed since Alice's escape (Lewis' would-be rescue). It was a hot and sunny Friday. It had become a running joke as to what they could do in the future, seeing as both of them were now unemployed…

Alice had not gone back to Clear Minds. Her 'proper chat' with Eric had not transpired, although admittedly she had not pushed very hard to arrange it. Eric had seemed determined to avoid her, and in fact to keep her away from the clinic. She wanted to do proper handovers of her patients – she felt terrible about leaving them all so suddenly – but he insisted that all was well and that they were all transitioning successfully to new therapists. She hadn't asked him, yet, about the subject of a reference.

Lewis meanwhile had resigned from SmartLab the next day. It had come as a big surprise to everyone there although not, perhaps, Kevan Monk. His boss had consulted with Kevan and informed him that in fact he could leave at the end of that week. They'd pay him a full month's notice. He had some holiday owing in any case. It was a hurried affair and Lewis didn't get to say proper goodbyes to a lot of his colleagues.

"It feels really bad, but it's the way it is," he said to Alice. "I just can't stay there at a company run by him. He's completely blanked me this week. And I can't get him on his own because there's always his PA there or another director or someone else…"

Another reason for leaving so quickly was that he couldn't do much work anyway – he had gone to A&E the next day because his hand was so swollen and sore. It turned out that he had a broken finger, a sprained wrist and severe bruising to several knuckles. They put a cast on his hand.

"My hero, breaking a bone for me!" Alice joked with a wry smile.

"Well, someone had to come and rescue you," Lewis replied.

"Except I'm a modern woman who can look after herself and was already gone," she said.

Behind the jokiness there was however a shadow. "Did you sleep with Monk then, that night?" Lewis asked. "I had to," Alice replied. "I didn't want to, though! I want nothing to do with him ever again." Lewis, though smarting, was prepared to leave it at that…

Also the next day, there had been a long insistent ringing on Alice's bell early in the morning. There was no one on the end of the intercom so she went down. She saw an envelope posted through the door – inside were her phone, her watch and her car keys. She looked outside – her car sat there, neatly parked. That was the only 'communication' she had had with Kevan Monk since her incarceration at Reacher's Point.

She was relieved to get her car back quickly, because she had an overpowering urge to get down to Weymouth to see her mother. She wasn't worried that Monk would actually do anything to her but after the things she'd been through, she felt a need to be close to her for a while. The revelation about her lost sibling had also, to her surprise, made her want to get closer to her mother, rather than stay further apart. So she phoned Valerie, who said she'd be delighted to have her. She could stay in her flat no problem – because in fact she'd been spending increasing amounts of time at Bill's. "We're peas in a pod really, my dear. Corks from the same bottle. Who knows, maybe I'll surprise you one day and become a newlywed pensioner! What do you reckon?"

It certainly seemed to be coming... And why not, Alice thought. Bill was a nice old guy and they fitted well together. They cared for each other. They tried to keep each other on the right side of pissed. Let them sozzle and cuddle and keep each other company in their advanced years!

Alice saw the news about DI Sharp when it was reported in the local press. There was a line from the police saying how shocked and saddened everyone at the force was, but that they weren't looking for anyone else in connection with the death. A couple of days later, there was another report in which a police spokesperson was quoted saying there were "no suspicious circumstances" and DI Sharp's death was being treated as a "private matter".

It was all highly strange – but, as Alice saw, ranks were clearly being closed. Why would DI Sharp commit suicide so suddenly out of the blue? There was something weird behind this, something that didn't add up. There needed to be a proper investigation. But it appeared that nothing public would ever transpire.

Meanwhile, Alice and Lewis considered their futures... Lewis had come down to spend a bit of time with her in Weymouth this week. They had so much to think about. A friend of Lewis' in London had an empty double room in the house he lived in and there was an offer there at quite a low rent. Should they go? What would they do? They both had notice periods to run down on their present accommodation in Knott. And they had to be careful about money. Alice had a modest sum put by in savings that would see her through several months; Lewis had little more than he needed to get through to the next pay cheque.

"Hell, we're young, Al – well, I am! – we can find something, we can get by," Lewis said cheerily. "Bar work, delivery work, office temping – we can make ends meet while we get our shit together. I'm sure you could find something in the counselling and therapy line. They have to give you a fair reference, don't they? And there are other people you can get references from too."

"Yeah, true... So, are we gonna do it? Leave Knott, make the leap?"

"Slip Knott, you mean, ha ha? I'm up for it, Alice. I've been clinging to safety for too long. It's now or never is how it feels."

"Right..."

"I mean, like, you know when you found out about your lost brother or sister?" Lewis said, gently, musingly, eyes on the sea. "And I spent all those years wrestling with myself over Dan? I don't know... I know they're very different, but even so, it feels like they tell us something. There's no room for holding yourself back, brooding on the past, what might have been. We've got to keep on going, moving forwards, into the future... you know?"

"I know," Alice said, squeezing his hand, dropping her head, briefly, onto her boyfriend's shoulder.

So, it seemed that the dice was cast. They both wanted to move on, and they both wanted to do so *together* – even though it would be a shame to leave Jane Silverwood, amongst other people. She and Lewis had met up; Alice had chatted to her on a video call. They were set to be good friends. Jane was doing well, too. She had got through Martin's funeral in one piece. He had been respectfully and peacefully laid to rest. Now, she was intent on moving forward. She was even considering buying some furniture for the house.

Alice and Lewis sat on their bench and surveyed the passers-by, the kids, the families, the tourists, the seagulls. It was therapeutic to have some time on their hands and no rush to do anything with it. Alice breathed in the clean sea air – she was enjoying being Mng-free, and felt an uplift in her health and wellbeing overall. She hadn't even realised what a shadow it had cast. Now, she felt up for the future, whatever that might bring. She also knew that Lewis was the person she wanted at her side to face it with. She could almost say – could she? – that she loved him. The admission was a novelty for her, through all the relationships she'd had. And it felt good. The glow it gave was *way* better than anything you could get from Mng!

They sat side by side, they browsed their phones. Then Lewis, notwithstanding his struggles to browse left-handed, let out an exclamation. "You've gotta have a read of this!" he said.

Alice took his phone – a story on a national newspaper website:

Donald & Donald throws its weight behind Mng

By Steve Strange

Multi-national pharmaceutical giant, Donald & Donald, is set to take a major stake in the development of anti-addiction wonder drug Mng, manufactured by Somerset-based SmartLab Pharmaceuticals, the chief executives of the businesses have jointly announced.

Donald & Donald is ready to invest up to £500m to support the development of a sequel drug to Mng which according to John Starkly, CEO, could have "game-changing properties."

"We have seen the potential for Mng2 which SmartLab are already a significant way down the track in

developing. I don't think I have ever been so excited by a new product. We believe everyone will want some Mng2 in their lives. It will be a revolution."

The executives said that Mng2 would induce a powerful sense of wellbeing without any trace of intoxication or addiction.

"It will be like taking paracetamol," Kevan Monk, CEO of SmartLab said. "Except that it will make you feel whole dimensions better than that. Mng2 will be simply transformative."

Mng has been a notable success in helping those addicted to other substances to reduce their dependency. However, there have been reports of some cases of addiction to Mng itself, leading the UK medicines regulator to recently open a review. Both CEOs were bullish about this.

"We're not worried. If we were, we wouldn't be investing," Mr Starkly said. "We have absolute confidence the review will conclude with no adverse findings. In any case, Mng2 will completely move the game on. They're two different products."

At the end of the press conference, Mr Monk of SmartLab was asked about a local press report claiming that he'd been interviewed by police in connection with a local murder.

He confirmed that was the case, adding: "I have nothing whatsoever to do with this. It's been a simple misunderstanding. I was pleased to help the police clear the issue up. They have assured me that the matter is *closed. As you probably know, another man has confessed to the crime. I believe his sentencing is imminent."*

Investors responded positively to news of the tie-up, with Donald & Donald shares rising by 15% in a matter of hours.

Specific details of the terms of Donald & Donald's investment are due to be published in the coming days. It is understood that Mr Monk will continue as CEO of SmartLab, which will remain an independent business "affiliated" with the Donald & Donald empire.

"Woah," Alice said, scrolling through the article, re-reading it, digesting. "So Monk's got an open road... Mng is going to take over the world... What a shitshow."

"Good news for you though," Lewis remarked. "Doesn't look like that review is going to go anywhere?"

"No, too many vested interests, my dear. Politicians, policy makers, corporations, investors – everyone is just determined Mng should be a good thing. Determined not to see any problems that could get in the way."

"Perhaps it *will* be a good thing, in the end?"

"Yeah right, when we're all automatons popping our happy pills... Give me a break, Lou, you great sap!" Alice stood up, slipped on her shades. "Come on! Let's get an ice cream and then have a stroll on the beach."

Hand in hand they walked back, along the seafront, towards the glimmering ice cream van, bathed in the light of the booming midday sun.

Printed in Dunstable, United Kingdom

COUNTRY COTTAGES

MANCHESTER
UNIVERSITY PRESS

Country cottages

A CULTURAL HISTORY

Karen Sayer

Manchester University Press
MANCHESTER AND NEW YORK

distributed exclusively in the USA by St. Martin's Press

Copyright © Karen Sayer 2000

The right of Karen Sayer to be identified as the author of this work has been asserted by her in accordance with the Copyright, Designs and Patents Act 1988.

Published by Manchester University Press
Oxford Road, Manchester M13 9NR, UK
and Room 400, 175 Fifth Avenue, New York, NY 10010, USA
http://www.manchesteruniversitypress.co.uk

Distributed exclusively in the USA by
St. Martin's Press, Inc., 175 Fifth Avenue, New York,
NY 10010, USA

Distributed exclusively in Canada by
UBC Press, University of British Columbia, 2029 West Mall,
Vancouver, BC, Canada V6T 1Z2

British Library Cataloguing-in-Publication Data
A catalogue record for this book is available from the British Library

Library of Congress Cataloging-in-Publication Data applied for

ISBN 0 7190 4752 8 hardback

First published 2000
07 06 05 04 03 02 01 00   10 9 8 7 6 5 4 3 2 1

Typeset in Goudy
by Graphicraft Limited, Hong Kong
Printed in Great Britain
by Bookcraft (Bath) Ltd, Midsomer Norton

CONTENTS

	Acknowledgements	*page* vii
	Introduction	1
1	The ideal home	19
2	The imperfect home	49
3	The English cottage garden	79
4	The cottage and national identity	113
5	Middle-class luxury, working-class necessity	142
6	The country and the city	172
	Concluding remarks	201
	Select bibliography	211
	Index	221

To Matthew

ACKNOWLEDGEMENTS

I would like to thank the staffs of the following libraries and archives: the British Library, at Great Russell St., Kings Cross, and Colindale; the Fawcett Library; University of Bristol Library; University of Sussex Library; University of Luton Library; Trinity College Library; and the Norfolk and Norwich Records Office.

Karen Sayer
University of Luton

INTRODUCTION

1. A dwelling-house of small size and humble character, such as is occupied by farm labourers, villagers, miners etc.
2. A small temporary erection used for shelter; a cot, hut, shed, etc. *Obs.*; late C18th
3. a. A small or humble dwelling-place; the cell of a bee etc. *clay* or *earthen cottage*: the 'earthly tabernacle' of the body. *Obs.* late C17th; b. A public lavatory or urinal, *slang*, homosexual, first use 1909.[1]
4. a. 'The term cottage has for some time past been in vogue as a particular designation for small country residences and detached suburban houses, adapted to a moderate scale of living, yet with all due attention to comfort and refinement. While, in this sense of it, the name is divested of all associations with poverty, it is convenient, inasmuch as it frees from all pretension and parade and restraint' (*Penny Cyclopaedia*, supp. 1845). In this sense, the appellation *cottage orné* (*ornée*) was in vogue, when picturesqueness was aimed at . . . b. In US, a summer residence (often on a large and sumptuous scale) at a watering place or a health or pleasure resort. c. A house which has only one storey. *Austral.*[2]

HOBBIT HOLES

The cottage is 'familiar', a 'familiar' sight – a family site[3] – to us, both ontologically and etymologically. It (em)bodies (frames, binds, fetters, confines the soul of) English national identity and ideal domesticity, representing 'true' femininity as 'natural', domestic (in terms of both domesticity and nationality), white, wise, and thoroughly desirable/pleasurable, through a constant reassertion of values which are seen to be at once unchanging/stable but also lost/in need of rescue.[4]

The cottage comes back to haunt us in this way through (hi)stories/narratives about children who eat gingerbread houses, adverts which try to whisk us away on country holidays, or which want us to buy a secluded, idyllic retreat (after we have already/simultaneously bought into the structures, dreams, ideas associated with it) and glimpses of little thatched roofs round village greens on our summer tours. Here, I am on my way to arguing that the cottage becomes, not just a microcosm of society/social mode (as it was proclaimed in the nineteenth century, through representations of family life), but also a reproduction/ copy/repetition of the way the English have used/still use their past to sell themselves – with little distinction between memory, nostalgia (derived from 'homecoming') and history – within the construction of their national identity.

What is the country cottage? As can be gathered from the epigraph, this is surprisingly hard to pin down. Even architecturally, 'cottage' can include anything from a one-storey 'hovel' to a small country house, while even the division between country and city is ill-defined, given that 'cottage' can be used to refer to a millworker's or miner's terrace. But, what seems to be key to the fantasy is that the 'country cottage' in particular be 'homely', as characterised by its small size, its almost organic unevenness shaped by time and weather, its cheery aspect within a rural community and its unpretentious interior. In this respect, its location and the influence of the picturesque and Victorian sentiment are central to the myth.[5]

The opposition between the country and the city is long-standing and today usually revolves around competing definitions of the country as site of health and well-being, the city as site of culture and sophistication, or diseased city vs. country tedium and idiocy.[6] Within this series of oppositions, the countryside always remains Other. If we look at the rural working class, for instance, it has been steadily politically and culturally marginalised since the nineteenth century. This is both because the city, against which the rural is tested, is the centre of power,[7] and because those who should be the labourers' political allies saw, and still largely see, them as the willing subjects of semi-feudal relations; Hodge has not yet been boiled in the factory pot.[8] In the nineteenth century, the city/metropolis mapped out and tamed its domestic territory as carefully as it mapped out and tamed its empire. The countryside was assumed to be subordinate to the needs of the city, empire and industry. At the same time, the rural working-class home was colonised by the (urban) bourgeoisie who, creating new cottages *ornée*, came to make them their own, ideal homes.

The cottage became a utopian space, a Beau Ideal,[9] for the middle class in the nineteenth century, formed through a peculiarly powerful mix of the discourses of Englishness and domesticity. There was and still is a desire for a lost territory here, an idealisation of the family relationship that binds us to the home and of the home itself as 'Woman/ Mother/Lover'.[10] The hunt for the organic community, then, took the English to the village, where they hoped to find their lost inner child, Hodge, who still lived in a close relationship to (mother) Nature.[11] The

English still seem to idealise a life that Tolkien's Hobbits would find comfort in; a pre-industrial and 'very ancient' people, the Hobbits 'love peace and quiet and good-tilled earth . . . a well-ordered and well-farmed countryside was their favourite haunt'. Like the English yeomen, they look: 'good natured rather than beautiful, broad, bright-eyed, red-cheeked, with mouths apt to laughter, and to eating and drinking . . . fond of simple jests . . . of six meals a day . . . hospitable and delighted in parties and in presents'.[12] 'Growing food and eating it occupied most of their time',[13] but, like Hodge (in Tolkien's world all the Hobbit actors are male) they are marginal, shy and increasingly 'hard to find'.[14] As capitalism replaces feudalism, so the Hobbits are reduced. Hobbits become both 'unobtrusive' and mysterious as the 'big folk' propel their machines into the countryside. At the same time, the Hobbits are reduced in size: 'They seldom now reach three feet', we are told, 'but they have dwindled, they say, and in ancient days they were taller.'[15] So reduced, the Hobbits become hidden and begin to haunt the landscape of the big folk. Where the Hobbits may be read as English peasants, so the big folk are representative of invasive, inimical capital.[16]

What Said says of the Orient, that it is 'a form of surrogate and even underground self'[17] is equally true of the British countryside. As the West 'gained in strength and identity by setting itself against the Orient',[18] so the metropolitan set itself against the rural. In both cases, however, the Other became mysterious and enchanting. As we see of Hobbits:

> They possessed from the first the art of disappearing swiftly and silently, when large folk whom they do not wish to meet come blundering by; and this art they have developed until to Men it may seem magical. But . . . their elusiveness is due solely to a professional skill that heredity and practice, and a close relationship with the earth, have rendered inimitable by bigger and clumsier races.[19]

The earth is the Hobbit's natural environment:

> All Hobbits had originally lived in holes in the ground, or so they believed, and in such dwellings they still felt most at home; but in the course of time they had been forced to adopt other forms of abode. Actually in the Shire in Bilbo's days it was, as a rule, only the richest and the poorest Hobbits that maintained the old custom. The poorest went on living in burrows of the most primitive kind, mere holes indeed, with only one window or none; while the well-to-do still constructed more luxurious versions of the simple diggings of old. But suitable sites for these large and ramifying tunnels (or *smials* as they

called them) were not everywhere to be found; and in the flats and the low-lying districts the Hobbits, as they multiplied, began to build above ground . . .

The craft of building may have come from Elves or Men, but the Hobbits used it in their own fashion. They did not go in for towers. Their houses were usually long, low, and comfortable. The oldest kind were, indeed, no more than built imitations of *smials*, thatched with dry grass or straw, or roofed with turves, and having walls somewhat bulged. That stage, however, belonged to the early days of the Shire, and hobbit-building had long since been altered, improved by devices, learned from Dwarves, or discovered by themselves. A preference for round windows, and even round doors, was the chief remaining peculiarity of hobbit-architecture.[20]

The *smial*, then, is a home that is comfortable, thatched, and was built in a golden age of prosperity. Inhabited only by the richest or the poorest of the community, *smials* provide a womb-like retreat from the invasions of the big folk that even in their modern form recycle ancient architectural details. The cottage is a *smial*, or, rather, the *smial*, especially of the older kind, is the most ideal of ideal country cottages. These homes embody the 'oldie worldie' values of community that the modern 'Englishman', just like Wemmick,[21] seems to want to find in 'his' castle. Inhabited by large families, *smials* are cluttered, full of 'mathoms' (gifts and artefacts that can never be thrown out, for sentimental, practical or thrifty reasons), throw-backs to the ancient English hall-house, built of sticks rather than bricks. As Tony Rivers argues, the English

> have seldom risen far above the earth. It has been observed that they have wallpaper like tapestries and carpet patterns whose earthy splodges bear no resemblance to any geometric culture of pattern-making. They like to get back down home, go to earth where it is cosy, as in burrows, dens, safe havens. If this impulse is not folk memory it is certainly rooted deep in English culture.[22]

Quoting *The Wind in the Willows*, he goes on:

> Mole tells Badger about what constitutes 'home': 'Once well underground' he said 'you know exactly where you are. Nothing can happen to you, and nothing can get to you. You're entirely your own master, and you don't have to consult anybody or mind what they say. Things go on all the same overhead, and you let 'em, and don't bother about 'em.'[23]

'Home' for the English is about embeddedness, the vernacular, folkways, heritage, tradition and the native. As we will see, these are loaded concepts, but suffice to say at the moment that it is difficult to separate the organic community of family and village from the 'imagined community' of England.[24]

CONDITIONS IN THE COUNTRYSIDE

'Real' cottages were, of course, known to be less desirable than the 'Ideal'. Though circumstances varied widely from region to region, there was nonetheless a widespread housing shortage during the nineteenth century and those cottages that were available were often dilapidated or poorly constructed. Many of the poor lived in adapted farm buildings and houses, split up into tenements by thin walls, while others lived in properties thrown up by speculative builders. Usually overcrowded and consisting of two rooms, most labourers' cottages were damp, cold, draughty, dark and unsanitary. Their water was often polluted by middens, if it came from a well, or by general waste, if came from a pond. Fuel was generally in short supply, due to the loss of common rights and the high cost of coal. Most strikingly of all perhaps, most fresh food went to the towns and actually had to be bought back by those who lived in the country, unless they had access to a garden or allotment. The provision of an allotment or garden itself varied from region to region. In Northumberland, farmers tended to provide cottages on their farms for their labourers, with payment in kind, permission to keep a pig, a garden for growing potatoes and some land on which to keep a cow, as part of the hiring agreement. This guaranteed the farmers labour for the year in a sparsely populated county. The cottages in the north tended to be well built, of stone, with pigsties. In the south and east of England, however, where the standard of building was much lower, labourers were paid in cash, were often not allowed to keep a pig or to garden on an allotment and had to find the money to rent their own cottages.[25]

These conditions persisted in part because improvement initially took place in the rapidly expanding and increasingly overcrowded towns and cities, where the need for sanitary and housing reform was simply more obvious. The fiction and art that attempted to promote reform always tended to understate the social ills and difficulties experienced by those who lived in the country, which, as Tristram argues, certainly demonstrates the inadequacies of the social theories of the period,[26] but is more broadly indicative of the representation of the countryside at that time. It was not that social observers were entirely oblivious to the experiences of the rural poor. It was just that industrialisation and urbanisation in and of themselves gradually came to be seen as the problem, while the rural, its villages and way of life came to be held up variously as a radical solution to that problem,[27] or as an escape from it. As the middle class became sensitive to the widening gap between rich and poor, as the condition of England debate gained currency, and as the middle class began to celebrate domesticity and the home as the sacred centre of society and social stability, so the cottage became the focus of artistic and literary attention.[28] But, the idealisation of the country militated against it and its people being seen as subject to the same problems as the urban environment. This continued into the twentieth century. As the labouring population declined, thanks to the dual impact of agricultural depression and increasing mechanisation, so the population of commuters, owners of second homes, George Bourne's 'Resident Trippers', and other 'incomers'[29] seeking the ideal rose. 'Ironically, as "agriculture" declined as a part of the national economy so a mythologized version of its remnants became desirable to the urban elite.'[30]

BACK TO THE LAND

Ethnographers, sociologists and social geographers have recently begun to look at why people move to the country, what they seek in such a move and what they find when they arrive. One thing that is certainly clear from such studies is that the number of people moving to rural areas is still rising, and that, given shifts in government policy and constraints imposed by banks and building societies in the 1980s, the vast majority of these 'incomers' are salaried. Nonetheless, as David Phillips and Allan Williams suggest, though the search for housing is often characterised as an unequal battle between certain groups and individuals, where those who are 'stronger' will win out, not all those competing in the market are after the same homes for the same reasons.[31] James Garo Derounian, for instance, highlights the important aspirational aspect of owning a house in the country as a high status acquisition.[32] Nonetheless, many people who move to the country are retired and have different needs and expectations of country life to those who commute, while the retired themselves are heterogeneous and can vary considerably in terms of housing needs and available resources. Though those who rent and those who seek to buy are competing in different markets, with rising prices, incomers invariably outbid locals in the housing stakes.[33]

When Michael Mayerfield Bell visited Childerley, a Hampshire village which had 475 inhabitants in 1994, just over half of the population owned their own home, and a third of the residents commuted, though many still worked in agriculture and there were a number of retired people. There were 'more than a dozen cottages and farmhouses from before the 1800s (including some from before 1700)'. There were also smatterings of nineteenth-century and more recently built cottages, most of which were once or still were tied.[34] As the old tied cottages went on the market in the 1980s, and two or more cottages became knocked through to make one – a result of a decline in local employment – so working-class villagers either left the country or moved into council housing. At the time of writing, typically a fifth of the rural housing stock was publicly owned. At the height of the property boom, many quite ordinary houses in Childerley sold for over £200,000 and none went for under £125,000. In 1988, before the housing crash, a three-bedroom Victorian cottage would have cost around £250,000. As a result, though house prices had fallen by the time he carried out his study, most home-owners in the village were still wealthy 'incomers' which generated a clear class divide between these 'moneyed' newcomers and the 'ordinary' villagers.[35]

The following is the classic statement on the different housing classes: 1) 'the outright owners of large houses in desirable areas', 2) 'mortgage payers who "own" their houses but on a mortgage', 3) 'council tenants in purpose-built council flats and houses', 4) 'council tenants in slums awaiting demolition', 5) 'tenants of private landlords', 6) 'resident landlords who take in lodgers to meet repayments', 7) 'lodgers in rooms'. However, this is based on a survey of Birmingham in the 1960s, so some modifications – the addition of large landowners, 'salaried immigrants', 'reluctant commuters', local traders and small business proprietors, tied-cottagers – might be expected in rural areas.[36] What it is particularly important to bear in mind here is that the availability of local authority housing in rural areas has always been lower than that in urban districts. Between 1968 and 1973, in England and Wales, there was double the number of council houses being built per 1,000 population in urban than rural areas. In 1984, they comprised on average 21 per cent of the rural housing stock; however, since the 1980s, this has fallen with the sale of council houses.[37]

The expectation of policy makers has often been that rural employers will supply their workers with housing, yet, by the mid-1970s, Ruth Gasson has shown, there were on average only 40 to 50 tied cottages per 100 members of the regular agricultural workforce. These were mostly let to full-time employees engaged in skilled work, cowmen, foremen and bailiffs, stockmen, and tractor drivers; 50 per cent of general farm labourers got a tied cottage as compared to 91 per cent of farm managers. At the time she was writing, there were probably only about 120,000 tied cottages in England and Wales. This included old cottages, purpose-built cottages and old farm buildings converted into labourers' dwellings. About two-thirds of these were over 100 years old, a quarter over 200 years, i.e. on average older than the rest of the housing stock. However, these cottages did tend to be better than average in the provision of basic amenities: 98 per cent had a bath, 97 per cent had hot water, 97 per cent had indoor toilets. Most had electricity, 80 per cent had three or more bedrooms, over 50 per cent had garages, one in seven had central heating.[38] Where the rural population has risen since the 1970s, therefore, this has been in parallel to the rate of home ownership and the ownership of second homes. In fact, the number of second homes rose from 101,100 in 1968 to 154,700 in 1979, which comprised on average one per cent of the British housing stock. As a result, over a half of rural homes were owner-occupied by 1984, a figure that was slightly higher than the national average. Within the Lake District, 52 per cent of houses were bought as holiday homes, second homes or retirement homes in 1981; in the south-west of England, on average 1–5 per cent of the housing stock consisted of second homes, rising to 10 per cent in north Cornwall.[39]

Meanwhile some areas have developed much higher landscape value than others – it is in these regions that leisure often becomes as economically important as agriculture. In the 1970s–80s, Dunn, Rawson and Rogers discovered most of the high status housing was to be found in the Home Counties, through the Midlands and on into the areas in and around the National Parks. Retired owner-occupation, on the other hand, was dominant around the east coast, along the south coast and on into the south-west. Farmers and farm-workers remained predominant in the north and north-east of England, and in the inland areas of Cornwall, Devon and most of East Anglia.[40] In the south of England you will therefore tend to find 'established' – sometimes referred to as 'traditional', 'occupational', 'working class' or 'estate' – villages with small populations of about 350 people, a quarter of whom commute while the rest work in agriculture or service. There are also 'metropolitan' villages of 3–4,000 residents, 46–70 per cent of whom commute. Unlike the 'established' villages, these usually have local services, a school, rail links and are often close to a neighbouring city or town, which they resemble. Between these lie 'encapsulated' – otherwise known as 'uniform' or 'two-class' – villages. Normally about $1\frac{1}{2}$ to $2\frac{1}{2}$ hours away from a major metropolitan centre, though closer to a smaller city, they have the highest retired population, which at 15 per cent is in line with the national average.[41]

These patterns may shift; however, one constant remains: the search for a 'real' cottage home. Despite rumours of its demise, vernacular architecture does survive, but (as discussed in Chapter 5) it is 'interpreted' and 'reinterpreted' by each new generation. In the twentieth century, historic preservation societies have occasionally tried to put this process into reverse, while the moneyed, seeking to buy into the rural idyll, remodel their cottages in such a way as to make them more 'authentic'. On one level, this means that there is very little material culture left to read; little material evidence of the life of the rural poor remains untouched. But all buildings change/learn, with or without architects,[42] and this process in itself alongside the contemporary use of buildings, can be read in terms of the new social and gendered meanings given domestic space.

APPROACH

In his case study of Swiss tenement buildings from 1860 to 1960, R. J. Lawrence discovered that physical barriers were realigned to separate public, collective and private space. Symbolic markers were redefined, suppressing those that the residents themselves used. Judicial borders were established through tenancy agreements and, finally, administrative limits were maintained to regulate the space. As a result, what was once a collective interior space – the transitional space in and around the tenement flats, used much as the working class used the thresholds and areas outside their cottages – was redefined into an empty, repressive passage used only for circulation. At the same time, the public space outside, designed as a garden, no longer acted as a barrier between the flats and the street, but became eventually an alienating 'no man's land'. The landlords intended to provide low-cost, low-maintenance, clean housing for multiple families in autonomous flats, but the use and redefinition of boundaries, coupled with spatial regulation, and the prescription of activities and surveillance transformed this kind of popular housing into a coercive environment. As he notes, 'the meaning and use of space cannot be prescribed by deterministic associations between behaviour and built form. Yet this is what was intended by the introduction of tenancy agreements and the redefinition of the architecture of the interior collective spaces.'[43]

This exemplifies the kind of complex architectural, economic and socio-political factors that need to be taken into account when considering the production and re-production of buildings. It is also an example of how, since the mid-nineteenth century, the built environment has become explicitly regulated and specialised. Given that most clients are now collective bodies, such as the state, it also points toward the role that architects have played in the production of a model metropolitan environment that has erased older (sometimes rural) social relations and meanings established by shared history and usage. What is therefore needed is a better understanding of the social meanings of domestic space and the bodily interaction of those who dwell in it with the form of the house, rather than its simple description as a text. In order to achieve this, Lawrence, following Lefebvre, believes it is necessary to look at the way the meaning and the use of domestic architecture has been transmitted from the past to the present through lived experience and by language. The use of oral history, novels, autobiographies, ethnography and other language materials is, he believes, therefore vital; such sources can help reconstruct the layout and use of domestic space and allow its analysis. And, 'unless all possible sources of data and diverse methods are used, vernacular architecture will not be fully understood'.[44]

It is equally important, Lawrence argues, to ask how people live in and think about the design of their houses. What do different house types, even different rooms mean? How is household life related to the spatial order and furnishing of the rooms? Whose 'ideas and values are being employed to define and delimit space'? How are these ideas expressed in the design and use of household space?[45] Lawrence ends by asking when architects will break away from the production of 'coercive' space that cuts across and begin instead to design 'evocative' space which will open up to the user.[46] In reforming housing and attempting to dictate cottage design, the elite were similarly attempting to impose their own values, in built form, on the rural poor. In this sense, the model cottage once built became a coercive space that, though it embodied community, also came to be overwritten by privacy.

Space reproduces ideology. It defines status and it shapes domesticity. In the nineteenth century, there was a gendered division of space that can still be seen in the original structure of houses and other buildings, and men and women moved through the same spaces in different ways. In terms of social status, for instance, class overwrote all domestic spaces. To go into a house, a visitor had to cross several, clearly defined processional boundaries: gate, path, portico, door. Servants within the homes of the wealthy had their own inferior means of access, thereby avoiding the negotiation of processional entrances, plus their own quarters and workrooms. Their movement around other parts of the house was policed/controlled by locks and keys. In this way, servants and masters were literally, not just metaphorically, kept at a distance. The social construction of space – and with it, of material objects – is clearly incredibly complex and concomitantly hard to read. It is difficult to know, for instance, how women and men from different classes have used different spaces. One way of tackling this problem is to use autobiography, realist novels or art in comparison to social commentaries as Philippa Tristram has done, and though this has its hazards, it does mean that we can begin to see how space was represented/mapped in class and gendered terms at different points in time. The social geographer Doreen Massey has, however, taken this concept of space a step further.

Massey shows how space does not just reflect, but how it is actually made up of social relations:

> The view, then, is of space–time as a configuration of social relations within which the specifically spatial may be conceived of as an inherently dynamic simultaneity. Moreover, since social relations are inevitably and everywhere imbued with power and meaning and symbolism, this view of the spatial is as an ever-shifting social geometry of power and significance.[47]

In fact, there are multiplicities of intersecting, cross-cutting, parallel, paradoxical and antagonistic spaces within this model. The observer – the social actor – sees stability only as an act of consciousness, in which they are stationary relative to all other actors, so that each observer intersects with space–time in different ways. Massey therefore stresses that power is inherently spatial. The 'spatial organisation of society . . . is integral to the production of the social', i.e. it is not just an effect or mirror image of the social, rather, the spatial 'is fully implicated in both history and politics'. In her view, the spatial is a way of thinking.[48]

This model has some interesting implications for the idea of 'place'. The idea of a unique 'sense of place' has become a key issue within rural history and regional studies when discussing the impact of social and economic change, such as that which took place during the height of the enclosure movement in the late eighteenth and early nineteenth centuries. Certain places are also recognised as nostalgic sites where people divorce themselves from 'progress' or 'history' and this has been studied with particular reference to Englishness. According to Massey, however, the definition or labelling of any place is something that will always be highly contested. Nationalism, for instance, tries to fix the meaning of specific spaces, attempts to surround them, to give them fixed identities and to claim them. Place in this case is defined as bounded, which relies on a view of space as static, apolitical and ahistorical. Massey, on the other hand, sees place as defined by the articulation of specific social relations and contested identities; as defined by its links to the outside world beyond, not by its boundaries. All attempts to fix boundaries of any kind are in her view an attempt to fix social relations. Wherever there is an attempt to stabilise meaning in this way, there will, therefore, be a 'social contest',[49] because 'places are always already hybrid'.[50] Hence, Fiona Bowie has observed that:

> Wales presents to the rest of the world a coherent picture of cultural self-sufficiency and a firm sense of identity. What outsiders see, however, is not so much Wales as their own reflection, or stereotypes of Welshness... As one begins to penetrate beyond this refracted image of Welshness, not least by learning the Welsh language, the unproblematic and monolithic nature of Welsh identity begins to fragment. One is left not so much with a coherent notion of Welshness... as with a sense of many conflicting and interlocking definitions of identity which actively compete for symbolic space and public recognition.[51]

In practice, one account is no more 'authentic' than another, rather they express disparate experiences and distinct ways of seeing, and when dealing with the 'rural', one is effectively dealing with similarly contesting, culturally constructed countrysides. Meanwhile, different visions of the 'rural', and the practices that result, work to include and exclude; the rural idyll that has become hegemonic marginalises as it places the privileged at its 'centre'. As Jan Marsh notes with reference to the Arts and Crafts movement of the late nineteenth century, for instance, William Robinson,[52] 'contested local residents' rights to age-old footpaths through Gravetye [Manor], which had previously been a farm... there were often conflicts between different manifestations of pastoralism'.[53] Paul Cloke and Jo Little's edited collection, *Contested Countryside Cultures*, is important here as bringing together a number of essays on these 'other' countrysides and advancing our understanding of how cultural constructions of rurality are deployed.[54]

Beyond these issues, the definition of space and time is, Massey has argued, also connected to definitions of gender, i.e. the polarisation of social roles into masculine and feminine. She accounts for the division of space and time into two opposite poles as part of the wider system of oppositions in Western thought, in which one half of the equation is always privileged over the other, e.g. masculine is always privileged over feminine. Time is privileged over space, in this case, and is also associated with masculinity, space with femininity. Time 'is aligned with history, progress, civilisation, politics and transcendence and coded masculine. And it is the opposite of these things which have, in the traditions of Western thought, been coded feminine.' Where space is in a position 'of stasis, passivity, and depoliticization',[55] Massey is interested in the way in which this is related to other dualisms and how these dichotomies might be challenged. In particular, she relates this to her concept of place, which of course for her is defined by interrelations, rather than fixed boundaries and the opposition of identities against each other. The need to fix borders, to secure identity is, she argues, inherently patriarchal.[56]

I will be using some of these concepts in relation to smaller 'spatial scales' – the cottage and the cottage garden – within the nineteenth and twentieth centuries. In particular, I am interested in the cottage as sign, as trope, icon, myth and (cultural) product. The cottage garden, for example, is supposed to be defined by its difference from nature, by the act of enclosure as a work of culture, so that the work done within it is nearly always referred to in masculine terms, yet it is also seen as a peculiarly feminine location. It is thought of as essentially English, as bounded by walls, hedges and fences, but it always contains some 'alien' plant species. How can a place that is apparently so simple have so many identities? And, what have they come to mean, what does the cottage connote?

This book will therefore cover a range of issues, from health – physical and moral – to gardening, to the representation of rural decay in picturesque modes; there will be less here about actual cottages, more about their representation. But, this is not a simple matter of art failing to offer up an accurate image of the countryside to its urban, middle-class audience. The myth of the country cottage gradually became an essential component within many key middle-class debates in the nineteenth century, as an icon or sign that carried with it a variety of meanings, which in turn shaped the way that rural housing came to be designed and built. This book therefore aims to explore some of the apparent contradictions which arose from this, and consider the wider issues the construction of the image of the country cottage raises about the countryside as site of both Nature and Culture, the formation of new national identities, and the definition of femininity, masculinity and childhood around an idealised site of domesticity/place. In order to do this I will be drawing on a range of sources, from parliamentary reports to novels, through to newspaper articles and art.

The cottage and the cottage woman were, indeed are, both in part defined by their opposition to the world outside. By the mid-nineteenth century, the world of economics, politics, industry, agriculture was not supposed to be a fit place for women, who were to maintain the home as a haven for their husbands. A woman, especially a married woman, who stepped outside her 'natural' sphere was automatically condemned as unfeminine unless she trod specific paths (parades and promenades) or engaged in suitably feminine tasks (shopping). Otherwise she was, in the parlance of the time, 'unsexed'. Again, this is partly about space, but as Ruth Swartz Cowan has argued in *More Work for Mother*, this is also about the development of industrialisation. History, economics, sociology still refer to the 'impact' of industrialisation on the home, as if work was something which was entirely removed from that space. In the gradual separation of home and paid work that is supposed to have taken place during industrialisation, the inherent opposition of home and industry is taken as a given. In our 'textbooks of history and economics and sociology', she argues,

> the terms *industrialization* and *home* are usually connected by the word *impact* . . . industrialization is conceived as being not just *outside* the home but virtually in *opposition* to it. Homes are idealized as the places to which we would like to retreat when the world of industrialization becomes too grim to bear; home is where the 'heart' is; industry is where 'dogs are eating dogs' and 'only money counts.' . . . Under the sway of such ideas . . . we resolutely polish the Early American cabinets that hide the advanced electronic machines in our kitchens and resolutely believe that we will escape the horrors of modernity as soon as we step under the lintels of our front doors.[57]

Though she is writing about America, what she says is just as true of England. To believe that industrialisation has not occurred within the home is, as she puts it, a 'form of cultural obfuscation'. Our homes are 'as much a locus for industrialized work as factories or coal mines are, and washing machines and microwaves are as much a product of industrialization as are automobiles and pocket calculators'.[58] When industrialisation removed some forms of work from the home, other kinds of work remained,[59] hidden by the increasingly widespread cult of the domesticity. Though Ann Romines has discussed the literary tradition of valuing this work, in what she calls 'the home plot', a plot that celebrates the repetitive rhythms and rituals of housework and subordinates the individual subject 'to an ongoing, life-preserving, and, for some women, life-threatening process',[60] history has continued to be written through the lens of separate spheres ideology. What this means is that an attempt must be made to look at the range of work undertaken by the cottage woman, and the material changes that have taken place within the cottage itself. The book will therefore include some autobiographical material on housework as well as an analysis of the representation of the home and what it has come to mean.

Chapters 1 and 2 draw largely on material from the nineteenth century to argue that there have been two major constructions of the cottage home – as Beau Ideal and its opposite the 'imperfect home'. In these chapters I touch on the picturesque, the issue of Nature vs. Culture and notions of childhood and poverty. I also begin to consider the intersection of rural idyll with domesticity and Englishness, and the social construction of domestic space within separate spheres ideology with reference to parliamentary reports, Victorian genre art and 'Condition of England' texts. Chapter 3 analyses the construction of the cottage garden as haven, and gardening as rational pursuit. Moving from the late eighteenth through to the twentieth century the chapter includes a survey of cottage gardening, its toils and pleasures, and readings of more rhetorical texts on the necessity of gardening as well as references to art and literature. Chapter 4 engages in a closer analysis of the relationship between the cottage as vernacular structure and Englishness. Moving from the nineteenth to the twentieth century, the chapter turns to a consideration of the rural and its relationship to national identity and here I begin to pick up on some of the issues raised within Cloke and Little. In Chapter 5, an attempt is made to open up readings of middle-class and working-class domestic space, with particular reference to the issues addressed by Lawrence, and a consideration of the available methods and sources. The chapter includes reference to autobiographical material and texts that address the reform of the cottage for the working class, both structurally and aesthetically. Chapter 6 looks at the modern commodification of the cottage and its meaning for those who 'buy into' the myth. Focusing on the twentieth century, the materials used include advertising, and the approach incorporates references to Raymond Williams' work and two recent key ethnographic studies undertaken at a local level. Here there is a return to issues of domesticity and national identity.

Currently our taste for the country cottage, or at least country-style, is waning. Style gurus on popular TV programmes such as the BBC's *Home Front* seem to be turning their back on cosy chintz in favour of a revived modern aesthetic. In its first edition, the gardening magazine *New Eden* had this to say:

> Now is an exciting time for garden design. The old-fashioned cottage-garden approach is being edged off the pinnacle it has occupied since the Edwardian era. It is being replaced by contemporary styles that celebrate colour, form and texture in a new way. Your garden space can be anywhere, on any scale – right down to the size of a window box.[61]

In the war between sticks and bricks, the bricks currently seem to have the upper hand. However, cottage-style will no doubt make its return, while our current taste for the modern interior does not seem to have cooled our ardour for the country cottage as a place in which to seek refuge.

As Jonathan Glancey argues:

> No great insights are needed to understand why we are so enchanted with the idea of the perfect village, with its doll's house homes. A return to childhood, a retreat into innocence. A chance for townies to dress up, learn to ride and take up hunting as if to the manor born. The desire to grow old conservatively, to grow pears, plant a kitchen garden, make fires, keep dogs and to wear a sexless uniform chosen from a rack of thick woollen tights, fisherman's hats and muddy boots.[62]

But, to what extent is a 'return to childhood' coterminous with a return to, or the retrieval of, a particular kind of femininity? To what extent might we begin to recognise the control that has to be exercised by a woman over her environment in creating this idyll? Are country people 'sexless'? What is the fisherman's ethnic identity, his class, his sexuality – if the answers seem 'obvious', why are they obvious? Is playing house the same as cleaning house? And, is this inevitably conservative?

NOTES

1. The gay slang 'cottaging' is reputedly derived from the appearance of certain public toilets on Hampstead Heath. These conveniences were apparently designed to look like cottages. We may wonder if this was 'really' the case, but, as noted in the *Oxford English Dictionary*, the word 'cottage' could also mean urinal c.1900–1912. Cottage, in gay slang, is also rumoured to derive from an eccentric will, which left money for the fabrication of public 'cottages', as meeting places. According to Neil Bartlett: 'Gay men have been cottaging and being entrapped by the police at least since the eighteenth century. "1742 *Select Trials*, London: In a little time the prisoner passes by and looks hard at me, and, at a small distance from me, stands up against the wall, as if he was going to make water. Then by degrees he fiddles nearer and nearer to where I stood, 'till at last he came close to – 'Tis a very fine night' says he, etc. You know the rest."' N. Bartlett, *Who Was That Man? A present for Mr Oscar Wilde* (London, 1988), pp. 88.
2. *Oxford English Dictionary* (Oxford, 1989).
3. **family** xv. – L. *familia* household, f. *famulus* servant; . . . So **familiar** xiv. Early forms *familier, famuler* are – (O)F . . . but forms in *-iar(e)* are also early and reflect the orig. L. *familiāris*. **familiarize** xvii. – F. **familiarity**. Xiii. – (O)F – L. *Oxford English Dictionary*.
4. See R. Sales, *English Literature in History 1750–1830: pastoral and politics* (London, 1983).
5. See C. Payne, *Rustic Simplicity: scenes of cottage life in nineteenth-century British art* (Nottingham, 1998).
6. See R. Williams, *The Country and the City* (London, [1972] 1985), pp. 1–8.
7. A. Howkins, *Reshaping Rural England: a social history 1850–1925* (London, 1991), pp. 292–3.
8. J. Marsh, *Back to the Land: the pastoral impulse in Victorian England from 1880 to 1914* (London, Melbourne and New York, 1982), p. 6. 'Hodge' was a pejorative

nickname applied to any male agricultural labourer/peasant in the nineteenth century.
9 See L. Davidoff, J. L'Esperance and H. Newby, 'Landscape with figures: home and community in English society' in Mitchell, J. and Oakley, A. (eds), *The Rights and Wrongs of Women* (Harmondsworth, 1986).
10 D. Massey, *Space, Place and Gender* (Cambridge, 1994), p. 10; G. Rose, *Feminism and Geography: the limits of geographical knowledge* (Cambridge, 1993), p. 47.
11 Marsh, *Back to the Land*, pp. 60–71.
12 J. R. R. Tolkien, *The Lord of the Rings* (London, [1955] 1979), p. 14.
13 Tolkien, *Lord of the Rings*, p. 21.
14 Tolkien, *Lord of the Rings*, p. 13.
15 Tolkien, *Lord of the Rings*, p. 14.
16 Williams, *Country and City*, pp. 288–91.
17 E. Said, *Orientalism* (London, [1978] 1995), p. 3.
18 Said, *Orientalism*, p. 3.
19 Tolkien, *Lord of the Rings*, p. 13.
20 Tolkien, *Lord of the Rings*, pp. 18–19.
21 In Dicken's *Great Expectations* (1860–61) Wemmick lives in a cottage *ornée* which has its own moat and drawbridge; he has a pig and grows vegetables and is therefore self-sufficient. Tristram notes that such a home was truly Victorian, i.e. individualistic, domestic, privatised; a literal refuge from the world and defined against that world, yet without taste. P. Tristram, *Living Space in Fact and Fiction* (London, 1989), p. 25.
22 T. Rivers, D. Cruickshank, G. Darley, M. Pawley, *The Name of the Room: a history of the British house and home* (London, 1992), p. 15.
23 Rivers et al., *The Name of the Room*, p. 10.
24 B. Anderson, *Imagined Communities: reflections on the origin and spread of nationalism* (London and New York, [1983] 1991). The 'imagined community' for Anderson refers to the construction of the nation.
25 Howkins, *Reshaping Rural England*, pp. 19–21.
26 Tristram, *Living Space*, pp. 66–115.
27 Marsh, *Back to the Land*, pp. 3–5.
28 C. Wood, *Paradise Lost: paintings of English country life and landscape, 1850–1914* (London, [1988] 1993), p. 129; Cf. Tristram, *Living Space*.
29 This includes those who sought to go 'back-to-the-land' at this time, i.e. those who found the idea of leaving the city to set up in a commune or as a 'cottage farmer' attractive enough to try it for themselves. Marsh, *Back to the Land*, pp. 4, 27, 93, 112–13.
30 Howkins, *Reshaping Rural England*, p. 290.
31 D. Phillips and A. Williams, *Rural Britain: a social geography* (Oxford, 1984), pp. 97, 100–1.
32 J. G. Derounian, *Another Country: real life beyond Rose Cottage* (London, 1993), p. 13.
33 Phillips and Williams, *Rural Britain*, p. 99.
34 M. M. Bell, *Childerley: nature and morality in a country village* (Chicago and London, 1994), p. 12.
35 Bell, *Childerley*, pp. 66–7.
36 Phillips and Williams, *Rural Britain*, pp. 97–8.
37 Phillips and Williams, *Rural Britain*, pp. 112–19.
38 R. Gasson, *Provision of Tied Cottages* (Cambridge, 1975), pp. 8–17, 60–9.
39 Phillips and Williams, *Rural Britain*, pp. 107–11.

40 M. C. Dunn, M. J. C. Rawson and A. W. Rogers, *The Derivation of Rural Housing Profiles* (Birmingham, 1980), pp. 11, 13–15, Fig. 2.
41 Bell, *Childerley*, pp. 14–15.
42 See S. Brand, *How Buildings Learn: what happens after they're built* (London, 1997).
43 R. J. Lawrence, *Housing, Dwellings and Homes: design, theory, research and practice* (Chichester, 1987), pp. 73–4.
44 Lawrence, *Housing, Dwellings and Homes*, pp. 18–19, 25–31, 54. As well as Lefebvre, Lawrence draws on Fillipetti and Trotereau, Eliade, Fox and Raglan, Lévi-Strauss, Rapoport (who lists the following as socio-cultural factors that might influence vernacular buildings: 'family', the 'position of women', 'privacy', 'social intercourse', 'genre de vie'), Hunziker, Innocent, Ladurie. Tristram reads space in exactly this way, drawing on plans, art and literature, though not field studies. Cf. Tristram, *Living Space*.
45 Lawrence, *Housing, Dwellings and Homes*, pp. 18–54.
46 Lawrence, *Housing, Dwellings and Homes*, pp. 74–6.
47 Massey, *Space, Place and Gender*, p. 3.
48 Massey, *Space, Place and Gender*, intro.
49 Massey, *Space, Place and Gender*, intro.
50 D. Massey, 'Places and their pasts', *History Workshop Journal*, No. 39, p. 183.
51 Fiona Bowie, quoted by J. Murdoch and A. C. Pratt, 'From the power of topography to the topography of power: a discourse on strange ruralities' in Cloke, P. and Little, J. (eds), *Contested Countryside Cultures: otherness, marginalisation and rurality* (London and New York, 1997), p. 64.
52 Author of *The Wild Garden: Or our Groves and Gardens made beautiful by Naturalisation of Hardy Exotic Plants; being one way onwards from the Dark Ages of Flower Gardening, with suggestions for the Regeneration of the Bare Borders of the London Parks* (1870).
53 Marsh, *Back to the Land*, pp. 179–80.
54 P. Cloke and J. Little, 'Introduction: other countrysides?' in Cloke, P. and Little, J. (eds), *Contested Countryside Cultures: otherness, marginalisation and rurality* (London and New York, 1997), p. 1.
55 Massey, *Space, Place and Gender*, p. 6.
56 Massey, *Space, Place and Gender*, p. 7.
57 R. Swartz Cowan, *More Work for Mother: the ironies of household technology from the open hearth to the microwave* (London, 1989), p. 4.
58 Swartz Cowan, *More Work for Mother*, p. 4.
59 Swartz Cowan, *More Work for Mother*, p. 5.
60 A. Romines, *The Home Plot: women writing and domestic ritual* (Amherst, 1992), p. 293.
61 T. Richardson, Editor, *New Eden: the contemporary gardens magazine*, No. 1 (May/June, 1999), p. 7.
62 J. Glancey, 'Visions of Albion', the *Weekend Guardian* (27 March 1999), p. 45.

CHAPTER 1

The ideal home

The Cottage Homes of England
   How beautiful they are;
In nooks and corners see them stand,
   Dotting the country near and far,
Down to the ocean strand.
   Sweet cottages of calm content
   From John O'Groats to lovely Kent.

By hill sides on the upland height;
   Down by the pleasant stream,
Where woodlands wave in joyous light,
   And thrushes sing and poets dream,
When summer's smile is bright,
   Where'er we stop, where'er we roam,
   We find the English Cottage Home.

The garden border's all in bloom;
   And climbing overhead,
The honeysuckles rich perfume,
   Mingles with roses white and red,
And shades the cottage room;
   While in the porch with fluttering wings,
   The gentle skylark hangs and sings.

'Dada is coming,' shouts a child,
   And toddles out to greet him,
While baby screams with gladness wild,
   And spreads his arms to greet him;
And mother's voice in accents mild,
   With matron-love, makes daily toil,
   Delightful by her placid smile.

The Cottage Homes of England,
   Are happy homes indeed,

Where love is the strong household band,
  And God is worshipped with due heed,
And cottage altars stand,
  For morning and for evening prayer —:
  God's blessing is for ever there.

(Benjamin Gough, 1876)[1]

THE COTTAGE HOMES OF ENGLAND

We meet the first (decorative) cottage homes of England in an age that favoured the picturesque over the sublime, a period when informality was valued over formality. A time when a new anti-authoritarian politics was developing within landscape gardening; a politics that was rooted in the validation of 'English' virtues, and a Whiggish kind of freedom – the 'freedom', as Pugh puts it, 'to transpose sites, to control random promiscuous nature'.[2] Those who favoured these 'wild', free gardens, in contrast to the fountains, parterres and straight lines of Versailles, began to design in such a way that their estates conformed to scenes painted in the picturesque mode and to require that their audiences progress from one 'picture' to another. And soon, their landscapes included temples dedicated to ancient gods and virtues, statues, obelisks and other built references to the fashionable values of the day.[3]

The picturesque has since become the spatial embodiment of individualism, and continues even now as the dominant way of seeing. Even the roads we drive, where traffic is a form of communication grounded in and expressive of capitalism,[4] is structured by its knowledge. 'Knowledge' was conceived spatially in the mid- to late-eighteenth century as 'an accretion of freedom' and as '*the* knowledge: of designed routes, a circuit usually marked by seats with classical inscriptions'.[5] Such an 'accretion of "freedom",' Pugh observes, 'anticipates the automobile and comes with new regulations: speed limits (inscriptions, "stay a while"), instructions to stay in lane (guide books), diagrams showing the shape of the road ahead (maps), and the need to keep an eye on the road ahead ("objects" to run the eye over)'.[6] It was within this paradigm that the odd (ornate but uninhabitable) cottage, tucked away in a corner of a wood, or dropped into a valley, became a, if not *the*, most delightful model of rural simplicity.[7]

By the late eighteenth century, the secular had begun to replace the divine. Just as individualism was beginning to take hold within the nascent middle class, so there was an increasing acceptance of the idea that the human mind could transcend Nature, even God. That which takes 'the Name of *Sublime*', John Ballie argued, is everything which thus raises the Mind to fits of *Greatness* and disposes it to soar above her *Mother Earth*; Hence arises that *Exultation* and *Pride* which the Mind ever feels from the *Consciousness* of its own *Vastness* – That *Object* only can be justly called *Sublime*, which in some degree disposes the Mind to this *Enlargement* of itself, and gives her a lofty *Conception* of her own *Powers*.[8]

The sensation of the sublime, represented architecturally by the neo-classical movement, elevated the individual's mind to a sense of wonder; for Burke, to a sense of terror or awe: 'Whatever is fitted in any sort to excite ideas of pain, and danger . . . whatever is in any sort terrible, or is conversant about terrible objects, or operates in a manner analogous with terror, is a source of the *sublime*.'[9]

The picturesque, on the other hand, valued the pastoral, and in 'pastoral form, nature is not much depraved'.[10] Opposing, yet parallel aesthetics, where sublime Nature overwhelmed and inspired picturesque Nature pleased its audience. And, though the sublime was closely linked to the Gothic in literature,[11] it was those that preferred the picturesque who sought to give what they saw as an organic, native architecture a new validity. For those who loved the picturesque, Nature was like a painting; they cultivated a framing gaze and applied painterly ways of seeing to the world around them; they sought out decayed ruins and fragments, and it influenced their taste. They had an objective eye and sketched, landscaped, mapped and classified the natural world around them. In the eighteenth century, to know of and practise the picturesque, whether in the form of natural history, writing, gardening, diary keeping or painting, at home or abroad, was to show one's education and breeding.

In the form of botany, for example, it permitted elite women to draw on skills and interests that were thought of as innately feminine, and provided them with a legitimate field of expertise on which to write – there were a number of women, according to Charles Bryant, whose 'fondness for plants seems to be blended in their very natures'.[12] Those who favoured the picturesque therefore looked on Nature rationally as something that might be tamed and cultured. When abroad they looked to Nature's fore-, middle- and back-ground to provide them with scenes that could be illustrated and described as if they were views found at home. The picturesque was a very English aesthetic – like agrarianism[13] and the Ordnance Survey,[14] it travelled everywhere with the English – which defined and thereby exercised control over new colonial territories as 'landscapes'. Hence, while her husband undertook to map Canada as part of the military survey of the territory, and thereby legitimise British rule, Mrs Simcoe – who travelled to Canada with her husband in the late eighteenth century – walked, sketched, wrote a diary and letters, collected seeds, copied maps and gardened. After the woods caught fire – which happened regularly both as a natural and as an agricultural process – she walked among the ashes admiring the effect of stark trunks and residual flames against the sky.[15] Those figures that simply did not seem to fit in with this aesthetic – native peoples, for instance – were simultaneously erased or idealised as those landscapes were re-produced. As a result, they were expected to simultaneously vanish from actual sight. US policy was to de-agriculturalise American Indians and this has been incorporated into idealised views of these peoples, as well as the landscape they farmed. At the same time, the changes native peoples made to the landscape were often erased before settlers moved into a region, because of the spread of disease, the activities of hunters and the promulgation of government policy removing native peoples from lands coveted by white immigrants. As well as thereby erasing what would have been recognised as signs of culture, contradictorily, this also diminished 'the imagined menace of both "savages and beasts"'.[16]

In art as in landscaping, cottages were added as a detail in the background, pictured at a distance. The taste for the picturesque made audiences look at the cottage from the outside as part of the landscape. Cottages did not (yet), to borrow Tristram's phrase, symbolise 'living space' but rather the values of 'old England' and as such it was the decorative details – thatch, smoke rising from the chimney, Gothic windows and doors, trees, peasants, cows and pigs – taken from pastoral poetry that dominated their design.[17] As Michael Reed puts it, 'cottages were discovered to be picturesque' at the end of the eighteenth century. As a result, John Nash[18] built several quite florid examples for J. S. Harford at Blaise Hamlet 1810–11, and several cottages *ornée* complete 'with half timbering, thatched roofs and wrought-iron balconies with verandas', the last a feature imported from India.[19] And as Tristram points out, the taste for the picturesque cottage led to the building of large cottages *ornée* as country retreats by and for the elite. James Malton's[20] designs for instance included conservatories, vines trained over trellis, at least two parlours and three or four bedrooms per 'cottage'. The biggest built by Nash – the King's Cottage, i.e. the Royal Lodge at Windsor – was designed for King George IV and cost £200,000.[21]

Nash's verandas illustrate how the English country cottage is not always as 'English' as it first appears. He typically combined the neo-classic with the Gothic, Chinese, Egyptian and Indian. In this way, we can see his work as typical of the nascent political, economic and aesthetic influences of the period, which absorbed the architecture of colonised peoples. And, these details remind us of the extent to which the desirability of the cottage originated within a construction of Englishness that was itself formed within and through imperialism. The further the English tried to reach in terms of empire, the more popular the 'countervailing sentiment for cosy home scenery, for thatched cottages and gardens in pastoral countryside' became.[22] 'Landscape imagery is not merely a reflection of, or distraction from, more pressing social, economic or political issues', observes Stephen Daniels, 'it is often a powerful mode of knowledge and social engagement.'[23] The landscape, as much as art, literature or architecture, is a construct, and as such can and should be read.

As P. Oliver notes, this elite treatment of the cottage of course persisted into the twentieth century and shaped its popularity as a second home. However, according to Oliver, who in common with many commentators in the 1970s argued for sustainability and a recognition of the cottage as folk history, the popularity of the cottage *ornée* meant that neither local materials nor vernacular architecture came to be valued. The irony of the landscapers' practice of demolishing 'real' villages to make way for 'ideal'/model villages has been widely commented on. But, he goes on to note, even now, when vernacular cottages are restored, they are still mostly done up using imported industrial materials to conform to a '*kitsch*' twentieth-century picturesque.[24] For Stewart Brand, writing in the 1990s, this constant adaptation by buildings to their environment, fashion and the needs of those who live in them is something in itself worth valuing and studying. As he says,

> you can't fix or remodel an old place in the old way. Techniques and materials keep changing... Buildings keep being pushed around by three irresistible forces – technology, money, and fashion... The march of technology is inexorable, and accelerating. Form follows funding. If people have money to spare, they *will* mess with their building... A building is not primarily a building; it is primarily property, and as such, subject to the whims of the market... As for fashion, it is change for its own sake.[25]

In R. J. Lawrence's view, by considering the interaction of sociocultural factors, design, decorative details and the way houses are 'zoned' or ordered, it is possible to move beyond simple narratives of these spaces to a 'semantic analysis of space and construction elements', an understanding of the language, syntax, and spatial organisation of the building and adaptation of houses:[26]

> the morphology of a vernacular building is inseparable from its social meaning and its use. A reinterpretation of vernacular architecture would stem from an understanding of the interrelationships between the spatial

and material organisation, as well as the meaning and the use of buildings and adjoining spaces ... buildings ought to be defined in relation to their own tradition: here tradition is not just a repertoire of historical building forms but the ways in which they have been used and regarded by people in specific social, cultural, geographical and historical contexts ... In architecture the relationship between space and time is a dialectical process between building form and social factors, between continuity and change, between permanence and flexibility. [Therefore the] information embodied in buildings cannot be understood solely by a synchronic investigation.[27]

This moves beyond the simple bid to freeze vernacular architecture in time, as attempted by preservationists like Oliver, to a treatment of domestic architecture as text with social meaning and an undertaking to map its contribution to the formation of identity and its impact on the body. It is an approach that is sensitive to the fact that buildings change over time, that they have many uses which will also change, that because they are experienced physically and symbolically they have many, contingent meanings, and that each time they are altered they are in a sense 're-interpreted'. We will return to this issue in Chapter 5, but given this process of continuity and change, it should not be surprising that the cottage, though remaining picturesque, also moved on. By the time Blaise Hamlet was built, the interest in the pastoral or the informal had already begun to decline and switch back to the rational and classical. By the 1820s a new kind of liberalism was emerging that favoured balance and control over organic disorder, leaving the latter-day Gothic revival to one-nation Tories and contemporary reformers like Ruskin[28] and Morris. Because critics like Richard Payne Knight, Edmund Bartell and John Wood began to suggest that there was more to a cottage than aesthetic effect, it gradually ceased working as a simple decorative feature within a wider landscape.[29]

The accommodation of the poor had in fact emerged as a pressing social issue well before the end of the eighteenth century, so that landscape architects had begun to plan and build model villages from about 1760; the first time that workers' housing had ever really been 'designed' in any formal sense. As S. Martin Gaskell comments, the symmetry and formalism of the final structures demonstrated both that the landowner had the power to control the landscape and that their 'wealth and taste could bring order to the living conditions of the lower orders'.[30] This is why, when he designed Blaise Hamlet, Nash was commissioned not just to create a pretty village, but also to build almshouses that would concretise the ideal of the village as stable 'organic' community. These cottages were to connote control not just in their picturesqueness, but also in the built imposition of social harmony. Cottage *ornée* became model cottage; in the end, it also became council house and suburban semi, while model village turned into council estate and new town.[31] Meanwhile, as Parker notes, even when a house was not designed strictly as a cottage, by the late nineteenth century its external detailing would often include pastoral effects taken from the picturesque, e.g. the use of timber or tiles on the walls, and diamond-paned windows. And, by the 1830s, the layout of a number of suburbs came to be based on picturesque conceptions of rural space, which dictated that plots be varied in size, several buildings be grouped together and that planting be used to break up straight lines.[32]

Architectural and landscaped space reifies ideology and concretises historically and culturally specific social relations. 'In the construction of [the] "country of the mind", the idea of domesticity as a general good was intimately tied to the powerful symbol of the home as a physical place.'[33] Even vernacular architecture is not simply influenced by the local physical environment of which it is a part, but is also subject to external (national) cultural and socio-economic forces. In Lawrence's view, therefore, houses, be they designed or vernacular, should never be simply classified formalistically or aesthetically. Rather, the wider uses of domestic space, such as religious practice, and the impact of social norms on the design and layout of the house ought also to be considered. Simply walking through and around a domestic space, crossing its public and private boundaries, is a form of systematic communication, which links together not only its internal rooms, but also the house as a whole to the public space beyond. A door, a path, garden walls all take on a variety of meanings and purposes when in use.[34] The model cottage, meanwhile, was nothing if not a deliberately executed ideal 'home'; a home valued for the honesty rather than the aspiration of its architecture and for the quiet habit rather than the ambition of its inmates.[35]

MAN'S REFUGE, WOMAN'S HOME

Just as the cottage entered the picturesque, so 'home' came to mean 'haven' in the eighteenth century. It therefore seems particularly apt that Gough should draw on the work of Felicia Hemans (1793–1835) in his evocation of comfort and content. Her poem 'The Homes of England' (itself inspired by a poem by Joanna Baillie) celebrated in turn the 'stately Homes of England', the 'merry Homes of England', the 'blessed Homes of England', the 'Cottage-Homes of England' and the 'free, fair Homes of England'.[36] But, though initially separated from the rough and tumble of the world in the eighteenth century,[37] it was thanks to the Victorians that 'home' became a place that we tend to look back to as having come from. It has since come to be constructed through the lens of nostalgia and the search for authenticity, whether that authenticity resides in national identity or history. Though it does not literally have to be a domestic space, it is associated primarily with both domestic and maternal imagery,[38] and it is that imagery that makes it 'comfortable'. This experience of bodily comfort cannot be separated from the association of femininity with nature, which – picking up on the mind–body dualism of the Enlightenment – was in turn linked to the association of femininity with the generative spaces of Woman's body. Likewise, the 'double association of women with reproductive activities and of these in turn with nature'[39] can account for the coding of Nature as feminine. In the nineteenth century that bodily comfort came to be established through women's naturalised (hidden) domestic work – inextricably linked to a woman's respectability and competence – and by men's cultured (conspicuous) acquisition of homely commodities.

A great deal depended on a woman's ability to generate an untroubled home, hence in 1887 Samuel Smiles[40] wrote:

> Where the mother is good and virtuous – no matter whether the father be reckless, profligate, or debased – she can by the influence of her example, and the coercive power of her gentleness and affection, save her children, and bring them up to virtuous courses in life. But when her character is bad – in spite of the excellence and goodness of the father – the cases are exceedingly rare in which any good comes of the children. No mere educational advantages, no surroundings of wealth or comfort, will compensate for the want of good mothers. It is they who mainly direct the influences of home – Home, which is the seminary not only of the social affections, but of the ideas and maxims which govern the world.[41]

Indeed, forty years earlier Andrew Combe[42] had already argued that to

> the right-minded mother, the management and training of her children ought to appear in the same light as the exercise of a profession. It is her natural and special vocation; and she is as much bound to fit herself for the discharge of its active duties, as the father and husband is to prepare himself for the exercise of the profession by which he is to provide for their support.[43]

Both Smiles and Combe were contributing to the formation and reformation of domesticity. Domesticity emerged within, but was quickly promoted beyond, the middle class – hence Gough's *Songs for British Workmen* (1876) was dedicated to 'the Editor of *The British Workman*' who, he said, had used 'indefatigable labours in promoting the wide circulation of pure literature, in a cheap and attractive form, among the masses of the people'.[44] Domestic literature like the Reverend T. H. Walker's *Good Servants, Good Wives and Happy Homes, illustrated by a series of characters and events sketched from actual life* (1862), in its sixth edition by 1888, promoted the symbolism of home as cornerstone of the nation's well-being.[45] Art, literature, architecture, sanitary reports all were engaged in this ideological work and though domesticity's apologists claimed that it was essentially static – because it was 'natural' – the ideology of domesticity was nonetheless frequently challenged, could seem contradictory and, despite its continuities, changed over time.

Domesticity in part arose as an effect of industrialisation. At the turn of the eighteenth to the nineteenth century, productive, economic 'work', for the middle and upper classes gradually came to be seen as something that both had and ought to take place outside the home. The home therefore became a place within which the family could supposedly quietly enjoy a few, normally 'rational', i.e. improving, leisure activities and the one place within which the head of the household could relax and gain some respite from the vagaries of competition. While he was absent, his wife was charged with the correct management of that home and the moral education as well as the physical well-being of his children. In this way, gender identities also shifted. Masculinity and femininity came to be constructed spatially, that is they were constructed in and through the nascent and soon-to-be dominant ideology of 'separate spheres'. While men 'went out' to engage in what were recognised as economically valuable employments within the public sphere, women were expected to remain 'at home' with their children in the domestic sphere.

Though transcendent by the Victorian period, this model of gender relations was hardly new. Leon Battista Alberti's fifteenth-century treatise *On the Art of Building in Ten Books* – a text which helped incorporate architecture into the liberal arts, and professionalised it in the long-term – is exemplary here as it defines what Wigley refers to as a specific 'intersection between a spatial order and a system of surveillance which turns on the question of gender'.[46] In it, we find the argument that women should be kept deep within the house's interior, while men be exposed to the outside world. Drawing on recollected Greek texts, Alberti treats the house as a mechanism for the domestication of women; the text is implicated in the production of 'Woman', though draws on the authority of displaced sources and custom. In other texts, Alberti suggests that if a man sits too long indoors he will be emasculated. If a woman goes outside, she becomes more feminine, in the sense that her sexuality begins to roam out of control as, drawing on the Greeks, only men have self-control. Stasis is figured as feminine, mobility as masculine – gender is spatialised – even though it is the woman who moves, at marriage, from her father's to her husband's house. Meanwhile, the house – also the law, marriage (the domestication of a wild animal) – controls the woman's sexuality for her. Architecture, was about the control of (Woman's) sexuality. Marriage was for reproduction and this required a house – marriage could not be conceived of outside a house, and was therefore itself spatial – while 'house' equally meant and still means family, of which the husband was the head, woman the body. The role of the house was therefore to protect the father's claims to his children, by protecting his property/access to his wife.[47]

In the fifteenth-century elite home, the housewife held the key to every room and chest (except that in her master's study, in which was housed the family's records), guarding the house and its nested, enclosed spaces, as her husband guarded her. A bride was trained to be a wife by learning where each possession was meant to be, in which room, what space within a room and in which part of what chest. The husband gave his seal of approval to this classification of spaces, which was in turn naturalised. If something were missing, then it would, supposedly, cry out; the house thereby monitored his possessions and stood in for the husband when he was away. While ordering his belongings, his wife was also classified as one of her husband's possessions – if she was absent, the house would expose that absence. Meanwhile, the doors between their bedrooms, while making their rooms private, differentiated between the sexes on grounds of physical difference. There were 'visible' and 'invisible' walls between husband and wife, part of the invention of the family begun in the fifteenth and dominant by the nineteenth century.[48]

The term 'housewife' itself originated in 1225 and rose in connection with the yeomanry. The housewife was originally the spouse of a husband; a man who had some right/was bound to the house in which they lived and the land which they farmed. Each contributed to the household's economy, the wife through housewifery, the husband through husbandry, though both would have been involved in work in and around the home. The term 'housewifery', was widespread between the thirteenth to the eighteenth century, but gradually changed to 'housework' in the nineteenth century, a change that can be seen as marking the rise of separate spheres ideology.[49] And, though a middle-class housewife never engaged in domestic work herself, even in the nineteenth century she was still expected to know where everything went and to be able to direct the servants.

By the mid-nineteenth century, then, these roles were represented as being entirely and equally 'natural' to both men and women, and in this way were promoted as being common to all classes and civilised peoples. Meanwhile, her innate fragility, placidity and comeliness in artistic and literary texts connoted a woman's respectability, which was in turn elided with her femininity.[50] Images of a wife waiting peacefully for her husband's return, a cottage mother who 'with matron-love, makes daily toil,/delightful by her placid smile' waits with her children to greet their father and receive him back into the refuge of home and family, can therefore be found throughout the genre art of the mid-to late-nineteenth century.[51] While her husband, whose point of view we share as readers, goes out to work, her love and guidance ensures that the 'The Cottage Homes of England,/Are happy homes indeed'. She waits, quite naturally, with the children for his return and thereby secures his home for God and England. Yet, as the quote from Combe suggests, a woman's value as a wife and mother rested not simply on her innate fitness for duty, but also on the 'right-minded', active, achievement of her 'vocation'. Her fitness was hard-won, and required a deal of education – an education Combe promoted.[52]

Different authors produced subtly different messages, interweaving the dominant discourses of the day to produce a complex pattern of argument even when, as here, they more or less agreed on approach. Combe's advice, for instance, drew on the latest medical and statistical evidence, and was clearly aimed at an audience who sought out self-improvement and had quickly come to elevate woman's role within the home as both active and expert. Indeed, though regularly updated and revised, Combe's *The Management of Infancy: physiological and moral, intended chiefly for the use of parents*, (c.1840), maintained its original urgent emphasis that women be educated in the scientific principles of infant management throughout all of its subsequent editions. Smiles, best known for his *Self Help* (1859), equally elevated woman's role and valued self-improvement, but placed less emphasis on the scientific or professional aspect of her vocation than on her virtue and, as Nead says, 'identified the home as the foundation of moral and social improvement'.[53] Gough, on the other hand, who seems to have believed in the innate morality of his subjects, certainly celebrated the mother's 'natural and special vocation', but drew on a more sentimentalised[54] and Anglican imagery to stress above all else the sanctity of a home bounded by love and worship.

During most of the working day, a man's position relative to the domestic sphere was supposedly peripheral and in pictures like F. G. Cotman's *One of the Family* (1880)[55] it is the children and women who form the focus of attention, even on his return. In this particular image of 'old England', the audience is encouraged to view the piece from the family's standpoint as if we too are 'one of the family' and in fact, the audience is physically closer to the family than the head of the household – a behatted and cheerful horseman who can only just be seen behind the door hanging up a rope in the back of the room. In *One of the Family*, the man looks on like we do, so that, though there is some suggestion of an ever-present male point of view, the man himself is actually in shadow. Only the tablecloth, which does not quite reach 'our end' of the table, ensures that we cannot quite step into the scene or take the ploughman's place.

By covering the right-hand side of the picture, in which horseman and horse are to be found, one is effectively left with an illustration of a neat bourgeois home and domesticity at its best. The table is laid for supper with quite pricey crockery and ample food, and two neatly dressed children are tucking in on their best behaviour. A dove-cote can be seen outside the window and a little painted wood panelling around the window-seat; otherwise there are few indicators that this home might actually house a labouring, not middle-class, family. On the right-hand side of the picture, which is much darker, we find many more signs of the rural community to which the home belongs.

When the poor or their homes were painted, a set of pastoral conventions around lightness and darkness came in to play in the eighteenth century; the rich and their dwellings had to be painted in light, while the poor and their cottages remained in the dark. This illuminated the relative social positions of rich and poor, while also linking the two, as both light and dark were dependent on each other. Allowing the deserving poor to come into the light seemed to offer the good poor some comfort and thereby reassured the rich.[56] Cotman has partially adopted this practice, while leaving the children, representative of the future, in the light. The ploughman and horse, plus the home's half-open 'stable' door, make it clear that this particular domestic scene is set in the country. Here the rest of the family are to be found – including another child, a grey-haired woman who clasps a loaf as she cuts a slice, and a younger woman who leans over to feed the horse, plus begging dog. They are obviously well fed, neat and tidy, but their casual postures and bond with the horse make their class clear. Again, Cotman is playing with older conventions here, in which it was common to represent the peasantry as being in close communion with their animals, thereby placing them on the animalistic side of the Enlightenment binary human/animal.[57] The two halves are linked via the three fair-haired, rosy-cheeked children, who form a radiant triangle at the centre of the piece and, along with their mother, catch the most light. Through the mother and children, the cult of the country and the cult of the home meet.[58]

What we can see from both Cotman and Gough is that by the second half of the nineteenth century, domesticity had intersected with both Englishness and the rural idyll. Indeed, the 'very core' of the nineteenth-century ideal of domesticity, as Davidoff, L'Esperance and Newby remark, 'was home *in* a rural village community'.[59] Sentimental poets like Gough were able to draw on a large number of literary and artistic antecedents that generated what Davidoff, L'Esperance and Newby have referred to as the 'Beau Ideal' – defined by the *Oxford English Dictionary* in 1820 as 'that type of beauty or excellence, in which one's idea is realised, the perfect type or model'[60] – of the nineteenth century. In fact, Gough's and many other's lines all owe something to Burn's *The Cotter's Saturday Night* (1786) which, along with other pastoral poetry, often lent its title to the visual arts that went to construct the Ideal:

> His wee bit ingle, blinkin bonnily
> His clean hearth-stane, his thrifty wifie's smile
> The lisping infant prattling on his knee
> Does a' his weary carking cares beguile
> And makes him quite forget his labour and his toil[61]

At this point, the cottage became coded as a feminine space that belonged to women and children and which men only entered when they were returning from the masculine world of work.

Though the sentiments outlined here were often satirised by *Punch*, which contrasted the ideal with the horrors of the 'real' cottage, we find illustrations of old men throughout the nineteenth and into the twentieth century who, having given up the masculine sphere of work altogether, have come home to rest in a final retreat from the world. Examples include William H. Snape's *A Cottage Scene* (1891) in which an old man reads to a girl as they sit by the window surrounded by the paraphernalia of everyday cottage life – cats, geraniums and a tattered picture of Queen Victoria on the wall – and James Hayllar's '*As the Twig is bent, so the Tree is inclined*' of an old smock-frocked man praying with a little girl and *The Invalid* (c.1889) of an old man waiting on his wife. While, in Henry Spernon Tozer's *The Evening Meal* (c.1900–10) an old man and his wife sit quietly by the fire having tea.[62] We also see numerous instances of the head of the labouring family relaxing at home on a Sunday (suggested by his Sunday best) or in the evening (implicit in the family's meal or prayers). Sir David Wilkie's *The Cotter's Saturday Night* (1832–37) – in title and subject certainly based on

Burns' *The Cotter's Saturday Night* – provides us with one such example of 'the sire' of the family turning 'o'er, wi' patriarchal grace,/The big ha'-bible, ance his father's pride'(lines 103–4). Later pieces include Thomas Webster's *Sunday Evening* (no date) in which, again, a man is seen reading to his family; and Arthur Hughes' *Bed-time* (1862) which, with considerable pathos, shows a man utterly exhausted sitting at table as his family say their prayers and retire to bed.[63] And later, Henry Peach Robinson was able to combine the theme of old age with the broader connotations of the day's labours complete in his photograph *Day's Work Done* (1877). Here, the title, age of the sitters and their costuming – they both wear clothes that were only worn by the elderly by this point, despite collectors' interest in preserving such pieces as 'typical' of rural dress[64] – and the postures of man and wife as he reads out of their bible while she knits, combine to suggest that they have reached the end of a laborious but respectable life, as well as the end of a literal working day.[65]

As allegories of patriarchy or religious sentiment, paintings like these served to treat the cottage as a model home, 'Where love is the strong household band,/And God is worshipped with due heed.' For these men the cottage home was represented as a self-contained, leisured, easeful space. Certainly, middle-class men might visit the cottage in an official capacity as illustrated by Luke Fildes' *The Doctor* (1891). Fildes' images of the rural, often published as engravings in the periodical press, were frequently full of pathos, representing middle-class life transposed to the village, and *The Doctor* was suggested to him by the death of his own first child on Christmas day 1877. But, in this (social realist) painting – in which a sick child at the centre of the piece is visited by a troubled physician, its father looking on with a hand on its mother's shoulder as she weeps – the relationships shown are quite different to those depicted in the compositions just mentioned. In *The Doctor*, as in *One of the Family*, for example, the labourer's child forms the centre of attention. But, unlike Cotman's painting, Fildes' is not of a rural family self-possessed and contented in their lot, because the same shaft of light that falls on the child also captures the physician's expression, linking them and making them *both* the focus of the painting. Meanwhile, the father stands in shadow and the mother is traced by a little light from the window. Excluded, the parents are as subject to the expertise of the doctor as their child; all are equally dependent upon his prognosis. This draws in, or rather, legitimises the entry of the painting's urban middle-class audience visually excluded from *One of the Family*. The father's proud stance and attempt to comfort the mother in her distress prompts the audience's sympathy, but that audience knows that he is powerless to effect any change in his child and are encouraged to remain intent upon the doctor's concern for his patient who lies, like little Nell, waiting for resolution.[66]

Again, in direct contrast to the exemplary family men discussed, were those men described as poachers. Represented as having returned home illegitimately – during the working day or with stolen rabbits – these men were pathetically shown to be forever ill at ease, even in their own homes. Of these, Thomas Wade's *The Poacher's Home* (c.1868) and Alfred Downing Fripp's *The Poachers Alarmed* (1844) – originally called *The Poacher's Hut* – are exemplary. In the former, a man glances over his shoulder as he lights his pipe and his children work at preparing some food. In the latter, two young men, having dropped their flagon of beer/cider, hover nervously at the door while one, possibly drunk, continues to sleep near a woman breast-feeding a baby. The latter may have been set in Ireland, but like Wade's piece, highlights the harshness of the game laws for those who were sympathetic.[67] The homeless for their part might also generate compassion but were much more likely to generate fear. Marcus Stone's *Silent Pleading* (1859), of a man and child sleeping rough in the snow and about to be arrested except for the intervention of a passing squire, for one provides an excellent example of pathos. Exhibited at the Royal Academy it carried the quotation 'Him and his innocent child' from Shakespeare's *The Tempest* to drive the point home and was well received. Yet Fred Walker's *The Vagrants* (no date) represents homelessness in a much harsher vein as he employs a social realist mode and places his figures in monumental stance.[68] Migrant labourers or gypsies remained outside of both home and community when men, women and children, but especially men, were supposed to have a 'place', a rank that they knew, a position in the form of paid work and a home.[69] For good family men, old and young alike, the cottage as refuge from the world, was a place of relaxation, not action, their restfulness in turn signifying that they were honest labouring men, good husbands, caring fathers. In this way, the Beau Ideal produced new forms of family-oriented and community-minded masculinity in parallel to the dominant idealising vision of (feminine) domesticity.

This Beau Ideal, Davidoff et al. observe, was thrown up by the search 'for stability and order in a changing society' and was consequently 'an attempt to manage the tensions that arise out of any social hierarchy'.[70] Where the city and the world of commerce intersected as sites of overwhelming aggression, in which a man had to strive to stay ahead of the mob (be it the working-class population that lurked on street corners, or his creditors), the home and family came to constitute an ideal community within which he might find peace. And it was because the communal came to be charged with standing firm against the worst vagaries of capital and the maintenance of older values such as social stability, that the intersection of the cult of the home and the cult of the country became paradigmatic. This model encompassed the gradual shift of political and economic influence away from those with land towards those in industry, the professions and commerce, and also the evolution of the 'two nations', the supposed physical separation of 'home' and 'work' and the effects of urbanisation.[71]

Both home and village community were conceived of as 'organic', as was reinforced by the continuing metonyms of head, heart and hands. Moreover, as 'head' of the household the husband and father was positioned as the equivalent of the local landowner; husband and squire both had the right to make decisions for their subordinates without consultation. In village and home, a full set of limbs/organs was required – which for the middle-class family meant servants (hands), as well as husband, wife and children. Each territory had its own physical and conceptual boundaries that separated it from the world at large and both home and village were characterised as being dependent on knowable face-to-face relations enacted on a daily basis within those bounds. 'The resulting ignorance of the outside world', Davidoff et al. maintain, 'was then used as a reason for not giving them responsibility. They could be ridiculed as country bumpkins, the "little woman", or cute children',[72] which, though it fails to take into account the derision that may still take place even when knowledge of the outside world is acquired, still largely holds true.

There were some differences between the construction of 'home' and 'village'. Firstly, the home, unlike the village as we have seen, was the site of legitimate sexual relations between the 'master' and one of his 'subordinates'. Secondly, the home's separation from the public sphere of economics, politics and competition was much greater than the village's, due to the additional physical barriers of walls, garden and fence/hedge. This second point is closely related to the first, as sexual relationships might only be legitimately enacted within the private sphere. And, as Davidoff et al. observe, this may seem to be at odds with seeing the home as a community, but the home's high degree of privacy was really only ever applicable to or used by the husband/head of the household. It was only masculinity which required such a strict maintenance of identity; the home ensured that the individualism of the husband remained sacrosanct.[73] Otherwise, within the home as in the village, subordinates 'knew their place'. In other words, the concept of community was vested with paternal authority, whether that authority be exercised in the home or on the estate, and became the ideal model for working through the new social relations that were emerging as a result of industrialisation.

Because the Beau Ideal was in origin a bourgeois idyll, as Davidoff et al. observe, it is difficult to know the extent to which the working class accepted the cult of the home, or indeed the cult of the country. But, in the form of the married woman ideally giving up paid work to look after her family, we can see that it was appropriated – at least in part – as an element within working-class definitions of respectability.[74] This was widespread enough to result in numerous campaigns for a 'bread-winning wage' by unions, including the National Agricultural Labourers' Union,[75] in the second half of the century, while Martha Vicinus has outlined the extent to which the industrial working class partly coped with urbanisation by turning to increasingly nostalgic visions of the rural that evoked the idea of home as refuge.[76] By the end of the nineteenth century, the country cottage, as Beau Ideal, had therefore probably become as potent an image for the working as it had for the middle class.

Working-class dialect poets – and those like Gough who emulated them – celebrated domesticity by highlighting the many pleasures of returning to a spotless, warm and, above all, hospitable home. But, as Susan Zlotnick notes, the attraction of domesticity lay not just in its comforts. It was the 'mythic quality of the moment, its historical indeterminateness',[77] the way in which it had the power to banish the gloom of the industrial present, that was key to its success among the working, not just the middle, class. The dialect poets of the mid-nineteenth century rarely paid attention to the industrial milieu in which they wrote. Zlotnick goes on to argue: 'In the closed world of dialect domesticity, the home became not only an antidote to modernity but the repository of working-class traditions, as if the lost village community, abandoned in the nascent moments of industrialisation, had been resurrected inside the worker's cottage.'[78] Certainly, the dialect poets were aware of the mundane minutiae of life for the poor and therefore adapted the cult of domesticity to the 'realities' of working-class life, but, according to Zlotnick, in the end 'the ideal seems to have held emotional and imaginative sway over the British working classes'.[79] At the same time, the visual arts became a discursive site within which the home was 'domesticated'; 'emptied of its association with work',[80] and became instead a symbolic haven or shelter from the world which contained nothing but leisure, accord and quiet family moments. The domestic scenes found in pieces like *One of the Family* belong to a point of interchange between the dominant forms of the eighteenth century, which had attempted to hide many social issues, and the artistic era of the Victorian period in which the distanced representation of painful and complex social issues became generalised. Through art the countryside became 'a universal stage on which the dramas of poverty and financial ruin, sexual desire and transgression, illness and death could be played out to their fullest'.[81] Urban and industrial problems could be dealt with via representations of the countryside,[82] meanwhile, the new middle class were seeking to assert their own taste in the production and meaning of art and to appropriate the cultural capital of the old elite; the relationship between culture and class was contested.

As they battled it out through the 1840s to the 1860s, as accessibility to art and the potential universalism of its appeal were debated, middle-class patronage and modern-life subjects came to be seen by both sides as the defining features of modern art. The Royal Academy's creation of a separate category of paintings in 1852, 'Domestic Pictures', to accommodate the increasing number of homely scenes it was being offered, therefore marked a shift in the relative positions of 'high' academic art, as patronised by the aristocracy and landed classes, and the new British school favoured by the emergent bourgeoisie. Hence, as well as possibly performing an ideological function for the urban middle class, wherein it provided them with a repository of ideas through which urban experience was perceived – simultaneously supplying the urban bourgeoisie with the myths to sustain itself[83] – it should be born in mind that, in tackling everyday domestic subjects, art equally had a role to play in the struggle of the middle class for cultural dominance.[84] As Nead points out: 'Modern life painting was perceived as middle-class art. It was criticised for being vulgar and undiscriminating and was celebrated for its patriotism and morality – it could teach the public and its appeal was universal. These debates surrounded the representation of femininity in nineteenth-century art.'[85] The inclusion of 'human incidents' like those seen in *One of the Family* meant that many rural paintings were deemed to be especially appealing as was argued, re farmyard scenes, by Huish, editor of Allingham's collection *Happy England* (1903).[86] Moreover, this way of seeing leapt discourses and once universalised, was prevalent enough to be treated as an observable indicator of the moral and physical welfare of the agricultural labourer. The fact that a visitor could leave a cottage in Northumberland realising that 'he has been in the presence of a thoughtful, contented, and unselfish woman' who was free to focus on her 'home duties' went a long way to convincing Joseph Henley that these women 'are not to be excelled as wives and mothers',[87] which in turn suggested that there was no need for reform when it came to women's paid employment in that county. In 1893 it was again noted, this time by Wilson Fox, that married women did not work in Northumberland and that, therefore, the children 'have the advantage of their mother's care at home, and the husband has the comfort of a tidy house and properly cooked meals'.[88] In fact, a woman's adeptness at housework and childcare were used throughout every report on women's work in agriculture and all other reports on the condition of the agricultural labourer – always figured as an adult male – to measure both her respectability and her husband's well-being. This was Beau Ideal in action.

NATURE VS. CULTURE

According to the most common images of rural life, the cottage was full of shining – either pewter or copper – pots and pans, slip-ware jugs and bowls, and children playing on a freshly-swept or newly-scrubbed brick floor. Often there is a blazing hearth in a crisp-blacked grate, on which a pot or kettle boils, and over which a simply-decorated mantel hangs. If there is no fire, this is because the picture hopes to capture 'summer's smile', in which case bright light streams in through a large, often open, window or door, (though there was often still a glowing fire, even in high summer). There is nearly always some kind of fuel by the fireplace, and a rug or two. Cats are a common feature, as are small caged birds, vases of flowers, pot plants, floral prints, and pictures of the King/Queen or other appropriate, usually biblical, subjects. The furniture is always simple, but sturdy, even when sparse. If the whole family is present, they are often, as in Cotman's picture, taking a meal, and if this is the case, there is always plenty of good, simple food on the table, itself usually covered in a rudimentary yet clean white cloth. It is normally apparent that the whole family have to socialise within one room, which serves as kitchen, dining room and parlour, yet everyone has room to move about, read, talk, do some small work, play, or warm themselves by the fire. We see children reading, prayers being said, the bible being studied, stories being told, romantic interludes, and mothers with new-born children. In Thomas Faed's *Home and the Homeless* (1856) there is even room enough for the family to take in some strangers, who crouch in a darkened corner more for effect than necessity.[89]

In these pictures, the hustle and bustle of daily life is given deliberate significance. Each detail is vested with its own contingent meaning. The limited quarters of the cottage home signify communality and mutual sympathy, not poverty. The work being done connotes industry. Whitewashed walls and well-scrubbed floor demonstrate the housewife's virtue; we know the wife is 'thrifty' because we can see the results of her work. Cats and birds secure the cottage's domesticity; food on the table and happy children playing suggest contentment. However, each material object within the cottage can be read on several different levels. Shining pots and pans certainly denote cleanliness and therefore connote industriousness, good housekeeping, and thereby the thrift of the housewife and the (moral as well as literal) orderliness of the family, yet as tools they also delineate what could and could not be achieved by the housewife when she cooked. Household tools like these could command their users. If one became worn, the housewife would have to get it patched by a passing craftsman or the local smithy, thereby linking her housework into the wider economy. Whereas today – if she actually has her copper pots in use at all, most now being purely decorative rather than functional – she would probably go and buy a new one. As Swartz Cowan points out, 'the history of household technology cannot be written without the history of the social and economic institutions that have affected the character and the availability of the tools with which housework is done',[90] because these tools 'are not passive instruments, confined to doing our bidding, [they] have a life of their own'.[91]

Housekeeping belongs to the wider economic context and though one might not expect this to appear in art or literature, given the ideological separation of the domestic from the public sphere, there are in fact genre pieces illustrating many of the interactions that regularly took place between local women and traders. In Myles Birket Foster's *The China Pedlar* (no date), for instance, a woman displays her wares on the road outside the cottage tempting the inhabitants – a young woman holding a baby, three older children and a man who hovers in the background at the door – to buy her blue and white. While in his *The Chair Mender* (no date) a man sits at a cottage gate mending the rush-weave on a chair seat and a young woman, who holds a baby, and two girls look on.[92] These scenes, together with other (high art) representations of village incidents such as Fildes' *The Village Wedding* (1883)[93] helped create a sense of the embeddedness of, and naturalised the face-to-face relations that took place within, the organic community. In fact, if we move outside, we find that the exterior of the cottage is, unsurprisingly, as significant as the interior in generating a sense of this embeddedness. To start with, it is always already old. The walls are usually made of timber, sometimes covered over in plaster, or filled in with brick. The roof might be tiled, but is often thatch, and the windows are frequently diamond-paned. Doors, and often windows, are usually open and surrounded by vines or roses growing up from the garden. The garden itself usually contains a variety of objects, not just plants, as we will see. Through such representations, the cottage homes of England were treated as belonging to the natural and, again, as being an essential part of their communities. Each element connotes an age-old, organic linkage between the (native) soil of the garden and the (vernacular) structure of the house, between the foundations and the building, as if it had grown up out of the land on which it stands. In the nineteenth century the cottage, though now a home with inhabitants, continued to *belong* within and to its landscape, it and everything it contained remained organically, inherently English.

Cottage women, like their husbands, had a 'place', which they were expected to know and to which they naturally and timelessly belonged. Moreover, the cottage woman came to personify that place called home.[94] Often situated near, rather than inside their cottages in genre art, it was enough for a woman to be present for the place being represented to become a home and there was never any doubt that she would always be there, waiting. That was the certainty sought by the Beau Ideal. Fildes' *The Farmer's Daughter* (1868)[95] like many stands just inside the wall of the farm garden, watched by a cat on a chair in the house. She genteelly feeds her fowl, which mill around just beyond the gate. Her garden blooms as an extension of her home, and though active, her work comes within the bounds of household management. For her at least, the garden path leads back through the open door into the house, not out into the road. She stays firmly within the bounds of the domestic sphere, signified by the garden wall. The farmer's daughter as a woman who never really steps outside the domestic/into the public sphere is idealised. Her position, it seems, will never vary, her identity is unchanging; there is an illusion of stasis, as if she were pinned to the page, kept in her place. Her life is bounded and enclosed by a series of nostalgic social relations, which are made to seem timeless. Meanwhile, the garden itself is worth a second look. It is flourishing, full of tall flowers, with a backdrop of climbers, which are beginning to meld with the building, which also has a young rose bush starting to grow up by the door. Like the home, it is a haven, a sanctuary that guarantees eternal peace and stability. The fecundity we see in any cottage garden picture promises to return through the course of the seasons and the actions of those figures placed within it.

Because the garden in *The Farmer's Daughter* is pleasant, prosperous and introspective, and connotes self-contained, contented thriftiness, we know that the interior of the house is clean, tidy, neat, and decorated with shining pots and pans. It is an ideal of domesticity that can contain growth within the bounds of ongoing, stable, organic social relations. Again, the farmer's daughter is fixed, pinned within these relations. She, like the rose, may grow up, but she will always be perfect. Parallel to this, the house itself is absorbed by the process of growth into the garden and Nature, while the garden, through the expansion of the climbers, will enter the house. This was something that was actively sought by nineteenth-century architects, who wanted to bring Nature into the houses they designed through the use of large windows, pot plants and conservatories. Where the large-scale formal garden had once been the site of controlled Nature and public display, i.e. the extension of Culture out from the house into the landscape, by the Victorian period the garden had become that much more homely, private and vernacular. And in generic representations of country life, the doors that always stood open onto perpetual summer, as if the garden was simply another room in the house, helped this reversal.[96]

This system of representation had special significance for the construction of femininity in the Victorian period and helps explain why the cottage garden came to be seen as an innately domestic space in the nineteenth century. Sherry B. Ortner has shown that the construction of gender centred on the polarity of Culture vs. Nature at this time. The feminine was seen to be closer to or having a greater affinity with Nature than the masculine, so the domestic sphere, as female space, was also seen to be more natural than the Cultured public sphere in which men operated. This had and still has political implications as both the woman and the cottage garden can take on equally compensatory or transcendent and evil aspects via this marginal status. The woman can be seductive and corrupting as well as morally pure; the enclosed, introverted cottage garden, like a house, can become a prison as well as a sanctuary. Both Woman and cottage garden are therefore in a position where they are inferior to Culture, restricted and restricting because they mediate between Nature and Culture, or inverted because of their ambiguity. There are key issues here for the spatial construction of Woman's role, and for the representation of domestic pastoral. If, as Ortner suggests, women mediate between Nature and Culture, by socialising children for example, and are therefore subject to contradictory meanings within this dynamic in which they act to ring-fence a small enclosure of Culture within a wilderness of Nature, then they are clearly acting out the same role as that associated with a home in the country. The wall around a cottage garden stands, or mediates, between Nature and Culture; it creates a small, defensive clearing of Culture, or tamed Nature, as a haven within the wilderness of the wider world.[97] Similarly, we can relate this to Massey's theory of the polarised relationship of dead Space, associated with the feminine, and active Time, associated with the masculine. For the girl in *The Farmer's Daughter* the passage of time is meaningless, she will stay in her place, her movement is and always will be arrested.

But, the farmer's daughter's position is also ambiguous and therefore unstable, she must move at some point. She occupies a liminal position between public and private, between Culture and Nature. She is not actually inside her home, or even her garden, she is somewhere in between, on the margins where public (Cultural) and private (Natural) space intersect. Though her position is meant to seem entirely peaceful and natural, the farmer's daughter stands on the threshold of adulthood, her garden and the world beyond – she is about to cross over the boundary between innocence and experience, and as discussed in Chapter 4 her class identity is blurred. She must at some point go to market, she may not even grow up there in the end, if competition from capitalist agriculture, or agricultural depression drives her father's farm out of business. The picture tries to recreate the division between the spatial and the temporal by freezing the woman into the deadness of space – where no action can or will happen – even as she grows up. But, though her garden seems to unite Nature and Culture in a domestic idyll, as a place its identity depends on the history it is given and on how we may care to read it. Like other places, it never achieves, can never achieve its identity; its character is always in formation, it is fluid.[98] The farmer's daughter's position is also, therefore, dynamic; she can therefore break her bounds.

What we are also interested in here, however, is the *act* of enclosure; the use of the garden wall as boundary through which the labourer returns and through which his wife or daughter never steps. And what should be borne in mind here is that within the codes of nineteenth-century genre painting, the wall, hedge[99] or fence provided an image of a physical and an ideological boundary between (sexual) innocence and experience, between wider social relations and the individual family unit, and between the competitive, masculine, world of work and the comfortable, feminine, world of domesticity. As such it was often used in courtship scenes, which had their own, frequently heady, implications of egress and congress. In Frederick Smallfield's Pre-Raphaelite-influenced *Early Lovers* (1858) for instance, we see a young girl sitting at a stile, gazing up into the eyes of and clasping hands with her young man as he ventures to climb over. Early summer blooms – dog roses, honeysuckle, bluebells and vetch – surround the two, the sky suggesting an early-morning meeting. Charles Keene, one of *Punch's* regular cartoonists, similarly represented the population of the countryside (if in a comic vein) in 1867 by parodying this kind of sweet rural courtship.[100] It was thus the garden wall/gate that secured the cultured continence and domesticity of the cottage's inhabitants. The 'mellowed wall', picket fence or privet hedge demarcated the boundaries of their 'home' and reassured a Victorian middle-class audience that within they would find stability, security and a timeless backyard-England. Because of this, according to Eleanor Rhode who was writing nostalgically in the 1930s, cottage gardens were intrinsically associated

> in one's memories with cathedral and remote little country towns – gardens with *mellowed walls* where the broad, generous beds were full of fine old hardy plants and flowers with rich soft colours and delicious scents and hoary with traditions of centuries. Each garden had its characteristic atmosphere and the owner knew every tree and flower as a shepherd knows his sheep. It is to those gardeners and to cottagers that we owe the preservation of many treasures among the old herbaceous plants despised by the enthusiastic admirers of bedding-out plants.[101] [my emphasis]

Here, every cottage garden is a unique space/place, while their historical authenticity is particularly emphasised in an evocative description of Englishness and vernacular domesticity. Their ability to remain distinct and to preserve treasures is dependent on each gardener's remote old-fashionedness and each garden's 'mellowed walls'. The walls around each cottage garden stand, or mediate between Nature and Culture; the gardens themselves create a small, defensive clearing of Culture, or Nature tamed, as a haven within the wilderness of the wider world.[102] The stress is on the peace and tranquillity of the country, its homeliness and privacy. It is this that the Beau Ideal captured. But, this is also a feminine Englishness, one less interested in the heroic exploits of official masculinity centred on 'Great Britain' and 'more inward-looking, more domestic and more private'.[103]

The cottage garden was accordingly constructed as an idealised, leisured and feminine space, which had little or nothing to do with the masculine world of politics or (paid) work. Its 'mellowed' walls were treated as a frame for domesticity. Its open gate invited the casual visitor from the village to step on through, thereby linking the cottage to the wider community, and called the husband back home to his wife and family while they waited patiently inside.

In Edwin Cockburn's *The Return from Market* (no date),[104] for instance, we see an agricultural labourer step through his garden gate to be greeted by his child, while its mother holds up a baby and a toddler stands on tiptoe to see him out of the cottage window. That window physically determines that the woman's sphere is within the home while the man's is outside. 'Woman', as Nead points out, 'is shown fulfilling her natural roles of wife and mother within the natural unit of the family home, situated in the natural domain of the countryside'.[105]

However, what we can also see in the eldest child's rush to greet its father is that the conceptual boundary of the 'home' extended out into the garden and only actually finished at the picket fence. The labourer reaches 'home' and safely escapes the grasp of capital before he even reaches the cottage door. By the late-nineteenth century the cottage homes of England had come to provide an idyllic focus for the cult of domesticity, set in an equally idyllic, i.e. still picturesque countryside valued for its healthfulness and moral purity. Within these largely nostalgic and paternalistic constructions of rural felicity, comfort – which could be politically loaded[106] – was seen as a prerequisite to happiness, while neatness and cleanliness became indicators of the moral superiority, physical health and industriousness of the inhabitants. A degree of contentedness that could thwart revolt was sought, at least in art if not in life,[107] and, as Gough's 'The Cottage Homes of England' (1876) suggests, that contentedness to a large degree rested on the thrift, diligence and continence of the cottager's waiting wife.

NOTES

1. B. Gough, 'The Cottage Homes of England' in *Songs for British Workmen* (London, 1876), p. 42. Similar poems by Gough (1805–77), who was keen to promote the moral well-being of the poor through domestic verse as well as good deeds, can be found in *Kentish Lyrics: sacred, rural and miscellaneous* (London, 1867).
2. S. Pugh, 'Received ideas on pastoral' in Mosser M. and Teyssot G. (eds), *The History of Garden Design: the western tradition from the renaissance to the present day* (London, 1991), p. 253.
3. M. Reed, *The Landscape of Britain: from the beginnings to 1914* (London, 1990), pp. 251–3.
4. R. Williams, *The Country and the City* (London, [1972] 1985), p. 296.
5. Pugh, 'Received ideas', p. 253.
6. Pugh, 'Received ideas', p. 253.
7. Pugh, 'Received ideas', p. 256; cf. P. Tristram, *Living Space in Fact and Fiction* (London, 1989).
8. J. Ballie, *An Essay on the Sublime* (1747), quoted in Fred Botting, *Gothic* (London and New York, 1996), p. 40.
9. E. Burke, *A Philosophical Enquiry into the Origin of Our Ideas of the Sublime and Beautiful* (London, 1757), p. 36.
10. Pugh, 'Received ideas', p. 255.
11. The term 'Gothic' initially developed in the eighteenth century as a criticism of medieval architecture. It emerged just as new conceptions of the bourgeois home as a site of comfort and privacy were developing in connection with the creation of new forms of individuality. L. Weissberg, 'Gothic spaces' in V. Sage and A. Lloyd Smith (eds), *Modern Gothic: a reader* (Manchester, 1996), pp. 104–5.
12. Charles Bryant, quoted in M. Hoyles, *Bread and Roses: gardening books from 1560–1960*, Vol. 2, (London, 1995), p. 79. Nonetheless, it was still thought

best by some to help women along a little. 'Yet,' Bryant goes on to ask, 'where are the Ladies who have made any great progress in the scientific knowledge of plants? They certainly are as capable as the opposite sex. But where are the books proper for teaching them?' What was needed, he thought, was a text that simplified the terms. Bryant's *A Dictionary of the Ornamental Trees, Shrubs, and Plants, Most Commonly Cultivated in the Plantations, Gardens, and Stoves of Great Britain* (1790) 'intended for the use of ladies' aimed to do exactly this. Priscilla Wakefield, a Quaker, drew on this knowledge to write for young people (*Introduction to Botany* (1796)) and in a later text (*Reflections on the Present Condition of the Female Sex* (1798)) suggested ladies ought to take up gardening (supervision) as a means of supporting themselves if left without a husband or father.

13 So much has been written on the cultural, political and economic intersection of the picturesque and the rise of large-scale capitalist agriculture 1730–1840 since the publication of Raymond Williams' *The Country and the City* that it can now virtually be taken as a given, but Williams' work has been added to. John Barrell, for instance, has considered changing representations of the rural poor in light of this shift in his *The Dark Side of the Landscape: the rural poor in English painting 1730–1840* (Cambridge, 1980). And Stephen Daniels in *Fields of Vision: landscape imagery and national identity in England and the United States* (Cambridge, 1993), has subsequently drawn attention to the large number of picturesque and agricultural 'improvements' that were funded and informed by colonialism, and the ways in which they have contributed to the formation and defence of national identity.

14 See Daniels, *Fields of Vision* for a valuable analysis of the formation of English national identity, imperialism and representations of the landscape, and the ongoing impact of the picturesque.

15 Karen Landman. See paper delivered to *Gendered Landscapes: an interdisciplinary exploration of past place and space* conference held at Penn State University, USA, 29 May–1 June 1999.

16 A. Kolodny, *The Land Before Her: fantasy and experience of the American frontiers, 1630–1860* (Chapel Hill and London, 1984), p. 96.

17 P. Tristram, *Living Space in Fact and Fiction* (London, 1989), pp. 73–5.

18 John Nash (1752–1835) was the architect who laid out Regent's Park, Regent Street, Carlton House Terrace, Trafalgar Square and St James's Park, and designed Marble Arch, in London. He also worked for the Prince Regent in rebuilding Brighton Pavilion and turning Buckingham House into Buckingham Palace.

19 Reed, *The Landscape of Britain*, p. 251.

20 See J. Malton, *Essay on British Cottage Architecture*, (London, 1798).

21 Tristram, *Living Space*, pp. 205–9.

22 Daniels, *Fields of Vision*, p. 6.

23 Daniels, *Fields of Vision*, p. 8.

24 P. Oliver, *English Cottages and Small Farmhouses: a study of vernacular shelter* (London, 1975), pp. 5, 23, 27. In 1975, most cottages and small farmhouses were not listed.

25 S. Brand, *How Buildings Learn: what happens after they're built* (London, 1997), p. 5.

26 R. J. Lawrence, *Housing, Dwellings and Homes: design, theory, research and practice* (Chichester, 1987), pp. 18–19, 25–31, 54; Cf. Tristram, *Living Space*.

27 Lawrence, *Housing, Dwellings and Homes*, pp. 31–2.

28 It was John Ruskin (1819 1900), a supporter of the Gothic and the picturesque, who finally linked the picturesque to the sublime in his essay 'The poetry of

architecture; or the architecture of the nations of Europe considered in its association with natural scenery and national character' in the *Architectural Magazine*, 1837–8.
29 Tristram, *Living Space*, pp. 73–4, 83.
30 S. M. Gaskell, *Model Housing: from the Great Exhibition to the Festival of Britain* (London and New York, 1987), p. 6.
31 L. Davidoff, J. L'Esperance and H. Newby, 'Landscape with figures: home and community in English society' in Mitchell, J. and Oakley, A. (eds), *The Rights and Wrongs of Women* (Harmondsworth, 1986), pp. 144–5, 170–5; Tristram, *Living Space*, p. 115. There is a large body of material on the history of the model village. Suggested reading includes: Gaskell, *Model Housing*; G. Darley, *Villages of Vision* (London, 1975); M. Havinden, 'The model village' in Mingay G. E., (ed.), *The Rural Idyll* (London and New York, 1989).
32 V. Parker, *The English House in the Nineteenth Century* (London, 1970), pp. 26–8.
33 Davidoff et al., 'Landscape', p. 153.
34 Lawrence, *Housing, Dwellings and Homes*, pp. 18–54.
35 Terms adapted from Brand, *How Buildings Learn*, p. 158.
36 F. Hemans, 'The Homes of England' in Ashfield, A. (ed.), *Romantic Women Poets 1770–1838* (Manchester, 1997), p. 124.
37 Weissberg, 'Gothic spaces', p. 106.
38 G. Rose, *Feminism and Geography: the limits of geographical knowledge* (Cambridge, 1993), pp. 53–5.
39 K. Soper, *What is Nature? Culture, politics and the non-human* (Oxford, 1995), p. 99.
40 Samuel Smiles was a biographer and essayist, a doctor and a journalist. He was a well-known proponent of self-reliance and industriousness, and his best-known work is *Self-Help: with illustrations of character and conduct* (1859).
41 S. Smiles, *Life and Labour: or characteristics of men of industry, cultures and genius* (London, [1887] 1910), p. 213.
42 Andrew Combe M. D., with his brother George Combe, is best known today as an expert on phrenology, but he was also a populariser of medical knowledge.
43 A. Combe, *The Management of Infancy: physiological and moral, intended chiefly for the use of parents* (London, [c.1840] 1860), p. 57.
44 Gough, *Songs*, p. vii.
45 Rev. T. H. Walker, *Good Servants, Good Wives and Happy Homes: illustrated by a series of characters and events sketched from actual life* (London, [1862] sixth edition 1888). See Preface.
46 M. Wigley, 'Untitled: the housing of gender' in Colomina, B. (ed.), *Sexuality and Space* (Princeton, 1992), p. 332.
47 Wigley, 'Untitled', pp. 332–9.
48 Wigley, 'Untitled', pp. 340–4, 348.
49 R. Swartz Cowan, *More Work for Mother: the ironies of household technology from the open hearth to the microwave* (London, 1989), pp. 16–18.
50 There is now a large body of material on the history of separate spheres ideology and what it meant for both men and women of different classes in the nineteenth century. See L. Nead, *Myths of Sexuality: representations of women in Victorian Britain* (Oxford, 1988); L. Davidoff and C. Hall, *Family Fortunes: men and women of the English middle class 1780–1850* (London, 1987); M. Poovey, *Uneven Developments: the ideological work of gender in mid-Victorian England* (London, 1989); J. Goode 'Women and the literary text' in Mitchell, J. and Oakley, A. (eds), *The Rights and Wrongs of Women* (Harmondsworth, 1986); C.

Hall, *White, Male and Middle Class: explorations in feminism and history* (Cambridge, 1992).
51 For example, Joseph Clark's *The Labourer's Welcome*, n.d., reproduced in Nead, *Myths*, in which a man returning from work can just be seen walking through the door in a mirror hanging above his wife's head.
52 A man's value as a husband and as an individual rested, similarly, on the active and successful prosecution of his profession. See Hall, *White, Male and Middle Class*.
53 Nead, *Myths*, p. 33.
54 In the eighteenth century, 'sentiment' (sensibility) embodied a loose philosophy of benevolence and a belief that the natural emotions (sentiments) were good, kindly and innocent, in opposition to culture which was seen as a corrupting force. By the Victorian period, however, writers like Hannah Moore, Mary Wollstonecraft and Jane Austen had attacked it so that the word 'sentimental' came to develop its current associations with artificial, forced and self-indulgent feelings.
55 F. G. Cotman (1850–1920), *One of the Family*, 1880; Walker Art Gallery, Liverpool (Medici Society postcard).
56 See Barrell, *Dark Side*.
57 See R. R. and C. R. Brettell, *Painters and Peasants in the Nineteenth Century* (Geneva, 1983).
58 Domesticity is often referred to by critics as 'the cult of the home'. Similarly, Englishness and the rural idyll might be called 'the cult of the country' – this term is used by J. Marsh in *Back to the Land: the pastoral impulse in Victorian England from 1880 to 1914* (London, Melbourne and New York, 1982).
59 Davidoff et al., 'Landscape', p. 140.
60 Cited by Davidoff et al., 'Landscape', p. 144.
61 R. Burns, *Poems chiefly in the Scottish Dialect* (1786). Burns (1759–96) was celebrated as 'a heaven-taught ploughman' by Henry Mackenzie but was better labelled 'self-taught'. He became a well-known and popular poet thanks to this volume.
62 William H. Snape (working 1885–92), *A Cottage Scene*, 1891, oil, Christopher Wood Gallery. James Hayllar (1829–1920), 'As the Twig is bent, so the Tree is inclined', n.d., oil, Christopher Wood Gallery; and *The Invalid*, c.1889, oil, City of Nottingham Museums: Castle Museum and Art Gallery. Henry Spernon Tozer (working 1900–10), *The Evening Meal*, n.d., watercolour, Sotheby's Bond Street. All bar *The Invalid* are reproduced in C. Wood, *Paradise Lost: paintings of English country life and landscape, 1850–1914* (London, [1988] 1993). *The Invalid* is reproduced in C. Payne, *Rustic Simplicity: scenes of cottage life in nineteenth-century British art* (Nottingham, 1998).
63 Sir David Wilkie (1785–1841), *The Cotter's Saturday Night*, 1832–37, oil, Glasgow Museums: Art Gallery and Museum, Kelvingrove, reproduced in Payne, *Rustic Simplicity*. Thomas Webster (1800–86), *Sunday Evening*, n.d., oil, Proby Collection, Elton Hall, reproduced in Wood, *Paradise Lost*. Arthur Hughes (1832–1915), *Bed-time* exhibited 1862, oil, Harris Art Gallery, Preston.
64 R. Worth, 'Rural labouring dress: the boundaries of representation', paper delivered to *The Dress of the Poor 1750–1900: Old and New Perspectives* conference held at Oxford Brookes University, 27 November 1999.
65 Henry Peach Robinson, *Day's Work Done*, taken 1877, photograph, Royal Photographic Society of Great Britain.
66 Sir Samuel Luke Fildes (1843 1927), *The Doctor*, 1891, oil, Tate Gallery, reproduced in Wood, *Paradise Lost*.

67 Thomas Wade (1828–91), *The Poacher's Home*, exhibited 1868, oil, Harris Museum and Art Gallery, Preston. Alfred Downing Fripp (1822–95), *The Poachers Alarmed*, 1844, pencil and watercolour, The Whitworth Art Gallery: University of Manchester. Both reproduced in and discussed by Payne, *Rustic Simplicity*, pp. 68–9, 81–2.
68 Marcus Stone (1840–1921), *Silent Pleading*, 1859, oil, Calderdale Museums, Halifax. Fred Walker (1840–75), *The Vagrants*, n.d., oil, Tate Gallery. Both reproduced in and discussed by Wood, *Paradise Lost*, pp. 105, 125–6.
69 A. Howkins, *Reshaping Rural England: a social history 1850–1925* (London, 1991), p. 97.
70 Davidoff et al., 'Landscape', p. 146.
71 Davidoff et al., 'Landscape', p. 146.
72 Davidoff et al., 'Landscape', p. 144.
73 Davidoff et al., 'Landscape', pp. 140–1. Hall, *White, Male and Middle Class*, pp. 256–8.
74 Davidoff et al., 'Landscape', p. 169.
75 For a discussion of their attitude to women's agricultural work, see K. Sayer, *Women of the Fields: representations of rural women in the nineteenth century* (Manchester, 1995).
76 M. Vicinus, 'Literary voices of an industrial town, Manchester, 1810–70' in Dyos, H. J. and Wolff, M. (eds), *The Victorian City: images and realities* (London, 1973). This nostalgia for the lost rural community was also influential in cultivating socialist dreams of going 'back to the land'. Cf. Marsh, *Back to the Land*.
77 S. Zlotnick, '"A thousand times I'd be a factory girl": dialect, domesticity, and working-class women's poetry in Victorian Britain', *Victorian Studies* (Autumn 1991), p. 10.
78 Zlotnick, 'A thousand times', pp. 10–11.
79 Zlotnick, 'A thousand times', p. 16.
80 Nead, *Myths*, p. 32.
81 A. Bermingham, *Landscape and Ideology: the English rustic tradition, 1740–1860* (London, 1986), p. 184.
82 Bermingham, *Landscape*, pp. 191–3.
83 Bermingham, *Landscape*, p. 193.
84 Nead, *Myths*, pp. 165–8.
85 Nead, *Myths*, p. 168.
86 M. B. Huish (ed.), *Happy England* (London, 1903), p. 150.
87 'Reports from the commissioners on the employment of children, young persons and women in agriculture' *Parliamentary Papers* (*PP*), 1867–70, pp. 54, 58.
88 'Reports from the Royal Commission on labour', *PP*, 1892–94, p. 55. In the reports on women and children's work, in all industries, there was often a metonymic slippage between woman and child.
89 Thomas Faed (1826–1900), *Home and the Homeless*, 1856, oil, National Gallery of Scotland. Reproduced in and discussed by Payne, *Rustic Simplicity*, pp. 64–5.
90 Swartz Cowan, *More Work for Mother*, p. 11.
91 Swartz Cowan, *More Work for Mother*, pp. 9–10.
92 Myles Birket Foster (1825–99), *The China Pedlar*, n.d., watercolour, Fine Art Photographic Library; and *The Chair Mender*, n.d., watercolour, Bridgeman Art Library/Victoria and Albert Museum. Both reproduced in Wood, *Paradise Lost*.
93 Sir Samuel Luke Fildes (1843–1927), *The Village Wedding*, 1883, oil, the Manney Collection, reproduced in Wood, *Paradise Lost*.
94 D. Massey, *Space, Place and Gender* (Cambridge, 1994), pp. 10–11.

48 Country cottages

95 Sir Samuel Luke Fildes (1843–1927), *The Farmer's Daughter*, c.1868, engraving, published in the *Sunday Magazine* 1868. NB 'farm' and 'cottage' were often confused, a slippage that will be discussed in a subsequent chapter.
96 Tristram, *Living Space*, pp. 239–43.
97 S. B. Ortner, 'Is female to male as nature is to culture?' in Mitchelle, Z. et al. (eds), *Woman, Culture and Society* (Stanford, 1974), pp. 67–87.
98 D. Massey, 'Places and their pasts', *History Workshop Journal*, No. 39, p. 186.
99 Fast-growing quick or privet hedges were commonly used to demarcate a piece of newly-enclosed ground by labourers who wished to become cottagers with right of settlement.
100 Frederick Smallfield (1829–1915), *Early Lovers*, 1858, oil, Manchester City Art Gallery, reproduced in Wood, *Paradise Lost*. Cf. Brettell, *Painters and Peasants* and Sayer, *Women of the Fields* on images of women who stand near farm gates.
101 Quoted in M. Hoyles, *The Story of Gardening* (London, 1991), p. 214.
102 Ortner, 'Is female to male', pp. 67–87.
103 Alison Light, quoted in J. Taylor, *A Dream of England: landscape, photography and the tourist's imagination* (Manchester, 1994), p. 123.
104 Edwin Cockburn, *The Return from Market*, n.d., reproduced in Nead, *Myths*.
105 Nead, *Myths*, p. 42.
106 A commentator in the *Labourers' Union Chronicle*, concluded one piece by saying, 'We now take our leave of the Royal Academy, sincerely hoping that another year we may see some comfortable cottages.' *Labourers' Union Chronicle* (28 June 1873), pp. 2–3.
107 See Barrell, *Dark Side*.

CHAPTER 2

The imperfect home

A stranger cannot enter the village without being struck with surprise at its wretched and desolate condition. Look where he may, he sees little else but thatched roofs – old, rotten, and shapeless – full of holes and overgrown with weeds; windows sometimes patched with rags, and sometimes plastered over with clay; the walls, which are nearly all of clay, full of cracks and crannies; and sheds and outhouses – where there are any – looking as if they had been overgrown very early in the present century, and left in the hopeless confusion in which they fell.
(*Norfolk News*, 1863–64)[1]

I think we deserve to be beaten out of our beautiful houses with a scourge of small cords – all of us who let tenants live in such sites as we see around us. Life in cottages might be happier than ours, if they were real houses fit for human beings from whom we expect duties and affections . . . oh what a happiness it would be to set the pattern about here! I think, instead of Lazarus at the gate, we should put the pig-sty cottages outside the park gate.
(George Eliot, *Middlemarch*, 1871–72)[2]

THE 'QUESTION OF THE HOUR'

Domestic pastoral provided the Victorian middle class with a cognitive map, a moral conscience that permitted their constant re-assessment of the ever more fluid and competitive 'real world' in which they were engaged. As Parker suggests, the history of housing broadly reflects cultural, economic, even political change and the houses of the nineteenth-century bourgeoisie, their design and siting, reflected the changing needs of the Victorian family, not just its resources, but also its status and ideals. Hence, whereas in the first half of the century, fashionable society had tended to adopt the older forms of classical architecture, new designs suited to a new elite began to emerge from the early 1850s. By the end of the century the middle class aspired to a 'modest, compact semi-detached suburban house with picturesque tiled roof and mullioned bay windows, set in leafy surroundings of well-tended gardens, neat and clean within and without'.[3] Architecture gave expression to wealth, lifestyle, attitudes and values, and builders' copy-books of 'polite' architecture provided the standard.[4]

By the 1870s Eliot had no need to provide her audience with Dorothea's plans for 'real houses', as she could be confident that they would already be familiar with the best known designs, as provided in Loudon's *Encyclopædia of Cottage, Farm and Village Architecture* (1833). It didn't even matter that Dorothea was reading Loudon's *Encyclopædia* before its publication; his principles had been so widely adopted by novelists and philanthropists alike that the slip could pass unnoticed.[5] As Richard Heath put it in 1893, the imperfect cottage had become the 'question of the hour'.[6] With increasing concern that rural homes were overcrowded and decaying, the state attempted to improve conditions by working with landowners, as well as by imposing higher building standards through by-laws. Model dwelling associations, such as the Model Cottage Society of Leeds, guaranteed loans to help artisans build their own homes, using plans provided by the Society. Meanwhile, competitions were run by journals such as the *Builder* to encourage estate owners to adopt more philanthropic designs. The Royal Agricultural Society's (RAS) own competitions included several subsections covering labourers' dwellings, and building societies were established to facilitate the erection of new homes – the Leeds Permanent lent money to the Cottage Society of Leeds and to the Society for the Erection of Improved Dwellings. However, this often failed to result in any significant change. In 1860, Caffyn notes, most of the designs submitted to the RAS were urban, or for classes higher than the agricultural labourer's cottage, and none were handed in for West Yorkshire.[7]

The Beau Ideal clearly competed with the 'imperfect' home in the Victorian imagination, and, given the oft-mentioned gap between 'ideal' and 'real life', still does. In the 1988 English House Condition Survey, 22 per cent of dwellings in rural areas were classified as being in poor condition and lacking basic facilities, as compared to 14 per cent of those in urban areas. Owner-occupiers in the countryside were one and a half times more likely to live in houses that could be classified as being in poor condition, while 48 per cent of private rented accommodation in rural areas was in bad shape, as compared to 40 per cent of that in the cities. It has also been found that the 100 most rural counties have housing that is in a worse state than the 97 most urban counties. In addition, a rise in the number of incomers, coupled with demographic change has meant that the kinds of houses needed in the countryside and those available no longer match up. The worst hit groups are those on low incomes, young couples and the elderly. Each of these groups has found it more and more difficult to rent, due to a drop in the number of privately and council-let properties. James Garo Derounian found that between 1980 and 1991 there was a 20 per cent drop in the public housing stock due to the widespread sale of council houses. On average 33 per cent of council houses were sold in rural areas over this period, as compared to 25 per cent nationally.[8] At the same time the high cost of owner occupation has largely priced those who would have let these properties out of the market in the most (visually) attractive areas. Hence, of the registered homeless in England in 1991, 14 per cent lived in rural areas. The Rural Development Council noted in 1992 that homelessness had increased at a much faster rate in the countryside than in the cities, though, in the same year, Mintel estimated that 4.5 million people planned to move into the countryside within the next five years. They wanted to move in order to get away from noisy, dirty towns, because they liked open spaces and because they believed that the countryside was less stressful. This is why Greater London, the Metropolitan districts and large cities all experienced a net loss of population between 1981 and 1991, while remoter, rural areas experienced a net gain of 6.1 per cent.[9]

As Derounian comments, even today 'image-makers protect, conserve and sanitise the way we look at country life'.[10] This is despite the publication of an increasingly large number of official and non-governmental reports on the subjects of rural deprivation, housing and demography such as the Church of England's report *Faith in the Countryside*, which found, for example, that elderly women living on their own constituted the single largest category of rural poor in the late twentieth century. It also noted that 60 per cent of women in the countryside do not drive and that this, coupled with very limited public transport, means that they do not have access to many essential services. Similarly, a report published in 1991, *Women and Employment in Rural Areas*, outlined how relatively few rural women participate in paid work due to this transport scarcity and the lack of affordable, accessible childcare. Those who did take on jobs, the report said, tended to go into part-time work, which at that point lacked the benefits of full-time work, and was in addition low-paid and casual.[11] Derounian therefore quotes Liz Rigby, a former producer of *The Archers*, as saying: 'I fear too much of the truth would prove painful to our listeners.'[12]

But, this, as in the nineteenth century, is not just a matter of 'truth' vs. 'fiction', rather it is a question of competing discourses/ narratives struggling for dominance. Such a struggle is always political at its heart, moreover, as Derounian himself notes, the victorious narrative – or 'misconception' as he calls it – has a very real impact on country people and country life in terms of both government funding and policy-making. Hence, in 1993, there was a disparity in funding, which meant that farmers, who made up just 10 per cent of the population, received the majority of grants in the countryside. Whereas urban areas received £775 million for development during 1989/90, the country received £26 million; as a fifth of the population lived in rural areas at this time, this should have stood at £193 million, on a pro rata basis. Quoting Brian McLaughlin, Derounian insists, 'rural areas contain a deprived population, the extent and intensity of whose disadvantage is perhaps of greater magnitude than is normally recognised'.[13] It is simple to set the idyll against an apparently more 'factual' or realist image of the countryside, but it is more useful to ask 'What does the imperfect cottage mean?' and to see what work the trope of the decayed cottage does in the imaginative and 'official' literature of the time, rather than just chart its horrors.

'WE HAVE REMOVED WOMAN FROM HER SPHERE'

Let's begin by taking Alfred Austin as an example; what was at stake when he wrote about the condition of rural housing in 1843? A firm believer in *laissez faire*, an expert who had already served on two previous Commissions – the 1838 Handloom Weavers Commission and the 1840–43 Children's Employment Commission – Austin contributed a report on the west country to the 1843 'Reports of Special Assistant Poor Law Commissioners on the employment of women and children in agriculture'. He disliked charity in all its forms and wanted the poor to rely on their own self-help organisations rather than the state. A professional within the nascent, early nineteenth-century bureaucracy, Austin carefully weighed up the pros and cons of women's work and saw occasional part-time employment, at harvest for example, as something which had to be accepted, because their earnings contributed to the family's wage.[14] However, like many of the new cadre of official reporters, he would also have preferred them to stay at home. Though he occasionally showed considerable sympathy for the women and children who laboured in agriculture, he nonetheless criticised them for not living up to the emergent standards of domesticity, femininity and morality to be found within his own class.[15] It therefore seems that while Austin tried to accept the gap between the experiences of his own class and those he wrote about, like many he found that acceptance hard and came to regret it. Domesticity was in the process of being universalised at this time and the definition of respectable femininity that originally gave the middle-class professional a moral edge over both the labourer and the aristocrat was coming to be seen as something that all women ought naturally to share.

Austin began by looking at dairy work and, like many commentators, exhibits some confusion over the issue of paid vs. unpaid work, what is 'domestic' work, i.e. part of the woman's home duties, and what is not. His report is unusual in that he emphasises the sheer hard labour of this 'work that is never finished'[16] and its physical impact on women's health. Having seen them at work, he rejects the commonplace image of the dairymaid grounded in bucolic bliss. Instead, he stresses the economic importance of the dairy to the farmer and strikingly, he represents the women who do dairy work, mostly unpaid farmers' wives and daughters who undertook the labour as part of their domestic duties, as highly skilled.[17] For Austin, the farmer's wife had economic worth aside from simple household management and reproduction. But, Austin did not describe those further down the social scale in such a positive fashion. He was caught in a class and gender divide in which it was only acceptable for women to do profitable work within their own dairy, an extension of the middle-class home, for their own family. Working-class women who had to leave their homes and go to work were criticised by him purely because they did not conform to the spatial norm being established by separate spheres ideology. Not only they, but also their husbands apparently suffered in consequence of their going out to work; when the man came home, Austin stated, there was 'no fire, no supper, no comfort, and he goes to the beer shop'.[18]

The issue is neatly summarised by Disraeli in *Sybil, or the Two Nations* (1845) when he draws on the 1843 report to provide Mr St Lys with the following declaration:

> But what is a poor man to do ... after his day's work, if he returns to his own roof and finds no home: his fire extinguished, his food unprepared; the partner of his life, wearied with labour in the field or the factory, still absent, or perhaps in bed from exhaustion, or because she has returned wet to the skin, and has no change of raiment for her relief? We have removed woman from her sphere; we may have reduced wages by her introduction into the market of labour; but under these circumstances what we call domestic life is a condition impossible to be realised for the people of the country; and we must not therefore be surprised that they seek solace or rather refuge in the beer-shop.[19]

At this point, a man's respectability was increasingly being linked to the quantity and frequency of his drinking. Medical practitioners and the clergy, in particular, took this very seriously for economic, physical and moral reasons, all represented under the catch-all word 'evil'. As one witness, the Rev. J. S. Toogood put it, 'of all the curses that the country at present labours under, one of the greatest seems to be the beer-house – it is impossible to say the extent of evil they do'.[20] Cobbett had advocated the need for beer, as something that would sustain a working man, but was less enthusiastic about letting women drink too much, unless they were engaged in physically hard labour. In his *Advice to Young Men* he stated: 'There may be cases among the *hard*-labouring women, such as *reapers* for instance, especially when they have children at the breast; there may be cases where very *hard*-working women may stand in need of a little *good* beer . . . I deny the necessity of any strong drink at all in every other case.'[21] This use of beer as sustenance was generally accepted when Cobbett was writing in the 1820s, but by 1843, religious men like Toogood – whose name is strikingly Dickensian, but apparently genuine – were beginning to turn against the practice. In fact, he wanted the landowners to build cottages on the farms to remove the temptation. Horatio Nelson Tilsey Esq., surgeon and medical officer of the Bridgewater Union – presumably a man of young middle age, named during the Napoleonic wars – agreed. He argued that the labourers had to go to the villages to find accommodation and therefore 'often congregate to the injury of their morals' in the local public house. Many of them would, otherwise, 'be better members of society'. One agricultural labourer, George Small, who was said not to have drunk alcohol for five years, was wheeled in as a witness in order to disprove the farmers' and labourers' argument that the men worked harder if given drink. He said he was still able to work as hard as the other men were. He had been persuaded to give up his cider by the offer of a strip of potato ground, which his wife and family helped work, even though his peers 'call me all kinds of names and laugh at me for not going to the cider-shop'. Drink, he thought, wasted the labourer's money and encouraged 'young men and women . . . [to] get together in a very improper way'. Another, Daniel Cox, who drank rarely, agreed.[22] The ideological overlap between the nascent medical profession and the Anglican clergy in the production of 'medico-moral discourse' and a new set of identities around the concept of respectability has been discussed by Frank Mort,[23] but what is also interesting here is the adoption of a working-class voice in support of this discourse, in direct opposition to the collective culture, articulated via peer pressure, of the man's own class and place. The comfort of the cottage home was therefore juxtaposed with that of the beer-house in much of the literature, imaginative and official, and in this way her husband's morality as well as her family's physical well-being were assumed to lie in the hands of the labourer's wife. If she were not at home, all would run to rack and ruin, and the man would inevitably turn to an alternative refuge. It would therefore be better, in an ideal world, if women did not go out to work.[24]

Austin's report, like Disraeli's novel, shows us how, by the 1840s, the ideology of separate spheres – articulated through a discussion of domesticity – was beginning to influence the public representation of both women's paid and unpaid work and enter official discourse as the norm against which to judge the circumstances and living conditions of all classes. Both, despite their different political allegiances, thought woman's proper sphere was the home, and Austin was shocked to find that even women who knew that it was dangerous, would out of necessity leave their children alone to take work.[25] Equally significantly, however, Austin, who followed his professional witnesses closely, though he distrusted the farmers and labourers sent to him,[26] also used the countryside as a stage on which to project the wider debate about public health and social welfare.

Like several other observers in the 'Reports of Special Assistant Poor Law Commissioners', Austin railed against the condition of cottages belonging to the poor far more than against the women and children's paid farm work he had been asked to investigate. In Cheshire, Gloucester and Worcestershire, he noted that the cottages often had a garden and a pigsty, while many had an allotment or potato ground too, all of which was seen to be good for the labourer. But, in Dorset, Devon and Somerset most of the cottages, Austin observed, were old and decaying; they mostly only had two bedrooms, sometimes only one, therefore both sexes, and all ages, slept together, often three or four to a bed. The only separation that was possible was by use of a shawl or blanket hung as a curtain. The living/day room floors were mostly made of stone and were wet and damp in the winter, as most of them were lower than the soil outside. The vast majority of cottages, he found, were poorly situated and badly drained. Thanks to overcrowding, and to pigsties and rubbish heaps being kept close to the houses, and because of inadequate sanitary arrangements, disease and immorality spread as quickly as each other. The following is an example of his findings, and is worth quoting at length as it is typical of the kinds of detail which observers like Austin sought to record, and the language that they used:

> At Stourpain, a village near Blandford, I measured a bed-room in a cottage consisting of two rooms, the bed-room in question upstairs, and

a room on the ground-floor in which the family lived during the day. There were 11 in the family: and the aggregate earnings in money were 16s.6d. weekly, (December 1842), with certain advantages... They had also an allotment of a quarter of an acre, for which they paid a rent of 7s.7d. a year... The room was 10 feet square... The roof was thatch, the middle of the chamber being about 7 feet high. Opposite the fireplace was a small window, about 15 inches square, the only one to the room.
[He provides a sketch in which there are three beds, two at right angles and one, in a corner, opposite the fireplace.]
Bed A. was occupied by the father and mother, a little boy, Jeremiah, aged 1½ years, and an infant aged 4 months.
Bed B. was occupied by the three daughters, – the two eldest, Sarah and Elizabeth, twins, aged 20; and Mary, aged 7.
Bed C. was occupied by the four sons, – Silas, aged 17; John aged 15; James, aged 14; and Elias, aged 10.
There was no curtain, or any kind of separation between the beds.
This, I was told, was not an extraordinary case; but that, more or less, every bed-room in the village was crowded with inmates of both sexes, of various ages, and that such a state of things was caused by the want of cottages... Everywhere the cottages are old, and frequently in a state of decay, and are consequently ill-adapted for the increasing number of inmates of late years... In the village of Stourpain, in Dorsetshire, there is a row of several labourers' cottages, mostly joining each other, and fronting the street, in the middle of which is an open gutter.
Behind the cottages the ground rises rather abruptly; and about 3 yards up the elevation are placed the pigsties and privies of the cottages. There are also shallow excavations, the receptacles apparently of all the dirt of the families. The matter constantly escaping from the pigsties, privies, &c., is allowed to find its way through the passages between the cottages into the gutter in the street, so that the cottages are nearly surrounded by streams of filth. It was in these cottages that a malignant typhus broke out about 2 years' ago, which afterwards spread through the village. The bed-room I have described is in one of them.[27]

His references to the small size of the bedroom window, the open gutter and proximity of pigsties and rubbish show us that Austin was attuned to the medical theories of his day. An ample supply of fresh air was seen as being crucial to health at the time, while many medical practitioners believed the foul air, or 'miasma', generated by waste might propagate disease. And having picked on the example of a house subject to typhus, the topography of the village and the domestic interior of the cottage are naturally overlain by the health/disease issue. But, given the diagram he provides and details of how the interior space is used, in his view the crowded sleeping conditions found in the cottage were at least as, if not more, pressing an issue than poor drainage. They ruined the self-respect of the poor and stripped them of their morality. The women, he said, lost all 'sense of modesty and decency ... [the men lost] ... respect for the other sex'.[28] As a result, incest, depravity and bastardy were said to be running rife in the region; men, women and children were morally corrupted in the home before they even got to work. The only good women came from detached cottages,[29] according to Austin, and though he did not say why, we can see that these homes came closest to fulfilling middle-class ideals of housing. The effectiveness of occasional attempts by the poor to maintain respectability were largely discounted. In his description of Stourpain, he makes no comment about the fact that the family have in fact divided their sleeping arrangements by age and sex. Their arrangements, split across three beds, simply did not count because they were not spaced out over three bedrooms; as far as Austin was concerned, they did not respect 'the family relationship'.[30]

The cottage, moated by physical filth, became an object of fascination, wherein the images of dirt and disease became symptomatic of immorality. As in the city, discussions of the sewer were 'unstable, sliding between social, moral and psychic domains';[31] Austin believed, as did Edwin Chadwick (the report's secretary), that immorality, rebellion and criminality were said to be rooted in physical disorder.[32] In having their pigsties so close to their cottages, the poor were placed at risk of behaving like pigs; the proximity of the pig/pigsty endangered the cottage and its inhabitants physically and morally. This was despite the fact that how it was handled largely induced the pig's behaviour. As Soper points out, following Stallybrass and White, though the pig was kept for meat, it was also used for human hygiene, the 'pig's "dustbin" habits provided its owner with a primitive form of sewage and refuse disposal, [therefore] a voraciousness and filthiness imputed to pig "nature" was enforced in the interests of human appetites and cleanliness'.[33]

In the nineteenth century, 'dirt' was closely associated with (improper) sexuality and the racial Other. 'As the bourgeoisie produced new forms of regulation and prohibition governing their own bodies, they wrote ever more loquaciously of the body of the Other – of the city's "scum".'[34] That Other, who might include the undeserving and the prostitute, both conflated with the 'black' Other within imperial discourse, was then observed and surveyed from a 'superior position'. The body of the Other had to be 'penetrated' and 'subjugated' through new proprieties. New ways of training the body were therefore sought, while constant reference to the unspeakable horrors of the city meant that architectural barriers were desired by those who wished 'decency and propriety' to be protected. New communication links, and the constant growth of the city, which granted promiscuous access, threatened to overwhelm the suburb and contaminate its pure spaces. More and more boundaries between the 'high' and the 'low' were therefore imposed, but these boundaries were constantly crossed in order that the 'immoral' might be observed and inspected. The mapping of the city in the nineteenth century via dirt/cleanliness mirrored the methodologies and structures of knowledge used within colonial anthropological discourse. The topography that separated slum (like the fair, a 'landscape of darkness, drunkenness, noise and obscenity') and suburb (the private domain of the self-controlled bourgeoisie), the respectable from the 'nomad', the 'division between cleanliness and filth, purity and impurity, is that between Christian and pagan, the civilised and the savage'.[35] Meanwhile, the bourgeois child, as it grew up was cleaned up, and taught the postures of civilised adulthood – not squatting, slouching, kneeling: the postures of servants and savages.[36]

In 1843, though the labourers themselves apparently accepted the conditions they lived in 'as a fact', those who wrote about them increasingly did not; it was no longer acceptable for the whole family to sleep in one room – even with a curtain between the beds. Even Doyle, who was otherwise quite positive about the state of the agricultural poor in the North, felt the need to state that, given their sleeping arrangements, 'any degree of indelicacy and unchastity ceases to surprise'.[37] The report's general findings were therefore picked up on by authors like Disraeli, Kingsley and Gaskell when seeking sources on the condition of England,[38] and, as might be expected, some public interest ensued. One clergyman wrote in to *The Times*, to declare that if the practice of employing women and children in agriculture were not brought to an end, then English cottages would be reduced to the 'standard of the Hottentot'.[39] As in the cities, the sanitary mapping of filth and cleanliness, alongside the employment of women, acted in parallel with colonial and anthropological discourse to map the distinctions of civilisation and savagery.[40]

However, the response to and production of the 1843 report must also be seen in the context of a broader political battle which ostensibly centred on the issue of housing, but which additionally came from an attack by industrialists on the paternalists who seemed to be hell-bent on clipping their wings.[41] For once, the emergent industrialists seemed to say it is the aristocracy that is to blame and the reports' authors agreed. The labourers themselves were defined as passive within this whole discussion; never rebellious, not even capable of immorality through their own initiative, they were corrupted in their cottages because they simply knew no better. This, it was said, was largely the fault of the landowners whose job it was both to maintain the cottages and keep a paternal eye on the labourers. If peasants were known for their ignorance and immorality, then it was the ruling class who should help them by building more cottages and giving them a better education. Doyle's comment was that 'useful knowledge . . . [is the best] . . . antidote against idle and vicious habits', while Denison believed that the landowners of Norfolk were 'a spirited body of agriculturists, and have only to be told to correct the evil'.[42] Moreover, the 'Special Reports' were notably produced after the 7th Earl of Shaftesbury had been highly critical of factories in the North of England and these attacks led very quickly to some unfavourable comparisons being made between the mills of the North and his estates. And certainly, looking at his diaries, he believed that the 1843 report was designed to attack him.[43]

Austin for one was specifically engaged in producing a report that took some implicit pot shots at Shaftesbury, whose estate in Dorset was shown to contain some very shoddy cottages indeed. Austin's report, along with criticisms from commentators like Harriet Martineau – who declared that the 'agricultural labourers of his own county were in a state of desperate ignorance and reckless despair', unlike those of the manufacturing districts, who were, 'the class, which was actually the most enlightened and the best able to take care of itself, of any working class in England'[44] – and the Anti-Corn Law League, finally drove Shaftesbury to state at the end of 1843 that: 'I ought not to be lynx-eyed to the misconduct of manufacturers and bend to the faults of landowners.'[45] Taking this and subsequent speeches into account, he can clearly be seen as having come round to the idea that reformers like himself had to look into the plight of the agricultural, not just the industrial, poor. And, by the time the next major report on women and children's employment in agriculture was published, in 1867, his estate had considerably improved – most of its housing was mentioned quite favourably, even though others largely got the credit.[46] Shaftesbury's final enthusiasm in tackling the plight of the rural poor, incidentally, destroyed his relationship with his father, but he tellingly wanted to show that landowners could look after their tenants and their labourers. Turning to the discourse of paternalism, refreshed as it was by apologists like Carlyle, he hoped to establish 'a model Estate, almost a garden for the culture and comfort of the Peasantry' to help 'the Constitution'.[47] What Austin's report therefore demonstrates, is not so much how terrible conditions were, but the way in which the trope of the decayed cottage, so desirable in picturesque discourse – though never so shabby as not to seem 'sufficient and independent' and therefore 'attract attention to the distress of the actual poor'[48] – could be converted by political economists and the ascendant, liberal and industrial bourgeoisie into anti-agrarian political capital. It also demonstrates how the image of rural *in*felicity became particularly powerful when coupled with the new boundaries of the civilised body being established by the bourgeoisie, within which the topography of the body was mapped onto domestic space.

A similar thing can be seen happening in the connection made between poor housing and the 'open' and 'close' village issue, which, Sarah Banks argues, was itself a 'scandal exaggerated by advocates of settlement law reform'.[49] 'Historians', she argues, 'have generally taken reports of the "open" and "close" parish problem at face value', any attempt to apply this model to rural society is therefore 'misconceived'. However, looking at the issues around 'open' and 'close' parishes can, she says, 'give some insights into the contrasting size, ownership, and occupational patterns of different parishes; into the interactions between neighbouring parishes in terms of movements of population and labourers'.[50] In the 1843 special report on Norfolk, Denison made great play of the 'open' village of Castle Acre and its failings. Like Austin, he placed the blame for the misconduct of those employed in agricultural gangs on the quality and quantity of cottages in the village, rather than the work itself, and this feeds into a discussion of the roles and responsibilities of the aristocracy, who have, he observes, been demolishing cottages in the region without replacing them, in order to avoid the poor rates. The cottages of Castle Acre, he consequently argued, had been built by speculative builders to accommodate those who could not find a home in a 'close' village; the 'evils existing in Castle Acre', he says, are not due to the gang system per se, but rather from it being an 'open' parish.[51]

The very fact of its 'openness' meant that it could be equated with the uncivilised, undisciplined and unbounded practices of the city. Here we begin to see an additional nuance to Dorothea's declaration that 'we should put the pig-sty cottages outside the park gate', i.e. outside the 'close' village over which the landowner, reputedly, has control. The condition of the cottages is used as a sign of the corruption of the 'open' parish and the failure of landowners; hybridised as a human and animal space, it adds to the scandal. And, though the 1843 report, as a whole, was widely ignored, this aspect of it was picked up and used within the wider debate about the relief of the poor. Disraeli, for example, uses Denison's argument in *Sybil* when he makes Lord Marney say: 'I will take care that the population of my parishes is not increased. I build no cottages, and I destroy all I can; and I am not ashamed or afraid to say so.' To which Mr St Lys replies, smiling: 'You have declared war to the cottage, then . . . It is not at the first sound so startling a cry as war to the castle.'[52] Though, the end result is indeed, war to the castle.

That the rural working-class home was not perfect was well known in the city. Imaginative literature, as well as formal social surveys, gave expression to widespread concern about the state of the poor. Charles Kingsley's *Yeast* (1847), for one, blames tumbledown cottages for their degenerate condition, and declares that any woman, of whatever class, would be corrupted if she lived in one.[53] He aimed to shatter the hegemonic dream of rural life as idyllic, naturally innocent and happy, by drawing on dominant concerns about the state of the poor in the towns and projecting them onto the country. Like most social commentators, the concerned yet naive protagonist, Lancelot, reads 'blue books, red books, sanitary reports, mine reports, factory reports; and came to the conclusion, which is now pretty generally entertained, that something was the matter – but what no man knew'.[54] Like *Sybil*, a typical 'condition of England' novel, *Yeast* is a deliberately provocative text that re-presents the findings of official reporters and social commentators of the 1840s. In writing it, Kingsley, if not Lancelot, presumed that he already knew what 'the problem' was, and sought to pass this on to his audience who were none to happy to hear his ideas. The story was found to be too challenging for *Fraser's Magazine*, and its readers nearly bankrupted the journal by withdrawing their subscriptions; Kingsley was forced to conclude the tale prematurely, and we can find signs of his distress in the novel where the author intrudes to tell us he is not a 'Plymouth Brother' or 'Communist' as the papers are suggesting; he is just trying to put on paper the concerns of the young and to shed light on the facts as they stand.[55] For a start, following Disraeli's 'two nations' thesis, with a dash of Carlyle's dislike for capital, he suggests that bourgeois expectations of the rural working class, especially working-class women, are partial. Hence, when Lancelot is spoken to rudely by a young elite woman he thinks to himself: 'If a country girl, now, had spoken in that tone . . . it would have been called at least "saucy" – but Mammon's elect ones may do anything.' In this way, he universalises the dominant construction of femininity. Secondly, he contrasts cultural 'image' with lived 'reality'. 'Arcadian dreams of pastoral innocence and graceful industry, I suppose, are to be henceforth monopolised by the stage or the boudoir?' Lancelot muses.[56] The two points come together when he finally feels

> utterly down-hearted about [everything he has seen at a fair] ... He had expected ... at least to hear something of pastoral sentiment and of genial frolicsome humour; to see some innocent, simple enjoyment: but instead, what had he seen but vanity, jealousy, hoggish sensuality, dull vacuity, drudges struggling for one night to forget their drudgery? And yet ... in these poor creatures too, lay the germs of pathos, taste, melody, soft and noble affections.[57]

Lancelot, a representative if concerned member of the upper class, expects to see certain things in the countryside based on his absorption of the picturesque, but learns that life in the country isn't all pastoral frolic. As this dawns on him, so he comes to regret the gap between rich and poor and to implicitly criticise those who refuse to see what they might, if they were not so quick to condemn, by appropriating the poor for pathos. As John Lucas says: 'The picturesque aims not at tragedy, but at pathos, and the pathetic is inseparable from a certain complacency precisely because it invites us to consider that nothing else can be other than what it is.'[58] However, in this instance, the poor are both without pathos and unable to feel pathos. A change of sentiment was required; for the true condition of the poor to be seen, detail was needed.

For Kingsley, the process of observation, the acts of going to the country, then looking and noticing what was there were as significant as what might actually be seen. Tregarva, a Wesleyan gamekeeper who teaches Lancelot to reflect on what he witnesses, notes at one point that 'everybody sees these evils, except just the men who can cure them – the squires, and the clergy'.[59] Where cottages are visible to passers by, they are kept up; in more out of the way places they fall down.[60] Kingsley, based on his experiences as a curate in Hampshire, reworked the material reality of rural life through the ideology of Christian socialism and the picturesque in order to shift the burden of moral welfare onto the shoulders of those men who protected their own women while others suffered. He drew on empirical material, images of pastoral, the declining language of taste and the emergent language of observation to attack what he saw as a distanced vision of the countryside that hid the causes of poverty. Within *Yeast*, the cottage is treated as a site where the delicate female frame might be shattered rather than made complete.[61]

Inferior housing continued to be seen as the cause of working-class immorality by subsequent Victorian commentators. When responding to a later report on women and children's paid work in agriculture, for instance, in 1869 an article in the *Saturday Review* argued, exactly as in 1843, that overcrowding was far more likely than field work to be morally corrupting. 'It is not', the *Review* observed, 'the solitary fact of adult female labour or of juvenile female gangs, which causes female immorality. It is the concurrence of this with home training, which precedes and accompanies the field work.' The country cottage was held up as Beau Ideal, the goal, in this article. But, the cottage as it stood did not secure the moral or physical welfare of the poor as it was meant to do; in fact, it actively caused their degradation. The result of the 'herding together of girls and boys, young men and women, in [a single room in a small cottage] . . . is the enforced and unnatural suppression of the native instinct of modesty. It is the foul and incestuous life in the cottage which generates the open and flagrant immorality in the fields'.[62] Sometimes, as a result, it was better to be out than in, and this horrified those who went to the country with certain pastoral expectations. In a second article, which seems to resonate with George Eliot's essay on the German peasantry, the *Review* refers to 'poets and painters' from every age who

> have amused the world by their conceptions of Corydons and Phyllises to whom the male and female peasants of working-day life have not the faintest resemblance. At no period of human history have the labouring rustics of Norfolk and Yorkshire . . . had anything in common with the rustic lovers of Poe's and Ticknell's pastorals or the picturesque impersonations of Watteau's fancy. And it must ever remain a problem why artists of the pen and the brush have conspired to throw over the homely incidents of rural life an imaginary grace which was never borrowed for the inhabitants of towns. [It seems that] . . . there is something in agricultural work at once so necessary, so useful, and so primitive, that we sympathize with the condition of those who perform it more than we do with the agents of other industries. The instinctive wish of those who examine it is that all the men engaged in it should be sturdy, vigorous and intelligent, and all the women comely, virtuous and decorous.[63]

When discussing the impact of housing upon the inhabitants, the *Saturday Review* therefore aimed to emphasise the differences between the lives of the working class and those who reported on them. It notes, for example, that 'the description of one class of people by an entirely different class is liable to exaggeration'. And that even 'the dullest and stupidest of them [the labourers] hates to be preached at. And we are not sure that he is wrong'. Indeed, 'inspectors and clergymen are generally prone to . . . forget', it declared, 'that at best the whole weft of agricultural life is almost necessarily coarse'.[64] And, in slightly satirical vein, it sought to see the world from the (male) labourer's point of view:

If he could only find the words in which to vent his indignation, he might ask his critics whether a man who was labouring hard the greater part of the year from morning to night for his family was not to be excused some breaches of manners and some outbreaks of gaiety. If, too, he were taunted with the temptations and corruption to which his daughters were exposed by field labour, might he not retort that the work of moral corruption had been begun by the insufficient and ill-constructed houses in which he and they were compelled to live?[65]

This sympathetic edge allowed the agricultural working class to become objects of pity and laid any blame for their condition firmly at the feet of those who provided the houses. In this way, the *Saturday Review* – which was critical of the official reporters' fastidiousness[66] – argued against intervention on women and children's employment as an ineffective tool of change. Though quite wretched in some areas, things wouldn't improve, it argued, until 'machinery does the work, not only of women and children, but also of men'. Only when the 'agricultural population of England has been diminished [will] . . . women and children . . . be relegated to the duties of home and the labours of school'.[67] In the meantime, why shouldn't a labourer want 'his wife and children to help him by their labour when they can'? It was only human nature, after all. It was only reasonable.[68] Why 'relegate' them to home and school when they could be productive? The *Saturday Review* was engaged in the widespread yet careful *laissez faire* balancing act of seeking better conditions for everyman, a man as reasonable as any other, but arguing that progress, which was to be encouraged, could not be forced. In its second article on the subject, the journal attacked the idea of legislating to remove women from the fields and railed against 'all the dangers which result from meddling with the free agency of individuals', and went on to warn of the financial distress that this would cause, unless some other employment were provided in the home.[69] The legislation that was already in place limiting the employment of children, coupled with the work of landowners and the clergy, would have to do. The poor man would just have to wait for things to get better, viz. for his wife to stay home, and his children to go to school.[70] But, in engaging in this debate and defending the poor, the *Saturday Review* nonetheless slips into the use of colonial and sanitary discourse.

The findings of the reports from the 1860s are summed up as follows: the labourer's 'children are untaught, his home slovenly, his wife and daughters half brutalized by excessive toil, and his own earnings barely sufficient for the purposes of ordinary subsistence'.[71] In Northumberland, the *Saturday Review* points out, where their homes are in good condition and their wages high, 'the conduct of the peasant woman is substantially virtuous and correct . . . The women talk the language of their own caste, which is not that of drawing rooms. [But,] they expiate their precocious slips from virtue by irreproachable fidelity as wives and mothers.'[72] In East Anglia, however, where living conditions were particularly bad, 'the women and girls act and speak like the harlot-caste of a savage race'.[73] Here, the homes and language of the poor are not just used to signify their moral condition, as was the case in the original parliamentary report, they are also used as a sign of difference in the experiences of the two classes. The cottage is used as a marker for, a sign of, the lamentable gap between rich and poor while the language of the poor – and Other 'savage' races – is placed in direct contrast to that of the 'drawing room', in other words the languages and homes of the official observers. However, in apparently transgressing the moral and physical, indeed the physiological, boundaries established by the middle class, the poor – as in 1843 – also transgress the boundary between civilised and savage, as signified by their speech.

The discourse of (physical and moral) health and disease, as well as running parallel to colonial discourse, drew on the Enlightenment distinction: humanity–nature. In describing the 'brutalization' of the women and the 'herding together' of the poor, the boundary between human and animal is crossed, and, in its sympathy for the agricultural labourer, the *Saturday Review* goes on to suggest that with education he couldn't be made to live like a 'pig with his family in [a] hovel'. No one, it argued 'can deny that his actual position in many counties tends to degrade him, not only as an English citizen, but even as a human being'.[74] Not only is the labourer's home a pigsty, 'he' has become a pig. By this point the pig had become encoded as an animal that lived in the working-class slum, but which was killed to feed the middle class, while its breeders worked for the wealthy, removing the filth from the suburbs back into the slums where it belonged. The pig, like the rat, had become representative of all that was Other in the symbolic city, an Other which troubled the identity of the discreet bourgeois body and which symbolised the filth and misery of the slum. Representations of the pig, as Soper discusses, only became really hostile as it was taken in to breed up in the slum, at which point it was treated with revulsion and hatred because it could eat garbage, contributed to the slum's dirt and thereby stood in for the slum dweller. It is then that the term 'pig' becomes a simple form of abuse, and comes to be associated with policing the bounds of respectable society.[75] In a sense then, the urban pig writes back to more 'innocent' rural versions of itself. Meanwhile, the pig was one of many symbols that helped re-map the bourgeois body and in this instance, the agricultural labourer becomes subject to the same metonymic slip as can be found in representations of the urban poor, whereby rather than being likened to their animals, they become their animals. Here the poor were written up in terms of 'bestiality', in the country, as in the town, because they transgressed the boundaries of the civilised body. As Stallybrass and White observe, the animal–human transgression is not simply an inversion, it is a hybridisation, a 'mixing of binary opposites'.[76] It was therefore hoped that in improving the working-class home, the working-class body could be re-formed, yet as a member of the working class, the agricultural labourer – already associated with the essential 'earthiness', the necessary coarseness of country life – could never escape this imaginary slippage. As Soper argues, that which

> is distinctively human is defined by exclusion of the carnal (more 'bestial') dimension, this being conceived as a 'lower' aspect or region. Such an exercise serves a number of functions, notably to preserve class and gender hierarchies. Where the distinctively human is identified with the aesthetic sensibilities and intellectuality whose acquisition is the privilege of an educated elite, the 'lower orders' of society necessarily figure as something less than human: as an uncouth, simple peasantry or proletariat, whose closeness to the earth and its animals also places it nearer to nature.[77]

It is again the poor's apparent passivity that stands out in the *Saturday Review*, especially the male labourer's ventriloquism. If anything, it is the cottage that determines how the poor live their lives; the (male) labourer is given a breadwinner's script, but he is not able to act. As Tristram notes: 'Houses may be determined by the life we lead, but to some extent they also determine our lives.'[78] This is assumed to be the case in the *Saturday Review*. It is the cottage that removes the women's *natural* modesty; the cottage that forces the family to sleep together and break the rules of privacy and morality they know exist – rules established by the cult of domesticity to guarantee the man's individuality. Alternatively, if the cottage itself is not culpable, then those who build them are. For all its defence of the 'free agency'[79] of the agricultural labourer, all the poor man can do is try to express his anxieties to any 'well-fed, well-dressed gentleman'[80] who steps across his threshold, which he will never be able to do without the efforts of a middle-class spokesman/translator. His wife and children, meantime, remain resoundingly silent; as chattels, their labour at his disposal, they do not even have words put into their mouths. In direct contrast to 'the agents of industries', the journal sees the rural labourer as profoundly inarticulate. As a result, 'his' home becomes a space, not just emptied of visible work, but also of political sentiment.

'A MOST DESPOTIC PARSON'S WIFE'

At the turn of the eighteenth and nineteenth century, Barrell observes, the poor 'as a class' came to be seen 'as the distant generalised objects of fear and benevolence'.[81] At the same time, the 'widespread and continued necessity of keeping the labouring poor alive by supplementing their wages with public or private charity made the line dividing the poor from the rest of society brilliantly if misleadingly clear.'[82] Charity had its own conventions and through their widespread adoption, the poor, though clearly Other, could no longer be treated as a homogenous unified mass at odds with the rich. In a children's poem from the 1830s, for instance, a character called 'Old Sarah', who wears a 'gipsy (sic) hat' and colourful yet tattered clothes, has 'No blazing fire, no cheerful home'; a migrant, outside the community 'She goes forlorn about to roam'. Like a ghost, she follows passers-by 'with a doleful cry,/ Of poverty and woe.' But, she does not care to work, she doesn't even sell 'laces gay, and wooden wares,/And garters blue and red.' Rather 'To stroll about and drink her gin,/She loves far better than to spin,/Or work to earn her bread.' Old Sarah is widely known and never pitied, 'For people do not like to give/Relief to those who idle live,/And work not when they might.'[83] Drunks and the idle are not to be comforted or helped, especially if they are migrants – in this case resembling the 'savage' gypsy.

The simplicity and conservatism of the form reinforce the simplicity and conservatism of the message, but, just to make sure that that message is not missed, it is followed by 'Old Susan', an identically-structured description of a woman who is the direct inverse of Old Sarah. Unlike Old Sarah, Old Susan lives in a cottage, and 'Though low the roof, and mud the wall,/And goods a scanty store,' she is happy and does not 'covet more'. Despite her 'aches and weaknesses' she 'daily plies her spinning-wheel,/Within her cottage-gate' which work brings in her 'homely fare' – a 'wholesome crust of barley-bread'. Not only is she content – she does not envy 'the great' – she is also neat and tidy in her person and knows how to keep her house in order:

> A decent gown she always wears,
> Though many an ancient patch it bears,
> And many a one that's new;
> No dirt is seen within her door,
> Red sand she sprinkles on the floor,
> As tidy people do.

As before, every one knows Old Susan, but in this case 'every one respected too,/Her industry and care'. So, when she's a little short 'Her neighbours gladly would bestow/Whatever they could spare.'[84] Domesticity, placidity and industry bring their own reward. Just as in visual representations of the poor, the 'good' poor – 'simple, laborious, honest', the legitimate subjects of pastoral[85] – naturally elicit compassion, even respect. In the meantime, the 'bad' – who were potentially more threatening by virtue of their deviance from the established norm – could be contained as characters within a moral narrative[86] in which they got their just deserts. There is also an interesting slippage in the two poems wherein those giving the charity are not Old Susan's betters, but her 'neighbours'; any hint of class conflict is therefore erased as the concepts of community and self-help are writ large.

Where industrious Old Susan, safe within the bounds of her cottage or garden, is cared for by the village, the more threatening figure of (homeless) Old Sarah is ostracised by that community and exists feebly on its margins. Its interests divided and feminised – where a woman like Old Susan might elicit greater sympathy than a poor man, a woman like Old Sarah was simultaneously a less threatening figure than a poor man – 'the poor' became less intimidating, more easily subject to a naturalised elite control. Meanwhile, the two poems contributed to the formation of two new identities: the 'deserving' (good Old Susan) and the 'undeserving' (bad Old Sarah) poor, created in part through their attitude to home. While in her homeliness Old Susan resembles the urban middle class, in her wandering at the edges of her community Old Sarah echoes the figure of the improvident nomad. This figure, Stallybrass and White argue, was constructed by observers like Mayhew 'via his desires ("passion", "love", "pleasure") and in terms of his rejections or ignorances'. In other words, the 'bourgeois spectator surveyed and classified *his own antithesis*', that antithesis being the nomad. But this is a figure that can also be seen emerging in the literature of the early nineteenth century and 'as the nomads transgress all settled boundaries of "home",' Stallybrass and White go on, 'they simultaneously map out the area which lies beyond cleanliness'.[87] In this instance, the rural poor were being used to map the boundaries of acceptable and unacceptable behaviour, and of class identity.

Metropolitan journals like *Punch* used similarly distanced images of the rural poor to stress the 'universal' (bourgeois) values of religion, deference and patriotism. 'The countryside was conceived of', Susan and Asa Briggs observe, 'as an adjunct to the city or, sometimes ... as a prelude to city life; and the best jokes about the countryside dwelt on the dangers which still lurked there for the well-bred townsman.'[88] In the case of the poor cottager, we see the themes of industry, piety, family and community being addressed, which when coupled with domesticity reinforced the Beau Ideal for an educated urban audience wary of the idiocy of country life. This negotiation of identity was often achieved through the inversion of dominant, well-known images of the rural idyll. In 1867 for instance, Charles Keene, one of *Punch*'s regular artists,[89] parodied rural courtship in 'Artful-Very!', a line drawing in which a young woman sits demurely on a stile as a puzzled youth, looking at her intently, leans on the fence behind. They are given the following script:

> Mary. 'Don't keep a screougin' o' me, John!'
> John. 'Wh'oi bean't a screougin' on yer!'
> Mary (*ingenuously*). 'Well, y' can i' y' like, John!'[90]

The visual component of the illustration used many of the elements to be found in commercial art, such as a landscape framed by stile, climbers and hedge flowers, quaint if cast-off quality dress, and a physical barrier between the two lovers. But, in its representation of rural dialogue, it went on to exaggerate and ridicule the pathos that might be found in most genre paintings. The bastardised dialect makes both characters look bumpkin-like, their rural setting enabling them to be easily turned into figures of fun, while the pretty young woman, pictured at a distance from the audience, is represented as beguiling in her 'artfulness'. The young man is slightly coarse-featured and though her flirting might not fool *Punch*'s urbane readership, it is implied that *he* will certainly be duped. However, as she sits on her pedestal aloof and remote, the audience is also encouraged to idolise her, just like her young man does. He has much more character in his faintly quizzical expression than she does and because he stands on the audiences' side of the fence, they are invited to identify with his point of view and empathise with his situation. They too are perplexed by her, or rather, by all women's behaviour. John, like the labourer in the *Saturday Review*, is everyman; puzzled by womanly wiles, he is understandable, reachable. Mary is everywoman; a puzzle, she is objectified and as easily condemned for her ingenuity as she is revered for her beauty.

As the Briggs point out, *Punch*'s 'masculinity', to be found in its management and approach, 'was at least as pervasive as its metropolitanism'. It always made fun of independent women, satirised middle-class women's clothes and attacked women's education. Though, being sensitive to its family readership, much of this was toned down,[91] the satirical male gaze caused the metropolitan bourgeoisie's construction of womanhood to be projected onto and reinforced via images of the working class in the country. In his use of a classic image of rural felicity, Keene therefore writes back to dominant constructions of rural life and universalises both masculinity and femininity. Old women, on the other hand, revised versions of 'Old Sarah' and 'Old Susan', were used in *Punch* as the main recipients of philanthropic relief to tackle the complex social relations inherent in charitable giving and the negotiations that took place between rich and poor.

Keene, in 'Legitimate Criticism' (1873), illustrated an old cottage woman showing a young lady a book as she sits opposite her by the fire:

> Aged Village Matron (*to Sympathising Visitor*). 'It's a "Cookery Book," as Mrs. Penewise, our "District Lady," give me this Christmas, Miss. I'd a deal sooner a' had the ingredients, Miss!!'[92]

It is possible to overstate, as Gerard seems to do, the idea that the poor might be especially deferential to the rich because of the 'undeniable glamour and authority about the aristocracy and gentry'.[93] However, it appears that many elite women such as the 'sympathising visitor' in the cartoon enjoyed visiting the poor, because, though the gap that existed between the visitor and the visited always remained, it was an opportunity to move beyond the normal daily round. Being 'Lady Bountiful' was a traditional duty for any female member of the landed gentry that, with the rise of Evangelicalism, went through something of a revival in the Victorian period and was additionally adopted by the urban bourgeoisie who adapted the model and developed the role of 'District Lady'. Most well-to-do women in the country therefore belonged to charitable societies, in some cases managing the society, in others simply donating either money or handcrafted items like baby clothes, while many others engaged in personal visiting and stopped to talk. 'Lady Bountiful' in particular, by virtue of her rank, established clubs and mothers' meetings, taught in Sunday school, provided school treats and children's parties. As a result it was these women who established the material link between rich and poor, who put the supposed face-to-face relations of the rural community into practice.[94] But, the young lady in this instance, who is in the foreground, says nothing, thereby leaving the reader to commiserate with the deferential, if pointed, old woman. The old woman's exposition allows the young lady and the audience to reflect on the pros and cons of aristocratic vs. bourgeois, rural vs. urban, private vs. state relief. As *Punch* was aware, the cottage threshold was not imposed simply in the form of bricks and mortar, it was also constructed through satire, observation and social control. Hence, Lawrence argues, 'boundaries are not just created physically but are also ordered by symbolic and juridical parameters which are transient in kind'.[95]

When in 1841, Sarah Miles, a spinster aged 60 who had taken no relief, knitted 230 oz of yarn and about 45 pairs of stockings, received £1, Susan Groom, the wife of an agricultural labourer, won £1 for the neatness of her cottage and raising six children under 14, and Elizabeth Howell got 15s (she only had five children), and the wife of A. Francis (who had four) received 10s,[96] the display of paternalism helped ensure conformity to the ideals specified in and realised by the large sums of money expended. These kinds of prizes, given out at shows or dinners, ensured a public display of paternalism in action and speeches on duty or the naturalness of the social order. Diverse in structure as well as membership, the agricultural societies that were established in the late eighteenth century had experienced resurgence in the 1840s, by which point they were playing a major part in the paternal structure of village life, organising dances, meetings and charitable help for the poor. Their annual awards helped drive many of the celebrated causes of the day, such as good cottage design, while the rewards given to labourers were intended to chivvy the poor into adhering to the correct forms of social behaviour, deference and loyalty.[97] But, if charity could reward, it could also punish; when a woman did not conform to the domestic standards laid down by 'Lady Bountiful' she would not get her extra coal, soup or clothing. Charity was meant to keep the poor in line – a mentality that influenced the development and application of the New Poor Law – in other words, as a form of social control, this apparent benevolence was designed to ensure stability. The Anglican Church, for example, often required regular attendance before help would be given and thereby hoped to encourage faith and discourage dissent,[98] and as with the prize-givings, bastardy or an overreliance on poor relief would normally result in the withdrawal of aid.

Joseph Arch's mother provides the best-known example of resistance; a woman who 'was shrewd, strong-willed, and self-reliant', she refused to give way to 'a most despotic parson's wife' who decreed that

> all the girls attending school were to have their hair cut round like a basin, more like prison girls than anything else. My mother put her foot down, and said she never would allow her daughters to have their hair cut in such an unsightly way . . . [The parson's wife made] things very uncomfortable for my mother; but she had met her match, and more, in the agricultural labourer's wife . . . she went out and did battle, but from that time my parents never received a farthing's-worth of charity in the way of soup, coals or the like.[99]

Cutting a girl's hair might seem like a slight thing, but long hair at the time connoted looseness and moral laxity. Charlotte Brontë questions this kind of action when she shows the evangelical Mr Brocklehurst, the proprietor of Lowood school, to be morally flawed and hypocritical when he picks on one of the girls, Julia Severn, for having naturally curly hair. His own daughters curl theirs artificially, but he insists that it be cut off.[100] But, beyond the literary text, it is hard to tell how the poor themselves felt about Lady Bountiful and their other visitors. Early nineteenth-century riots can be seen as a demand that paternalism be put back in place, rather than as a demand that they be given new rights and freedoms, given that it was the erosion of customary rights that gave rise to them. Where charity was seen as a right, Lady Bountiful might, therefore have been welcomed.[101] However, charitable relief was not the same as a customary right, while resistance can be seen in the poor's refusal to take charity. The poor might shun 'begging' from the wealthy by borrowing money or goods from members of their own class; a favour which they could return.[102] As one character says to her grandson in Charlotte Yonge's 'Quack, Quack' (1882), a children's story about saving, 'My dear, you never went begging to the quality for it [30s rent]? I never begged in my life, nor none of mine ever did.'[103] Though the story contains a clear-cut moral about self-help, it also reflects the complex emotions, hostility and pride in independence, generated by the power relations vested in philanthropy and poor relief. It was, after all, relatively simple to subvert the strictures of respectability by simply putting a white apron on to give the appearance of cleanliness. Thomas Hardy quoted one woman, in 'The Dorsetshire Labourer' (1883), as saying 'I always kip a white apron behind the door to slip on when the gentlefolk knock, for if so be they see a white apron they think ye be clane.' He thought her standards of cleanliness pretty poor, but 'by a judicious use of high lights, shone as a pattern of neatness in her patrons' eyes'. Another woman who kept house very well, but had painted her house in burnt umber and wore clean but faded snuff-coloured clothing never got a penny. In his opinion, 'One of the clearest signs of deserving poverty is the effort it makes to appear otherwise by scrupulous neatness.'[104] The significance of charitable giving – the consequence of controlling what was given – was therefore clearly understood by the recipients, not just historians, philanthropists or *Punch*. With the gradual removal of customary rights, as Barrell argues and Hardy's article suggests, the poor had come to be well aware of their need, and of 'the postures of cheerfulness, submission and gratitude they had to take up to receive' charity. This was important in helping create class-consciousness among the rural poor: 'us the poor, them the rich'.[105]

In *Punch*'s 'Troubles of our Clergy' (1873) and 'Helping Him On' (1874) – by an artist signed 'LB' – this resistance is satirised. The old woman in the former, Mrs Smith, says she has not collected her soup from the rector that day because 'there wasn't no taste in it last week; and they tell me there be hardly enough seasoning in it today!'[106] In the latter the 'oldest inhabitant' explains to the new curate visiting her 'you may sit down and read a bit to me, and then you may give me a shilling, and then you may go'.[107] Bundled up in serviceable aprons, shawls and bonnets, in contrast to the artful girl on the stile and the young lady visitor, each of the old women represented in *Punch* have 'character'. Marked by the passing of the years, all are in their own way garrulous renderings of 'Old Sarah'. Drawing not just on cottage imagery, but also on fairy-tale reflections of Hansel and Gretel, with hooked noses and pointed chins, they huddle up to their fires, cauldrons cooking, or mysteriously wander through woods near the church to poke fun at their superiors. At a remove from *Punch*'s readership in terms of class, gender and space, potentially quaint and quite funny, these old women are, if not well-off, at least not ragged; in this sense they are not threatening to their audience. Yet, they are lone women, worldly-wise, above social niceties and ungrateful to their betters. Set against an opposing 'respectable' figure, in each case they seem to get one up or talk back to them and transgress the boundaries of deference. This gives each picture an authenticity that it would otherwise lack, thereby securing the power of the image. Here, the rural poor are shown to be 'naturally' independent at a time when agitation was increasing in the country. The 1870s saw heightening agricultural depression, falling wages, casualisation, mechanisation, depopulation, widening education (a double-edged sword that might civilise and therefore control, but also teach the poor their rights), the loss of power by the clergy and the rise of the chapel and union. 1873–74 was the period of the National Agricultural Labourers' Union's (NALU) greatest power. Founded in 1872–73, the Union organised a strike in 1874, often called 'the revolt of the field'. There was also widespread union activity beyond the bounds of the NALU while considerable comment about the state of the agricultural poor was being published at the time.[108]

As before, the iconography comes from genre art, while the text in each case, as dialogue, directs the audience to select the preferred reading of country life for that image. Text and image therefore complement each other and come together to realise the message at a higher level, that of the story being told.[109] The story *Punch* is trying to narrate is a shift in rural social relations that clearly puts the lie to the Beau Ideal, whereby the 'peasantry' suddenly seems to be as ugly as the industrial working class. By focusing on little old women, the clergy and Lady Bountiful – all that are left of the rural community – the journal could continue to represent the countryside as stable, paternal and communal, the rural poor as self-reliant and therefore without need. On the other hand, these images also work at a political level to throw up a series of fears about that independence, which effectively criticise the old, rural elite for their failings. The implication in these illustrations, even 'Legitimate Criticism', seems to be that the poor are ungrateful and cheeky, while the clergy are stupid and weak – the social issues of the city are projected onto the country. This suggests that both the rural poor and elite are in a sense 'naturally' undeserving – of money, attention or respect – even though there is a resistant reading that suggests the poor are self-assured, autonomous and know the true cost of philanthropy.

In its early days, the 1840s, *Punch* was quite radical. But, the Briggs point out, this was a very well-to-do kind of radicalism – like that of the condition of England novels – and by the 1860s the journal had become well established. It exposed scandals, highlighted abuses and exploited panics 'but its concerns and angles were very much middle class concerns and angles'. By this point it was pro-Crimea, anti-Cobden, anti-strike and unsure about parliamentary reform.[110] In 'Legitimate Criticism' the old woman therefore has a book and can read well enough to know that she hasn't the ingredients, as she emphatically states – perhaps paternalism ought to come in the form of food, not book-learning, wouldn't that be safer? In 'Troubles of our Clergy' and 'Helping Him On' Mrs Smith and the oldest inhabitant seem deferential enough, but the clergy have lost control – what has become of the old forms of power, the old face-to-face village relations so admired by the city? The city knows better, but will not help out, why should it, the rural poor are far away; it's up to the clergy to deal with them. In this instance, the city, by turning its back on and marginalising the uncertainties of the country, displaces and refuses to confront the difficulties of the social relations thrown up by mature capitalism; difficulties that existed in town and country.

As Lawrence suggests, 'human relations are not merely expressed or communicated by, but are embodied in, the spatial configuration of the built environment, particularly the interface between public and private domains, that is spaces with liberal and controlled access'.[111] Its apparent boundedness and isolation have made the cottage desirable as a controllable space[112] (housework in this case is a pleasurable expression of that control), a haven from external threats, and a place where the family can be at peace, secure from the promiscuous contamination of the city. Topographies of the rural – including the constructions of the rural deployed by realist discourses, such as traditional academic disciplines – have 'reified "the village" as a bounded, sealed space and [have] ignored the flows of social relations across boundaries'.[113] Yet, places, communities, including villages, 'are always constructed out of articulations of social relations . . . which are not only internal to that locale, but which link them to elsewhere. Their "local uniqueness" is always already a product of wider contacts . . . to the geographical beyond, the world beyond the place itself.'[114] This is recognised in images of the country cottage in which all the dirt and the filth of the (city) sewer permeates the village and in which the labourer becomes a 'pig'. In its association with feminine nature (and therefore the corporeality of reproduction) and its vernacular embodiment of the folk (and therefore their coarse earthiness and bestiality) the topography of the cottage has been overwritten by the topography of the (animal) body. The resulting construction – a hybridisation of human and animal – has often been treated as the material reality that lies behind the idealised image of country life discussed in Chapter 1. However, it is more pertinent to consider the imperfect cottage as the other face of rurality, the inverse of the Beau Ideal – which defined what was in fact desirable – and therefore as a trope deployed within those realist discourses that continue to obscure or conceal 'the topographies of power'.[115] In the discussion of what is 'real' vs. what is 'imagined', the Enlightenment division of body vs. mind is perpetuated.[116]

NOTES

1 *Norfolk News*, quoted in R. Heath, *The English Peasant; Studies: historical, local and biographic* (Wakefield, [1893] 1978), p. 69.
2 G. Eliot, *Middlemarch* (London, [1871–72] 1994), pp. 31–2. Dorothea wants to do good to/for the poor in the local village by designing better, healthier cottages, and is discomfited by the lack of opportunity she has for this after her marriage.
3 V. Parker, *The English House in the Nineteenth Century* (London, 1970), p. 4.
4 Parker, *The English House*, pp. 3–5.
5 P. Tristram, *Living Space in Fact and Fiction* (London, 1989), pp. 69–70.
6 Heath, *The English Peasant*, p. 70.
7 L. Caffyn, *Workers' Housing in West Yorkshire, 1750–1920* (London, 1986), pp. 82–6.
8 J. G. Derounian, *Another Country: real life beyond Rose Cottage* (London, 1993), p. 87.
9 Derounian, *Another Country*, pp. 81–8, 92–4, 39, 23.
10 Derounian, *Another Country*, p. xi.
11 Derounian, *Another Country*, pp. 40–6.
12 Derounian, *Another Country*, p. 5.
13 Derounian, *Another Country*, pp. 16–23.
14 'Reports of Special Assistant Poor Law Commissioners on the employment of women and children in agriculture', *Parliamentary Papers* (PP), 1843, p. 28.
15 'Reports of Special assistant Poor Law Commissioners', pp. 5, 12, 22–4.
16 'Reports of Special Assistant Poor Law Commissioners', p. 5.

17 'Reports of Special Assistant Poor Law Commissioners', p. 5.
18 'Reports of Special Assistant Poor Law Commissioners', p. 27.
19 B. Disraeli, *Sybil, or the two nations*, (London, [1845] 1995), p. 95.
20 'Reports of Special Assistant Poor Law Commissioners', p. 118.
21 W. Cobbett, *Advice to Young Men and (incidentally) to young women in the middle and higher ranks of life* (London, [1830] 1856), p. 85.
22 'Reports of Special Assistant Poor Law Commissioners', pp. 118, 122, 123, 124.
23 F. Mort, *Dangerous Sexualities: medico-moral politics in England since 1830* (London, 1987).
24 'Reports of Special Assistant Poor Law Commissioners', p. 28. This was though, as noted, outweighed by the necessity of adding to the family wage.
25 'Reports of Special Assistant Poor Law Commissioners', p. 26.
26 'Reports of Special Assistant Poor Law Commissioners', p. 1.
27 'Reports of Special Assistant Poor Law Commissioners', pp. 19–21.
28 'Reports of Special Assistant Poor Law Commissioners', p. 24.
29 'Reports of Special Assistant Poor Law Commissioners', pp. 19–17, 24–5.
30 'Reports of Special Assistant Poor Law Commissioners', p. 24.
31 P. Stallybrass and A. White, *The Politics and Poetics of Transgression* (London, 1986), p. 130.
32 Stallybrass and White, *Politics and Poetics*, pp. 130–1.
33 K. Soper, *What is Nature? Culture, politics and the non-human* (Oxford, 1995), p. 87.
34 Stallybrass and White, *Politics and Poetics*, p. 126.
35 Stallybrass and White, *Politics and Poetics*, p. 131.
36 Stallybrass and White, *Politics and Poetics*, pp. 125–45.
37 'Reports of Special Assistant Poor Law Commissioners', p. 299.
38 Charles Kingsley drew on it to write *Yeast – A Problem* (1847), as did Elizabeth Gaskell for her passages representing the poverty of the agricultural labourer in *North and South* (1854).
39 *The Times* (30 December 1843), p. 5.
40 Stallybrass and White, *Politics and Poetics*, pp. 130–2.
41 The Corn Law debates also played their part.
42 'Reports of Special Assistant Poor Law Commissioners', pp. 302, 280.
43 See E. Hodder, *The Life and Work of the 7th Earl of Shaftesbury, KG* (London, 1888), pp. 236–7.
44 Quoted in Hodder, *Life and Work*, p. 279.
45 Speech made at Sturminster Agricultural Society's annual cattle show, November 1843. Quoted in G. B. A. Finlayson, *The 7th Earl of Shaftesbury, 1801–1885* (London, 1981), p. 199.
46 Finlayson, *7th Earl of Shaftesbury*, pp. 198–201, 499–500. Hodder, *Life and Work*, pp. 4, 279–82, 236–7, 484, 624, 693.
47 Quoted in Finlayson, *7th Earl of Shaftesbury*, p. 500.
48 J. Barrell, *The Dark Side of the Landscape: the rural poor in English painting 1730–1840* (Cambridge, 1980), p. 19.
49 S. Banks, 'Nineteenth-century scandal or twentieth-century model? A new look at "open" and "close" parishes', *Economic History Review*, XLI, I (1988), p. 51.
50 Banks, 'scandal or model?' pp. 51, 71.
51 'Reports of Special Assistant Poor Law Commissioners', p. 280.
52 Disraeli, *Sybil*, p. 95.
53 C. Kingsley, *Yeast – A problem* (London, [1847] 1895), pp. 36–40, 61, 177, 191.
54 Kingsley, *Yeast*, p. 98.

55 Kingsley, *Yeast*, p. 199; B. Collins, *Charles Kingsley: the Lion of Eversley* (London, 1975), pp. 105–9.
56 Kingsley, *Yeast*, pp. 44, 181.
57 Kingsley, *Yeast*, p. 194.
58 J. Lucas, 'Places and dwellings: Wordsworth, Clare and the anti-picturesque' in Cosgrove, D. and Daniels, S. (eds), *The Iconography of Landscape* (Cambridge, 1992), p. 83.
59 Kingsley, *Yeast*, p. 172.
60 Kingsley, *Yeast*, p. 191.
61 See K. Sayer, *Women of the Fields: representations of rural women in the nineteenth century* (Manchester, 1995), Chapter 2.
62 *Saturday Review of Politics, Literature, Science and Art* (16 January 1869), Vol. 27, p. 79.
63 *Saturday Review*, (13 February 1869), p. 212.
64 *Saturday Review*, (16 January 1869), p. 79.
65 *Saturday Review*, (16 January 1869), p. 79.
66 Of the women's language, for example, it said it 'may not suit the requirements of clerical inspectors or fastiduous censors, but it will satisfy the expectations of most reasonable men'. *Saturday Review*, (16 January 1869), p. 79.
67 *Saturday Review*, (16 January 1869), p. 79.
68 *Saturday Review*, (16 January 1869), p. 79.
69 *Saturday Review*, (13 February 1869), p. 213.
70 *Saturday Review*, (16 January 1869), pp. 79–80. In its second article, it championed the use of allotments and the education of the labourer who would then need to be told to send his boys to school and keep his 'girls wholly out of the turnip or the gleaning field'. *Saturday Review*, (13 February 1869), p. 213.
71 *Saturday Review*, (13 February 1869), p. 212.
72 *Saturday Review*, (16 January 1869), p. 79.
73 *Saturday Review*, (16 January 1869), p. 79.
74 *Saturday Review*, (13 February 1869), p. 213.
75 Soper, *What is Nature?* pp. 87–9.
76 Stallybrass and White, *Politics and Poetics*, pp. 131–2, 147–8, 44–59.
77 Soper, *What is Nature?*, p. 91.
78 Tristram, *Living Space*, p. 228.
79 *Saturday Review*, (13 February 1869), p. 213.
80 *Saturday Review*, (16 January 1869), p. 79.
81 Barrell, *Dark Side*, p. 3.
82 Barrell, *Dark Side*, p. 3.
83 Anon, *Original Poems for Infant Minds*, Vol. I (London, 1836), 'Old Sarah', pp. 87–8.
84 Anon, *Original Poems*, 'Old Susan', pp. 88–9.
85 Barrell, *Dark Side*, pp. 19, 23.
86 Barrell, *Dark Side*, p. 19.
87 Stallybrass and White, *Politics and Poetics*, p. 128–9. (Emphasis in the original).
88 A. and S. Briggs (eds), *Cap and Bell. Punch's Chronicle of English History in the Making 1841–1861* (London, 1972), p. xxix.
89 Briggs, *Cap and Bell*, pp. xxi–xxii.
90 *Punch, or the London Charivari* (28 September 1867), p. 132.
91 Briggs, *Cap and Bell*, pp. xxix–xxx.
92 *Punch*, (25 January 1873), p. 41.
93 J. Gerard, 'Lady Bountiful: women of the landed classes and rural philanthropy', *Victorian Studies*, Vol. 30, (Winter 1987), No. 2, p. 192.

94   Gerard, 'Lady Bountiful', pp. 183–209.
95   R. J. Lawrence, *Housing, Dwellings and Homes: design, theory, research and practice* (Chichester, 1987), p. 53.
96   Docking Union Association, posters and minutes, 1841 (Norfolk Record Office, SO17/1 488x).
97   A. Howkins, *Reshaping Rural England: a social history 1850–1925* (London, 1991), pp. 78–81.
98   Howkins, *Reshaping Rural England*, pp. 81–3.
99   J. Arch, *Joseph Arch: the story of his life told by himself*, (Countess of Warwick (ed.), London, 1898), pp. 7–8.
100   C. Brontë, *Jane Eyre* (1847), Vol. I, Chapter 7.
101   Gerard, 'Lady Bountiful', p. 200.
102   An anonymous navvy, whose memoir was originally published in *Macmillan's Magazine*, Vol. V, 1861–62, reprinted in J. Burnett (ed.), *Useful Toil: autobiographies of working people from the 1820s to 1920s* (London, 1976), p. 62.
103   C. M. Yonge, 'Quack, Quack' (1882) reprinted in G. Avery (ed.), *Village Children* (London, [1846–82] 1967), p. 123. Charlotte Yonge (1823–1901) was a novelist who lived in Otterbourne, Hampshire, for the whole of her life and taught in the parish school. She edited *The Monthly Packet*, a girls' magazine, and wrote 160 books consisting of fiction, histories, biographies and text books. She also wrote a number of children's stories about a village called Langley, the first published in 1846 in the *Magazine for the Young*. These early stories were reprinted as a collection called *Langley School* (1850), the rest were written and published in the 1880s. *Village Children* includes five of these stories and one other.
104   T. Hardy, 'The Dorsetshire Labourer', *Longman's Magazine*, Vol. 2, (1883), p. 255.
105   Barrell, *Dark Side*, p. 3.
106   *Punch*, (17 May 1873), p. 199.
107   *Punch*, (28 November 1874), p. 223.
108   For further detail, See Howkins, *Reshaping Rural England*, pp. 166–94.
109   R. Barthes, *Image, Music, Text*, trans. S. Heath (London, 1982), p. 41.
110   Briggs, *Cap and Bell*, pp. xxv–xxvii.
111   Lawrence, *Housing, Dwellings and Homes*, p. 52.
112   Tristram, *Living Space*, pp. 264–5.
113   J. Murdoch and A. C. Pratt, 'From the power of topography to the topography of power: a discourse of strange ruralities' in Cloke, P. and Little, J. (eds), *Contested Countryside Cultures: otherness, marginalisation and rurality* (London and New York, 1997), p. 53.
114   D. Massey, 'Places and their pasts', *History Workshop Journal*, No. 39, p. 183.
115   Murdoch and Pratt, 'Topography', p. 53.
116   See Soper, *What is Nature?* for a discussion of the consequences.

CHAPTER 3

The English cottage garden

When we return from visiting other lands, we notice with gratified eyes these homely wayside gardens, which are peculiarly English. Englishmen have always loved their gardens, and all classes share in this affection.

(P. H. Ditchfield)[1]

The cottage garden is Nature tamed. Quintessentially English, evocative of stability, childhood and homeliness, cottage gardens with their resident flowers, whether cultivated or self-seeded, vegetables and livestock, have conjured up powerful and nostalgic associations of the Beau Ideal since the mid- to late nineteenth century. As discussed in Chapter 1, an appendage to the country cottage, the cottage garden has come to be seen as an extension of the domestic sphere, and, like the cottage itself, as a private space or retreat, rather than as a place of visible work, or of wider social relations.[2] At the same time, the cottage garden has also gained its own connotations of comfort, thriftiness and permanence. The image of the cottage garden has come to be used as an indicator of what is 'natural', what values we should mourn the loss of and how we might resurrect them.[3] It works at the level of the small scale, the communal and is associated with the useful and the pleasurable.[4]

The modern idea of a 'cottage garden' is a construct created in part through art, literature and related discourses, and in part through the efforts of landscape gardeners and designers like J. C. Loudon,[5] William Robinson[6] and Gertrude Jekyll.[7] And there was a direct relationship between the ascendancy of the ideal cottage and the development of the ideal cottage garden. For instance, the images of rurality celebrated in the late nineteenth century by Helen Allingham[8] – the domestic idyll, the vernacular, tradition, authenticity, romance, nostalgia – were put into gardening practice by Gertrude Jekyll. Jekyll campaigned against formal garden structures in favour of informal planting and became the foremost proponent of the cottage garden for use in town and country. Earlier, Loudon had wished 'to see fruit-trees, ornamental shrubs, climbers, and flowers in every Cottager's garden, with bees, poultry, rabbits (if only for the children), pigeons and a cat'. And, though keenly interested in the welfare of the labourer, in his view the 'cultivation of a few Brompton and ten-week stocks, carnations, picotees, pinks, and other flowers ought never to be omitted: they are the means of pure and constant gratification which Providence has afforded alike to the rich and the poor.'[9]

Comments like this mean that both contemporary designers and garden historians often feel driven to search for a wilder working-class authenticity and to set this against a cultivated bourgeois counterfeit. As one garden historian writes, the 'cottage garden... can be seen to express a spirit of community. It is in short, a "folk" entity and harks back to a time when the community in which men have to live and are probably meant to live was not obscured by the cult of the individual mind and spirit.'[10] There are apparently economic and social distinctions to be made between those idealised gardens constructed by garden designers (who use the cottage garden as a motif), the creations of small-scale yet middle-class gardeners (whose gardens are the result of growing prosperity) and the plots of those who have planted up their gardens out of economic need.[11] Jekyll, they note, claimed that her inspiration was the labourer's cottage garden. 'I have learnt much from little cottage gardens that help to make our English wayside the prettiest in the temperate world', she believed. 'One can hardly go into the smallest cottage garden without learning or observing something new.'[12] But, it appears, she 'simply did not see the yard-cum-garden of the average cottager, with its chicken-house, rabbit-hutches and outdoor earth-closet'.[13] And this is why Geoff Hamilton feels able to say that her

> influence, and that of other great gardeners of her time and a little later, while masquerading as 'cottage gardening', in my view missed the essence... Great gardeners, talented artists and original plantswomen they certainly were, but were they really cottage gardeners? For me the answer has to be no—the cottage garden is an *artisan's* creation, not an artist's.[14]

Gillian Darley's assessment that the 'cottage garden is an odd mixture of myth and reality'[15] is currently the most commonplace. Looking at the history of the cottage garden is not just a matter of setting 'image' against 'reality', which Darley writes off as failing to recognise 'the less picturesque truth that history can provide'.[16] As Lynda Nead argues, in the case of the rural idyll the 'work of representation should not be seen in terms of a false construction of country life. Rather than a manipulation of reality, images of rural domesticity were the site where an ideological category designated the "rural labouring class" was defined and given visual form.'[17] The same can be said of gardens and the work of garden designers.

This is now increasingly recognised, hence even Hamilton goes on to assert that the 'cottage garden "style" was not invented; it simply evolved. So you can just step into that process of evolution to make a traditional, romantic cottage garden – wherever you live.'[18] It seems that there is a certain fluidity to the cottage garden style, which allows the cottage garden itself to be re-created using up-to-date materials, in any location, without losing any of its 'authenticity'. This is a view which highlights not only the fashion-driven nature of most gardening,[19] but also the garden's intrinsic hybridity.[20] Nonetheless, we should still note the particular stress on the 'traditional' in Hamilton's statement, the organic 'evolution' of the cottage garden 'style', and the passing reference to the 'romantic', which takes us back to the pre-industrial, the 'folk' and the village community. The cottage garden remains essentially 'rural', even when its location is materially urban, and it is this unique ability to transform city-space into country-space that currently forms part of its allure, as Geoff Hamilton suggests, in 'a frenetic, stressful world we *need* our "rural idyll" more than ever'.[21] The cottage garden 'style', like the cottage itself, is as desirable today as it was in the nineteenth century because, ideologically, it is still supposed to provide a tranquil haven, a stable sanctuary from the world at large and safety from the vagaries of capital.

SETTING THE BOUNDS

As we have already seen, the combination of domesticity with a privileging of organic communal relations provided a particularly powerful and persistent Beau Ideal in the nineteenth century. As the lives of the new middle class became less fixed, so they looked to a past and for a present that would provide them with both independence and the stability of long-standing tradition.[22] The cottage garden, like all gardens, therefore appeared within most nineteenth-century literature and art to be a place that was socially neutral, psychologically fixed and physically bounded by hedges, fences and walls.[23] However, as Reed notes, the

> fields, farms, churches and cottages, castles and gardens of the landscape are not discrete entities, but the constituent elements of a dense historical matrix, linked in the minds of men and women by assumptions, values, and preconceptions, sometimes formally codified, often nothing more than practices informally recognised through custom and long usage.[24]

Its links, both concrete and cultural, to and its relationship with, the outside world therefore also overwrote it. There is, in fact, some irony in the etymology of the word 'garden' derived as it is from the Old English 'geard', i.e. yard or enclosed ground.[25] Even on the most literal level, many of the cottage garden's most popular plants were originally imports,[26] thereby demonstrating the power of the English garden to take in, naturalise and domesticate what was once essentially alien to it.[27] The auricula, for instance, a common cottage plant by the mid-nineteenth century, 'was brought to our sheltered lawns from the snowy moss of the Swiss Alps,'[28] while the humble ranunculus[29] was spread about by Mahomet IV's vizier – who demanded that every Pacha should 'send seeds and roots of the finest species of the Sultan's favourite to Constantinople.' In 'the process of time,' clergyman and critic R. A. Willmott suggests, 'the ambassadors at the Turkish court procured specimens for their prospective sovereigns, and the ranunculus reared its head in all the royal gardens of Europe. Next to the rose, it seems to be the most expansive name in botany.'[30] Here we find an uneasy mix of the celebration of empire and the more home-spun act of (cottage) gardening. Meanwhile, the imposition of a country garden on a native landscape worked as visible demonstration of the civilising impact of the English, while the cottage garden could be read as a tangible expression of the imperial project. In this respect the history of gardening, even quintessentially English cottage gardening, is immutably bound up with the history of trade and the growth of empire, which highlights the need to avoid what the geographer Doreen Massey has called 'internalist and essentialist constructions' of place.[31] As Martin Hoyles points out in *The Story of Gardening*, an examination of international relations and colonialism is essential to an understanding of garden history.[32]

Indeed, even today there is often an uneasy tension in gardening literature between the fantasy of the English garden as enclosed space, and the celebration of the English garden as harbour of exotic trophies. As Agyeman and Spooner have noted, there are often powerful associations to be made between 'alien' and 'native' peoples, and 'alien' and 'native' plants.[33] Gardening and gardeners are far from being 'innocent' and when in *The English Garden* (1966) Edward Hyams notes that William Robinson aimed to '"naturalise" into an English landscape plants more spectacular than any which the native temperate flora could furnish',[34] one can see in process not simply the writing of botanical history, but also a naturalising of the colonial language of the 'exotic' and 'alien', the 'temperate' and 'native' into gardening discourse. Earlier on he describes Loudon as the gardener who defined the 'English Garden', 'which by that time had a definite meaning for foreigners;

yet ... was far from clearly defined ... [Loudon helped establish it as] the English dream, the re-created paradise'.[35] When looking at the story of the cottage garden we therefore need to recognise that the politics of its border crossings have largely remained hidden within subsequent histories of the 'natural' and leisured act of gardening,[36] which, for the nascent middle class, came to be seen as a singularly rational and profoundly apolitical occupation in the nineteenth century.[37]

In Britain at least, gardening came initially to be seen by the nascent middle class as an ideal use of their new-found leisure time, one which crucially allowed them to avoid the pitfall of idleness. According to the journals of the day, such as *The Gardener's Magazine of Rural and Domestic Improvement* established in 1826 and edited by Loudon, or Joseph Paxton's *Horticultural Register* published from 1831, gardening required diligence and application, was physically and morally healthy, and stimulated the mind. In addition, the garden was thought of as a private space, as a part of the house, while as an activity gardening was supposed to be a domestic occupation, home-centred and focused on the family.[38] This rational recreation, it was assumed, would have an equally beneficial effect on rich and poor alike. In particular it would ensure that the working class were employed in thrifty, healthful work, stop them from going to the pub and strengthen their ties to home and family. The net result, according to those who promoted gardening among the poor, would be that the labourer would turn away from the dangers of community-based politics and mob rule.[39]

Clearly, this rhetoric was focused on the male labourer, so that the condition of any cottage garden came to signify the thriftiness, industriousness, honesty, sobriety and continence – i.e. the respectability – of the man who worked it. As one mid-century author in the *Cottage Gardener* put it, there 'is moral beauty ... in the cultivated cottage garden. Neatness and attendance bespeak activity, diligence, and care; neglect and untidiness tell of the *beer-house*'.[40] This kind of construction represented the cottage garden as a male domain and, at one and the same time, wrote off the political resonance/radical potential of gardening for Geoff Hamilton's pet artisan:

> The labourer who possesses and delights in the garden appended to his Cottage is generally among the most decent of his class; he is seldom a frequenter of the ale-house; and there are few among them so senseless as not readily to engage in its cultivation when convinced of the comforts and gain derivable from it. When the lower order of a state are contented, the abettors of anarchy cabal for the destruction of its civil tranquillity in vain, for they have to efface the strongest of all earthly associations, home and its hallowed accompaniments, from the attachment of the

labourer, before he will assist in tearing them from others, in the struggle to effect which, he has nothing definite to gain, and all those flowers of life to lose.[41]

Loudon agreed: 'Give the Cottager land that will reward his labours,' he pleaded, 'it will stimulate his industry, and ultimately tend to link each class of society in inseperable [sic] bonds for the preservation of national order and tranquillity.'[42] The labourer's cottage garden, then, secured (male) working-class respectability and became a defence against agitation; it stood between chaos and civilisation, between licence and order. The country was secure as long as the labourer returned home to tend his flowers (metaphorical and literal) and dig over his quarter of an acre. The male labourer was domesticated through useful toil.

THE ARTISAN'S GARDEN

The 'folk', or 'artisan's' cottage garden, historically consisted of a small plot of land, normally, though not always, attached to the labourer's house, mostly used for growing vegetables, fruit and herbs, and sometimes for keeping a pig, a few chickens or ducks, bees and, occasionally, some rabbits. Loudon suggested that a rood, i.e. a quarter of an acre, would be needed to supply the labourer, his wife and three small children, plus pigs and poultry, with the requisite vegetables and potatoes. He thought they should grow: onions, leeks, carrots, beans, parsnips, cabbages and potatoes, currants, gooseberries, cherries, apples, pears and other soft fruit.[43] One such, tended by Britton Abbot, was described in 1797:

> Two miles from Tadcaster, on the left-hand side of the road to York, stands a beautiful little cottage, with a garden, that has long caught the eye of the traveller. The slip of land is exactly a rood, inclosed [sic] by a cut quick hedge; and containing the cottage, fifteen apple trees, one green gage, and three winesour plum-trees, two apricot-trees, several gooseberry and currant bushes, abundance of common vegetables, and three hives of bees.[44]

Not that the productive labourer's garden necessarily lacked flowery interest.[45] Geoff Hamilton for one believes that a few hedgerow flowers were also grown purely for pleasure even in medieval cottage gardens, though it is clear that the practice of gardening as a form of recreation really only began in earnest in the Elizabethan period. The sixteenth century, for example, saw the rise of topiary, an oft-maligned craze adopted by cottage gardeners which persisted into the twentieth century when Ditchfield was writing, examples of which can still be seen dotted around the country.[46] The auricula was quickly adopted and grown competitively by enthusiasts from the same period; by the time that Willmott was writing, these 'florists' had clubs all over the country.[47] When tended by an enthusiast, a nineteenth-century English cottage garden might include dahlias, hollyhocks, delphiniums, sweet peas, roses, pinks, clematis, fritillaries, lilies, geraniums, mignonette, and border carnations among its plant-stock, as well as the requisite fruit, herbs and vegetables. Plants from the big house probably made their way to the small as fashions that became popular among the wealthy were adapted and adopted by the poor, who were therefore just as likely to plant up the rows of carpet bedding detested by the proponents of wild gardening, as they were to use 'traditional' cottage garden plants.[48] Similarly, in the nineteenth century the majority of private urban and suburban gardens were planted up by the speculative builders who constructed the houses they belonged to, and because of this often contained a strange amalgamation of quite ordinary plants and expensive exotics. As was noted at the time:

> The late Mr Loudon drew attention to the costly plants often found in them. He gave this explanation:– The gardens of suburban streets are planted by speculative builders, and chiefly from nursery sales, which have been very frequent during the last twenty or thirty years. It is quite the custom at these auctions to mix rare with common plants, that the former may sell the latter. In this way, the choicest specimens have found their way into the grass-plots of cottage-villas or the humbler row.[49]

But, the evidence from the proponents of cottage gardening makes it clear that this small plot of land primarily had to provide the labourer's family with additional food, or a surplus, to help them spin out their wages. A garden, or an allotment, was in fact widely supposed to be essential to the survival and comfort of the rural labourer. Arthur Young was typical in identifying an absence of land for gardening as problematic in 1804 when he surveyed Hertfordshire for the Board of Agriculture:

> SECT. II. – COTTAGES
> I am sorry not to find any minutes in my notes upon this head, which is so truly important, except the remark so often recurring, that the cottagers have no where any land, more than the small amount of insufficient gardens. I twice went out of my way to make inquiries; where I was told that one or two labourers possessed enclosed land enough to support a cow; but the intelligence was unfounded ... The present system of supporting the labouring poor is certainly erroneous, both in practice and theory.

It appears to me as a matter of demonstration, from a multitude of facts, that the granting them land for cows, and an ample garden, is the only cheap mode of assisting them materially.[50]

It is difficult to assess what a cottage garden might be worth to the labourer, but, it was suggested that Britton Abbot, who earned 12s to 18s a week as an agricultural labourer, managed to get 'from his [quarter acre] garden, annually, about 40 bushels of potatoes, besides other vegetables'; while 'his fruit, in a good year [was] worth from £.3 to £.4 a year'.[51] Nearly a century later, Susan Silvester's mother, who her daughter says was a thrifty manager, helped keep her children well fed and well clothed in part because of the family's garden and allotment, pig and chickens. 'Mother grew hyssop and horehound in the garden and made "tea" with them when we had colds.' On moving with her (blacksmith) husband to a cottage in 1902 that had a large garden in which they could grow fruit and vegetables, and had room for pigs, chickens, a pony and trap, Susan Silvester found herself well off.[52] It is equally hard to establish exactly how many rural homes actually had gardens.[53] Despite enclosure, common land, or land used as such, often survived and this, plus small areas of sub-let land, edges and corners of fields, were also frequently available to the labourer for grazing or planting up with potatoes, carrots and other staples in most regions. In fact, many artisans and labourers held small acreages of land, worked on by the whole family, which were as important to their subsistence as their cash wages, and which blur the occupational divisions in the countryside, especially between small farmers, artisans and farm workers.[54]

When provided, the size of a garden plot varied considerably from region to region and for 'garden' we might more appropriately read 'allotment' in many instances, especially as many 'allotments' were themselves attached to the labourer's house. According to *The Penny Cyclopædia of the Society for the Diffusion of Useful Knowledge* (1843):

> COTTAGE ALLOTMENTS may be considered as such portions of land hired by labourers, either attached to, or apart from, their dwellings, as they, assisted by their families, may be able to cultivate without ceasing to let out their services daily to others ... Various experiments have been tried, and the opinion of the persons best informed upon the subject appears now to be, that a quarter of an acre is about the quantity which, without prejudice to his other employments, a labourer can in general thoroughly cultivate, and consequently derive the greatest profit from.[55]

Meanwhile, *Chambers's Information for the People* (1842) defined what it called 'spade husbandry', otherwise known as 'cottage-farming', or 'field-gardening' in terms of the labourer's requirements. The actual tools required to engage in 'spade husbandry' were: 'two or three spades of different sizes, a pickaxe, three-pronged digging fork, hoes, rake, light harrow which he can draw, scythe, reaping hooks, hay-forks, flail, wheelbarrow, &c., according to means'. It was useful if the labourer could sharpen his tools himself, but he would not keep a horse. 'All the work is done by the manual labour of the farmer and his family. The only live stock is a cow or cows, pigs and poultry. The homestead consists of a cottage with several apartments – a cow-house, pig-stye, and barn. The size of the farm is supposed to vary from four to six acres, and to be laid out in six or eight distinct fields, properly fenced.'[56] *Chambers's* then elaborated as to the best methods, likely value of produce and difficulties that might be experienced. It also referred to the Labourers' Friendly Society, founded in London, 1833, as a 'beneficial' body that was attempting to secure 'allotments' for the 'labouring poor', and copies part of its publication on keeping a cow and pig on an acre of land.[57] In subsequent numbers – each cost $1\frac{1}{2}d$ – it outlined best practice in 'The Kitchen Garden', 'The Flower Garden', 'The Fruit Garden', 'Arboriculture', 'Cattle and Dairy Husbandry', horse, sheep, pig, caged-bird and bee management; later it covered dogs and field sports, angling, and 'Out-Of-Doors Recreations'. In other words, it provided complete guidance on the best use of rural space, as well as advice on the management of the land, for the aspiring (upper working-, or lower middle-class) reader.

In the west of England, as for Britton Abbot, a cottage 'garden' could be as large as a quarter of an acre and include a pigsty, while in Northumberland labourers and their families were often provided with a cottage, pigsty and garden rent-free, including an additional 1,200 yards for planting potatoes and summer grazing rights.[58] Tom Mullins, a Staffordshire farm labourer rented a smallholding of seven acres for £15 when he married in 1886 – totalling a rent of £20 a year for house and land.[59] Conditions varied, however, and by the mid-nineteenth century many labourers were left without either garden or allotment, especially in the south and east of England. This was in part because cottages were increasingly being built without any land attached to them – especially those thrown up by speculators – and because, according to campaigners, the land that had originally surrounded many older cottages was gradually being taken away.[60] As Britton Abbot said, when offered his cottage free for the work he had done, 'Sir, you have a pleasure in seeing my cottage and garden neat: and why should not other squires have the same pleasure, in seeing the cottages and gardens as nice about them? The poor would then be happy; and would love them, and the place where they lived: but now every little nook of land is to be let to the great farmers; and nothing left for the poor, but to go to the parish.'[61] Though some commentators thought the cottage garden could tame the labourer, it nonetheless remained a contested site.

During the late-eighteenth to early-nineteenth century, the enclosure of a piece of land as a garden was the first stage in a labourer's bid to become a squatter, build his/her own cottage and thereby gain possession, or title, to the land.[62] Social reformers and clergymen campaigned throughout the nineteenth century for the extensive provision of allotments, in order to improve the overall condition of the labouring class. *Chambers's* itself engaged in this battle, finishing off its essay on 'spade husbandry' by rebutting accusations in the *Encyclopædia Britannica*'s entry on the 'Cottage System' that cottage farming increased the number of paupers and distracted the labourer from his proper labour.[63] But, like the difference between 'garden' and 'allotment', the distinction between a smallholding and an allotment was itself a nice one. In keeping with the move towards large-scale capitalist agriculture, even the most vociferous supporters of allotment gardening were often highly critical of the idea of small-scale subsistence farming supported by *Chambers's* and the *Penny Cyclopædia*. 'It has also been urged against the system of cottage allotments', the *Penny Cyclopædia* noted for instance,

> that it tends to encourage early marriages, and to the production of a race of beggars. That cottage allotments may have this effect is true, but the objection is mainly applicable, and perhaps has been mainly applied, to cottage allotments which are of such magnitude as to render it impossible for the cottager to cultivate them without exchanging his character of a labourer for that of a farmer without adequate capital ... The multiplication of small farms is quite a different question from that of cottage allotments as here understood, and opinions can hardly be much divided as to the inexpediency of such increase.[64]

As we might glean from the statement that an allotment was a piece of ground that could be cultivated by the labourer 'without ceasing to let out their services daily to others', large farmers were generally found to 'have strong prejudices against the system'.[65] Whereas small farmers could get away with paying less than a subsistence wage if their labourers had an alternative source of income, at least until the mid-nineteenth century,[66] many larger farmers were apparently reluctant to allow their hands land which might distract them from their paid work on the farm, or make them less dependent on a cash wage. There therefore seems to have been considerable confusion between peasant/yeoman farming and cottage gardening. This confusion has historically elided the difference between work and leisure and currently provides the cottage garden, which most histories trace back at least to the Norman period, with its 'authenticity' within the discourse of Englishness.[67] And a tension has remained in the language of gardening – wherein gardening might lead to the labourer's independence.

The idea of setting up in a self-sufficient farming community or on an independent smallholding was given serious consideration within radical circles throughout the nineteenth and on into the twentieth century. There were any number of radical land schemes proposed from the 1820s onwards, Malcolm Chase notes, the Chartist Land Plan being one of the largest of its kind, with a peak of 70,000 weekly subscribers, each of whom hoped to live on a cottage smallholding rented from the Plan. In 1843 the Chartist Convention accepted Feargus O'Connor's plans to restore the land to the labourer. As Chase argues, the Chartist Land Plan has often been written off by historians as 'absurd', 'unquestionably reactionary', 'crack-brained', 'harebrained', 'utopian', 'nostalgic' and as a 'distraction'.[68] But, though the Chartist Land Plan itself failed, the concept persisted. In July 1900, The *Labour Leader* exclaimed, 'England cannot live without agriculture. Her harvests and her fruit and vegetable supplies are as important to her as her mineral wealth. The cry must go forth "Back to the land!"'[69] With the rapid rural depopulation that took place at the close of the nineteenth century, the campaign for the allotment system and for the provision of smallholdings was given wider credence. As Marsh argues, this 'back to the land' movement was prompted by a desire to return 'to cultivation, to agrarian life and a closer, intimate relation with the earth', in direct contrast to 'the competitive, commercial world of the city'.[70] However, even at the end of the nineteenth century, and despite Jesse Collings' Small Holdings Act of 1892 and subsequent Small Holdings and Allotments Act of 1907 – consolidated in 1908 – which resulted in the creation of over 14,000 allotments of anything between 1 to 50 acres, resistance towards this kind of reform continued.[71]

As Hoyles suggests, it always seems a little odd to talk of politics in reference to gardening. Gardening should be an escape from politics, a refuge; yet, if we mean the theories and practices of power relations between people when we talk of politics, then gardening has everything to do with it.[72] The politics of gardening, he argues, have simply been hidden because the activity of gardening has come to be seen as 'natural',[73] i.e. as universal and unchanging. The supposedly essential, innate domesticity of the cottage garden, its enclosed introspection, coupled with the moral benefits, natural and leisured aspects of the act of gardening itself have written off the political meanings of cultivation in dominant discourse. As Robert Willmott noted, in his *A Journal of Summer Time in the Country* (1864), when suggesting that a history of gardening should be written, the 'moral influence of a garden . . . is lively and lasting'.[74]

Hence Denison for one felt able to recommend the adoption of allotments when making a return for the 1843 'Reports of Special Assistant Poor Law Commissioners on the employment of women and children in agriculture'. In Beccles, Suffolk, the allotment system, which he reported largely employed women and children, had been found to be the best way to improve the moral, economic and social condition of the poor. The aim being to 'dispauperize' them, each cottager was provided with 40–60 rods of land, and despite the loss of employment in the area, the condition of the labouring class was found to be good. The holders of allotments were industrious and orderly, cottage gardens were better looked-after, because the young had begun to emulate their elders, and neighbours had begun to compete with each other for the quality and quantity of their produce.[75]

Though demands by labourers like Abbot that the poor have access to small plots of land in order to remain materially independent were partially permissible, because property-centred and individualist aspirations were always preferable to mass action,[76] they were still inevitably glossed over unless reference to them was thought expedient. For instance, in stating 'now every little nook of land is to be let to the great farmers', Abbot seems to have been attacking the process of enclosure, but the author who quotes him is only interested in criticising the poor laws as then constituted. His argument is premised on a considerable loss to national efficiency and encompasses some morally debilitating side effects, but bypasses Abbot's own concerns about the rise of large-scale agriculture. While the garden was seen as a private space, as part of the house, gardening was seen as a domestic occupation, home-centred and focused on the family:

> Were they properly and universally encouraged to industry and economy, we should soon find thriving and happy cottagers in every part of the kingdom. Let only a tenth of the money, now spent in workhouses, in what is usually called '*the relief of the poor,*' be applied in assisting and encouraging them to thrive and be happy in their cottages, the poor rate will be lessened, and a national saving made in both labour and food . . . *Domestic connections, property, liberty, the hope of advancement,* those master springs of human action exist not in a workhouse . . . Of the different modes of aiding and animating the poor, none would have more tendency to raise them above the want of parochial aid,

than that of enabling them progressively to follow his [Abbot's] example, in such a manner, that the most deserving might in their turn become the owners of comfortable cottages and productive gardens.[77]

He goes on to declaim:

> Let us consider what must be the effect of this system [of poor relief] on the cottager. Tenant to the farmer who has taken his cottage over his head, he is aware that his new landlord will require as much rent as he can contrive to pay. He has a young and increasing family; and, when times are at the best, he often finds it as much as he can do to go on, from one day to another, in their support . . . If the hour of adversity arrives, he knows the rule of his parish, that *'no assistance is to be given to the labourer, while he possesses any thing of his own;'* . . . Is it perfectly clear, that [in the same circumstances] we should not spend every penny that could be spared from the daily nourishment of our families, in self-indulgence at an ale-house?[78]

The emphasis on the cottager's 'industry and economy', the stress on the 'national saving . . . in labour and food', and the reference to '*property, liberty, the hope of advancement,* those master springs of human action' all smack more of self-help and political economy than of an attack on the enclosure movement *per se*. This is why even Arthur Young, proponent of large-scale capitalist agriculture, favoured allotments and was critical of the landowners of Hertfordshire who generally failed to supply cottagers with any more than the most meagre of gardens. He was relieved to be able to find one labourer who had a pig and the use of six acres – cropped with $1\frac{1}{2}$ acres each of wheat, barley, turnips and $1\frac{1}{2}$ acres lying fallow – for which he paid 10s an acre ploughing and £10.10s rent. While he noted that at least the Earl of Clarendon provided 'nooks and corners of fields to his labourers for planting potatoes; which they most thankfully cultivate, and find of singular use to them'.[79] This point was pursued in 1843 by the *Penny Cyclopœdia* which asserted that the

> object of cottage allotments is to increase the resources of the labourer; firstly, by supplying him with many necessaries and comforts which he would have a difficulty in purchasing from a portion of his wages, and which, if even he could do so, he would purchase at a great disadvantage; secondly, by enabling him to turn everything to profit, so that nothing need be lost.[80]

By arguing that the labourers 'were become reckless, devoid of skill, and incapable of taking care of themselves'[81] from the loss of land, a neat sidestep away from any explicit radicalism, the *Penny Cyclopœdia* was able to pursue the argument that every labourer should be given an allotment in order to mitigate against poverty. The cottage garden, like the labourer's home, became a defence against (male) anarchy; it stood between chaos and civilisation, between Nature and Culture.

'ALL THOSE FLOWERS OF LIFE TO LOSE'

Historically, despite the rhetoric, the bulk of cottage gardening often fell to the woman of the house. The large amount of garden work that could be done by a labourer's wife is outlined in an *Account of the Produce of a Cottager's Garden in Shropshire* (1806) published alongside the *Account of Britton Abbot's Cottage and Garden*. In this instance the labourer's wife largely managed the land – 1 and 1/16 acres – herself, planting most of it up with wheat and potatoes in rotation, fertilising it by keeping a pig and mostly cultivating it with her own labour. Her husband, a collier, apparently 'always assists in digging, [and harvest] after his hours of ordinary labour',[82] which legitimised, because it limited, her work on the land. Her methods, the commentator noted were sound; her potatoes and wheat apparently being grown 'in a way which has yielded good crops, and of late fully equal, or rather superior, to the produce of neighbouring farms, and with little or no expense'.[83] Her work included manuring, hoeing, raking, planting and harvesting the crops. She also planted up peas, beans, cabbages, early potatoes and turnips on some of the land – used as a garden – and sold her early potatoes, peas and cabbages at market.[84] This kind of very physical and dirty labour was rarely given public recognition, however, especially later on in the century, because it increasingly came to be seen as an unfeminine and hence an inappropriate occupation, even for working-class women.[85]

As Hoyles maintains, there 'is a kaleidoscope of cultural meanings attached to gardening'[86] and within this kaleidoscope gardening as an activity was gendered.[87] Even in the work of social realists, the one place where we do see women at work on the land, the garden itself carries gendered connotations. In Clausen's *The Allotment Garden* (1899)[88] for example, we are presented with a bleak, brown, muddy landscape, the scene almost heroic as a young couple struggle to unearth their potatoes. The picture has considerable movement; the man digging, on the left of the canvas and a little way from the audience, the woman stooping busily to pick up the potatoes she has just forked. Though similar to Millet's *The Angelus*, as was noted when it was originally exhibited, in this instance the couple do not show their piety by stopping to pray; figured as a part of the land they work, their labour is their prayer. As he digs to one side, she picks up the fruits of their labour; placed in the foreground, she is as important to and active in her task as her husband is. Here, Clausen celebrated the productive unity of man and wife working together, and a foreshadowing of the results of another kind of co-operative effort, a haystack, like a full breast, looms above the woman in the middle of the canvas. This appears to be the central connotation: rural womanhood as active fruitful motherhood, the garden/allotment as generative female space, the linking of Woman with Nature.

Thomas Hardy used the same Edenic associations to shock his audience in *Tess of the d'Urbervilles* (1891). When Alec d'Urberville approaches Tess on her family plot, it is over a year since Tess has been home and she is setting about planting up the garden and allotment with her father. Late one evening, she finds Alec d'Urberville working beside her disguised in a smock frock; after refusing his aid she returns to the house to find that her father has died and her family have to quit the cottage. At this point in the novel, the pressure is building for Tess, who needs Alec's help as soon as she has refused it. This is Tess's third and final return home, this time in darkness, and it is seen through her own eyes; as she works, the world around her feels unreal, the landscape reflects her history, mingled with its own, and her perceptions are subtly altered. Alec's sudden reappearance by firelight, holding a pitchfork, reminds us of his devilish aspect, which is reinforced when he calls her 'Eve' and names himself 'the old Other One'. In this instance, Alec takes the position of observer, spying on Tess as she works, objectifying her, while he plays out the tension that existed between garden as property and garden as common. His invasion of this intensely private and female space is figured as another kind of rape.[89]

The scene echoes that in which Tess creeps through the farm garden to listen to Angel playing his harp, in which we see how Tess is subject to and driven by nature's rhythms. Tess is described animalistically, and the garden's red stains, sticky profusion and clouds of pollen are symbolic of abundant fertility, desire and insemination. But, it is also reminiscent of the scene in which Alec makes Tess swear on a stone commemorating a man who had sold his soul to the devil. It brings together the imagery of fire, and of the Fall – through which Tess has been figured both as Eve and the snake – which have dogged her throughout the novel. And, because he watches her, Alec is fascinated by what he sees; as observer he not only watches, but also identifies with the observed. The 'person gazing puts a spell on his victim', Victor Burgin argues, but 'the person watching is also fascinated by that which he sees'.[90] Tess is not simply subject to Alec's gaze; engaged in productive work and caught in her own reverie, she also becomes a figure with whom he seeks to empathise. 'Eve' to his 'Old Other One', he makes her transcendent and the pair symbolically move rapidly beyond the minutiae of spadework.

In high art and literature, then, women's employment on the land might take on a series of metaphysical connotations that seek to exceed the material, or even the domestic, through the use of the mythic image of garden as Eden/Paradise. However, the meaning of 'paradise' has historically had dramatically different connotations for women and men. As Annette Kolodny suggests with reference to the use of this concept in the American West at the turn of the nineteenth and twentieth centuries:

> For men the term (with all its concomitant psychosexual associations) echoed an invitation for mastery and possession of the vast new continent. For women, by contrast, it denoted domesticity. Thus, while men sought new Edens and created new Arcadias for themselves, working 'the keen adze' and altering the landscape to make it comply with their dreams of receptive and bountiful realms, women patched Pine Tree quilts, appliquéd counterpanes with brightly colored Rose of Sharon designs, and cultivated small gardens in order 'to render Home a Paradise.'[91]

A century earlier, in England, Humphrey Repton, on buying a cottage in 1786, by 1816 had taken some land around it and argued,

> by this appropriation of twenty-five yards of garden, I have obtained a frame to my landscape; the frame is composed of flowering shrubs and evergreens; beyond which are seen, the cheerful village, the high road, and that constant moving scene, which I would not exchange for any of the lonely parks that I have improved for others.[92]

The garden 'framed' both the view of the cottager and the cottager's view; it shaped the way in which the countryside might be seen and turned an active agricultural setting into a landscape.

By the mid-nineteenth century, in perfect form it was full of tall, colourful flowers, healthy vegetables, trees weighted down with fruit and a backdrop of climbers covering a wall or the cottage itself. Roses were, of course, commonplace in these scenes, signifying both a very English idyll and an idealised femininity. The resident cat and, commonly, caged bird as ever stood in as signs of domesticity, while chicks and kittens equated with childhood and a nostalgic sense of passing years. The remaining vegetables, occasional pig, bee hives and farm/garden implements, were suggestive of the cottager's thrift and industry, and assured the audience that the absent man of the family would soon be home. The female occupants of these lush gardens were normally engaged in some kind of domestic work, or occupied in other suitably feminine activities such as flower-picking, convalescing, nursing, feeding ducks and fowl, kitten-taunting, courting or visiting. The same imagery was used in literary texts:

> Granny Woodfall had a nice garden... with double daisies and thrift and violets along the paths, and vegetables beyond, also three or four stocks of bees... She would not keep fowls, because she said they would scratch up her garden and ruinate it, but she had ducks – which ate the slugs and did no harm.[93]

Where, for the Georgians, cottage gardens were, as Repton's statement implies, human, self-conscious,[94] landscapes on the small scale, the Victorians went on to figure them as domestic spaces and ideal playgrounds. Children were meant to play in gardens, to enjoy their surroundings under the watchful eye of their mother or grandmother. The countryside itself was often represented as a single continuous garden in which children might roam freely – the countryside was figured more often as Nature tamed rather than a wilderness, so it was safe to leap the garden fence. Drawing on Romantic constructions of childhood (which saw children as creatures of Nature, requiring a slight channelling in the right direction rather than strict mechanistic control), parental or other adult constraints always lay in wait in the background, but were given the lightest possible touch. The garden fence, the stile, hedge and gate provided a frame for rather than a physical barrier to the child's play.

William Collins' *Rustic Civility* (1832)[95] is an early case in point; drawing on picturesque conventions to show three submissive children holding a gate open for a gentleman, he is present only in the form of his shadow, which falls across the foreground. Painted in response to mounting agitation over the Reform Bill (Collins was a Tory and the piece can be read as an allegory of the relationships that were supposed to exist between squire and peasant[96] in which the child becomes archetypal peasant, naive and profoundly unthreatening), *Rustic Civility* also demonstrates a growing interest in childhood as a period of leisure. As such, it marks a distinct shift in the representation of peasant children who had been predominantly painted at work rather than at play by artists like Thomas Gainsborough. As Barrell points out, though a late-eighteenth and early-nineteenth century audience would be sympathetic to the plight of a child who had to work not play, it was necessary to show them at work in order to generate that sympathy in the first place. In literature, too, poor children were sent out to work to learn good habits, as much as to earn a crust. The plight of the poor was therefore naturalised. However, where ideologically the need had been to demonstrate the industry of children, especially poor children, thereby guaranteeing the sympathy of the audience and the children's honesty,[97] by 1832 this was beginning to change; it was enough to show their simple deference.

During the early Victorian period, then, the idea that children automatically had some economic worth for their parents was widely challenged. By the latter half of the nineteenth century, childhood was supposed to be entirely happy, free from want and leisured, regardless of the child's place,[98] and the countryside, in the form of the rural idyll, provided its perfect setting. In one beautiful example of this, Charles James Lewis's *Mother and Child* (no date),[99] we see a mother holding up her baby playfully as she sits in the garden outside her cottage. Mother and child are on the edge of a path leading from the garden into the house, and this path then leads straight out of the house again into a wood lit up with the early summer sun and suggestive of playtimes to come. Surrounded by chicks and elder flowers, as well as industrious beehives and hay-rake, masculine wood block and axe, she is a picture of flushed youth and maternal joy. In this sense she is like so many of the wax doll figures of idealised motherhood seen at this time. Their physical fragility and youth, Nead argues, was indicative of their innocence, respectability and moral strength, established in direct contrast to the physical robustness of actual working-class women often seen at the time as morally weak.[100] The gentle shadows that criss-cross the scene bisect the cottage interior, which is literally central to the picture, and the moment of leisure that mother and child enjoy is bounded by the gaze they share. Together, they are framed by both the cottage home (which extends to the edge of the picture) and its garden (which dominates the foreground and penetrates the house).

In *Mother and Child*, the title and subject of which clearly draws on the theme of Madonna and child, we find the almost perfect expression of the English countryside as site of natural domesticity, physical health and childhood pleasure. As Nead notes, the 'image of the Madonna and child was a paradigm of maternal devotion and purity and during the nineteenth century the image could be drained of its associations with Catholicism and taken up with English ruling-class culture as a sign of respectable Protestant values'.[101] And this removal of Catholic associations worked particularly well when scenes like this were placed within the countryside which carried its own powerful connotations of Englishness. Moreover, we can see the same representational system at work in Charles Kingsley's *The Water Babies* (1861–62) and in William Howitt's *The Boy's Country-Book* (1880), as well as in pictures like Myles Birket Foster's *The Wild Flower Gatherers* (no date) or *Cottages at Amersham* (no date).[102] Sometimes the children in question are seen at work, though in such instances they could be more appropriately described as being engaged in 'constructive play'. Girls are often pictured tending flowers, feeding geese, chickens and ducks, while boys are mostly shown catching fish, cultivating vegetables and watching over sheep. There were clearly gendered divisions at work here,[103] but it was this kind of unpaid employment that was also seen by many early nineteenth-century reformers as being the best education a child could get. These older conceptions of childhood lingered for a while, linked to pleasing thoughts of future adult thrift so that the late nineteenth-century image of playful work continued to draw on older notions of useful childhood toil such as those espoused by Cobbett.

Cobbett, like many early nineteenth-century authors, saw labourers' children as bringing both 'pleasures and solid advantages' to their parents, and he saw their education as a key factor in determining the well-being or otherwise of the labourer's family. To him, children were 'assistants and props', an investment against the troubles of old age and 'sure and safe friends' who, working together as brothers and sisters, might 'set what is called misfortune at defiance'. He believed that children ought to learn from books, but only 'after ... all the measures are safely taken for enabling them to get their living by labour'. As far as he was concerned, nothing was taught in schools, especially church schools, 'but the rudiments of servility, pauperism, and slavery'.[104] Hence, it was

> more rational for parents to be employed in teaching their children how to cultivate a garden, to feed and rear animals, to make bread, beer, bacon, butter, and cheese, and to be able to do these things for themselves, or for others, than to leave them to prowl about the lanes and commons, or to mope at the heels of some crafty, sleek-headed pretended saint, who while he extracts the last penny from their pockets, bids them be contented with their misery.[105]

It was with this in mind that he wrote *Cottage Economy* (1822). While he believed that parents ought to teach their children how to look after themselves by bringing them up according to his methods, those parents would initially have to do some 'book-learning' in order to follow this plan. Cobbett was a radical who drew on the supposed skills and knowledge of the past in order to fight the vagaries of the present. His was not an entirely nostalgic mode, but his writing did have its ironies. However, for most Victorian authors it was the very idea that cottage children might be able to 'prowl about the lanes and commons' that fascinated them. Hence, Howitt declared that 'the life of village children seems to me quite heavenly, compared to that of thousands of town children'.[106] This became so accepted that societies were established to take poor city children out to the country on holidays and outings, and though by the early twentieth century there was more interest in teaching children about country life than taking them to see it, even during the Second World War, evacuees were said to benefit from being in the country.[107]

The cottage, the cottage garden, the allotment, and, to some extent, the field and hedgerow, were construed as ideal spaces for children, just as childhood itself was constructed as a time of pleasure and as a safe haven from the cares of the world. The Victorians maintained and expanded on the Romantic idea of childhood as a place where the attributes lost in adulthood remained. As with the rural idyll and domesticity, so it was with childhood; the more that society seemed to undergo change, and the more alienating that change, the more childhood came to be seen as a timeless, static place of refuge. Childhood was conceived of as a protected garden, a place that had links to Nature and the virtues, such as community and natural friendship, that now seemed to be lost to the adult and to the modern world. It was thought of as a sanctuary, and though it was a place to which the adult could never really return, this emergent conception of childhood became the guiding force behind the vast bodies of protective legislation that were eventually passed in the nineteenth century.[108] The 'sensibility and rhetoric' of the factory movement, Cunningham observes, 'was unquestionably informed by an internalised acquaintance with the Romantic poets'.[109] The concept of childhood, was idolised like Woman and Home. Hence, Cunningham points out, from the late 1860s we see an increased volume of material written for and about children. Childhood was turned to in place of Christianity as a focus for worship. Kingsley, MacDonald, Carroll, Alcott, Barrie, Grahame, Nesbit, Potter, Hodgson Burnett and Milne, all doubted or rejected Christianity and turned to childhood as a form of heaven, either by looking back to their own childhoods, or projecting their fantasy of it onto children.[110] This idealised childhood also intersected with domesticity, Englishness and the rural idyll, and was therefore quite clearly part of the Beau Ideal. This continued on into the twentieth century wherein, the consolatory role of the country continued to be linked nostalgically to childhood, 'since the countryside is associated not only with "the past" but also with the personal past of childhood'.[111]

Caring for a garden in itself was equated with caring for a family in the nineteenth century; 'some people', the *Sunlight Year Book* for 1898 observed, 'seem to have the faculty of making flowers thrive in the most unlikely places. And why? Flowers, it is said, are like children, they require love. In other words, they require care and attention and an interest in their welfare.'[112] George Johnson's organic metaphor for the family as 'all those flowers of life', was commonplace. The garden was therefore figured as feminine, so that home and garden together formed the locus of female authority for the elite woman in particular; arranging, cultivating and writing about gardens and gardening were all part of middle-class women's lives. But, to be more precise, it was *flower* gardening that was represented as peculiarly feminine; in treatises on the cottage garden, while the man of the family would be expected to dig the vegetable patch, his wife would tend her blooms and their children would help. Where cottage garden flowers connoted contemplative passive femininity, vegetables, beehives, and garden implements like spades and hoes were suggestive of self-contained, contented masculine thrift and activity. Unsurprisingly, a class division also becomes apparent here. Though Jane Loudon encouraged 'ladies' to engage in some light digging for the benefit of their 'health and spirits',[113] the elite oversight of a garden, or the suburban hobbyist's experience was very different to that of Tom Mullins' wife, who 'managed the holding and our three cows, while I worked as a labourer for neighbouring farmers'.[114]

Meanwhile, though (flower) gardening was (and still is) seen as a peculiarly feminine activity, under the control and direction of the woman of the house, it has mostly been men who have published gardening texts and have been paid for gardening work. Looking at the official enumeration of the employed and unemployed, we find that the recognition of women's work, paid or unpaid, was steadily eroded during the nineteenth century, especially if it appeared to belong to the realm of domestic duty, or was undertaken for the family. Because a woman's domestic duties were supposed to override their paid employment, especially if they were married and the work was part-time, that work was only ever recorded piecemeal.[115] As Eddie Higgs argues, the collection of data for the record was and is far from being a value-free exercise, while the production of the censuses as texts provides us with a clear demonstration of separate spheres ideology in formation.[116] The difficulties of recording even women's paid work continued into the twentieth century, as is suggested by Mrs Daisy, born in 1904, who remembered that, though she and another woman worked on a farm in Kent, 'there was never anything official said about us women'. The arrangement was entirely informal and she recalled that though she liked the work, she never received a man's wage for it.[117] Nor is this simply an historical issue, as Joni Seager and Ann Olson argue, even today: 'Because much of women's agricultural work done in or near the home, is small in scale, part-time or seasonal, it is considered unimportant by official agencies. As a result, women are often left out of economic development schemes. Women are at the bottom of the pay and power scales in agriculture.'[118] The unpaid labour of a woman for her family, on an allotment or smallholding, could therefore always be captured for domesticity, because of the form it generally took and the treatment of gardening as rational recreation, and because the exact nature of the work women did was usually glossed over.[119] Hence, even with the material on the collier's wife, the commentator recommended the cultivation of the garden 'to the cottager and *his* family for their vacant hours . . . The practice will tend to promote domestic habits, – will attach the labourer to *his* own possessions and family, – will supply interesting occupation for *his* vacant hours, – and leave no space for the dissipation and idleness of the ale-house and the tap-room'[120] (my emphasis). We do not know her name and her work is repossessed.

The traditional history of gardening has likewise become 'a story about men, written by men. Women are usually completely absent, in a supporting role to men, or relegated to weeding.'[121] The centrality and skill of women's work is thereby erased. And though this is gradually being corrected,[122] the tendency is still for gardening historians to slip into a celebration of individual gardening women, rather than to undertake a reassessment of the gendered relationships within gardening. It is therefore really only in autobiographic material that we find any evidence of the work that women did in their gardens, or the meanings they attached to that work. And, what this material suggests is that in England working-class women gradually learned to refuse to work on their family's allotments or vegetable gardens using the rhetoric of separate spheres. By the time Flora Thompson[123] was growing up, allotment work such as that undertaken by the collier's wife – like all outdoor work – was in the view of women 'men's work'. What the women hoped to have was a flower garden and 'herb corner' in which to keep bees and grow herbs for cooking, laundry, medicine, mead and tea, and most homes 'had at least a narrow border beside the pathway'.[124] Then, when tea had to be offered to

> an important caller, or to friends from a distance, the women had their resources. . . . Thin bread and butter . . . with a pot of homemade jam, which had been hidden away for such an occasion, and a dish of lettuce, fresh from the garden and garnished with a little rosy radishes, made an attractive little meal, fit, as they said, to be put before anybody.[125]

What we can see here is that the cottage garden could generate high status products suitable for a visitor, as well as serviceable items for home use, but that seeds and plants were expensive, therefore most women collected cuttings and roots from their neighbours. This meant that though their range was limited,

> they grew all the sweet old-fashioned cottage garden flowers, pinks and sweet williams and love-in-a-mist, wallflowers and forget-me-nots in spring and Michaelmas daisies in autumn. Then there was lavender and sweetbriar bushes, and southern-wood, sometimes called 'lad's love, but known there as 'old man'.
>
> Almost every garden had its rose bush; but there were no coloured roses among them. Only Old Sally had those; the other people had to be content with that meek, old-fashioned white rose with a pink flush at the heart known as the 'maiden's blush'. Laura used to wonder who had imported that first bush, for evidently slips of it had been handed round from house to house.[126]

In Thompson we see a working-class woman reworking the experience of domesticity into literary form,[127] and conjuring up an English idyll for an urban reader during the Second World War.[128] Her account is nonetheless particularly striking in that the use of plants comes to stand in as a kind of material communication that takes place between gardens and ordinary (women) gardeners. Where Eleanor Rhode treated the garden a few years later as an expression of (masculine) individualism and the last preserve of the native, Flora Thompson, more like Willmott, treats it as a fluid space. The garden is part of the village, a chronicle of resources and a communal, public space where the gardener swaps plants and gossips with her neighbour. The garden, as well as producing tangible benefits like jam (with the addition of hedgerow fruits), lettuce and radishes, could therefore be read as the visible expression of her community's history. It is this understanding of the 'artisan's' cottage garden that has continued to fascinate commentators and garden historians.

PINKS AND SWEET WILLIAMS: HOW DOES YOUR GARDEN GROW?

In his recent ethnographic study of Childerley – the name he gives a small village in Hampshire – Michael Mayerfeld Bell observed that the gardens of the well-to-do were always more formal and restrained than those of ordinary villagers. These gardens, he suggests, reflect the different social attitudes of incomers and local Childerleyans, rich and poor. One moneyed villager, John Lane, who had an acre and a half of land that he worked himself, particularly enjoyed guiding the visitor round his garden:

He likes to take people out into it through the solarium, with its antique leaded glass. The door opens onto the stone patio, with its fountain, Grecian marble statue, and border of boxwood topiary. In the centre of the garden is a section of grass, as green as could be imagined, perfectly rolled and edged, smoother and fuller than any indoor carpet. The grass merges into massed plantings of flowers, scented clouds of carefully harmonized colors. First are the low borders of annuals – marigolds, ageratum, pansies – which round away into such taller perennials as delphinium and iris.

John also grows a lot of vegetables. His patch is away in the back, discreetly screened from the patio and solarium by a bank of high perennials. He keeps a lot of fruit trees back there too, as well as gooseberries and currants, nestled amid the winding grassy paths he maintains. One of these paths leads unexpectedly to a picture-perfect pool of water flowers, with an arched bridge, another Grecian statue, and a shady bench where one can sit in individual contemplation and seclusion. The rest of the back is devoted to a small wilderness of bushes and fruit trees that John has let go wild for the birds (he's an enthusiastic birdwatcher), his equipment shed, and two large compost piles. The whole serves as a fit setting for the jewel that dominates the scene – his seventeenth-century thatched house with antique varieties of roses round the door.[129]

In middle-class gardens, entrances remained transitional and public in the twentieth century; family spaces, gendered neutral and visible from the house, were used for socialising, sport and display; private spaces, gendered female, were set aside for individual contemplation; front gardens were designed as a setting/frame. Meanwhile, though changing fashions in garden design have had their impact, the use of this space varies with the age and needs of the family, and alters during weekdays, evenings and weekends. The gardens of wealthy Americans, for example, have grown to accommodate a variety of zones, some for looking in, some for looking out, some for holding large parties, some (tennis courts, for instance) for marrying off daughters, some for retreat. The Western American garden, David Streatfield notes, has often been figured female while the surrounding ranch and paddocks were coded male. These room-like spaces therefore echo the domestic interior of the middle-class home and its gendered boundaries, but they are nonetheless negotiated and contested; the control and use of garden space reveals the fault lines of class, race and gender beyond the simple distinction 'public'/'private'. The middle-class woman's garden, for instance, exists within surrounding male space, which ebbs and flows with the working day.[130]

In contrast, Rose and Ed Lambton, a working-class couple who had lived in Childerley all their lives, had a garden of roughly five thousand square feet which they used as a social space. When Bell visited:

> Rose was sitting on the little patch of lawn in front of the house, mending a dressing gown at an old metal garden table with a big umbrella. Their lawn is shaded by a huge old ash tree, around which they have built a circular bench. As I opened the creaky gate she looked up from her work and welcomed me in. Ed was a little late returning from an errand, so she took me around for a tour of the garden until his arrival, when we would have tea...
>
> The principal outdoor seating area was in front of the house... The view of their house from the road was obscured by the big ash tree and several smaller ones. In full view in the front garden was an old caravan... up on blocks, faded, dented, and somewhat rusty, as well as a retired auto in similar condition...
>
> In place of controlled formalism, the garden was fairly bursting with a kind of dense activeness. Every bit was not only used, but doing something. Instead of massed plantings separated by wide grassy spaces calculated for the framing of the house, there were many small centres of activity and interest. Here the fish pond (an old bathtub sunk into the ground), there the caravan, here the tea table, there the vegetable garden, here a pile of construction debris, there a flourishing bank of roses...
>
> And rather than creating a still, silent backdrop for the house, the Lambtons have filled their garden with a foreground of animation and talk. The pond water is alive with tadpoles and goldfish. Clustered about the pond, but also scattered everywhere, are arrays of little statues of dogs, leprechauns, children, kittens, badgers, foxes, an old man, and a pair of smiling boots, all brightly painted. Nearby is Ed's aviary, in which there are about sixty-five birds. In back of the house, there's a run with chickens and ducks, cackling and quacking, fillings the air with the sounds of liveness.[131]

Most of the ordinary villagers followed the practices of 'formal' gardening – 'the careful panning of overall effect, within the "picturesque" language of the English gardening tradition'[132] – but few took this to the extreme of the moneyed incomers. Though the Lambtons' plot is seen through Bell's American eyes – the 'leprechauns' are probably garden gnomes and he is a little prone to over-sentimentalising the lives of the poor – it is still clear that this, as he says, is not the 'intentional aesthetic space' of John Lane's garden. This might be a function of making do, of not having the money and time to spend on gardening, but the Lambtons do, Bell reports, pass all their spare time in their garden, growing 'nearly all their own fruits and vegetables – potatoes, swedes, beetroot, beans, peas, lettuce, cabbage, carrots, gooseberries, plums, and pears'.[133] Their principles of gardening, Bell therefore argues, are more informal, more active and interactive than Lane's,[134] and it is clear that their understandings of what a garden is for are quite different.

Lane's ordered garden has its own carefully-structured narrative which moves from the domestic interior, to the public formality of patio and lawn, through into a less rigid secluded 'room' of (partially ornamental as well as productive) fruit trees and scheduled contemplative pool, to a 'natural' wilderness and functional space. His gardening is based on the eighteenth-century pictorial technique mentioned in Chapter 1, which required the (educated) garden visitor to read the garden, to pause at selected points and appreciate the rationale of the design. The garden as a whole is meant to enhance and display the beauties of the owner's home, while maintaining its privacy and distance from the world at large. This is the kind of garden seen in stately homes; Lane's is an eighteenth-century picturesque garden on the small scale in which his guest becomes a tourist. On the other hand, the Lambtons' garden is closer to the vernacular than the architectural and this is why (according to moneyed eyes) it is less aesthetically pleasing. Both Lane and the Lambtons welcome visitors, but rather than a teleological tour of the garden, the latter present their company with many contingent spaces in which a range of activities take place.

As in Flora Thompson's testimony, gardening in this instance is grounded on an explicit identification with the community, and an ability to manage, to make do; the Lambtons' garden is about self-esteem, self-efficacy and continuity. The garden itself is a workspace as well as a site of leisure; in fact, it encompasses several different kinds of work, including flower-gardening, spade-husbandry, the care of fowl, construction and sewing – Bell meets Mrs Lambton engaged in (private) domestic work out in her (public) front garden. Where his conservatory frames Lane's garden, the Lambtons treat the garden as productive of (informal) relationships that override the built division between interior and exterior space. The myth of the English cottage garden outlined in the epigraph was originally produced by and for a newly-urbanised middle class. That myth reworked the ideological categories of its day so that spadework came to be seen to be masculine, rational and apolitical, while the garden itself remained 'naturally' feminine. In this way, the cottage garden became a haven to which both the honest labourer and the weary Englishman abroad could always return. But, it is this informal 'folk' aspect of cottage gardening, the garden's links to the community at large that work alongside its enclosed introspection, that helps maintain the cottage garden's popularity.

The topography of class, race and sexuality, grounded in the division of slum from suburb and what Stallybrass and White call 'new thresholds of shame', overwrote the country and the city in the nineteenth century through a metonymic chain that linked purity and ethnicity via the 'native'. This linkage continued into the twentieth century when the purity of rural areas came to be contrasted with the pollution of the urban and physical degeneration. From the turn of the nineteenth and twentieth centuries, as the aesthetic and spiritual aspects of the 'back to the land' movement began to take precedence in the national imagination, so anti-urbanism and anti-industrialism became associated with the wild, and the stewardship of the earth. As Lowe argues, this enabled the emergence of a concern for the fragility of the environment as a web of life, but it also led to the strengthening of the patriotic through a celebration of the indigenous and the native. There was a concern that the fragile environmental balance might be all too easily disturbed by the invasion of aggressive alien Others, 'human and non-human'.[135] There was a direct link, therefore, between the British back-to-the-land movement of the early twentieth century and the formulation of fascist ideology in 1930s Germany. And, as Kate Soper notes, when discussing the Romantic conception of nature as an innocent power for good, which might be liberated, 'we should not forget the irrationalities and repressions to which this "nature libertarianism" can also lend itself': 'Romantic conceptions of 'nature' as wholesome salvation from cultural decadence and racial degeneration were crucial to the construction of Nazi ideology, and an aesthetic of "nature" as source of purity and authentic self-identification has been a component of all forms of racism, tribalism and nationalism.'[136] In the postcolonial period, this division has continued in the Right's use of the rural idyll as 'green and pleasant land', and in the adoption of the language of soil by more recent Fascist organisations, such as the National Front and the British National Party. Not, as Agyeman and Spooner stress, that all those who adopt the rural idyll or the language of nature are fascists, but, this does highlight the slippage that can occur between the indigenous/native, the folk and the race.[137] The understanding of the cottage and its garden as natural, embedded and vernacular expression of the community might also be read in this light.

As Gillian Darley argues, the Victorians chose the cottage garden as a symbol, 'as a repository of rustic values and rural simplicity. As an image it did not have to contend with the realities of poverty.'[138] Treated as a private space, the conventions that applied to the representation of cottages applied equally to their gardens. Meanwhile, the trope of the sweet-smelling cottage garden helped inform the image of the country as full of light, purity; the city as congested, dark and foul.[139] The cottage garden consequently came to represent an ideal of private family life and English domesticity that could contain growth within the bounds of ongoing, stable, organic and 'natural' social relations. Within the language of gardening, 'order' became a keyword. The garden offers an opportunity for the maintenance of order and thereby security; through the traditional practices and morality of gardening, (social, political, spatial) order can be reasserted and a distance put between the gardener and the rest of the world.[140] Moreover Geoff King is right to assert that: 'Tending to the pastoral garden in modern industrial societies might appear to be a digging down, literally, to a more real ground, the earth itself, as if it were not overlain by cultural strata.' However, the garden is itself a product of culture, a 'controllable, mappable space in which a multiplicity of clear boundaries, fences and hedges can be maintained'. It can be cultivated, following the forms suggested by gardening books, or it 'can be left to run wild, to go to seed, safe in the knowledge that any such chaos remains strictly bounded and contained'.[141]

The grand landscapes of the picturesque were meant to be interpreted, but the 'nice social distinctions implied by the total absence of front gardens, small front gardens to terraced houses, large front gardens to semi-detached ones ... and the seclusion of large detached houses in tree-filled gardens'[142] identified by Michael Reed can equally be read as giving expression to the politics and meanings of space. As he notes, the

> fields, farms, churches and cottages, castles and gardens of the landscape are not discrete entities, but the constituent elements of a dense historical matrix, linked in the minds of men and women by assumptions, values, and preconceptions, sometimes formally codified, often nothing more than practices informally recognised through custom and long usage.[143]

In this sense, the garden's use and meaning inevitably reflects the patterns and relations of advanced capitalism and patriarchy. To borrow Raymond Williams' point about the nature of modern society: 'It is not only that the specific histories of country and city, and of their immediate interrelations, have been determined ... by capitalism. It is that the total character of what we know as modern society has been similarly determined.'[144] When faced with uncertainty and distanced forces that are out of our control, we retreat for comfort into subjectivity or seek 'social pictures, social signs, social messages, to which, characteristically, we try to relate as individuals but so as to discover, in some form, community'.[145] The garden might be used either way as introspective shelter, or to grow relationships alongside the fruit and vegetables. Gardens themselves always do a range of cultural work too; they may have a social, economic and biological function – as suggested in reformers' attempts to give labourers allotments and the ever-present necessity of producing food – but they can also generate a sense of place and reinforce identity. In memoirs, letters, oral testimony, we find gardens and their plants linked to memories of other gardens; these recollections, alongside the traditions of gardening, help mould both the garden and the gardener's sense of self.[146] And, the garden's plants can be put to ideological use to propagate notions of the native/domestic vs. the alien/foreign.

William Robinson, and Gertrude Jekyll and her followers 'began from a premise in which a delight of the natural sets the scene'. Admiring of cottage gardens, and in parallel to the Arts and Crafts architects who mirrored vernacular architecture and followed 'traditional' building techniques, these garden designers sought out the gardens of country people and their old-fashioned plants. The traditional cottage garden flowers, seen as gentler in their colouring and growth were juxtaposed to the (urban) artificiality of hothouse bedding and the climbers, roses, clematis, jasmine and honeysuckle, became indicative of the natural abundance of the English countryside. In the late nineteenth century the cottage garden became 'the model, even the justification' for those rebelling against the formality of conventional bedding out. Today the cottage garden is preserved through the activities of organisations which see historic gardens as living monuments so that 'the conceptual, the ethical and political vacuum surrounding gardens' has become filled up with heritage projects and interests. As Darley observes, the cottage garden has become 'a vehicle for aspirations of many sorts';[147] among those aspirations can be found the desire to seek out the 'native' white space of the country, the search for order and security.

NOTES

1 P. H. Ditchfield, *The Charm of the English Village* (London, [1906] 1994), p. 84.
2 S. Constantine, 'Amateur gardening and popular recreation in the 19th and 20th Centuries' in *Journal of Social History* (1981), Vol. 14, No. 3, 387–406; also, P. Tristram, *Living Space in Fact and Fiction* (London, 1989).
3 For 'the famous five Rs: refuge, reflection, rescue, requiem and reconstruction' of pastoralism, see R. Sales, *English Literature in History 1780–1830: pastoral and politics* (London, 1983), pp. 15–18.
4 M. Hoyles, *The Story of Gardening* (London, 1991), p. 228.
5 John Claudius Loudon (1783–1843) was a well-known and widely read British journalist and architect with a social bent, who produced a large number of

gardening books and edited *The Gardener's Magazine*. Admired by Robinson, he had a considerable impact on all aspects of gardening practice in his day.

6 William Robinson (1838–1935), originally an assistant gardener in Ireland and eventually herbaceous foreman in Regent's Park, London, became a prolific garden writer and founded his own magazine, *The Garden: an illustrated weekly journal of horticulture in all its branches*, in 1871. His best-known works are probably *The Wild Garden* (1870) and *The English Flower Garden* (1883). He disliked artificiality, including topiary and carpet bedding, and looked back to 'pre-bedding' cottage gardening as an ideal.

7 Gertrude Jekyll (1843–1932), originally an artist, became a professional garden designer (the first woman to do so in Britain) when her eyesight began to fail. She wrote for and later became joint editor of *The Garden*, and often collaborated with architect Edwin Lutyens (1869–1944).

8 Helen Allingham, nee Paterson, was born in 1848 in Derbyshire. Her aunt (Laura Herford) was a professional artist. Allingham attended the Royal Academy School in 1867 and then worked as an illustrator for a range of novels, magazines and periodicals – she was the illustrator for Thomas Hardy's *Far From the Madding Crowd*, serialised in the *Cornhill Magazine*. She also began painting watercolours in the 1870s and exhibited at the Royal Academy in 1874. She was elected a full member of the Royal Society of Painters in Water Colours in 1890. In 1879, she began painting the subjects that she became best known for, viz. cottage gardens, country cottages and their inhabitants. For the latter, she often used professional models, including Mrs Stewart who sat for du Maurier.

9 J. C. Loudon, *The Cottager's Manual of Husbandry, Architecture, Domestic Economy, and Gardening*. Originally published in the *Gardener's Magazine*, this was reprinted for the Society for the Diffusion of Useful Knowledge in 1840, (London, 1840), p. 45.

10 E. Hyams, *The English Garden* (London, 1966), p. 153.

11 Hyams, *English Garden*, pp. 153, 271.

12 Jekyll quoted in Hoyles, *Story*, p. 225.

13 Ronald King, quoted in Hoyles, *Story*, p. 225.

14 G. Hamilton, *Geoff Hamilton's Cottage Gardens* (London, 1995), p. 31 (emphasis in original). *Geoff Hamilton's Cottage Gardens* was published to accompany the highly popular six-part TV series of the same name.

15 G. Darley, 'Cottage and suburban gardens' in John Harris (ed.), *The Garden: a celebration of one thousand years of British gardening* (London, 1979), p. 151.

16 Darley, 'Cottage' p. 151.

17 L. Nead, *Myths of Sexuality: representations of women in Victorian Britain* (Oxford, 1988), p. 42.

18 Hamilton, *Cottage Gardens*, p. 5 (caption).

19 'Fashion has been as fickle in gardening as in architecture – if anything more so.' Hugh Johnson, Introduction in Harris, *The Garden*, p. 4.

20 D. Massey, 'Places and their pasts', *History Workshop Journal*, No. 39 (Spring 1995), p. 186.

21 Hamilton, *Cottage Gardens*, p. 32 (emphasis in original).

22 Tristram, *Living Space*, pp. 203–4; L. Davidoff et al., 'Landscape with Figures', in Mitchell, J. and Oakley, A. (eds), *The Rights and Wrongs of Women* (Harmondsworth, 1976), pp. 139–75; Nead, *Myths*, pp. 40–4.

23 L. Davidoff and C. Hall, *Family Fortunes: men and women of the English middle class 1780–1850* (London, 1987) p. 361.

24 M. Reed, *The Landscape of Britain: from the beginnings to 1914* (London, 1997), p. 265.

25 Hoyles, *Story*, p. 1. The *Oxford English Dictionary* defines a garden as 'enclosed cultivated ground', or 'an enclosed piece of ground devoted to the cultivation of flowers, fruit, or vegetables'.
26 Reed, *The Landscape of Britain*, p. 253.
27 Susan Zlotnick makes a related point in 'Domesticating Imperialism: curry and cookbooks in Victorian England', *Frontiers*, Vol. XVI, No. 2/3, pp. 51–68.
28 R. A. Willmott, *A Journal of Summer Time in the Country* (fourth edition, London, 1864), p. 165.
29 The *Ranunculus* family includes the meadow buttercup, the lesser celandine, and 'bachelor's buttons' ('fair maids of France' or 'fair maids of Kent'). *Ranunculus – ranunculus acris; ranunculus ficaria; ranunculus aconitifolius*. Bulbs cost between four and six pence per dozen, depending on the variety, in 1897. *Webbs' Spring Catalogue* (London, 1897), p. 99.
30 Willmott, *Journal*, p. 165.
31 Hoyles, *Story*, p. 78; Massey, 'Places', p. 183.
32 Hoyles, *Story*, p. 55.
33 J. Agyeman and R. Spooner, 'Ethnicity and the rural environment' in Cloke, P. and Little, J. (eds), *Contested Countryside Cultures: otherness, marginalisation and rurality* (London and New York, 1997), p. 212.
34 Hyams, *English Garden*, p. 129.
35 Hyams, *English Garden*, p. 120.
36 Hoyles, *Story*, pp. 1, 5, 21. Hence he stresses the importance of the labour, paid and unpaid, involved in the production of a garden.
37 Constantine, 'Amateur gardening', pp. 389–90; Davidoff and Hall, *Family Fortunes*, p. 373.
38 Davidoff and Hall, *Family Fortunes*, pp. 373–5.
39 Constantine, 'Amateur gardening', pp. 389–91.
40 Cited in Hoyles, *Story*, p. 16.
41 G. Johnson, *A History of English Gardening* (1829), quoted in Hoyles, *Story*, p. 16.
42 Loudon, *The Cottager's Manual*, p. 56.
43 Loudon, *The Cottager's Manual*, pp. 4, 41, 45.
44 Anon, *Account of Britton Abbot's Cottage and Garden; and Account of the Produce of a Cottager's Garden in Shropshire: to which is added Jonas Hobson's Advice to his Children: and the Contrast between a Religious and Sinful Life* (London, [written 1797] 1806), p. 5.
45 Hamilton, *Cottage Gardens*, p. 14.
46 Hamilton, *Cottage Gardens*, p. 14. See Ditchfield, *Charm*, pp. 92–3.
47 Hoyles, *Story*, pp. 52–3. A mixed packet of auricula seed cost 6d and 1s in 1876. *The Illustrated Guide for Amateur Gardeners* (Norwich, 1876), p. 62.
48 Hamilton, *Cottage Gardens*, pp. 26–9; Hoyles, *Story*, pp. 77, 226.
49 Willmott, *Journal*, p. 155.
50 A. Young, *General View of the Agriculture of the County of Hertfordshire, Drawn up for the Consideration of the Board of Agriculture and Internal Improvement* (Newton Abbot, [1804] 1971), pp. 21–2.
51 *Account of Britton Abbot's Cottage*, p. 8.
52 S. Silvester, *In a World that Has Gone* (Leicester, 1868), pp. 3, 5, 27.
53 Constantine, 'Amateur gardening', p. 392.
54 M. Reed, 'The peasantry of nineteenth century England: a neglected class?' *History Workshop Journal* (Spring 1984), pp. 57–9.
55 *The Penny Cyclopædia of the Society for the Diffusion of Useful Knowledge* (London, 1843), Vol. VIII, p. 88.

56 W. and R. Chambers (eds), *Chambers's Information for the People* (Edinburgh, 1842), Vol. II, p. 345.
57 *Chambers's Information*, pp. 345–8.
58 A. Howkins, *Reshaping Rural England: a social history 1850–1925* (London, 1991), pp. 20–1.
59 J. Burnett (ed.), *Destiny Obscure: autobiographies of childhood, education and family from the 1820s to the 1920s* (Harmondsworth, 1982), p. 67.
60 *Penny Cyclopædia*, Vol. VIII, p. 89.
61 *Account of Britton Abbot's Cottage*, pp. 8, 9.
62 This process is detailed by R. Jefferies, *The Toilers of the Field* (London, [1892] 1981), p. 56. Abbot, for one, only paid rent after negotiating for a piece of land that he could enclose and within which he could build his own cottage.
63 *Chambers's Information*, p. 352.
64 *Penny Cyclopædia*, Vol. VIII, p. 89.
65 *Penny Cyclopædia*, Vol. VIII, p. 89.
66 Reed, 'Peasantry', pp. 60–9.
67 See, for example, Hoyles, *Story*, p. 215.
68 M. Chase, 'We wish only to work for ourselves: the Chartist Land Plan' in Chase, M. and Dyck, I. (eds), *Living and Learning: Essays in honour of J. F. Harrison* (London, 1996), pp. 133–5.
69 *Labour Leader*, 7 July 1900, p. 216. The *Labour Leader* was a radical working-class publication that focused on agricultural issues.
70 J. Marsh, *Back to the Land: the pastoral impulse in Victorian England from 1880–1914* (London, Melbowne and New York, 1982), pp. 93–122.
71 J. Thirsk, *Alternative Agriculture: a history from the Black Death to the present day* (Oxford, 1997), pp. 204–16.
72 Hoyles, *Story*, intro.
73 Hoyles, *Story*, pp. 1, 5, 21.
74 Willmott, *Journal*, p. 155.
75 'Reports of Special Assistant Poor Law Commissioners on the employment of women and children in agriculture', *Parliamentary Papers* (PP), 1843, pp. 220, 259.
76 Constantine, 'Amateur gardening', pp. 391–2, 401.
77 *Account of Britton Abbot's Cottage*, pp. 11–12 (emphasis in original).
78 *Account of Britton Abbot's Cottage*, pp. 14–15 (emphasis in original).
79 Young, *Hertfordshire*, pp. 224–5.
80 *Penny Cyclopædia*, Vol. VIII, p. 88. NB published after the passing of the Poor Law Amendment Act of 1834.
81 *Penny Cyclopædia*, Vol. VIII, p. 89.
82 *Produce of a Cottager's Garden*, pp. 7–10.
83 *Account of Britton Abbot's Cottage*, p. 6.
84 *Account of Britton Abbot's Cottage*, pp. 5–12.
85 Davidoff and Hall, *Family Fortunes*, p. 374.
86 Hoyles, *Story*, p. 8.
87 Davidoff and Hall, *Family Fortunes*, pp. 310, 374–5.
88 Sir George Clausen (1852–1944), *The Allotment Garden*, 1899, oil, Fine Art Society, reproduced in C. Wood, *Paradise Lost: paintings of English country life and landscape 1850–1914* (London, [1988] 1993).
89 T. Hardy, *Tess of the d'Urbervilles – a pure woman* (London, 1891), p. 431. There is reference to a kind of natural justice in the family's subsequent removal from their cottage which echoes that in Chapter 11, and the reference to eviction reminds us of the cottage in which Tess worked in Chapter 9.

90 V. Burgin, 'Perverse space', in Colomina B. (ed.), *Sexuality and Space* (Princeton, 1992), p. 233. Burgin argues that 'scopophilia' as used by Laura Mulvey, while recognising the commodification of woman that takes place in and through objectification, fails to take account of the unconscious.
91 A. Kolodny, *The Land Before Her: fantasy and experience of the American frontiers, 1630–1860* (Chapel Hill and London, 1984), p. 54.
92 Quoted in G. Darley, 'The English cottage garden' in Mosser, M. and Teyssot, G. (eds), *The History of Garden Design: the western tradition from the renaissance to the present day* (London, 1991), p. 424.
93 C. M. Yonge, 'Quack, Quack' (1982), reprinted in Avery, G. (ed.), *Village Children* (London, [1846–82] 1967), p. 112.
94 Darley, 'The English cottage garden', p. 424.
95 William Collins (1788–1847), *Rustic Civility*, 1832, oil, the Duke of Devonshire and Chatsworth House Trust, reproduced in C. Payne, *Rustic Simplicity: scenes of cottage life in nineteenth-century British art* (Nottingham, 1998).
96 Payne, *Rustic Simplicity*, pp. 57–8.
97 J. Barrell, *The Dark Side of the Landscape: the rural poor in English painting 1730–1840* (Cambridge, 1980), pp. 82–6. H. Cunningham, *The Children of the Poor: representations of childhood since the seventeenth century* (London, 1991), p. 3.
98 Cunningham, *Children*, p. 3.
99 Charles James Lewis (1830–92) *Mother and Child*, n.d., oil, Bridgeman Art Library/Christopher Wood Gallery, reproduced in Wood, *Paradise Lost*.
100 Nead, *Myths*.
101 Nead, *Myths*, p. 26.
102 Myles Birket Foster (1825–99), *The Wild Flower Gatherers*, n.d., watercolour, St Peter's Fine Art Gallery Ltd., Chester; *Cottages at Amersham*, n.d., watercolour, M. Newman Ltd., London. Both reproduced by the Medici Society Ltd., London.
103 See Davidoff and Hall, *Family Fortunes*, on the gendered history of childhood.
104 W. Cobbett, *Cottage Economy* (Oxford, [1822] 1979), pp. 4–6.
105 Cobbett, *Cottage Economy*, p. 9.
106 W. Howitt, *The Boy's Country Book* (London, 1880), p. 129.
107 Cunningham, *Children*, pp. 147–51, 222–3, 230.
108 Cunningham, *Children*, pp. 3–5, 23, 29–31, 50, 63, 65, 70–6, 84–9, 91–103.
109 Cunningham, *Children*, p. 90.
110 Cunningham, *Children*, p. 152.
111 K. Halfacree, 'Contrasting roles for the post-productivist countryside: a postmodern perspective on counterurbanisation' in Cloke and Little, *Contested Countryside Cultures*, p. 80. They also point out that many attitudes to the countryside are formed in childhood. This issue is developed by O. Jones, 'Little figures, big shadows, country childhood stories' and S. Harper, 'Contesting later life' in the same collection.
112 *Sunlight Year Book* (1898), p. 270.
113 J. Loudon, *Gardening for Ladies* (London, 1840).
114 Quoted in Burnett, *Destiny Obscure*, p. 67.
115 E. Higgs, 'Women, occupations and work in the nineteenth century censuses', *History Workshop*, 1987, p. 60.
116 Higgs, 'Women, occupations and work', pp. 60, 63.
117 C. Kightly (ed.), *Country Voices: life and lore in farm and village* (London, 1984), pp. 37–9.
118 Quoted in Hoyles, *Story*, p. 191.
119 Higgs, 'Women, occupations and work', pp. 60, 63.

120 *Produce of a Cottager's Garden*, p. 11.
121 Hoyles, *Story*, p. 187.
122 Martin Hoyles has himself begun to recoup this hidden history in *Bread and Roses: gardening books from 1560 to 1960*, Vol. 2 (London, 1995), pp. 75–109. He also cites, for example, J. Tabaroff, 'Wife unto thy garden: the first gardening books for women' in *Garden History*, Vol. 11, no. 1 (1983).
123 B. English, 'Lark Rise and Juniper Hill: A Victorian community in literature and history', *Victorian Studies*, Vol. 29, No. 1, (1985). Barbara English discusses the status of Flora Thompson's writing as fact or fiction in some detail and stresses that much of *Lark Rise* ought to be seen as having been written through the lens of nostalgia; the most painful memories are erased. *Lark Rise* therefore belongs to the genre of literary autobiography, written to adhere to the dominant forms of the day.
124 F. Thompson, *Lark Rise to Candleford: a trilogy* (Harmondsworth, [1939, 1941, 1943], 1979), pp. 114–16.
125 Thompson, *Lark Rise*, p. 118.
126 Thompson, *Lark Rise*, pp. 114–15.
127 See A. Romines, *The Home Plot: women writing and domestic ritual* (Amherst, 1992).
128 See J. Taylor, *A Dream of England: landscape, photography and the tourist's imagination* (Manchester, 1994). This issue will be discussed in greater detail in Chapter 4.
129 M. M. Bell, *Childerley: nature and morality in a country village* (Chicago and London, 1994), pp. 175–6.
130 D. Streatfield, 'Garden Herstories: West Coast women as patron and designer, 1920–1970', paper delivered to *Gendered Landscapes: an interdisciplinary exploration of past place and space* conference held at Penn State University, USA, 29 May–1 June 1999.
131 Bell, *Childerley*, pp. 176–7.
132 Bell, *Childerley*, p. 178.
133 Bell, *Childerley*, p. 178.
134 Bell, *Childerley*, pp. 175–8.
135 Agyeman and Spooner, quoting Lowe, 'Ethnicity and the rural environment', pp. 199–200.
136 K. Soper, *What is Nature? Culture, politics and the non-human* (Oxford, 1995), p. 32.
137 Agyeman and Spooner, 'Ethnicity and the rural environment', p. 201.
138 Darley, 'The English cottage garden', p. 424.
139 Darley, 'The English cottage garden', p. 424.
140 For a discussion on the link between 'order' and counter-urbanisation, see Halfacree, 'Contrasting roles'.
141 G. King, *Mapping Reality: an exploration of cultural cartographies* (London, 1996), pp. 67–8.
142 Reed, *Landscape*, p. 288.
143 Reed, *Landscape*, p. 265.
144 R. Williams, *The Country and the City* (London, [1972] 1985), p. 295.
145 Williams, *The Country and the City*, p. 295.
146 T. Fritze, 'Growing a home', paper delivered to *Gendered Landscapes: an interdisciplinary exploration of past place and space* conference held at Penn State University, USA, 29 May–1 June 1999.
147 Darley, 'The English cottage garden', pp. 424–6.

CHAPTER 4

The cottage and national identity

Home can be about architecture or a place in geography; or it can be about the sense of permanence we come to know through habit: an article of clothing repeatedly worn, a favourite turn of phrase, a melody of which we are fond, or the many visits to see a friend. Home is about the familiar, about gravity, about falling back into the self after being dispersed and overextended in the world.

(Andrew Bush, *Bonnettstown*)[1]

THE COTTAGE AND THE LAND

In 1906, P. H. Ditchfield could state confidently that:

> No country in the world can boast of possessing rural homes and villages which have half the charm and picturesqueness of our English cottages and hamlets. Wander where you will, in Italy or Switzerland, France, or Germany, and when you return home you will be bound to confess that in no foreign land have you seen a village which for beauty and interest can compare with the scattered hamlets of our English land.[2]

And the origin of this charm? Stability and variety. 'Nothing changes in our country life.' He went on, the 'old tower of the village church that has looked down upon generation after generation of the inhabitants seems to say, "*Je suis, je reste.* All things change but I." . . . [but] there are no two villages exactly the same. Each one possesses its own individuality, its own history, peculiarities, and architectural distinction.'[3] Architecture for Ditchfield was utterly indicative of place. Moreover, for Ditchfield, each village was a self-contained community, watched over by the Church, fixed, immutable, a microcosm of old England

– and the irony of his use of French to evoke this 'oh so English' image is as sweet as Gough's 'From John O'Groats to lovely Kent' in reference to the cottage homes of England.

The word 'vernacular', a term taken from linguistics in the 1850s, meaning 'the native language of a region', captures the supposed nativism, the authenticity and rootedness of the country cottage perfectly. Sometimes 'vulgar' and sometimes referring to the 'folk', the term vernacular refers to the common – ordinary, widespread, mean – but, in opposition to high architecture designed by an educated urban elite, also connotes the communal – shared roots, original knowledge and traditional work. Though, in 'the eyes of tastemakers, old vernacular is lovely [and new] vernacular . . . is unlovely',[4] the vernacular always belongs to and emerges from the people, and is set against the transitory and 'dispursive movements of industry, urbanisation and capitalism'.[5] In architecture, art and criticism, the West, especially the English, has historically turned away from modernity, and sought out 'radical alternatives in the assumed continuities of folk cultures, "authentic" habits and "genuine" communities'.[6] Any understanding of the cottage as folk architecture is as much about establishing what values ought to be preserved, as it is about the buildings themselves.

This is why Paul Oliver argued in 1975 for the preservation of more cottages and small farmhouses. For Oliver, small farmhouses and cottages were the largest and least appreciated component of Britain's housing stock, but it was only vital to save them because they were 'indigenous'. He explains:

> The qualities that are expressed in the cottage are not those of high-rise buildings, of blocks of flats, of suburban development or of housing projects . . . [They were] built by the populace as expressions of community needs, rather than as the conceptions of the individualist acting on behalf of society.[7]

As Daniels says of the 1970s, this was a period of racial tensions, of sharp, bitter social relations, of unrest and riots. These tensions, which embraced the country as well as the city (but which were seen as essentially urban), troubled definitions of Englishness and the dominant fantasy of English national identity. Spatially, the countryside of the south was not yet quite remade into comfortable commuter belt. Culturally, Raymond Williams was questioning the literary, artistic and social construction of pastoral.[8] Meanwhile, in the view of commentators and preservationists like Oliver, city space was full of the modernist architecture, epitomised by the high-rise flat, that was an expression of disjointed individualism. Rural space on the other hand was made up of the vernacular, epitomised by the cottage, as an expression of the popular.

Within the Victorian Beau Ideal, cottage women were established as belonging to, were part of and embedded within their villages and cottages. The cottage homes of England were likewise treated as occupying and sitting at the heart of their community and nation. The village connoted the nation on the small scale while, in genre art, the cottage's walls, roof and (timber) frame connoted an age-old, fundamental link between soil and house, nation and village, as if the cottage had grown up out of the land on which it stood. Amongst those who applaud the vernacular tradition today, this is as it should be. If there are architectural plans, then the native culture from which the house is drawn must be weakening; 'the more minimal the plan, the more completely the architectural idea abides in the separate minds of architect and client.'[9] Since the eighteenth century the cottage has *belonged* in and to its landscape and people, it and everything it contained has been seen as naturally, organically, inherently English. The intersection of rural and domestic idylls that creates domestic pastoral has therefore remained a metaphor for stability in a changing society.

The nineteenth-century's Beau Ideal, a house in the country, celebrated and sought to reify a sense of home, as domestic sphere and as a place, that was construed to be authentic, static, organic and embedded, at one with its community. Today, the peaceful, unchanging cottage 'nestled in the heart of the British countryside'[10] stands in for 'the hidden beauty of England',[11] and has come to symbolise both freedom from capital/disorder and a return to the homely/ordered. Nash's eighteenth-century verandas, on the other hand, illustrate how the English country cottage was and is not always as 'English' as it first appears. They remind us of the extent to which the desirability of the cottage originated within a construction of Englishness that was itself formed within and through an outward-looking and accumulative imperialism, itself a form of capital. The further the English tried to reach in terms of empire, the more popular the 'countervailing sentiment for cosy home scenery, for thatched cottages and gardens in pastoral countryside' became.[12] The cottage as either settled haven or rural retreat belongs to a vocabulary of national identity that has grown up within and in reaction to capitalism and colonialism.

Meanwhile, England itself is meant to exhibit timeless continuity and the English a steady and quiet certainty in their own conservative traditions:

> Symbolically elaborated around consecrated relics, traditions, and shrines – Westminster, the monarchy, Oxbridge, the Royal Navy, the public school system, the syllabus of 'English' – it is as though, through an undisturbed continuity, the very spirit of 'History' has laid its blessing on the nation.[13]

This is nation as 'imagined community'[14] and as 'home'. As Brand says, the home is the place 'where you fall back into the self *from* the world, a place of honesty instead of aspiration, habit instead of ambitious striving. Returning to it you say with a sigh and a double meaning: I'm home. (I've come home and I *am* home.)'[15] 'Home' can be a building, a place, a community, a nation and a feeling, but it is always consecrated by age.

> In its neo-Gothic architecture, pre-Raphaelite paintings, chivalric poetry, fourteenth-century socialist utopias, and its insistence on the earlier harmonies of rural life and artisan production, Victorian intellectuals of the most varied political persuasions sealed a pact between a timeless and mythical vision of the nation and their selection and installation of an acceptable heritage. British 'culture', and its profound sense of 'Englishness' (the narrowing of the national nomenclature was not accidental), was found . . . to exist beyond the mechanical rhythms and commercial logic of industrial society and the modern world.[16]

This has continued into the twentieth and early twenty-first centuries and history in the form of 'heritage' is the keyword here; a package that intersected with the rural and the domestic in the nineteenth is now commodified in the twentieth and twenty-first centuries. Within this paradigm, 'landscape' is treated as if it belongs in a binary opposition with 'wasteland'; the wasteland, despoiled land in turn accentuates and frames the 'beauty spots' we hold dear as markers of 'our' national heritage and which might be 'spoiled' by large-scale agriculture and industry.[17] Doreen Massey's point that predominantly we wish to see a place called home as providing 'stability, oneness and security', that the very concept 'place' is similarly associated 'with stasis and nostalgia, and with an enclosed security'[18] is well-taken here. 'Home' as 'place' was, and still is, meant to be a refuge from change, from the loss of identity brought about by competition and innovation. And, as we have seen, the cottage homes of England, still part of the grammar of heritage, are meant to embody steady vernacular domesticity in contrast to the progressive expression of individualism found in the city. Yet, as Brand argues, the home exhibits continual change, its inhabitants constantly respond to new wants with what he calls 'direct, vernacular action'.[19] Though we may like to think buildings are immutable, they are, in fact, far from static; old buildings are made to adapt to new standards and emergent aspirations. This goes somewhat against the grain, of course, when we value the very agedness of what is built:[20]

> 'What makes a building come to be loved?' A thirteen-year-old boy in Maine had the most succinct answer. 'Age,' he said. Apparently the older a building gets, the more we have respect and affection for its evident maturity, for the accumulated human investment it shows, for the attractive patina it wears – muted bricks, worn stairs, colorfully stained roof, lush vines.[21]

This is an American idyll, but it is just as applicable to the UK and it is as powerful among critics of Victorian sentimentalism as it is among the users of domestic space. Oliver himself admits that many cottages, 'simple, sturdy, built for a purpose', remain in use, but he nonetheless urges that they need saving from planners and architects who, because they see them as nothing but the shoddy embodiment of old England, knock them down. He also laments that they have been bought up and converted into second homes using industrial materials and a 'kitsch' image that has altered their original form. He adds a dose of tough realist history – he mentions the rushes on the floor that trapped insects and disease, the poor sanitation and wattle walls – to counteract what he calls 'the popular romantic picture of Britain' and authenticate his own perspective.

But, he goes on to celebrate the cottage's 'enduring capacity to meet housing needs through the intelligent and creative use of renewable or natural available resources' and grieves that villages have been 'spoiled' by speculation, new housing developments, the remodelling of old houses, the 'juxtaposition of incompatible buildings'.[22] Cottages for Oliver are like folk art and song and what we see here, exactly as with the nationalist preservation of folk art and song, are several intersecting, seemingly contradictory, values centred on contamination. Though hoping to avoid a 'romantic' understanding of the rural, he nonetheless wants to preserve the British landscape for the educated eye. He values what is 'indigenous' and aged yet distrusts the image of old England. His use of history naturalises and verifies his own mythology of the cottage as expression of the sustainable rural community that endures and which, though it might organically evolve over time, is 'spoilt' by the intrusion of rapid change, industrial materials and commerce, all 'alien' to the country. This is not simply about contradiction, what we see here are the parries and thrusts of competing narratives of Englishness. Access to the land is still policed. It is quite telling for instance that an advertising campaign aimed at encouraging black and Asian visitors to the countryside used the image of an open gate, implicitly revealing and thereby reinforcing the existence of barriers that had gone before.[23] Within this binary 'the (mis)representation of England as a Blessed, sceptred isle' is contrasted with 'the (mis)representation of the country as septic or spoiled'.[24]

It is in this way that the cultural battle lines between country and city, continuity and change are drawn, as will be seen in Chapter 6. However, during the mid-eighteenth to mid-nineteenth century, the rate of rural population growth was just as great as that in the towns – despite migration from the former to the latter. Agricultural 'improvement' was as much Mammon's child as the Industrial Revolution; in fact, industrialisation could not have begun without the Agricultural Revolution. During the nineteenth century, old, established, patterns of work altered in the country; more and more labourers worked for a cash wage. Though the widespread and wholesale use of machinery in agriculture, as in manufacturing, was yet to come, one of the biggest changes in farming, as in industry, was the increased need for cheap 'unskilled' casual labour – and this meant women and children.

The extent of their employment varied between arable, pastoral and mixed farming, and as they were often employed on a part-time or casual basis, they do not necessarily appear in either farm books or censuses. Eddie Higgs stresses that the numbers in the censuses are far from being value free, and that the empirical data must be seen as a construct. For instance, as of 1881, farmers' female relatives did not count as being employed in agriculture, even though, as Alun Howkins argues, this was a serious misrepresentation of the nature of farming at the time, which means that women's removal from farm work towards the end of the century has been overstated. However, we do know that 'high farming' was labour-intensive and that their employment rose and fell alongside it. In 1851, Howkins suggests, 9 per cent of farmers were women, while women constituted 8 per cent of full-time outdoor farm labourers. Of the total employed population – men and women – 21.5 per cent were employed in agriculture in 1851.[25]

Arable agriculture, which had always been labour intensive, required more employment more often as fashionable crops and techniques were adopted. Turnips had to be weeded several times in a growing season, also thinned, then dug up and trimmed; likewise farmers found that higher yields could be produced by weeding other crops, such as wheat, more intensely. They began to employ labourers to clear the land of stones, and though it is debatable whether this really resulted in higher levels of production, as was claimed, it did produce a good supply of material for the roads which in their turn were also 'improved'.

Larger crops, finally, required more sweat during harvest. All of this meant increased employment for what might be called the reserve army of labour – that body of workers who spend their time either unemployed waiting for work, or going from job to job, as needed – but, it also meant that the land itself was remade. As always, change in agriculture meant change in the landscape. As Reed argues,

> the landscape today is a palimpsest, a text upon which men and women have written their own social autobiography, without, however, being able to erase entirely the contribution of their ancestors ... every human activity, however base, grubby, altruistic, or refined, finds its reflection in the external world, and the ways in which many of these human activities have been provided for have created institutions and structures which have proved to be astonishingly durable.[26]

The land itself, Reed maintains, shapes and is equally shaped by human activity. Take place names, for example, made tangible by road signs and represented in maps. They may appear ahistorical, they may seem to outline distinct boundaries that somehow already exist around predetermined places, yet, they are an historical attempt to create order, to write boundaries across the land, to establish this place as being different to that place. Some of them, such as 'Westminster', but also 'Stonehenge' and 'the Lake District', have ancient origins and seem to belong to the timeless narratives of national identity, but their basis in history becomes obvious when we come to realise that even these names have changed over time.[27] Place names are an exercise in power, a bid to control and make sense of what would otherwise be an incomprehensible terrain in constant flux. This is why Anderson discusses the European habit of naming recently settled places with old place names. This could only work, given that the old settlements still existed, because of the feat of imagination that placed the settlers in parallel to the 'old country'.[28] The landscape, for all its supposed constancy, is as much a construct as literature or architecture.

OLD ENGLAND

One way of getting to know that landscape is to walk through its villages and hamlets, and, during the early nineteenth century, this became well established both as a form of country writing and mode of reading. One of its best-known proponents, Mary Russell Mitford[29] contributed a series of literary sketches on the subject to the *Lady's Magazine* from 1819. Collected together in five volumes as *Our Village: sketches of rural life, character and scenery* (1824–32), her illustrations of country life became enormously popular and took the (urban middle-class) reader on a tour of the 'Berkshire hamlet in which I write'. Described as a 'delightful' place to live by Mitford, who liked 'a confined locality... even in books', the site of her expedition:

> Is a little village far in the country; a small neighbourhood, not of fine mansions finely peopled, but of cottages and cottage-like houses... with inhabitants whose faces are as familiar to us as the flowers in our garden; a little world of our own... where we know everyone, are known to everyone, [and are] interested in everyone.[30]

Her village was the very model of the idealised (closed) rural community, made up of cottages and based on naturalised and organic – note the likening of its inhabitants to flowers in a garden – face-to-face relations through which everyone knew everyone. Written in a gently humorous style, with a dash of pathos and the occasional moment of moral interjection, it was a text that set out to offer verisimilitude and, thereby, consolation to the reader trammelled by disorder. Through the detailed characterisation of each household and recuperation of her few references to the hardships of rural life – she excuses the women and children who go bean setting from 'dumping'[31] – all is shown to be well.

This was the time when artists and agricultural experts began to agree on the favoured image of the rural. Where painters and visitors to the country had once valued wild heathlands in opposition to agriculturists who preferred cultivated landscapes, by the 1820s the former had come round to the latter's point of view. Now enclosed fields and harvesters came to the fore as deer parks succumbed to the plough.[32] The English village and its people were likewise there for the taking, or rather, ready for absorption into an emergent fantasy of English national identity grounded in familiarity and prosperity. Yet, Mitford was also writing in a period of growing social unrest; as the Napoleonic wars came to an end and plunged Britain into depression, so the enclosure movement and game laws robbed the poor of that which they needed to subsist. The landless were beginning to fight back, while sympathetic commentators like Cobbett were highlighting the fundamental poverty of rural life. As new definitions of property emerged, so the rural poor came to be seen as increasingly dangerous.

Barrell notes how eighteenth-century painting dawdled, in comparison to literature, when it came to introducing realism, but argues that poets, painters and writers of prose were all involved in trying to make conventional pastoral fit what they saw as 'real' rural life. As the realist tradition became dominant, so the rural became represented as the site of social tension and the poor as objects of pity. By the 1780s, it had already been tacitly accepted in literary and artistic circles that the poor ought to be represented as industrious, honest and content in order to maintain a peaceful image of the land. As Barrell puts it, the 'painter of sensibility, in selecting the images that will conjure up this mood [of pastoral serenity], must no more choose to portray the hinds as idle than to show the surface of the lake whipped up by a violent storm'.[33] Not that she or he would necessarily be conscious of this choice, this was just the inescapable, or at least the most profitable, convention of the day. The number of pieces depicting rural life exhibited at the Royal Academy, in which all kinds of rural industries and crafts were illustrated, increased dramatically at this time. These were more often than not genre pieces, familiar and, with the growing tension between Britain and France, patriotic.

By the end of the century, Barrell observes, there was a growing interest in the minutiae of rural life, be it in the form of landscape or genre painting, and its popularity continued at least through to 1818. Rural subjects, he suggests, came to be seen, at least for a while, as somehow peculiarly evocative of Britain's national identity – something that appears to be the case again around the two world wars – while the figures we see in them provided the rich with some kind of reassurance that the rural poor were inherently English and therefore trustworthy. But, what was required for this reassurance to work was that labourers be laborious; images of the poor who were not obviously at work were seen as unpatriotic and dangerous. They might only relax after a hard day's work, after the harvest, on their way to church, or during a meal break and their tools always had to be close by. The way in which they are shown to be working changes – from blithely in the mid-eighteenth century, to cheerfully at the end of the century, to automatically at the beginning of the nineteenth century – but they must work. For most of the Victorian period, it was the industrial labourer who came into the foreground as labourer and carrier of English progress, while the peasant faded into the rural community, and was offered up as the alternative to disorder. By the 1830s–1840s, therefore, the rural labourer could be shown as being at one with their surroundings and this is what we see in the work of artists like Linnell – in whose paintings labourers always seem to do whatever comes naturally to them, be it rest, work or play.[34]

In this respect, Mitford was not unusual in focusing on the village as a rural landscape peopled by figures; if slightly late, she simply followed the trend for patriotic images of peasants that Barrell discusses. But, more significantly, we can also see that Mitford represents the village as a whole as a living place, as a neighbourhood and familiar community within which people know and help each other; she links people and places. In this, like a realist novelist, she constructs a desirable 'knowable community'[35] and, to a large extent, follows the tradition established by Wordsworth and Clare of an interest in dwelling; of introducing prosaic details, like ordinary everyday language, into images of pastoral. Living and working, for Wordsworth and Clare, were linked and key to the concept of dwelling. To 'dwell' meant 'to inhabit, to live in a place, to reside'; while 'occupation', as 'the art of taking possession' could be linked to 'abode'. As John Lucas puts it, the key terms 'occupation', 'abode', 'dwelling', generated pleasure and love for the surrounding landscape in those who dwelt in a place. Landscape might, at the same time, be read through these three terms as being connected with 'work, love and aspiration'. Memories of the land and the landscape could in this way be intimately connected to a domestic sensibility that became increasingly important in the nineteenth century. Wordsworth and Clare were, in different ways, both critical of industrialisation and urbanisation, which removed men from their wives and people from the land, and which therefore destroyed the signs of occupation and abode.[36] Mitford drew on this conception of land, used her own intimate knowledge of place, to reassert the importance and continuity of home in the village, and therefore helped establish the village as separate and distinct from the town.

Writers like Mitford claimed the rural for the emergent Beau Ideal and English national identity by laying out the rural community for the observation of the elite armchair 'tourist' who, like Lady Bountiful, was always welcome in the ordered labourer's home. What and whom they saw were invariably 'pretty' and hard working. Hannah Birt, for example, has a 'pretty garden' and the village visitor would see her daily, 'sallying forth from the cottage door, with her milk-bucket in her hand, and her little brother following with the milking stool'. Her father was a drover and had three children, and since their mother had died, the eldest had become 'accustomed to take the direction of their domestic concerns, to manage her two brothers, to feed the pigs and the poultry and to keep house'. Mitford goes on, 'she was a quick, clever lass, of a high spirit, a firm temper, some pride, and a horror of accepting parochial relief'. So, when her father had to stop work, she asked his employer for a cow and was given permission to keep it on some common land. She got some utensils together 'and speedily established a regular and gainful trade in milk, eggs, butter, honey and poultry . . . Her domestic management prospered equally.' Now seventeen, she has a 'rustic grace' and eyes 'softened and sweetened by the womanly wish to please'.[37] What happened to Hannah Birt after enclosure, at which point she probably lost her piece of common, we do not know, but she is held up as a model of industrious self-help, and aided by paternalism she becomes the very model of a contented peasant woman, as is written upon her body. We do not step in through the door of Hannah Birt's cottage, but as elite readers we are assured that her domestic management is as good as her economy; given her 'womanly wish to please', we do not need to see it in practice to be sure that this is true.

As Tristram says, the taste for the picturesque, still current in 1819, made the rich look at the cottages of the poor from the outside. As the homes of the poor were knocked down (to avoid the poor rates) so the rich came to love their image. It was only in the Victorian period, in condition of England novels like Disraeli's *Sybil* (1845), that the cottage really came to be seen as a 'living space'.[38] But, the antipicturesque, as written by poets like Clare, established a highly particularised sense of place in which the home, as house, neighbourhood and people were treated as being familiar. The loss of that home was through external forces, the pain that resulted was homesickness for what was known, and disorientation in the face of unfamiliar landscapes ordered by strangers. In Clare's case, this allowed a radical criticism of the social and economic changes that were taking place at the time.[39] Mitford, of course, was not the radical that Clare was and this is significant:

> For what is knowable is not only a function of objects – what is there to be known. It is also a function of subjects, of observers – of what is desired and what needs to be known. And what we have then to see, as throughout country writing, is not only the reality of the rural community; it is the observer's position in and towards it; a position which is part of the community being known.[40]

In addition – and what Williams fails to note but what Davidoff et al. do point out – any such knowledge/observation is gendered. When the community in question is the household, for example, then even 'when the writer was a woman, the underlying imagery is the unacknowledged master of the household looking *in*, so to speak, at the household he has created'.[41] And, though the domestic idyll was aimed squarely at the urban middle class, the community of the home, as we have seen, always awaits the master's return. To extend this point, given that this master is ideally the country gentleman who is going about his business in the rural landscape,[42] when the community is the village, it awaits its squire as expectantly as the members of his household do. It is his estate as well as his home to which he rushes after a foray abroad. The village is therefore invariably laid out for and constructed, even in Mitford's writing, through an elite male gaze – Lady Bountiful is only his most humane representative. This is why we suddenly find that Hannah Birt's honesty is written on her flesh; as we pause to look at her labour, so we pause to look at her body, her physical frame becomes a metaphor for the ideal community in which she labours.

Mitford similarly describes the daughter of a shoemaker as

> a light, delicate, fairhaired girl of 14, the champion, protectress and playfellow of every brat under 3 years old, whom she jumps, dances, dandles, and feeds all day long. I have never seen any one in her station who possessed so thoroughly that undefineable charm, the lady-look. See her on a Sunday in her simplicity and her white frock, and she might pass for an earl's daughter. She likes flowers too . . . as pure and delicate as herself.[43]

She, like the flowers she is drawn to, is physically 'light, delicate' and 'pure', her blond hair and white dress mark her out as simple, while her maternal instincts and youth would make her a perfect model for one of C. W. Cope's later images of young motherhood. What Mitford is outlining in this instance is an emergent image of English femininity grounded in (white) frailty and purity. She is describing a girl who, though she might have a 'lady-look', is nonetheless explicitly not an 'earl's daughter'; in describing her 'undefineable charm', Mitford is elevating this (working-class) girl above her 'station' and thereby universalising and naturalising the 'lady-look' that she seems to possess. In other words, her physical frailty and appearance are indicators of her moral and social respectability, which in turn secure her (normative) femininity.[44] It was through authors like Mitford, that the village eventually became the perfect site in which to find such a girl/'lady', even if it might also contain, as in another house, 'a plump, merry, bustling dame with four fat, rosy, noisy children, the very essence of vulgarity and plenty'.[45] The bustling dame being 'the very essence of *vulgarity*' is clearly a figure of the past, the fairhaired girl with her 'lady-look' a figure of the future, and indeed it was the latter who came to take precedence in Victorian literature and domestic pastoral. The use of the word 'vulgarity' here is indicative of the influence of an older, eighteenth-century aesthetic and her elite position as an observer of a distanced picturesque landscape, despite her use of detail, makes her more like Wordsworth than Clare. Mitford's writing sits between several traditions, between the realist vision of the rural as site of social tension and the pastoral understanding of land as site of stability, between picturesque depictions of the labourer as vulgar but cheerful and anti-picturesque images of their community as a particularised place. However, by the end of the nineteenth century, we see new narrative emerging; one that valued the old over the contemporary or the new.

The mid-1870s saw agricultural depression, caused largely by foreign competition, but also poor growing conditions, hurting rural employers and employed alike, especially in the arable regions of the south and east. There were widespread labour disputes in town and country, a steady rise in rural depopulation, and an increasing number of reports and commentaries on rural deprivation. Under the circumstances, one might expect the rural idyll to have been abandoned. Yet, if we look at the prose of this period we can see a new genre emerging, one that sought to reprise rurality as the solid centre of old England. As in Mitford's time, the distance that still existed between writer and subject was hidden by a fantasy of little details for the reader. Authors maintained an expert knowledge of their characters' habits, dialect and dress, but these characters were, by the 1870s, more likely to be of times gone by than of the present. Village characters came to stand in as signs for those values that had been lost rather than those that were emerging. In this way, they became part of the mechanism that enabled the rescue and reconstruction of ideology from the past in the present,[46] while as the carriers of ancient English folklore and bearers of national history, they became metaphors for the land, the nation and the race. George Bourne was one of the most popular writers in this new genre.[47]

As Bourne goes out for a walk one summer evening, he reports in *Change in the Village*, (1912), he overhears the following conversation:

> The people were out late that night, and indeed, it was pleasant to be out. Not as yet were there any of those street lamps along the road which now make all nights alike dingy; but one felt as if walking into the unspoiled country. For though it was after ten, and the sky overcast, still one could see very clearly the glimmering road and the hedgerows in the soft midsummer twilight. Enjoying this tranquillity, I passed by a man and a woman with two children, and heard the man say invitingly: 'Shall I carry the basket?' The wife answered: "E en't 'cavy, Bill, thanks... Only I got this 'ere little Rosy to git along.'
>
> Her voice sounded gentle and cheerful, and I tried to hear more, checking my pace. But the children were walking too slowly. I was getting out of earshot, missing the drift of the peaceful-sounding chatter, when presently the woman, as if turning to the other child, said more loudly: 'Come along! You'll be left behind!'
>
> The children began prattling; their father and mother laughed; but I was leaving them farther and farther behind. Then, however, some other homeward-goer overtook the little family. For the talk grew suddenly louder, the woman beginning cheerily: 'Hullo, Mr. Weatherall! 'Ow's your poor wife?... I didn't see 'twas you, 'till this here little Rosy

said...' What Rosy had said I failed to catch. I missed also what followed, leading up to the woman's ending remark: 'This 'ere little Rosy, she's a reg'lar gal for cherries!' The neighbour seemed to say something; then the husband; then the neighbour again. And at that there came a burst of laughter, loudest from the woman, and Mr Weatherall asked: 'Didn't you never hear that afore?'

The woman, laughing still, was emphatic: 'No; I'll take my oath as I never knowed that.'

'Well, you knowes it now, don't ye?'

'I ain't sure yet. I ain't had time to consider.'

After that the subject changed. I heard the woman say: 'I've had 6 gals an' only one boy – one out o' seven. Alice is out courtin'; and then they seemed to get on to the question of ways and means. The last words that reached me were 'Fivepence ... tuppence-ha'penny'; but still, when I could no longer catch any details at all, the voices continued to sound pleasantly good-tempered.[48]

The conversation and Bourne's observation of it is worth quoting at length because it exemplifies the relationship that existed between rural authors and their subjects and, on closer inspection, it appears that the distance that existed between Bourne and his characters allowed him to slip into pastoral mode. The country seems 'unspoiled', 'soft', tranquil; it is 'pleasant' to be there and its 'people' are inviting, 'gentle', 'cheerful'; their 'chatter' is 'peaceful-sounding' and 'good-tempered'; they laugh and walk slowly among family and friends. This was a language of land as cultivated, feminine, open. But there is also a sense in which the construction of childhood and the loss of the rural overlap in this extract. It is the slow pace of the child which dictates the speed at which the other adults walk, yet Bourne, as external observer cannot match his step to theirs and is forced to walk past without quite being able to catch the girl's words to enjoy the companionable spirit of the group. The passage therefore works metaphorically to connote the slower pace of rural life as compared to the heightened speed of modernity (signified by the street lamps that come to 'make all nights dingy'), which has taken reader and author out of reach of its gentler ways.

Because he was largely sympathetic to the poor, and generally scathing of urban visitors who moved to the countryside to regain a lost golden age, Bourne's work has often been taken to provide some of the most authentic material of the period. But, as Marsh notes, it was a simple matter for an account like this, written as it was in dialect, to be read as heroic by its audience, regardless of its author's intent.[49] A book like *Change in the Village* offered its readers a temporary excursion into a rural world that was constantly slipping away.[50] Bourne was a realist who sought mimesis in his writing and his use of dialect, embedded in an apparently faithful account of a conversation that he cannot quite catch, gives the book authenticity. Yet, he is eavesdropping and the reader can only ever hear what he hears. As he moves through the discussion and passes along the lane, he brings a citified elite sensibility to what he discerns, and his reader must follow him. He frames the scene – contrasting the rural lane with the urban street – and interprets the conversation. Though they get onto 'ways and means' their talk never seems to be anything other than pacific, and this he states at the outset is 'a sample of what is normal'.[51] Texts like this performed the spatial relationship of the urban or moneyed observer to the rural working class and sought to recuperate the country from commentaries like D. C. Pedder's *Where Men Decay: a survey of present rural conditions* (1908)[52] by evoking a timeless (yet unreachable) English idyll reassuringly untroubled by decay or, more importantly, disorder.

HAPPY ENGLAND

It was order as opposed to disorder, far more than country vs. city, which came to determine images of English national identity at this time and it was exactly this sense of harmony, in the design and function of its architecture as well as social relations, that was at stake for those who sought to preserve the rural against botched renovation and commerce. It was the 'aesthetic of clear order and truth to materials', rather than domestic pastoral *per se* that lay behind many early twentieth-century attempts to save vernacular architecture. Thoughtful planning and sensible preservation, as found in the national parks, would ensure that an 'orderly England would replace decay and chaos with sweetness and light'.[53] What was sought was the clarity of vision found in Georgian England. However, with the re-emergence of this aesthetic, a new negotiation took place between those who valued Englishness envisioned as picturesque imperfection and those who desired 'fair' open landscapes and regularity.

Helen Allingham's work was described by Ruskin, who systematically rejected the foul, polluting products and corruption of industrialisation in favour of the natural and the native landscape, as 'bursting out like one of the sweet Surrey fountains, all dazzling and pure'.[54] Whereas Marcus Huish's commentary on her work, as collected in Allingham's biography *Happy England* (1903), described how she painted to preserve a vernacular tradition being destroyed by the orderliness of modernity. Take, for example, his description of the cottage depicted in 'In Witley Village' (1884). Knocked down by the owner soon after Allingham had painted it, it was, according to Huish,

> replaced by buildings whose monotonous symmetry to his eye no doubt, appeared in better taste. The cottage was still far from the natural term of its existence, as evidenced by the troublesome piece of work it was to dislocate the sound, firm old oaken beams of which its framework was built up.[55]

Similarly 'The Fish Shop, Haslemere' (1887), also subsequently demolished, was a 'picturesque little tenement' thanks to its 'diamond-paned lattices, its projecting shop front, and its spoutless eaves, which had allowed the damp to rise up from the foundations and the green lichen to grow upon its walls'.[56] Moreover, Huish stressed, as she had only ever travelled to Venice, her portrayal of each scene was quintessentially English; in this, she never strayed. Her aim was 'to illustrate in colour an artist's impressions of a particular country'. As a 'commentary [the book] ... is throughout, a mirror of halcyon days'.[57] According to Huish, Allingham, whose work replaced/stood in place of 'reality', therefore provided her audience with a respite from the world of commerce, and solace in exile:

> What does the worker, long in city pent, desire when he cries
>   'Tis very sweet to look into the fair
>   And open face of Heaven'?
> And what does the banished Englishman oftenest turn his thoughts to, even although he may be dwelling under aspects of nature which many would think far more beautiful than those of his native land? ...
>   'Oh to be in England' [Browning]
>   'Happy is England!' [Keats][58]

As the embodiment of 'England' and as 'home', the image of the country cottage might rescue the Englishman from the perils of exchange and the lure of foreign lands. In this way, he argued, Allingham sought to re-present England as she saw and hoped to see it. Allingham, like Oliver, tried to freeze her cottages in historical time, to conserve them by capturing a snapshot of a particular view of her cottages at a particular moment, and thereby define a particular place. And this, according to her editor was a patriotic necessity, as:

> It would, perhaps be a low estimate, however, to say that a thousand ancient cottages are now disappearing in England every twelvemonth, without trace or record left – many that Shakespeare might have seen, some Chaucer; while the number 'done up' is beyond computation ... Had Mrs Allingham done nothing else for her country, she has justified

her career as a recorder of this altogether overlooked phase of English architecture – a phase which will soon be a thing of the past.[59]

The cottage, naturally part of its landscape, organically of the tradition to which Shakespeare and Chaucer belonged in 'halcyon days', had, in Huish's view, to be saved for the nation. Yet, as the book starts with a highly self-conscious move in the discussion of its title, the editor of *Happy England* was clearly not unaware of the imperfect cottage or of Ruskin's preferences. The prefix 'Happy', apparently, occasioned

> the disapprobation of certain of the artist's friends, who, recognising her as a resident of Hampstead, have associated the title with that alliterative one which the northern suburbs have received at the hands of the bank Holiday visitant; and they facetiously surmise that the work may be called 'Appy England! By a Denizen of "Appy" Ampstead!'[60]

But, this working-class touristic intrusion was smoothed over by the assertion that Allingham had, in Huish's view, sought to provide her audience with a revised way of seeing, one in which illness might become convalescence, agedness rest, where the pedlar 'finds a ready market for her wares', and 'the tramp assistance by the wayside'. She had avoided 'dales, crags and fells' – the sublime – and preferred the 'South Downs, cottages, farmsteads and flower gardens' – the picturesque. As a result, she had 'catered for the happiness of the greatest number' – in good Liberal tradition – including the 'worker', and 'in strong opposition to the tendency of the art of the later years of the nineteenth century, the baser side of life has been studiously avoided', in an entirely deliberate way. Consequently she seemed to assert that 'happiness' as cleanliness and order, in some fashion, is as real as 'the sterner realities'.[61]

As Stephen Daniels points out, this kind of Englishness as domestic pastoral, the counterweight to imperialism, came in two versions, the yeoman's farmhouse and the country cottage, and many paintings of country houses can be read as either or both.[62] For instance, Fildes' *The Farmer's Daughter* (1868), discussed in Chapter 1, is ambiguous in social as well as spatial terms. The girl is supposed to be a *farmer's* daughter, but the house itself looks as if it must be a cottage; covered in vines, it is simply too small to be a farm at the height of the 'golden age' of agriculture. Its garden is picturesque, its chickens charming; this is not a working farmyard. This ambiguity slips in because Fildes is representing an older, smaller-scale, independent yeoman farming celebrated by Cobbett, not the large-scale capitalist agriculture that is supposed to have been dominant by the middle of the nineteenth century.

Though very English, this was also one of two competing images of America at the end of the eighteenth century. Codified by Jefferson,

America was envisioned as 'an expanding agricultural republic of small, family-sized farms, their yeoman owners the backbone of democracy and proof against the corruption of greedy commerce'.[63] Cobbett, who lived in the US for nearly twenty years, took this image of self-sufficiency back with him and re-invigorated it. In fact, in *Cottage Economy* he makes many passing references to the Americans, both learning from and hoping to teach them something – 'I like the Americans very much;' he says 'and that, if there were no other, would be a reason for my not hiding their faults.'[64]

The second competing image of America as wilderness, peopled only by the solitary white man, had no place in the UK – unless one reads the aristocratic use of the country for the pursuit of hunting/ shooting/fishing in this way. But, what Kolodny says of the two images, that what was at stake was 'the new nation's choice of a defining fantasy for itself . . . and competing and contradictory strategies for being in and relating to' nature, is equally applicable to England and definitions of Englishness. Moreover, as in the US, each image had its own gendered characters, which could be used within the context of their symbolic and mythic narratives to hold up 'a mirror to contemporary reality'. In some narratives, where men were the white hunters, women were used to represent the subtler forces of cultivation. Meanwhile, agriculturists/ homesteaders, including women, were represented as pushing back the frontier and claiming the wilderness, while it was hoped that old colonial relations centred on commerce might be substituted by 'the more benign economic organisation of a nation of cultivators'.[65] In America as in England, women pushed back wild Nature to claim a small clearing of Culture.

Through the image of independent yeoman farming associated in this instance with the freeborn Englishman, the essence of old England, Fildes manages to suggest that organic social relations have survived in the country, if not in the town. The elements of the picture that make it a cottage scene, on the other hand, work through the elevation of domesticity captured in the Beau Ideal and the presence of the farmer's *daughter*, not the farmer himself, to elevate those relations and set them against the rigours of (male, urban) commerce. It was exactly this combination of naturalised, peaceful domesticity within a paternalistic rural setting, connoting ongoing organic communal relations in the home and the country, which generated the Ideal's appeal. *The Farmer's Daughter* therefore looked to a past that supposedly provided independence and the stability of long-standing tradition, and Fildes' audience is reminded of the tenacious persistence and homeliness of Old England. This picture is exemplary of the defining fantasy of Englishness that came to be adopted by the urban bourgeoisie and in painting it, Fildes was following a tradition established at the beginning of the century.

As Daniels notes, Constable's paintings are equally ambiguous. Willy Lot's house in *The Haywain*

> could be seen as a sturdy farmhouse, neatly tiled and plastered, as plain and durable as the farmer who inhabited it. Or it could be seen as a pretty cottage, by focusing on the creeping foliage, the puff of hearth smoke, and the woman washing or drawing water from the stream.[66]

This two-fold way of seeing domestic pastoral continued through to the end of the Victorian period, and became a fantasy that was 'compelling across the whole political spectrum from the later nineteenth century'. However, the weight gradually shifts so that Constable Country, which as metaphor of 'the South Country' has remained the 'essential England',[67] becomes predominantly a country of cottages, rather than farms, and therefore of homeliness rather than productivity.

Allingham's water-colours work in the same way – she painted cottages, farms and deliberately ambiguous homes that might be either – but most significantly, she saw Constable as a painter of homely cottages, not farms, and in this he had, she thought, never been surpassed. The old English cottage 'was the most typical thing in England' in her view. In contrast to great houses or modern homes 'the cottage prefers to nestle snugly in shady valleys. The trees grow closely about it in an intimate familiar way'.[68] They blended in so well that, in *Happy England*, Huish noted it was all too easy to pass them by, 'without a thought to their structure, or an idea that it is an evolution which has grown on very marked lines from primitive types, and that almost every instance is influenced by local surroundings.'[69]

What was being valued here was an old England that knew its roots and could hold its head up with pride in a world that had by this point, passed 'new', industrial England by. By the 1880s, the industrial north was losing out to competition from Germany and the US and it is at this point that the rural south really comes to the fore. The productive 'North Country', previously figured as the 'metaphor of England as the workshop of the world', came to be seen as essentially unEnglish. Meanwhile, the snug domestic south, supported economically by the imperial and financial clout of London, emerged as a site of safety – from overseas expansion, aggression and competition – and as a retreat from the (figurative and actual) metropolis. With the decline of agriculture and therefore of agricultural interests, the 'South Country' came to be remade in the image of metropolitan concerns. However, this fantasy was not easy to secure. Given that the decline of agriculture also led to fears about the state of the nation as a whole, the rural population was equally vulnerable to sudden urban invasion and 'slow internal decay'. There was constant concern that country people and places, and their native (folk) traditions, were being either contaminated or erased.[70]

The increasing number of books which catalogued the lost peasantry of England, like Bourne's *Change in the Village*, in mourning what was being lost, sought to reveal and thereby recoup the true strength of the nation. They therefore carried reassuring connotations of robust health and morality, not just images of peace and tranquillity. According to Bourne, for one, the cottager was now well off enough to have a rabbit for dinner and a fire to cook it on, while the cottage woman, and even her husband, could be held up as models of stalwart domesticity. Cottagers, Bourne declared, couldn't get 'a man' or 'a woman' in to do the worst or even ordinary household tasks. The wife of a labourer could not

> call in 'a woman' to scrub her floor, or to wash and mend, or to skin a rabbit for dinner, or to make up the fire for cooking it. It is necessary for her to be ready to turn from one task to another without squeamishness, and without pausing to think how she shall do it. In short, she and her husband alike must practice, in their daily doings, a sort of intrepidity which grows customary with them; and this habit is the parent of much of that fine conduct which they exhibit so carelessly in moments of emergency.[71]

This, he went on to say, was not down to Nature or instinct, but had emerged out of 'time-honoured tradition'. It no longer mattered that cottage women were rough, what mattered was that they were capable. They had their own standards, their own ways of doing things and these he held up as valuable models of behaviour that should be preserved. Moreover, thanks to their innate strength, 'during the South African War there was many a woman in the village keeping things together at home while the men were at the front'.[72] The practical domesticity of the countrywoman, though learnt, meant that the nation could send its men to war, could defend itself against the foreign interests and aggression that were so much a concern of the time. By this time, a reading of the rural could never be separated from the celebration of hereditary Englishness, or reference to the Empire. Together, the discourses of imperialism, gender and place combined to re-form the 'South Country' as the site of a newly hardy, comfortable, 'snug' and native English idyll. The Surrey cottages painted by Allingham therefore became metaphors of this re-formed national identity.

Belonging to the 'lower classes' and, according to Huish, built of local materials, each cottage painted by Allingham had a twist that made it suitable to and revealed it as being rooted in its site. 'The roofs,' he declared, 'like the framework, testify to the geological formation and agricultural conditions of the district.'[73] But, Huish goes on to lament, their demise is almost inevitable because of 'lack of sympathy, time or interest'.[74] There is no 'sense of pride' in, no attempt to 'deal reverently with' these cottages. Their 'workmanship' was therefore steadily being lost because of landlords who, worried that they were 'tumbling down' or 'falling to pieces', got in agents, who sent in

> a scratch pack of masons or joiners [who] between them . . . supplant fine old work, most of it firm as a rock, with poor materials and careless labour, and rub out a piece of old England, irrecoverable henceforth by all the genius in the world and all the money in the bank.[75]

The well-repaired old cottage, on the other hand, would 'last for generations to come' and

> be more comfortable than the new or the done-up ones, to say nothing of the 'sentiment' of the cottager. An old man, who was in a temporary lodging during the doing-up of his cottage, being asked, 'When shall you get back to your house?' answered, 'In about a month, they tell me; but it won't be like going home.'[76]

Though Huish is a little prone to archaism in securing the nostalgic reading he intends, this sounds remarkably like Oliver's plea for the preservation of the cottage/small farmhouse sixty years later. An example of Williams' escalator[77] (see Chapter 6), like *Change in the Village* this was nostalgia by requiem.[78] In *Happy England*, the cottage as a place acquired an assured organic and inseparable relationship to its community and the English landscape of the 'South Country'. 'Old England' and 'home' as the dual centres of human sentiment both needed to be treated with reverence, and once effaced they could never be replaced. Being embedded in the folk, no amount of architectural fakery[79] could make up for their loss. Yet, given the expectations of Williams' escalator, they were in a sense always already ruined.

The cottage homes of England, characterised by age and tradition, were constantly in danger of erasure, of destruction by modernity and progress. What was therefore needed was 'a real feeling of wise conservatism',[80] but the form and nature of this 'conservatism' – which might mean preservation, restoration, renovation, the conservation of land, place or values – was up for debate by the inter-war years. This is why a struggle emerged between two competing images of the nation.

One image (itself cut across by the nature vs. nurture debate), which was grounded in the necessity of preserving the nation's physical health, tended to pick up on the language of science, individualism and the modernist aesthetic. The other – exemplified by Huish's commentary – was grounded in the need to sustain what was left of its traditions before they were lost and gone forever, and employed the language of nature/ the natural, the communal and the aesthetics of old pastoral. However, both images saw the nation through the lens of decay, drew on 'conservatism'/conservation, deployed the rhetoric of organicism and placed England in opposition to its western competitors and eastern Other.[81]

STROLLING THROUGH COTTAGE ENGLAND

Tourists and tourist imagery require repetition; guidance, routine, predictability are the basis of successful tourism, on a practical and an ideological level. This repetition offers reassurance to the tourist, ensures that they avoid unsettling experiences and that they get what they came for.[82] Tourists use familiarity to guarantee that pleasure will overcome anxiety; 'repetition is crucial, since it returns to tourists whatever they are looking for. Repetition not only smothers the unexpected but also reliably re-presents the already known.'[83] Tourism relies on the mass, which becomes fixed in place, queuing for the opportunity to see what it came for. Meanwhile, photographers like Martin Parr who have played with this experience and produced pieces that though they ostensibly criticise these ways of seeing, rely on their existence in order to engage with and write back to them. 'Trippers', 'tourists' and 'travellers' belong to a hierarchy of seeing in which the tripper barely observes what is around them, the tourist glances around and slips into the clichés with a sigh of relief and the traveller casts an expert and weather eye over the whole.[84] Country writing might be classified in the same way; Mitford being a tripper, W. S. Percy a tourist, Bourne a traveller.

W. S. Percy's *Strolling Through Cottage England* (1936), like the heritage industry and its texts, fixes the armchair tourist to the spot, and though not strictly a guidebook, secures a specific way of seeing. Indeed, the idea of the armchair tourist is peculiarly apt as the criticism of tourism that arises from the highlighting of repetition might also be read in light of the patriarchal response to housekeeping and other 'women's work' as routine, repetitive, unfocused, static. In this way, where tourism is homely and feminine (static/repetitive), travelling (mobile/focused) is outward-looking and masculine. To begin with, by exhorting one to 'stroll' through 'cottage England' – outlined as 'The South-East Corner and Wessex', 'The Cotswolds', 'Devon and Cornwall',

'The Midlands', 'Lancashire', 'The Lake Country, Yorkshire and the North', 'The Eastern Counties—And some Windmills', and 'The Home Counties' – Percy thereby recoups the English landscape for the rambler-tourist. Secondly, this is one of a series of 'strolling' books, which relies on a tried and tested form that the reader will know and trust. Thirdly, it provides numerous illustrations, as well as descriptions, of representative cottages highlighting, teaching, mapping out and determining what the reader ought to see. The book begins with 'A Little History', which takes us back in time to the round huts of early Britons excavated at Glastonbury – likened to the Kaffa huts in contemporary Africa, and those of charcoal burners, who, it is suggested, 'are too lazy to build' anything other than 'this old form of home'.[85] And, follows on with 'The Evolution of the Cottage'. 'History' and 'evolution' together tell the cottage's story and are both important to the placing of the text in its national context. The history chapter refers to the early Britons and the Kaffa, also to Australian colonists and aborigines, New Zealand colonists and the Maori, Romans, Saxons, Normans, Elizabethans, Flemish and Dutch. Throughout, the British reveal their potential in contrast to these Others – hence the early Britons are praised for their many skills and are therefore distanced from barbarism. And, at the end of Elizabeth I's reign, England is said to be 'already on the way to being the leader of industry and finance'.[86] This is a book that works to colonise the past as well as the Kaffa.

It is during Elizabeth I's reign that the English move into modernity. Moreover, the cottage is described as in essence Elizabethan, and as such as 'part of the country', (viz., nation) whereas Georgian architecture is declared to have 'contributed little to the art of the cottage. Its spirit was directed more towards building homes for the newly rich created by the Industrial Revolution.'[87] Manufacturing (production) is said to have destroyed the English landscape; the nation's identity and heritage is grounded firmly in the great days of Elizabethan pastoral, not the muck and grime of the nineteenth century. The root of this particular evil is placed at the door of the factory system which, when it came into being, destroyed the

> home industries of the spinners and weavers created in Queen Elizabeth's time... This in its turn brought about a new class distinction; the mill workers inhabited ugly houses built in mean, sordid streets. The mill owners were able to build huge, pretentious Georgian houses.[88]

Here, we hear echoes of Disraeli, Carlyle and Cobbett. This is a well-worn historical track that sets the modern and neo-classical against the indigenous, the vernacular, the Gothic, and the Conservative against the Liberal. But, it is also a track which suddenly takes a domestic, if nationalistic turn as the 'continental style, mostly German' of the 'Hanoverian kings' is derided as foppish. 'Beau Nash and Beau Brummell' it seems, hated anything 'old English' while the 'Italian classic was glorified and worshipped'. This, Percy concludes, 'was a false age – picturesque, certainly, but nevertheless false'.[89] It took, apparently, Ruskin and Morris in their dislike of the industrial and love of the natural, to rescue England from this architectural mire and set the English back on the true path of cottage building – to be seen in suburbs up and down the country[90] – *pace* Englishness. Though 'not a socialist' himself, our guide believes Morris has been misremembered as a 'mad socialist'. He was really 'a man who imagined the world would be put right by men being happy in their work. In the light of present day conditions was he far wrong?'[91] Percy is writing to rescue the English reader of the 1930s from both the disorder of the depression and the aggressions of a new German state. A tour of cottage England at a strolling, pre-industrial pace, through familiar territory and comfy 'corners', reassures that all is well; the stress is on the peace and tranquillity of the country, its homeliness and privacy. But this is also a feminine Englishness, one less interested in the heroic exploits of official masculinity centred on 'Great Britain' and 'more inward-looking, more domestic and more private'.[92]

This form of Englishness, Taylor and Alison Light both argue, became dominant after the First World War, covered for a loss of masculine nerve in the face of real aggression, and helped articulate a peacetime focus on home and family. The English came to define 'themselves in terms of sentiment and memory . . . "throttled emotion" or conservative nationalism – "a politics which eschews politicking; a system of beliefs and values without systematisation; an organic and inevitable way to be".'[93] In its self-reflexive irony, it lingers in today's advertising for cottage holidays, discussed in Chapter 6, and though it might seem to value the distant past above all else, was a firmly modern form. This feminised England became the centre of a new national history envisioned as stability. A middle-class voice of responsibility, steadiness and femininity as reliability, it found its feet in commerce – it 'was as much a product of modern retailing as the masculine adventure rhetoric of the Victorians'.[94] Its modernity can be seen in its provision of commercial novels for the middle class, by writers like Agatha Christie who stuck to a formula and constantly evoked an idealised pre-war England of country houses and stable class relations. Feminised England could be reproduced reliably according to a set pattern. Dependable and honest, it could be found in all cultural arenas, from magazines like *Weekly Illustrated* and *Picture Post* to the radio and cinema.[95] Largely an inter-war phenomenon, this highly nostalgic, closed version of Englishness can be seen emerging in Huish's 'real feeling of wise conservatism' and stress on the cottage as labourer's home, but is epitomised in the renewed linkage of Elizabethan 'cottage home' and 'England' seen in Percy's stroll and 1930s Tudorbethan.

Though, as a myth, national identity can take the form of either geographical territory or genealogical descent, national identities are always characterised by 'both a historical and a geographical heritage', and are defined by

> 'legends and landscapes', by stories of golden ages, enduring traditions, heroic deeds and dramatic destinies located in ancient or promised home-lands with hallowed sites and scenery. The symbolic activation of time and space, often drawing on religious sentiment, gives shape to the 'imagined community' of the nation. Landscapes, whether focusing on single monuments or framing stretches of scenery, provide visible shape; they picture the nation. As exemplars of moral order and aesthetic harmony, particular landscapes achieve the status of national icons.[96]

It is in this context that we ought to see the country cottage, as part of the lexicon of Englishness as narrated by artists and authors, historians, tourists, cartographers, geographers, geologists, architects and commentators since the late eighteenth century. But it takes work to maintain this identity, it has to be constantly redone, revised. Ditchfield has to tiptoe uneasily between the need to stress continuity and individuality when discussing how each 'church, manor-house, farm and cottage, differ somewhat in each village . . . It is true' he says,

> that the style is traditional, that each son learned from his sire how to build, and followed the plans and methods of his forefathers; but he never slavishly imitated their work. He introduced improvements devised by his own ingenuity and skill, created picturesque effects which added beauty to the building.[97]

Heaven forbid that the freeborn Englishman follow his forebears slavishly. This contradiction lies at the heart of the Beau Ideal. Just as the home is a community, yet secures the privacy of its head, so each village must be timeless, yet have a story. Every attempt to fix identity is an attempt to distinguish between many competing representations of a particular geographic region or to lay claim to a particular history, as inflected through other forms of cultural identity based on ethnicity, class, gender and faith. And, in the process of making the attempt, the histories and identities of others living in that territory are necessarily excluded. Myths of national identity use homeliness to delineate what is worth fighting for, what must be defended, and they are created by keeping the Other out. When taken abroad, imperialists use their preferred fantasy of national identity to place an embargo on the identity myths of Others' places and to create a space called home for themselves in which they might belong, while they remain separate from that which surrounds them. 'For every magnificent, even multi-cultural, prospect of national identity,' Daniels observes, 'there is a more homely ethnic enclosure';[98] it is in this way that the countryside becomes a 'white space'.[99]

Within the context of globalisation, a place called 'Home' is at the centre of a search for identity. The current characterisation of globalisation as an ever-increasing compression of space–time, is a white, Western, way of seeing.[100] Here, 'Home', whether this be a building or a geographical place, is implicated in a search for a long-lost 'authenticity', 'stability', 'reliability', and 'reactionary politics'. 'Woman' and 'Home' are treated as if they have no relationship to history, to everyday labour, or wider connections to the rest of the world, but are both used purely as symbolic centres by and for others.[101] In which case, the cottage as a 'safe' space, embedded in its community, might offer a retreat not just from the aggressions of exploitative capitalist relations, but also from attempts to shunt the 'white, Western, middle-class, heterosexual, male' from his 'position of absolute power' at the 'cultural centre'.[102] The country cottage is after all ideal home, site of authentic, romantic, vernacular architecture, while the cottage garden, as extension of that home, is figured as a metaphor for the lost and sheltered innocence of childhood.

NOTES

1. Andrew Bush, *Bonnetstown* (New York, 1989), p. 12, quoted in S. Brand, *How Buildings Learn: what happens after they're built* (London, 1997), p. 158.
2. P. H. Ditchfield, *The Charm of the English Village* (London, [1906] 1994), p. 1.
3. Ditchfield, *Charm*, p. 2.
4. Brand, *How Buildings Learn*, p. 132.
5. I. Chambers, *Migrancy, Culture, Identity* (London and New York, 1994), p. 71.
6. Chambers, *Migrancy*, p. 71.
7. P. Oliver, *English Cottages and Small Farmhouses: a study of vernacular shelter* (London, 1975), p. 5.
8. S. Daniels, *Fields of Vision: landscape imagery and national identity in England and the United States* (Cambridge, 1993), pp. 225–7.
9. Henry Galssie, quoted in Brand, *How Buildings Learn*, p. 132.
10. Country Holidays advert, ref. GA193, (c.1997).
11. Advertisement for English Country Cottages, *The Guardian*, 7 January 1995, p. 3.
12. Daniels, *Fields of Vision*, p. 6.

13 I. Chambers, 'Narratives of nationalism, being "British"', in Carter, E., Donald, J., Squires, J. (eds), *Space and Place: theories of identity and location* (London, 1993), p. 146.
14 B. Anderson, *Imagined Communities: reflections on the origin and spread of nationalism* (London and New York, [1983] 1991).
15 Brand, *How Buildings Learn*, p. 158.
16 Chambers, 'Narratives of Nationalism', p. 147.
17 J. Taylor, *A Dream of England: landscape, photography and the tourist's imagination* (Manchester, 1994), pp. 262–83.
18 D. Massey, *Space, Place and Gender* (Cambridge, 1994), pp. 167, 171.
19 Brand, *How Buildings Learn*, p. 159.
20 Brand, *How Buildings Learn*, pp. 2–3, 10–17.
21 Brand, *How Buildings Learn*, p. 10.
22 Oliver, *English Cottages and Small Farmhouses*, pp. 5, 7, 23.
23 W. J. Darby, 'Access/ability: geographies of exclusion' paper delivered to *Gendered Landscapes: an interdisciplinary exploration of past place and space* conference held at Penn State University, USA, 29 May–1 June 1999.
24 Taylor, *A Dream of England*, p. 264.
25 A. Howkins, *Reshaping Rural England: a social history 1850–1925* (London, 1991), pp. 7–14; E. Higgs, 'Women, occupations and work in the nineteenth century censuses', *History Workshop Journal*, (1987).
26 M. Reed, *The Landscape of Britain: from the beginnings to 1914* (London, 1997), pp. xii–xiii.
27 Reed, *The Landscape of Britain*, pp. xiii–xiv, 101, 340–1; Interestingly, Herman Muthesius thought that the English habit of naming their houses was indicative of the Englishman's love of his home. H. Muthesius, *The English House*, Sharp, D. (ed.), Seligman, J. (trans.), (London, 1904), p. 7. The maps that historians use to trace landscape history are another exercise in power, a deliberate evocation of territory in documentary form. Reed, *The Landscape of Britain*, pp. 127, 239.
28 Anderson, *Imagined Communities*, pp. 187–9.
29 Mary Russell Mitford (1787–1855) was the daughter of a country doctor. *Our Village* was set in and around Three Miles Cross, near Reading.
30 M. R. Mitford, *Our Village: sketches of rural life, character and scenery* (London, [1824–32] 1893), pp. 3–4.
31 Mitford, *Our Village*, pp. 64–5. 'Dumping': planting more than one bean at a time.
32 H. Prince, 'Art and agrarian change, 1710–1815' in Cosgrove, D. and Daniels, S. (eds), *The Iconography of Landscape* (Cambridge, 1992), pp. 98, 107.
33 J. Barrell, *The Dark Side of the Landscape: the rural poor in English painting 1730–1840* (Cambridge, 1980), p. 19.
34 Barrell, *Dark Side*, pp. 19–33.
35 R. Williams, *The Country and the City* (London, [1972] 1985), pp. 165–81.
36 J. Lucas, 'Places and dwellings: Wordsworth, Clare and the anti-picturesque' in Cosgrove, D. and Daniels, S. (eds), *The Iconography of Landscape* (Cambridge, 1992), pp. 83–8.
37 Mitford, *Our Village*, pp. 233–45.
38 P. Tristram, *Living Space in Fact and Fiction* (London, 1989), pp. 71–4.
39 Lucas, 'Places and dwellings', pp. 89–96.
40 Williams, *The Country and the City*, p. 165.
41 L. Davidoff, J. L'Esperance and H. Newby, 'Landscape with figures: home and community in English society' in Mitchell, J. and Oakley, A. (eds), *The Rights and Wrongs of Women* (Harmondsworth, 1976), p. 154.

42 Davidoff et al., 'Landscape', p. 154.
43 Mitford, *Our Village*, pp. 7–9.
44 L. Nead, *Myths of Sexuality: representations of women in Victorian Britain* (Oxford, 1988), pp. 26–32, 125–30.
45 Mitford, *Our Village*, pp. 9–10.
46 R. Sales, *English Literature in History 1750–1830: pastoral and politics* (London, 1983), pp. 15–18.
47 In *Women of the Fields* I discuss his representation of Lucy Bettesworth, a working-class woman who was a field labourer all her life. In his 'Bettesworth Books' he describes her work and likens her to the land on which she has worked. Ultimately, she is dehumanised and mythologised as part of the land, and by extension the nation itself. K. Sayer, *Women of the Fields: representations of rural women in the nineteenth century* (Manchester, 1995).
48 G. Bourne, *Change in the Village* (London, [1912] 1989), pp. 31–2.
49 J. Marsh, *Back to the Land: the pastoral impulse in Victorian England from 1880 to 1914* (London, Melbowne and New York, 1982), pp. 61–4.
50 By the 1890s the interested traveller could get a Cook's tour to see the 'real' Constable Country of the Stour Valley. Those who were called 'pilgrims' were expected to have a detailed knowledge of Constable's work. Daniels, *Fields of Vision*, p. 212.
51 Bourne, *Change in the Village*, p. 31.
52 D. C. Pedder, *Where Men Decay: a survey of present rural conditions* (London, 1908). This was based on a series of articles originally published in the *Nineteenth Century Review*, the *Contemporary Review* and the *Monthly Review*. Lt-Col. Pedder claimed that his commentary was based on observation and wanted wider publicity for the plight of the rural poor as only publicity could help improve their conditions. 'Let Labour arise,' he cried 'and let his enemies be scattered.' Pedder, *Where Men Decay*, p. viii. This was one of many accounts at the time which highlighted the degraded state of the agricultural poor and sought to improve their condition.
53 Daniels, *Fields of Vision*, pp. 217–21.
54 J. Ruskin cited in M. B. Huish (ed.), *Happy England* (London, 1903), p. 4.
55 Huish, *Happy England*, pp. 76–8.
56 Huish, *Happy England*, pp. 79–80.
57 Huish, *Happy England*, pp. 2, 4.
58 Huish, *Happy England*, pp. 5–6.
59 Huish, *Happy England*, p. 129.
60 Huish, *Happy England*, pp. 2–5.
61 Huish, *Happy England*, pp. 2–5.
62 Daniels, *Fields of Vision*, pp. 6, 214.
63 A. Kolodny, *The Land Before Her: fantasy and experience of the American frontiers, 1630–1860* (Chapel Hill and London, 1984), pp. 62–3.
64 W. Cobbett, *Cottage Economy* (Oxford, [1821] 1979), p. 48.
65 Kolodny, *The Land Before Her*, p. 63.
66 Daniels, *Fields of Vision*, p. 214.
67 Daniels, *Fields of Vision*, p. 214.
68 H. Allingham, *The Cottage Homes of England* (1909) quoted in Daniels, *Fields of Vision*, p. 214.
69 Huish, *Happy England*, p. 119.
70 Daniels, *Fields of Vision*, pp. 214–15.
71 Bourne, *Change in the Village*, p. 18.
72 Bourne, *Change in the Village*, p. 30.

73 Huish, *Happy England*, p. 123.
74 Huish, *Happy England*, pp. 126–7. He also confesses here that: 'One of the few alterations that Mrs Allingham allows herself is the substitution of these diamond lattices throughout a house where she finds a single example in any of the lights, or if, as she has on more than one occasion found, that they have been replaced by others, and are themselves stacked up as rubbish. She has in her studio some that have been served in this way, and which have now become useful models.' Allingham was obviously a bit of a recycler on the sly.
75 Huish, *Happy England*, pp. 126–7.
76 Huish, *Happy England*, p. 128.
77 Williams, *The Country and the City*, p. 10.
78 Sales, *pastoral and politics*, pp. 15–18.
79 Huish goes on by pointing out that no natural, basically picturesque, feature remains after renovation, though just along the road 'perhaps on the very next property an architect is building imitation old cottages with lattices!' Huish, *Happy England*, pp. 127–8. Jan Marsh discusses the history and impact of this fakery in Marsh, *Back to the land*, pp. 171–83. The aim was for the newly-built cottage to look 'as if it had always been there', as if it had 'roots'. Marsh, *Back to the Land*, p. 171.
80 Huish, *Happy England*, p. 129.
81 Daniels discusses the way in which the two images came together during the preservation of Willy Lot's house in 1926. Daniels, *Fields of Vision*, pp. 217–19.
82 Taylor, *A Dream of England*, p. 242.
83 Taylor, *A Dream of England*, p. 243.
84 Taylor, *A Dream of England*, pp. 242–4, 274.
85 W. S. Percy, *Strolling Through Cottage England* (London, 1936), p. 11.
86 Percy, *Strolling*, p. 20.
87 Percy, *Strolling*, pp. 22, 23.
88 Percy, *Strolling*, p. 24.
89 Percy, *Strolling*, pp. 25–6.
90 Percy, *Strolling*, pp. 27–30.
91 Percy, *Strolling*, pp. 28–9.
92 Alison Light, quoted in Taylor, *A Dream of England*, p. 123.
93 Taylor, *A Dream of England*, p. 124.
94 Taylor, *A Dream of England*, p. 124.
95 Taylor, *A Dream of England*, pp. 123–6.
96 Daniels, *Fields of Vision*, p. 5.
97 Ditchfield, *Charm*, pp. 2–4.
98 Daniels, *Fields of Vision*, pp. 5–7.
99 J. Agyeman and R. Spooner, 'Ethnicity and the rural environment' in Cloke, P. and Little, J. (eds), *Contested Countryside Cultures: otherness, marginalisation and rurality* (London and New York, 1997), p. 212.
100 Massey, *Space, Place and Gender*, pp. 147–8.
101 Massey, *Space, Place and Gender*, intro, and p. 180.
102 Agyeman and Spooner, 'Ethnicity and the rural environment', p. 200.

CHAPTER 5

Middle-class luxury, working-class necessity

> Buildings and dwelling-places have been dressed up in monumental *signs*: first their facades, and later their interiors. The homes of the moneyed classes have undergone a superficial 'socialisation' with the introduction of reception areas, bars, nooks and furniture (divans, for instance) which bespeak some kind of erotic life. Pale echoes, in short, of the aristocratic palace or town house.[1]

The relationship between the producer/architect and user/inhabitant[2] of a building has altered dramatically since the late eighteenth century. Industrialisation and improved communications systems have allowed the use of new or imported materials in building or rather have reduced the material limitations of building in a particular place. During the nineteenth century, architecture was professionalised and the attributed meaning, if not the intended meaning, of buildings changed. Architecture was historicised, the sensation of atmosphere was promoted, and the suggestion of wear and tear became a sign of age and long-standing tradition. Grounded in expert knowledge, architecture as a profession came to value the individual genesis of design, while capitalist economic and social relations began to shape the process of building. New modes of production meant that, by the end of the nineteenth century, construction specialists had generally replaced the local 'craftsman', or indeed the 'user' of the home, as builders. From a populist and conservationist point of view, these new forms of building and design were much less sympathetic to their environment and less efficient, as they required the moving around of more resources and the neglect of local topographical and material restrictions. It also meant that older ways of planning, building and using houses were replaced by a more distanced set of social relations. From the late eighteenth century, therefore, new methodologies and technologies transformed the production of buildings and, as a result, (new) houses acquired a modern set of economic, use, aesthetic and exchange values. However, as buildings are not 'static', 'objects' or 'fixed', it is also important to ask how the meaning and use of (old) houses has changed over time rather than simply mourn what has been lost.[3]

Designed and built in model villages, planned in official reports, mimicked in suburban estates, country houses large and small gradually reflected the wealthy's attempts to realise the Beau Ideal, whether that be in the form of domestic pastoral or, in the twentieth century, feminised Englishness.[4] Even farmers sought to adopt the styles of polite architecture, as evidenced by G. H. Andrews *Modern Husbandry* (1853), when, with reference to the farmer's residence, he states:

> The house must be a question entirely for its occupier and his architect, for certainly those who have embarked their fortunes in agriculture are not less entitled to the refinements and elegancies of life than those who may have embarked a similar amount in spinning cotton. The dwelling-house of the farmer will therefore be such a one as may be required for any English gentleman of similar income from whatever source it may be derived.[5]

The main building phases for aristocrats remodelling their country seats, based largely on agricultural incomes, took place between 1800–35 and the mid-1840s–1880. At the cheapest end of the spectrum, such a building might cost between £1,200–£1,500, often in a Tudor or Gothic style, and include a minimum of three reception rooms and five or six bedrooms. A middle-of-the-range country house would cost about £40,000, while at the upper end, a landlord might spend £400,000. It was these properties that the urban middle class sought to emulate. If possible, they made sure that they had a drawing room, in which would be found, c.1920, according to Flora Thompson when she visited her wealthier, urban friends,

> a piano . . . palms in pots and saddlebag suites of furniture and hand-painted milking stools and fire-screens, and cushions and anti-macassars in the latest art shades; but beyond bound volumes of the *Quiver* and the *Sunday at Home* and a few stray copies of popular novels, mostly of a semi-religious character, there were no books to be seen.[6]

Also, a dining room, and second sitting room, library or study – though at the lower end of the building scale they settled for a parlour in which to take calls – and eight bedrooms. If living-in servants were to be hired, then servants' quarters were required, such as an attic bedroom; though a servants' stair was desirable, a kitchen and scullery were requisite. By the late nineteenth century, water closets might be placed on the ground and first floors, but bedrooms were generally supplied with matching sets of wash jug and bowl, plus chamber pot and the use of these items was gendered and incorporated in the disciplining of the middle-class body.[7] As one man remembered:

> One morning my uncle came into my bedroom and found me sitting on the chamber pot. He told me that I must not sit on it because it was unmanly and I was a little boy. Girls and women sat on chamber pots. If I could not stand up and hold the pot in front of me for fear of spilling its contents, I had better kneel down in front of it to use it.[8]

As the bourgeois child grew up, it was 'cleaned up, the lower bodily stratum [was] regulated or denied, as far as possible, by the correct posture ("stand up straight", "don't squat", "don't kneel on all fours" – the postures of servants and savages)'.[9] Meanwhile, the body of the boy child was separated from that of the girl.

In order to escape the hazards of town life, and gain the prestige of owning some land, many of the middle class moved to the country and sought advice on the best site to choose, how and what to build there. Always, 'fitness for purpose' was stressed. For a household with an income of £1,000, a house of sixteen rooms, at a building cost of £1,500 was recommended. The terrace town house persisted as a cheaper alternative to the country house until the end of the nineteenth century, though the scale and detailing varied. The main layout was of two to three rooms per floor, a staircase running from the front to the back, a kitchen on the ground floor or at the back, and a little private space for a garden at the rear. What it was gradually replaced by was a compromise between town and country. Irregular plots, extensive planting and building plans featuring groups of houses were sought, as straight thoroughfares were replaced by winding roads. Mimicking a rural environment and the layout of villages, this design grew in popularity from the 1830s and evolved into the garden suburb. However, though the detailing changed with the fashion of the time – at first classical, then Gothic, then picturesque and vernacular, including timber and diamond-paned windows – the interior layout nonetheless remained very similar to the old terrace. A suburban semi, which might cost about £800–£1,000, would have three storeys and an attic, with two or three rooms per floor, and a kitchen built in the basement or as an addition at the rear.[10]

The history of (normative) domestic architecture is, in a sense, the history of privacy. As individualism became hegemonic, so the houses of the well-to-do were divided into ever-smaller spaces, each with its own use, and each for the use of specific individuals – though as such they required constant, conspicuous consumption and work.

The passage from street through gate along path to front door and into front parlour was a processional that delineated public and private space. As Lawrence says, it was always possible to identify a 'stranger' in any household. In fact, there were subsets of 'strangers', e.g. visitors as compared to the inhabitants of neighbouring flats. Though renting altered much of the common sense of public/private relationships, owner-occupied homes additionally had strict legal boundaries, regardless of how the space was used or the actual physical demarcation between public and private space.[11] Moreover, while the Madonnas occupied the home, domain of the pure, the whores could be seen on the streets, domain of the fallen. Servants were given their own, distanced entrances and exits, their own back-room and back-stairs spaces that protected the bourgeois family from the taint of dirt and decay. Children and adults, men and women were kept apart. Only those who had keys had access to rooms, and the doors of those rooms swung inwards to guard the occupants at the moment of entrance. Where possible, the rich moved away from the poor, or in the case of 'emparkment', moved the poor out of sight. As the wealthy increasingly regulated their own bodies, so they sought to control the body of the Other, whether this be by throwing up architectural barriers, or simply removing them from sight.[12] As Davidoff et al. argue:

> The home became both setting and symbol of the domestic community. In the upper-income ranges, the house's carefully guarded entrances with drives, gates and hedges, its attended portals and elaborate rituals of entrance created a sense of security as well as preserving its inmates' rank from pollution by inferiors. Throughout the middle class and in respectable working-class homes, the front privet or iron fence, whitened doorsteps, clean curtains and shining brass door furniture presented the household to 'the World'.[13]

In the bourgeois home, there was therefore a social division of space that can still be seen in the original structure of Victorian terraces. This space was also gendered; middle-class men and women moved through the same spaces in different ways, while the furniture in their public rooms, especially the objects associated with domesticity, helped signify their owner's status. Not that moral and political messages that challenged old hierarchies and tradition could not be inscribed onto interior space. The possession of anti-slavery texts and decoration of one's home with anti-slavery prints, pin cushions, china, pottery, stationary or art, for instance, deliberately revealed the political stance of the home-owner.[14] It was at this point that novelists became interested in interior space, and as authors began to step across the threshold, so living spaces took on character. For the Victorians, each object had its own story to tell; the contents of each interior were dictated by feeling not taste. In this way each 'house' became an expression of individualism and at the same time a 'home'.[15]

Manuals guided the owner on running the house and hiring his/her servants, but the domestic technology at the heart of that home went largely unchanged – hence the range, though it was difficult to operate, hard to clean, and wasteful of heat and fuel, stayed. It was not until the end of the nineteenth century, once servants had become scarce, that much thought was given to labour saving or the most efficient use of space. Even in America – despite Catherine Beecher's research from the 1840s – over half of the population still did not live 'comfortably' by the turn of the century. In other words, by 1900 most Americans cooked on a coal or wood stove, did not have running water, a bathroom, connection to the gas/electric mains, central heating, an iron, vacuum cleaner or fans. 'The matriarch of a hypothetical hard-pressed family [at this time] might have lived in a tenement in a large urban area, a dilapidated frame house in a small city, a row house in a company town, a collapsing farmhouse on a small plot of land, or even a log cabin in the woods.'[16] Davidoff et al. therefore stress the housework, the sheer physical, yet hidden, 'drudgery' required of the children, wife and servant(s) of a middle-class family just to keep up appearances. 'The "temple of the hearth" became a powerfully evocative image, not only in literature but in house design, and in spending resources of servants, labour and income in the lavish use of open coal fires in a deliberately wasteful manner.'[17]

The maintenance of the domestic idyll therefore necessitated having a considerable income, probably from commerce, the very thing from which the head of the household sought refuge. Moreover, the back-room nature of much household management facilitated the invisibility of sexuality, and gave tacit permission for illicit encounters to take place not only between the master and sons of the house and the servants, but also between the men and girls of the family. The Beau Ideal had a tangible, material contradiction at its heart,[18] centred on thresholds of disgust. The home came to embody the shame and embarrassment of the body, as the body's senses were publicly reformed. The wider discussion of the city and its contents – its sewers, rats and savages – helped constitute the meaning of home. Maids belonged literally and imaginatively 'both to the bourgeois family and to "the nether world" of the city, they mediated between the home and the lure of the city'.[19]

The servants as well as the home's owners consequently generated meanings within the domestic spaces of the middle class. The cleanliness of the bourgeois home required the servants to become tired and dirty, and the association of dirt with carnality left them open to sexual exploitation – the topography that separated the middle-class home from the urban slum equally separated the middle-class family from the servant. The rhetoric of spatial and physical opposition hid what were intimate relationships between the maid and the bourgeois child, indeed the supposed separation between the two helped construct a topography of adult desire traversed by a series of oppositions: low maid vs. high status gentleman.[20] It is therefore important to consider the values embodied by buildings, not as 'autonomous objects' but as 'complex artefacts, which are endowed with meanings'.[21]

BUILDING THE IDEAL

During the 1850s to 1860s, the expected outlay on farm buildings and farmhouse, excluding cottages, was on average £7 to £9 an acre and agricultural writers discussed in detail the benefits of this expenditure, in part because, having taken on board the financial commitment, landowners then had to be persuaded to bear the cost of investing in High Farming. Despite its practicability, the actual pattern of farm building provision varied across the country compared to that urged in advice books. Farmers and landowners were more likely to invest in the reorganisation and renovation of what was already in place than to build their farms anew. 'Mid nineteenth-century agriculturists were primarily concerned with describing best practices in the design, plan and function of farm buildings, and irrespective of cost urging their adoption, paying little attention to buildings supplied on the ground.'[22] While Victorian architects' plans represent ideal, picturesque, philanthropic cottages or prize-winning designs, farmer's advice books contain cheap blueprints with which they hoped to recoup their investments while fulfilling their social duty. In 1853 Andrews, for example, only ever dabbled in a taste for the picturesque and the rhetoric of self-help:

> *Labourers' Cottages* are of two kinds, those erected about the estates of noblemen and gentlemen and which are of an ornamental character, and those which should exist on, or in the vicinity of all farms, merely to accommodate the labourers employed upon them, the tenant of the farm being charged for them, and he again charging a rent to his labourers who inhabit them. Now if these cottages are to be expected to pay interest for the money spent in erecting them, they must be of the simplest possible form, and of the cheapest materials, for it is quite impossible that labourers can pay a rent equal to the most moderate

> rate of interest for such costly and ornamental buildings as are designed by architects generally.
>
> A labourer's cottage must not cost more than £75, and should be built in pairs, as the cost is less than when placed singly; each cottage should contain a kitchen, or house-place, in which the family live, a wash-house or back office, and two bedrooms. A water-closet and pig-stye should adjoin; each cottage should have about a quarter an acre of garden. An oven and copper should exist in every cottage. [A plan is provided of a single-storey example] . . . of a cheap labourer's cottage; many were constructed in a similar manner, looked very picturesque, and gave satisfaction to their inhabitants.[23]

He then went on to advise that the farmer look first of all for the best local materials that might be obtained and draw on 'local knowledge in the manner of working them', in order to ensure cheapness and durability, even though they should buy all timber from abroad and use zinc-coated cast iron elsewhere on the farm.[24] In referring to the 'satisfaction' that the cottage might give to its inhabitants and dispensing with architects, Andrews based his design on the old Board of Agriculture's two-bedroom standard,[25] and preferred to adopt a slightly more vernacular approach alongside the latest practices in farm management. Less interested in the mores of urban reformers, it is clear that his advice centred on cost and workable common custom. In fact, it was probably more cost effective to adapt older properties than to build new ones. Today the rehabilitation of a building, Brand notes, even if this is extensive, costs between 3 and 16 per cent less than demolishing it and starting again. This was, he argues, well known in the nineteenth century.[26]

Nonetheless, the newly built, three-bedroom cottage gradually became the standard by which all housing was to be judged. By the end of the nineteenth century, urban philanthropists believed in the value of two-storey privacy, of parlours to receive visitors and three bedrooms to prevent incest: the application of middle-class architecture to working-class homes. Prince Albert for one designed several model cottages that divided the family along the lines of what came to be known as 'decency' and new by-laws came to codify what was perceived to be best practice, as taken from model housing and medical discourse. There was a range of legislation on housing during the nineteenth century, most of which centred on the needs of the urban, not the rural community. The Towns Improvement Clauses Act, passed in response to cholera in 1847, was the first to give local authorities the power to tackle urban sanitation, followed by subsequent acts in 1867–68, 1875 and by the Royal Commission on Housing in 1884. The law on housing was consolidated in the Housing of the Working Classes Act, 1890.[27]

Meanwhile, experts like Andrew Combe combined architectural with medical guidance for parents anxious to find the best location to bring up their children:

> SITE OF THE HOUSE. – The first and most essential requisite in a nursery is the constant supply of pure air. To obtain this, a residence should be selected in a dry and rather elevated situation, removed from humidity and all sources of contamination, and, at the same time, sheltered from the violence of the wind. When a choice can be made, the country should be preferred to the town; as one of the clearest results for which we are indebted to the late statistical returns and sanitary reports is the fact of the superior healthiness of the country, especially for the young. The close vicinity to the house of trees or thick shrubbery, of ponds, undrained meadows, or sluggish water-courses, ought to be scrupulously avoided; for, however ornamental they may be, they are invariably prejudicial to health, not only from the humidity and in many cases the impurities which they diffuse through the air, especially at night, but also from the obstruction which they present to free ventilation. For the same reason, narrow valleys, and localities shut up by thick woods or overhung by hills or mountains, ought never to be chosen as the sites of houses or villages. From overlooking the unfavourable influence of a stagnant humid air, families going to the country in pursuit of health often sustain serious injury, by settling in situations which a better acquaintance with the laws of the animal economy would have taught them to be very ill suited to the infant constitution.[28]

The concerns found in the parliamentary reports of the 1840s were thereby disseminated as advice to the educated middle class who learned that it was best to avoid living the picturesque for the sake of their families' health. Standardisation in pattern books and by-laws equally reduced the influence of vernacular traditions, and the model cottage, which worked as an evocative reminder of community and the open spaces of Nature, became the exemplar of improvement, both aesthetic and social. As noted, this model housing, whether it focused on the appearance of the cottage, its quality, layout, numbers of rooms or construction, had the social role of demonstrating to the poor what was good for them. Moreover, though it reflected fashions in morality and reinforced the socio-economic values of the time, the model house, unlike the ideal, was always realisable. It was a 'demonstration of the way the domestic situation of the working class could be improved within the economic expectations of society'.[29]

By 1913, Lawrence Weaver, author of *The 'Country Life' Book of Cottages*, advised of the need to provide housing that was cheap, as well as being 'of a sort that shall not disfigure the countryside'.[30] Drawing on a modernist aesthetic and domestic Englishness of the inter-war years, when there was a widespread interest in the provision of workers' cottages and allotments,[31] Weaver looked to new building materials such as concrete, suggested that all cottage builders use architects, and that the design be kept simple.[32] Cost was always central to the provision of model housing.[33] The architect must therefore be:

> Both practical and artistic, who knows the needs and habits of cottage-folk, and yet has an eye for the unpretentious, gracious qualities that make an old cottage a delight to the eye and an ornament to the countryside.[34]

Happy to suggest the moderation of building regulations and the restoration of older cottages, he nonetheless insisted that

> the preservation of precious little bits of our building history must not be the excuse for stereotyping unhealthy or cramped accommodation. Very often a pair of old cottages provides no more floor space and cubic space than is proper for a single cottage, and should be converted into one. Many a single cottage can be made a decent habitation by tacking on a little wing or even a single storey back addition, but it is very desirable that even such small works shall be supervised by architects who have a feeling for the old craftsmanship and judgement in devising additions in the same spirit.[35]

In Weaver, the rhetoric of preservation met the forward-looking language of health and good order.[36] The vernacular could now only be saved by the expert architect, who would 'feel' their way through the 'old craftsmanship'. And, the designer had to look ahead; 'it is important to lay stress on the recent sudden rise in the standard of comfort, and on the probability that it will rise still more rapidly during the next fifty years. Cottages should be financed and built to last eighty years at least'.[37]

REFORMING THE COTTAGE

In *The Cottage Register*, a sanitary table of what to account for in the labourer's home, H. W. Acland,[38] required observers to count every fireplace, window, door and room in the cottages they visited. They had to give the dimensions of all bedrooms and living rooms, specify the location of all windows and their size, and determine if there were porches, back doors, an earth-closet, privy or drainage, a pigsty and lodgers. The form-filler had to describe the surrounding ground's drainage, the cottage's state of repair, the likely cost of any repair and if this was worth it. He asked: 'Is it wanted in the neighbourhood, or had it better be placed elsewhere; and where?' As well as being interested in whether or not the cottage had a well, spring, tank or conduit, Acland finally expected anyone using the form, be they a vicar or carpenter, to make some closing remarks and to jot down 'any social or other memoranda'. This architectural accounting was the first step, in his view, 'to a complete reform of the condition of Cottages, of Villas and of Artisans' dwellings'.[39] But, his interest in the cottage extended beyond the mapping of its structure to a delineation of its decorative, interior space. A friend of the secretary of the Book-Hawking Union, Acland presents us with a classic example of that union of medical and religious expertise that Frank Mort has referred to as belonging to 'medico-moral discourse'.[40]

Evidence that the elite was aware of the gap that might exist in the experience of the cottage home can be discerned in high and low cultural, not just official, political or architectural discourse. George Eliot called for a detailed examination of the lives of the rural poor and wrote an urgent social critique of pastoral in 1856.[41] Even the *Art Journal* carried a review which said of Mark Anthony's *The Pedlar's Visit to an Old Cottage* (1860) that the 'building... is of the class which looks very well in pictures, but that forms very indifferent habitations'.[42] And, Frederick Daniel Hardy's *The Dismayed Artist* (1866)[43] followed in this tradition, evidencing a distrust both of the artist's impression of rural life and a conflicting set of values around the use of the cottage's interior. In it, Hardy is shown arriving at a cottage with his brother, ready to continue a painting of its interior – he carries a half-finished canvas in his hand and an easel rests against a wall to one side of the foreground – only to find that the woman of the house and three of her children are industriously limewashing the walls. Its humour is carried in this self-parodying contrast between the painters and their subject; while the effete artists are horrified at the loss of their brick and stone fireplace, the whitewash, as we have seen, might make the difference for the family between charitable relief and hunger. But it also suggests that the cottage looks very different according to which side of the window one looks through, the experiences and the values one brings to it. A self-reflexive piece, which may or may not be based on Hardy's actual experience, as Christiana Payne argues, *The Dismayed Artist* 'dramatises the contrast between the artist's attitude to picturesque cottages and the more practical approach of those who actually lived in them'.[44] Nonetheless, the art attacked by artists like Hardy, and meant for the consumption of the rich, was easily appropriated for the edification of the poor. In 'Cottage-wall Prints' (1862), Acland sets out his ideas for the most educative and morally uplifting illustrations that might be adopted by the labourer.

All classes and ages, Acland argued, loved '*ornament*', though this love is especially strong in 'the gentler sex' and in infancy – whether that infancy be in 'years', 'race' or 'education'. The decoration of rooms, he thought, was much less harmful than 'personal adornment' and this is why the society ought indeed 'minister to a right and rational decoration of the humbler homes of England'. A wall print might be anything placed on the wall more or less permanently, it might be an engraving, a woodcut, photograph, a piece of text, more or less anything 'that may be affixed ... to cottage walls, in frames or out of them'.[45] What Acland suggested was a range of possible subjects that The Book-Hawking Union might like to promote. These included patriotic illustrations of the Queen, the army or navy, and images of 'family life and incidents; the church path, the sick child; the vacant fire-side; the flowers on the grave.... Domestic and truly English scenes' such as those taken from Wordsworth, Tennyson, Stothard, Wilkie and Morland. Religious subjects, he thought, were also useful, especially those taken from the early Italian and German schools or Blake. Scenes showing common qualities 'from history or from imagination [such as] deeds of daring in a good cause – love, filial duty; devotion; penitence' and scripture passages were to be valued, as were more scientific subjects such as 'maps of the world', geological sections, sections of steam engines. Useful knowledge might be provided through tables of advice. All of these ought to be well produced, but not too academic. Overall, it was the images of the Queen, family life, bible subjects and common qualities that were in his view the most useful, but they had to have 'a certain firm but tender quaintness, as of the early Italian school, and [be] clearly coloured in strong colour'. Finally, he provided a list of suggested scenes and artists, but stressed that what was required were images 'full of earnestness and pathos, which a skilful artist, and one with a large knowledge of mankind, would think it feasible to dispose through the cottages of England'. And, he praised The Book Hawking Union for its previous lithographs, which he considered 'careful' and therefore not too 'popular'.[46]

The labouring class, along with the 'gentler sex' and infant, though unnamed, races, are likened here to children who not only enjoy decoration, but, unable to appreciate the finer points of artistic expression, respond best to bright colours. Having found the perfect form, Acland is intent on taking genre art back to the poor as a kind of distorting mirror through which they will see what they ought to be. As Lawrence suggests, the analysis of documents such as tenancy agreements 'reveals the power and strategy of landlords and estate agents' who saw the space they managed as site in which they might regulate the behaviour of their tenants.⁴⁷ The prizes donated by agricultural societies for good housekeeping and the negotiations that took place around charitable giving discussed in Chapter 2 might be read in the same way. But, given Acland's tract, the attempt to police working-class space clearly extended beyond the judicial and the socio-economic to include the cultural. Meanwhile Acland, who hopes to develop the sentiment of the poor through 'firm but tender' education, is given the tacit right to rewrite the cultural space of the working-class home. As more and more barriers were thrown up to protect the decency and propriety of the elite from the transgressions of the poor, so the rich increasingly crossed those barriers in order to police the poor body.⁴⁸ By effectively defining his own class as those who understood art and knew best, in opposition to the poor who needed their guidance, he takes scopophilic paternalism to its logical conclusion. Rather than just passively observing the poor as Hardy might, or simply supplying the poor with religious tracts, Acland is effectively arguing that the Book-Hawking Union ought to step across the boundary of the cottage and turn its interior into a reforming text. What it is also important to note, is that this art was deliberately selected to be put on display in a private/domestic, rather than a public/museum, setting. This assumes the universalised accessibility of bourgeois art, and by implication (beyond the values and intentions of those who were in a position to make this kind of move), moral and social doubt is thrown on the poor's own decorations.

Equally, though it is possible to see cottage interiors decorated with pictures of the Queen in some genre pieces, this offers more of an indication of what elite audiences found comforting – pictures of the Queen suggest an innate patriotism among the poor – than any clue as to what the poor actually put on their walls. Because the values and ideals of those other than its residents overwrote the cottage as a domestic space, it was not in any way a private, untroubled retreat; it was always open to inspection and criticism. Reformers like Acland, architects and designers of model housing were thus engaged in a wider dialogue, which gave rise to planning regulations and by-laws, and included the concrete construction and rewriting of (respectable) working-class space. But, what meanings and uses did the residents themselves confer upon the domestic vernacular?⁴⁹

READING THE DOMESTIC VERNACULAR

The houses themselves, of course, have been constantly altered. This is not just a rural phenomenon as Caffyn, like many housing historians, notes, for instance, most workers' houses, urban and rural, have been destroyed, altered or have decayed.[50] Therefore, there is little material evidence left of the decorative treatment of cottage interiors, though it was through this that 'the occupier of a vernacular dwelling expressed his (or more likely her) decorative wishes and turned a house into a home'.[51] Other than Acland's designs on the interior, all that we know of it is that wallpaper was a luxury item until at least the mid-nineteenth century. Wood panelling remained in use throughout the nineteenth century, though plaster was often preferred as it could help conserve heat and reduce drafts. Limewash was commonly used to renew, clean, lighten and disinfect the wall. Where the exterior frequently experienced little change, the interior was often altered to suit the contemporary lifestyle of the building's residents, and their use and adaptation of that space changed with them. Though vernacular architecture does survive, it is therefore 'interpreted' and 'reinterpreted' by each generation that lives in it. Wall paintings, hangings and mouldings are often lost in subsequent modernisations, and wall decoration is probably more subject to fashion than any other aspect of interior design.[52]

In the twentieth century, historic preservation societies occasionally tried to put this process into reverse, while the moneyed, seeking to buy into the rural idyll, remodelled their cottages in such a way as to make them more 'authentic'. The 1970s found modernism being treated as pariah; but, as a 'quiet, populist, conservative, victorious revolution', preservation attracted far less publicity than 'its sibling, the environmental movement'.[53] Preservationists ask: '"What makes some buildings come to be loved?" and they act on what they learn. The result is a coherent, still-evolving ethical and aesthetic body of ideas.'[54] As a building is preserved, older modifications are stripped away and earlier practices become known; the stripping away of old wallpapers, plaster, and bricked-up fireplaces and windows produce a narrative of the building's use.[55] Preservationists, be they public bodies or private individuals, take a keen interest in the organisation of buildings and they work their way back through the history of the structures they hope to save for the future. Preservationists, Brand argues, have learned the pragmatic language of property development; they therefore often succeed where those who rely simply on aesthetic and cultural arguments fail. There is a hierarchy in the language of building rehabilitation. 'The French archaeologist A. N. Didron', Brand reminds us, 'stated in 1839 the slogan that still guides all preservationists: "It is better to preserve than to repair, better to repair than to restore, better to restore than to reconstruct."'[56] However, because much preservation relies on the political-economic-design device 'adaptive use',[57] the vast majority of the built evidence is still written, or rather over-written, from above and thereby comes to reflect elite rather than working-class values and intentions. So, little material evidence of the life of the poor remains untouched, and on one level, this means that there is very little material culture left to read.

Even when a building has been stripped to the bone, its internal design is not always clear, at which point, as Brunskill says, it becomes necessary to turn to documentary evidence such as contemporary descriptions by travel writers, novels and visual evidence such as photographs or paintings.[58] M. W. Barley, for example, who looks at the history of the English farmhouse and cottage from the sixteenth to the eighteenth century, notes that records were often kept of who took on each property as it changed hands. Indeed, like Oliver, Barley asserts that the necessity of recording cottage architecture has become urgent, as folk culture has been neglected in this respect. Only the rural provides historians with any remaining evidence of peasant society before the industrial and agricultural revolutions. The cottage, in this respect, is referred to as providing evidence of 'the native, the traditional, the submerged elements of British culture'.[59] However, using the detailed inventories based on probates and estate surveys from the late seventeenth to early eighteenth century,[60] we can see that the possessions of a seventeenth-century cottager might include at least one bedstead and stand, bed linen, clothes, some chairs, stools or seats and often one large or two smaller tables. Other items included cupboards and chests, brass and pewter pieces such as candlesticks, cups and plates, wooden platters and trenchers, pots and a frying pan, spit, dog irons, tongs, bellows, dishes, knives, spoons, labouring tools, and 'other trifles unthought of'. There might also be some livestock, such as a pig or a cow, and money – though the goods and chattels of yeomen and husbandmen were generally much more numerous.[61]

The neighbours who listed the items in the house and gave them a value prepared these probates. Though they do not describe the interior in detail, they do, Brunskill argues, follow a logical route through the house enabling us to imagine the layout and use of each room. Though the cottage itself had little in the way of prestige to communicate, the more prominent the room, the more likely a stylish display. Carved bread and spice cupboards suggest that the symbolic value of fixed furnishings was as great as their practicality, but the fireplace and hearth took on a particularly powerful set of connotations that made the structure into a 'home'. The type of fire indicated the room's use, its fabric taking on a corresponding symbolic importance, while its mantle, as well as being a utilitarian addition, provided opportunity for extra decoration. A gradation in social meaning was attributed to the washhouse copper, the range and the fireplace that led to scullery, kitchen and parlour being attributed variant relative statuses.[62] In some instances, a loom is mentioned, or a cart, also gardening tools and brewing equipment,[63] suggestive of the kinds of occupation that went on in the house, the uses to which the domestic space was put. And, though these probate lists do not continue into the nineteenth century, documentary photographs suggest that this kind of list would have held true.

In one photograph of a Dartmoor cottage kitchen, taken in 1890,[64] a settle, some cushions, a rug and a small table constitute the room's furnishings. The fire contains a range, kettle, sticks, spit, fire dogs, bellows and poker. Above the fireplace, there is a mantle on which sit articles in china, pewter and brass, including vases, candlesticks, plates and mugs. On shelves and hooks around the room, a dinner service, tankards and cups can be seen, while on the wall there are some small-framed pictures. Given that what governed the working-class home was largely necessity, rather than choice, it is not surprising that the inventory has not changed substantially. Yet, there are significant, if subtle, differences. The loss of wooden trenchers and introduction of fine china into the working-class home, for instance, especially the 'best' dinner service kept on display on a high shelf in the corner, is indicative of new values based on aspiration and respectability, as well as the widespread adoption of new production techniques in the potteries. What has also changed are the kinds of work that go on in the home; the demise of weaving for instance, and the gradual removal of brewing to specialist public houses have probably resulted in the absence of loom and brewing kit. Though there is what looks like a sewing basket on the settle, there is little indication that anything other than the simplest of household tasks takes place in this space.

As Brunskill states, it is therefore possible to use photography to see how the copper fitted into the scullery, 'or the tea caddy onto the mantelpiece of a worker's cottage'.[65] However, a distinction needs to be made between readings that follow 'the language of intention', what the photographer, author or painter said he/she wanted to portray in representing the 'labourer', what the polite expected to see or believed about the countryside, and what his or her texts 'cannot help admitting about the actuality of their condition'.[66] Tristram for instance notes that there was a shift in the middle of the nineteenth century when, the excessive privatisation of the home and its utter separation from community came to be read as an abdication of responsibility. As a result, the middle class began to look back to the eighteenth century, its values and hence its vernacular architecture as a model for order within the community. Charles Eastlake's *Hints on Household Taste* (1868) helped stimulate this return to the cottage by illustrating rural interiors like the one in the photograph, as superior to those of urban houses. Together with the rise in the Arts and Crafts movement – of which Eastlake was a part – so novelists like Hardy began to celebrate household objects for their *use*. Displayed objects, such as the crockery on the shelf, became tangible evidence of domesticity through their connection with farms and cottages; they were no longer just material 'things'. Useful objects were equated with useful lives; such objects therefore required contemplation and interpretation, and transcended the material. The vernacular and images of the vernacular began to guide the Victorians and Edwardians towards a more spiritual search for quality within their own homes wherein a harmonious relationship between the human and the natural was sought.[67]

A similar impulse can be seen in the urge to collect and preserve domestic items and pieces of rural dress such as the smock frock and sunbonnet. As Rachel Worth suggests, what is required here is a consideration of the reaction to change in, say, rural dress, as much as a study of the material culture itself. There was a specific cultural significance attached to rural dress in the late nineteenth century that came from the perception of change at this time. Artists and novelists used sunbonnets and smocks as signifiers of timeless rural life, when both had long been passed over by those who were supposed to be wearing them. Worth therefore goes on to observe that the handcrafted production of smocks meant that they came to be associated with rural tradition, itself associated with continuity as against rapid social change. The smocks themselves, in their cut and stitching, demonstrate the care required in their making and the value placed on both the material and the final product by those who made them. Each of these factors needs to be taken into account when attempting to write a history of material culture such as that of dress.[68]

Equally, just because many photographs seem to confirm what can be seen in genre painting does not mean that what they depict is any more accurate or 'true'. Indeed, in another photograph,[69] the same Dartmoor kitchen as that described above can be seen in much more homely and prosperous vein. This time the fire forms the central feature, its mantle and table covered in swags of material, with the addition of some iron cooking pots on the stove, two scuttles full of coal, a ladder-backed chair and tea laid out on the table. The addition of decorative materials and coal in the fireplace is suggestive of modernity and plenty, meanwhile, despite ongoing criticism in some quarters, knowledge of teatime etiquette has become a sign of domesticity. Cobbett for one had hated 'the gossip of the tea table', which he observed for girls, 'is no bad preparatory school for the brothel. At the very least, it teaches them idleness.' He equally believed it weakened men. It caused 'a softness, an effeminacy, a seeking for the fire-side, a lurking in the bed, and, in short, all the characteristics of idleness, for which, in this case, real want of strength furnishes an apology'.[70] This second photograph connotes that universalised domesticity, femininity and well-being that made the cottage particularly desirable as Beau Ideal. But, the Ideal was contested, while the absence of any visible sign of work, other than the most small-scale of domestic occupations, does not necessarily mean that the kitchen was not used productively, or for large-scale work such as laundry which took over the whole space.

Rural life, Barrell notes, generally appears stable in the pastoral mode, untainted by conflict or change. Painting, Barrell maintains,

> offers us a mythical unity and – in its increasing concern to present an apparently more and more actualised image of rural life – attempts to pass itself off as an image of the actual unity of an English countryside innocent of division. But by examining the process by which that illusion is achieved – by studying the imagery of the paintings, the constraints upon it, and upon its organisation in the picture-space – we may come to see that unity as artifice, as something made out of the actuality of division.[71]

This goes for all subsequent representational systems, including photography, which seek to reify what they represent. In particular, all realist texts, whether 'imaginary' or 'factual', reflect, respond to and hope to contain the actuality they try to re-present, and in the process produce a variety of readings. What it is then necessary to remember, is that all sources need this degree of examination. Where the probate inventories give an impression of the layout, use and meaning of the house and its contents, they are nonetheless structured within legal discourse for judicial usage; similarly, documentary photographs are re-presentations of reality and not necessarily as trustworthy as we might like to think. Likewise, as Calder notes, though the middle class constantly urged the working class to labour and good housekeeping, and monitored the cleanliness of their homes, 'it could be a soul-destroying task for the working-class housewife to keep her home homely'.[72] Photographs, like paintings, are objects that capture a way of seeing and, as Tagg warns, they have come to be seen as reliable evidence of the past due to a specific 'social, semiotic process'. 'The very idea of what constitutes evidence has a history', a history of specific power relations, real institutions and procedures. The use of photographs as historical evidence should be placed within this context.[73]

What remain to us are diaries, letters and autobiographies. In the vast majority of this material we find evidence of some intimidation at using middle-class forms and style, while most working-class authors find wealthy representations of themselves 'both unflattering and disturbingly untrue to their experience'.[74] Nonetheless, because there is so little evidence from the women themselves about, for instance, their daily round, something like the 'poetic testament' of Mary Collier is particularly valuable.[75] In essence a political document which aimed to prove that women were not idle (she was 'writing back' to Stephen Duck, a labouring poet who had dismissed women's work as leisure), *The Woman's Labour; an epistle* (1739) charts women's life from dawn to (beyond) dusk.[76] As Donna Landry argues, Collier represents housework as hard physical labour, but as labour to which she and other working women were accustomed and that ought to be valued. Women like Collier, Landry argues, wrote 'poems that strive to provide an alternative to the existing sexual order'.[77] We ought, Landry therefore argues, to assess Collier and those like her in terms of their own position and ours. By recognising the material value of and skill inherent in unpaid domestic work, Landry proposes that an alternative reading of that work, in all representational systems, might be opened up.[78] Working-class autobiography insists on working-class history, self-definition and values, while, according to Gagnier, 'their judgements make reference, often explicitly, to the norms of morality' to which they are subject.[79]

Through working-class autobiography, we can see how the residents[80] put the cottage to a variety of economic and cultural uses. In the more literary examples of working-class writing, for instance, the cottage was often used as a sign of poverty or well-being, especially in the more political texts like that by Joseph Arch. Where Collier used Duck's bucolic imagery and rural grammar, and borrowed additional classical references to reinforce her own identity and gain authority,[81] Arch in part laid claim to his right to speak for the (male) agricultural labourer by stressing that his family had used the cottage he had been born in for 150 years. His grandparents, who he said were thrifty and hardworking, saved up and bought the freehold for £30. When he married, his father brought his mother to the same place, where they lived, had four children, and died. By using the rhetoric of Englishness and tradition – this cottage home, 'right in the very heart of old England', in Shakespeare's country[82] – as well as self-help, Arch sought respectability and permission to speak for the rural working class. But, autobiography also provides evidence of the more mundane physical adaptations the country poor made to their own homes. George Baldry, for one, records that his grandmother excavated her dairy herself, dropping the floor by two feet in order to keep it cool in the summer, though the excavation caused the dairy to flood one winter after particularly bad weather.[83] It was quite common for cottagers to take structural items, such as glazed windows, with them from house to house when they moved,[84] and where floors were earthen, neighbours might be invited to a dance to pack them down when they were established or renewed.[85] It is only through autobiography that can we find that women read and discussed novellas, which they passed around – but which they saw as a vice and therefore as something to be hidden from men, children and non-readers – while the Sunday paper was lent and borrowed freely.[86]

The exact layout of a cottage varied quite widely,[87] but most, by the Victorian period, whether one or two-storey, had no more than three or four rooms. Of these, as most of the dwelling's winter heat and light[88] came from the kitchen range or stove – a cheap and practical solution to the difficulties of getting fuel and the necessity of watching over children while working – the kitchen was always the most-used room. Some cottages had sculleries or wash houses at the back, in which wet work was done, but the bulk of the cooking and other household tasks and odd jobs took place in the kitchen or 'house-place'. The bedroom(s), meanwhile, divided up by curtains and blankets, were generally shut up and only used at night. If upstairs, a simple ladder or a straight flight of stairs would reach them, often hidden away downstairs by a door, as if placed in a cupboard. These normally led straight into the room above – in Victorian and Edwardian three-bedroom cottages, the dog-leg, which gave opportunity for a landing and passageway, was preferred as permitting more privacy. Outside, many cottages obviously had pigsties, but the oven might also be found in the garden[89] – Baldry says that many villagers had their own windmill and ground their own corn.[90]

The basic requirements in a labourer's home were supposed to be a place in which to live (for cooking, eating and socialising), a place in which to retire (to sleep, store things and seek privacy) and at least one source of heat for warmth and cooking. These activities generated the layout of the cottage, while vernacular builders 'made decorative what could have been merely utilitarian'.[91] In addition, as well as the division of space along the lines of privacy, architectural history also incorporates the spatial delineation of 'human' and 'animal'. While those animals permitted to remain within human space were generally given the identity 'pet' and attributed with those human characteristics that we value, the remainder of 'domesticated' animals were distanced and seen as the alien embodiment of those human characteristics deemed 'lower'/'bestial'.[92] Here, we see the development of (exterior) architectures, both formal and vernacular, designed specifically for the (domesticated) animal; the built expression of the Enlightenment human–nature/animal dualism.

However, though this layout reflected the ordinary organisation of domestic space, it did not necessarily dictate how that space was to be used. Non-conformists, for instance, would sometimes gather in a cottage for prayers and hymns, adopting it for religious use.[93] It was also quite common for members of the household to do handwork outside where the light was good, as well as for the door to the house to stand ajar in all but the worst of weather. As water was normally available from a communal source, and because ovens and other resources, like mills, were often shared, the physical delineation of public and private space was rarely as sharp as that seen in middle-class homes. Tom Mullins, for example, a farm labourer from Staffordshire, remembered that in the 1870s 'few houses had an oven and the women used to make their own dough and take it to the bakehouse; baking cost a halfpenny per quartern loaf.'[94] Similarly, Elizabeth Ashby, who lived in a three-room cottage, got her garden dug and fuel brought to her in exchange for writing letters, cutting shirts, whitewashing ceilings and looking after the sick. In late September, after the harvest, she would count her leasings (gleanings), tidy the house, buy footwear and calico, and pay off her debts.[95] When a pig was killed, neighbours would participate in the event and hope to benefit from some largesse.[96]

The garden gate and entrance to the house therefore acted as figurative, much more than physical, barriers; the garden path and doorway acted as links to the wider community rather than as processionals. Doors, gates, even roadsides were the point at which people stood and talked, where children played, where work – paid and unpaid – got done. Gossip created a community of and for women, in and through language, spoken in public places, at home and at work. Collier for one defends gossip as both a reasonable activity and as something that is absolutely necessary to women at work. Women's work goes on all day, she says and they have no other opportunity to talk but in the fields and lanes. And, as Chamberlain notes in *Fenwomen*: 'The village women field workers have always been renowned for the volume and roughness of their voices – seasons of experience in carrying on conversations across the crop to where their fellow workers were working ensured that they could be heard in all weathers.' In 1975, paid work was still seen as a way of getting out and meeting people.[97] At home, women sought to get along with their neighbours and kept up good relations by chatting over tea, in some cases beer.[98]

In the country cottage, social convention and use overwrote the clear-cut built boundaries of the garden wall or front door. Ordinary country people are still more likely to use the back rather than the front door and to pop round for a chat, than their middle-class neighbours are. This is not simply a difference in the use of the built environment, Bell contests, it is about different styles of living and identities; the *back door* style being 'more informal, group-oriented, local, interactive, and experiential', the *front door* style 'more formal, individualistic, far-flung, private, and distanced'.[99] Historically, when the poor have transferred this use of space to the urban environment the moneyed have been none too happy. Though Victorian genre art meant for elite consumption evidences a fascination with ordinary communality, it was the working class who put it into practice and it was the working-class body that came under scrutiny when this practice was transferred to the town. The Victorian middle class felt threatened when it came to the use of public space by the working class who 'milled' around on street corners. In the city, the use of space described in a rural context as 'communal' suddenly became 'irrational' and 'disorderly', and required regulation.[100]

The front room/'parlour' and front door were treated as high status; if there were two rooms on the ground floor, the one at the front went largely unused while the front door remained closed, except on special occasions. And, that status was conferred not just through (dis)use but through women's work. Margaret Penn recalled that her third-person alter ego, Mrs Winstanley, circa 1909 'scrubbed and polished her front room for days before' her aunt's wedding party came back to her home for tea. The wedding tea itself consisted of a three-tier cake from her aunt's employer, cold ham, large pork pie, piccalilli, red cabbage, pickled onions, cakes, jellies, tinned fruit, white bread and butter, current bread and butter, tea and port wine.[101] Like the American frontierswoman, the cottage woman had to tackle 'tainted water supplies, rancid food, soot and skin burns from open fires, and full chamber pots'[102] on a daily basis. As Zlotnick observes:

> A yawning and unbridgeable gap existed between the domestic ideal ... and the necessities of survival for working-class families in Victorian Britain. The ideal demanded that working-class women reproduce, albeit in a less opulent form, the bourgeois world inside the worker's cottage, a demand that the working-class wife could rarely achieve, and then only through small acts of daily heroism.[103]

The constant physical exertion required to maintain control of the domestic environment, to prevent the almost inevitable slide into chaos, and make a 'house' into a 'home', was rarely if ever recognised. Whereas in official publications it simply was not described, in imaginative literature, especially that written by men, housewives and housework were represented as oppressive (to men and boys), humorous, nostalgic or transcendent.[104]

Yet, the autobiographical evidence suggests that women's daily round could be diverse. They answered the door and dealt with peddlers, sewed, knitted and mended the family's clothes, made rag rugs, cared for fowl and butchered pigs, bought, bartered and sold goods at market, took in paid work, and were employed extensively within agriculture and its related industries. In Northumberland, once the pig had been killed in the winter, it had to be shaved and scalded. The carcass had to be hung from nine o'clock in the morning to six in the evening, it would then be salted, cut down the backbone and saltpetre put in the joints. After a further covering of salt, the 'corpse' would be wrapped in a linen sheet and put in the pantry. The brine that ran off it had to be cleaned up every morning. After three weeks, the curing would be complete, but it had to be turned half-way through. Once cured, it would be removed from the salt, rubbed down and hung up in the kitchen to dry. In East Anglia, the pig was pickled in brine. And, though a butcher might do some of the work, the women of the family had the responsibility to at least oversee the process.[105] Kate Taylor, born in Suffolk in 1891, records her mother as taking in washing and needlework, acting as a midwife and wetnurse. She taught her and her sisters sewing, knitting and crochet. She treated her husband for a nasty wasp-sting on his tongue, dressed and bandaged an axe-wound. She cooked Sunday lunch that was eaten by her family and her husband's friends who belonged to the Salvation Army band. Kate herself helped her father when she was older by writing out his speeches when he was a political agent, and his estimates and accounts when he went sheep shearing. And, when Kate's grandmother became 'feeble', the family took her in.[106]

As seen in Chapter 1, in engaging in housework, the housewife ensured that everything was in its place; she regulated the home for her husband. Though this was in origin an elite ordering of space, by the nineteenth century it had been naturalised and, through the ideology of separate spheres, in adapted form cut across all classes – e.g. it was normally the working-class woman who managed the home's finances and other resources. As Romines observes with reference to nineteenth-century America, the woman of the house was meant to manage effortlessly a variety of day-to-day unpaid tasks that were often pushed to one side because they were repetitive, circular, 'ordinary' or 'everyday', unworthy of attention.[107] Housework, she says, therefore 'commands low wages, or none, and is often considered trivial or demeaning, "shitwork". What these women do is essential yet impermanent and invisible ... The culture consumes the products of the housekeeper's labor; the fact and the process of that labor are suppressed.'[108] The clergyman Richard Cobbold expressed the ideal in the following terms: 'Poor people require a help-meet for their condition of life. The wives are in general the managers of their affairs. The wisest and best wives learn to have the fewest wants and to make their husband's wages to the farthest, not the fastest.'[109] Later, Arch went on to state in his memoirs that 'the working man's home is no home at all, if there is not a good housewife within doors'[110] – Arch was never averse to using the language of the elite to further his cause, in this instance, a bread-winning wage. Domestic work preserved the order of the house as 'home'; it prevented a gradual descent into decay – Nature. It transformed the Natural order, making it safe for Culture. While the messiness of house-work, the casting of litter outside the back door, the free-ranging fowl and mud, were repugnant to many male authors[111] (to urban, middle-class men like Austin, this chaos threatened to turn inwards and con-taminate the ordered home), to women, housekeeping was 'a constant of everyday life ... a sacramental activity that provide[d] essential cul-tural continuity.'[112]

The weekly wash took priority; if the laundry took less time, because the weather was fine or the family had fewer clothes, then a woman who started early might have a bit of time for other household tasks, yet the washing always came first. Markets, for instance, were held on Thursdays or Saturdays and household labour had to be fitted in around the important business of buying and selling as dictated by external forces – hence in Lark Rise, cleaning could take place on Saturday. This might include whitewashing the walls, but normally encompassed the tasks of scrubbing the floor and table, and polishing the grate.[113] But, laundry had its own day fixed early on in the week, usually a Monday or Tuesday, because whatever the number of clothes to be washed, whether or not the wash was weekly or fortnightly, it could still take the rest of that week to complete. Just the washing itself took all day; the scrubbing might begin at eight o'clock in the morning and not be finished until nine or ten at night – and when washing day came round, the men were turned out of the house to work in the garden. For the women and girls who remained, the scrubbing would result in chaffed and raw hands as well as being physically tiring.[114] However, and this was important, if all the women did their laundry on the same day, it also meant that they were all doing the work at the same time and had company.[115]

Holding back the natural process of decay, domestic work gained a ritualised aspect and these domestic rituals exhibited the qualities found in all rituals: 'regular recurrence, symbolic value, emotional meaning and (usually) a "dramatic" group-making quality'.[116] A woman who washed on her own would make herself into an outsider. Likewise, the evidence suggests that the working class (woman) had a formalised, not simply functional, conception of interior/domestic space. In *Country Voices*, Cissie Elliot and Mary Watson, born in Northumberland in 1904 and 1898 respectively, describe how bad luck could be brought on a house 'if an unchurched woman or an unchristened baby was brought into it'.[117] 'After I'd had my child,' Mary Elliot remembers,

> I couldn't go out until I'd been 'churched'. I could go out in our yard of course, but I couldn't go into anybody's house, it wasn't allowed. I had to go to church, to thank God for the safe delivery of the child: that would usually be about a month after it was born. But, before you did that you couldn't go into anybody's house: it was unclean and it was unlucky.[118]

The boundaries of the cottage and the meanings conferred on its interior spaces were symbolic, not just utilitarian or physical; moreover, the symbolic barriers could be more concrete than those of the built environment. Housework was productive of these thresholds of control, and though it was certainly materially significant,[119] much of this work also had a sacramental overtone rooted in the corporeal boundaries of the housewife's body. If they were in the middle of a period, for example, a woman would not be allowed to salt a pig as this was said to turn the meat bad. This may be derivative of the associative link between women's reproductive organs and 'pig', the traditional Germanic link between the menses and woman's 'sowish' behaviour, but within scientific discourse, the study of menstruation has also been used to highlight the link between Woman and (animal) Nature.[120] To adapt Mark Wigley, housework acted as a form of surveillance over the domestic space and the fluid female body:

> The capacity of the house to resist the displacing effects of sexuality is embedded within a number of systems of control – mythological, juridical codes, forms of address, dress codes, writing styles, superstitions, manners etc. – each of which takes the form of surveillance over a particular space, whether it be the dinner table, the threshold, the church, the fingertips, the bath, the face, the street.[121]

In the same way, the act of washing ensured that the body and home remained clean, just as domestic vernacular established built boundaries of purity based on bodily cleanliness (the privy down the garden path, the scullery/wash-house outside the kitchen). Order was therefore maintained and pollution was avoided, in and through the housewife's work. In the instigation of order (which depended largely on an ordering of the body, the development of modesty and privacy, and therefore the division of ever more discreet spaces), architecture effected the possibility of the individual subject and actively constituted the private subject.[122] Meanwhile, as the old rhyme suggests,[123] there was a weekly rhythm and pattern to this work to which any experienced housewife would adhere.

NOTES

1. H. Lefebvre, *The Production of Space*, Nicholson-Smith, D. (trans.), (Oxford, 1991) cited in N. Leach (ed.), *Rethinking Architecture: a reader in cultural theory* (London and New York, 1997), p. 141.
2. It should be recognised that both of these are loaded terms within architectural discourse. Lefebvre outlines how the architect primarily represents space – in plans, blueprints etc. – and produces a conception of space which appears neutral and objective. Whereas the space of 'users'/'inhabitants' is 'lived', 'the space of the everyday activities of users is a concrete one, which is to say, subjective'. The two kinds of space are normally placed in opposition to each other; the one related to the public sphere the latter to the private. Lefebvre, *The Production of Space*, pp. 144–5.
3. P. Tristram, *Living Space in Fact and Fiction* (London, 1989), pp. 117–18; K. Soper, *What is Nature? Culture, politics and the non-human* (Oxford, 1995), p. 203; R. J. Lawrence, *Housing, Dwellings and Homes: design, theory, research and practice* (Chichester, 1987), pp. 32–50.
4. V. Parker, *The English House in the Nineteenth Century* (London, 1970), p. 5.
5. G. H. Andrews, *Modern Husbandry: a practical and scientific treatise on agriculture illustrating the most approved practices in draining, cultivating and manuring the land; breeding, rearing and fattening stock; and the general management and economy of the farm* (London, 1853), p. 91.
6. F. Thompson, *Lark Rise to Candleford: a trilogy* (Harmondsworth, [1939, 1941, 1943] 1979), p. 497.
7. P. Stallybrass and A. White, *The Politics and Poetics of Transgression* (London, 1986), pp. 144–5.
8. David Garnett, c.1896, quoted in I. Stickland (ed.), *The Voices of Children 1700–1914* (London, 1973), p. 198.
9. Stallybrass and White, *Politics and Poetics*, p. 144.
10. Parker, *The English House*, pp. 5–28; L. Davidoff, J. L'Esperance and H. Newby, 'Landscape with figures: home and community in English society' in Mitchell, J. and Oakley, A. (eds), *The Rights and Wrongs of Women* (Harmondsworth, 1986), p. 162; J. Marsh, *Back to the Land: the pastoral impulse in Victorian England from 1880 to 1914* (London, Melbowne and New York, 1982).
11. Lawrence, *Housing, Dwellings and Homes*.
12. Tristram, *Living Space*; Davidoff et al., 'Landscape'; T. Rivers, D. Cruickshank, G. Darley and M. Pawley, *The Name of the Room: a history of the British house and home* (London, 1992); S. Brand, *How Buildings Learn: what happens after they're built* (London, 1997); Stallybrass and White, *Politics and Poetics*, pp. 125–6.

13 Davidoff et al., 'Landscape', p. 153.
14 L. Walker and V. Ware, 'Political pincushions: decorating the abolitionist interior, 1780–1860, paper delivered at *Reading the Nineteenth-century Domestic Space*, King Alfred's College, Winchester (April, 1996).
15 Tristram, *Living Space*, pp. 23–5.
16 Parker, *The English House*, pp. 20–1; R. Swartz Cowan, *More Work for Mother: the ironies of household technology from the open hearth to the microwave* (London, 1989), pp. 155–6, 160.
17 Davidoff et al., 'Landscape', p. 153.
18 Davidoff et al., 'Landscape', pp. 164–5.
19 Stallybrass and White, *Politics and Poetics*, pp. 148–50.
20 Stallybrass and White, *Politics and Poetics*, pp. 150–65; L. Davidoff, 'Class and gender in Victorian England' in Newton, J. L., Ryan, M. P. and Walkowitz, J. R. (eds), *Sex and Class in Women's History: essays from feminist studies* (London, 1985) pp. 18–29.
21 Lawrence, *Housing, Dwellings and Homes*, p. 76.
22 A. D. M. Phillips, 'Landlord investment in farm buildings in the English Midlands in the mid nineteenth century' in Holderness, B. A. and Turner, M. (eds), *Land, Labour and Agriculture, 1700–1920: Essays for Gordon Mingay* (London, 1991), pp. 191–2, 209–10.
23 Andrews, *Modern Husbandry*, pp. 93–5.
24 Andrews, *Modern Husbandry*, pp. 95–6.
25 The Board of Agriculture's competitions to stimulate cottage building at the beginning of the nineteenth century originally stipulated that all designs ought to include two bedrooms, so that the male and female members of the family would not sleep together. L. Caffyn, *Workers' Housing in West Yorkshire, 1750–1920* (London, 1986), p. 49.
26 Brand, *How Buildings Learn*, pp. 92–4.
27 Caffyn, *Workers' Housing*, p. 88. Quiney, gives an extensive chronology of legislation on housing up to 1984. A. Quiney, *House and Home: a history of the small English house* (London, 1986), pp. 191–3.
28 A. Combe, *The Management of Infancy: physiological and moral, intended chiefly for the use of parents* (London, [c.1840] 1860).
29 S. M. Gaskell, *Model Housing: from the Great Exhibition to the Festival of Britain* (London and New York, 1987), p. 9.
30 L. Weaver, *The 'Country Life' Book of Cottages* (London, [1913] 1919), p. 1.
31 Caffyn, *Workers' Housing*.
32 Weaver pointed to Mr Strachey of the *Spectator* who could build houses for £150 using concrete blocks, no living room – unnecessary, according to the labourer – and three bedrooms and an earth closet. He disliked the omission of a porch, but otherwise saw this as paradigmatic. Weaver, *The 'Country Life' Book*, pp. 9–11.
33 Gaskell, *Model Housing*, pp. 5–10.
34 Weaver, *The 'Country Life' Book*, p. 3.
35 Weaver, *The 'Country Life' Book*, p. 7.
36 S. Daniels, *Fields of Vision: landscape imagery and national identity in England and the United States* (Cambridge, 1993), for a broader analysis of this theme in inter-war discussions on preservation, especially of Constable's landscapes.
37 Weaver, *The 'Country Life' Book*, p. 25.
38 H. W. Acland, *The Cottage Register; or Forms for Registering the Sanitary Conditions of Villages: for the use of Landowners, Officers of Health, Guardians and Others* (London, 1861) which had run to a fourth edition by 1872. Henry W.

Acland M.D., D.C.L., FRS, was Regius Professor of Medicine at Oxford and Hon. Physician to HRH, Prince of Wales.
39 Acland, *The Cottage Register*, p. iii.
40 F. Mort, *Dangerous Sexualities: medico-moral politics in England since 1830* (London, 1987).
41 G. Eliot, 'The natural history of German life' from *Westminster Review* (July 1856), in Byatt, A. S. (ed.), *George Eliot: selected essays, poems and other writings* (Harmondsworth, 1990).
42 *Art Journal* (1860), p. 80.
43 Frederick Daniel Hardy (1826–1911), *The Dismayed Artist*, 1866, oil, Wolverhampton Art Gallery Collection, reproduced in C. Payne, *Rustic Simplicity: scenes of cottage life in nineteenth-century British art* (Nottingham, 1998).
44 Payne, *Rustic Simplicity*, p. 70.
45 H. W. Acland, *Cottage-wall Prints* (London, 1862), pp. 3–4.
46 Acland, *Cottage-wall Prints*, pp. 4–8.
47 Lawrence, *Housing, Dwellings and Homes*, p. 72.
48 Stallybrass and White, *Politics and Poetics*, pp. 126–30.
49 Lawrence, *Housing, Dwellings and Homes*, p. 73.
50 Caffyn, *Workers' Housing*, p. 1.
51 R. W. Brunskill, *Traditional Buildings of Britain: an introduction to vernacular architecture* (London, 1992), p. 120.
52 Brunskill, *Traditional Buildings of Britain*, p. 121.
53 Brand, *How Buildings Learn*, p. 88.
54 Brand, *How Buildings Learn*, p. 90.
55 Brunskill, *Traditional Buildings of Britain*, p. 107.
56 Normally cited to *Bulletin Archeologique*, Vol. 1 (1839).
57 Brand, *How Buildings Learn*, pp. 89–93.
58 Brunskill, *Traditional Buildings of Britain*, p. 107.
59 M. W. Barley, *The English Farmhouse and Cottage* (London, 1961), p. xxii.
60 Brunskill, *Traditional Buildings of Britain*, pp. 107–8; Barley, *The English Farmhouse*, pp. xvii–xxi.
61 Barley, *The English Farmhouse*, p. 281.
62 Brunskill, *Traditional Buildings of Britain*, pp. 106, 110–20.
63 Barley, *The English Farmhouse*, pp. 276–87.
64 The photograph is reproduced in J. Calder, *Victorian and Edwardian Society from Old Photographs* (London, 1979), Fig. 8.
65 Brunskill, *Traditional Buildings of Britain*, p. 107.
66 J. Barrell, *The Dark Side of the Landscape: the rural poor in English painting 1730–1840* (Cambridge, 1980), p. 18.
67 Tristram, *Living Space*, pp. 26–8.
68 R. Worth, 'Rural labouring dress: the boundaries of representation' paper delivered to *The Dress of the Poor 1750–1900: Old and New Perspectives* conference held at Oxford Brookes University, 7 November 1999.
69 Calder, *Victorian and Edwardian Society*, Fig. 35.
70 W. Cobbett, *Cottage Economy* (London, [1821] 1926), p. 20.
71 Barrell, *The Dark Side*, p. 5.
72 Calder, *Victorian and Edwardian Society*, p. ix.
73 J. Tagg, *The Burden of Representation: essays on photographies and histories* (London, 1988), pp. 4–5.
74 R. Gagnier, 'Social atoms: working class autobiography, subjectivity and gender', *Victorian Studies*, No. 3, Vol. 30, p. 341.

75 S. Rowbotham, *Hidden From History: 300 Years of women's oppression and the fight against it* (London, 1974), p. 24.
76 M. Collier, *The Woman's Labour: an epistle to Mr Stephen Duck in answer to his late poem called the Thresher's Labour, to which are added the Three Wise Sentences taken from the First Book of Esdras, chapters III and IV* (London, 1739).
77 D. Landry, *The Muses of Resistance: Labouring-class women's poetry in Britain, 1739–1796* (Cambridge, 1990), p. 29.
78 Landry, *The Muses of Resistance*, pp. 26, 56–76.
79 Gagnier, 'Social atoms', p. 342. Here she is drawing on Bouderieu's contention that where the elite believe in the representation rather than what is represented, working people believe that each image performs a function, so that they expect 'representations and the conventions which govern them to allow them to believe "naively" in the things represented'. Bouderieu, quoted in Landry, 'Social atoms', p. 342.
80 These might be a widow and children, several women living together, a married couple, a nuclear or extended family and could include lodgers, etc.
81 Landry, *The Muses of Resistance*.
82 J. Arch, *Joseph Arch: the story of his life told by himself*, Countess of Warwick (ed.), (London, 1898), pp. 3–5.
83 G. Baldry, *The Rabbit Skin Cap: a Tale of a norfolk countryman's youth*, Haggard, L. R. (ed.), (London, [1939] 1950), p. 113. This autobiography, in the form of a narrative, records his early life as the son of a shoemaker. His father was born in 1800, as one of eight children, and often took work on local farms as well as making shoes, to make ends meet. The family kept two cows, some pigs and birds, which his grandmother looked after, as well as making gloves and buskins by candle light. Baldry, *Rabbit Skin*, p. 22.
84 Anon, *The Autobiography of one who has Whistled at the Plough* (London, 1848), p. 3. Though this refers specifically to south Scotland, c.1770, this practice continued in the north of England well into the nineteenth century.
85 Brunskill, *Traditional Buildings of Britain*, p. 117.
86 Flora Thompson describes the value of gossip, i.e. of women visiting each other for a chat in the afternoon in *Lark Rise*, pp. 105–13.
87 Vernacular architecture obviously varied across different regions, but it is important to remember that many cottages were in addition adapted spaces. A large house might decline in status to farmhouse and then further divided into a set of cottages. See Brunskill, *Traditional Buildings of Britain*.
88 Light in the evening might come from candles or rushlights, but household mending and paid glove-making were also done by firelight. For instance, Baldry, though not necessarily representative, says his mother resisted using anything other than rushlights, as she was wary of new ways or extra expense. His grandmother kept a ragbag of pieces of cloth for repairs and would work by the fire mending clothes. Baldry, *Rabbit Skin*, pp. 37, 208.
89 D. Smith, *No Rain in Those Clouds: being an account of my father John Smith's life and farming from 1862 to the present day* (London, 1943), p. 110.
90 Baldry, *Rabbit Skin*, pp. 209–10.
91 Brunskill, *Traditional Buildings of Britain*, p. 106.
92 Soper, *What is Nature?*, p. 84.
93 S. Silvester, *In a World that Has Gone* (Leicestershire, 1868), p. 11.
94 Quoted in J. Burnett (ed.), *Destiny Obscure: autobiographies of childhood, education and family from the 1820s to the 1920s* (Harmondsworth, 1982), p. 67.

95 M. K. Ashby, *Joseph Ashby of Tysoe, 1859–1919: a study of English village life* (London, [1961] 1974), pp. 5, 26. Born 1837, Elizabeth Ashby is the mother of Joseph Ashby, an illegitimate child, fathered by her employer while she was in service. Most women, even if they never went into the fields at any other time of year, would go gleaning. Though this was a contested privilege, the practice continued in many areas well into the twentieth century. D. H. Morgan, *Harvesters and Harvesting 1840–1900: a study of the rural proletariat* (London, 1982), pp. 152–62; P. King, 'Gleaners, farmers and the failure of legal sanctions in England 1750–1850', *Past and Present* (1989).

96 C. Kightly (ed.), *Country Voices: life and love in farm and village* (London, 1984), pp. 75–8.

97 Landry, *The Muses of Resistance*, pp. 65–6; M. Chamberlain, *Fenwomen: a portrait of women in an English village* (London, 1975), pp. 91–2.

98 Thompson, *Lark Rise*, pp. 105–113; Baldry, *Rabbit Skin*, pp. 209–10.

99 M. M. Bell, *Childerley: nature and morality in a country village* (Chicago and London, 1994), p. 52.

100 F. Barret-Ducrocq, *Love in the Time of Victoria: sexuality, class and gender in nineteenth-century London*, Howe, J. (trans.), (London, 1991), pp. 7–13, 39–43. In one way this harks back to the conception of space discussed by Wigley, in which man is meant to be mobile, woman static, yet in which the man is self-controlled while the woman's sexuality roams outside the house. Cf. M. Wigley, 'Untitled: the housing of gender' in Colomina, B. (ed.), *Sexuality and Space* (Princeton, 1992).

101 M. Penn, *Manchester Fourteen Miles* (Firle, [1947] 1979), pp. 30–3.

102 Susan Strasser, quoted in A. Romines, *The Home Plot: women writing and domestic ritual* (Amherst, 1992), p. 10.

103 S. Zlotnick, '"A thousand times I'd be a factory girl": dialect, domesticity, and working-class women's poetry in Victorian Britain', *Victorian Studies* (Autumn 1991), p. 15.

104 Romines, *The Home Plot*, p. 11.

105 Kightly, *Country Voices*, pp. 75–8; Stickland, *The Voices of Children*, p. 194.

106 Burnett, *Destiny Obscure*, pp. 288–94.

107 Romines, *The Home Plot*, p. 131.

108 Romines, *The Home Plot*, p. 6.

109 R. Fletcher (ed.), *The Biography of a Victorian Village: Richard Cobbold's account of Wortham, Suffolk, 1860* (London, 1977), p. 120.

110 Arch, *Joseph Arch*, p. 45.

111 Romines, *The Home Plot*, p. 131.

112 Romines, *The Home Plot*, p. 6.

113 Thompson, *Lark Rise*, p. 114.

114 Gladys Otterspoor, quoted in Chamberlain, *Fenwomen*, p. 32. This chaffing and being rubbed raw was also recorded by Collier, *The woman's labour*.

115 C. Davidson, *A Woman's Work is Never Done* (London, 1986), pp. 149–50.

116 Romines, *The Home Plot*, p. 12.

117 Kightly, *Country Voices*, p. 227.

118 Kightly, *Country Voices*, p. 227.

119 See Soper, *What is Nature?*, pp. 87–90, 92, 94.

120 Ethel Gotobed, quoted in Chamberlain, *Fenwomen*, p. 104. Cf. Soper, *What is Nature?*.

121 Wigley, 'Untitled', p. 338.

122 Wigley, 'Untitled', p. 345.

123 Traditional rhyme:

*They that wash on Monday
Have all the week to dry;
They that wash on Tuesday
Are not so much awry;
They that wash on Wednesday
Are not so much to blame;
They that wash on Thursday
Wash for shame.
They that wash on Friday
Wash in need;
They that wash on Saturday,
Oh, they're sluts indeed!*

In Barker, C. M. (ed.), *A Little Book of Old Rhymes* (London, c.1930), p. 29.

CHAPTER 6

The country and the city

It is a common opinion that a love of natural scenery is a purely modern passion [of one race, but the] middle class multitude in their selection of a home and in their regard for the beauties of nature . . . do not wish to get quite beyond the busy world. They like flowers, parterres, shrubberies, lawns, vineries and peach-houses, just as they like lace-curtains, glowing carpets, brilliant furniture and burnished grates. Both represent to them comfort and culture combined, are the signs of monied ease and elegance, and create a velvety sensation in the atmosphere by which they are surrounded. It is not a wrong taste in itself; it is a good one if not carried to excess, but indulged in exclusively, as we every day see it, it is the taste of a Sybarite, and anything but a proof of the love of nature. Take most people for a day into the real natural scenery and they will be at no loss for well-known epithets expressive of admiration. Leave them there, however, for a few days, and admiration will yield to weariness. There can be no genuine love here. Love of change, excitement, novelty, will make even mountains delightful, but custom make them detestable.

(*Daily News*, 9 July 1869)

THE COTTAGE AS COMMODITY

By the 1900s a love of domestic pastoral over-determined English architecture. Hermann Muthesius for one was able to state that the Englishman's love of his home was well known by 1904 and to equate it with his love of independence and his hatred of the city. The Englishman, Muthesius declared, did not and could not live in the city. He flew from the metropolis, always sought to regain his bond with nature and lived for his return to home.[1] Where, during the nineteenth century, the city was figured as a site of public excess and promiscuity, the country was figured as safe, self-contained and bounded, like the home, by its own timeless, natural moral order. As a result, by the late nineteenth century the country home came to appear 'in every guise. It was the unmistakable message of sermons, hymns, poems, popular song, wall texts, household manuals, annuals, tracts, magazines and novels, ... periodicals, advertisements and calendars'.[2] Nearly a century later, Glancey makes the same point, maintaining that: 'The weekend motorway set and most of the rest of us, too, remain, at the tail end of the 20th century, either in love or bemused by [the] rural idyll that, if it never really existed ... certainly doesn't today.'[3]

As more people begin to resist the imposition of bypasses and other new roads in their own back yards, Williams' point that traffic 'is a form of consciousness and a form of social relations' is worth bearing in mind here.[4] We see the countryside in part through our spatial relationship to it as we pass by. The idea of rural retreat, which implies some form of social and physical mobility, has remained dominant, alongside the celebration of wild unspoiled nature more generally set against capital.[5] The signs of country-living (bramble-covered toasters, oaken beams, chintz and country kitchens – mass-produced commodities designed to re-present the house as 'home'), are still 'imported' on a vast scale into the towns. Likewise, as Oliver notes, the cottage today can be found on calendars, cards, puzzles; it can be made into 'teacosies and firescreens, distorted into teapots and marmalade jars', while the 'real' cottage has been bought up and modernised as holiday or commuter home.[6] According to the property advertisements that we can see everyday in the paper – but especially in the Sunday supplements – it is now relatively easy to buy a comfortable cottage. Alternatively – and this is cheaper – the cottage and other components of the rural idyll can be bought up as collectable small-scale ornaments. But is this the simple 'distortion' of a 'traditional English domestic building'[7] that Oliver suggests?

Take Wedgwood; they sell several series of 'collector plates' depicting a variety of natural and rural incidents, often represented in their advertising as authentic country scenes based on the artists' childhood memories. In one recent sequence, *The Farm Year*, the artist is quoted on the back of one application form: 'The little boy in the picture is me,' confesses artist Michael Herring, 'I remember every detail of the bright November day when I took my new toy tractor into the fields to watch the threshing – it was magical!' The series of plates are sold as 'golden memories'; the artist 'transports us back to a bygone age' by bringing 'an enchanting rural scene' to life. He depicts 'exquisite period detail: the working horse and lovingly crafted wooden cart, the milkmaid with her apron and scarf' – though how we know she is a milkmaid is unclear as she has none of the tools of her trade with her, she just holds the boy's hand. The boy himself is 'a picture of innocence'; overall, the piece is described as 'a glorious celebration of childhood and the golden age of farming' and this is the real pleasure of the piece.[8] The first in the series was 'Hay-making'; advertised in the same way, the scene on this plate was of a collie, two girls and their mother watching the hay being carted from the field at 4 o'clock in the afternoon. Cottages – tile rather than thatched – can be seen in the background near a church. In this instance, Herring is said to have 'spent many happy hours on his grandparents' farm, and he uses his knowledge' of this to paint the scene.[9] Though 'Threshing', like 'Hay-making', employs details taken from childhood memory, the actual historical period is obfuscated by the written text, which sets the scene vaguely in a 'bygone', 'golden age of farming' and it is painted from the distanced view of the adult painter gone back to watch his childhood. Given the clothes the threshers wear, the scene is set probably no more than fifty years before it was painted, viz. the 1940s, but the copy's stress on 'golden' makes the scene seem 'timeless' and therefore especially charming. The written text teaches the purchaser what to see, but it also authenticates and naturalises the myths of the rural idyll and childhood as homely places that remain unchanged, sources of 'stability, reliability and authenticity. Such views of place,' Massey points out, 'which reverberate with nostalgia for something lost, are coded female.'[10] And, it is the little boy's mother who stands at the centre of the piece.

As Williams argues in *The Country and the City*, there is a common formula in representing country life and ways as lost and gone, usually within the last fifty years or so. He describes an 'escalator' of constant nostalgic regret. If you go back fifty years, you will find a text that evidences sorrow at the loss of a better way of life, a 'golden age' that existed fifty years ago. This regret can even be seen in More's *Utopia* in which the noblemen are accused of knocking down houses and putting sheep in the churches, and in much earlier texts as well. 'Where indeed shall we go', Williams asks, 'before the escalator stops?'[11] This is not, however, a matter of 'historical error, but historical perspective'.[12] The unreachable past can be used to criticise the present. Nostalgia is not inherently conservative or Conservative; as in the Wedgwood ad, it resides in the author's childhood. But, more importantly: 'Old England, settlement, the rural virtues – all these, in fact, mean different things at different times, and quite different values are being brought into question.'[13] In other words, the retrospect for each period has a different nuance. The country retains its imaginative power, its persistence relies on pastoral, but the images, forms and ideas change to some extent over time. They are there to interpret different kinds of experience to those of previous eras. In the nineteenth century, for instance, there was a preoccupation with the mob. At the same time, a focus on mobility and isolation that only became dominant in the twentieth century began to emerge with the widespread growth of the cities. Today, the sixteenth-century linkage of the city with money and law persists in occasional concerns about corruption and the celebration of commerce, yet, when someone says 'city', they more often mean capitalism, bureaucracy and centralised power.[14] These ideas, therefore, 'express . . . human interests and purposes for which there is no other immediately available vocabulary'.[15] Today, as well as being coded female, rural spaces are constructed in commercial texts as offering an escape from the materialistic, the corrupt and the limiting world of the city – for 'city' read 'capital'.

The 'Property Now' section of *The Herald*, and the 'Property Guide' from the *Citizen* (which proclaims itself 'The area's No 1 Property Guide'), both carry a front page leader every week on especially choice houses that have just become available in the area – viz. Bedfordshire. These leaders are given extravagant headlines, such as 'A Touch of Class', or 'Five Bedroom Delight', and frequently provide details of desirable cottages. Headlines in recent years referring to cottages include: 'Period cottage full of charm', 'Cottage full of character', 'Cottage with charm', and one that has particularly stuck in my mind 'Cottage even has snooker room!' To be especially charming, or to become engraved on our hearts, it has become helpful for the cottage to be 'listed', i.e. to have gained a certain protected status as a historic building, according to the law, and to be in some degree haunted by history. This gives it stability, continuity and authenticity. For example, the following advert appeared in 'Property Now' on 25 May 1995, accompanied by an artist's impression of what the building *would* look like when renovated. The illustration included blue-birds flying overhead, climbing roses and a steep roof, a sure sign that this was once a thatched building:

> *Cottage full of character*
> Currently under complete reconstruction and refurbishment, this detached listed cottage is reputed to be one of the oldest properties in the village of Cranfield. When complete the property will comprise of a cloakroom, sitting room, dining room, kitchen, three bedrooms and bathroom.[16]

Though it is listed, the developer hasn't provided a realist photographic image of the house, as is normal when selling an older property, but an artist's impression of the idyllic finished product that is akin to estate agent's adverts selling unbuilt houses on modern estates. In the written text, it is convenience, comfort and cosiness, all the advantages of modernity with a light touch of historic interest that is relied upon as much as picturesque detail to sell the cottage. Notice also the dining room and sitting room, in addition to the kitchen, the three bedrooms and its detached position. Though 'reputed to be one of the oldest properties in the village', it conforms to the bourgeois Beau Ideal, rather than the one-up, one-down vernacular dwellings condemned by men like Kingsley. It is the larger properties that are so much in demand. Where smaller cottages remain standing, they too are normally converted – two or three smaller buildings often being knocked through to form one living space – to conform to the three-bedroom detached bourgeois standard. The building's total reconstruction – to the buyer's specification, as the ad goes on to say – and its historic reputation within the law, apparently sets up an inherent and undisguised contradiction within the text. But, this ad allows the buyer to have it all – the freedom to choose and the unspoiled continuity of country life. They can transpose the benefits of the city to the country, rescue those values lost and mourned and thereby reify the Beau Ideal of the twentieth century: a compromise between the 'old ways, human ways, natural ways' and 'progress, modernisation, development'.[17]

If you cannot afford a cottage for life, of course, you can still buy a Cottage Holiday, such as those advertised in the *Guardian*, 7 January 1995. Playing on the highly contemporary self-awareness/consciousness of the chocolate-box image that the *Guardian* readership might be expected to share with Oliver, this advert seduces us with a peculiarly sweet image of the Cottage Homes of England, à la Benjamin Gough:

> A *Selection of chocolate box cottages (from English Country Cottages)*
> Let us tempt you to an English Country Cottage. To the romance of Rosemullion, set in one of Cornwall's prettiest villages, close to Frenchman's Creek. To the magic of Martin's Cottage, complete with oak beams and lavender scented garden. Or perhaps the charm of The Old Lodge, surrounded by magnificent walking country – and opposite the local inn! . . . Choose from a Lakeland farmhouse, a Norfolk barn – even a castle . . . An English Country Cottage puts you in touch with the hidden beauty of England.[18]

The utter desirability of the cottage as retreat can be seen in this use of the chocolate box image in which the cottage becomes consumable, literally eatable/edible – as it is in Hansel and Gretel. All are thatched, all have roses round the door, all are set in the summer sunshine of the English countryside, yet are – probably – not too far from the pub, something which nineteenth-century, middle-class social commentators would have definitely frowned upon. We are left with a charming, saccharine yet knowing vision of England and its 'hidden beauty' – England's beauty is always hidden, awaiting discovery by the intrepid tourist as if the nation like a bashful virgin was awaiting penetration on her wedding night.

The advert draws on a faintly left-wing embarrassment about consumerism, plays with irony to distance readers from their political fears, draws them in to think about how they might use their time and finally hopes to clinch the deal with a small turn to nostalgia. This last move comes across as equally conservative and radical, it might be celebrating Englishness, or it might be satirical; it is indeterminate, again allowing the purchaser to choose. Anyway, as Mary Douglas suggests, in *Purity and Danger*, the crossing of one bodily frame can come to mean/ substitute for the crossing of other bodily frames, hence the ease with which advertisers can smuggle sex into almost anything. And the crossing of boundaries through these frames is always a transgression. This makes what crosses the boundary offensive; the act of crossing through the frame generates disgust.[19] While playing with as much of the myth of the country cottage as possible in 115 words, the text seems to have no preferred reading other than the commercial denotation: 'we have cottage holidays for sale'.

This allows the cottage to become available for momentary, instant gratification, in an advertising campaign that sells it 'simply' as part of a chocolate selection. It flatters the reader that he or she is an individual with the freedom to read, see and do what they want. Moreover, our choice of 'cottage' extends to farmhouses and castles; paradise is, it seems, dependent on our preferred 'style, character, and location', not our income, nor any other restraint. Here, the picturesque apparently fixed, feminine cottage reveals its fluidity; the model of stability, listable, subject always to long-term paternalistic authority, it is equally transient, expendable and mutable. Nostalgia is thereby harnessed in service of a discourse that seeks to reassure the consumer that they are always free. Another company, Country Holidays, headlines its advertising with: 'Choose a Country Holidays Cottage and you choose the freedom to do what you want'. The next line, presented as a banner inside the advert, is: 'The freedom to choose from over 6,500 Country Holidays Cottages'. The copy goes on to stress that there will be no 'one to bother you', 'overcrowded hotels', or 'set timetables to keep to', instead there is just 'complete freedom from Land's End to John O'Groats and everything that's between'.[20]

The cottage homes of England that stretched 'from John O'Groats to lovely Kent'[21] in Gough's poem housed contented settled families. In the 1990s, though they continue to offer a 'warm welcome', they have come to symbolise retreat into the unspoiled 'peace and tranquillity' of the country and a naturalised freedom from restraint, for the urban tourist who wants to 'get away from it all'. The advert contains several pictures of families on holiday, with the following captions: 'The peace and tranquillity of an English country village could be the perfect retreat – whatever the time of year.' 'Children will love the freedom of lazy summer days spent getting back to nature. An unforgettable holiday.' 'A quaint thatched cottage could be your "home-from-home", nestled in the heart of the British countryside.' 'Getting away from it all is a breath of fresh air. After a relaxing day you can return to a warm welcome.' The penultimate line is: 'In one of our home-from-home cottages or houses you can start discovering the Britain no one knows.'[22] In picturesque mode, it seems that it is appropriate to tag any cottage with labels such as 'charm',[23] or 'character',[24] and this adds a certain value. But, it is peace, freedom, discovery, leisure, time with the family, the space to relax, a movement away from the crowded spaces of the city, that are – according to commercial discourse – really in demand. Settlement, continuity and 'unspoiled' nature, i.e. the 'pre-capitalist' countryside, is sought, but it is retreat, which requires mobility, money and movement, the 'benefits' of capitalism, that takes precedence in the advertising.

MONIED EASE AND ELEGANCE

In 1973, Raymond Williams observed that:

> We live in a world in which the dominant mode of production and social relationships teaches, impresses, offers to make normal and even rigid, modes of detached, separated, external perception and action: modes of using and consuming rather than accepting and enjoying people and things.[25]

While, retrospect is celebrated,

> it is not so much the old village or back street that is significant. It is the perception and affirmation of a world in which one is not necessarily a stranger and an agent, but can be a member, a discoverer, in a shared source of life.[26]

Though not expressed by Williams in this way, the negotiation of these two impulses, or perceptions, leads to the creation of many contesting, culturally constructed countryside*s* and multiple, contingent rural space*s*. Moreover, Doreen Massey argues, these spaces are implicated in social relations; the way space is thought of, the way it is organised is 'integral to the production of the social, and not merely its result. It is fully implicated in history and politics'.[27] As Stephen Daniels observes in discussing landscape as 'a mode of knowledge and social engagement', the many discourses and practices that come into play and run through any image mean that an 'apparently simple picture of a country scene may yield many fields of vision'.[28] One account is no more 'authentic' than another, rather they express disparate experiences and distinct ways of seeing; when dealing with the 'rural', one is effectively dealing with many contesting, culturally constructed countryside*s*. Meanwhile, different visions of the 'rural' and the practices that result work to include and exclude; the rural idyll that has become hegemonic marginalises as it places the privileged at its 'centre'.[29]

The association of national identity with certain landscapes 'negotiates many other forms of identity: local, regional and international; social, religious and familial',[30] and as spaces and places are given symbolic meaning, so they become gendered. The symbolic meanings given to spaces and places in turn reflect, help to construct and reify gender. The attempt to define particular places as 'home', for instance, in which 'mum' awaits 'a stable symbolic centre – functioning as an anchor for others', is an attempt to limit the numbers of ways in which those places can be seen. But, given the 'unutterable mobility and contingency of space–time' any such attempts are 'constantly the site of social contest, battles over the power to . . . impose the meaning to be attributed to a space'.[31] As Annie Hughes – a feminist geographer who looks at the 'lived experiences of non-farming women' – puts it, neither gender nor rurality ought to be treated as 'fixed unchanging categories, but as "unstable and interactive reference points" constructed through social and cultural practices which have given them meaning in everyday life'.[32]

A recognition that country life is only really accessible through books, or the disposal of vast sums of money, has led critics like Glancey to attack the chocolate box village and thatched cottage as the province of the deluded tripper or the rich.[33] There is a vast amount of publishing on country cottages and their gardens at the moment. Each seeks to combine watercolours, photographs, brief historical sketches and literary extracts to conjure up the charm of the cottage; some contrast image and reality in a claim to veracity.[34] Likewise, in 1988, domestic visitors generated £7,850 million; 'Britain's architectural heritage "is almost certainly England's most valuable tourism asset", according to Save Britain's Heritage.'[35] But, as ethnographer Michael Mayerfeld Bell observes in his study of Childerley there are many ways of seeing the rural, even among those who live in the country. He found that moneyed incomers, for example, had an elaborate and highly discriminating aesthetic language for describing the land as landscape, while ordinary villagers who were less critical about the quality of the scene, had a more restricted descriptive vocabulary, but valued the land as place. The moneyed were especially interested in who had 'nice views' from their houses. Those who 'owned' a nice view – these could cost tens of thousands of pounds – took great pride in it, explained that this was why they had bought that particular house and remembered each subtle change in it.[36]

While he was there, one view was 'threatened' by a development of four new houses and a discussion took place about their possible visual impact on neighbouring properties:

> 'Will it affect your view?' Laura asked her [Jane].
> 'No. Not ours,' Jane replied. 'If it did, you can be sure I'd be making a loud noise about it.'
> 'You do have a nice view there,' said Laura, commiserating...
> 'Yes, it is a nice view. That's why we bought the house. We looked at a lot of places, but when we saw that view, we knew we had to have that house... Our view is one of the best around.'[37]

Jane's explanation of her reasons for buying her house is quite typical of a moneyed response to land as landscape. For moneyed Childerleyans, Bell records, landscape is in part about the value of property. Because they buy a home for its view, its destruction would mean not simply the loss of a picturesque and aesthetically pleasing scene, but a fall in the monetary value of their home. They therefore have a sense of entitlement to the 'peace and quiet' or the view they have in a sense bought.

Nice views are rare – open views are the most valued – and the view that the moneyed own therefore confers status. There is a cultural expectation that other moneyed people will share their way of seeing and therefore recognise the ranking of their view as compared to others, in order for it to be evaluated. Nevertheless, this is not just a matter of money and education, it is also about form, the cultural knowledge taken from the picturesque that permits and requires an objective eye and the objectification of the land as landscape. This objectification allows the appropriation of what is seen, an appropriation which contests the use of the land for farming. Another moneyed villager, Ed Laws, was annoyed that a local farmer had built a new dairy and some silos in sight of his house. Though the farmer had responded to a local 'outcry' against the installation by planting trees around it, Ed was still unhappy because the screen was incomplete and the trees were not native.[38] The picturesque and agrarian capitalism have been at loggerheads in this way since the late eighteenth century and while in art they have gradually come to accommodate each other,[39] the old tension it seems has re-emerged in the late twentieth century; ploughed fields are one thing, sheet-metal dairies are another. This is a political battle over land/landscape ownership, an attempt to secure the identity of the place and stabilise its meaning[40] as separate from capital. As Bell puts it, 'seeing land as landscape is a bit of a power trip, a mental taking possession of all one sees – something that feels right to the socially powerful'.[41]

In sharp contrast to the moneyed way of seeing the land in and around Childerley, Audrey and Ted Spencer, two working-class Childerleyans, took a very different approach to the whole idea of 'views'. When having tea with Audrey, Bell asked her about a hedge at the back of their tied cottage. He discovered that though to his (moneyed) mind the cottage should have a magnificent view, they had planted the hedge across the end of their garden because of the wind. They preferred to sit in their garden than to look at the fields. Another working-class man took great care to observe the village and its surrounding land in detail when he arrived, in order to know it, to get a sense of place.[42] Hence, Bell suggests that what ordinary Childerleyans 'see around the village is still very important to them. But instead of putting mental pictures around village views, villagers like Ted Spencer (who has lived in Childerley since he was nine) speak of village places more as where things have happened – as sites of story and memory'.[43]

Massey identifies a continued 'tendency to identify "places" as necessarily sites of nostalgia, of the opting-out from Progress and History', which she believes, is related to a specific conceptualisation of 'place' as 'bounded'. Certainly the moneyed understanding of Childerley fits in with this understanding of place 'as in various ways a site of authenticity, as singular, fixed and unproblematic in its identity' which relies on seeing space as itself something that is fixed and immutable, separate to time which is about change. But, the narrativisation of place undertaken by ordinary villagers, in which every place is subject to a constant re-writing based on experience seems closer to her preferred model of space as space–time, 'formed out of social interrelations at all scales'. In this instance place becomes 'a particular moment in those networks of social relations and understandings', which relationships may extend beyond the bounds of the place itself to encompass the wider social relations of the world:[44]

> Such a view of place challenges any possibility of claims to internal histories or to timeless identities... The particularity of any place is,

in these terms, constructed not by placing boundaries around it and defining its identity through counter-position to the other which lies beyond, but precisely (in part) through the specificity of the mix of links and interconnections *to* that 'beyond'.[45]

As the commercial material might suggest, moneyed incomers seem to value places like Childerley for the sense of isolation that the land in and around the village confers. They look for privacy in the landscape and they don't want to see other houses nearby or to live close to other people. A small place like Childerley therefore offers them the advantages of open space with the services and accessibility they require. This privacy is, of course, increasingly elusive; as more people move into the countryside, so it disappears or, rather, so it becomes more exclusive and pricey. But, isolation is not just a material pleasure or about status, it is also cultural; in a sense, it comes from the Romantics as well as Mammon and it is reflected and reified in the well-to-do's use of their houses. Where the working-class villagers have an 'open-door' policy and go in and out through the back, the wealthy use the front door and expect a phone call before anyone visits.[46] Rather than a celebration of the settled communality found in nineteenth-century representations of rurality, it is privacy, individuality, distance and freedom that seem to have come to the fore.

Many of those who live in the country see this freedom as coming from nature; drawing on pastoral, nature is linked to the countryside and, vested with a special morality, is used to criticise the modern condition. The words 'nature' and 'natural' are loaded, as always, but Bell suggests that those who live in the country,

> find in nature a kind of moral preserve in a landscape of materialist desire, an alternative region of moral thinking I will call the *natural conscience*. They discover this other moral landscape with the help of their pastoral and interest-free conceptions of what nature is. On this more solid, more fertile inner ground they seek to build their house and plant the garden of their identities.[47]

Natural freedom from social constraint is valued above all, but this freedom can alternatively be described as abstracted isolation or alienation, the very thing that so many seek to escape in reaching out to the 'unspoiled' countryside.

COMFORT AND CULTURE COMBINED?

Any study of the rural is made more complex by the variation of experience by region,[48] so that as Alun Howkins observes, we must recognise that the notion of 'one' rural England is in itself problematic. Although we have been accustomed to seeing the United Kingdom as the first 'modern' economy with a unified market and productive system, it is clear from even the most cursory examination that this was simply not so for all of the nineteenth century and much of the twentieth. Rather England was an amalgam of regional economies each with its own often distinctive social and economic structures.[49]

This has been highlighted by regional studies encompassing the economic and social history of rural England, as well as social studies, anthropology and ethnography. Within any one region, Anthony Cohen has argued, a degree of cultural 'localism' can emerge, which often overrides the supposedly homogenous and overarching conceptions of British culture peddled in the media.[50] Moreover, Hugh Kearney has noted, what often appears 'national' can, on closer inspection at the level of the local, fragment into distinctive regional cultures, 'with their own perceptions of the past, of social status ... of religion' and so on.[51] In some instances such regionality has been reinforced by policy making and regional studies consequently came into much sharper focus when changing levels of unemployment and so called 'uneven development' came under scrutiny during the 1970s and 1980s. Massey therefore argues that social geographers and politicians set 'individual spaces (in this case the regions) within the larger spaces of capitalism' at the time and goes on to note that this 'involved introducing the notion of power relations between regions (through spatial structures, or spatial divisions of labour)'.[52]

During the 1960s and 1970s, regionalism therefore fed into the spatial reorganisation of the relations of production, yet, Massey observes, there still remained cross-cutting issues such as British economic decline, in part dependent on political allegiances, which brought all regions together. In this way regionality should be understood as a social and cultural construct which relates not just to literal geographic space, but also economic space and the relations of production.[53] Massey goes on to argue that the 'geography of social structure is a geography of class *relations*, not just a map of social classes; just as the geography of the economy should be a map of *economic relations stretched over space*, and not just, for instance, a map of different types of jobs' (emphasis in original).[54]

In addition, many of these relationships, the connections made between dominant British culture and the countryside have been understood in such a way as to re-create a singularly white, male, middle-class story of rural life. Hence Philo states:

> There remains a danger of portraying British rural people ... as all being 'Mr Averages', as being men in employment, earning enough to

live, white and probably English, straight and somehow without sexuality, able in body and sound in mind, and devoid of any other quirks of (say) religious belief or political affiliation.[55]

In fact, we still know very little about many women's experiences of or reasons for moving to the country. As Annie Hughes[56] argues, though rural sociologists and feminists have begun to trace the experiences of those women involved in farming, be they farmers' wives, farmers themselves or farm labourers, those of women outside of agricultural production have largely been neglected. She therefore looks at women's domestic experiences and the construction of women's domestic identities within the category 'rural'.[57] Hughes, like Williams, treats rurality as a social construct that is itself dynamic and unstable, and sees the rural as a category that has significance in everyday life, constructed in and through culturally and spatially specific social practices. She therefore makes the point that,

> the multiple meanings attaching to rural areas must be uncovered if contemporary rural experiences are to be fully understood and explained. Rurality is culturally defined and, as a result, the social, economic and cultural meanings inferred in relation to, and embedded in, rural places need to be addressed if we are to understand how these discourses inform contemporary experience.[58]

In other words, like Bell, she argues that we ought to 'read' the significance of the rural, its images and spaces, for different people at different times in order to understand what it means for them and how they put it to use. Rural women may take on board elements of the dominant construct 'domestic woman', but they may also contest it. Equally, they may adhere to and/or contest dominant constructions of rurality. Rural women construct their identities from their experiences of the rural and these experiences are diverse.

In her study of Ditton and Llangeley, two small villages on the Welsh border,[59] Hughes found that rural women's lifestyles had changed over the last ten to fifteen years. For a start, more women were taking paid work. However, the 'general attitude prevailing was that it was a woman's duty to stay at home with her children . . . [and this] was felt by both younger and older women, by incomers and locals, by the well off and less well off'.[60] Physical barriers to paid work (which are greater in the country than in the city, viz. shortages of public transport and formal childcare facilities, plus a lack of employment), the family's expectations, personal motivation and confidence were all important factors. But many, especially younger women, also felt that they had to conform in order to be accepted. Hence, one woman said: 'You have to work hard to prove yourself to feel you belong. There is a lot of pressure, whereas in the city . . . you don't have to make such an effort. You have to conform to their expectations or they will gossip . . . about you'.[61] Hughes therefore observes that a rejection of traditional modes of femininity is readily identifiable in a small rural community, while women's lives are constrained by the physical characteristics, social attitudes and moral order of that rural community. Though the rural community is, in her view, changing so that the women in the villages she studied have begun to take on a less family-oriented lifestyle, she points out that this change is contested. This might seem to support the oft-stated point that small, especially, rural communities are more restrictive than large urban conurbations, and that spatial control is easier to maintain 'through the power of convention or symbolism' in villages than cities. Interestingly, though Childerley is a bit bigger, Bell similarly noted that most women who took paid work only did so part-time and though some younger women did hold professional jobs, these were talked about critically by other women, as were young professional couples who were not married. 'As a resident described one such couple . . . "They're, shall we say, 'partners'. And that's not the village way."'[62] However, what is equally significant here is that the limits placed on women who want to work are the limits that other women have outlined for them.[63]

The moral order of the village, Hughes suggests, placed women within their homes and the local community and those women who took paid work put their domestic duties first, and thereby maintained that order. However, it was only the well-to-do, who never took paid work, who really stayed at home as expected. The retired farmwomen in the two villages Hughes studied, like the younger incomers, used to adopt a traditional, domestic role, but they saw this as a necessity. Their housework included dairying and making bread, not just washing – without washing machines or electricity. Any paid work was part-time or casual, close to home and followed on from their domestic duties. A negotiation therefore took place that revolved around domesticity, the village moral order, womanhood and material need. Women who had to work maintained their respectability by working their way through a complex set of interlocking expectations. The older women Hughes interviewed also gained self-worth – by taking pride in and gaining a sense of fulfilment from – the achievement of unpaid domestic tasks.[64]

Domesticity was and still is held in high regard by women in Ditton and Llangeley. To be a countrywoman, in the view of the incomers, you have to be a good housewife too. Rose, an incomer of a few months, commented: 'Some of these country ladies, I just do not know how they do it... One particular lady, she cooks, and if there is something going on in the village she will pull her weight and she will bake her few cakes and she will, you know, always do her bit to help. She is a wonderful cook, a real countrywoman.'[65] Mary, an incomer of two years, observed:

> Even though most of them [rural women] work they are very talented ... They are marvellous cooks and I have learned a lot from them, it amazes me... I don't know too many that don't work even if it is only the odd thing... but they bake a lot and they knit and they do tapestry... they are very talented... I don't think they [rural women] have changed as much as in the town. Take Catherine... I can't see her changing. She is a very solid good woman... she is always baking.[66]

Hughes notes the stress on the skill of housework in these quotes, how this is celebrated, 'even though [they] work'. She comments that housework is seen as something that is praiseworthy and provides the women with self-worth; it is not something that is experienced as oppression.[67] It is also noticeable that the nineteenth-century conceptualisation of housework as the effort of creating order out of chaos is reduced here to baking and creative work, suggesting that this focus is more symbolic than actual, in which we see the elevation of housework to domestic ritual. As Romines notes, the vision of domesticity as connection/communication is something valued by many women. Quoting Bettina Aptheker, she refers to the 'dangers and the promise of' seeing this as a way in which 'the daily and the domestic voices that speak to and through all of us' might be written:

> Sometimes it produces in women an inability to focus anywhere but on their own house, their own culture, their own problems in ways that divide women from each other. Yet the dream of connection, the need for ritual and beauty, the drive to nurture the human spirit continually rekindle these patterns of resistance in women's everyday lives.[68]

Domesticity, Romines argues, ought to be interrogated and re-valued; while avoiding essentialism, 'women's traditional lives are worth thinking about, worth writing about, worth reading... housekeeping may be one of our common human languages'.[69] However, as Hughes says, what is also interesting in these quotes is the way in which the 'rural women' are referred to in the third person. The incomers do not include themselves in this understanding of country life. Hughes comments that this occurs in many of her interviews with the women of the village. The 'rural women' are 'them' not 'us'.[70] Clearly, taking the model of the countrywoman who always does her bit, participation in village events is valued as a communal, not simply a domestic activity and in part this might be because it enables the newcomer to feel that they belong.[71] An uneasiness therefore remains that they are really outsiders and by using the third person, they are accepting the greater legitimacy of these women's claims to be countrywomen, as compared to themselves.

In Childerley, Bell found that simply living in a village does not necessarily mean that you are accepted as a 'real country' person. There were four main criteria in the village he studied: localism and ruralism, (both based on the lived experience of rural place), communalism (participation in village life) and what he calls '*countryism*', (knowledge of rural 'rules' and ways). This last might include knowledge of farming, but also local knowledge, pet care, botany, riding, walking, country manners, ways, dress and food – cooking and eating 'rural' dishes like jugged hare. The formation of rural identity was about class and power, however, not just geographic place or the borders of rural space. The working-class villagers stressed the importance of localism and had a higher standard of ruralism than the better off. The moneyed, on the other hand, stressed the effort that is put into remodelling houses, skills like riding, and participation in local events and drives to tidy up the village. Distinct versions of rural identity therefore emerge, often set against city life, but also based on criteria that sought to exclude or include those who lived in the village based on money and the manipulation of its space. Talking about country identity becomes a way of talking about class and class conflict. Long-standing 'ordinary' residents contested the right of wealthy newcomers to claim they were 'countrymen'. But, Bell argues, it is also about defining the self in such a way as to avoid the embarrassment of conflict and to gain a sense of pride, status and authority when this would otherwise be unavailable. The polite avoidance of the word 'class', the use of phrases like 'countrywomen', reveals the social positioning of those who are talking, but they also permit a more positive and deferential world-view of the poor by the rich. The claim to a rural identity is always contested because being a real country person confers power. 'The implications of being a country person, power and identity are linked.'[72]

What we see in the passages quoted by Hughes is that 'real countrywomen' are also perceived to be older, as having come from the country and as women who would never buy convenience foods. Though at times they are figured as long gone they also become the living ideal against which the incomers measure themselves and several women incomers said that they moved to the country in order to be more 'homely'. In other words, a direct link is drawn between domesticity and the rural as a lifestyle;[73] the domestic community is still figured as the ideal, but this is aspirational for them, something that is sought out by moving to the village. The countrywoman is equated with the country home and the countryside, each of which contains values that are supposedly lost in the city and may even be ebbing away in the country. Regret is therefore being used to rescue those values that are supposed to be dead or are constantly slipping away, in which case nostalgia for what this older generation have done and still achieve becomes a sign of the moral order that ought to be current. Nostalgia can authenticate a golden age within which women remain in their traditional place; a 'rhetorical practice . . . the battleground is representation itself'.[74] But, the countryside is also being feminised, domesticated. Most of the incomers, Hughes found, had moved to the village to get away from what they saw as the pressures of modern life. Some sought an 'authentic rural lifestyle' and this 'authenticity' included getting back to the domestic[75] almost as a kind of secular salvation.

Though the home is no longer described in terms of religious sanctity, the language of 'peace and salvation' maintain some currency as a form of secular morality within the domestic idyll. Davidoff et al. argue that domesticity as daily round and weekly ritual emphasises the cyclical and timeless quality of family life which, in the nineteenth century, was set against the linear progress and instability of commerce, as embodied in city life. These qualities were seen to be an essential, natural part of family life, as compared to the unnaturalness of industry and the family was though of as entirely natural; the natural setting for the family was therefore the country.[76] This appears to have maintained its significance for many late twentieth-century incomers. Homeliness was not always the prime, or indeed the only, motive for moving, nor did all manage to fully reify their domestic idyll, but more and more people, Hughes suggests, seem to be moving into the country to enjoy what they see as this 'authentic' country life. As Lizzy, a woman who had moved to Llangeley thirteen years before said:

> I bake my own bread . . . I enjoy baking and I do those sorts of cookery things. I make my own puff pastry and jams and pickles . . . I go shopping for what I call real things. I don't usually get a lot of frozen precooked things, we used to make our own sausages and things like that . . . Still, sometimes I am envious of people that pop into Iceland . . . and stock up their freezers . . . whatever I cook I start from scratch *but that is what we came for* [emphasis added].[77]

Part of the dream of country life, she thinks, is to get back to nature and be more home-centred; this is more 'real' than shopping. City life is equated with paid work, commerce – in the form of Iceland – and the pressures of a career, and many of the women stated that they wanted to get away from this. One woman, Pauline, said she wanted to spend more time with her family; though she did not want to spend all day doing housework, she still wanted to be more 'homely'. Her husband, meanwhile, kept his job and commuted. For Pauline, being at home with her family was part of getting back to nature; giving up work and staying where they were would not have 'been the same'. In the city, she felt there were more pressures on her to maintain a career – the city, though not as 'real', has its own pressures to conform. Lizzy thought that 'urban-minded' women would not want to move to a village, because they would want to fill their freezers with ready-meals, and that is different to the way things are done in the country. In other words, she thinks 'urban-minded' women are just not home-centred. Jenny, another incomer, thought rural life attracted only certain kinds of women: those who were married with families. If you were a young career woman, she assumed, you would not fit in, nor would you want to.[78]

This contrast between the 'urban-minded' woman and the countrywoman, though less explicitly pejorative, is uncannily similar to the late-eighteenth/early-nineteenth century opposition between 'women of the town', who engaged in the promiscuous life of tavern and street, with 'pure country girls', who had never experienced the temptations of sin.[79] Indeed, the number of moneyed women who stay home with their families is not so much to do with lack of opportunity for work, or even income, as attitude; they are there because they do not want to work. All those who stated that they had moved in order to live a more homely life were well off, married and had children.[80] As in the nineteenth century, the nuclear family becomes its own 'private' community. But, there is a negotiation that has to take place for the incomer between the desirability of peace as privacy, domesticity, freedom, and the urge to live a country life that is both communal and watchful.

Though all seem to share some interest in domesticity, the women interviewed by Hughes perceive and apply it in different ways depending on their age, class and understanding of rurality. Older women, retired farmers' wives, clearly valued the skill and material worth of their work in the domestic sphere. Domesticity was central to their construction of their femininity and sense of self-worth. This and the dominant construction of the rural as idealised site of domesticity influenced younger farmwomen. Dominant discourse has coded the home as woman's natural sphere/place and those who live in the country reinforce this. Those who do not conform in small villages are both seen and judged by other women. Many incomers also linked domesticity and rurality when defining the authentic 'rural woman' and 'rural life'. In the instances quoted by Hughes, Bell would say that the countrywomen are recognised as such because of their exhibition of authentic countryism, in the form of cooking, as valued by the moneyed. 'The vocabulary of rural identity also carries class messages.'[81] They took what they saw in the village as confirming the images of rural life they brought with them. However, the divisions of age and class were also found to wend their way through the linkages being made between rurality, womanhood and identity.

Some women had to take paid work and therefore had to negotiate the dominant moral code of the village in order to maintain their respectability. Given that this was often done out of choice, however, Hughes argues that some women contested and challenged their place in the home even while they fitted their paid work in and around their families. In the end, it is the well-to-do incomers who are best able to make use of the idealised linkages that can be made between femininity, rurality and domesticity. The incomer seeking refuge from modernity (as careerism) in this case is in part reinforcing any apparent 'conservatism' on the part of rural women; it is not simply innate to the small rural community. As Hughes rightly notes, it would be wrong to generalise from her findings to other kinds of village and regions where the local farming practices and demography were very different.[82] However, many of the points she makes are equally applicable to Childerley. What Bell goes on to observe is that in Childerley, women would use a language of nurturing, with reference to nature, when men never do. He comments that the women experienced nature 'as a realm of mothering and nurturing'. 'Do you know what nature is, to me?' one women asked him, 'Nature is caring. It's taking care of others.'[83] The natural and the homely can come together for some to form an identity that allows a criticism of the modern condition, or rather produces a moral language, which remains separate from the material.

A LOVE OF NATURAL SCENERY

Unsurprisingly, the freedom that is supposed to exist in accessing the country is often limited in practice. For a start, not all of those who would like to move to the country can do so. Whereas in 1992, Mintel found that 4.5 million planned to move to the country within five years, 8.5 million wanted to do so but could not, most because they were young, semi-skilled manual workers on a low-income; 54 per cent wanted to leave the towns because they were dirty and noisy, 45 per cent liked open spaces and 22 per cent thought the country would be less stressful. This clearly highlights an ongoing opposition between country and city in terms of perception, and supports the advertising materials' stress on fresh air and space to roam. But, Derounian also outlines the material difficulties thrown up by the influx of incomers for those who were born in the country: the lack of services, employment and scarcity of government aid due to misconceptions about who lives there and in what conditions.[84]

If a bank or building society prefers to lend to a salaried 'white-collar' worker who wants to buy a modern house, the opportunity for an hourly-paid agricultural worker to buy an old cottage is going to be restricted. Restrictions are often placed on older properties, so that only those with the available cash will be able to make a purchase. Opportunity deprivation (limited jobs, recreation, poor health, education, low income) and mobility deprivation (lack of public transport) are also important factors in the degree of choice that a purchaser can exercise. Income, status, stage in life cycle, accessibility (car ownership), employment, quality of life (education, health, services, recreation), housing tenure and conditions are all linked.[85] It is therefore unsurprising that the apparent 'influx' of 'incomers' can lead to explicit and implicit conflict between those who are materially less well off and those who are moneyed. The very language used highlights how this clash might be played out across space as much as across class, and class is not the only relationship that might be written up in this way.

Racial prejudice is partially perpetuated in the country by the complacency of the majority white community and because government bodies do not recognise the need for rural anti-racist or equal opportunities policies.[86] Though the black or Asian figure is highly visible in the rural community, resulting in close observation and sometimes violence, the presence of the black figure in the country is viewed in and of itself as a form of penetration. In this way, because the countryside is a white space, 'race' slips out of sight; racism becomes an urban problem.[87] While whiteness, as Agyeman and Spooner suggest, has rarely been treated as an ethnic signifier – the ethnic Other is defined against whiteness, so that whiteness has been largely taken for granted as the 'norm' – the representational boundaries between ethnicities and places have converged. Viz. 'for white people the "inner city" has become a coded term for the imagined deviance of people of colour', while '"ethnicity" is seen as being "out of place" in the countryside, reflecting the Otherness of people of colour':[88]

> In the white imagination people of colour are confined to towns and cities, representing an urban, 'alien' environment, and the white landscape or rurality is aligned with 'nativeness' and the absence of evil or

danger. The ethnic associations of the countryside are naturalised as an absence intruded upon by people of colour.[89]

Estate agents have been entirely willing to play on this image. Deborah Phillips, cited by Derounian, found some 'estate agents made openly racist remarks even though we were taping them. They tried to discourage black or Asian custom, for example by failing to send out details relating to "higher status" properties.' This research was carried out in Bedford, where estate agents were covering not simply the town, but also the wider area detailed in the adverts quoted above. Estate agents, Phillips continues, aimed to preserve the 'traditional character' (whiteness) of the countryside and 'associated black minorities with the inner city'.[90] Surveys have also shown that at least a third of white people living in the countryside express racist attitudes. However, as with the imposition of domesticity, this racism is as likely to have been brought with the 'incomer', as to be innate to the country. In leaving the city, many white people hope to leave not only the noise and dirt, but also the supposed racial aggressions of city life behind, and they do not want 'blacks' to 'follow' them into the country.[91]

The 'heritage' – national history, countryside and buildings – we are sold is white, while a sense of ownership of that heritage is largely constructed through a language tying the people to the land. Meanwhile, all others are written out of the history. Just as the building of country-house landscapes in eighteenth-century America, based on the European picturesque, involved the direct use of slave labour, so slavery and imperialism played in the financing of country-house landscapes and architecture in England. But, this is a rewriting of history that confronts the perception of the rural and its past as 'quaint' or 'charming' and which sees history as a process, an expression of wider cultural practices.[92] The key factors in preventing black and ethnic minorities from visiting or moving to the countryside, Agyeman believes, are: culture, time, the economics of getting out and about, poor publicity and fear. Many immigrants to Britain fled rural poverty and therefore have no interest in travelling to rural areas. This may change with the second and third generations, who will probably come to see it as a recreational resource through school trips, however, positive action from bodies like the Countryside Commission is also, he believes, required. But, there is a related issue here of seeing all black and ethnic minority groups as the same. Punjabi Sikh emigrants came from middle income groups; they were not attempting to escape poverty, but to improve the standing of their families in the Punjab through land purchase there. Moreover, rural Punjab is not an 'economic backwater'.[93]

The conservatism – be this embodied in gender or ethnicity – of the country, as compared to the city, in many ways seems to have turned into a self-fulfilling prophecy, which belongs to the chain of meaning that links country life to conservation, the native, and the 'natural'. By identifying with 'country people' and the natural interests of the countryside the incomer and the tourist can sidestep some of the more painful moral thinking arising out of social relations and turn to that based on 'self-evident' moral 'truths', free from the contaminating influences of social life.[94] Using the *natural conscience*, the imaginary 'unspoiled' countryside is mobilised to resist actual, material change – usually termed 'progress' – and to fight the invasion of the 'alien'. The language of 'native' and 'alien' can be traced in discussions of wildlife, plants,[95] architecture, family life and bypasses. It is constantly used in the negotiation between material reality and the perception of rural life and through it we can see how images of the country and the city represent social and cultural responses to change. The rhetoric of this 'native', 'natural order', reinforces the construction of country as white, (inner) city as 'black'. The way to tackle this, Agyeman and Spooner argue, is to recognise 'representations of rurality and rural life [as] replete with . . . devices of exclusion and marginalisation by which mainstream 'self' serves to 'other' the positioning of all kinds of people in the socio-spatial relations of different countrysides'.[96] It is not enough to simply set city against country, it is necessary to look at the way they interrelate, and address the construction of whiteness, its relationship to power and exclusion.[97]

The underlying shift, or 'crisis' in Williams' view was an inability to deal with the present – where the country connoted the past and the city connoted the future. Williams saw capitalism as the history of country *and* city, and he called for resistance to it. However, he noted, while Marx and Engels 'denounced what was being done in the tearing progress of capitalism and imperialism' and insisted on struggle, they nonetheless believed that 'the bourgeoisie had "rescued a considerable part of the population from the idiocy of country life"' and celebrated modernism as against uncivilised barbarism. The urban proletariat was then, according to Marxism, destined to create a higher form of society, a society with 'values higher than "rural idiocy" or "barbarism"'. In radical discourse, city (again) equated to progress, country to backwardness.[98]

This way of seeing persists not only in advertising, but also in rural social studies and social geography. Though Massey analyses the 'power geometry' of the networks that criss-cross space–time,[99] even she refers to the country as 'Conservative – politically and socially'.[100] Indeed, many critics still take the assumed division between (conservative) rural and (radical) urban on board without question, albeit in footnoted form, especially with reference to issues associated with sexuality. Heterosexuality and domesticity, it appears, are easier to police in the country. Lesbian women, it seems, feel the need to leave the country for the city in order to express/explore their sexuality. Sue Golding and Elizabeth Wilson for instance have therefore 'celebrated the possibilities ... of life in the big city as opposed to that of the small "community"'.[101]

Massey likewise associates 'going out to work' with the difficulty of 'keeping track of women in the city'. She argues that 'metropolitan life itself seemed to throw up ... a threat to patriarchal control'.[102] Like the women Hughes has interviewed, Massey creates an equation which links the rural with 'home' and the urban with 'going out'; i.e. the country with the supposedly limiting domestic sphere and the city with the apparently more radical public sphere. On the whole, feminist social geographers like Massey offer us a useful analysis of space, in relation to and as one with time, and of spaces/places as reflecting and affecting gender relations. But, even they can be tripped up by the particularly powerful dualism between country and city, in which the cottage and the garden act as important, often idealised, symbols of spatial control, as opposed to the dangerous freedoms of the urban locale, and the urge to see the repetitions of women's domestic life as implicitly less valuable than more directed (masculine) exploits.

As Jonathan Murdoch and Andy C. Pratt observe, academic writing on the rural therefore often perpetuates images of harmony, consensus, timelessness, by presenting the rural as a social space that is homogenous:

> One which seems in many ways to exist in some timeless zone where old-fashioned virtues and their associated forms of life still linger. And while in the past thirty years or so a more critical approach to the countryside has been evident ... even these accounts have sometimes thrown up new versions of the same old rural myths.[103]

The maintenance of this boundary leads to generalisations about 'rural' and 'urban' experience, it perpetuates a way of seeing which refuses to recognise the fluid and cross-cutting relationships, the deep geographies, of class, race and gender. The myth of the thatched cottage, within which the rural is sold as England's heritage, a 'peaceful' 'pure' safe space, itself helps perpetuate this way of seeing. As Tony Rivers argues:

> Pre-Renaissance England is the period to which the English constantly return. It is the authentic 'olden times' re-remembered in the elaborate rural constructions of the Gothick revivalists and the Victorians. It is also recalled in ersatz medieval banquets during which late twentieth

century clerical workers throw chicken bones over their shoulders in a belated contribution to the enduring English mulch. This remembrance of communality is of course a dream of a Merrie England that never quite was. We constantly perfect the past.[104]

Meanwhile, 'the Western demand for the "mythical uncontaminated space" of an authentic "native" culture perpetuates the imperial gesture', as the West turns to its Others to find authenticity.[105]

HODGE AND A COLLECTION OF PICTURES

In 'The Royal Academy and the Labourer', published in *The Labourers' Union Chronicle*, 28 June 1873, a leading question is asked on behalf of the reader: 'What has a collection of pictures to do with Hodge, or Hodge with a collection of pictures?'[106] Our guide, as the author turns out to be, quickly assures us that the answer will become clear and that we will not be bored because, 'we are no critics; we have not the smallest intention of talking about the depth and breadth of colouring, about the effects of light and shade'. A tour then proceeds round the Royal Academy's latest exhibition, with particular attention being paid to the cottages and other country scenes hanging on its walls. Room by room, the rhetorical observations and impressions of the author, and comments from bystanders, are recorded for us in conversational style while 'image' is contrasted with 'reality'.

In the first room there is 'a hovel', which is supposed to stand 'near Aldborough, in Suffolk': 'Very true to nature we thought it – a tumble down old place, sure enough; but what on earth can possess people to buy a picture like that? Surely all the world and especially his wife, must know that such a house cannot shelter anything but misery.' The author hopes that the buyer will purchase it for this reason, 'that he may be constantly reminded of the miserable holes in which poor folks have to hide their heads'. Overall:

> There are several pictures of English scenery which we liked very much, only every one of them is spoilt in our judgement by the insertion of a cottage. Perhaps, as a sweet-looking, gushing creature in our hearing, observed of a cottage in a picture by Cotman, called 'summer noon,' 'It's cleverly painted!' But so the cottage may have been; we have seen some medical pictures of horrid deformities, and sores and sears, which were very cleverly painted, but for all that we did not care to look at them. In the same way we cannot bear to look at these cottages; they are exactly like the realities, but to us they are most painful likenesses, because they are exactly like. Does that young lady so elegantly dressed know what she is speaking about when she exclaims, 'What a pretty

little cottage! How delightful to live in that charming place! So picturesque! Look at the mossy thatch, and the dear little windows, and the smoke curling up from the chimney!' It sounds pretty; but we who know that mossy thatch means old thatch with a good many holes in it; that little windows mean a stifling atmosphere; that a little cottage means four little rooms at most, and from two to ten people living in them; – we who have entered into these hovels and seen how destitute they are, for the most part of those three requisites to comfort – a porch, a tank, and a well; – we who feel the innumerable drafts [sic] which compel the smoke to go up the chimney, we turn from these pictures with a saddened heart as we think of the wretched inhabitants, of whom it has been said, that their greatest misfortune is that they don't enough feel their wretchedness.

Finally, our guide asks, how much longer will it be before these 'signs of misery are swept from the land?' And parts with us, 'sincerely hoping that another year we may see some comfortable cottages'.[107] According to its critics, the price of buying what the cottage represents can be high. The National Agricultural Labourers' Union (NALU) wanted to show that there was a moral cost in obtaining a picturesque scene; in their view, both comfort *and* beauty were required if the cottage was going to embody delight.

Unsurprisingly, the psychic space of and meanings suggested by the cottage vary according to the (class/sex) position of its observer. For some, the thatched cottage is always a 'hovel', for others, like Huish and Allingham, it must always contain 'Appiness'. This is not just a matter of interior vs. exterior, or of the 'real' vs. the mediated. The cottage, like other living spaces, can after all be sanctuary and prison, the site of domestic control and the location of squalor; it can contain both pleasant memories and ghosts at one and the same time, because the ideal and imperfect home are one and the same place.[108] Domestic/living space is a fluid manifestation and aspect of dynamic, lived social relations. Individual homes can house a variety of relationships, individuals and identities. Novelists have expressed this through the sudden change that common objects undergo during moments of emotional crisis; the familiar suddenly becomes the unfamiliar and the homely becomes uncanny. The materials that go to make up living space – walls, doors, gardens, windows, furniture, ornaments, hearth – can represent altered states of mind.[109] And, as Lawrence says, 'the relationship between habitat and resident is dynamic or changeable and it includes factors which may remain unresolved over a relatively long period of time . . . a building can have many meanings at a specific time, and/or through its history'.[110] The cottage – both real and mediated

– was (and is) a space that could be simultaneously loathsome and delightful.

Likewise, the meanings vested in any visual representation of the cottage, like those of the cottage itself, are inherently unstable because they depended on different, sometimes contested, ways of seeing. Hence, the NALU article recognised that 'gushing young creatures' would look at the art it decried with quite a different eye. This article, however, is not simply about class, it is also about the way in which city sees country. This is equally captured in the written text of Allingham's biography, which admits that the owner of the freshly built brick cottages she detested would probably see them as superior to the old buildings she had painted. The cottage, like other places, is 'always already hybrid',[111] but it also a marker for the difference that is supposed to exist between what we categorise as urban and what is decreed rural. In English, the word 'country' is derived from *contrada/contrate* (Latin), meaning 'that which lies opposite'. This despite the fact that it is in the French language that the word for cottage, *la chaumière* (from *chaumage*, a clearing of stubble), is explicitly linked to the word for thatch, *chaume*. And it is in England that the thatched cottage is sold to us as ideal 'living space'[112] through the enchained devices, images and phrases of the Beau Ideal that still go to make up the myth we buy to escape the city.

NOTES

1. H. Muthesius, *The English House*, Sharp, D. (ed.), Seligman, J. (trans.), (London, 1904), pp. 7–11.
2. L. Davidoff, J. L'Esperance and H. Newby, 'Landscape with figures: home and community in English society' in Mitchell, J. and Oakley, A. (eds), *The Rights and Wrongs of Women* (Harmondsworth, 1986) p. 163.
3. J. Glancey, 'Visions of Albion' in the *Weekend Guardian*, (27 March 1999), p. 45.
4. R. Williams, *The Country and the City* (London, [1972] 1985), p. 296.
5. Williams, *The Country and the City*, pp. 288–91.
6. P. Oliver, *English Cottages and Small Farmhouses: a study of vernacular shelter* (London, 1975), p. 5 – note the word 'distort' here, the commodification of the cottage for Oliver is a corruption.
7. Oliver, *English Cottages*, p. 5.
8. Wedgwood advert for 'Threshing' by Michael Herring, ref. BSD1234, (c.1996).
9. Wedgwood advert for 'Hay-making' by Michael Herring, ref. HUL 12345, (c.1996).
10. D. Massey, *Space, Place and Gender* (Cambridge, 1994), p. 180.
11. Williams, *The Country and the City*, pp. 10–11.
12. Williams, *The Country and the City*, p. 10.
13. Williams, *The Country and the City*, p. 12.
14. Williams, *The Country and the City*, pp. 9–12, 289–91.

15 Williams, *The Country and the City*, p. 291.
16 'Property Now', (25 May 1995), Leader.
17 Williams, *The Country and the City*, p. 297.
18 *The Guardian*, (7 January 1995), p. 3.
19 Mary Douglas, *Purity and Danger*, (1966), quoted in Nead, L. *The Female Nude: art, obscenity, and sexuality* (London, 1992), p. 5.
20 Country Holidays advert, ref. GA193, c.1997.
21 See Chapter 1.
22 Country Holidays advert, ref. GA193, c.1997.
23 Charm, (F.-L.) M.E. *charme*, sb. – O.F. *charme*, an enchantment – L. *carmen*, a song, enchantment, the use of magic/occult powers.
24 Character, (L.-Gk.) L. *character*, an engraved or stamped mark, to furrow, scratch, engrave. The cottage is given character through the process of decay.
25 Williams, *The Country and the City*, p. 298.
26 Williams, *The Country and the City*, p. 298.
27 Massey, *Space, Place and Gender*, p. 4.
28 S. Daniels, *Fields of Vision: landscape imagery and national identity in England and the United States* (Cambridge, 1993), p. 8.
29 See P. Cloke and J. Little, 'Introduction: other countrysides?' in Cloke, P. and Little, J. (eds), *Contested Countryside Cultures: otherness, marginalisation and rurality* (London and New York, 1997), p. 1.
30 Daniels, *Fields of Vision*, p. 8.
31 Massey, *Space, Place and Gender*, pp. 179–80, 5.
32 A. Hughes, 'Rurality and "Cultures of womanhood": domestic identities and moral order in village life' in Cloke and Little, *Contested Countryside Cultures*, p. 124.
33 Glancey, 'Visions of Albion', pp. 44–5.
34 Three of the most popular titles are: T. Evans and C. L. Green, *English Cottages* (London, 1982); A. Clayton-Payne, *Victorian Cottages* (London, 1993); P. Drury, *The Cottages of Britain: a heritage of country life* (London, 1997).
35 Cited in S. Brand, *How Buildings Learn: what happens after they're built* (London, 1997), p. 94.
36 M. M. Bell, *Childerley: nature and morality in a country village* (Chicago and London, 1994), pp. 166–8.
37 Bell, *Childerley*, p. 168.
38 Bell, *Childerley*, pp. 168–9, 170–2.
39 H. Prince, 'Art and agrarian change, 1710–1815' in Cosgrove, D. and Daniels, S. (eds), *The Iconography of Landscape* (Cambridge, 1992), p. 107.
40 Massey, *Space, Place and Gender*, pp. 4–5.
41 Bell, *Childerley*, p. 172.
42 Bell, *Childerley*, pp. 168–70.
43 Bell, *Childerley*, p. 170.
44 Massey, *Space, Place and Gender*, p. 5.
45 Massey, *Space, Place and Gender*, p. 5.
46 Bell, *Childerley*, pp. 52, 66–8, 173–4.
47 Bell, *Childerley*, pp. 137–8.
48 See C. H. Lee, *The British Economy Since 1700: a macroeconomic perspective* (Cambridge, 1986).
49 A. Howkins, *Reshaping Rural England: a social history 1850–1925* (London, 1991) p. 1.
50 A. Cohen, *Belonging: identity and social organisation in British rural cultures* (Manchester, 1982).

51 H. Kearney, *The British Isles: a history of four nations* (Cambridge, 1989), p. 7.
52 Massey, *Space, Place and Gender*, p. 20.
53 Massey, *Space, Place and Gender*, pp. 19–22.
54 Massey, *Space, Place and Gender*, p. 22.
55 C. Philo, 'Neglected rural geographies', *Journal of Rural Studies*, 1992, Vol. 8, No. 3, p. 200. Philo is cited and discussed extensively in Cloke and Little, *Contested Countryside Cultures*.
56 Hughes' study focuses on what Raymond Williams has called the 'border country'. In fact, in his novel, *Border Country*, Raymond Williams links together the experiences of class, childhood, place and social mobility, as he notes in *The Country and the City* (pp. 298–9), that are pertinent in any discussion of identity, regionality and rurality.
57 Hughes, 'Rurality and "cultures of womanhood"' pp. 123–4, 135–6.
58 Hughes, 'Rurality and "cultures of womanhood"', p. 125.
59 Both villages had experienced considerable in-migration of, mostly, retired English couples during the 1980s and 1990s.
60 Hughes, 'Rurality and "cultures of womanhood"', p. 130.
61 Hughes, 'Rurality and "cultures of womanhood"', p. 131.
62 Bell, *Childerley*, p. 213.
63 Massey, *Space, Place and Gender*, p. 180.
64 Hughes, 'Rurality and "cultures of womanhood"', pp. 127–9.
65 Hughes, 'Rurality and "cultures of womanhood"', p. 132.
66 Hughes, 'Rurality and "cultures of womanhood"', p. 132.
67 Hughes, 'Rurality and "cultures of womanhood"', p. 132.
68 A. Romines, *The Home Plot: women writing and domestic ritual* (Amherst, 1992), p. 294.
69 Romines, *The Home Plot*, pp. 292–6.
70 Hughes, 'Rurality and "cultures of womanhood"', pp. 131–2.
71 J. G. Derounian, *Another Country: real life beyond Rose Cottage* (London, 1993), p. 13.
72 Bell, *Childerley*, pp. 101–14. Localism: having lived in the village for 'a substantial portion of his or her life'. Ruralism: number of years someone has lived in rural areas and holding a rural job, e.g. farmer or labourer. Communalism: participation in communal activities, doing things that demonstrate a commitment to the community, e.g. church-going, sitting on parish council, belonging to darts team or Women's Institute, using village shop and pubs, visiting neighbours.
73 Hughes, 'Rurality and "cultures of womanhood"', pp. 130–2.
74 J. Doane and D. Hodges, *Nostalgia and Sexual Difference: the resistance to contemporary feminism* (London, 1987), p. 3.
75 Hughes, 'Rurality and "cultures of womanhood"', p. 132.
76 Davidoff et al., 'Landscape', pp. 155–6.
77 Hughes, 'Rurality and "cultures of womanhood"', p. 133.
78 Hughes, 'Rurality and "cultures of womanhood"', pp. 133–4.
79 Davidoff et al., 'Landscape', p. 158.
80 Hughes, 'Rurality and "cultures of womanhood"', p. 134.
81 Bell, *Childerley*, p. 107.
82 Hughes, 'Rurality and "cultures of womanhood"', pp. 135–6.
83 Bell, *Childerley*, p. 220.
84 Derounian, *Another Country*, p. 39.
85 D. Phillips and A. Williams, *Rural Britain: a social geography* (Oxford, 1984), pp. 101–2.
86 Derounian, *Another Country*, pp. 70–1.

87 J. Agyeman and R. Spooner, 'Ethnicity and the rural environment' in Cloke and Little, *Contested Countryside Cultures*, pp. 202–3, 212.
88 Agyeman and Spooner, 'Ethnicity and the rural environment', p. 199.
89 Agyeman and Spooner, 'Ethnicity and the rural environment', p. 199.
90 Derounian, *Another Country*, p. 70.
91 Derounian, *Another Country*, pp. 70–1.
92 Agyeman and Spooner, 'Ethnicity and the rural environment', pp. 201–2.
93 Derounian, *Another Country*, pp. 67–8; Agyeman and Spooner, 'Ethnicity and the rural environment', pp. 198, 208–11.
94 Cf. Bell, *Childerley*, also cited by Cloke and Little, who argue that rural researchers might similarly engage in this sidestep. Cloke and Little, 'Introduction', p. 10.
95 Agyeman and Spooner, 'Ethnicity and the rural environment', p. 207.
96 Cloke and Little, 'Introduction', p. 1.
97 Agyeman and Spooner, 'Ethnicity and the rural environment', pp. 205–12.
98 Williams, *The Country and the City*, pp. 297–303.
99 J. Murdoch and A. C. Pratt, 'From the power of topography to the topography of power: a discourse on strange ruralities' in Cloke, P. and Little, J. (eds), *Contested Countryside Cultures: otherness, marginalisation and rurality* (London and New York, 1997), p. 62; Massey, *Space, Place and Gender*, pp. 3–4, 164–7, 265.
100 The phrase 'Conservative – politically and socially' is taken from a paper 'A woman's place?' (Massey with Linda McDowell, 1984) that discusses the experiences of women in the Fens in contrast to those in the coal-mining regions of Durham, the cotton factories of the North, and the sweat-shops of London. Massey, *Space, Place and Gender*, p. 200.
101 Massey, *Space, Place and Gender*, p. 11.
102 Massey, *Space, Place and Gender*, p. 180.
103 Murdoch and Pratt, 'Topography', p. 51.
104 T. Rivers, D. Cruickshank, G. Darley and M. Pawley, *The Name of the Room: a history of the British house and home* (London, 1992), p. 15.
105 I. Chambers, *Migrancy, Culture, Identity*, (London and New York, 1994), p. 72.
106 'Hodge' was the generic, familiar name given to the (male) peasant from the mid-nineteenth century.
107 *Labourers' Union Chronicle* (28 June 1873), pp. 2–3 – this was the publication of the National Agricultural Labourers' Union. NB 'John Bull' is the generic familiar name given to Englishmen (yeoman).
108 D. Massey, 'Places and their pasts', *History Workshop Journal*, No. 39, (Spring 1995), p. 185.
109 P. Tristram, *Living Space in Fact and Fiction* (London, 1989), pp. 229–32.
110 R. J. Lawrence, *Housing, Dwellings and Homes: design, theory, research and practice* (Chichester, 1987), p. 51.
111 Massey, 'Places and their pasts', p. 183.
112 Tristram discusses the formation of 'living space' in Tristram, *Living Space*.

◌℞ CONCLUDING REMARKS

It is not unlikely that the meanness, the squalor, and the arid character of much of modern life may ever and anon provoke a yearning for something better, broader and purer; for refreshing fountains of water, for the scent of heather, and even for the clamour of storms. But, on the whole, we see no sign of any general disposition in our contemporaries to leave the flesh-pots of the City and the suburbs for the manners and the splendid melancholy of the desert.
(*Daily News*, 9 July 1869)[1]

Now, if only a publisher was to offer a scratch-and-sniff book of the most beautiful villages in England – the scent of thatch-eave roses on page 26, potpourri on page 94 – we could happily sit in our towns and cities, secure in the knowledge that rural perfection existed somewhere without us having to drive along motorways and new bypasses, past distribution depots, to find them.
(Jonathan Glancey, *The Weekend Guardian*, 27 March 1999)[2]

When we see images of children sitting or standing in the road outside a cottage, and women feeding fowl or even doing a little paid work like glove-making, their presence signifies that that cottage is a 'home'. Even now, that 'home' is supposed to have crystal-clear and utterly fixed boundaries. 'Home', as a concept, relies on a very specific view of space that is static: habitual, apolitical and ahistorical.[3] 'Home' as an ideal belongs to continuity; like 'family' and 'country' it is 'natural' and enduring.[4] In the face of social flux and rapid change, the observer/social actor simply prefers to see permanence,[5] and 'home', we have come to assume, is the one sure link that we have between past and present in a world that otherwise values constant innovation. Yet, homes, Stewart Brand observes, 'are the domains of slowly shifting fantasies and rapidly shifting needs'.[6]

The connection between a nation and its architecture that was supposed to exist in the nineteenth century cannot be overstated. To take Cassell's *The Popular Educator: A complete encyclopaedia of elementary, advanced, and technical education* (c.1881) as an example, architecture as an art was clearly believed to be an expression of individualism and civilisation. While uncivilised peoples were thought to have achieved something in this direction, their buildings could not properly be thought of as formally architectural. 'The word *architecture*', it began,

> is derived from the Greek ... *I command*, and ... *a workman*. This etymology indicates the operatives engaged in the building on the one hand, and the leader or chief, the man of science and practical skill, putting in action all his resources in order to execute his plan on the other ... According, therefore, to the literal meaning of the etymology, mankind must have, at the origin of architecture, possessed a degree of civilisation sufficient for the organisation of different kinds of industrial operations, and acquired a degree of skill in the art, which enabled some men by their experience to be the leaders or directors of others ...
>
> Before arriving at this point, mankind must have overleapt ages. One of the first wants of society was a covering or shelter ... Simple was the art employed in constructions of this kind. Grottoes or caves hollowed square to make them more habitable, and cottages constructed of branches of trees and blocks of stone – such were the primitive constructions in wood and stone which formed the rudiments of architecture ...
>
> Proceeding at first from the high table-lands of Asia ... the early fathers of our race could have but little idea of architecture, or of a well-established system of construction. As wandering and pastoral tribes, like the Hottentots of the present day, they lived in tents or wretched huts, which had no pretensions to architecture. It was not until they became more settled that they sought the means of rendering their buildings more durable, by employing in their construction wood or stone, and bricks baked in the sun.
>
> From the differences in the materials, and from the variety of tastes and feelings, are the varied appearances which the monuments of different nations present, and which constitute their peculiar style of architecture ... The very different character exhibited in local architecture enable us to judge of a country by its monuments, inasmuch as the buildings themselves are the expression of the various wants of the people who constructed them ... In these we see it in its primitive, refined, or degraded state, as civilisation arose, approached to perfection, or decayed.[7]

In the nineteenth century, a nation was its 'monuments'; a nation's architecture, though under the direction of a single educated man of science, was representative of the whole nation. Even lowly 'constructions', because they were built of local materials based on need, were taken to be indicative of both the degree of civilisation and the character of the people.[8]

Architecture, then, because it was treated as having emerged from within the primitive culture of the nation, was assumed to provide (civilised) 'man' with an intimate knowledge of a nation's history and of the people who gave it form. Or, rather, the architecture allowed him to imagine the community from which it had emerged.[9] This suggests a degree of sensitivity to buildings as things that change over time, but predominantly buildings were assumed to be fixed markers of culture and of race. Building as an activity might have a history, but ideologically buildings were treated as the immutable trace of that history. In this way they were used to tell stories, to map out and define places, and as markers they fitted an entirely static, imperial and Eurocentric way of seeing space, a way of seeing which more broadly valued the solidity of stone to the seeming transience of the Hottentots' huts. In this way the cottage homes of England, as examples of vernacular architecture 'Dotting the country near and far', were not just signs of the stability and 'calm content' that the Victorians came to desire, but emblematic of those values seen as innately/naturally English. The cottages we see represented in and through the Beau Ideal had always been there, they would always be there; they, like the values they represented, were timeless and unchanging. The very agedness of the buildings ensured their ideological import in a changing world.[10]

For Massey, all places are 'always already hybrid'.[11] No place has ever had a single rooted identity, every community has always been characterised by diversity – of class, age or sex, for instance – and by the links between it and the rest of the world. In one sense or another, most apparently distinct, bounded communities are 'meeting places' and this has always been the case. There are always multiple routes through any particular 'place' and many favourite haunts within it. Each individual or group therefore has to make up their own conceptual map. But, this hybridity is traditionally denied by a) those who wish to see a place called home as providing 'stability, oneness and security' and b) those who associate the concept of place 'with stasis and nostalgia, and with an enclosed security'.[12] This is exemplified by the Beau Ideal. The mythos of the country cottage celebrated and sought to reify a sense of home as authentic, natural and embedded, and, by the beginning of the twentieth century, the English country cottage had come to be widely admired as a natural 'frame' for its inmates.[13] It was seen to provide them both with a setting in which to live and with an organic support that could shore them up against the rigours of commerce and industry. As a result, 'new' cottages were increasingly being built by architects like M. H. Ballie-Scott for the well-to-do in Surrey.

But, despite the rhetoric, there's nothing special about the country cottage. As a simple domestic or vernacular structure, building and architectural historians have actually found it quite hard to define – they tend to find it easier to say what it is not, than what it is. This despite the fact that it is constantly sought out, bought up, sold and captured by tea cosies and plates, on notelets and greetings cards, in calendars and books. In the late nineteenth century, social mobility was thought to be putting the countryside at risk. Today, the late Victorian period is used to create an image of order, peace and calm.[14] To turn it around, then, the country cottage is only special because of the rhetoric, the fantasies it feeds, the stories we tell about it. Through these, the cottage has gained an incredible capacity to drive those who love 'heritage' into bombastic statements about architectural vandalism, and to incite critics to scathing retorts that the only people who buy cottages get to them 'by Mercedes estate down the M3 or M4, turning off at the A59765 intersection'.[15] The English in their constant search for 'charm' and 'character', in desiring a return to a childish Eden, seem homesick for a past and place that never was.

As Tony Rivers observes:

> There is a sense in which the natural development of English domestic architecture ceased in the sixteenth century. Our nostalgia for the golden age is perhaps prompted by a feeling of incompleteness. The asymmetrical, coincidentally picturesque nature of medieval houses is referred to architecturally again and again. It is in the joke-oak gables of semis, in the love of a steep and sheltering roof, the idyll of any country cottage, in the suburbs and the garden cities, our connection with the earth, all that is rural and ideal in mullioned, wainscotted bowers and flowery doorways and lots of wood – the persisting idea of something sturdy and no-nonsense.[16]

The English love of sticks over bricks continues as the 'big folk' seek to recover the Hobbits' small-scale, communal, pre-industrial relationship with the earth. The (vernacular) cottage, nestled safely within landscape seems constantly at risk, and sits contrasted alongside the 'doll's house' commuter homes Glancey detests. But, as I have argued, in the discussion of what is 'real' vs. what is 'imagined', the Enlightenment division of body vs. mind, Nature vs. Culture is perpetuated.[17] While the sources of renewal draw on the same key signs and sites of Englishness as they did in the 1890s, such as Stonehenge or the Lake District, there are now new kinds of loss. Newspapers, oppositional photographers, artists, all have thrown up new 'pictures of discord'. Where tourist materials envision an England 'at peace with itself' and seek reassurance, other texts have become critical of a self-satisfied 'Little England' in which everything and everyone remains in its/his/her place.

In each instance, as Taylor says, the idea of landscape is used, 'to define ... and establish ... security and [a] sense of belonging and nation'.[18]

The focus today, while often still centred on the picturesque, has come to include a renewed concern with the environment and access to the land; the meeting of landowners – both individual and collective – at the boundaries of their territory.[19] The dream of the cottage is based on the deferential organic hierarchy of pre-consumer, fairy-tale, (once-upon-a-time) days. Model cottages 'consciously created artefacts',[20] were built to embody the dream, while 'the cumulative effect of ... widespread preservation ... is a country that feels solidly rooted in its own history, culture and place'.[21] They mark the boundaries. What often seems to be at risk, therefore, is not so much the countryside or the environment itself, as a 'way of life' as embodied in the vernacular cottage – beautiful, peaceful, community-oriented, 'natural', sustainable. And, it is this defence that can seem unpalatably moneyed; it is certainly political. 'Preservationists might be thought of as tourists-in-place',[22] Brand notes, but, the layering of interrelations and connections between these sites and what lies beyond them means that to try and fix their identity by suggesting that they are in some fashion quintessentially, authentically and always English is effectively fruitless. Any attempt to maintain the fantasy is always based on an expedient need to achieve some form of authority.[23]

Allingham's attempt to preserve individual (vernacular) cottages before they were destroyed, and thereby stabilise a specific representation of place, is therefore best understood as an attempt to define and (re)establish a particular set of social relations valued by the urban middle class. The article from *The Labourers' Union Chronicle*, which challenged her definition of place, testifies to the political implications of her intentions. Thomas Hardy and William Morris experienced a similar conflict of interests when first of all trying to restore old buildings (a process which often destroyed them, as 'misinterpretations' of the English past and favoured forms of architecture were layered onto them), then trying to preserve them, to fix them in time with all their marks, chips, faded wallpaper and wear-and-tear. Tristram argues that this meant buildings came to be seen as living entities,[24] but, the attempt to freeze them in time failed to do exactly that; it failed to grasp that the houses which were preserved would continue to change. This urge to preserve in itself leads Adrian Tinniswood to declare,

> ours is a living village, not a theme park ... And all that the cottagers have done is what cottagers have always done – move with the times, as changing taste dictate and their means allow. It may be sad that

parked cars and power lines dominate the landscape, or ironic that the exposed stonework and stripped pine interiors owe more to myth and magazines than to architectural correctness. But at least the English cottage is alive and well here. And for the cottage to have a future, it *must* adapt. Otherwise it will be relegated to a museum of rural life, an object of curiosity rather than what it should be – a home.[25]

In his conclusion to *The Country and The City* (1985), Williams argued that capitalism has overwritten all our relations, our identities, our communication, and our perception of country and city. Where the city is seen as the embodiment of those alienating social relations over which we have no control, the country is treated as a retreat from capital into subjective isolation or sought-for communal relations.[26] Images and ideas of the country and the city are 'forms of response to a whole social development. This is why, in the end,' he states, 'we must not limit ourselves to their contrast but go on to see their interrelations and through these the real shape of the crisis.'[27] Williams also highlights how, 'Old England, settlement, the rural virtues – all these, in fact, mean different things at different times, and quite different values are being brought into question'.[28] These different ruralities 'express . . . human interests and purposes for which there is no other immediately available vocabulary'.[29]

As Bell observes, there are two kinds of moral thinking, one which is 'socially derived' and painful, and another which looks to 'truths' that fly above social life in order to make comment. Opting to be a 'country' person or claiming to be of the village can allow the critic to find an identity, the confidence to speak out and a way of integrating those social distinctions that cause unease into the motivation and social power to act.[30] There are, as we have seen, dangers in idealising the rural, the natural and the native (what Halfacree calls 'counterurbanisation as nostalgia'); there are also dangers in succumbing to the consuming pleasures of following the trend, the style and aesthetic of counterurbanisation for its own sake (what Halfacree denotes 'counterurbanisation as lifestyle dalliance').[31] These tensions can be seen in a report from *The Big Issue* (July 1999) on 'low-impact living', i.e. the building of ecologically thought-through and sustainable housing in the country. The Hockerton project– requiring 16 hours work a week from each resident – consists of clusters of homes covered in earth so that they cannot be seen from the road (an interesting choice of viewpoint). Each home has its own allotment, non-chemical sewage plant, heat drawn from conservatories at the front and – if they ever get planning permission – the possibility of turbine power. What is holding up that permission is the hostility of other local residents who feel entitled to the clean and open skyline they've bought.[32] However, Halfacree believes, if both postmodern relativism and premodern essentialism can be avoided, then counterurbanisation, might emerge as a critique of contemporary capitalism.[33] 'The major hurdle to overcome is the selective representation of the countryside – the rural idyll – with which the counterurbanisers' hopes and fears are typically enmeshed.'[34]

Soper is equally optimistic. Even 'conservative' conservation projects, she argues, have the ecological benefit of freezing resources in place and thereby preventing further waste of energy and materials, while right-wing neo-monetarists bemoan the break put on 'progress' by preservationists and environmentalists. The difficulty with both industrial 'progress' and environmental conservation, she observes, is that, both 'are inserted within the existing relations of production, and both will reflect the class structure and inequalities that these relations sustain and reproduce'.[35] What is needed Soper argues, is an approach to heritage and environmentalism that is more dialectical. A dialectical approach will reveal that both are politically closer to (green) socialism than neo-monetarism, but that environmentalism is nonetheless 'caught up in the same mythologies about "our" heritage and the "common land" that have developed to sustain the property of those most directly responsible for ecological destruction'. She goes on:

> Even less will it deny the hypocrisy of those whose concern for 'nature' extends no further than the environs of the rural retreat to which they resort at week-ends in order to refresh themselves for the Monday assault upon its resources . . . the love of the countryside by no means confined to those best placed to enjoy it, and the environmental movement includes within its ranks many whose 'backyard' is a strip of urban cement . . . None of this complexity is registered by the simple dismissal of the preservationist impulse as 'elitist' or by treating it as an 'ideological' – and hence in principle dispensable – urge.[36]

Environmentalists must learn to think about human needs and how, 'in preserving the countryside we are preserving the inscription of a very unequal access' to its 'beauty spots', species and resources. Ecocentric critics should, meanwhile, recognise that 'a simplistic anti-human speciesism that treats all human beings as equal "enemies" of nature covers over the social relations responsible for the abuse of nature' while its policies might hit those least to blame the hardest. In dealing with the environment, it is therefore important to recognise that there are a variety of responses to nature, ranging from the aesthetic to the utilitarian. To be truly progressive, eco-politics needs to be scrupulous in considering the validity and implications of 'both the delight in nature and the obligation to the future', and 'the discourses in which they have been promoted'.[37]

As representative of 'nature' it is therefore important to consider what the cottage means. The cottage as a domestic space has come to embody a set of values that link it to the rural and to femininity. In the nineteenth century as Beau Ideal, it reified separate spheres ideology and embodied those values of paternalism and stability sought out by the new middle class as they moved further and further 'away' from 'home'. In the twentieth century, it still embodies domesticity, but embedded in the English village (as the built expression of native Englishness), in the form of vernacular domestic it has come to offer shelter from the aggression and disorder of post-colonialism. In both instances, it has been treated as an exclusive space, and as a sign that has marked the 'boundary' between rural and urban space; indeed, in some instances it has helped re-create the exclusivity of the rural (associated with the communal) in urban space. In the process, it has contributed to the formation of Otherness.

The cottage has, however, also been subject to cross-cutting social relations. The agricultural labourer's home has been subject to architectural alterations resulting from decisions taken at a considerable (metric) distance from it, which have treated it as any other labourer's home. In this way, rural and industrial cottages have been brought closer together. Both have been exposed to the same complex of power relations – incorporating paternalistic and interventionist regulation of housing – based among other things on a regret at the gap in the experience between rich and poor, the economic and productive necessity of having a fit workforce and the emergence of environmentalist medical practices. In this instance, the agricultural labourer's home becomes tied into a network of 'vertical' and 'horizontal' relations that go beyond the local or regional. Similarly, local preservationists have allied with groups in geographically distant regions to take political action by pooling their resources and by building on the experience of others.

By mapping these relationships it is possible to move beyond the rural as having an 'inside' and an 'outside', so that places which share a similar set of experiences are brought closer together.[38] In the sense that the cottage belongs to the matrices that surround the loaded concepts 'Englishness', 'Nature', 'community', 'country', 'domesticity', and that the boundaries between inside and outside are not always as sharp as they seem, the cottage can also, finally, be read as a fluid space. This demands the recognition that there is no single vantage point from which to capture and assess the rural, because the rural 'is no longer one single space, but a multiplicity of social spaces . . . each of them having its own logic, its own institutions, as well as its own specific network of actors'.[39] When we look at the country cottage, then, or the cottage garden, what we are in effect considering is an 'understanding of . . . a particular envelope of space–time'.[40] But, the more we think we know what the cottage is and what it means, the harder it is to catalogue. It is a *mise en abyme*, an ever-regressing image, sometimes desirable, but always unattainable. The very essence of stability, the cottage and its image is a constantly contested sign built on the shifting sands of nostalgia, time, sex, sexuality, gender, class and race.

NOTES

1. The *Daily News* was a radical paper, set up in 1846, which took most of its readership from the middle class. Its nearest rival, the *Morning Chronicle*, was more expensive and in decline by the time that the *News* was set up. *Daily News*, (9 July 1869).
2. J. Glancey, 'Visions of Albion' in the *Weekend Guardian*, (27 March 1999), p. 45.
3. D. Massey, *Space, Place and Gender* (Cambridge, 1994), intro.
4. L. Nead, *Myths of Sexuality: representations of women in Victorian Britain* (Oxford, 1988), p. 40.
5. Massey, *Space, Place and Gender*, p. 3.
6. S. Brand, *How Buildings Learn: what happens after they're built* (London, 1997), p. 10.
7. Cassell, *The Popular Educator: A complete encyclopaedia of elementary, advanced, and technical education* (c.1881), pp. 319–20. Again, this is a text written for those who sought self-improvement, in this case aimed at the upper working and lower middle class.
8. Lefebvre engages in a detailed discussion of the meanings of monuments and monumental space in H. Lefebvre, *The Production of Space*, Nicholson-Smith, D. (trans.), (Oxford, 1991).
9. See B. Anderson, *Imagined Communities: reflections on the origin and spread of nationalism*, (London and New York, [1983] 1991).
10. Brand discusses the cultural value and therefore the price placed on age re buildings in *How Buildings Learn*, p. 10.
11. D. Massey, 'Places and their pasts', *History Workshop Journal*, No. 39 (Spring 1995), p. 183.
12. Massey, *Space, Place and Gender*, pp. 167, 171.
13. Based on Voysey. Voysey was a late nineteenth-century architect who was strongly influenced by the Arts and Crafts movement. He sought to combine traditional materials and techniques with modern design. His principles were: 'Repose, Cheerfulness, Simplicity, Breadth, Warmth, Quietness in a Storm, Economy of Upkeep, Evidence of Protection, Even-ness of Temperature, and making the house a frame for its inmates'. Quoted in J. Marsh, *Back to the Land: the pastoral impulse in Victorian England from 1880 to 1914* (London, Melbourne and New York, 1982), p. 175.
14. J. Taylor, *A Dream of England: landscape, photography and the tourist's imagination* (Manchester, 1994), pp. 5–6, 240–2.
15. Glancey, 'Visions of Albion', p. 45.

16 T. Rivers, D. Cruickshank, G. Darley and M. Pawley, *The Name of the Room: a history of the British house and home* (London, 1992), p. 15.
17 See K. Soper, *What is Nature? Culture, politics and the non-human* (Oxford, 1995) for a discussion of the consequences.
18 Taylor, *A Dream of England*, pp. 5–6, 240–2.
19 Taylor, *A Dream of England*, pp. 276–83.
20 S. M. Gaskell, *Model Housing: from the Great Exhibition to the Festival of Britain* (London and New York, 1987), p. 135.
21 Brand, *How Buildings Learn*, p. 95.
22 Brand, *How Buildings Learn*, p. 94.
23 See Massey, *Space, Place and Gender*.
24 P. Tristram, *Living Space in Fact and Fiction* (London, 1989), pp. 125–9, 143–57.
25 A. Tinniswood, *Life in the English Country Cottage* (London, 1995), p. 209.
26 R. Williams, *The Country and the City* (London, [1972] 1985), pp. 289–306.
27 Williams, *The Country and the City*, pp. 296–7.
28 Williams, *The Country and the City*, p. 12.
29 Williams, *The Country and the City*, p. 291.
30 M. M. Bell, *Childerley: nature and morality in a country village* (Chicago and London, 1994), pp. 85–116.
31 K. Halfacree, 'Contrasting roles for the post-productivist countryside: a postmodern perspective on counterurbanisation' in Cloke, P. and Little, J. (eds), *Contested Countryside Cultures: otherness, marginalisation and rurality* (London and New York, 1997), pp. 84–5.
32 *The Big Issue*, 12–18 July 1999, No. 343, pp. 6–7.
33 Halfacree, 'Contrasting roles', pp. 70–89.
34 Halfacree, 'Contrasting roles', pp. 70–89. What he requires is that counterurbanisers move away from the premodern and towards the postmodern pole, then he believes they and environmental protesters might find that they have something in common; together they might harness a progressive and critical response to modernity.
35 Soper, *What is Nature?*, pp. 203–4.
36 Soper, *What is Nature?*, p. 204.
37 Soper, *What is Nature?*, pp. 208–9.
38 J. Murdoch and A. C. Pratt, 'From the power of topography to the topography of power: a discourse on strange ruralities' in Cloke and Little, *Contested Countryside Cultures*, pp. 61–3.
39 Marc Mormont, quoted by Murdoch and Pratt, 'From the power of topography', p. 57.
40 Massey, *Space, Place and Gender*, pp. 2–4.

SELECT BIBLIOGRAPHY

ARCHIVAL MATERIAL

Material held in the Norwich and Norfolk Records Office, Norwich
Docking Union Association for Promoting and Rewarding Good Conduct and Encouraging Habits of Industry and Frugality Amongst Servants, Labourers, and Cottagers, Minutes
Society of Ministers of the Church of England in Little Latham, Minutes
Loddon and Clavering Board of Guardians, Minutes
Norfolk Agricultural Association, Minutes
Norwich Sick Poor Society, Minutes
St. Peter's Mancroft Ringer's Benefit Society, Minutes
Snettisham Friendly Society, Minutes

PUBLIC DOCUMENTS

British Parliamentary Papers
'Census of Great Britain' **1801**: 1801, 140.VI.813. – 1801–2, 9., 112. VI.VII; **1811**: 1812, 316., 317. XI; **1821**: 1822, 502. XV; **1831**: 1831, 348. XVIII.1; **1851**: 1852–53 [1631]. LXXXV.1., [1632]. LXXXVI.1., [1691-I]. LXXXVIII. pt.I.1., [1691-II]. LXXXVIII. pt.II.1., **1861**: 1862 [3056]. L.1., 1863 [3221]. LIII. pt.I.265., pt.II.1., [3221]. LIII.1.; **1871**: 1873 [C.872]. LXXII. pt.I.1., [C.872-1]. LXXI. pt.II.1.; **1881**: 1883 [C.3797]. LXXX. 583., [C.3722]. LXXX.1.; **1891**: 1893–94 [C.7058]. CVI.1., [C.7222]. CVI. 629.; **1901**: 1905 Cd.2660.CII.1., 1904 Cd.2174.CVIII.1.; **1911**: 1913 Cd. 7018., Cd.7019. LXXVIII.321. LXXIX.1., 1917–18 Cd.8491.XXXV.483.; **1921**: Cmd.1485.XVI.257.
'Report from His Majesty's Commissioners on the administration and practical operation of the Poor Laws' *Parliamentary Papers* (PP) 1834: 44.XXVII; 44.XXVIII; 44.XXIX; 44.XXX; 44.XXXI; 44.XXXII; 44.XXXIII; 44.XXXIV.
'First report of the Factories Inquiry Commission, employment of children in factories' PP 1833: 450.XX; 519.XXI.
'Sixth report of the Children's Employment Commission', 1862, PP 1867: [3796]XVI.
'Reports from Select Committees on the Act for the Regulation of Mills and Factories' PP 1840–41: 203.X.
'Reports from the Royal Commission on labour' PP 1892–94: [C.6708]XXXIV; [C.6708-V]XXXV; [C.6708-II]XXXIV; [C.6894-I]XXXV; [C.6894-III]; [C.6894-V]; [C.6894-XIII]; [C.6894-XXV]XXXVII pt. II; [C.6894-XXIV].
'Reports of Special Assistant Poor Law Commissioners on the employment of women and children in agriculture' PP 1843: [510]XII.
'Reports from the Commissioners on the employment of children, young persons and women in agriculture' PP 1867–70: [4068]XVII; [4068-I]; [4202]XIII; [4202-I]; [C.70]XIII; [C.221]; [C.221-I].

212 Select bibliography

'Reports of the Royal Commission on the depressed state of the agricultural interest' *PP* 1880–82: [C.3309]XIV; [C.3309-I]; [C.3309-II]; [C.2678]XVIII; [C.3375-I]XV; [C.3375-II]; [C.3375-III]; [C.3375-IV]; [C.3375-V]; [C.3375-VI].

'Reports from the Select Committee and others on allotments and small holdings and peasant proprietors with proceedings' *PP* 1888–94: C.358.XVIII; C.313.XII; C.223.XVII; [C.6250]LXXXIII; C.122.LXVIII.

'Reports of the Royal Commissioners on the agricultural depression' *PP* 1894–97: [C.7400]XVI pt. I; [C.7400-II]; [C.7400-II] pt. II; [C.7400-III]XVI pt. III; [C.7981]XVI; [C.8021]XVII; [C.8146]; [C.8540]XV; [C.8541]; [C.8300]; [C.7365]XVI pt. I; [C.7372]; [C.7334]; [C.7374]; [C.7342]; [C.7728]XVI; [C.7691]; [C.7671]; [C.7755]; [C.7623]; [C.7624]; [C.7735]; [C.7842]XVII; [C.7871]; [C.7764]; [C.7915]; [C.7915-I]; [C.7625]; [C.7742]; [C.8125]XVI.

'Sixth report of the Medical Officer of the Privy Council' *PP* 1863, 3416 XXVIII.I.

'Report on wages and earnings of agricultural labourers in the United Kingdom' *PP* 1900, Cd.346 LXXXII. 557.

'Report of wages, earnings and conditions of employment of agricultural labourers in the United Kingdom' *PP* 1905, Cd.2376 XCVII. 335.

'Reports of the Inter-Departmental Committee on physical deterioration' *PP* 1904, Cd.217 XXXII. 1 I; Cd.2210 XXXII. 145 II; Cd.2186 XXXII. 655 III.

'Report on the decline in the agricultural population of Great Britain 1881–1906' *PP* 1906, Cd.3273 XCVI. 583.

'Reports on the wages and conditions of employment in agriculture' *PP* 1919, Cmd.24 IX. 1 I; Cmd.25 IX. 207 II.

COUNTRY BOOKS, ADVICE BOOKS AND LITERATURE

Acland, H. W., *Cottage-wall Prints* (London, 1862).

Acland, H. W., *The Cottage Register; or Forms for Registering the Sanitary Conditions of Villages: for the use of Landowners, Officers of Health, Guardians and Others* (London, 1861).

Allingham, H., *The Cottage Homes of England* (London, 1909).

Andrews, G. H., *Modern Husbandry: a practical and scientific treatise on agriculture illustrating the most approved practices in draining, cultivating and manuring the land; breeding, rearing and fattening stock; and the general management and economy of the farm* (London, 1853).

Anon, *Account of Britton Abbot's Cottage and Garden; and Account of the Produce of a Cottager's Garden in Shropshire: to which is added Jonas Hobson's Advice to his Children: and the Contrast between a Religious and Sinful Life* (London, [written 1797] 1806).

Anon, *Original Poems for Infant Minds*, Vol. I (London, 1836).

Anon, *The Standard Cyclopedia of Modern Agriculture and Rural Economy in 12 Volumes*, London, 1912.

Bacon, R. N., *The Report on the Agriculture of Norfolk, to Which the Prize was Awarded by the Royal Agricultural Society of England* (London, 1844).

Barker, C. M. (ed.), *A Little Book of Old Rhymes* (London, c.1930).

Bourne, G., *Change in the Village* (London, [1912] 1989).

Cobbett, W., *The Poor Man's Friend: a defence of the rights of those who do the work and fight the battles* (London, 1826).

Cobbett, W., *Advice to Young Men and (incidentally) to young women in the middle and higher ranks of life* (London, [1830] 1856).

Cobbett, W., *Rural Rides* (London, [1830] 1957).

Cobbett, W., *Cottage Economy* (Oxford, [1821] 1979).
Combe, A., *The Management of Infancy: physiological and moral, intended chiefly for the use of parents* (London, [c.1840] 1860).
Ditchfield, P. H., *The Charm of the English Village* (London, [1906] 1994).
Fletcher, R. (ed.), *The Biography of a Victorian Village: Richard Cobbold's account of Wortham, Suffolk, 1860* (London, 1977).
Fordham, M., *The English Agricultural Labourer 1300–1925* (London, 1925).
Garnier, R. M., *Annals of the British Peasantry* (London, 1908).
Gilly, W. S., *The Peasantry of the Border: an appeal in their behalf* (Edinburgh, [1842] 1973).
Gough, B., *Kentish Lyrics: sacred, rural and miscellaneous* (London, 1867).
Gough, B., *Songs for British Workmen* (London, 1876).
Gould, S. B., *Old Country Life* (London, 1890).
Green, F. E., *A History of the English Agricultural Labourer 1870–1920* (London, 1927).
Green, F. E., *The Tyranny of the Countryside* (London, 1913).
Gretton, S. M., *Burford Past and Present* (London, [1920] 1946).
Haggard, H. R., *Rural England: being an account of agricultural and social researches carried out in the years 1901–1902* (London, 1902).
Hamilton, G., *Geoff Hamilton's Cottage Gardens* (London, 1995).
Hardy, T., 'The Dorsetshire Labourer', *Longman's Magazine*, Vol. 2 (1883).
Heath, F. G., *Peasant Life in the West of England* (London, 1880).
Heath, F. G., *The English Peasantry* (London, 1874).
Heath, R., *The English Peasant; Studies: historical, local and biographic* (Wakefield, [1893] 1978).
Holdenby, C., *Folk of the Furrow* (London, 1913).
Howitt, W., *The Boy's Country Book* (London, 1880).
Howitt, W., *The Rural Life of England* (Shannon, [1844] 1971).
Hudson, W., *A Shepherd's Life: impressions of the South Wiltshire Downs* (London, 1910).
Hudson, W., *Nature in Downland* (London, [1900] 1925).
Jefferies, J. (ed.), *Field and Hedgerow: being the last essays of Richard Jefferies* (London, [1889] 1948).
Jefferies, R., *Hodge and His Masters* (London, [1880] 1966).
Jefferies, R., *The Toilers of the Field* (London, [1892] 1981).
Jessopp, A., *England's Peasantry and Other Essays* (London, 1914).
Kay, J., *The Peasant Proprietors*, Vol. 1 of the *Social Condition and Education of the People in England and Europe; Shewing the Results of the Primary Schools and of the Division of Landed Property in Foreign Countries* (Shannon, [1850] 1971).
Kearney, H., *The British Isles: a history of four nations* (Cambridge, 1989).
Kebbel, T. E., *The Agricultural Labourer: a Short Summary of his Position, Partly Based on the Report of her Majesty's Commissioners Appointed to Inquire into the Employment of Women and Children in Agriculture, and Republished from the 'Pall Mall Gazette' and the 'Cornhill Magazine'* (London, 1870).
Kingsley, C., *Yeast – A problem* (London, [1847] 1895).
Loudon, J. C., *An Encyclopaedia of Gardening* (London, 1822).
Loudon, J. C., *The Cottager's Manual of Husbandry, Architecture, Domestic Economy, and Gardening* (London, 1840).
Marshall, W., *Review and Abstract of the County Reports to the Board of Agriculture* (London, [1811] 1818).
Marshall, W., *The Rural Economy of Norfolk* (London, 1795).
Masterman, C. F. G., *The Condition of England* (London, [1909] 1910).
Matthews, A. H. H., *Fifty Years of Agricultural Politics, Being the History of the Central Chamber of Agriculture 1865–1915* (London, 1915).

Mitchell, G., *The Skeleton at the Plough, Or the Poor Farm Labourers of the West; with the Autobiography and Reminiscences of George Mitchell, 'One from the Plough'* (London, 1874).
Mitford, M. R., *Our Village: sketches of rural life, character and scenery* (London, [1824–32] 1893).
Muthesius, H., *The English House*, Sharp, D. (ed.), Seligman, J. (trans.), (London, 1904).
Pedder, D. C., *Where Men Decay: a survey of present rural conditions* (London, 1908).
Percy, W. S., *Strolling Through Cottage England* (London, 1936).
Perry, G. W., *The Peasantry of England, an Appeal to the Nobility, Clergy and Gentry on Behalf of the Working Classes, in which the Causes which have Led to their Present Impoverishment and Degraded Condition, and the Means by which it May Best be Permanently Improved are Clearly Pointed out: the whole Drawn from Personal Observation and Patient Research and Illustrated by Numerous Interesting Facts, and Copious Statistical Data* (London, 1846).
Pringle, A., *General View of the Agriculture of the Country of Westmoreland, with Observations for the Means of Improvement, Drawn up for the Consideration of the Board of Agriculture and Internal Improvement* (London, [1793] 1805).
Raymond, W., *English Country Life* (London, 1910).
Rowntree, B. S., and Kendall, M., *How the Labourer Lives: a study of the rural labour problem* (London, 1913).
Smiles, S., *Life and Labour, or characteristics of men of industry, cultures and genius* (London, [1887] 1910).
Somerville, A., *The Whistler at the Plough: Author of Letters 'One Who Has Whistled at the Plough' and Agricultural Customs in Most Parts of England, with Letters from Ireland: Also 'Free Trade and the League': a Biographic History* (Manchester, 1852).
Stephens, H., *The Book of the Farm, Detailing the Labours of the Farmer, Farm-Steward, Ploughman, Shepherd, Hedger, Farm-Labourer, Field-Worker, and Cattle-Man, in Six Divisions* (Edinburgh, [1844] 1891).
Thomas, E., *The South Country* (London, [1909] 1984).
Tuckett, J. D., *A History of the Past and Present State of the Labouring Population; Including the Progress of Agriculture, Manufacture and Commerce* (Shannon, [1846] 1971).
Walker, T. H., *Good Servants, Good Wives and Happy Homes: illustrated by a series of characters and events sketched from actual life* (London, [1862] six edition 1888).
Weaver, L., *The 'Country Life' Book of Cottages* (London, [1913] 1919).
Whitehead, C., *Agricultural Labourers* (London, 1870).
Willmott, R. A., *A Journal of Summer Time in the Country* (fourth edition, London, 1864).
Young, A., *General View of the Agriculture of the County of Hertfordshire, Drawn up for the Consideration of the Board of Agriculture and Internal Improvement* (Newton Abbot, [1804] 1971).
Young, A., *The Farmer's Kalendar* (Wakefield, [1871] 1973).
Yonge, C. M., 'Quack, Quack' (1882), reprinted in Avery G. (ed.), *Village Children* (London, [1846–82] 1967).

DIARIES, BIOGRAPHY, AUTOBIOGRAPHY, AND MEMOIR

Anon., *The Autobiography of one who has Whistled at the Plough* (London, 1848).
Arch, J., *Joseph Arch: the story of his life told by himself*, Countess of Warwick (ed.), (London, 1898).

Ashby, M. K., *Joseph Ashby of Tysoe 1859–1919: a study of English village life* (London, [1961] 1974).
Baldry, G., *The Rabbit Skin Cap: a tale of a Norfolk countryman's youth*, Haggard, L. R. (ed.), (London, [1939] 1950).
Bourne, G., *A Farmer's Life, With a Memoir of the Farmer's Sister* (Firle, [1922] 1979).
Bourne, G., *A Small Boy in the Sixties* (Cambridge, 1927).
Bourne, G., *Lucy Bettesworth* (Firle, [1913] 1978).
Bourne, G., *Memoirs of a Surrey Labourer: a record of the last years of Frederick Bettesworth* (London, 1907).
Bourne, G., *The Bettesworth Book: talks with a Surrey peasant* (London, 1902).
Bourne, G., *William Smith: potter and farmer, 1790–1858* (London, 1919).
Burn, J., *The 'Beggar Boy' An Autobiography: Relating Numerous Trials, Struggles, and Vicissitudes of a Strangely Chequered Life, With Glimpses of English Social, Commercial and Political History, During Eighty Years 1802–1882* (London, 1882).
Burnett, J. (ed.), *Useful Toil: autobiographies of working people from the 1820s to 1920s* (London, 1976).
Burnett, J. (ed.), *Destiny Obscure: autobiographies of childhood, education and family from the 1820s to the 1920s* (Harmondsworth, 1982).
Chamberlain, M., *Fenwomen: a portrait of women in an English village* (London, 1975).
Cole, G. D. H., *William Cobbett* (London, 1925).
Collier, M., *The Woman's Labour; an epistle to Mr Stephen Duck in answer to his late poem called the Thresher's Labour, to which are added the Three Wise Sentences taken from the First Book of Esdras, chapters III and IV* (London, 1739).
Collins, B., *Charles Kingsley: the Lion of Eversley* (London, 1975).
Davies, M. L., (ed.), *Life as We Have Known it, By Co-Operative Working Women* (London, [1931] 1990).
Evans, G., *Ask the Fellows Who Cut the Hay* (London, 1977).
Evans, G., *From the Mouths of Men* (London, 1976).
Evans, G., *The Days That We Have Seen* (London, 1975).
Evans, G., *The Farm and the Village* (London, 1969).
Evans, G., *The Pattern Under the Plough: aspects of the folk-life of East Anglia* (London, 1966).
Evans, G., *Where Beards Wag All: the relevance of the oral tradition* (London, 1970).
Finlayson, G. B. A., *The 7th Earl of Shaftesbury, 1801–1885* (London, 1981).
Fletcher, R., (ed.), *The Biography of a Victorian Village: Ruth Cobbold's account of Wortham, Suffolk 1860* (London, 1977).
Hardy, S., (ed.), *The Diary of a Suffolk Farmer's Wife: a woman of her time* (Basingstoke, 1992).
Harman, T., *Seventy Summers: the story of a farm* (London, 1987).
Hodder, E., *The Life and Work of the 7th Earl of Shaftesbury, KG* (London, 1888).
Huish, M. B. (ed.), *Happy England* (London, 1903).
Jermy, L., *The Memoirs of a Working Woman* (Norwich, 1934).
Jessopp, A., *The Trials of a Country Parson* (London, 1894).
Kightly, C. (ed.), *Country Voices: life and lore in farm and village* (London, 1984).
Langdon, R., *The Life of Roger Langdon: told by himself with additions by his daughter Ellen* (London, 1909).
Luty, M., *A Penniless Globe Trotter* (Accrington, 1937).
Mackerness, E. D., (ed.), *The Journals of George Sturt 1890–1927, in Two Volumes, a selection* (Cambridge, 1967).
Mitchell, G., (ed.), *The Hard Way Up: the autobiography of Hannah Mitchell, suffragette and rebel* (London, 1968).
Penn, M., *Manchester Fourteen Miles* (Firle, [1947] 1979).

Pentecost, E., *A Shepherd's Daughter* (Petworth, 1987).
Reid, R. D., (ed.), *The Diary of Mary Yeoman of Wanstrow, Co. Somerset* (Wells, c.1926).
Rose, W., *Good Neighbours: some recollections of an English village and its people* (Cambridge, 1942).
Silvester, S., *In a World that Has Gone* (Leicester, 1868).
Smith, D., *No Rain in Those Clouds: being an account of my father John Smith's life and farming from 1862 to the present day* (London, 1943).
Smith, I., *A Hired Lass in Westmorland: the story of a country girl at the turn of the century* (Penrith, 1982).
Somerville, A., *The Autobiography of a Working Man, By 'One Who Has Whistled at the Plough'* (London, 1848).
Stickland, I. (ed.), *The Voices of Children 1700–1914* (London, 1973).
Thompson, F., *Lark Rise to Candleford: a trilogy* (Harmondsworth, [1939, 1941, 1943] 1979).
Unwin, C., *The Hungry Forties: life under the bread tax, descriptive letters and other testimonies from contemporary witnesses* (Shannon, [1904] 1971).
Williamson, Mrs., 'The Bondage System', in Anon., *Voices From the Plough* (Hawick, 1869).

SECONDARY SOURCES

Agyeman, J. and Spooner, R., 'Ethnicity and the rural environment' in Cloke, P. and Little, J. (eds), *Contested Countryside Cultures: otherness, marginalisation and rurality* (London and New York, 1997).
Anderson, B., *Imagined Communities: reflections on the origin and spread of nationalism* (London and New York, [1983] 1991).
Banks, S., 'Nineteenth-century scandal or twentieth-century model? A new look at 'open' and 'close' parishes', *Economic History Review*, XLI, I (1988).
Barley, M. W., *The English Farmhouse and Cottage* (London, 1961).
Barrell, J., *The Dark Side of the Landscape: the rural poor in English painting 1730–1840* (Cambridge, 1980).
Barret-Ducrocq, F., *Love in the Time of Victoria: sexuality, class and gender in nineteenth-century London*, Howe, J. (trans.), (London, 1991).
Barrett, M., 'Ideology and the cultural production of gender' in Newton, J. and Rosenfelt, D. (eds), *Feminist Criticism and Social Change: sex, class and race in literature and culture* (New York, 1985).
Barthes, R., *Image, Music, Text*, Heath S. (trans.), (London, 1982).
Bartlett, N., *Who Was That Man? A Present for Mr Oscar Wilde* (London, 1988).
Bell, M. M., *Childerley: nature and morality in a country village* (Chicago and London, 1994).
Bermingham, A., *Landscape and Ideology: the English rustic tradition, 1740–1860* (London, 1986).
Brand, S., *How Buildings Learn: what happens after they're built* (London, 1997).
Brettell, R. R. and C. R., *Painters and Peasants in the Nineteenth Century* (Geneva, 1983).
Briggs, A. and S. (eds), *Cap and Bell. Punch's Chronicle of English History in the Making 1841–1861* (London, 1972).
Brunskill, R. W., *Traditional Buildings of Britain: an introduction to vernacular architecture* (London, 1992).
Caffyn, L., *Workers' Housing in West Yorkshire, 1750–1920* (London, 1986).

Calder, J., *Victorian and Edwardian Society from Old Photographs* (London, 1979).
Chambers, I., 'Narratives of Nationalism, being "British"' in Carter, E., Donald, J., Squires, J. (eds), *Space and Place: theories of identity and location* (London, 1993).
Chambers, I., *Migrancy, Culture, Identity* (London and New York, 1994).
Chase, M., 'We wish only to work for ourselves: the Chartist Land Plan' in Chase, M. and Dyck, I. (eds), *Living and Learning: essays in honour of J. F. Harrison* (London, 1996).
Cloke, P., and Little, J., 'Introduction: other countrysides?' in Cloke, P. and Little, J. (eds), *Contested Countryside Cultures: otherness, marginalisation and rurality* (London and New York, 1997).
Cohen, A., *Belonging: identity and social organisation in British rural cultures* (Manchester, 1982).
Constantine, S., 'Amateur gardening and popular recreation in the 19th and 20th Centuries' in *Journal of Social History* (1981), Vol. 14, No. 3.
Cunningham, H., *The Children of the Poor: representations of childhood since the seventeenth century* (London, 1991).
Daniels, S., *Fields of Vision: landscape imagery and national identity in England and the United States* (Cambridge, 1993).
Darley, G., 'The English cottage garden' in Mosser, M. and Teyssot, G. (eds), *The History of Garden Design: the western tradition from the renaissance to the present day* (London, 1991).
Darley, G., *Villages of Vision* (London, 1975).
Davidoff, L., 'Class and gender in Victorian England' in Newton, J. L., Ryan, M. P. and Walkowitz, J. R. (eds), *Sex and Class in Women's History: essays from feminist studies* (London, 1985).
Davidoff, L., L'Esperance, J. and Newby, H., 'Landscape with figures: home and community in English society' in Mitchell, J. and Oakley, A. (eds), *The Rights and Wrongs of Women* (Harmondsworth, 1976).
Davidoff, L. and Hall, C., *Family Fortunes: men and women of the English middle class 1780–1850* (London, 1987).
Davidson, C., *A Woman's Work is Never Done* (London, 1986).
Derounian, J. G., *Another Country: real life beyond Rose Cottage* (London, 1993).
Doane, J., and Hodges, D., *Nostalgia and Sexual Difference: the resistance to contemporary feminism* (London, 1987).
Dunn, M. C., Rawson, M. J. C. and Rogers, A. W., *The Derivation of Rural Housing Profiles* (Birmingham, 1980).
Dyck, I., 'William Cobbett and the farm workers 1790–1835', PhD dissertation, Sussex University, 1986.
English, B., 'Lark Rise and Juniper Hill: A Victorian community in literature and history', *Victorian Studies*, Vol. 29, No. 1 (1985).
Gagnier, R., 'Social atoms: working class autobiography, subjectivity and gender', *Victorian Studies* Vol. 30, No. 3 (1987).
Gaskell, S. M., *Model Housing: from the Great Exhibition to the Festival of Britain* (London and New York, 1987).
Gasson, R., *Provision of Tied Cottages* (Cambridge, 1975).
Gerard, J., 'Lady Bountiful: women of the landed classes and rural philanthropy', *Victorian Studies*, Vol. 30 (Winter, 1987), No. 2.
Halfacree, K., 'Contrasting roles for the post-productivist countryside: a postmodern perspective on counterurbanisation' in Cloke, P. and Little, J. (eds), *Contested Countryside Cultures: otherness, marginalisation and rurality* (London and New York, 1997).

Hall, C., 'The history of the housewife' first published in *The Politics of Housework* (1980), reproduced in *White, Male and Middle Class: explorations in feminism and history* (Cambridge, 1992).
Hall, C., *White, Male and Middle Class: explorations in feminism and history* (Cambridge, 1992).
Harper, S., 'Contesting later life' in Cloke, P. and Little, J. (eds), *Contested Countryside Cultures: otherness, marginalisation and rurality* (London and New York, 1997).
Harris, J. (ed.), *The Garden: a celebration of one thousand years of British gardening* (London, 1979).
Havinden, M., 'The model village' in Mingay, G. E. (ed.), *The Rural Idyll* (London and New York, 1989).
Higgs, E., 'Women, occupations and work in the nineteenth century censuses', *History Workshop Journal*, (1987).
Howkins, A., *Reshaping Rural England: a social history 1850–1925* (London, 1991).
Hoyles, M., *The Story of Gardening* (London, 1991).
Hoyles, M., *Bread and Roses: gardening books from 1560–1960*, Vol. 2 (London, 1995).
Hughes, A., 'Rurality and "cultures of womanhood": domestic identities and moral order in village life' in Cloke, P. and Little, J. (eds), *Contested Countryside Cultures: otherness, marginalisation and rurality* (London and New York, 1997).
Hyams, E., *The English Garden* (London, 1966).
Jones, O., 'Little figures, big shadows, country childhood stories' in Cloke, P. and Little, J. (eds), *Contested Countryside Cultures: otherness, marginalisation and rurality* (London and New York, 1997).
King, G., *Mapping Reality: an exploration of cultural cartographies* (London, 1996).
King, P., 'Gleaners, farmers and the failure of legal sanctions in England 1750–1850', *Past and Present* (1989).
Kolodny, A., *The Land Before Her: fantasy and experience of the American frontiers, 1630–1860* (Chapel Hill and London, 1984).
Landry D., *The Muses of Resistance: labouring-class women's poetry in Britain, 1739–1796* (Cambridge, 1990).
Lawrence, R. J., *Housing, Dwellings and Homes: design, theory, research and practice* (Chichester, 1987).
Leach, N. (ed.), *Rethinking Architecture: a reader in cultural theory* (London and New York, 1997).
Lee, C. H., *The British Economy Since 1700: a macroeconomic perspective* (Cambridge, 1986).
Lefebvre, H., *The Production of Space*, (trans.), (Oxford, 1991).
Lucas, J., 'Places and dwellings: Wordsworth, Clare and the anti-picturesque' in Cosgrove, D. and Daniels, S. (eds), *The Iconography of Landscape* (Cambridge, 1992).
Marsh, J., *Back to the Land: the pastoral impulse in Victorian England from 1880 to 1914* (London, Melbourne and New York, 1982).
Massey, D., *Space, Place and Gender* (Cambridge, 1994).
Massey, D., 'Places and their pasts', *History Workshop Journal*, No. 39 (Spring 1995).
Morgan, D. H., *Harvesters and Harvesting 1840–1900: a study of the rural proletariat* (London, 1982).
Mort, F., *Dangerous Sexualities: medico-moral politics in England since 1830* (London, 1987).
Murdoch, J. and Pratt, A. C., 'From the power of topography to the topography of power: a discourse of strange ruralities' in Cloke, P. and Little, J. (eds), *Contested Countryside Cultures: otherness, marginalisation and rurality* (London and New York, 1997).

Nead, L., *Myths of Sexuality: representations of women in Victorian Britain* (Oxford, 1988).
Oliver, P., *English Cottages and Small Farmhouses: a study of vernacular shelter* (London, 1975).
Ortner, S. B., 'Is Female to Male as Nature is to Culture?' in Mitchelle, Z. et al. (eds), *Woman, Culture and Society* (Stanford, 1974).
Parker, V., *The English House in the Nineteenth Century* (London, 1970).
Payne, C., *Rustic Simplicity: scenes of cottage life in nineteenth-century British art* (Nottingham, 1998).
Phillips, A. D. M., 'Landlord investment in farm buildings in the English Midlands in the mid nineteenth century' in Holderness, B. A. and Turner, M. (eds), *Land, Labour and Agriculture, 1700–1920: Essays for Gordon Mingay* (London, 1991).
Phillips, D. and Williams, A., *Rural Britain: a social geography* (Oxford, 1984).
Philo, C., 'Neglected rural geographies', *Journal of Rural Studies*, 1992, Vol. 8, No. 3.
Pinchbeck, I., *Women Workers and the Industrial Revolution, 1750–1850* (London, [1930] 1985).
Poovey, M., *Uneven Developments: the ideological work of gender in mid-Victorian England* (London, 1989).
Prince, H., 'Art and agrarian change, 1710–1815' in Cosgrove, D. and Daniels, S. (eds), *The Iconography of Landscape* (Cambridge, 1992).
Pugh, S., 'Received ideas on pastoral' in Mosser, M. and Teyssot, G. (eds), *The History of Garden Design: the western tradition from the renaissance to the present day* (London, 1991).
Quiney, A., *House and Home: a history of the small English house* (London, 1986).
Reed, M., 'The peasantry of nineteenth century England: a neglected class?' *History Workshop Journal* (Spring 1984).
Reed, M., *The Landscape of Britain: from the beginnings to 1914* (London, 1997).
Rivers, T., Cruickshank, D., Darley, G. and Pawley, M., *The Name of the Room, a history of the British house and home* (London, 1992).
Romines, A., *The Home Plot: women writing and domestic ritual* (Amherst, 1992).
Rose, G., *Feminism and Geography: the limits of geographical knowledge* (Cambridge, 1993).
Rowbotham, S., *Hidden From History: 300 years' of women's oppression and the fight against it* (London, 1974).
Said, E., *Orientalism* (London [1978] 1995).
Sales, R., *English Literature in History 1750–1830: pastoral and politics* (London, 1983).
Sayer, K., *Women of the Fields: representations of rural women in the nineteenth century* (Manchester, 1995).
Soper, K., *What is Nature? Culture, politics and the non-human* (Oxford, 1995).
Stallybrass, P. and White, A., *The Politics and Poetics of Transgression* (London, 1986).
Swartz Cowan, R., *More Work for Mother: the ironies of household technology from the open hearth to the microwave* (London, 1989).
Tagg, J., *The Burden of Representation: essays on photographies and histories* (London, 1988).
Taylor, J., *A Dream of England: landscape, photography and the tourist's imagination* (Manchester, 1994).
Thirsk, J., *Alternative Agriculture: a history from the Black Death to the present day* (Oxford, 1997).
Tinniswood, A., *Life in the English Country Cottage* (London, 1995).
Tristram, P., *Living Space in Fact and Fiction* (London, 1989).
Vicinus, M., 'Literary voices of an industrial town, Manchester, 1810–70' in Dyos, H. J. and Wolff, M. (eds), *The Victorian City: images and realities* (London, 1973).

Wigley, M., 'Untitled: the housing of gender' in Colomina, B. (ed.), *Sexuality and Space* (Princeton, 1992).
Williams, R., *The Country and the City* (London, [1972] 1985).
Wood, C., *Paradise Lost: paintings of English country life and landscape, 1850–1914* (London, [1988] 1993).
Zlotnick, S., '"A thousand times I'd be a factory girl": dialect, domesticity, and working-class women's poetry in Victorian Britain', *Victorian Studies* (Autumn, 1991).

INDEX

Literary works and works of art can be found under authors' and artists' names.

Note: 'n.' after a page reference indicates the number of a note on that page. Page numbers given in **bold** refer to main entries.

Acland, H. W. 154, 167–8n.38
   Cottage Register, The 150–2
   'Cottage Wall Prints' 151–3
Africa 135
agrarianism 21, 181 *passim*
agricultural societies 71, 153
   see also names of societies
agriculture 118–19, 129, 132, 143
   women's employment in 99–100, 118, 184
      bean setting 120
      gleaning 170n.95
   see also work
Alberti, Leon Battista 27–8
   On the Art of Building in Ten Books 27
Allingham, Helen 36, 79, 108n.8, 127–9, 131, 132–3, 141n.74, 196, 197, 205
   Happy England 36, 127, 133
allotment 56, 85, **86–92**, 93, 98, 100, 150
   see also Clausen, George; garden; potato ground
Alps, Swiss 82
America *see* United States
Andrews, G. H. 147–8
   Modern Husbandry 143, 147–8
animal(s) 60, 80
   and domesticity 37
   /human 30, 65–6, 75, 160–1, 165
   see also Nature; pigs; pigsties
anon.
   'Old Sarah' 67–8, 70, 73
   'Old Susan' 67–8, 70
Anthony, Mark
   The Pedlar's Visit to an Old Cottage 151

Anti-Corn Law League 59
Arch, Joseph 71, 159, 164
Archers, The 51
architects 9, 142, 148, 150
architecture 27, 142–3, 166, 193, **201–3**, 204, 208
   see also Alberti, Leon Battista; buildings; conservation; house; Lawrence, R. J.; space; Weaver, Lawrence
Art Journal 151
Arts and Crafts 12, 107, 157, 209n.13
Austin, Alfred 52–60, 164
Australia 135

'back-to-the-land' 17n.29, 89, 105
Baillie, Joanna 25
Baldry, George 160, 169n.83, 169n.88
Ballie, John 20–1
baking 185–6, 187–90 *passim*
Banks, Sarah 60
Barley, M. W. 155
Barrell, John 67, 72, 95–6, 120–1, 158
Bartell, Edmund 24
bathroom 146
   baths 8
   see also earth-closet; toilet; water closet
Beau Ideal, the 2, 14, **31**, **33–9**, 42, 50, 63, 69, 73, 75, 79, 81, 98, 115, 122, 130, 137, 143, **146**, 158, 176, 197, 203, 208
Bedfordshire 175–6
   Bedford 192
bedrooms 8, 28, 55–7, 144, 148, 150, 160, 167n.32, 176

beer 161
  house 54, 83
  see also brewing
Bell, Michael Mayerfeld 6, 101–4, 162, 179–80, 181, 184, 185, 187, 190, 199n.72, 206
Berkshire 120
Big Issue, The 206–7
black
  access to countryside 117–18, 192, 193
  figure 191
  minorities 192
  see also identity; race; racism
Blaise Hamlet 22, 24
Board of Agriculture 85, 148, 167n.25
body, the 24, 28, 57–8, 60, 65–6, 75, 144–7 passim, 153, 162, 165–6, 177, 204
  able in 184
  Woman's 26, 123, 124, 165
Book-Hawking Union, the 151, 152, 153
Bourne, George 6, 125–7, 134, 140n.47
  Change in the Village 125, 126, 132, 133
Bowie, Fiona 12
Brand, Stewart 23, 116–17, 148, 154, 201, 205, 209n.10
brewing 156
Britain 117, 120, 121, 136, 178, 192
  British 116, 155, 183
  see also England; Englishness; national identity; United Kingdom
British National Party 105
Bryant, Charles 21, 44n.12
Builder 50
building materials 142, 148, 150
  industrial 23, 117
buildings 23–4, 116–17, 202, 203, 205
  adapted 169n.88
  farm 143, 147
  heritage 192
  use of see Lawrence, R. J.
Burgin, V. 93, 111n.90
Burke, Edmund 21
Burns, R. 46n.61
  The Cotter's Saturday Night 31, 32
Bush, Andrew 113

Canada 21–2
Carlyle, Thomas 59, 61, 135

Castle Acre 60
Chadwick, Edwin 57
chamber pots 144
Chambers's Information for the People 86–7, 88
character 178, 198n.24, 204
charity see poor, the
charm 178, 198n.23, 204
Chartist Land Plan 89
Chase, Malcolm 89
Cheshire 55
child 58, 147
childcare 184
childhood 15, 16, 79, **94–6**, **98**, 111n.111, **126**, 138, 173–4, 199n.56
children 26, 32–4 passim, 47n.88, 52, 57–9 passim, 64, 66, 90, **95–9**, 118, 120, 125, 145, 146, 152, 160, 161, 169n.80, 178
  images of 29–30, 37–8
Church of England
  Faith in the Countryside 51
Citizen 175
city 162, 178, 185, 201
  versus country 118, **Chapter 6**, 206
  space 114
Clare, John 122, 123
Clark, Joseph
  The Labourer's Welcome 46n.51
class 10, 11, 30, 36, 53, 54, 66, 73, 99, 102, 105, 187, 191, 194, 196, 197, 199n.56, 203, 209
  conflict 68, 72
  relations 183
  see also identity; poor, the; work
Clausen, George
  The Allotment Garden 92–3
clothes see dress
Cobbett, William 54, 97, 120, 129–30, 135
  Advice to Young Men 54
  Cottage Economy 97, 130
Cockburn, Edwin
  The Return from Market 42–3
Collier, Mary 161
  The Woman's Labour; an epistle 159, 170n.114
Collins, William
  Rustic Civility 95
Combe, Andrew 26, 29, 45n.42, 149
  The Management of Infancy 29

comfort **26**, 43, 53, 54, 59, 85, 150, 172, 176
   comfortable cottage/home, the 133, 173, 196
   to live comfortably 146
conservation 142–3
   see also Brand, Stewart; Huish, Marcus B.; Oliver, P.; preservation; Weaver, Lawrence
Constable, John 131, 167n.36
   The Haywain 131
Constable Country 131, 140n.50
Constantinople 82
Cope, C. W. 124
Cornwall 8, 134, 176
Cotman, F. G. 31, 32, 37, 195
   One of the Family 29–31, 32, 35, 36
Cotswolds, the 134
cottage garden *see* garden
Cottage Gardener 83
   see also garden
Cottage Society of Leeds, the 50
cottaging (*slang*) 1, 16n.1
council 51
   estate 25
   house 25, 51
   housing 7
counterurbanisation 206–7, 210n.34
Countryside Commission, the 192
Cowan, Ruth Swartz 38
   More Work for Mother 14
Culture *see* Nature
Cunningham, Hugh 98

Daily News 172, 201, 209n.1
Daniels, Stephen 23, 114, 129, 131, 138, 141n.81, 179
Darley, Gillian 80, 105
Dartmoor 156, 157
Davidoff, Leonore 31, 33, 123, 145, 146, 188
Denison, S. 58, 60, 90
Derounian, James Garo 6, 51–2, 191, 192
Devon 8, 55, 134
dialect poems 35
Dickens, Charles
   Great Expectations 17n.21
Disraeli, Benjamin 55, 58, 61, 135
   Sybil 53, 60–1, 123
Ditchfield, P. H. 79, 84, 113–14, 137

door 28, 30, 39–40, 145, 161, 196
   back 150, **162**, 164, 182
   front 145, **162**, 182
Dorset 55, 56, 59
Doyle, F. H. 58, 59
drainage *see* sanitation
dress 32
   smock frock 157
Duck, Stephen 159

earth-closet 150, 167n.32
East Anglia 8, 65, 163
east coast, the 8
Eastern Counties, the 135
Eastlake, Charles
   Hints on Household Taste 157
Eliot, George 63, 151
   Middlemarch 49, 60, 75n.2
empire/Empire 2, 23, 82, 115, 132
   colonialism 115, 135 *passim*
   imperialism 115, 129, 132, 192, 193
   see also slavery
enclosure 11, 41, 86, 90, 91, 120
   see also garden
Encyclopædia Britannica 88
England 5, 14, 20, 29, 38, 42, 59, 89, 94, 100, 113–41 *passim*, 176–8, 183, 194, 203, 204
   condition of 6, 15, 58, 61, 74, 123
   the East/east of 5, 87, 125
   feminised 136–7
   the North/north of 8, 58, 59, 135, 169n.84
   old/Old 22, 113–41 *passim*, 159, 174, 206
   the South/south of 5, 87, 125
   the west of 87
   see also south-west, the
English 22, 39, 65, 79, 96, 101, 113–41 *passim*, 184, 203, 205
   domesticity 106
   syllabus 116
   see also Englishness; garden; national identity
English, the 20, 21, 23, 82, 113–41 *passim*
English House Condition Survey 50
Englishness 2, 11, 23, 31, 42, 46n.58, 89, 96, 98, 113–41 *passim*, 150, 159, 177, 204, 208
   feminine/feminised **135–7**, 143

environmentalism 207
  see also animal(s); counterurbanisation; native; Nature
exterior 38–9

Faed, Thomas
  Home and the Homeless 37
fence 68–9
  see also garden
Fildes, Luke
  The Doctor 32–3
  The Farmer's Daughter 39–41, 129–31
  The Village Wedding 38
florists 85
folk 80, 81, 84, 104, 105, 114, 117, 132, 133, 155
Foster, Miles Birket
  The Chair Mender 38
  The China Pedlar 38
  Cottages at Amersham 97
  The Wild Flower Gatherers 96
Fox, Wilson 36–7
France 113, 121
Fraser's Magazine 61
freedom 20
Fripp, Alfred Downing
  The Poachers Alarmed/The Poacher's Hut 33

garden 5, 9, 16, 20, 40, 50, 59, 81, 92, 97, 98, 104, 106, 107, 108n.25, 120, 122, 129, 160, 161, 164, 165, 196
  gates 10, 39, 42, 103, 145, 161
  cottage 13, 15, 39, 40, 42, **Chapter 3**, 138, 209
  designers 79–81, 107
  English 82–3, 103
  images of 39–41
  implements 94, 99
  plants 13, 21, 42, **82**, 85, 101, 107, 193
    auricula 82, 85, 109n.47
    Ranunculus 82, 109n.29
  provision of a 5, 55, 144, 148
  suburb 144
  walls/fences/hedges 25, 34, 39, 40, **41–3**, 48n.99, 81, 84, 95, 106, 145, 162, 181, 196
  see also allotment; Cottage Gardener; Garden, The; Gardener's Magazine, The; gardening; Horticultural Register; Nature; New Eden;

picturesque; potato ground; space; work
Garden, The 108n.6, 108n.7
Gardener's Magazine, The 83, 108n.9
  see also garden
gardening 15, 21, 44n.12, 81, **82–3**, 85, 89–90, 92, 99, 103, 106, 108n.19
  see also garden
Gaskell, Elizabeth 58
  North and South 76n.38
Gaskell, S. Martin 24
Gasson, Ruth 7
Germany 113, 131
  German school of art 152
  German state 136
  German style 136
Glancey, Jonathan 16, 173, 179, 201, 204
Glastonbury 135
Gloucester 55
golden age 4
  see also England; nostalgia
gossip 161
Gough, Benjamin 26–7, 29, 31, 35, 43n.1, 176
  'The Cottage Homes of England' 19–20, 43, 114, 178
  Kentish Lyrics: sacred, rural and miscellaneous 43n.1
  Songs for British Workmen 26
Grahame, Kenneth 98
  The Wind in The Willows 4
Guardian, The 176

Hamilton, Geoff 80, 81, 83, 84, 108n.14
Hampshire 62
Hardy, Frederick Daniel 153
  The Dismayed Artist 151
Hardy, Thomas 157, 205
  'The Dorsetshire Labourer' 72
  Far From the Madding Crowd 108n.8
  Tess of the d'Urbervilles 93–4, 110n.89
Hayllar, James
  'As the Twig is bent, so the Tree is inclined' 31
  The Invalid 31
hearth 37, 146, 155–6, 196
Heath, Richard 50
Hemans, Felicia
  'The Homes of England' 25
Henley, Joseph 36
Herald, The 175

Hertfordshire 85, 91
Higgs, Eddie 99, 118
Hobbits 2–4, 204
Hodge 2, 16–17n.8, 195, 200n.106
home 2, 4–5, **25–7**, 29, 31, 33, 34, 35, 39, 43, 53, 54, 68, 90, 93, 98, **116**, 113–41 passim, 145, 146, 154, 155, 162, 164, 172, **179**, **201**, 203
   cult of the 31, 34, 35, 46n.58
   homely 187–8, 189, 190, 196
   see also Beau Ideal, the; house; household; housewife; housework; place; privacy; Royal Academy, the; space
Home Counties, the 8, 135
Home Front 15
homeless, the 33, 51
   nomad 68
Horticultural Register 83
   see also garden
Hottentot, the 58, 202, 203
house, concept and function of 27–8, 165
   see also home; household; housewife; housework; place; privacy; space
household
   management 39, 53, 122, 146
   tasks 156, 160
   technology 38, 146
housekeeping see household; housewife; housework; work
housewife **28**, 37, 38, 158, 164, 166, 185
housework 14, 28, 37, 38, 74, 132, 146, 159, **162–6**, **185–6**, 189
   images of 67, 163
   and paternalism 70–1, 72
   see also baking; laundry; Romines, Ann
Housing of the Working Classes Act (1890) 148
housing stock 8, 114
Howitt, William 97
   The Boy's County-Book 96
Howkins, Alun 118, 182–3
Hoyles, Martin 82, 89–90, 92, 109n.36, 112n.122
Hughes, Annie 184–90, 194, 199n.56
Hughes, Arthur
   Bed-time 32
Huish, Marcus B. 36, 127–9, 131, 133, 134, 137, 141n.74, 141n.79, 196
Hyams, Edward 82

identity 13, 107, 179, 199n.56, 206
   class 41, 68
   domestic 184
   ethnic 16, 138, 191
   regional 179
   see also black; class; national identity; race; rural; sexuality; white
imagined community 5
incomers 6, 7, 50, 180, 185, 188, 190, 191, 192, 193
India 22
individualism 20, 101, 113–16 passim, 134, 144–5, 146, 201–2
   of the husband 34, 66
industrialisation 14, 27, 35, 118, 122, 142
inhabitant 142, 166n.2
   see also architects; resident
interior 37–8, 39, 56–7, 102, 153, 157
   decoration 151–3, 154, 156
   design 155
   space 145–6, 151, 154, 165
   layout 155, 158, 160
Ireland 33
Italy 113
   Italian school of art 152
   Italian style 136

Jefferies, Richard
   The Toilers of the Field 110n.62
Jekyll, Gertrude 79–80, 107, 108n.7

Keene, Charles 41, 69–70
   'Artful-Very!' 69
   'Legitimate Criticism' 70, 74
Kingsley, Charles 58, 98, 176
   The Water Babies 96
   Yeast 61–2, 76n.38
kitchen 37, 143, 144, 148, 156, 157–8, 160, 163, 176
'kitsch' 23, 117
Kolodny, Annette 94, 130
Knight, Richard Payne 24

Labourers' Friendly Society, the 87
Labourer's Union Chronicle, the 195–7, 205
Labour Leader 89
'Lady Bountiful' 70, 71, 72, 73, 122, 123–4
Lady's Magazine, the 119
Lake Country/District, the 8, 119, 135, 204

Lakeland 176
Lancashire 135
landscape **118–19**, 122, 135, 137, 179–81, 182
  value 8, 180
  'views' of 180–1
laundry 158, 164–5
  represented in traditional rhyme 171n.123
Lawrence, R. J. 9–10, 15, 23–4, 25, 70, 74, 145, 152–3, 196–7
Leeds Permanent 50
Lefebvre, H. 166n.2, 209n.8
Lewis, Charles James
  Mother and Child 96
limewash 151, 154
  see also Hardy, Thomas; whitewash
Linnell, John 121
listing 176–7
London 51, 87, 131
Loudon, Jane 99
Loudon, John Claudius 79, 80, 82–3, 84, 85, 107n.5
  Encyclopædia of Cottage, Farm and Village Architecture 50
Lucas, John 122

male
  gaze 69
  point of view 30, 63, 69
Malton, James 22
Marsh, Jan 12, 89, 126, 141n.79
Martineau, Harriet 59
Massey, Doreen 11–13, 40, 82, 116, 174, 179, 181, 183, 193, 194, 200n.100, 203
Mayhew, Henry 68
men 94, 100, 145, 146, 160
  and masculinity 33
  representations of 31–3, 38, 130
  and respectability 53–5, 83–4
  see also house; individualism; work
Midlands, the 8, 135
Mitford, Mary Russell 119–24, 125, 134, 139n.29
  Our Village: sketches of rural life character and scenery 119, 139n.29
Model Cottage Society of Leeds 50
Morris, William 24, 136, 205
Mort, Frank 54, 151
Muthesius, H. 139n.27, 172, 197

Napoleonic wars 120
Nash, John 22, 24, 44n.18, 115, 135
National Agricultural Labourers' Union/ (NALU) 35, 73, 196–7, 200n.107
  see also Arch, Joseph
National Front, the 105
national identity 1, 2, 13, 44n.13, 44n.14, **Chapter 4**, 179, 183
  English *see* Englishness
  Welsh 12
nationalism 11, 105
National Parks, the 8
native 4, 22, 82, 101, 105, 107, 113–41 *passim*, 155, 193, 206, 208
  versus 'alien' 193
  'nativeness' 191
natural conscience 182, 193
Nature/nature 2, 21, 26, 40, 79, 93, 95, 98, 105, 132, 134, 149, 165, 178, **182**, 190, 207–8
  back to 188–9
  and Culture 13, 41, 42, 92, 164, 172–200 *passim*
  versus Culture 15, 40, 130, 172–200 *passim*, 204
  see also animal(s); pigs
Nead, Lynda 29, 36, 42, 80, 96
New Eden 15
  see also garden
New Poor Law, the 71
New Zealand 135
Norfolk 59, 60, 63, 176
Norfolk News 49
North Country, the 131
Northumberland 5, 36–7, 64–5, 87, 163, 165
nostalgia 2, 26, 47n.76, 79, 112n.123, 133, 174, 177, 181, 188, 203, 209
  see also home; Beau Ideal, the
nursery 149

O'Connor, Feargus 89
Oliver, P. 23, 24, 114–15, 117, 128, 133, 155, 173, 176, 197n.6
'open' versus 'close' parish/village 60–1, 120
Ordinance Survey 21
Ortner, Sherry B. 40

parlour 37, 143, 144, 148, 156, 162
Parr, Martin 134

Paxton, Joseph 83
Payne, Christiana 151
Pedder, D. C.
  Where Men Decay 127, 140n.52
Penny Cyclopedia of the Society for the Diffusion of Useful Knowledge 86–7, 88, 91–2, 108n.9
Percy, W. S. 134, 136, 137
  Strolling Through Cottage England 134–5
philanthropy *see* poor
Picture Post 136
picturesque 2, 15, **20–5**, 43, 44n.13, 44n.14, 44n.28, 50, 59, **62**, 63, 103, 104, 106, 123, 129, 144, 147, 178, **180–1**, 192, 205
pigs 5, 57, 65–6, 75, 84, 86, 87, 91, 92, 94, 122, 155, 161, 162, 165, 169n.83
pigsties 55–7, 65, 87, 148, 150, 160
place 11, 13, 33, 34, 39, 40, 42, 54, 75, 82, 113, **116**, 121–2, 124, 128, 132, 134, 179, 199n.56, **203**
  names 119
  narrativisation of 181
  sense of 11, 107, 123, 181
  see also home; space
poachers 33
poor, the 30, 44n.13, 59–66 *passim*, 83, 85, 90–1, 95, 101, **120–1**, 123, 140n.52, 145, 151–3, 155, 160, 187, 208
  charity/philanthropy, and **67–75**, 122–3, 151
  respectability and 57, 124, 156
  see also class
Popular Educator, The 201–2, 209n.7
potato ground 54, 55
preservation 154–5, 205
  preservationist impulse 207
  preservationists 208
  see also conservation
privacy 34, 42, 144, 148, 160, 166, 182, 189
  private rooms and 28
  suburb and 58
  see also door; garden; home; house; place; space
privy *see* bathroom; earth-closet; toilet; water closet

Punch 31, 41, 68–70
  'Helping Him On' 72–3, 74
  'Troubles of our Clergy' 72–3, 74
  see also Keene, Charles

race 64–5, 117–18 *passim*, 125, 152, 191–2, 194, 203, 209
  ethnicity and 137–8
  see also black; empire; identity; native; racism; savage; slavery; space; white
racism 192
  racial prejudice 191
  racial tensions and 114
Reed, Michael 81, 106, 119, 139n.27
region, concept of 182–3
Repton, Humphrey 94, 95
resident 159
  see also architects; inhabitant
Rhode, Eleanor 42, 101
Rivers, Tony 4, 15 *passim*, 194–5, 204
Robinson, Henry Peach
  Day's Work Done 32
Robinson, William 12, 79, 82, 107, 108n.5, 108n.6
Romines, Ann 14, 163–4, 186
Royal Academy, the 33, 48n.106, 108n.8, 121, 195
  and 'Domestic Pictures' 36
Royal Agricultural Society, the (RAS) 50
Royal Commission on Housing (1884) 148
Royal Navy 116
rural 180, 182, 184, 194, 208–9
  identity 187
  idiocy 193
  places 184
  ruralism 187, 199n.72
  rurality 183–4, 189, 190, 193, 199n.56
  spaces 178–9
  topographies of the 74
  women and the 184–90
Rural Development Council 51
Ruskin, John 24, 127, 129, 136
  'The poetry of architecture' 44n.28

Said, E. 3
Sales, R. 107n.3
sanitation 55–8, 146–7, 150
Saturday Review 62–6, 69, 77n.66, 77n.70

savage 58, 65, 67
scullery 143, 156, 160, 166
sentiment 46n.54
servants 28, 145, 146–7
servants' quarters 143, 144
servants' stair 143
sewers *see* sanitation
sexuality 184, **194**, 209
Shaftesbury, Anthony Ashley Cooper, 7th Earl of 59
Shakespeare, William 128, 129
  Shakespeare's country 159
  The Tempest 33
slavery 192
Smallfield, Frederick
  Early Lovers 41
Small Holdings Act (1892) 89
Small Holdings and Allotments Act (1907) 89
Smiles, Samuel 26, 29, 45n.40
  Self Help 45n.40
Snape, William H.
  A Cottage Scene 31
Society for the Diffusion of Useful Knowledge *see* Penny Cyclopedia of the Society for the Diffusion of Useful Knowledge
Society for the Erection of Improved Dwellings 50
Somerset 55
Soper, Kate 57, 65, 66, 105, 207
south coast, the 8
'South Country', the 131–2, 133
South Downs, the 129
south-east, the 134
south-west, the 8
space 40, **74–5**, 106, 123, 145–6, 191, 194, 197
  attempt to police 153
  and capitalism 183
  as concept **10–13**, 41, 166n.2, 181
  domestic 26, 40, 60, 117, 153, 156, 161, 165, 196, 208
  female 93
  feminine 31
  garden 102
  picture 158
  private 41, 79, 83, 90, 145, 161
  public 25, 41, 101, 145, 161, 162
  rural 115, 175, 179, 187
  time and 12, 24, 40, 137, 138, 179, **181–2**, 209

white, countryside as 107, 138, 191–2
  see also black; class; interior; place; privacy; rural; white
Staffordshire 87, 161
Stone, Marcus
  Silent Pleading 33
Stonehenge 119, 204
strangers 37, 145
  see also visitors
Sturminster Agricultural Society 76n.45
Sublime/sublime, the 20–1, 44n.28
suburb *see* garden; privacy
suburban semi 144, 204
Suffolk 90, 163, 195
Sunlight Year Book, the 98
Surrey 127, 132, 203
Switzerland 113
  Swiss tenement buildings 9

Taylor, John 136, 205
tea 161, 162
  -time 100–1, 157–8
Thompson, Flora 100–1, 104, 143
  Lark Rise to Candleford 112n.123, 169n.86
tied cottages 7–8
time and space *see* space, time and
Times, The 58
Tinniswood, Adrian 205–6
toilet 8, 165–6
  see also bathroom; earth-closet; water closet
Tolkien, J. R. R. 3
  The Lord of the Rings 3–4
tools 38, 87, 94, 99, 121, 156
  see also gardening; household
tourism 134–5
tourists 104, 122, 129 *passim*, **134**, 135, 137, 178, 193, 205
  armchair 122, 134
  materials 204
Towns Improvement Clauses Act (1847) 148
Tozer, Henry Spernon
  The Evening Meal 31
traffic 20, 173
  road signs 119
transport, public 184, 191
Tristram, Philippa 5, 11, 17n.21, 18n.44, 22, 66, 123, 156, 205

United Kingdom 183
  see also Britain
United States (US) 1, 14, 22, 94, 102, 117, 129–30, 131, 146, 162, 163–4, 192

Vicinus, Martha 35
Victoria, Queen 31, 152, 153
visitors 145, 148
  see also door; strangers

Wade, Thomas
  The Poacher's Home 33
Wales 12
Welsh border 184
  see also national identity
Walker, Fred
  The Vagrants 33
Walker, T. H.
  Good Servants, Good Wives and Happy Homes 27
War, South African 132
washing *see* laundry
water closet/water-closet 143, 148
  see also bathroom; earth-closet; toilet
Weaver, Lawrence 167n.32
  Country Life Book of Cottages 149–50
Webster, Thomas
  Sunday Evening 32
Wedgwood 173
Weekly Illustrated 136
Wessex 134
Westminster 116, 119
white 1, 107, 124, 130, 138, 183–4, 191–3
  community 191
  immigrants 22
  see also identity; race; racism; space

whitewash 37
  whitewashing 161, 164
  see also limewash
Wigley, M. 27–8, 165, 170n.100
Wilkie, Sir David
  The Cotter's Saturday Night 31–2
Williams, P. and A. 6
Williams, Raymond 15, 106, 114, 123, 133, 174, 178–9, 184, 193, 199n.56, 206
Willmott, R. A. 82, 101
  A Journal of Summertime in the Country 90
Women and Employment in Rural Areas 51
Wood, John 24
Worcestershire 55
Wordsworth, William 122, 124, 152
work 27, 34, 64, 66, 79, 83, 88–9, 97, 104, 156, 161, 185
  dairy 53
  domestic 26, 94, 104, 159, 165
  farm 55
    women 185, 189
  and home 35, 144, 158, 163
  images of labourers at 121
  'occupation', and 122
  women's 92–4, 99, 100, 134, 162
  see also agriculture; class; gardening; household; housewife; housework; servants

yeoman 3 *passim*, 88–9, **129–31**, 155, 200n.107
Yonge, Charlotte 78n.103
  'Quack, Quack' 72
Yorkshire 63, 135
  West 154
Young, Arthur 85, 91